THE STONE COLD THRILLER SERIES - BOOKS 1-3

A Stone Cold Thriller Boxset

J. D. WESTON

WESTON MEDIA

STONE COLD

The
Stone Cold Thriller Series
Book 1

CHAPTER ONE

TWO MEN SLIPPED SILENTLY THROUGH THE DOOR OF warehouse twenty-four. It was a generic warehouse building, typically found in business parks all over the world. This particular unit was in Beckton, East London, and the park was aptly named 'The East London Business Park.' Harvey Stone closed the door behind them, careful to make no sound. He turned to his companion, Julios, and nodded. The movement was barely discernible in the pitch darkness, but Julios understood the signal and moved forward, listening for any change in noise from the room beyond.

They had entered through a narrow door that opened into a small hallway. Stairs on their right led up to a row of mezzanine offices, and a door directly in front of them led out to the large warehouse space, where several men could be heard loading a truck. They listened to the whirr of a heavy battery-powered forklift and the hiss of hydraulic rams lowering its cargo onto the truck. The sounds were clear in the otherwise silent warehouse.

Julios chanced a glance through the gap in the semi-open connecting door. He watched intently for a while before holding three fat fingers up to Harvey, who stood behind him in the darkness, still and alert.

The three men in the warehouse worked in silence. There was no banter and no casual insults to pass the time. There was no sound at all save for the whirrs, hisses and metallic rattles of the machinery.

Julios and Harvey had a plan they would carry out precisely. It was the only way to ensure a one-hundred percent chance of success. According to Julios' tried and tested methodology, deviation from any plan caused variants in possibilities. Julios did not like variants. They led to mistakes, and in their line of work, mistakes often ended in death.

Harvey and Julios heard the sliding tailgate of the truck followed by the light, metallic click of a padlock. As the diesel engine fired up, then came the twin thumps of the closing truck doors, which boomed around the large warehouse. The screeching of the sliding concertina shutters began their banshee-like cry as they were pulled open to allow the truck to leave. Once it had pulled out and the sound of its engine had faded away, the sliding shutter was closed with a crash. Chains were dragged through a series of steel rings then padlocked, marking the end of the audible warehouse performance.

Every detail played out in Harvey's mind. A lifetime of working in the dark had tuned his senses to noise, allowing him to visualise minute details. He and Julios remained in the shadows, blocking the one remaining exit for the one remaining man. There had been three men in the warehouse, and two truck doors had been slammed, which left only one. Exactly as they had planned.

Julios moved further into the blackness, ready for the door to open, and gave a silent signal for Harvey to follow suit. They waited in practised silence, listening to sounds and imagining their meanings.

A new noise. Four digital clicks of a smartphone being unlocked followed by a stutter of taps, indicating a message being sent. Then the warehouse lights turned off. There were six switches in two rows of three, according to Harvey's interpretation of the timing of each click. Total darkness ensued. But Julios didn't need light to carry out the job.

A familiar lift in Harvey's heart rate sent a thrilling warmth through his body. His eyes pulsed once as the adrenaline released and he rolled his neck from side to side, waiting for the two satisfying clicks.

He was ready.

The sound of footsteps and jangling keys grew closer until, at last, the little door creaked open and their target stepped into the trap. The man hadn't taken two steps into the hallway when Julios' huge black shape emerged from the darkness and slipped a steel wire around his neck.

As Julios had instructed, Harvey remained where he was, watching with awe at the panicked struggle in the darkness. The only sounds were a few feeble squeals of the man's trainers skidding on the painted concrete floor and the sickly, choking sound of his few last breaths.

Julios was a pro. Harvey admired his control and composure during these moments and looked on with admiration. Emotion was not a factor in the transaction. No anger, spite, or bitterness tainted his methods. He was, in Harvey's eyes, a master of his trade.

Their instructions had been simple. *Leave no clues. Make a statement.*

Julios waited his standard one minute after the moment he believed his work to be done. The one-minute rule applied to nearly every aspect of the job. Above all else, it added an element of control when instinct might favour haste.

Julios' gloved fingers tugged at the wire trace then pocketed the weapon.

Leave no clues.

He looked up at Harvey, who was waiting in the shadows on the second step of the staircase, and nodded at him in the darkness, signifying that it was Harvey's turn to perform.

Make a statement.

Harvey stepped over the body and, using a small, two-cell torch, found the light switches on the wall of the warehouse. Two rows of three, exactly as he had guessed. He used the point of his knife to turn on just one switch then pocketed the torch. The knifepoint wouldn't rub off any existing fingerprints and certainly wouldn't leave his own.

He glanced at the front end of the warehouse. There was an electric chain hoist on a running beam fixed to a series of overhead gantries roughly ten metres high. The running beam led from above the large shutters all the way to the rear of the warehouse where the mezzanine floor stored large machinery and crates. Presumably, the hoist was used for loading and unloading flat-bed lorries.

But Harvey had another use for it in mind.

A yellow console with two buttons marked with up and down arrows hung from the hoist by a thick cable. Harvey hit the down button and the hoist jumped into life, lowering a large hook on the end of its chain. He waited for it to reach knee level then released the button.

The dead man's body slid across the painted concrete floor with little effort. As Harvey dropped him beside the hook, he saw an angry red line across the man's throat.

Beside the doors, Harvey found a broom that he smashed against the wall until he was left with just the handle. He slid it through the dead man's jacket sleeves then wrapped the chain around his limp body before connecting it to the large hook. The hoist jumped into life once more and, inch by inch, the man rose into the air with his head rolled forwards and his lifeless limbs hanging free.

Harvey stopped the hoist when the hook reached its maximum height and stepped back to admire his work. Ten metres in the air, hung like a crucified sacrifice, their target stared back at Harvey and Julios.

An ill-feeling crawled across Harvey's skin, unfamiliar and tense. He stared back at the statement he'd been told to make and knew in the deepest, darkest pit of his gut that they'd crossed the line.

He and Julios had just started a war.

2

CHAPTER TWO

DRIVING IN SILENCE AFFORDED FRANK CARVER A RARE opportunity to think clearly without the background noise and interruptions of office life. He drove at a slow but steady sixty miles an hour on the M25 motorway and prepared to take the next exit, which would lead him onto the M11 then subsequently onto the North Circular Road and into Beckton. It was late morning, so the roads were clearer than during the rush hour madness.

One of the cases he'd been working on was building up. He had a feeling it was all going to come crashing down soon enough, and in his experience, he would need to be there when it did. He'd need to ensure the rewards came his way and the right suspects were locked up.

If he left it to anyone else, the lead investigator would settle for prosecuting anybody involved, but with no hard strategy. To nail a big fish, you needed a strategy, an infallible plan that produced irrefutable evidence. Anything less and big fish would sink below the surface of their legitimate operations for a few years until it's all blown over and their smart lawyers found a loophole. Only then would they commit themselves to another big job. By then, Frank planned on being retired.

Frank wouldn't let Terry Thomson slip away this time, and he'd take down anyone who stood in his way.

Frank had been informed of a body found inside a warehouse of an East London business park. One of his team had designed a computer tool to sniff for tags in the Metropolitan Police database. It had flagged the case as soon as it was logged. The warehouse was leased by an affiliate company of Thomson.

In the old days, links between cases and new information were easily missed, and he'd likely never have heard about it. But these days, not a lot was missed. In fact, too many leads were generated, of which only a handful were useful. The trick was to sift through the pile and identify the ones that *would* lead somewhere.

He took the next exit and followed the slip road onto the dreaded A13, the main artery into London from the east, which was notorious for its heavy congestion. Then he turned off into Beckton and drove slowly down the road to the business park, which was bumpy from years of fully laden lorries driving in and out.

At the far end, he could see the spinning lights of the local police. Frank switched off the sat-nav and rolled to a stop beside a bored-looking policeman, who stood by two traffic cones and a roadblock. He hit the button to lower the passenger window.

"You'll have to turn around, sir," said the officer with a Manchester twang. "The road is closed for the morning, I'm afraid."

Frank flashed his ID before the officer could finish and continued to drive forwards, squeezing his Volvo through the small gap between the police car and the traffic cone. Outside the warehouse, he parked between a forensics van and an ambulance. Inside, he pulled on a pair of blue shoe protectors and ducked beneath the red and white tape, flashing his ID once more to an officer guarding the single door.

In Frank's mind, a murder scene broke down into stages: the entry, the act, and the exit.

The warehouse doors showed no sign of a forced entry, suggesting they were left unlocked or the killer was invited inside. The kill was clean with no sign of struggle, but the killer had gone to great lengths to humiliate the victim, which suggested that time was not an issue. Due to the location, the exit would've been made using a vehicle.

A mark across the victim's throat identified the probable cause of death as strangulation, garrotting, to be precise. Given the immaculate crime scene and lack of evidence, Frank knew the weapon was taken by the murderer. But when Frank pulled on a pair of synthetic gloves and used the bright yellow console to lower the hook, the case became truly interesting. Inside the victim's jacket, he found a smartphone and a brown leather wallet, which held a few hundred pounds in twenty-pound notes, three credit cards and a driving license.

The name on the front of the license was Bradley Thomson.

If two and two equalled four, the white-faced and stone-cold body that hung from the hook like a centre piece in a museum was the son of the renowned East End villain, Terry Thomson. The very man he wanted to put away.

Pieces of a hazy puzzle fell into place in Frank's mind. Bradley had been garrotted with zero mess. There was no blood and no damage to the immediate environment. This all suggested that the killer was old school and a pro. These days, killers had no style. Too many Hollywood films made dealing with a messy murder an all-too-frequent part of the job. But a messy murder leaves clues. Bradley Thomson's killer left no trace.

Hanging Bradley's body was either a message or a statement. Either way, the murder was suicidal. The killer would need an army to stop Terry Thomson's retaliation, and despite Thomson's numerous enemies, there weren't many people who had that amount of manpower.

It wasn't often that Frank saw the work of a pro anymore. Not in a murder anyway. He hadn't officially worked a straight murder case for years. He missed the challenge. He'd enjoyed his work back then, but it hadn't left much room for talk over dinner. Instead, he would listen to his wife rattle on about the neighbour's dog or the local shop being bought out. Yet, given the chance, he would give everything to hear Jan rattle on one more time.

Forensics were hunting for fingerprints on the surrounding environment and footprints in the dust. They spoke of having the body checked for third-party DNA. The local investigators were following a standard procedural template, which rarely left room for common sense and creativity. It was more like data collection. Later, somebody lower in the ranks would feed the information into a computer and hope for it to spit out the right answer. It rarely did.

Frank thought it was pointless to hunt for clues on the scene when the killer had clearly been carrying out a job for someone else. Time could be more efficiently spent hunting the man who gave the order, or checking the surrounding areas where the perpetrator may have been less diligent about leaving traces of evidence. Pros like this were hired men.

Using his phone, Frank took a photo of the abrasions on Bradley Thomson's neck and face before heading back outside. He'd been inside the warehouse for less than ten minutes. He walked past two women who were standing nearby, both stifling tears. It was cold out and they hugged each other for warmth and comfort.

"Excuse me, ladies," said Frank. "Did either of you know the victim?"

The elder of the two women dropped her face into her hands and whined. The other offered Frank a stern look and pulled her friend closer.

"We both did," she said. "We found him this morning. Who would do something like this?"

"That's what we're going to find out. Have you both given a statement?"

The woman nodded.

"Good," said Frank. "Don't worry. We'll catch them."

He left the women and moved along the row of warehouses. Cameras were fixed to tall poles at the entrance. Another was fixed to the side of the building and pointing down the road at oncoming traffic. But there were no cameras facing into the park. It was as if the security designer had deemed it unnecessary because all traffic had to come in through the gates.

Frank continued his walk along the front of the neighbouring units, many of which had people standing outside them in the cold, trying to get a look at the commotion. He wore jeans and a loose-fitting button-up shirt under a long jacket that hid the paunch he'd been developing for the past few years. Onlookers turned and watched him walk by, but he didn't look back.

At the far end of the units was a small copse of trees with a steel fence marking the perimeter of the business park. It had two-inch steel bars running vertically every four inches. A person might get their hands between the rails but not much else, and the sharp, angled tops of each bar would certainly prevent anybody climbing over.

But at the end of the fence, closest to the warehouses,

Frank found a gap. Two bent steel bars had been forced off, probably with a car jack, and were laid on the grass outside the perimeter.

There were no footprints to disturb, so he stepped through the hole, careful not to rip his jacket. Then he walked among the trees until he found himself at the dual carriageway which ran behind the estate and up to the North Circular Road.

He'd found the exit.

The section of road was fast-moving by day as it bypassed the A13. But at night, Frank knew it would be empty save for the odd taxi or night-worker. It would give the killer ample opportunity to get away unseen.

A single tire track was barely visible in the long grass, but at the right angle and in the right light, it was clear as day. Frank looked closer. He traced the faint path and found a small patch of mud between two clumps of grass.

He smiled to himself.

Got you.

The print wasn't very clear but clear enough for Frank to take a photo. He lay a ten-pound note on the ground and snapped a shot. The ten-pound note would provide accurate scaling for Tenant, his tech research guy, to identify the tire tracks.

Returning to the investigation with a positive sense of accomplishment, Frank found the inspector in charge, who was requesting camera footage from a security guard. The guard wore an ill-fitting, bright yellow, high-visibility jacket and, judging by the way he was shrugging, was of little use.

"A word in your ear," said Frank in his soft Scottish accent. "Those cameras won't show anything. That's a waste of time." He turned and nodded towards the fence. "He came from that way. There's a gap in the railings and a motorbike track in the dirt. You can dust the fence for prints. You won't find any, but send me the results of the track analysis as soon as you have them. I'll need a list of motorbikes that tire might belong to." He handed the bemused inspector his card. "I'll be waiting for your email."

Frank stepped away from the scene. He hadn't mentioned that he'd already identified the victim and knew the significance of the murder; the investigator could waste precious time figuring that out. Frank would be well ahead by that time. Besides, as Bradley was heir to the Thomson throne, as it were, the case would land on Frank's lap anyway. His team of organised crime specialists were far more likely to get to the bottom of it.

He returned to the warmth of his car and sent the photos to his small team. He glanced back at the hive of activity, knowing that the uniforms would glean less from the crime scene in an entire day than Frank had in less than half an hour.

3

CHAPTER THREE

SERGIO WOKE EARLY, AS HE DID EACH MORNING, TO THE soprano melody of Strauss' Epheu. The crisp tones from the inbuilt ceiling speakers flowed throughout his small but lavish apartment one mile from John Cartwright's estate in the village of Theydon Bois in Essex. The hardwood floors gave resonance to the sound. Sergio smiled at the dexterity of the vocalist and slid from the smooth, black, silk sheets into the cold bite of the air-conditioning.

He glanced back at the girl who had stayed overnight. She slept naked and quietly. Her mouth was open just a fraction, showing the tips of her perfect young teeth beneath her full lips. The smooth sheets lay across her body and her arm was exposed, revealing one soft and firm breast. Her nipple stood proud and hard, exposed to the cool air that circulated the apartment. Sergio checked his email and messages on his phone then took a sly video of the sleeping girl. He hardened at the thought of watching it later that evening when she had left. He would add it to his collection.

He showered in the tiled, black, en-suite bathroom and dressed in a black tailored shirt and suit. Saville Row's finest.

His shirt was ring spun and smooth to the touch like silk. But the material retained a masculine look with its matte finish, unlike Italian materials, which, in Sergio's opinion, were cheap-looking.

For breakfast, he ate yoghurt with banana and drank fresh coffee made with Ethiopian beans direct from the source. He placed his dish, cup and spoon in the dishwasher. The maid would turn it on and empty it when she arrived later. He saw an upturned martini glass from the previous night. It was tainted with the lipstick of the sleeping girl, and he remembered her lips fondly.

His mornings were clockwork. Disruption to his patterns caused disruptions to his thinking, which led to mistakes. And John would not tolerate mistakes. Sergio walked across to the bedroom and woke the girl by cupping the breast that was offered in the cool air. She breathed in deeply and murmured in a sleepy voice. He squeezed a little harder until she gasped.

"Does daddy want to play some more already?" The girl smiled and opened her eyes. Seeing Sergio fully dressed, she said, "Oh, so early. You have to leave?"

"It's *you* that has to leave, I'm afraid," he replied coldly.

She ran her hand up his leg and found what she was looking for growing in excitement as she returned the squeeze.

"Are you sure you can't stay a little longer?" she asked, finding the zipper and giving it a soft tug.

He considered the thought of being ten minutes late. He was technically an hour *early* each day anyway, so a ten-minute delay would not actually result in him being *late*. The girl reached inside and gripped him between finger and thumb. Her gaze followed his body up to his eyes as she moved her mouth closer to him and ran her hands across the smooth material of his shirt.

Desire overcame his rigid professionalism, and he let her touch him. He enjoyed toying with women. He enjoyed the power, the power to say no, the power to stop them when he commanded. To be the boss for once. He enjoyed the girl a moment longer, then pulled away.

"Now get up. You're leaving."

She sat back on the bed and looked at him incredulously. "Is that how you treat such a nice gesture?"

"Are you dressing?" he asked, as he paced around the bed. "In one minute, you are leaving this apartment, dressed or not."

He left and heard the pillow bounce softly across the room behind him.

"Pig!"

The view from the kitchen looked out over Epping Forest. Sergio enjoyed watching the trees sway gently in the breeze. Birds flew from one branch to another in a restless state of fear and hunger, just like workers in the city.

The front door slammed as the girl left and Sergio smiled to himself. She had been expensive, but worth every penny.

His Mercedes waited for him in the small basement car park of the apartment building. It seemed to wake like a happy puppy with a push of the key fob. The headlights and indicators flashed on then dimmed, the locks popped open, and the soft inner light gently brightened the plush leather interior.

The expensive car stereo picked up from where the apartment stereo had left off and continued with the delights of Strauss as the large saloon pulled out of the car park and onto the back streets of Theydon Bois. Sergio turned up the volume as he drove past the hooker, ignoring her gesture, and headed towards the office to hear the news from Julios and Harvey.

Sergio's day had started well.

4

CHAPTER FOUR

ONLY THE WIND WHISTLING THROUGH THE WINDOWS AND the tapping fingers of the old oak tree against the misted glass accompanied the bright flashes of lightning that lit the boy's room long enough to set his wild imagination spiralling. Dark shadows of friendly toys teased his fear with their large, crooked noses, pointed chins and long, gnarled fingers. The black spaces between objects grew deeper and darker with each crack of thunder. With the bedsheets pulled up to his eyes, he waited for dawn, when daylight would banish the shadows and the songs of birds would ward off the wind.

He began to hum a tune his foster father often played on his record player. The melody began with the high and innocent cry of a scared and lonely violin as if it walked unaccompanied through a deep forest. Slowly, the orchestra grew, as if strangers stepped from behind the trees to face the darkness together. The strength and confidence of the violin grew with each additional sound and the dark shadows faded with each instrumental entrance. The volume rose to an almighty high to break through the canopy of trees and let the sunlight shine down to guide the way of the orchestra. The tempo, chaotic yet rhythmic, fought the resilient darkness whose desperate talons clung to the fat trunks of gnarled trees. Then the beating heart of a timpani, strong and bold, fell in line, bringing up the rear, pumping life into the ensemble, and casting the deathly shadows back to where they belonged.

And then there was light.

A single violin sang its soulful tune, confident and unafraid.

The sheets slipped from the boy's face and cold air breathed across his skin. Hard patters of rain washed against the glass outside in waves, blown this way and that by the incessant wind. He rose from his bed, placed his bare feet on the cold, wooden floor and crept to the window, driven by wonder and hoping to see the tail of the banished storm.

But the storm lingered, waiting in the dark clouds high in the sky. Its tenacious claws gripped the old oak and at the peak of the wind, when the wash of rain threatened to break through the glass, it crashed its fist down with an angry crack of thunder. Lightning flashed in a series of strikes and the wind tore a huge branch from the old oak, which fell against the house, grinding and scratching its way to the dark ground.

The small boy turned and saw the foreboding shapes of his toys against the cold, hard wall, which seemed to rise above his own cowering shadow. He ran from the room and into the corridor, slipping on the wood until he crashed into his sister's room. Slamming the door, he leaned breathlessly against the wood as the wind circled the house, carrying with it a perpetual stream of leaves and rain.

He slipped into his sister's bed, shaking with fear but safe in her presence. They were together, and together, they could face anything. He lay with his back to her back and placed the soles of his cold, young feet against the warmth of hers. The anger of the storm faded away into the night.

He dreamed they were running along a beach through the

long, wild grass that bordered golden sand, laughing and rolling, and staring up at the sky, making shapes from its wispy formations. But then there were none. Grey sky pushed away the blue. White clouds grew darker like a cancer working its way through the shape and blackening its heart. The light was banished, unable to penetrate the evil gloom.

The boy woke with a start.

His feet searched for his sister's but found nothing.

He rolled and padded the bed, but she was gone. He was alone. There was only a warm patch where she had been laying and a hollow in the pillow. Once more, the cold floor nipped his feet as he padded across the room and opened the door a crack. The house was still. The invading storm had moved on, leaving a trail of destruction and fear.

He crept along the corridor to the great hallway where two grand staircases curved then met on the ground floor like evil arms welcoming guests into their lair. Keeping to the edge of the stairs to avoid the creaks and groans of the wood, he passed the oil paintings whose dull and unsmiling faces stared at him with contempt until he reached the hard, wooden floor below.

There was a sound. A murmur. It was shrill and out of place alongside the subtle moans of the old house.

He stepped through to the kitchen behind the stairs where the hard terracotta tiles bit his skin. Resting one foot on top of the other, he switched when the pain was too much, all the time, listening. The room ran across the width of the building with windows along its length that flooded the space with bright moonlight. It shone across the kitchen surfaces, licked at the sides of the old pots and pans that hung from the exposed beams, and lit the round, brass handle of the small cellar door.

That sound again. A rhythmic groan of pain and tears.

His hand, shaking with terror, reached for the brass

handle which seemed to beg to be touched, shining bright against the dark wood.

But there were footsteps on the stairs below, heavy boots and the cough of a man unafraid of the night, unafraid of anything.

The boy sank into the shadows, backing into a dark space beneath the kitchen surface, amongst sacks of potatoes and protected by the very shadows that had tormented him all night.

The cellar door opened with the creak of old wood, revealing the sound of that rhythmic grunting, tears, and agony, loud in the night. It was all wrong. So wrong. From the doorway emerged a man, tall, lean and gaunt, who stepped into the kitchen. Closing the door behind him, nothing more than a distant whisper was left of the pain below and the mournful sobs lost to the night.

Then came the metallic click of a cigarette lighter and the man's deep inhale of smoke. He rolled his head back and sighed with pleasure then allowed a soft, breathless release of poisoned air. From where the boy hid, he could see through the window beyond. The bright moon framed a large, crooked nose, a deep, pointed chin and the outline of a face that would change his life forever.

CHAPTER FIVE

5

FRANK'S PHONE RANG OVER THE CAR'S BLUETOOTH SYSTEM.

"Carver."

"Sir, we received your photos," said Melody Mills, his lead investigator. "You're on loudspeaker with me, Tenant and Cox. Did you find anything useful?"

"Did you see the victim?" asked Frank.

"We did, sir. Not sure what to think of that."

"Things are about to get messy, Mills," replied Frank. "Are you able to identify the bike from the picture of the tire track?"

"I can try, sir," said Reg Tenant. "I can get a list of bikes that might fit the bill. It'd give us a starting point."

"Good. Can we have it ready by the time I get back to the office?"

"I'm on it now, sir."

"Mills?"

"Sir?"

"Research. We need eyes and ears out there. There's a change in the air. I want to know which way the wind's blowing."

"I'll see what I can find, sir. Did the job look pro?"

"Clean as a baby's arse, Mills."

"Looked like a garrotting from the photos. Am I right?" asked Mills.

"Spot on. Neat job. Would have been over in seconds."

"We'll pull up all the garrottings then. Maybe there's a link in the method."

"Good. We need to know what the Thomsons are involved in right now, and what they're planning. Whoever did this is either stupid or has some serious balls."

"There are only two real main players, sir, the Stimsons and the Cartwrights," said Melody. "Killing is not Stimson's style, but let's not write him off."

"Agreed," said Frank. "But for John Cartwright to have a go at Thomson would be like poking a sleeping bear."

"You would need a big stick to poke that bear, sir."

"You would. Even then, you'd be asking for trouble. See what sticks Cartwright has in his arsenal. See if there's one big enough to take out Bradley Thomson."

"Will do, sir."

"Oh, and Mills?"

"Sir?"

"Have Cox sort out that van. I can see this going mobile," said Frank. "Find out where Thomson is holed up these days and plan for a recce."

"I'm right here, sir," said Cox.

Denver Cox wasn't an investigator or a tech research guru. He was an engineer assigned to the unit, and he came with a certain set of skills that had come in handy on numerous occasions. Denver was a first-class rally driver trained by the best. He'd also obtained his private pilot's license and CAA-approved helicopter license, which gave him a leg up over other drivers and engineers. It also meant that Frank rarely let him get seconded to other units. There had been a few times when Frank had to step in and block a request for Denver's time, much to the annoyance of other lead investigators.

"Good," said Frank. "We need that van up and running. You're going to be busy over the next few days, and we can't have it just sitting on the side of a road somewhere."

"The van is golden, sir," said Denver. "It won't be an issue."

"Good stuff."

"And Stimson, sir?" asked Mills. "Do you want me to bother with him? Or do you want me to concentrate on Cartwright? You know, process of elimination."

"The mythological Stimson? See what you can find. But don't hold your breath. I haven't laid eyes on him in the thirty years I've been on the job. Chances are you'll find people that work for him, but they'll have their mouths bound shut with fifty-pound notes. Anyway, you won't get no further than that. Better to find our killer. Find him and he'll lead us right into the hornets' nest."

6

CHAPTER SIX

Terry Thomson spoke quietly and slowly but never once raised his eyes from the framed photo on his desk.

"Why wasn't I told sooner?"

"We've only just found out, boss," said Lenny. "Apparently, the police took his..." He stopped and adjusted his sentence. "Took *him* away for examining. They didn't release the news until they had to officially."

"How?" asked Terry.

It was a question Lenny had been both expecting and dreading.

"Strangled, boss," he began. Lenny spoke with no fear or hesitation. He gave it to Terry straight. "Steel wire around his neck. It would have been quick."

Terry nodded and pondered on how his son might have looked in that moment. Then he wondered why he hadn't fought back. It wasn't as if Bradley was a pushover. He could look after himself.

"Was it a professional, Lenny?" asked Terry.

"It looks like it. No prints. No sign of anyone. No evidence."

"Who found him? Who else knows?"

"The woman who opens the yard saw him when she walked in. He was hanging from the hoist by a chain. So all the girls at the yard know. They've been told not to shout about it. Police closed the scene off pretty quick so no-one else got a look in."

"Any ideas about who it might be?"

"None, boss," replied Lenny. "Do you want me to put the feelers out?"

Terry nodded. "If you find him, Lenny, I want him alive. Make sure the boys know that this one is mine." He paused and fought to control his wavering voice. "Thanks, Lenny. Can you give me a bit? I need some time alone."

CHAPTER SEVEN

FOR HARVEY, THE DRIVE TO JOHN CARTWRIGHT'S OFFICE in nearby Chigwell was mostly country lanes free of traffic. John was originally from neither Chigwell nor Theydon Bois. But that part of Essex was, in his foster father's words, "*An affluent area where people aren't afraid to splash the cash.*" It was an ideal location for a man whose primary business required a legitimate way of cleaning up money.

John had several bars in various parts of London, and he even owned a little country pub on the South Coast that he visited every few months. John enjoyed the lord-like welcome he received when he arrived there with his flavour of the month, which usually came in the form of a blond half his age with a coke habit.

Harvey opened the door without knocking and walked into John's office.

"Alright, Son? Take a seat," said John.

Only three people were allowed to enter the office unannounced.

The first was Sergio, who acted as an adviser to the family. He kept the books and was often the face of the firm in their more legitimate business dealings. Occupying the office next door, Sergio typically used the no-knock rule because he was in and out of John's office all day. It was practical.

The second person was Donny, Harvey's foster brother. Donny worked in John's bars and kept the businesses running on the ground. He entered without knocking, not because his office was close by, but just because he could. It was a display of power in front of John's staff. And it fed Donny's ego.

Harvey didn't knock because he refused to feed people's egos, no matter who they were.

Hearing Harvey arrive, Sergio stepped out of his office into John's, settling into a seat at the side of the room with his laptop. Sergio was a lean man, bordering skinny, of Eastern European descent. His taste for immaculately crafted, tailor-made suits and fine Italian shoes gave off a strong impression. But it was countered by his small frame and spineless whisperings into John's ear. He also had a knack for knowing everything. By placing himself in the middle of any conversation, he guided the firm, whereas John only told it where to go. Sergio was the only one who had the power to coerce John into his way of thinking. John trusted him, as did the other, more silent, partners. He was a safe pair of hands with a massively intelligent head on his shoulders. Sergio was a strategist.

And Harvey loathed him.

Unlike the bar staff, managers, heavies and runners that all worked for John, it was only Harvey who *openly* detested Sergio. There were many who distrusted him, but Harvey had grown to hate the man. He had been around ever since Harvey was a child, always there in the background, sneaking around, whispering and manipulating.

Sergio always kept a sly and watchful eye on Harvey. Harvey couldn't explain his feeling. It was more of a gut instinct than a tangible reasoning. But Sergio shrank when

Harvey was around. He averted his eyes as if Harvey could see what he was thinking. That was what bothered Harvey the most; he was always planning.

"Did it go alright? Were there any problems?" Sergio asked Harvey with a little cock of his head.

"No problems. It was easy. In and out," replied Harvey without looking at him.

"Good, and what about the truck?" asked Sergio.

"It was loaded up and driven off. No questions. Two blokes drove off in it. I didn't see their faces," said Harvey.

"Perfect. And did you-"

"Make a statement, Sergio?" finished Harvey. "We did what we could with the resources available to us." Harvey continued to stare at John but could feel Sergio's eyes boring into him.

"There may be some backlash coming from this," warned Sergio. "It'll get noisy before it gets quiet. But not until after the funeral. We should be ready."

"It'll get noisy before it gets quiet? You just started a *war*," said Harvey. He was unable to look in Sergio's direction. Instead, Harvey looked up at the ceiling and took a deep breath, sensing the confusion growing on his foster father's face. "What do you think the Thomsons are going to do now? They're not going to sit on their backsides feeling sorry for themselves. They'll be planning a genocide and they certainly won't wait until after the funeral."

"Sergio, what exactly did you ask Harvey and Julios to do?" asked John, leaning forward. John sat in a large, leather, reclining office chair, and he commanded the room.

"You mean *you* don't know?" asked Harvey.

"Exactly what I told you, John," said Sergio. "We took care of one of Thomson's men. We need them busy. We need them distracted while we-"

"You *don't* know, do you?" said Harvey to John, cutting off Sergio.

"Someone is going to tell me in the next three seconds," John replied, his eyes widening. John kept his cool, a trait for which he was notorious. But he looked between the two men with a rage growing behind his calm exterior.

"My contacts assure me that Terry Thomson will be far too distraught to continue pursuing any other job while he is in mourn-"

"The man is a cold-blooded killer and a businessman, Sergio." The weak justification from Sergio for killing a powerful man like Bradley Thomson was too much for Harvey. "You could set Terry Thomson's mother on fire, and he'd still make time to shove your head up your backside *and* see that your family were all strung up by their balls before he even threw a bucket of water over her. You don't understand these people, Sergio. Why don't you go back to your office and do a spreadsheet or whatever the hell it is you do."

"Let me finish," said Sergio, his voice rising in pitch. "My contacts assure me that the family will be too busy running their legitimate businesses to even consider organising a job as big as the northern job."

"What northern job?" asked Harvey.

John slammed his hand down on his desk. The room fell silent, but his voice remained low and calm. "I want to know who it was we killed last night."

Harvey turned away.

Sergio looked defeated.

"It was Bradley," he said quietly.

"*Bradley Thomson?*" John said calmly.

He lifted the papers from his desk and straightened them before creating a neat pile on the corner of the table. He turned in his chair and looked out of the floor-to-ceiling window at the traffic on the street below. Average people driving average cars to average jobs.

"Sergio, leave the room, please. We'll discuss this later." John remained facing the window while Sergio stood and opened the door. But his voice betrayed the anger that was building inside. "Sergio?"

Sergio turned to face John but kept his head lowered like a scolded child.

"Get Donny to up the security on the bars. I imagine Thomson will be looking for blood. But he might decide to hurt my pocket before the bloodbath starts."

When the door was pulled closed, John turned back to face Harvey.

"I thought you'd know," said Harvey. "Sergio said it was all part of a plan."

"It's not your fault, Son. But you're right. Thomson is going be spitting fire right now, and we need to be crystal on what we're going to do about it."

"We?" asked Harvey. "I'd say that was a job for Sergio. *He* spilt the milk."

The two men locked stares until John broke away. Although his foster father held the power, Harvey was resolute and had no qualms about voicing his opinion, especially against Sergio.

"Listen, Harvey, there's something we need to take care of later this week," said John. His voice had dropped to a gravelly whisper. "It's an important job, but in light of all this, it'll be dangerous. I don't want to talk about it here, but you and Julios are going to have to handle it after Sergio's cock up."

John Cartwright always spoke about problems using the words '*we*' and '*us*,' but Harvey didn't pay any attention to it. It was just his foster father's way of trying to make Harvey feel included in the family business so that he might one day take on more of a leadership role. This was despite Harvey's attempts to remove himself as much as possible.

"Why don't you come over and have dinner with your old man? We can talk about it at home," said John.

"I have plans this afternoon," replied Harvey.

He felt the beast stir inside him at the thought.

"What plans?" asked John.

Harvey didn't reply.

"Shall we say eight o'clock then?" John asked cheerfully as Harvey stood to leave.

There was no point in nodding or agreeing. It wasn't an optional invitation; it was a decision made by his foster father with an informal agreement. Disobeying the instruction would have consequences. Harvey didn't care much for consequences. But he played along with John's games for an easy life.

Harvey respected the old man and admired his control. Deep down, Harvey loved him in his own kind of way. But their relationship was soured by a deep mistrust rooted in the past. It was clear to Harvey that John knew more than he let on. Whenever Harvey raised the topic of Hannah's death or his real parents, the same old story was recited, verbatim. John made no attempt to embellish it or make it believable. He just expected Harvey to carry on as usual. But Harvey could never be sure if the truth was hidden for his own protection or reasons John would rather forget. After all, John had raised Harvey and Hannah as his own, and Harvey wasn't blind to the affection in John's eyes.

It was the affection in John's eyes that had fuelled the rift between Harvey and Donny, his foster brother. Harvey had been twelve years old when his sister, Hannah, had killed herself, leaving Harvey alone and a target of John's attention. But John was a busy man. He'd had only so many hours in the day to dote on his kids, and Harvey started to get the lion's share of the two boys.

Donny had noticed the favouritism, and as siblings often do, he soon began an onslaught of sly attacks on his younger brother. Spitting in his dinner, pushing him down the stairs and locking him in the dark attic were all common occurrences. The incidents were small and Harvey grew resilient to them. But over time, the attacks built up to a mutual hatred. Then Harvey grew wiser and stronger, and with Julios' training, he put Donny in his place several times.

Since those days, it was rare that Harvey and Donny were in the same room. Donny, like Sergio, carried a look of fear in his weak eyes and had a knack for keeping away from Harvey. He preferred instead to enjoy his father's wealth and power with cocaine-fuelled nights in his bars with random women by his side.

Harvey left the first-floor office via the metal steps that led out the back of the building. He walked around the side street where his bike was parked and strode through the alleyway, staying close to the fence. It was another of Julios' rules: never create a pattern, never leave a trail, and never let *anybody* get one step ahead of you.

As he swung his leg over his bike, Harvey glanced up at the rear of the building and found Sergio staring back at him from his office window. Even from a distance, Harvey could see a wry smile on his face. Julios' words of advice played on repeat in Harvey's mind.

Sergio was one step ahead.

CHAPTER EIGHT

John Cartwright sat at his desk thinking about Terry Thomson's possible reactions. There was a light knock at the door. It was Sergio's knock. He only knocked when John was angry.

"Enter," said John. He sat up in his chair and straightened the papers on his desk. "Sergio, what's the news?"

John's mood had quietened enough for the monotonous weekly financial report. It was a sly way for Sergio to justify his worth in light of his recent mistake.

"Hello, John," said Sergio, hiding behind the door. "I have the weekly financial reports for you. Do you have time right now?"

The short time alone had given John time to think. Sergio had known John would be fearful of a war with the Thomsons and would have vetoed the hit on Bradley. But John also understood that the distraction was the best way of getting the Thomsons out of the northern job, leaving them to only deal with Stimson. The diamonds from the northern job were Sergio's key to success, and if it went wrong, it was his neck on the line.

"Is it that time already, Sergio?" replied John

He reached for his desk phone and asked his assistant to bring through two coffees. John eyed the tall, lean man in front of him whose long, bony fingers held the printed copies of the firm's financial reports, both the legitimate and the not-so-legitimate. His gaunt face was clean shaven with pale skin that stretched across high cheekbones, and his large Romany nose held thick-rimmed glasses that magnified his permanently bloodshot eyes.

"Okay, so let's start with the BVI report," began Sergio.

His faint Eastern European accent added a little romance to the otherwise dull conversation that was about to ensue. The British Virgin Islands report was a holistic view of the legitimate businesses that were grouped under a BVI holding company, which, being tax exempt, saved John thousands each year.

"We transferred clean assets-"

"Where's Donny?" John interrupted.

Sergio paused. "I haven't seen him since we landed from our trip."

"I want him to be here for the weekly reports. He needs to know what's going on. Does he even know you're here?" As he spoke, John was reaching for the desk phone. "Get me Donny, please. Call back is fine."

"You would like me to wait, John?" asked Sergio.

The door opened and John's assistant walked in with a tray holding two espressos in small cups sat atop two large saucers, each with an expensive-looking Italian biscuit on the side. They were a touch previously added by Sergio, and a sign of his impeccable taste.

"Thank you, May," said John as the door closed. "No, Sergio. Give me the BVI report then wait for Donny to give the rest."

"Okay. So July saw a ten percent-"

The desk phone rang. John answered and was connected to Donny by May.

"Where are you, Son?"

"I'm in Wembley, Dad. Just doing an audit of the stock here. Sergio gave me a heads-up that an FSA inspection is likely."

John was used to the Food Standards Agency showing up unannounced.

"Did Sergio also give you a heads-up that today was report day? And is that why you decided to saunter off to the other side of London? Sergio is here now. Why don't you come join us? You are, after all, the operations manager."

"What about the inspection?"

"You earned five hundred grand last year, Son. Did you earn that by counting bottles and frozen burgers or by making sure the fire extinguishers work? No. You earned it by making sure the business is profitable. I'll see you in less than an hour."

John replaced the handset and gestured for Sergio to continue.

"Okay. We transferred everything we could off-shore, but we still have the clean-"

The phone rang again. John answered.

"There's a gentleman on the line who would like to talk with you."

"Who is it, May?"

"I'm afraid he wouldn't give a name. But he said you'd be keen to hear from him."

"Alright. Put him through."

John motioned for Sergio to hold on and pushed the loud-speaker button. Sergio sank back in his chair, crossed his legs, and unlocked his phone. He tapped on the screen while John spoke, but he listened carefully. He always listened carefully.

"Cartwright," said John cautiously.

"The one and only John Cartwright?" On the other end of the line, the gravelly voice hinted at humour but the tone was far from it.

"That must be the one and only Terry Thomson. To what do I owe the pleasure?"

"Well, you know how it is, John. We're in the same game. I thought I'd give you a call and see how business is going."

"No, Terry. I don't know how it is. We seem to of managed to get this far without standing on each other's toes. Why change all that now?"

"Are you planning something, John? Be straight with me."

"The only thing I'm planning on doing, Terry, is putting the phone down and getting on with my busy day. Take care, Mr Thomson."

"Hang on, hang on," said Terry, the urgency in his voice betraying a momentary lapse of dignity and composure. "Are you there, John?"

"Yeah, I am."

"He's gone, John," said Terry. "Bradley. Did you hear?"

John waited a few seconds as if in shock. He sat back in his chair, lifted his feet to the edge of his desk, and closed his eyes, imagining Terry and the pain of his lifelong enemy. "No, Terry. I didn't hear."

"John, I've got to ask." Terry's voice was clear and strong but wounded. "Was it your lot? Cause if it weren't then it could only be one other firm, and this isn't their style."

"I'm going to be polite given the circumstance, Terry. But don't you ever dare to ask me that question again. I'll ask the boys to keep their ears to the ground. If I hear anything, you'll be the first to know."

John disconnected the call

"He fell for it?" asked Sergio.

"He did. Well, for your sake, Sergio, I hope he did."

CHAPTER NINE

TERRY THOMSON DISCONNECTED THE CALL AND SAT staring at the phone.

"Lying bastard," he said to the empty room.

He snatched open the top drawer of his desk and lifted the false bottom up to reveal his SIG Sauer P226. It was tucked neatly into a custom-made, felt-lined panel. He slid the handgun from where it had sat untouched for over a year, released the magazine to check it wasn't loaded, and slotted it back into place with a click. Sliding back the action, he looked inside the empty chamber then laid the handgun on his desk and placed his hands in front of him. He closed his eyes and breathed, slow and deep, controlling the whirlwind of scenarios that rushed through his mind. But each time he slowed his thoughts, a picture of Bradley came into view and his anger soared once more.

His meditation was disturbed by a gentle knock at the door. He wasn't in the mood for company, conversation or consolation and ignored the disruption, preferring silence so he could think about possible suspects and reasons for them to do this to him. It was, after all, an attack on him, even if he hadn't been the target. Bradley had been his eldest child and the only son in the business. Terry's other son, Spencer, had chosen to live a normal life removed from the money, adrenaline and risk, a normal life where paying off the police and putting hits on other families weren't topics of discussion over breakfast.

Terry would need to call Spencer and tell him the bad news about his brother. He hadn't spoken to him in years. Last time, their father and son chat had ended in a heated exchange of spiteful words, slammed car doors and unanswered calls. Terry had given up after several weeks of persistent attempts. Gradually, they'd drifted apart. He didn't even know where his son was now. But Lenny might. They had been fairly close when the boys were younger. He'd ask Lenny.

As if on cue, there was another gentle knock at the door.

"Who is it?" called Terry.

"It's Lenny, Terry. Just seeing if you're okay. Do you want a cup of tea or something?"

"Come in, Len, will you?"

Terry picked up his handgun once more and began to imagine a faceless man beaten beyond recognition, on his knees and crying for mercy with the muzzle of the Sig between his teeth. Somewhere close by, the door opened and closed, and Lenny sat in the chair opposite Terry.

"What is it, boss?" asked Lenny, snapping Terry from his distant musings on murder.

"Why would somebody kill *Bradley*? Why now?"

"We're trying to find out, Terry," said Lenny. "Honest, mate. I've got all the boys on it."

"What about the guns?"

"We're off-loading half of them to Cartwright in a couple of days. We were going to use the rest for the northern job then ditch them when we're done."

Terry nodded his slow, contemplative nod as he aimed along the barrel of his SIG at a small mark on the wall.

"Killing a man's son is something somebody does to initiate a war, Lenny," said Terry. "Any man worth his salt does not kill a man's flesh and blood as a mere distraction."

"Agreed, Terry."

"And we have to remember that Stimson is not a killer." Terry raised his index finger as if to support the statement.

"Unless that was the point, Terry," said Lenny.

"What do you mean?"

"Well, we're selling Cartwright a dozen MP5s in a couple of days. Why would he hit us so close to a deal?"

"That's what I was wondering," said Terry.

"So if Stimson thinks that all eyes would be on Cartwright because he's the obvious suspect, that would leave Stimson free to go and do the northern job."

"I see. Smart thinking, Lenny," said Terry. He sat back in his chair and let the weight of his head fall onto the headrest. "So you think Stimson *was* trying to start a war between us and the Cartwrights?"

"He must be," said Lenny.

"Smart bastard," replied Terry.

The theory did make perfect sense. Cartwright was supposed to be buying twelve Heckler and Koch MP5s from Terry later that week. There was no way John Cartwright would kill Bradley before they did a deal.

"John Cartwright and I weren't always enemies, you know?" said Terry. "We've always run our own firms and didn't always see eye to eye, but in the beginning, we weren't at war. He kept to his turf. I kept to mine. There was an understanding."

"So what happened?" asked Lenny.

Terry exhaled, long and slow.

"The usual," he replied. "Greed, I guess. He got in my way.

I got in his way. It was the eighties. Gang wars were kicking off all over the place. But before that, we'd trade all the time. He sold me a box of shotguns once in return for some inside information on a job he was planning."

"What's he like then?"

"He's as hard as they come and smarter than most," replied Terry. "The only thing he lacks is vision. That's why he still run bars and pubs. The real money is in the clubs. Everyone knows that."

"So why now?" asked Lenny. "Why is he buying guns from us now?"

"I wanted to see if he was planning the northern job, Lenny. A mutual friend of ours set it up for me. See, I knew that if I offered John Cartwright twelve of our lovely MP5s at a higher than average price, he'd be planning the northern job."

"But how does that help us, Terry?" asked Lenny. "I mean, if we sell Cartwright the guns, he'll be just as well equipped to do the job as us."

"Do you know how many years you'd get for possession of twelve automatic weapons, Lenny?"

"You're setting them up?" said Lenny with a smile and laughed out loud at the plan.

"Having them buy the guns from me was the only way I could be sure of them being in a certain place at a certain time with a box of guns. It's not rocket science, Lenny," said Terry, staring at the ceiling, pleased with his plan.

"What do you want to do now then?" asked Lenny, once more dragging Terry out of his own thoughts.

"Well, we can go back and forth like this all night, Lenny, and neither one of us can do anything but speculate, can we?"

"Not really, no, Terry. It could've been Stimson or Cartwright. They both have the method, means and motive."

"Right then," said Terry, pushing himself out of his chair.

He stepped to one side to view himself in the full-length mirror fixed to the wall beside the window then straightened his suit, admiring the contrast between his tan and the whiter-than-white shirt. "So there's only one thing we can do, isn't there, Lenny?"

"What's that, boss?"

Terry turned to face the much-younger man, adjusted his cuffs and collected the gun from the desk.

"We'll kill the bleeding pair of them. One of them wanted a war, and a war is what they'll get. If we don't retaliate, we'll be seen as weak."

He turned back to the mirror and continued to admire his reflection, now with the addition of the SIG.

"And Terry Thomson is not weak."

"What about the guns?" asked Lenny, recognising the fire in his boss' eyes.

"Here's what's going to happen. Step one, find me Donny Cartwright. Take him down and make it public. Make a mess but make sure he's recognisable. As long as John Cartwright denies the hit on Bradley, I'll deny the hit on Donny. It'll be a stalemate."

"Right."

But Lenny was a little unsure of the move.

"Step two, the gun deal is still on. John Cartwright won't back down. I know him. He'll send his best men and they'll want to take us out at the deal. If they do, we'll be ready. I've got just the man up my sleeve."

"What about Stimson?" asked Lenny.

"We won't see Stimson until the diamonds are in Britain. No doubt, he'll dig a tunnel or do something extravagant to steal them. And when he comes out, we'll be standing right there with twelve lovely MP5s ready to take those nice shiny diamonds off him, won't we? That's step three."

"That's a big risk, Terry," said Lenny. "Cartwright's men are pretty heavy."

"What are you saying? Don't you want the job, Lenny?"

"I'm not saying that at all. But if me and Rob get hit, the firm gets an awful lot smaller."

"I trust you, Lenny, and I trust Rob. That's why I'm sending you."

"What about if we had a driver? I'd manage him. All he'd have to do is drive the van, give them the guns and take the cash. If he doesn't get shot, he's a lucky boy. If he does, well, we'll still have twelve MP5s to do the northern job. Plus John Cartwright would have just started the war by openly killing our man."

"Kind of like a fall guy, you mean?" said Terry. "Expendable?"

"Yeah. Rob and I will be close by to see it all go down, but far enough away to survive."

"I like it," said Terry. "Who do you have in mind?"

"I'll find someone expendable. Who do *you* have in mind to take care of the Cartwrights?"

"Like I said, Lenny, I know just the man for the job." Once again, Terry sighted the mark on the wall along the stubby barrel of his SIG. "How about that cup of tea? I'm suddenly feeling quite rejuvenated."

Supportive to the core, Lenny nodded at the master plan and headed for the door to the kitchen. Terry checked he was out of earshot then picked up his phone and dialled a number from memory. It was a number he hadn't dialled for a very long time.

"Frank, my old friend, how have you been?"

CHAPTER TEN

"THERE'S BEEN A TOTAL OF FOUR DEATHS BY GARROTTING IN London during the past year, sir," said Mills. "Only one of the cases is closed and the suspect is currently serving fifteen years in Belmarsh."

"And the other three?" asked Frank.

"Unsolved, sir. Gang crime. Lots of tight lips and fat wallets."

"What about the motorbike? Did we find anything?"

"We did, sir," said Melody. But her tone had shifted; her competence had faded to insecurity.

"Go on, Mills."

"We matched the tyre tread to three unsolved murders."

"So that's good news," said Frank. "We have a lead?"

"Not so good, sir. We've been hunting the killer for more than a decade."

"What do we know about him?" asked Frank, intrigued by the potential new challenge.

"All we know is that he targets sex offenders."

"A vigilante?" said Frank.

"This is no ordinary vigilante, sir," continued Mills. "The man is sick."

"Dying sick?"

Mills shook her head.

"Twisted sick, sir. The cases were never made public. The top brass was worried the locals would support the killer if they found out. They'd give him a name and then, of course, the copycats would come out of the woodwork."

"So you're telling me there's some psycho out there murdering sex offenders and nobody is doing anything about it? How do we know it's the same guy?"

Mills hesitated then passed Frank a blue file. Inside were photographs printed on eight-by-six photo paper. The first showed the remains of a man lying on a forest floor with only stumps where his limbs had been. His remaining skin was charred beyond recognition. The second photo showed the peeled face of a skinless man.

Frank snapped the folder shut and passed it back to Mills.

"He's sick alright."

"Psychologist's report classes him as a primary psychopath. He'll exhibit no emotion and won't respond to punishment, possibly as the result of child abuse or traumatisation. He most likely grew up in a violent household. He's deeply scarred, sir."

"Aren't we all, Mills?" said Frank. But the look on Mills' face discouraged Frank's flippant response. "And we think this man killed Bradley Thomson, do we?"

"Can I be honest, sir?"

"Of course."

"I hope not. I really do."

The fear in Mills' eyes added a heavy sincerity to her words. But their shared moment was cut short by the flashing screen of Frank's phone, which began to vibrate on his desk.

"Would you excuse me?" said Frank. As she was closing the door, he called out to her. "Mills?"

"Sir?" she said, half in and half out of his office.

"Good work."

"Thank you, sir," she replied, and closed the door.

Frank hit the green button to answer the call.

"Carver."

"Frank, my old friend, how have you been?"

"I wondered when you'd call," replied Frank, feeling a wave of nausea wash over him.

"Yeah, well, it's been a bit busy. You know how it is, Frank," replied Terry. His thick East London accent suited his gruff tone, but somehow, he still managed to sound clear and articulate. "I've got a job for you."

"A job?" said Frank. "And what makes you think I'm for hire?"

"Well, Frank, there's still the matter of your little debt, and I know exactly how you can repay me."

"I repaid that debt a long time ago."

"You repaid nothing, Frank," said Terry. "I'll tell you when the debt is paid."

Frank was silent.

"Yeah. You remember, don't you?"

"It's been over a year, Terry."

"And now your time has come. I always knew you'd come in handy one day, Frank."

"What's the job?"

"Babysitter," said Terry.

"I'm a little long in the tooth for babysitting."

"Well, it's a little more than that if I'm being honest."

"Spit it out, Terry. I'm a busy man."

"I'm doing a deal. I want you to make sure it goes smooth and my boys don't get hurt."

"Where's the deal?" asked Frank.

"In the sticks somewhere. I'll have someone send you the location. It'll be discreet."

"What's the deal?"

"It's a box, Frank. Do you need to know any more than that?" said Terry.

"Who's the buyer?"

"That's a bit direct, Frank."

"Should I fluff it up a little for you?" asked Frank. "You want me to stroke your ego, Terry?"

"Why do you want to know who the buyer is?"

"Self-preservation, Terry."

"Self-preservation, Frank?"

"Self-preservation. If you tell me the buyers are three little old ladies, I'll know where I stand. But if you tell me you're doing a deal with the Essex arm of ISIS, then I might need to adjust my approach."

"It's neither."

"I was hoping for old ladies."

"You like old ladies, Frank?"

"They make good tea, Terry."

"It's not old ladies, Frank."

"So no tea then?"

"No tea."

"Are you going to tell me?" asked Frank. "You've built it up now."

"Did I build it up or did you?" replied Terry. "I recall it was you that asked the question, Frank."

"And it's you who's been avoiding the answer."

"Cartwright."

"John Cartwright?" Frank sat forward in his chair and lowered his voice. "Are you crazy?"

"The one and only. Feel better?"

"Well, I know where I stand. That's all I wanted." Frank paused. "Terry?"

"Yes, Frank."

"This is the last time. I've repaid the debt."

"Are you severing our relationship, Frank?"

"No, not severing. But I won't be in your pocket after this one."

"One of my men took the rap for you if you remember, Carver. You don't get to make demands."

"It's been long enough," said Frank. "I'm retiring soon. I'd like to actually live that long."

Terry was quiet for a moment.

"Alright, Frank. I understand."

"You do?" said Frank.

"Yeah, of course. I'd like to put my feet up one day myself."

His feet had never been down in the first place, thought Frank.

"Course, there's a price to pay for that kind of freedom," said Terry.

"A price?"

"For freedom."

"Is that right?"

Here it comes, thought Frank.

"That's the rules," said Terry. "How badly do you want to retire?"

"Don't play games, Terry. Spit it out."

"I suppose you know already, don't you?"

"Depends on what it is you suppose I already know, Terry."

"Bradley. My boy."

"What about him?"

"He was hit, Frank. Did you know?"

Terry paused to listen to Frank's reaction.

"No," Frank lied.

"Adam Stimson got him."

"You sure about that, Terry?" asked Frank. "That doesn't sound like Stimson's style."

"You came to that conclusion quickly, Frank. Sounds like you already gave it some thought."

"It's my job to see through the crap, Terry. I'm sorry to hear about it, anyway."

"Yeah, well. It doesn't end here."

"And this is where I come in, is it?" asked Frank.

"When the deal is done, I want you to off the Cartwrights."

"You want me to what?" Frank stopped himself from shouting it aloud and whispered into the phone, "You want me to kill John Cartwright? Are you insane?"

"Careful, Frank. We're friends but let's not throw insults around."

"We're not friends, Terry. We're two people on two very different paths if that's what you think I'm going to do."

"I don't need you to off John himself. But I do need his men sorted out. Just whoever turns up at the gun deal. My man gives them the guns. Their man gives my man the money. My guy drives off. You take the Cartwrights down. Plus, as a sweetener, you get to keep the guns. I imagine there's a whole team of you somewhere searching for them."

"So it's guns, is it?" said Frank.

"A box of them, Frank."

"And why do you have a big box of guns? You're planning a job, aren't you?"

"Our relationship doesn't go quite that far, Frank. Let's stay on track, shall we?"

"You make it sound so easy," said Frank. "But I thought you said it was Adam Stimson's boys that got to Bradley?"

"Well it's not rocket science, is it?" said Terry. "Stimson's trying to start a war, and Cartwright's buying my guns because he wants to play with the big boys."

"So you take out the Cartwrights and Stimson thinks you fell for it."

"You're learning."

"Meanwhile, Cartwright doesn't interfere in the job you're planning, and Stimson walks right into your hands."

"Everyone's a winner, Frank," said Terry. "Well, everyone that counts."

"Right."

"You know what to do, Frank?"

"I do now. Then we're done. That's it. This is over."

"Oh, Frank, I nearly forgot."

Terry wanted to add a final power play.

"What is it, Terry?"

"Don't try anything stupid."

"Of course not," said Frank.

But Terry had already hung up.

CHAPTER ELEVEN

In an interview room at Potters Bar police station in North London, Shaun Tyson held his hands out. A begrudging officer removed his handcuffs with a stony expression and rough manner that did little to mask his opinion of Shaun. As Shaun rubbed at the red marks on his wrists, he was led to a small stack of blue, yellow and white papers on the desk of the duty officer. A pen attached to a curled flexible cord was dropped beside them.

Three stars had been made beside the areas where Shaun was to sign. But he received no verbal instruction. Hate-filled eyes stabbed at his conscience from all corners of the room. The officer behind the duty counter, two more behind a meshed security, and another tall, dark officer were all watching him with silent loathing.

The conditional release form was justified in blue handwriting. It agreed that Shaun's court date was pending and insufficient evidence prohibited him from being detained any longer. But Shaun knew it wouldn't be long before the court heard what they needed to hear. The idea of a grim-faced judge slamming his hammer played over in his mind as Shaun signed his name with an unsteady hand.

"We'll be in touch, Mr Tyson."

The officer punched in a security code and shoved open the heavy door when its magnetic release sounded. The loud, buzzing alarm caught the attention of the few people waiting in a row of blue, plastic reception chairs.

"Mr Tyson?"

Shaun turned and stared up at the officer holding the door.

"I'd advise you to get yourself home as quick as you can."

He'd been locked up long enough for word to spread. His face had no doubt been on the local news. All it would take was for one angry local to recognise him and start an onslaught of retribution.

"Yes," he replied. "Thank you."

The cold afternoon and a heightened sense of fear sent a shiver through Shaun's core. His rapid heartbeat brought a thin layer of sweat to his pores, which caught the sharp wind and stiffened his shaking limbs. He pulled the hood of his sweatshirt up and around his face, both for warmth and to avoid recognition.

A small group of teenagers ambled past. They smoked cigarettes and laughed the loud, uncaring laughs of youths with nothing to fear. One of them glanced back at Shaun, catching his eye. But the look was fleeting and Shaun hoped he hadn't been recognised.

A steady stream of traffic passed left and right on the main road. But Shaun noticed a static shape among the movement. One hundred yards away on the far side of the street, parked beside an old, black taxi, a man was sitting on a motorcycle dressed in a black leather jacket and staring directly at Shaun. A curl of faint, grey smoke was hanging in the air beside the bike's exhaust. With one gloved hand, the rider lowered down his black visor.

The three teenagers who had passed him stopped further down the road. They huddled together as if in conference and stared back at Shaun, whose heart was working overtime. Inside the pockets of his hooded sweatshirt, his long fingers rubbed his sweaty palms with anxiety.

Shaun glanced back across the road at the rider, but he was gone. He searched the traffic left and right, but there was no sign of the bike. There were no exhaust fumes. No man in black was anywhere to be seen.

The teenagers began to walk towards Shaun, slowly at first. But it was enough for Shaun to start moving. He turned left, kept his head down, and worked out what route he would take to get home. A network of back alleys could be reached from the next side street. As he turned, he glanced back at the teenagers. They had quickened their pace. One of them was using his phone, maybe calling his friends.

With the empty side street ahead of him, Shaun started to run.

The fear that coursed through his body had taken control of his legs, slowing him. No matter how hard he pushed, his legs felt alien. He glanced back. The teenagers were running too, and they were fast. Shaun searched the road ahead, seeking an exit. Two more youths had turned into the street and were pointing at Shaun from just three hundred yards away. He looked back once more, but stumbled, fell and rolled onto the ground. It was just like a dream he'd had the previous night in the police cell.

He closed his eyes, preparing himself for the inevitable beating. But as the footsteps thundered closer and his heart beat like a drum, the growl of an engine came to a stop beside where he lay curled up in a ball.

"Get in," said a voice.

Shaun opened his eyes and found a white unmarked van parked in the road beside where he was standing. The side door was open.

"No," said Shaun. "No, please."

He scurried away from the road. The teenagers were closing in from both sides. The van was in front. It was over. A loud sob rose from his stomach and fell from his lips. It was like no other sound he'd ever made before.

"Get in the van, Shaun," said the man again. Shaun looked back at the running teenagers. "Seriously, mate, I won't ask you again. Get in the van. You've got about ten seconds." The man's voice was growing agitated.

"Who are you? How do you know my name? You can't expect me to just climb into the back of a van," said Shaun. His voice was high and loud. Maybe a neighbour would hear it and help him.

"Shaun, we are here to *stop* you getting into any more trouble. Do you *know* what those boys are going to do to you?"

Shaun nodded.

"Do you want help?"

Another nod and a flash of hope, warm and bright.

"So get in the van."

The man wound up his window as a sign that the discussion was over. The two groups of boys were closing in on either side, sprinting towards Shaun. It was now or never.

Three steps on shaky legs and Shaun fell into the back of the van. He dropped to the wooden floor in a corner and curled up, ready for the blows. But instead, the side door was slammed shut and the loud diesel engine roared into life, low and angry above the shouts of the teenagers, who had missed their target by just a few seconds. A few hurled stones at the sides of the van, but the driver didn't slow.

The pitch darkness in the rear cargo area offered a space of relief and calm. Shaun found a wheel arch to sit on and allowed his racing heart to wind down. Out of the frying pan and into the fire, he thought to himself.

The journey seemed endless, but at least the driving was calm. There were no sudden turns and only gentle braking. Imagining the network of roads, Shaun tried to guess where they were taking him, but small turns here and there blurred his imagination. Then they hit the M25 motorway and the back of the van filled with the grumble of the diesel engine and the incessant rumble of the road.

Shaun had spent more than an hour sitting alone in the darkness with his thoughts, regrets and wild imagination when the van slowed and pulled off the motorway. Then the turns were tighter and sharper and the hills were more defined. A part of Shaun, the coward that tugged at his heart and fed his mind with possibilities, hoped the journey would last longer, maybe forever. He was safe in the van. Nobody could touch him, and he could touch nobody.

But after a few more minutes of winding roads, Shaun felt the van slow once more. It then turned onto a bumpy surface where it finally shuddered to a stop.

The silence was agonising.

Once again, Shaun's tired heart started to beat wildly. The layer of sweat resumed its position on the palms of his hands and under his arms. He could smell himself. It was as if his carnal senses were heightened like that of a deer circled by wolves. He smelt the oily odour of diesel, the grain of the van's wooden floor, and most of all, the steely scent of his own fear.

Bright light filled the van as the door screeched open, breaking the security of silence.

"Out," said the dark silhouette of the man.

Shaun hesitated, afraid to move.

"Are you deaf or something? *Out!*"

Shaun heard the driver call from the other side of the van, "Come on, Lenny. What are you playing at?"

"It's not *me*. I can't get *him* out of the van. It took him bleeding long enough to get in and now he won't get out."

"Well tell him he can sleep in there if he wants. Or he can come inside and have a nice cup of tea."

The man at the door spoke quietly. Shaun's eyes were beginning to adjust to the light so he could see the man's face more clearly.

"Mate, we're not going to hurt you. We're going to help you. Trust me."

The man offered out his hand to help Shaun.

"Come on."

And then it came. Like a pressure valve releasing a cloud of angry steam into the atmosphere, all his hopes, prayers, and desperate clutches to possibilities succumbed to the bitter reality that there was no escape. Then it faded, leaving Shaun with a single choice.

He pushed himself to his feet with trepidation and dropped down onto the gravel. Unsteady on his shaking legs, he held onto the door and took in his surroundings.

"Where are we?" he asked, his voice more of a breath than a vocalised sound.

"You'll see. This way."

The man slammed the van door and headed towards a single-floor building. It was the right-most of three structures that had been built in a crude C-shape to form a courtyard. The centre building appeared to be an old farmhouse with two floors and eight large windows. The left-side building was a double garage.

"Come on, Shaun," called the man from the door of the building.

"I'm coming," said Shaun.

He allowed himself one more look at the endless sky above.

"I'm ready," he whispered to himself.

CHAPTER TWELVE

From the top of the hill, surrounded by fields and trees, Harvey watched the white van take a left turn off the quiet country lane. The driver slowed and pulled into the grounds of the only building in sight, which was an old farmhouse. Harvey killed the bike's engine and removed his helmet as Shaun Tyson was led from the van into the building on the right. It looked like a small barn that had been converted into living space or offices. Across the open fields, the sound of the slamming sliding door disturbed a few birds that took to the air. They circled once and then returned to the ground to nest or feed when the silence of nature resumed.

The autumn day was drawing to a close. The temperature was already dropping and long shadows of the bare trees reached across the fields like long fingers searching for warmth. A small gap in the hedgerow to Harvey's right opened onto a patch of mud beneath an elm tree. It was the perfect place to store his bike and wait for darkness while watching for movement in the farmhouse.

As time went by, lights from the building flicked on,

lighting the courtyard. Two men carried a large wooden crate from the van to the open garage. But Shaun Tyson was nowhere to be seen.

When darkness had fallen, Harvey made his way along the lane at the top of the hill to gain a better view of the small development. He passed the turning that led down the hill and continued on straight to see the rear of the house where a ten-foot brick wall and tall conifer trees blocked any view. But Harvey saw a single light shining in the rear garden.

The house backed onto fields, which may or may not have belonged to the property. It was common for small plots of farming land to be sold off. With no farming machinery in view or space to keep it, Harvey assumed the small plot of land was isolated. Keeping to the edges of the field and the clumps of grass alongside a drainage ditch, Harvey made his way to the rear of the house. Two large gates were locked with a chain.

He pushed on one of the gates and it opened to the extent of the chain. It allowed a twelve-inch gap, enough for him to slip through. Then Harvey began Julios' standard one-minute wait in case the noise had alerted somebody. The rear garden, shielded by tall conifers, enjoyed near darkness. Only the light from a single window shone across the tips of a row of wildflowers.

A full minute passed before Harvey made his way behind the trees, creeping along the wall towards the single light. It called to him. The window belonged to a small bedroom as wide as two beds and twice as long, which Harvey guessed to be a guest room for the farmhouse. It was furnished with minimal effort, hosting a single bed and a wall-mounted TV above a small desk.

A shadow danced across the room then disappeared.

Harvey waited.

Then, as if sensing Harvey's presence, the shadow gave

way to a human form, who moved to the window and searched the night with wondering eyes.

Harvey froze.

The man drew the thin net curtains to one side, glanced back at the door, then tried to open the window. But it was locked. He stared out into the darkness at the sky above and towards the trees as if it were all new. Then, without warning, he stared straight at where Harvey was standing in the shadows. The man's face was loathsome and red from tears. His eyes strained from lack of sleep and his tongue rested between his parted lips giving him a perverse yet naïve appearance.

"Found you," Harvey whispered.

CHAPTER THIRTEEN

"Not thinking of trying to run for it, are you?"

Shaun turned from the window and found Lenny standing in the doorway.

"No," replied Shaun. "I wasn't. I wouldn't."

"There's nothing stopping you," said Lenny. He took a step closer. A cruel smile spread across his gaunt face, and he gestured to the darkness outside. "But you're safer in here with us than out there."

"I won't run," said Shaun. "I don't even know where I am."

"You don't need to know," said Lenny, turning to leave the room. "Anyway, the boss wants to see you."

Taking slow, tentative steps, Shaun left the relative safety of his new accommodation and followed Lenny along the small hallway. At the end of it was the entrance to the central building. But Lenny disappeared through a door on the right then poked his head back into the hallway a few seconds later.

"Come on. Hurry up."

Shaun took a few deep breaths and walked through the door into a long room with soft, red, leather couches, a coffee table, and a large desk at one end. Behind the desk, sitting with his hands clasped together, a thin, older man wearing a white, open-collared shirt was sitting and staring at Shaun.

"Take a seat, Shaun," said the wiry old man whose thick horn-rimmed glasses magnified his dark eyes and suggested a calculating yet brutal intelligence. He offered Shaun the seat with an open palm. It was an indication that he should sit in that particular seat and no other.

"Lenny tells me you often need telling more than once, and that maybe you're a bit slow. Well, Shaun, my old son, I'll tell you this once, so listen very carefully." The old man cleared his throat, but his gravelly tones remained. "*I* do not intend on repeating *anything* I say just so that you can stand and stare at me. *Understood?*"

Shaun nodded.

"Good. Now sit down, shut up and listen."

Shaun sat in the offered seat and placed his hands on his lap as if he were being interviewed.

"Good. We're making progress," said the man. "Do you want a cup of tea?"

"No, thank you, sir," Shaun replied quietly.

"Lenny, get him a cup of tea, will you?" said the man, ignoring Shaun's response.

Lenny rose and left the room by another side door, leaving just the man and Shaun at the desk. The driver of the van sat on one of the red leather sofas in the corner of the room, playing with his phone. The old man sat forward, put his elbows on the surface of the desk, and linked his fingers, resting them against his mouth.

"Tell me about yourself, Shaun," he said.

"About myself?"

"Don't make me repeat myself, Shaun," the old man warned, and he raised a bony index finger.

"I'm twenty-four."

"That's a start. How about embellishing on that very detailed account?"

"I'm from North London, but I live in Potters Bar now. My dad left, and Mum moved us up there for a fresh start."

"You live with your mum, do you?"

"Yeah," said Shaun.

He was slightly embarrassed that he hadn't managed to leave the family nest at his age.

"And why did your dad leave, Shaun?"

"Dunno. I don't think he had another woman. But him and mum always argued. He just never came home one time."

"That's a shame, Shaun. Do you see him at all?"

"No. I haven't seen him since he left."

"And how do you feel about that? Would you like to see him?"

"I don't mind, really. I mean, I don't know if *he* wants to see *me*. Especially not now."

"Especially not now? But he's your dad, Shaun. Why wouldn't a father want to see his son?"

"Because of what I did, and because of who I am."

"Tell me about what you did, Shaun. Tell me why the police were holding you."

"You know what I did."

"Do I? All I know is what I read in the papers, and you can't believe everything you read in the papers, can you, Shaun?" The man sat back and folded his arms. "Tell me what you did."

There was an uncomfortable silence before Shaun leaned forward and rested his elbows on his legs. He stared at the wooden floor. His eyes didn't focus or blink. They just followed the intricate patterns of the hardwood's grain.

"Shaun, I'm waiting. Tell me *where* you did it. Let's start there."

"In the forest near our house by the lake."

The man nodded, encouraging Shaun to tell his story. Shaun's urge to tell it grew. It was as if vocalising the events would ease the pressure building inside him.

"I was out walking one time. I liked to walk there. It's quiet. Every now and then, I'd get a couple of beers from the off-license, and I'd sit there by the lake. If you sit long enough, the birds and squirrels get used to you, and you can watch them running around. One time, I'd finished my beers and was sitting near the lake looking at the swans. There was a voice behind me. A girl's voice. She asked me what I was doing."

CHAPTER FOURTEEN

"Stop snivelling, Shaun. You're going to mess the floor up," said the old man.

Lenny returned with two cups of tea. He handed the first cup to the old man. The second, a mug with the slogan '*World's Best Husband*' on it in bold red letters, he placed on a coaster in front of Shaun.

"Len, get him some tissues, will you? He's making a right old mess over there."

Lenny left once more to fetch a box of tissues from the kitchen. He returned a few seconds later, holding them out for Shaun, who took the box without looking up.

"Do you know what they do to people like you in prison, Shaun?"

Shaun shook his head and continued to stare at the floor.

"Well, put it this way, you wouldn't be doing much of what you did again, mate. Your old boy would be hacked off and fed to E-wing for their supper."

The old man laughed at his own joke. But even amidst the laughter, Shaun could feel his dark eyes burning into him.

"I don't know what would be worse though, to be honest,"

the old man continued. "They must be hunting you down in Potters Bar right now. I imagine crowds of them are sitting outside your mum's house with pitchforks. You're lucky we found you so easily. What do you reckon, Rob?" he called to the driver of the van. "Being locked up or being let out? Which one would you prefer?"

"I reckon I'd prefer to off myself, boss, in that scenario," said Rob from the other side of the room. "Let's face it, neither option is likely to make you many friends."

"Too right, Rob. Did you hear that, Shaun? Rob over there reckons you ought to *off* yourself. What do you say to that then?"

"I thought about it," mumbled Shaun through his phlegm-filled throat.

The talk of suicide only made his sobbing worse. His body convulsed as he tried to stop the inevitable. He closed his eyes tight, which screwed up his face, and a thick trail of snot ran down his nose far too fast for any tissue to stop.

"You thought about it, did you? Did you hear that, Rob? He thought about *offing* himself."

"Yeah, we heard, boss. We're amazed he didn't follow through with it. Aren't we, Lenny?"

"That's right. *Amazed*, we are," said Lenny.

"How would you do it, Shaun?" asked Terry. "Here, Rob, how would *you* do it if you was him?"

"Well, it would have to be quick, boss. I reckon jumping off a bridge is a pretty good way to go. They reckon you have a heart attack on the way down. So you don't even feel the bump."

"Jumping off a bridge." Terry said the words staccato. "Shaun, what do you say to that then?"

Shaun didn't reply.

"Lenny, what about you? How would *you* do it?"

Lenny sat opposite Rob on the couch, looking at his phone.

"Well, I always thought jumping in front of a train would be quick. But it's such a selfish way to go, you know? All those people late home from work. So I reckon it'd have to be drowning. That's it, yeah. They reckon it's quick and one of the better ways to go. Over in seconds. I saw it on a documentary."

"Do they now? One of the better ways to go? Drowning. Did you hear all that, Shaun?" He paused. "Shaun, don't make me repeat myself. I don't like repeating myself."

"I heard it. I heard it all."

The wiry man in the chair leaned forward and said quietly, "So, tell me, Shaun. Tell me how *you* would do it."

Shaun couldn't hold his emotion any longer. A loud whimper escaped from his throat along with a deep breath that culminated in a howl. He cried wildly, unable to restrain the tears that had built up behind his burning eyes.

"I was going to hang myself," Shaun said, mid-sob. "I was going to jump from the balcony in the library and snap my neck. I'd be *done* with it all."

"There we go," said the old man, sitting back in his winged chair. "You were going to *hang* yourself."

The old man sat forward again, intrigued by Shaun's choice of suicide.

"Have you ever seen a man die, Shaun?"

Shaun shook his head.

"No."

The man was silent for a moment.

"I have." He grinned. "I've seen many men die, and you know what, Shaun?" The man raised a single eyebrow. "Pretty much every single one of them pissed their pants. What a way to be remembered, eh? Pissing your pants? Not only would you be remembered for being the nonce that ruined that poor little girl's life, took away her innocence and caused devastation among her family, but they'll all remember that you pissed your pants as well. Not to mention, of course, the nightmares you'd have given the old Doris who unlocks the library every morning. She'd have walked in one day, probably slipped over in your piss, broken her hip, and laid in the stinking puddle looking up at your ugly mug swinging above her. What do you reckon, Rob?"

"I reckon you're right, boss. Slipped over, broke her hip and lay in his piss."

"What do you want from me?" Shaun asked.

"Lenny, tell Shaun the *first* thing I want."

"Courtesy, Shaun," said Lenny.

"That's right, Shaun," said the old man. "Courtesy. A little bit of respect for the man that got you off the street before you were lynched, castrated and set on fire by the locals with their pitchforks. Understood?"

Shaun nodded silently.

"So do me the courtesy of looking me in the eye when you talk to me. I'm fed up of looking at your ear. What's on the floor, anyway?"

"Nothing. There's nothing on the floor," Shaun said, lifting his head to meet the man's eyes.

"Right. Well, stop looking down there and look at me. Can you drive?"

"Eh?"

"A car, Shaun. Can you drive a car? Do you have a driving license?"

"Yes, I've got one."

Shaun searched for his wallet.

"I don't need to see it, just as long as you've got one. Right. I've got a job coming up and you, my perverted little friend, are going to be very useful to me."

CHAPTER FIFTEEN

"What is it you want me to do?" asked Shaun.

"Oh, it's just a little job. Drop something off for me. Collect something else. You'll know nearer the time. In the meantime, why don't you relax? Watch some TV. Go for a walk if you want. It's nice out there. Proper British countryside."

"What happens after I do this job for you?"

"Shaun, there are three possible outcomes. Being the nice man I am, I'm going to let you decide which one happens."

Terry was growing impatient, but he composed himself well. He explained things to Shaun in a childlike manner so the possibilities were communicated plain and simple.

"One."

Terry leaned forward on the desk and held up the skinny index finger of his right hand. It was often used to accompany his mouth when ordering people around.

"You try to run away, call the police, or mess things up for me in any way, shape or form, then Lenny and Rob will take you outside for a good kicking. After that, they'll dump your broken, pitiful, perverted body on your mum's doorstep.

Then either she or the locals can find you. Pitchforks, Shaun. Pitchforks."

He added a middle finger to the first without removing his eyes from Shaun's.

"Two. You ask too many questions. If that habit doesn't stop, the boys will see that my pigs are fed and that you are never seen again. Have you ever seen a pig eat a human body, Shaun?"

Shaun's jaw widened in horror. "No."

"It's quite fascinating. There's no grace to it. They don't care which part they eat first. They're not like you eating your mum's lovely roast dinner on a Sunday in front of the telly. You eat your greens first to get them out the way so you can savour the tender meat and succulent gravy. But no, Shaun. It's not like that at all. One or two of them will start on your feet or your hands, whichever is closest. Then they'll work their way up your body until nothing is left. They have to grind your bone down with their huge incisors and tear your flesh off. But they seem to manage it okay, and it doesn't take long."

Terry sat back in his chair and studied Shaun's reactions.

"Whereabouts along that process a man actually stops feeling pain and succumbs to death is different every time. Some blokes have survived for ages. Some even watch their knackers getting chomped off, unable to defend themselves because their hands are already eaten. Do you remember that one, Lenny?"

"Yes, boss. I remember. One of my favourites, that was," replied Lenny.

"It's a fascinating thing to watch."

Terry rearranged his finger configuration; he held up three digits, the pinkie, ring and middle, with his palm facing Shaun.

"Three. You relax. Thank God, or whoever you want, that

you're not being sodomised in Pentonville Prison right now. Be grateful to walk in the countryside with the fresh air and the chance at starting a new life. In a week, you'll take the van, do a delivery, pick up a bag for me, and come back."

"Then what?"

"*That's* another question, Shaun," said Terry. "Can you remember the outcome of asking too many questions?"

Shaun nodded. "Yes."

"Oink oink, Shauny." Terry turned to his boys. "Lenny, Rob, show him back to his room. Then sort out that box in the garage out, will you?"

"Yes, boss," replied Rob.

"Oh, and Shauny, my old son," said Terry.

Shaun looked back at the man at the desk, whose cruel smile had faded into a warning stare.

"No more questions."

CHAPTER SIXTEEN

JOHN CARTWRIGHT STOOD IN THE MIDDLE OF THE LARGE kitchen of his five-bedroom house in Theydon Bois. He was chopping onions and carrots with a practised hand at the centre unit. His workstation was neat and organised, a reflection of his controlled life and mind.

Harvey leaned on the far side of the island and sipped a glass of water.

"Fancy making yourself useful and getting your old man a brandy?" asked John.

Thankful for the break in monotonous silence and the excuse to leave the room, Harvey stepped into the lounge and walked to the drinks cabinet. He poured half an inch of brandy over three ice cubes in a crystal tumbler. Exactly how the old man liked it.

He sat the brandy by John's hand and resumed his position leaning on the counter.

"Thanks, Son."

"Is anyone else joining us?" asked Harvey.

"No. I thought we could have a night together, you know? Have a little chat."

Harvey didn't reply.

"So how's the bike?" asked John.

"It's fine."

"Why don't you get yourself a car? It must be bloody freezing on that thing."

"It's fine," said Harvey.

"What about the place, you know, in France?"

It was a typical conversation with John. The topic changed from one minute to the next, never delving into details unless, of course, John wanted to hear the details. Then there was no escaping it.

"I'm getting there. No rush."

"Well, there's a job coming up. You could earn big if you want it."

"I told you. I don't want to get involved in all that. I like the little jobs Julios and I do. It's enough for me."

"Yeah, but they're not frequent. You need a regular income. You *need* money so you can make *plans* and buy that little French farm you always wanted."

"The farmhouse will happen. Can we leave it there?"

"Alright, alright. I'm just trying to make sure you've got enough. I'm making sure you're sorted. That's all."

"I know. Where's Donny skiving off these days?" asked Harvey. He was keen to move the conversation away from his life plans. "I haven't seen him creeping around for a while."

"Your brother? He's off somewhere. He said he'd be back tomorrow. He better be. I need him on this job."

"What's the job?" asked Harvey.

"Thought you didn't want in?"

Harvey didn't reply. John smiled.

"There's a job up north next month and we'll need fire-power." John sipped his brandy and smacked his lips, a subconscious habit that Harvey had always noticed. "I'll need you and Julios to pick up something for me before then. The less you know, the better. I'll give you details nearer the time. But needless to say, you won't fit a crate of automatic rifles on the back of your bike. So you'll have a van. Sergio will make the arrangements."

Harvey took a breath at the mention of the name; putting his life on the line for a job arranged by Sergio was a risk.

"Sergio?"

"Leave him to me, Son."

"Aren't you concerned at all about the repercussions? Bradley was a major player in the Thomson empire."

"No. I'm not. Leave it to me," replied John.

It was enough to silence Harvey's cynicism. John's short words were a demonstration of his power, which Harvey neither feared nor had the patience to counter.

"A crate of rifles? I can handle that on my own. Why send Julios?"

"In case the job goes south, Harvey. I don't want you there on your own. Sergio will make the arrangements. It's his contacts."

Harvey frowned.

"What's going to happen? Cash in a bag, guns in the van, I check, they check, we both leave. What can go south?"

"It's the *Thomsons*, Harvey," said John, as he set the knife down and mirrored Harvey's position leaning on the island.

"You're buying *guns* from the *Thomsons*? Correct me if I'm wrong, but didn't Julios and I just off one of their main men and string him up?"

"You did, Harvey. But remember yourself. Don't question me." John often reminded people who he was, regardless of who they were. "Have a little faith in your old man. Think about it. Sergio's faux pas may just work in our favour." John tapped his temple with his index finger. "Right now, Terry Thomson is trying to work out who killed his boy. He probably thinks that whoever did it wanted the Thomsons out of the way for the northern job. Right?"

"Right."

"This gun meet has been lined up for a while now. Why on earth would I put a hit on his son so close to a deal? He knows we don't have the men to go up against him."

"So who's he going to think it was?"

"Who has the men to do the northern job and happens to have a weakness for diamonds?"

"The Stimsons," said Harvey. "This gets worse. But what we did to Bradley Thomson isn't Stimson's style."

"Yeah. But the Stimsons are the biggest jewel thieves in the country. If anybody is going to go after the northern job, it'll be Adam Stimson. Or Terry Thomson. We aren't even players." John took a swig of his brandy and puckered his lips. "If I'm right, which I normally am, Thomson will come to the same conclusion. He'll go after Stimson."

"Right."

"Which means *we* get the Thomsons and the Stimsons out of the way, *and* we get the guns. The job is ours for the taking, Son."

"So the job is jewels. You're going to start a war and then nick a load of diamonds. What happened to us running bars and doing over cash vans?"

"Slight correction, Harvey. I believe Sergio *already* started the war. I'm just making the best of a bad situation."

Harvey didn't reply.

John tipped the carrots into a saucepan of boiling water and banged the chopping board with the knife.

"You hungry, Harv? This'll be ready in five minutes."

Harvey didn't reply.

"So tell me what you're up to anyway," said John. "Is everything okay?"

"Everything is fine. I want to ask you something."

"Anything for you, Son. Take a seat. Ask away. I'd offer you a drink, but you'd only refuse."

Harvey didn't reply.

"You look like you've got something on your mind, Harvey. What's up?"

"Tell me again about how you found us."

"How what? How I found you? Oh, Harvey. I told you before. You need to drop it, mate."

"I need to hear it again. The small details."

"There *are* no small details, Harvey. You and your sister were left on a seat in my bar in East Ham."

"And my parents? I mean my real parents."

"Harvey, come on. We've been over this how many times?"

"I know. But something doesn't add up. None of it adds up. It never has done."

"You were found with a note from your mum. I'm sorry, Harvey. I've always hated saying this part. But they both killed themselves. I don't know why. I wish I still had the note. But I didn't know them. I just happened to own the bar nearby, I guess. I was well known, Harvey. Maybe they knew we'd take care of you." John had used that phrase countless times in response to the countless times Harvey had raised the topic. It was verbatim.

"Barb wanted to keep you both," he continued. He spoke slowly as if savouring the memory. "We couldn't have any more kids. You know, complications. We finished up in the bar one night. The staff had all gone home, and we were cleaning up. We did it all ourselves back then. We found you in a little hamper with your sister sitting by your side."

"Wrapped in blankets," finished Harvey.

"Wrapped in blankets," said John in confirmation.

Harvey stood in silence, replaying the scene over in his mind.

"Are we done, Harvey?" said John. "I need a favour."

"I guess we are."

"I need you to shadow Donny."

CHAPTER SEVENTEEN

HARVEY FOUND DONNY'S CAR TUCKED INTO AN ALLEYWAY behind one of John's bars. He stopped his bike outside a cafe opposite and selected a window seat inside with his back to the wall. He picked up a random newspaper left on a table as he entered, ordered a tea and settled in for the second monotonous day of shadowing his foster brother.

John hadn't issued a specific reason for tailing Donny. He only said that he should keep him in sight and report back with anything he deemed out of the ordinary. But in the sleazy world of fast cars, drugs and cheap women, everything in Donny's life seemed out of the ordinary.

From his seat in the cafe, the view of the bar's entrance was skewed only by passing traffic on foot and on the road. Harvey drank his tea slowly and watched as a contracted cleaning firm entered the bar. Three women armed with buckets, mops and bags of products went inside. Two hours later, they left in their small van. Nobody else walked in. Nobody else walked out.

"Are you going to order something, sweetheart?" said a shrill voice beside Harvey's ear. "It'll be lunchtime soon and the crowds will come in." As she spoke, the door opened and rang the small bell above it. Two tradesmen dressed in grubby jeans entered the cafe.

"Morning, boys," the woman said.

"Alright, Rose? Couple of bacon rolls please, love," said the larger of the two men.

"No problem, darling. Take a seat. I'll be right with you."

She turned to look back at Harvey, who was staring out the window. He felt her gaze and turned to face her.

"What takes the most time to cook?" said Harvey. "I'm waiting for someone. He's late."

"The all-day breakfast," said Rose.

"I'll take one," replied Harvey, already looking back out the window.

"*Please?*" said Rose.

Harvey turned to face her again but didn't say a word.

"One all-day coming up then," she said as she walked off.

One of the things Harvey had learned from Julios was how to communicate without words. Often a mere expression or gesture would convey his thoughts. It was a skill he had never been taught directly, but over time, he had improved it and it became natural. Of course, it was another reflection of Julios' techniques imprinted upon him. As Harvey sat at the table in the small cafe in East Ham staring out of the window, his own reflection stared back at him from the glass. It seemed to question who he was.

To the outside world, Harvey Stone didn't exist. He was a shadow raised by his criminal foster father. He was unknown to the world and trained to be a killer by London's finest hitman. But the reflection saw through his hardened exterior to a time when a young boy, angered by the deaths of his family and frustrated with loneliness, felt the first violent pang of the beast developing in the pit of his stomach.

At first, John had asked Julios to spend time with Harvey

to help him mourn. But as time went by, and Julios saw potential in the boy, their training sessions developed from fitness
to defence. And then finally, attack.

Julios and Harvey always trained in the large gym to the
rear of John's house. The gym was a standard oblong building
with a pitched roof and floor-to-ceiling glazing that ran
around the perimeter and boasted a view of the wooden deck
and swimming pool. It was separated from the main house by
a short walk across the lawns.

After training one day, man and boy had walked to the
house for some water. Inside, John had been holding a
monthly meeting. They were an opportunity for John to
demonstrate his power, show off his wealth, and get a feel for
the men who were running his various operations.

As Julios and Harvey filled glasses of water in the kitchen,
two of the men had walked in behind them. They lit cigarettes and asked the cook for coffee. Then they waited while
she boiled water, exchanging whispered comments in each
other's ears. Harvey watched them curiously.

The first man took a drag on his cigarette and moved
across to the sink to tap away the ash. Leaning on the counter
with his back to Harvey and Julios, he continued his hushed
conversation with the second man, using wild arm gestures to
emphasise his point. As he turned to tap his ash once more
and blow smoke up towards the open window, his profile was
framed in the sunlight that shone through the glass.

Harvey froze. He instantly recognised the large, crooked
nose, the pointed chin and the outline of the man who had
haunted his dreams since...

Hannah.

Harvey had seen the face profile before. He'd recognised
the movement as the man relaxed his head back to smoke.
He'd heard the sound of his breathing.

Only previously, it had been by moonlight.

A crash of crockery on the tiled floor snapped Harvey from his daydream. The two tradesmen slid their chairs across the tiled floor to help Rose pick up the smashed plates. Harvey looked back out the window.

Donny's car hadn't moved. There was no sign of life in the bar, but outside, school children ambled past with their heads buried in mobile phones. They walked in groups of twos and threes and sometime more, their voices loud and shrill as they called to friends across the street.

But one boy walked past alone. Ignoring stares and deep in his own troubled thoughts, he looked like the weight of the world hung from his shoulders. His head snatched to the left as if he felt Harvey's gaze and the two locked eyes for a brief moment. Then the boy passed out of sight but remained for a while in Harvey's thoughts. He recognised the suffering on the boy's face and was reminded of a time when he too wore the same haunted look.

The outline of the man's face in the sunlight all those years ago had stirred a dark memory in Harvey. It had been as if the sheer will of his conscience had suppressed the image beneath layers of camouflaged emotions. But Julios had picked up on Harvey's mood change with an almost parental instinct. That afternoon when they were training, he'd stopped and lowered his pads, leaving Harvey poised and ready for the attack.

"That man in the kitchen," began Julios. "You know him?"

Harvey didn't reply.

But a single silent stare from Julios elicited a response.

"What man?" asked Harvey, continuing to hold his guard up and offering no emotion.

Julios was an artist at communicating without words. He was the Da Vinci of facial gestures. He looked down at Harvey with understanding in his eyes.

"I thought he was someone else," Harvey lied.

His eyes diverted to the floor and his guard dropped.

But Julios continued to stare. The urge to blurt it out, to tell Julios, his only living friend, what he'd seen that night was so strong. But he couldn't. It would be weak. Julios wouldn't understand.

Instead, he returned Julios' stare with a look of his own.

Julios nodded.

"I think it is time for patience, planning and execution," Julios had said.

Harvey was dragged back to reality when the waitress cleared her throat.

"Are you going to stay much longer?" she said, staring down at the cold all-day breakfast. "You've been sitting here all day."

Behind her, on the wall above the kitchen door, was a clock. Harvey checked the alleyway.

Donny's car was gone.

He pulled a twenty-pound note from his pocket, which he slammed on the table, then jumped up and pulled on his helmet while walking to his bike. The late afternoon traffic was building up. Harvey glanced left then right, scanning the cars, and for the briefest of moments, he saw the tail end of Donny's Mercedes turning left at the Green Street traffic lights.

18

CHAPTER EIGHTEEN

"THERE'S SOMEONE FOLLOWING US," SAID DONNY, AS HE pulled off London's North Circular Road. "It's the same beaten-up old wreck we saw in East Ham."

From the passenger seat of Donny's Mercedes, Sergio leaned forward to look into the mirror. But he saw nothing.

"There's nobody, Donny. You're high and paranoid."

"I'm not paranoid, Sergio," spat Donny. A thin layer of sweat had formed on his brow and he chewed his lower lip with his front teeth. "Look. Three cars back."

They stopped at a set of lights with Epping Forest on their left.

"I'm going to turn left and see if they follow," said Donny. "If they do, we'll lose them in the country lanes."

"There's nobody there, Donny. Relax."

The seconds ticked by as the traffic flowed in the opposite direction, but as soon as the lights turned green, Donny floored the big saloon. The rear wheels spun, and the car screeched into the lane where a series of sweeping curves were followed by a long straight.

"Is he there? Did he follow?" said Donny, gripping the wheel and checking the mirror.

Sergio turned in his seat as they emerged from the last bend and Donny found fourth gear.

"I don't see anybody," said Sergio. "See, I told you. There's nothing to worry about."

But as soon as he'd said the words, the rust-coloured heap that Donny had spotted earlier nosed into view and entered the straight. Its body was twisted and its front end raised with the torque of the engine.

"Hold on," said Sergio.

"What?" said Donny, wiping his sweaty hand on his trouser legs. "Tell me what you see."

"It's that old car," said Sergio over the noise of the engine. "He's catching."

"He can't be catching. We're doing seventy miles an hour."

"Go faster, Donny. He's right behind us."

"I'm trying," said Donny.

"Faster, Donny."

Donny's eyes flicked to the mirror and back to the road. But it was too late. The front end of the rust bucket slammed into the rear of the Mercedes. Donny fought with the steering, but the force of the blow had already sent the car swinging from side to side. Sergio gripped the safety handle above the door with one hand and with the other, he held onto the smooth dashboard. As Donny slammed on the brakes, the wheels left the tarmac, found the forest floor, and sent the car into a series of rolls and spins.

Then silence ensued.

Sergio's head smashed the passenger window on the first roll and Donny's face bent into the steering wheel. Then, as the car flipped end to end, a weightless yet hopeless feeling came over the men as their world spun in slow motion. They were thrown around the front of the car. All around was chaos, which was brought to a bone-shattering stop with the aid of a fat tree that stood in the car's path.

Neither man spoke at first. The only sounds were the soft chinks of broken glass falling to the forest floor and the chattering of birds and squirrels in the trees above. And then a footstep on a snapped twig.

"Can you move?" said Donny, holding his broken nose.

"Shh," said Sergio, aware of the blood running from his forehead.

"What is it?"

Donny's red eyes glowed in the semi-darkness.

"Somebody's there," Sergio whispered.

Liquid sloshed inside a metallic container. A lid was being unscrewed. And then the smell of petrol.

"He's going to burn us," said Sergio, as he fought to remove his seat belt. "Get out."

"I can't," said Donny. "My foot is stuck behind the pedals."

"Well pull it out," said Sergio

Oily liquid began to drip into the front of the car.

"Faster, Donny."

"I'm stuck, Sergio."

The rush of flames across the vehicle and pop of air pockets finding heat silenced them both.

"Get *out*, Donny."

Sergio pulled himself through the passenger window, stinging his hands on the searing surface the car. He dropped to the forest floor and rolled away from the heat as the flames found a puddle of fuel and reached high into the air.

The car was on its side with the driver's door against the ground. Beyond the burning wreck on the tarmac a hundred metres away, the beaten-up old car roared away, a flash of rust between the forested shades of green.

"Sergio," screamed Donny. "Help me."

But Sergio was frozen to the spot. With his back against a tree and his ruined hands clamped around his body, all he could do was sit and watch. Pink fleshy hands beat against the windscreen as Donny strived to break free and find air. He was screaming at Sergio for help. But then the hands dropped. There was stillness. All Sergio could do was bury his head between his arms and let the tears fall as Donny succumbed to the fire.

19

CHAPTER NINETEEN

THICK BILLOWING SMOKE POURED FROM THE CANOPY OF dense forest, marking the spot. Harvey jumped the red lights, turned into the bend with his knees just inches from the tarmac, and powered up the road. Cutting a straight line through the long, sweeping bends, he entered the straight at high speed, just in time to see the tail end of an old car as it tore away from the scene.

A quick glance at the wreckage as he shot past told him it was serious, giving him just a fraction of a second to make his decision. Catch the car or make sure Donny was safe.

Harvey braked heavily and felt the tail end of his bike weave from side to side. Then, using the momentum, he opened up the throttle, turned the front wheel, and went into a wild wheel spin in the centre of the road. Once he'd turned one hundred and eighty degrees, he sped back to the crash.

Stopping twenty feet from Donny's car, he pulled off his helmet and searched the area to find Sergio wallowing in a guilt-ridden stupor.

"Where's Donny?" said Harvey

Sergio immediately appeared glad to see Harvey. But there

was no need for him to answer. The hope in Sergio's face dropped to dismay as he stared at the burning car.

"He's in the car?" asked Harvey, dropping his helmet and searching through the smoke for a sign of his foster brother. With his jacket pulled up to protect his face from the searing heat, he stepped towards the flames.

"Donny?" he called out and kicked at the upturned roof. "Donny, are you there?"

No answer came at first. But when Harvey was about to move away, a fist punched the windscreen from the inside. The effort was futile, but it was enough to let Harvey know Donny was alive. The hard sole of Harvey's boot cracked the windscreen on the second kick. The fourth punched a hole, emitting a waft of thick, foul smoke. Finding a broken branch, Harvey wedged it into the gap, hung all of his weight on the end, and levered the sheet of laminated glass from the car.

Flames licked at the fresh fuel and smoke filled the interior space, but Donny's hand reached out.

"I'm stuck," he called, coughing and fighting for air. "My foot is stuck in the pedals."

The fire had found the high side of the car, and the passenger seat had already begun to smoulder, sending hot drips of melted plastic onto Donny, who was powerless to avoid them.

With a single large stride, his knife in hand and his jacket pulled over his face, Harvey forced his leg through the empty window and into the car. He placed his legs on the back seat with his front laying across his foster brother, allowing him to reach down and cut the laces from Donny's leather shoes.

He pulled the foot free just as flames took the passenger seat and sent black smoke in every direction. Harvey shoved himself through the windscreen, reached back inside, blind in the poisonous fumes, and found Donny. Then with a final haul, he pulled him free and the two men rolled clear of the fire.

But Donny was unconscious.

Harvey dragged him aside, shouting at Sergio to move. Then he leaned Donny against the tree, loosening his clothes and feeling for a pulse.

"Is he alive?" said Sergio, his voice wavering and his eyes wide with fear.

"No thanks to you," Harvey replied. "Call John. *Now.*"

Sergio, in his traumatised state, barely spoke two words to John when Harvey ripped the phone from his hands.

"John, I need a car here now. Epping Road. Look for the smoke. Donny's hurt. We'll take him back to your house so get the doctor."

"Is he okay?" asked John.

"He will be. Just get me that car before the police turn up."

"I'm on it now," said John. "What else do you need?"

Harvey scanned the scene. There was no saving the licenses plates. The fire was too intense and Donny's belongings were in the car. The police would trace it for sure.

"I need a body," said Harvey.

CHAPTER TWENTY

"SIR, TRAFFIC JUST FLAGGED A RED LIGHT BEING JUMPED out near Chigwell in Essex," said Mills. "Vehicle is a BMW motorcycle matching the model that fits those tyre tracks."

"Chigwell, you say?" said Frank. "Do we have an ID?"

"Tenant is scanning the BMW database now."

"It's a bit wild, Mills, and unlikely our man would be as careless as that."

"Right now, sir, we need every lead we can get."

Behind Frank's desk was a large pin board. He turned in his chair to face the photos he'd pinned up on it. John Cartwright was on one side, along with all known accomplices. Terry Thomson was on the other side with his usual suspects. Below, Frank had left a space for Adam Stimson. There was no photo, just a placeholder with an avatar.

"Do you really think it's Stimson, sir?" asked Mills.

"You want the truth, Mills?" he replied. "I really don't know this time."

"Maybe we'll actually get to see his face if it is."

"You should go home, Mills," said Frank. "You don't need

to wait for me. Why don't you go and have a drink with the others?"

"Are you kicking me out, sir?"

"No, Mills. No. But you work hard enough," said Frank. His Scottish accent had lost its subtlety. He checked his watch. "Would you look at that? It's gone seven o'clock already."

"I'd rather stay and make some progress, sir," said Mills. "I've just got the database report from Tenant."

"Anything of interest?" replied Frank, staring hard at the black-and-white photo of Terry Thomson.

"Hold on," she replied.

Frank turned back to her. He knew the look on her face. He'd seen it a dozen times before, and with that look on her face, the girl was always right.

"You've found something?"

"It's just a name, sir. All the details are fake. His address, date of birth and national insurance number all belong to someone else."

"How do you know?"

Frank pulled open the bottom drawer of his desk and produced a small bottle of scotch and two glasses.

"Not for me, sir, thanks," said Melody.

Frank poured one for himself and watched his prodigy scan through the files on her laptop screen.

"Well for one, sir, he's dead."

"Who's dead?"

"The man who owns the motorcycle," said Melody. "He died four years ago."

"How?" asked Frank.

But the flow of conversation was broken by the ringing of her mobile phone.

"Mills," she answered, a little too abruptly.

A female voice spoke with a soft tone, but that was all

Frank could make out. He turned and faced his pin board while Melody took the call, imagining a link between the three families in front of him and rolling the glass of scotch between his fingers and thumb.

"Thank you," said Mills.

As soon as she put down her phone, the tapping of laptop keys resumed. Frank waited. He knew there would be news, but the trick with somebody as keen as Mills was to let them articulate it in their own time, rather than extract information through questions before they were ready.

"Sir, there's been an incident. It could be relevant."

It was a polite way to ask Frank to turn and face her. So he did. Mills placed the laptop on the desk so they could both see the screen. It showed an internet map of Essex with the M25 circling the city and thick patches of green depicting Epping Forest.

Using a pen, Mills indicated an area of road between Chigwell and Epping.

"This is Epping Road, sir," she said.

"Epping Road?" said Frank. His attention had been captured.

"Police just found a burned-out car there."

"So?"

"The car belonged to Donald Cartwright."

"Was it a crash?" asked Frank.

Mills nodded.

"It's over a hundred metres into the forest and laying on its side. He must have been travelling at speed."

"Is there..." began Frank. But he hesitated.

"A body? One, sir. Burned beyond recognition. All the local police know is that it's a male and the size and height match Donald Cartwright's description."

Frank turned back to his wall and started up at Terry Thomson.

"You couldn't just wait, could you?" he muttered.

"Sorry, sir?"

"Nothing."

Frank downed the remainder of his drink. He pushed himself out of his chair and reached for a red marker on his desk. Then, careful to keep the lines straight and neat, he drew a cross from corner to corner on Donny Cartwright's photograph.

"What does that tell you?" he asked Melody.

Her eyes flicked from side to side then to the avatar placeholder representing Stimson.

"Balance, sir."

"Nicely put," Frank remarked. "So we have Bradley Thomson dead. And our suspects are Cartwright or Stimson-"

"And now we have Donny Cartwright dead," said Melody. "And our suspects are-"

"Thomson and Stimson," Frank finished. "So either the Cartwrights and the Thomsons are at each other's throats, or Stimson really is starting a war."

"There's one more thing, sir," said Melody. She waited for him to glance back over his shoulder then pointed at her laptop. Using the pen again, she indicated a small area of road. "This junction here."

"Yes?" said Frank.

"This is where the motorbike jumped the lights."

"The dead guy," said Frank. "Who was he?"

"Well that's the interesting thing, sir," said Melody. "His name was Albert Small."

"It doesn't ring a bell," said Frank. "Should it?"

"He was found buried in a shallow grave four years ago deep inside Epping Forest."

"He was murdered?" said Frank, reaching for the bottle.

"Pathologist reports say he was buried alive."

Cogs began to fall into place in Frank's mind. But Mills hadn't finished.

"He'd just been released from Belmarsh Prison after serving seven years for aggravated sexual assault on several girls."

"He was–"

"A sex offender, sir," finished Mills. "He was one of the unsolved murders."

CHAPTER TWENTY-ONE

A GOLD BRACELET AND HEAVY WATCH WERE ALL THAT could be seen of John Cartwright's hands, which were forced deep into his pockets in agitation as his son lay on the bed in his old bedroom with an oxygen mask strapped to his face.

"Who did this, Harvey?" John turned at the end of his pace across the room then began again. "Was it Thomson's lot?"

"Never seen him before," said Harvey.

"So you got a look at him?"

"I got close, but not close enough."

"But you *saw* him? You could have got him?"

"From a distance. But I had to stop and turn back. I *could* have caught him and he *could* be strung up downstairs right now waiting to have his skin peeled off. But then we wouldn't be sitting here waiting for Donny to wake up, would we?"

The statement silenced John. From the corner of Harvey's eye, he saw Sergio shrink further into the chair beside Donny's bed. John caught it too; he glared briefly at Sergio in a demonstration of control then looked away.

"The body was a good idea, Harvey. It'll be at least a week before they realise it's not Donny."

"And when they do?" asked Harvey.

"By the time they realise it was just a lowlife scumbag who can't pay his debts, they'll have a whole new bunch of bodies to be sifting through."

John offered Harvey a wink just as Sergio jumped into life.

"He's moving. I felt his hand. He moved."

"Get the doctor," said John. "He's downstairs."

Sergio ran from the room, calling out for the doctor to come quickly. John leaned over Donny. With a rarely gentle hand, he brushed Donny's hair from his brow.

"Are you awake, Son?" he asked.

Searing hot metal had singed the side of Donny's face. The bandage was concealing one of his eyes. But the other opened slowly as if for the first time.

"That's my boy," said John. "Don't you move. You're alright. You just had a nasty accident, that's all."

The eye flicked around the room then settled on Harvey and moistened.

"Harvey, over here, before Sergio gets back," said John in his best conspiratorial whisper. "What happened?" he asked Donny. "Was it one of Thomson's lot? I need to know."

A single blink, long but meaningful.

"So you didn't get a look?" asked John. "At the driver? Did you see the driver?"

Donny's swollen lips parted like great cracks in the earth's crust. His tongue slid from his mouth but failed to bring moisture and retreated back inside.

"No," said Donny. His voice was more of a croak than a word, and his efforts fogged the oxygen mask in an instant.

"Don't talk, Donny," said John. "Don't worry. We'll get them. We just need a plan."

"What about the meet?" asked Harvey. "Is it still on?"

With both hands resting on the bed, John turned his head sideways to face Harvey and nodded.

"The gun deal is still on. Nothing changes."

Donny became restless. His legs twitched, and he tried to speak.

"Easy, Son," said John. "Just take it easy."

Using his forearm, Donny tried to pull the mask from his face, but only managed to push to it one side.

"The northern job," he croaked.

John repositioned the mask over Donny's mouth just as the doctor entered the room. Sergio walked in behind him, pleased that he'd been able to help.

"It's still on," said John, looking between his two sons. "Nothing changes."

The doctor began to assess Donny's condition, ordering Sergio to refill the water jug. The reprise offered John a chance to pull Harvey to one side.

But Harvey spoke first.

"You just lost a man for the northern job. Don't ask me."

The stare John returned was understanding yet frustrated. He knew not to push Harvey.

"Now Thomson and Stimson will think that Donny is dead. If it was Stimson who did this, he'll be under the impression that neither the Thomsons or us can do the job. We'll be too busy mourning."

"What if it was Thomson?" asked Harvey.

"Well, I guess we'll find out when you and Julios go and collect our guns, won't we?"

"We need to make sure they think Donny is dead. We need them both to think that we're out of the game for a while."

"I'll be back tomorrow," said the doctor with a raised voice to cut into the whispered conversation. He had his bag in his hand and was ready to leave. "He's stable, but his wounds will need cleaning and dressing twice daily."

"Thanks, doctor," said John. "I really appreciate you coming, and, of course–"

"You've known me long enough to know I won't talk, John." The doctor leaned forward, met John's eyes and spoke with the serious hushed tones of a surgeon practised at delivering bad news. "He'll be scarred for life. His hands will heal but the side of his face won't, I'm afraid."

"Understood," said John, nodding and staring at Sergio, who stood doting over Donny.

The doctor brushed past them but turned back at the door. "Make sure you keep him hydrated and call me if there's any change."

"What about a bit of sunshine and salt water?" asked John.

"I don't follow," replied the doctor.

"Would it do him any good relaxing by the sea?"

The doctor nodded.

"Yes. In a week or so, maybe."

"Thanks, doctor. I'll call if there's anything else."

Harvey and John moved to Donny's side. Sergio sensed the change in atmosphere and fell back into the seat. John removed the oxygen mask. The examination had woken Donny, and his eye waited for John to speak.

"Sergio," began John, "I want you to arrange a holiday for Donny. Somewhere hot. The Maldives, maybe?"

"But, Dad, what about the northern job?" Donny's voice was still cracked and broken but was clearer than it had been.

"Once you've done that, Sergio," continued John, ignoring his son's question, "I want you to arrange a funeral."

"Whose funeral?" croaked Donny.

John smiled the smile of a man who had a plan and would go any length to see it through.

"Yours, Son."

John's gaze switched between his two sons.

"But don't worry. It'll be an event to remember. We'll all be deeply sad. Won't we, Harvey?"

Harvey didn't reply.

CHAPTER TWENTY-TWO

"Morning, boys," said Terry as he entered his office. "I suppose you heard the good news?"

"What's that, boss?" asked Rob, removing his feet from the coffee table.

"Poor old Donny Cartwright was involved in a nasty accident. I hear it was fatal," said Terry. "Terrible shame."

"Old John Cartwright must be in a right old state," said Lenny, flicking the page of his newspaper.

"I hope so," said Terry, the joy lost from his voice. "Where's the nonce?"

"In his room, boss. I think he's saying goodbye to his testicles."

"Well, get him out here. I need to go over tomorrow's plan with you all."

The two men exchanged glances. In Terry's mind, they were both equal. But between them, an unofficial rank elevated Lenny above Rob. He had worked for Terry for a longer period of time, and therefore been involved in more jobs. Rob stood to leave the room.

"Get me a tea while you're up, Rob, will you?" said Terry.

"I wouldn't say no to a tea, come to think of it, Rob. Cheers, mate," said Lenny.

Rob left the room with an audible sigh. He returned a few minutes later with a sheepish-looking Shaun in tow.

"Take a seat, Shaun," said Terry. Shaun did as he was told and sat at the desk where Terry had broken him and reduced him to a snivelling wreck. "No. Not there. Let's join Lenny on the couches. I need to talk to you all, and I don't want to shout across the room."

Shaun stood and distanced himself by taking the furthest seat from Lenny. A few moments later, Rob returned, carrying a tray with three teas and a little plate of biscuits.

"Shaun, do you want a tea, mate?" asked Terry.

"Erm..." Shaun hesitated. His eyes flicked to the tray of steaming teas and cold cookies.

"Get Shaun a tea, will you, Rob? While you're up."

"*Him?*" answered Rob. "A tea?"

"We're going to have a civilised chat and Shaun's one of us now. So he needs a tea. You've got a tea. Lenny's got a tea. I've got a tea. Shaun needs a tea, and seeing as you clearly possess the tea-making skills in this band of merry men, you have my vote for tea maker of the year. The man of the hour goes to you. Now go and make Shaun a tea."

"Cracking tea, Rob," said Lenny, sipping at one of the mugs.

Rob turned to return to the kitchen, muttering to himself.

"Hold on, Rob," said Terry. "Shaun, how do you like it?"

At the mention of his name, Shaun looked up, slightly embarrassed but enjoying the banter.

"Like it?"

"Tea, Shaun. Tea."

"Oh, tea. White, please."

"White," said Rob.

"You want sugar, Shaun?" asked Terry.

"Have a sugar, Shaun," said Lenny.

"One please, Rob," said Shaun, doing his best not to smirk.

"So, let's get this straight. One cup of steaming-hot tea, white with one sugar," summarised Terry. "You got that, Rob?"

"It's not rocket science, boss," said Rob, trying to sound cheerful and not let the banter get the better of him.

He walked away.

"The British Empire was forged on good tea, Rob. Just remember that," called Terry.

"Yeah, I know," said Rob, as he reached the door. "I remember the time Alfred the Great stopped killing all the Vikings and made them tea instead. They all stopped fighting, sat down, and had a nice brew and a chat. Then the big ugly Viking pulled his great big sword out of the big ugly Englishman and produced a packet of bourbons from his pocket."

"That might be taking it a bit too far, Rob," said Lenny.

"Yeah, a bit far that, Rob," said Terry. "Vikings used to like custard creams, mate, not chocolate bourbons."

Lenny and Terry chuckled to themselves while Rob shook his head and walked away. He returned a few moments later with one more cup of tea, which he placed on the coffee table in front of Shaun.

"Thank you, Rob."

"Right, now that we've all got tea, finally, can we discuss the job tomorrow?" said Terry. "The meet is at six o'clock, and I trust you've been to check the place out." He looked at Lenny questioningly.

"Yeah, not a problem, boss," replied Lenny.

"Good. You'll be meeting Cartwright's boys and they'll be fired up. So be on guard. Shaun, you are our number one. You will be on your own. Lenny and Rob won't be far away, but you can manage it. You won't need them."

"On my own?" blurted Shaun. "But–"

"Don't worry. Lenny and Rob will be close by to make sure nothing happens."

"Why *me*? I don't know nothing about it. I don't even know *what* it is we're doing."

"Well, in that garage over there is a big box of guns, Shaun. When we're done talking, you three are going to load them all into the van. Then tomorrow, you're going to take them up to a cosy little spot in the pretty English country-side. You're going to sit, wait, and then sell them to the men that arrive at six o'clock."

"*Guns?* You want me to sell guns? But–"

"But what, Shaun? You could be sitting in a cell in prison. You *could* get eaten by pigs too, and you've managed to avoid that so far. But by the skin of your balls, I might add. It's easy. They rock up. You show them the guns. They nod their heads, give you the cash before they put the box in their own van, and you drive off."

"This is serious stuff. I don't know."

"Shaun, Shaun, Shaun. Calm down," said Terry. "Lenny?"

"Boss?"

"What would you rather, given a choice? Go to prison for selling guns to villains? Or go to prison for letting underage girls lick your lollipop?"

"Selling guns, boss. I imagine I'd have a much nicer time." Lenny continued to dunk his biscuit into his tea as he spoke.

"There you go, Shaun. See, we've given you options, son. If you were walking free now, waiting for your court date, you would have probably been lynched by the locals. Then you would have gone to prison as a nonce, and you'd have more fingers in you than a bucket of KFC. But now, you have options. You *could* always turn yourself in. Or you can do this job for me as a thanks. Yes, there is a small risk of getting caught and going to prison. But at least it won't be for dirty sex offences. Failing that, the pigs are hungry. So there's three options on the table, Shaun. You, mate, are a very lucky boy."

"What if they want to take the guns before they pay me the money? How am I going to stop them?"

"Just close the van doors, Shaun. Get in and drive off," said Lenny.

"If they want them that bad, and they do, I know they do, they'll soon hand over the cash," said Terry. "Done right, the deal will take fifteen minutes, tops."

"And do I go free after?"

"Free?" cried Terry. "Free? Shaun, you are free. I just told you. I should mention that you have now skipped bail and are wanted by the police, but you are *definitely* free to go."

Terry picked up his tea, dunked a biscuit, and took a bite.

"After the job, what then?"

"We'll see, Shaun," said Terry, swallowing his biscuit. "I could do with another pair of hands. Maybe we'll keep you on." He popped the other half of the biscuit into his mouth. "Clive on the farm needs help with the pigs. Maybe you could be his farm hand if the pigs don't mind the smell. We'll talk about that when you get back."

"Can I ask one more question, please?" Shaun sat forward, put his own tea on the table, and folded his hands. "How come I'm going to be on my own?"

Terry put down his tea, sat forward, and mimicked Shaun by folding his hands. "The men we're selling the guns to are..." Terry searched for the right words. "A little upset right now. They'll be a bit jumpy. And when men like that are jumpy, it can get dangerous."

"Dangerous?"

"These are very serious men, Shaun. They are the sneaki-est, most cunning, and deviant villains I know, and I happen to know a lot of villains. It would not surprise me in the slightest if they shoot you dead and take the guns. That's why Lenny and Rob will be close by, to make sure they don't get away without paying one way or another."

Shaun sat back. "So I'm..."

"Expendable, Shaun. Expendable is what you are."

CHAPTER TWENTY-THREE

IN A COFFEE SHOP ON A SMALL SIDE ROAD OFF EPPING HIGH Street, Harvey sat at a corner table with his back to the wall. He was waiting for Julios to arrive to discuss their plans. The location of their meets always varied. It was a stipulation of Julios to avoid regular patterns.

The tables inside the coffee shop were empty. Rush hour had been and gone, and the few customers that did come through the door ordered takeouts.

A few minutes passed before Julios' old Subaru drove past the first time. Harvey counted down from sixty, picturing Julios performing his routine check of the surroundings before the car passed by once more and parked facing the fastest way out of town. Julios ambled into the coffee shop as if time would wait for him, noting every person in sight with a discreet flick of his eyes. Constant voyeurism was another of Julios' habits born from years of looking over his shoulder.

The big man stepped up to the door wearing his long overcoat, thick pants and boots. He ignored the welcoming smile of the waitress and took a seat on the table next to Harvey's, also facing the door with his back to the wall.

They both ordered coffee, which was delivered with effortless manners and minimal disturbance. Menus were placed in front of the two men, but the waitress didn't offer the special of the day or push for a food order. Instead, she left her only two customers to talk in near silence, their gestures filling the gaps between their sparse words.

"They got to Donny," said Harvey.

A frown formed on Julios' brow.

"Either Thomson or Stimson. I didn't get a look," Harvey continued. "Donny's in a bad way and John is mad as hell. He's sending him away and faking the funeral. Give it six months and he'll be back with a new identity."

A sideways stare from Julios asked another silent question before his eyes returned to monitoring the traffic outside.

"I think it was Thomson. A revenge hit."

Julios nodded.

"Which makes tomorrow's deal slightly more complex," said Harvey.

The statement caught Julios' attention.

"But it's still on. John sent me the location," said Harvey.

Julios considered the response then nodded and raised an eyebrow in another silent question.

"It's a safe enough spot. In a small grass clearing along a country lane in the sticks," said Harvey. "I checked it all out."

But Julios' face remained the same. The question hadn't been fully answered.

"It looks like a turning space for tractors and farm machinery. It's no bigger than required, just enough for two vans to pull up side by side. It's protected from the road by big hedges, and it's one minute to the M11 motorway at high speed."

Harvey took a sip of his coffee before he continued.

"There are thick trees on three sides of the location. We'll need to be there first to do a recce and see anybody coming. So there's no real chance of an ambush."

A slight nod from Julios was enough to confirm his approval. He didn't need the details but just certainty that Harvey had done the research. Julios trusted Harvey's word. He believed that it was a safe place, and all risks were known.

"Sergio has arranged a van. Meet me at John's tomorrow morning. Given the circumstances, we'll travel separately. I'll take my bike. You take the van."

Julios gave another nod as he sipped at his coffee then placed the cup on the table. He played with the handle distractedly. It was an unusual behaviour for Julios. Something was on his mind. The big man sat motionless. A soft grumbling sound from the back of his throat was the only sign he was about to speak.

"Do you remember your first time?" asked Julios. His voice was cracked and hoarse, more from the lack of use than anything else. "The first time you killed?"

"I remember," said Harvey, nodding. "The boy in the woods."

"No, no, no," said Julios, his face screwing with distaste. "That was not a kill. That was you and your immaturity letting your emotions run away. It was anger in its purest form, seeking something that you'd never find. When I ask you if you remember your first kill, I'm asking about the first time I showed you. The first time you felt control. The first time you fed the beast inside you."

"Yes," said Harvey.

"I remember it also. Very well in fact," continued Julios. He gazed across the cafe in wistful thought. "I remember it as clearly as I remember my own first time. I watched from the shadows as Jack came home from one of John's meetings. I could see the light in your eyes. They were like two sharp diamonds in a soft blanket of shadow. Jack poured himself a drink and lit the small lamp beside the record player when you stepped out behind him. I urged you to get back, to wait. It wasn't time. But still, you stayed there. You seemed to take delight in his ignorance."

"There's not a day that goes past when I don't remember that, Julios," said Harvey.

"I thought he would catch you before you made your move. You stood too long." Julios laughed, singular and nasal, recalling the memory. "And as the music began, powerful and so full of life, Jack lay his head back as he so often did. You bent to one knee, sliced his Achilles then stepped aside to let your prey fall to the floor."

"He was taller than me. I had to get him down to my level."

"I've never seen a boy hold a knife the way you did that night, Harvey. As wrong as it was, I have never felt so proud."

"I needed to do it, Julios. I did it for Hannah."

"You needed to do it, Harvey, so you could continue with your life. You needed to do it so you could enjoy the blissful memories of her. And you needed to do it to feed your inner beast."

"I've been feeding it since," said Harvey.

A smiling exhale from Julios was more of a breath than a laugh.

"Yes, Harvey." He paused. "But your targets, those men you seek, they will never satisfy the hunger."

The two men shared a moment of silence. Harvey hadn't heard Julios speak so much for a long time. He took a deep breath and hung his head forward.

"I have these dreams. I can't sleep for weeks. My targets, my hunt for them, it's the only thing that helps."

"You will not find retribution in that way," said Julios. "You may feed your beast, but he'll just get hungrier. You need to find the man you've been looking for."

"The second man," whispered Harvey. Hate rose up like bile in his throat. He shook his head. "And until then?"

"When you killed Jack, when that boy sank his knife into Jack's eye, a part of you lived. A part of you rejoiced. Find that again, Harvey," said Julios. "Don't let the hunt for retribution take everything from you. Life will pass you by."

His striking dark eyes latched onto Harvey's. They felt as strong as the man's hands, and they wouldn't let go.

"Don't waste your time killing meaningless men, Harvey. Find the other man who attacked Hannah. Allow yourself true revenge. Give the beast its final meal. Then move on with your life."

CHAPTER TWENTY-FOUR

THE AUTOMATED NUMBER PLATE RECOGNITION SYSTEM used by the Essex police had flagged the motorcycle in less than twenty-four hours from when Mills had submitted the request. A series of emails and calls woke Frank at seven in the morning. By quarter past, he was in his car. By nine o'clock, he was cruising Epping High Street observing every motorcycle he passed, either parked or moving.

It was a small town, so the search didn't take long. When the suspect emerged from a cafe, Frank laid eyes on what could be the biggest catch of his career. If he could tie this vigilante with Bradley's murder, *and* put away Thomson or Cartwright, it would be like winning the lottery.

But what Frank hadn't counted on was the other man who emerged from the cafe about a minute later. Frank reached for the Nikon DSLR camera he kept in his glove box. Then he snapped three shots of Julios Saville getting into an old Subaru.

The motorbike passed, riding slowly down the narrow street. Frank indicated and pulled out into the road behind him. Maintaining a steady distance, Frank settled in for the tail. He accelerated as any normal driver would with a clear path ahead. Following a small bend beneath a railway bridge, he found himself on a wide country B-road. The suspect was in front by three hundred yards. There was no other traffic in sight.

He slowed.

The bike slowed too, turning right at a roundabout toward Stapleford Abbots.

Frank slowed further and dropped into third gear.

The bike pulled to the side of the road. Seeing no alternative, Frank eased to a stop twenty metres behind him. But the rider didn't move. He made no attempt to dismount or even turn to look at Frank. Instead, he just stared into his mirror.

With slow, deliberate movements, Frank reached for the door handle. The two men locked eyes in the reflection of the bike's mirror. Through the darkened helmet visor, Frank felt the burn of the man's stare.

The door clicked open.

Frank had committed. He lowered his foot onto the tarmac and pulled himself outside. The rider didn't flinch.

"Excuse me," said Frank. He kept one foot inside the car and used the door as protection in case the man turned to shoot at him. "I'm looking for Theydon Bois. Can you tell me where it is, please?"

But the rider didn't move. It was as if he hadn't even heard Frank's voice.

"Did you hear me?" called Frank. "I said I'm looking for Theydon Bois."

He leaned back into the car and reached for his phone. But as he did, without warning, the Subaru roared past, ripping the door from Frank's car with an explosion of twisting metal. Diving for cover and pulling his legs inside, Frank sprawled across the seats, cowering with fear, until the riot of noise had ceased and the whine of the motorcycle faded to nothing.

The car door finished its dizzying spin on the tarmac a hundred yards up the road as Frank pulled himself from the car. Dizzied and shaking from shock, he worked his way to the grass verge then emptied the burning acid contents of his stomach onto the ground.

A few minutes passed, allowing time for Frank's heart to settle, the perspiration to dry and his head to stop spinning. But as he climbed back into his car, he reached for the non-existent door and found only air where it used to be. With his seat belt in place, he indicated then pulled out onto the empty road. The wind whistled past his ear and whipped at his stained trouser leg. He rolled the scene over and over in his mind like a bad dream.

It had been an attack.

"Do they know who I am?"

He was so far behind both the bike and the car that giving chase would have been futile. So he cruised along at well below the speed limit while a plan formulated in his head and his shaking hands gripped the steering wheel.

The River Roding ran alongside the road. It was slow-moving with patches of long reeds dotted by fishermen. Collected beside a small weir, they enjoyed their own version of quiet time. He saw the gleeful arch of a fishing rod. One man stood on the river bank playing his catch. Frank turned in his seat to glance at the action as he passed. He was quietly pleased for the man.

Then he returned his attention to the road ahead, just in time to feel the silence that ensues before death lifts its head and marks a man's mortality with one foul sweep of its cruel hand. It was in that moment that Frank's entire world slowed to a crawl. It was as if he was falling from a cliff, but no matter how hard he tried to hold on, no matter what memory passed through his mind, of love, of life, of winning and losing, he couldn't help but fall.

The Subaru entered his peripheral vision.

Frank saw the spot where the two cars would collide.

He closed his eyes and remembered life.

He thought of love.

He had time for one last breath before the old Subaru slammed into the side of his Volvo.

CHAPTER TWENTY-FIVE

A REGULAR BEEPING SOMEWHERE FAR AWAY BECAME PART OF Frank's dream. It grew louder as consciousness weaved its way towards the daylight behind his closed eyes. Slowly opening his lids, Frank saw two nurses standing with their backs to him. Through the open door was a corridor with a lime-green floor and white walls.

The beeping was coming from behind his head. He turned to see it. But a sharp pain rose up like the tail of a scorpion and stung his neck muscles before scurrying away, leaving Frank to groan in pain.

"Mr Carver," said one of the nurses, a pretty redhead with a light blue uniform and professional smile. "How are you feeling?"

"A little confused if I'm honest," Frank replied.

"You've been in an accident, Mr Carver."

"Call me Frank."

"Okay. You've been in an accident, Frank. You're in St Margaret's Hospital in Epping. Are you in any pain?"

"No," he said, although he was conscious not to move his head.

"There are no broken bones, but you do have severe bruising. So we're going to keep you in for a while."

"What about the other guy?"

"What other guy, Frank? You were travelling alone."

"The other car," said Frank. "The one that hit me?"

"I can find out for you. But as far as I know, you veered off the road, rolled and landed in the river. Two fishermen pulled you out."

"There was another car."

"It's okay, Frank. You've had a nasty hit to your head. Just rest a while and if you need anything, you can press this button here." She showed Frank the little red button on a wire fixed to the side of the bed. Then she left the room, leaving Frank to admire her rear at it swayed from side to side. But the pleasure was short lived as Melody Mills stepped into view wearing a surprised but friendly smile.

"She's old enough to be your daughter, sir," said Mills.

"I wasn't-"

"It's okay, sir," she said. "I'm sure you're in a lot of shock and not quite yourself."

She placed a small sports bag on the floor and put a smartphone on the bedside table.

"Your replacement phone," said Mills. "I've had Tenant restore a backup. It should look and feel exactly like your last one, minus any messages you received since the last backup."

"Thank you, Mills," said Frank. "How did you know-"

"In case you've forgotten, sir, we work for the UK's finest. We were alerted as soon as your car's number plate was entered into the system."

"Good work." Frank paused. "No grapes?"

"No grapes, I'm afraid. I didn't take you for the grape type, sir. But you'll find a change of clothes in the bag. I had to guess your size so sorry if it's wrong."

"Thank you, Mills," said Frank. "I'm sure they will be fine."

"Is there anything else, sir? What were you doing out here?"

"My car?" said Frank, ignoring her second question.

"It's being pulled from the river and from what I hear, it's a write-off."

"My camera. Can you get my camera?"

"If it was inside, I think you'll be needing a new one, sir."

"See if Tenant can get the photos from it. Keep it confidential. The last few photos are of a man. Run some facial recognition and send me the results."

"I'll see what I can do, sir."

"Thanks," said Frank.

"Oh, before I forget," said Mills, placing a car key beside Frank's new phone. "Black Range Rover in the car park."

"A Range Rover?"

"We figured you needed an upgrade, sir. Denver managed to wrangle it from the car pool. I've put a parking sticker inside so you're good for two days. I'll be back before then to see how you're getting on."

"Thanks, Mills. What would I do without you?"

"Aside from walk home in a hospital gown?" said Mills. "I'll let you rest. But call me if you need anything."

"I need your weapon," said Frank.

"Sir?"

"I was forced off the road, Mills. They might come back for me."

"But, sir, the report says you came off the road and rolled. There was no-one else involved."

"I was there, Mills. I saw the car. It was a Subaru."

"Sir~"

"Just trust me, Mills. Leave your weapon."

All humour dropped as the two locked eyes. Then Mills

released her weapon from beneath her armpit, checked behind her for nurses, and tucked it beneath the pile of new clothes in the sports bag.

"Does this have something to do with the camera, sir?"

"Run the facial recognition, Mills. It's important."

"I'm all over it, sir," replied Mills. She made to leave then turned at the door, smiling. "Oh and leave those nurses alone."

The door closed behind her, allowing Frank a moment's peace. But his active mind was already piecing together a plan.

A dull pain seized his arm as he pulled the hydration drip free. A trickle of thin blood ran down his skin, but he wiped it away with his gown before pulling on the fresh t-shirt and trousers. Mills had done a good job guessing his size. Even the shoes were a perfect fit.

His body revolted against the movement. His bruises announced their presence with every effort, and each time, the warnings of his body slowed Frank. But by the time he was dressed and had tucked Mills' weapon into his waistband, he felt he could pass as a visitor. He glanced around the small room, collected his phone, car key and wallet, which was still damp, and eased the door open.

Nurses flitted from room to room in an endless state of controlled hurry. Seeing the reception to his right, Frank slipped into the corridor, walking slowly to minimise the limp from the bruise on his right leg.

As he walked, he diverted his eyes to his phone, trying to avoid the guilty look of a man escaping from prison. He saw the automatic doors ahead. Each second, he waited for a gentle tap on his shoulder or the sound of his name being called out.

Outside was damp. The sky was a dull grey blanket of cloud that filled the space from horizon to horizon. Rain had left a sheen across the surface of the ground. In the corner of the car park, standing alone with an almost conspicuous appearance, was the Range Rover.

Climbing into the car was tougher than Frank had anticipated. Raising his leg aggravated his bruises and the effort to haul himself inside sent stabs of pain through his neck. By the time he was sitting in the seat, he was breathless and questioning his own plan.

Searching his phone, Frank retrieved the message from Terry Thomson with the location of the gun drop. Thankfully, it hadn't been lost. Then he typed a message to Mills stating a fake plan. His finger hovered over the send button. But the intricate lies and tangled web of deceit bore more implications that his imagination could process.

He hit delete.

26

CHAPTER TWENTY-SIX

ANXIETY GRIPPED SHAUN'S CHEST WITH ITS STRONG CLAWS the moment he opened his eyes and recognised the small room. He dressed in the only clothes he had, baulking at the smell, and wandered outside. Through the door to Terry's office, Shaun heard three voices. Instead of walking inside, Shaun ventured back to the kitchen, made four cups of tea and found an old tray on which to carry them.

He knocked and walked into the office to find all three men standing around Terry's desk. They looked up as he entered.

"Tea?" he said, hopeful that the gesture would initiate a positive start to the day.

"Now that's what I call cognitive thinking. Well done, Shaun," said Terry. He appeared to be forcing a jovial mood, masking the lingering sadness for the loss of his son.

"Where should I put them?" he asked.

Lenny reached out, took a cup and passed it to the old man before reaching back and taking one for himself. Rob took one too and left Shaun holding the tray with both hands, unable to let go and remove his own cup. His nerves began to kick in. His hands began to shake and tea spilt onto the tray.

"Stick it on the table over there, Shaun," Lenny said.

The opportunity for a barrage of insults was open, but neither Terry nor Lenny took it. But Rob turned, staring at Shaun while sipping his tea.

"What do *you* want?"

"I…I thought we were planning," replied Shaun, realising he may have intruded.

"Yeah, *we* are planning, but *you* don't need to plan. All you need to do is-"

"Easy, Robby. The bloke just made you a cup of tea. Play nicely," said Terry. "Shaun, squeeze in, mate. You're going to need to know this more than any of us, anyway."

Shaun moved to an empty space around the table where a large map was opened out.

"Right. The drop is at six o'clock. Lenny, talk me through the sequence of events."

"We'll arrive just before six. Rob and me will get out and walk through these trees here." He pointed at the thick line of trees that surrounded the location on three sides. "Just in case Cartwright's lot are planning an ambush. Shaun will take the van in on his own. Rob and me will find-"

"Rob and I, Lenny. It's Rob and I," said Terry.

"Rob and you, boss?" said Lenny.

"No, it's English, Lenny. It's not Rob and *me*. It's Rob and *I*."

"Right. Okay. So Rob and I will find somewhere out of sight to keep an eye on things. If things go well, Shaun will drop the guns and get the money, and we'll be waiting on the road when he pulls out."

"What if things don't go well?"

"Rob and…*I* will be in a good place to step in and take

them out. We won't start shooting unless it looks like they're pulling one over on us," finished Lenny.

"Shaun, talk me through it," said Terry, moving his attention to the wiry, nervous kid.

"I'll drop Rob and Lenny off before the car park then drive in alone."

"Good. Then what?"

"I'll turn the van around so I'm facing the exit like Lenny told me to."

"Good."

"Then I'll wait for them."

"Okay. What happens if a nosy policeman comes sniffing around?"

"I'll tell him that I'm a delivery driver and I just stopped for a break or something."

"Have you got your driver's license on you?"

"Yeah, it's..."

Shaun reached for his wallet in his pocket and removed his license. Lenny took it from him, snapped it in half and tossed the two halves in the waste bin behind Terry.

"Don't be stupid, Shaun. You're all over the news. You're on the run," said Lenny.

"Lenny's right, Shaun. You show a copper that licence and not only will you be nicked for being the dirty, little nonce you are, but they'll also be slapping a fair chunk of time on you for what's in the back of the van." The old man opened the desk drawer to his right and pulled out a wallet. "*This* is your wallet. Throw the other one away."

Shaun opened his wallet again and began to search inside, but Lenny took it from him and tossed it in the bin with the license. He then took the new wallet from Terry and passed it to Shaun.

"So, you're all parked up, and they're there. Now what?"

"I show them the crate?"

"Exactly. Open the doors and step back. Let them work it out. You want to know why?"

"Why?"

"Because, Shaun, if I wanted a load of guns and didn't want to pay, and if the dopey bloke I was buying them off climbed into the back of the van of his own fruition, I'd shut the doors on him, drive off and have the lot for nothing. They'd have the van, the money *and* the guns, Shaun."

"Right."

"Then what?"

"They open the crate, have a look, give me the money then move the guns."

"Good boy, Shaun."

"Any questions?"

"No."

"Good. One more thing. Lenny, Rob, I've arranged to have a little bit of security attend. He won't get involved, but he will sit and watch. Don't do anything stupid. Just do what you have to do and everything will be fine," said Terry. "Shaun?"

"Yeah?"

"Don't yeah me, Shaun."

"Sorry."

"I've got a little surprise lined up for the Cartwrights. As soon as the deal is done, you need to get your pervy little backside out of there and don't look back."

"A surprise?" said Shaun. "What kind of surprise?"

"Oink oink, Shaun," said Terry. "Oink oink."

27

CHAPTER TWENTY-SEVEN

TWO HUNDRED YARDS FROM THE DROP, HARVEY PULLED OFF the narrow country lane and rode into the thick trees, finding a safe place to conceal his bike. Using long, bushy branches pulled from nearby trees, he covered it over. Then he walked through the forest to find Julios waiting in the van.

Darkness fell fast. As the two men waited, Harvey's pulse raised and fell with each sporadic passing car.

"John was asking about you," Julios said eventually. "I spoke to him this morning while you ran."

"What was he asking?"

"He's just concerned. You keep asking him about your parents."

"He knows something."

"That's not my concern."

"Tell me, Julios. Was you around when they found us?"

"I was. You know I was."

"Where did they find us?"

"What did John tell you?"

"That's not what I asked."

"What did he tell you?"

"In his bar, after closing. We were in a booth. I was in a hamper and Hannah sat beside me."

"Then you know. Stop chasing nothing. It's clouding your judgment."

"It's not the full story," said Harvey.

"I know nothing more," said Julios, attempting to end the conversation.

But Harvey had caught the thread between his teeth.

"You too? I thought I could at least count on you."

"You can count on me, as you have always done, to keep you alive," Julios snapped.

"You know something?"

"All I know is that if you do not get your head out of ancient history and into the game, we will both be killed. Snap out of it," Julios ordered.

Then he slid out of the van just as a black Range Rover nosed into the small space.

"Recognise him?" asked Julios, as Harvey climbed outside.

"The windows are tinted. I can't see his face," replied Harvey, joining Julios in front of the van.

The Range Rover parked in front of the entrance, leaving enough room for another van to enter and park.

"Do you think that's them?" asked Harvey.

"Why would they park over there?" said Julios. "No. It's a babysitter. He's there to make sure we don't try to rip them off."

Harvey checked his watch.

"Any minute now."

CHAPTER TWENTY-EIGHT

"I knew it," said Harvey. "They're up to something."

Julios looked at Harvey, whose eyes tracked the driver as he turned the van and reversed up alongside theirs.

"That's my *target*," said Harvey.

"Your target?" asked Julios.

"Shaun Tyson."

"Him?" said Julios. "He's a-"

"He's out on bail. Preys on little girls."

"We're here for the guns, Harvey. Keep your little hobby out of this," said Julios.

"But why is he working for Thomson?"

"I said keep your hobby out of this. Stay professional. Stay alert."

But deep inside Harvey's stomach, the beast had awoken at the sight of Shaun Tyson. A long finger reached up and clawed at Harvey's chest. The beast was hungry.

"*Harvey*," snapped Julios, bringing Harvey back from his stare. "I'll watch the Range Rover. You check the guns."

The driver's door opened and Shaun Tyson stepped down

to the ground. He glanced back at the Range Rover then returned his nervous eyes to flick between Harvey and Julios.

"Friend of yours?" asked Harvey.

Shaun nodded. He seemed reluctant to step past Harvey to open the back of the van.

"Open the doors," said Harvey. "And don't try anything stupid."

A growl from Harvey's stomach sent a wave of energy through his body as Shaun stepped past him. His eyes pulsed as a dose of adrenaline released into his bloodstream. Harvey pulled his handgun from the waistband of his cargo pants and aimed at the doors, ready for someone to jump out.

But nobody did. Inside was a wooden crate on a pallet and nothing else.

Having opened the rear doors, Shaun stepped back out of Harvey's way. They were all in full view of the mystery car. Harvey made the gun safe and tucked it away. Then he drew his knife.

The movement frightened Shaun, and he stepped back, his eyes wide with fear. Searching inside the boy's eyes, Harvey found nothing but the desire to tear him limb from limb. He found himself imagining how he would kill him. It would be slow and it would be painful.

Julios joined them at the back of the van and positioned himself where he could see both the boy and the Range Rover. He'd pulled his own handgun from his waist and let it hang at his side in clear view. A warning to whoever was in the car.

"Are you going to stand there looking at the boy? Or are you going to get the guns?" said Julios, once more snapping Harvey from his thoughts.

Removing the wooden lid of the crate required little effort. Using his knife to pry it from the box, Harvey let it fall to the van's floor with a deafening boom like a bass drum. Inside, as expected, were twelve Heckler and Koch MP-5s.

Harvey reached in to check the serial numbers had been removed as agreed. He tested the action and slotted one of the twenty-four magazines in and out.

"They're new. They're clean," he called out to Julios.

"Okay. Move them out," said Julios.

"I need the money first," said Shaun. His voice wavered. "You can't take them until you give me the money."

Shaun's voice was weak as if he were a lamb. And Harvey felt like a wolf. He stepped down with the rifle in his hands. Ignoring Shaun's weak request, he opened the door to his own van and lay down the gun at one end of a thick blanket inside. Then Harvey returned his attention to Shaun.

"They said I had to take the money or-"

"Or what?" said Harvey. "Or your friend will take the money from me?"

"I'm not looking for trouble," said Shaun. "I was just told-"

"Just pay the boy," said Julios. A wry and very rare grin crept onto his face beneath the bored expression. "Let's get this over with."

From his jacket pocket, Harvey produced an envelope. He held it at head height, weighing it in his hand and studying Shaun's face, remembering every minute detail. He took a step towards the boy, peering into his eyes and enjoying the fear that ran across his face like a stampede of weakness.

"Now, now," Julios cautioned Harvey. "Play nicely."

Harvey slapped the envelope of money against Shaun's chest. For the briefest of moments, as Shaun reached up to take it, their hands connected. It felt as if a pulse of electricity burst into his veins. Harvey reeled.

"Are you going to help or are you going to just stand there?" asked Harvey.

Shaun returned his look but did not speak. He took a step back, pocketing the envelope. His eyes darted from the van to the Range Rover and back to Harvey.

"You get them out and pass them to me," said Harvey.

"I'm not allowed," said Shaun, his voice stuttering. "They said I wasn't-"

But Shaun's refusal was broken by Harvey snatching his gun from his waist and placing the muzzle against Shaun's temple.

"In the van, now," he said.

One by one, Shaun passed Harvey the remaining eleven weapons, which Harvey covered with the blanket before slamming the doors to his van. Beads of nervous sweat had formed on Shaun's forehead. When he jumped down to close the doors of his own van, he seemed relieved to be out and for the episode to be over.

But as he moved to walk towards the driver's door, Harvey blocked his path. The urge to reach out and grab the boy's throat was strong. The beast inside him was ready.

"Are we done?" said Julios, breaking the tension.

Harvey stepped to one side, allowing Shaun to pass him and run to the front of the van. The engine started before the door had even closed. The wheels spun as Shaun, in his desperation to get away, fumbled with the pedals. Harvey and Julios watched the van disappear onto the lane and waited for the Range Rover to follow. But it remained stationary.

"Let's go," said Harvey, climbing into the van. "Drop me at my bike and I'll follow."

But something had caught Julios' attention. He walked to the centre of the clearing, staring into the Range Rover as if his gaze could cut through the tinted windows.

Every sense in Harvey's body came alive in an instant.

His eyes flicked from Julios to the car. The driver's window lowered.

Julios reached for his weapon.

A handgun emerged through the window.

Dropping to one knee, Julios raised his gun and aimed.

The two men opened fire.

Harvey leapt from the van, pulling his gun as the Range Rover lurched into action. Its wheels span as it sped from the scene. Harvey opened fire, shattering the car windows and bursting its tyres. The black bodywork was peppered with bullet holes. As Harvey released the magazine and slammed a fresh one into place, at the very edge of his vision, he saw Julios lying face-first on the ground.

CHAPTER TWENTY-NINE

THE HUGE SUV BOUNCED OVER THE BODY OF JULIOS Saville. All around Frank, glass shattered. A single bullet tore through the car's interior, ricocheted past Frank's ear and shattered the windscreen, leaving a sprawling web of finger-like cracks and a thumb-sized hole in the glass.

The two blown tyres hindered his turn out of the clearing. As Frank hauled on the wheel with his foot flat on the accelerator, the front end of the car tore through a hedgerow, kicking up dirt and sliding from side to side as the remaining rubber searched for grip.

Daring once to look up and check his rear-view mirror, Frank saw the dark shape of the surviving man run into the road. He raised his weapon and emptied the remainder of his magazine into the back of Frank's car. The rear window shattered. When the shooting finally stopped, Frank pulled himself up from where he was ducked below the line of fire. The two blown tyres pulled him to one side, forcing Frank to use all his strength to keep the car straight.

The end of the road was in view, but the ordeal had been too much for the car. Thick plumes of white smoke poured from the engine bay. With the windscreen shattered and full of holes, and every other window blown away, it soon began to fill the car. Hanging his head out the window, Frank managed to reach the junction where a left turn would take him onto the M11 motorway south, and a right turn would take him north. Straight on would take him into the Essex countryside.

The remainder of one of the tyres pulled free from the wheel and shot off to the left. A shower of sparks flew up into Frank's face as the wheel cut into the tarmac road. Seeing no other choice, he forced the car forward, knowing the man would be right behind.

The motorway passed below him and the darkness of the countryside closed in on all sides. But with no lights to see by and his eyes sore from the smoking engine, only glimpses of the tree line to the side of the road guided Frank onward.

Until the dark line of trees disappeared.

And the angry rumble of the wheels on the road stopped.

For the second time in two days, Frank's broken body was tossed around inside a rolling car. His head smashed into the door frame then the steering wheel. Broken glass rained down on him, and huge scoops of dirt ripped from the ground and flew into his face. The car came to a stop on its roof at the foot of a steep embankment in a wash of angry steam and smoke.

His body screamed at him, unable to tell old bruises from new. Frank gracelessly lowered himself to the roof amongst the shards of glass and dirt. A loud whining rang in his ear as if he'd just stepped from a loud nightclub, and a trickle of blood ran into his eye from a vague cut somewhere on his head.

Close by, an engine approached. The sound of tyres on gravel. A flicker of headlights.

Then nothing.

The desire to give up was overwhelming, but something inside Frank, something stronger than he knew, pushed him on. He reached for his gun, which lay among the broken glass and dirt.

A van door slammed. Frank recognised the sound.

With slow and tender movements, Frank eased himself into the prone position, aiming at the embankment through the rear window as footsteps made their way through the long grass.

In the darkness beyond the car, two legs appeared. They stopped, as if the owner was searching the scene, then eased forward.

In his mind, among wild thoughts of the killer's eyes and of the death he faced, Frank tried to recall how many shots he had already fired.

But the footsteps came closer. Just two legs.

The pulse of his heartbeat was deafening. The throb of his bruised legs and ribs was excruciating. The blood that flowed from a wound on his torn skin blinded him in one eye. His gun shook in his hands. His finger curled around the trigger, ready to squeeze, and at last, when the dark outline of a head peered into view through the empty window, Frank pulled the trigger.

But the hammer fell on an empty chamber.

CHAPTER THIRTY

THE MOTIONLESS FORM OF HARVEY'S MENTOR, BEST FRIEND and only companion lay still, face down in the mud. In his hand, the gun he'd cleaned with meticulous regularity was filled with the same dirt that stained the man's face. His fat finger still rested on the trigger and his strong hand still clutched the grip.

A single tyre mark ran across the width of his body and a hole in his neck identified the kill shot. Blood no longer oozed from the wound, but Julios' face and overcoat still wore the evidential spatter. It was inky black in the dark night.

Dropping to his knees alongside his friend and with his own gun in his hand, Harvey took in the sight as if he'd borne the brunt of the gunfire himself. A stab of pain in his chest tightened and a rhythmic pounding of anguish in his head created the urge to scream out loud into the silent sky above.

A familiar scratching of a long, hungry finger teased Harvey's mind with thoughts of retribution. It filled him with images of pain and suffering. Harvey knelt, indulging in the promise of revenge until, at last, he said goodbye to his friend.

"I'll come back for you."

Harvey cast a fleeting glimpse at the van and made his way toward his bike, fuelled by a deep craving. It was a craving he'd felt only once before as a child standing behind a man in the darkness.

Colliding with trees invisible among the shadows, Harvey made his way through the thick forest. Blinded by his desire to find the man in the Range Rover, Harvey stumbled into his bike. Drunk with passion, loss and fatigue, he manoeuvred onto the narrow country lane. The relentless beast inside him was scratching its way out, controlling his thoughts and guiding every action.

The rear wheel spun with a snatch of his wrist and release of the clutch. Harvey felt the beating heart of the bike as if it were a part of him. He worked through the gears, winding the engine up to full speed. Every sensory organ in his body was alive to his surroundings. The world shot past in a blur of dark shapes and darker shadows until light crept in and the winding snake-like motorway lay before him. It enticed his poisoned mind with an open space in which to ride and scream and shout at the top of his lungs. So fast that nobody could hear. So carefree that cars he passed were merely indistinct stationary objects.

The hot metal of the bike warmed the insides of Harvey's legs in a stark contrast to the bite of the cold air on his numbed fingers and face.

And without warning, the world appeared real once more.

He slowed to a crawl and moved across to the slow lane, allowing cars he had passed moments before in a heightened state of delirious mourning to speed by as if the world hadn't noticed the death of Julios Saville.

Coming to a stop on the shoulder, he switched off the engine and warmed his hands on the fuel tank. To his left, rolling fields and trees seamlessly met the dark horizon, masking where one ended and the other began. But somewhere in that layer of dark unknown, there was unfathomable beauty, a dawning of realisation. It struck Harvey as hard as the deaths of his best friend, Julios, and the only person he'd ever loved, Hannah.

A calm wash of cool blood filled his veins, easing the craving inside him and stroking the wild emotions that had run riot. It was then that he knew. In that moment. When a world of fields and trees and the massive expanse of sky joined hands hidden by shadows, the answer came to him.

CHAPTER THIRTY-ONE

"Sir? Are you in there? Are you okay?" asked Melody.

Her voice struck a chord in Frank, forcing him to exhale with audible relief.

"Sir, can you hear me? We're going to get you out."

Every muscle in Frank's body relaxed. His head dropped to the glass-riddled roof of the car. He let go of the weapon. His eyes, after all the fear, tension and adrenaline, released a single tear. Muffled voices approached and flashlights switched on to show the full extent of the damage. Shielding his eyes from the bright light, Frank reached forward to grasp the hand of Denver Cox.

"How did you know where to find me?" said Frank, ashamed to hear the tremble in his voice.

"Tenant tracked your phone, sir," said Melody. "We found a strange message from an unknown number when we restored your mobile."

"The location?"

"Yes, sir. So when we couldn't find you at the hospital, we figured this is where you'd be. I'm sorry if we overstepped the mark, sir. We were worried."

"Possibly the best police work you've done this week, Mills," said Frank with a laugh that sent a wave of sharp pain through his ribs. He grimaced, sucking in air through his teeth to control the agony.

"Let's get you to the hospital, sir," said Melody.

"No," said Frank. "We need to go back."

"To where, sir? We saw the van leave, and the motorbike."

"You'll see," said Frank.

With the help of Cox, step by step, he walked up the embankment to the team's old VW Transporter van. Frank was helped into the passenger side, Cox drove, and Mills and Tenant sat in the back. A workbench had been built along one side, where Tenant had fixed two computer screens. Below the bench was a computer and a network of cables splayed out in all directions, including along the chassis of the vehicle to the roof, where the VSAT antenna was fixed for mobile internet access. In a space behind the front seats, Melody stored her surveillance equipment and sniper rifle.

They drove back over the motorway and toward the scene of the crime where, less than thirty minutes previously, Frank had engaged in a shootout. The memory seemed a lifetime ago.

"Is this the right road?" said Frank. "I don't remember that bend and I don't remember that field."

"Shock, sir," said Melody from behind, as Cox turned the little van into the clearing and stopped at the entrance. "You'll be amazed at the things it can do to your mind."

In front of them, lit by the headlights and alien to its surroundings, was the body of Julios Saville.

The team were silent for a few seconds as they took in the sight. The van parked to the right had three bullet holes in the bonnet, which must have been from Frank, although he had no recollection of shooting them.

"Did you manage to find my camera?" Frank asked nobody in particular.

"We did, sir," said Tenant. "It was water damaged, but I recovered the files. The camera is a write-off, I'm afraid."

"Forget about the camera. Did you run the facial recognition?"

The team were silent once again.

"Sir?" began Melody. "What exactly happened here? That's Julios Saville. He's been wanted for more than twenty years. The rider, we strongly believe, is the vigilante that we've been hunting for over a decade. What's the connection?"

"Cox, Tenant, load Mr Saville into the back, would you?"

The two operatives acknowledged the order and got to work.

"Mills, help me out."

Every movement seemed to find a new nerve ending with a new feeling of pain. But with slow steps and the help of Melody, Frank walked to the back of the white van. Then he paused. Before he opened the door, he turned to face Melody.

"Mills, you're my number one," he began. "You're a credit to the force and I honestly don't know what I'd do without you. Without any of you. You, Cox and Tenant, you're what we used to call a dream team."

"Thank you, sir," replied Mills. She was maintaining her professionalism but unable to hide the perplexed expression in her furrowed brow.

"You've got a great career ahead of you. You all have. But while you might be the smartest person I ever met, sometimes, Mills, you need to trust your instinct. Even if your instinct seems to be leading you against the grain." He lowered his voice. "And sometimes you have to do things that are...questionable."

"Sir?" said Mills.

She was desperate to see inside the van to see what Frank was hiding.

"That man over there is a promotion, Mills. No question. He's been wanted for two decades, and although we have no proof, we know he's responsible for more murders than you can imagine."

"I saw on his file, sir. He's a catch, alright."

"And inside here," continued Frank, "is a god damn medal."

He pulled open the doors, tossed the blanket to one side, and stepped back to let Mills take in the view of twelve Heckler and Koch MP-5s, dark and heavy, but glistening in the moonlight.

CHAPTER THIRTY-TWO

"It's over. I'm out," said Harvey, slamming the door to John's home office.

The entrance was far removed from Harvey's usual silent approach, and John stood in surprise for a second before a lifetime of wealth and power helped him regain control.

"What do you mean you're out?" replied John, sinking back down. "What's happened?"

"It's all lies. There's no truth to any of it, is there?" said Harvey.

"What do you mean, Son?" said John. "And remember who you're talking to."

"I know who I'm talking to, John. I'm done with it. I'm done with the lies."

"I don't understand."

"The hamper, the pub, the blankets, and the made-up story about how you found us. It's all lies."

"Harvey," said John, "take it easy. What's brought this on?"

"I suppose you know about Hannah too, don't you?"

"Hannah?" said John, surprised to hear Harvey mention her name.

"You know what happened to her, don't you?" said Harvey. "That night. The night she cut herself to ribbons in shame."

"No, Harvey, I-"

"Well, I know. It was Jack. And if I knew, then you damn well knew too. And he wasn't alone, was he?"

"Listen, Son. I don't know what's happened. But you need to calm yourself down. Here, have a drink," said John, passing Harvey his crystal tumbler of brandy with the remains of three ice cubes floating on the surface.

Harvey took the drink then launched it across the room. Glass shattered to the hardwood floor and a golden stain edged its way across the flock wallpaper.

"You need to start telling some truths, John. You see all this?" Harvey swept his hand through the air. "I'll burn it to the ground and I'll take you with it."

With practised composure, John straightened the cuffs of his shirt, a habit he'd formed and a sign he was processing information. Walking from behind his desk, following a well-trodden path to his drinks cabinet, he poured himself a fresh brandy. Three chinks of ice against crystal preceded a gurgling decanter, which was then placed in its spot on the silver tray. With his back to Harvey, John sipped at his drink. He puckered his lips then returned to his place behind the desk and rested his forearms on the black leather inlay.

"Where's Julios?" he asked, his voice calm and controlled.

"Face down in the mud with a bullet hole in his neck," replied Harvey.

John sipped at his drink, not the faintest of emotions betraying his thoughts.

"That's why you're upset," said John. "It's natural."

A pulse of life bulged at Harvey's eyes.

"What about the guns?" continued John.

But it was too late.

In one smooth move, Harvey had reached over, grabbed

his foster father by his neck and dragged him across the desk to the parquet floor, gripping his throat with one strong hand.

"Give me one good reason why I shouldn't kill you right now," said Harvey, his voice hoarse with tension as he squeezed the life from John Cartwright.

But John stared back with a reproachful eye. Any sign of his struggle was masked by years of control, lies and deceit.

"I know who killed Hannah," he rasped.

A stab of the beast's sharp claws. Harvey released his grip.

"You want to know?"

John slapped Harvey's hand away and pushed himself to his feet. He smoothed his trousers, flattened his hair and straightened his cuffs then moved back to his place behind the desk where, once more, he took his seat.

"Sit down," said John.

Harvey didn't react.

"I said sit down," said John, louder and more forceful.

The two men locked eyes, daring each other to break, testing the other man's resolve.

"Have it your way," said John, sipping at his drink. "But be warned, what I tell you will destroy you."

"No, John," replied Harvey. "*You* destroyed me with your lies. You destroyed me when you had Julios train me. You bred me to be a killer because your own son was too spineless."

"You won't antagonise me, Harvey. I love you both. But as much as I love you both, you're both flawed."

Harvey didn't reply.

"I'll do a deal. It's a onetime offer."

"I know your deals well enough."

"It's a onetime offer," continued John, ignoring Harvey's comment. "You do one last job for me-"

"I told you. It's over," said Harvey. He pushed off the desk and paced the room, turning back to John only when the rage inside him showed a momentary lapse. "There will be no more jobs."

"You'll do one more job for me, Harvey Stone, if it's the last thing you do," said John. His voice had raised well beyond its normal volume and the fire in his wide eyes was burning with anger.

"And what?" said Harvey. "I do one last job for you, so you can screw me over one last time. Is that it?"

"You do one last job for your old man," replied John, his voice lower, calmer and the tone softer. "For me. Like the old days."

Harvey met his foster father's eyes with a raised eyebrow, waiting for the finish.

"And I'll tell you who raped Hannah."

CHAPTER THIRTY-THREE

"CAPONE, *HOW YOU DOING*?" ASKED ROB IN A MOCK ITALIAN accent as Shaun approached.

He and Lenny were unloading boxes and sacks from the van.

"I'm okay. Terry said to come and help you. He said he needs some time alone. What can I do?"

"Listen, Shaun. You're not really a people person, are you?"

"Eh?"

"You may have been *told* to come and help, but you don't need to tell us you've been told to come and help. Right, Rob?"

"That's right, Lenny."

Shaun looked confused.

"See, if you had walked up to us and said, 'Hey guys, can I help you?' we would've just thought it was your exceedingly good nature that brought you out into the cold, and we'd have appreciated the gesture. But being told to come out here means that you are, in fact, reluctant to help but will do it because the boss said so. Right?"

"I guess," replied Shaun, unsure if he should be helping or not.

"He *guesses*, Rob."

Lenny climbed into the rear of the van and pulled a few boxes to the edge before jumping down. Rob snorted at Shaun and then carried on shifting the boxes to a neat pile in the corner.

"What are you doing, anyway?"

"We're emptying the van, Shaun. What does it look like we're doing?" said Lenny, as he dropped another box carefully to the ground.

"What is all this stuff?"

"It's all the food for Bradley's wake," said Lenny. "Blimey, he don't stop asking questions. Does he, Rob?"

"No, mate, he doesn't stop asking questions."

"You know what, Rob?"

"What's that, Lenny?"

"I seem to *remember* something about questions," said Lenny. "It was something the boss said about asking too many of them."

Shaun looked at the floor. He'd thought he'd won some respect from the two men, but they were both still as mean as ever.

"Oh, *I* remember that," said Rob. He stopped and leaned on a large wooden crate. "What *was* it now? Was it, if you ask too many questions, you get to lay in a big cosy bed all day, and the boss would pay for hookers to come and keep you company?"

"No, I don't think so, Rob. That doesn't ring any bells. Was it, if you ask too many questions, the boss will make you a roast dinner with all the trimmings and serve it to you while you watch the football?"

"Hmmm, no, I don't think it was that either," said Rob.

He laughed as he took two sacks from Lenny. "I'm sure it had *something* to do with..."

"*Pigs*," they both said at the same time.

"That's it," said Lenny. "Pigs."

"If you ask too many questions, the boss will feed you to the pigs."

"Alright, alright. I get it," said Shaun, and turned away.

The two men laughed at his dejection and removed the last of the boxes from the van.

"Look, Shaun, if you really want to help, grab that sack over there and the roll of gaffer tape," said Lenny.

Shaun looked around and found an old hessian sack on the floor and the gaffer tape on a shelf above it. He passed them to Lenny who threw them into the back of the van.

"Is that it?" Shaun asked.

"Easy, eh?" said Lenny.

"One day you'll be as good as us at moving boxes and passing the gaffer tape," said Rob.

"Is that *more* guns?" said Shaun, pointing to a wooden crate.

"I don't believe it, Rob."

"I'm flabbergasted, Len."

"What?" said Shaun.

Shaun's world turned black as the sack was forced over his head and he was thrown into the back of the van.

CHAPTER THIRTY-FOUR

"I don't know how the old man does it. Imagine having your son killed and still being able to hold it together enough to plan the northern job, sell guns to Cartwright *and* arrange the funeral."

Harvey watched from the shadows to the side of the house as the larger of the two men spoke.

"Yeah, I feel for him," said the other. "I did ask if we could help, but he said he'd take care of it. He said he wanted to do it, like it was some kind of parental obligation."

"You think he feels guilty?"

"For what? Bradley? No. Bradley walked the line, and he knew it. We all do, right?"

"Yeah, I know what you mean. Do you ever think about getting out before it's too late?"

"What do you mean too late?"

"You know, getting killed. Seems like it's getting serious again. Bradley's dead. That guy at the gun deal. I even heard the old man talking to that bloke on the phone. You know he killed Donny Cartwright?"

"What bloke?"

"You know." The man began to talk in hushed tones. "The bloke he gets to *take care of business*."

"None of it makes sense, mate. As for getting out, do you really think you could walk away from all this with your knees intact? Do you honestly reckon Terry would let you?"

"Hold on. Keep it down, Rob."

Footsteps approached across the gravel, but from where Harvey was hiding, the newcomer was out of sight. An image of the scene formed in his mind.

"Capone, *how you doing?*" said one of the men.

"I'm okay. Terry said to come and help you. He said he needs some time alone. What can I do?"

In an instant, Harvey placed the weak voice. The image in his mind evolved to include Shaun Tyson. As the conversation between the two men and Tyson played on, Harvey's imagination digressed into scenes of twisted retribution.

"Is that *more* guns?"

The question snapped Harvey from his wild daydream. A rare smile crept onto his face as a plan formulated.

"I don't believe it, Rob."

"I'm flabbergasted, Len."

"What?" asked the simple voice.

Muffled, panicked screams and anguished cries were followed by gaffer tape stripped off a roll then the thud of Tyson's body hitting the wooden floor of the van. Rear doors slammed with thundering booms in the night. The scene played out with brutal attention to detail in Harvey's head.

"*Questions*, Shaun. We told you," said one of the men, and banged on the side of the van.

"Do you want to take him now or in the morning?" asked one man to the other.

"I'm bleeding knackered, Rob. But tomorrow's Bradley's funeral. It's going to be hell."

The van fired into life, coughing black diesel smoke from

its exhaust, and the driver found first gear with a crunch of the gearbox.

Harvey made his move.

Making almost no sound, he slipped behind the vehicle, placed one foot on the rear bumper and found two hand-holds. The moment the van lurched into action, Harvey put his full weight onto the bumper, timing the shift with the rising of the clutch and movement of the vehicle.

Clinging to the rear doors, his view was restricted. His plan was vague but options had been limited. The driver turned right out of the courtyard, steering the van along the empty country lane where overgrown trees scraped the sides and scratched his face. The driver stopped only once, at a T-junction at the end of the lane. The break gave Harvey precious moments to adjust his fingers and search for a better handhold.

But the journey was short. They had travelled less than a mile by Harvey's estimates when the van slowed and pulled into a working farm. It continued down a bumpy track between huge barns and machinery sheds.

The main house, which was set back from the rest of the buildings, appeared old, dark, and poorly maintained, while the barns seemed to be well kept. Fresh mud flicked from the wheels as the van passed through a field, sliding and fighting for grip. The driver stayed in first gear, keeping the revs low. It was as if he knew the track well, seeking the higher dry patches of ground amid the thick glutinous mud.

Their arrival created a disturbance in the livestock. Head-lights shone two bright beams of light onto the end of the track. The vehicle shuddered to a stop. Dropping to the ground, Harvey crawled beneath the van just as the two front doors opened.

"Time to meet your maker, Shauny," said the driver, banging the side of the van

Harvey heard muffled whines and screams followed by scuffled struggles on the van's wooden floor as the rear doors opened and the two men pulled out Tyson and dropped him into the mud. His hands were bound behind his back and his heavy breathing was loud through the sack over his head.

Both men delivered a few taunting kicks to their prisoner, seeming to enjoy the warm up to the main event. The hessian sack was ripped off Tyson's head, but the kicks had left him breathless and he lay face down in the mud, his eyes shining with the guilty tears of a condemned man. A strip of gaffer tape had been placed across his mouth and the muffled screaming began. It was high like the cries of a child.

"Right," said one of the men. "Let's get him up and into the pen so we can get out of here."

"Here, Lenny. How about a little wager?"

"What? Like last time?" replied Lenny.

"Yeah. How long do you reckon he'll last?"

The man called Lenny seemed to consider his answer, giving Shaun time to look around, hopeful for the smallest chance of survival. His eyes fell on Harvey, who raised his index finger to his lips in the international sign for silence.

"I reckon less than a minute," said the first man. "He's not exactly a fighter, is he?"

"Alright, you're on. Ten quid?"

"Done," said the man.

Behind them, a chorus of grunting pigs chimed in.

"Don't worry, Shauny. The noise excites the pigs. They love it. Gets them all horny or hungry. One of the two. I doubt young Shaun would mind if they get a bit frisky, would you? Dirty little perv would probably enjoy it."

With wide, pleading eyes, Shaun held Harvey's stare for a second longer before he disappeared from view, dragged out of sight by the two men.

Harvey set to work.

Sliding in the mud beneath the van, he turned to watch as the men dragged Tyson towards a huge pig pen a few metres away. With slow, deliberate movements, Harvey rolled from his hiding place and walked into the open until he was standing just five feet behind them.

"Here piggy," called one of the men.

"What are you doing?" asked the other.

"I'm calling the pigs over."

"Pigs don't respond to being called. They respond to being fed."

Shaun struggled harder. His muffled screams grew higher and louder. As if sensing the weakness in the air, one by one, the pigs came to the fence, fighting for the prime position. Their size was impressive. They were the biggest swine Harvey had ever seen, fat, bulky shadows wallowing in the dark mud. But it was the noise they made that impressed him the most. The loud grunts and snorts of the hogs gave no indication of their number, but the sound was chaotic. Harvey used it to mask the sound of his own attack.

Switching his gun to his left hand, Harvey drew his knife with his right. Then he stepped behind the larger of the two men, who were both leaning on the fence, antagonising the hogs with imitations of farm animals.

In one swift movement, Harvey reached around and sliced the big man's throat. Raising his gun hand, he aimed at the man's friend. Harvey forced the dying man up onto the fence until his weight carried him over. He fell to the ground inside the pen with a slap, trying in vain to hold the two flaps of his neck together and stem the flow of blood.

All the pigs silenced, stopped and stared at the twitching body.

As the alpha made his way through the mud, driven on by the irony scent of blood, the second man, in horror, slowly turned to face Harvey, who stood grim-faced with his weapon aimed at the man's chest.

In disbelief, the man's gaze flicked from his dying friend to Harvey and back again.

No words were spoken. Both men weighed their odds. The largest of the hogs took its first tentative bite of the dead man's flesh.

"Do you know what you've just done?" the surviving man said to Harvey, shaking his head, still dumbstruck by the turn of events.

"Put your hands on the fence where I can see them."

"Do you even know who we are?"

A wild and furious bout of grunting announced the hog's approval of the man's flesh and the whole pack descended on the body.

"I don't care who you are. Put your hands on the fence," replied Harvey, shouting to be heard above the grunts and crunching of bones.

"What are you going to do? Shoot me?"

The man placed both hands on the fence. The alpha hog caught the movement. He carried on with his meal but kept a watchful eye on the second course.

A single gunshot found the mud behind the man's boot.

"The fence," said Harvey. "Climb it."

"What? No."

Harvey didn't reply. He just locked eyes with the man, reading his next moves and drinking in his fear.

"No. No, you're going to have to shoot me."

The man searched the darkness around him for help.

"We're alone. And you can run but you won't get far," said Harvey.

Then he paused, allowing the man time to consider his options.

"What's your name?" asked Harvey.

"Rob," the man replied after considering a lie.

"Okay, Rob," said Harvey. "Do you think you can make it to the other side of the pen before the pigs get you?"

"Are you *crazy*? What? No."

"How about a wager? You do gamble, don't you?"

Wide eyes glistening with fear stared back at Harvey as he stepped closer.

"If you can make it to the other side, I'll let you live."

The man silently considered the distance.

"Keep your hands on the fence," said Harvey

Harvey glanced across at the remains of the man in the pen.

"Now is your chance," said Harvey. "I'd go while they're busy eating your friend. But there doesn't seem to be much of him left."

A hog grunted behind Harvey as if confirming the fact.

The rise and fall of Rob's chest was clearly visible. He psyched himself up with three loud exhales, his hands gripping the top bar of the fence like it was his only lifeline. Then, as the first of the pigs looked up from its meal, sniffing the air for fresh blood, Rob lunged upwards. He vaulted the fence, landing on both feet in the mud with a loud slap.

Before he could make a move, before his feet had stopped sliding, and before he'd let go of the fence, Harvey swung his arm in a wide arc and jammed the point of his knife through Rob's hand. It stabbed deeply into the soft wooden post, pinning Rob to the spot. His eyes flicked from his hand to Harvey and then to the pigs, who had reduced the dead man to nothing but a few gnawed bones in the mud.

"No. No. No," Rob said, his voice high like a child's.

"You lose," said Harvey.

"Let me go. No. Stop. Don't leave me here."

He gave constant nervous glances back at the increasingly interested hogs.

The biggest of the animals took a step towards him, sniffing the air for fear.

In desperation, Rob seized the knife with his free hand and tried to pull it from the wood, turning it left and right, his face contorting with every tiny movement of the blade. But the knife held fast. With a final effort, his bloodied hand slipped from the handle. The hogs took another step closer.

"Help me, you bastard," Rob breathed, his throat closed with fear and panic.

Harvey didn't reply.

A hog stepped closer, sniffing at the man's leg.

"Get off me," screamed Rob, kicking out at the animal, which only angered the beast and intrigued its appetite.

Seeing no alternative as the hogs closed in, Rob caught Harvey's stare, reminding him in that instant of the lengths a man will go to live. With his teeth bared and as the first of the hogs sank its jaw into the back of his leg, Rob pulled his hand from the blade.

He roared as if he'd become a beast himself as his hand split around the sharp blade until just a small slice of flesh and sinew held fast to the fence. He tugged his hand free with a whimper.

But it was too late.

The weight of the hogs bore down on Rob, and their razor-sharp teeth clamped onto any piece of his body they could find.

Harvey turned away, picked up Shaun's leg and dragged his own quarry to the van.

35

CHAPTER THIRTY-FIVE

No lights lit the courtyard of the farmhouse at the foot of the hill, but Frank knew it was the right place even in the darkness. He eased the door of the rental car closed, leaving it unlocked to avoid the brief flashing of lights. As if he were out for a late evening stroll in the countryside, he ambled along the lane towards freedom or death.

But the charade of a night time stroller was unnecessary. Not a single car passed or even drove near to the road. Frank had time to breathe the air, smell the fields, and admire the wide open expanse of nothing.

The darkness proved useful for his unobserved movements around the side of the three buildings and into the rear garden. Peaks of tall conifers reached high into the sky. The light from a single ground-floor window illuminated the grass and gravel garden.

Inside the house, a familiar shape passed by the window. The man leaned against a grand, brick-built fireplace with a solid oak mantle, which sat beneath a mirror framed with ornate mouldings of silver and bronze.

Terry Thomson stared at his reflection with a seething

look of contempt. It was the stare of a guilty man who had, at last, discovered a conscience amongst the rotting lies that blackened his heart.

Looking on with voyeuristic pleasure, Frank felt a connection to the broken man. Terry had held his career on a knife edge. He'd used blackmail to coerce Frank into diverting police resources, which had resulted in lie upon lie to compound, blocking promotions and opportunities while those around Frank had soared.

But the end was in sight and the path of freedom grew close.

Fingering the trigger of his weapon, Frank savoured each passing moment the way a hunter might relish his prey moments before taking a life. Foreplay before the act of death.

A rush of pleasure ran through his body unlike anything he had felt for years.

A sigh fell from his throat, involuntary and loud in the silence.

And a tingle twitched his fingers.

Terry, wearing a gown of deep red silk fastened with a similar belt, sank the amber contents of his glass in a single mouthful. The burn in his throat was masked by his already reddened eyes. A bottle of brandy stood nearby on a wooden drinks cabinet. The lid was off. Terry's current drink was neither his first nor last.

Enjoying the power, Frank allowed Terry Thomson one last drink, and Terry poured it with careless measure. Beside the bottle was an old record player, finished with synthetic wooden veneer and adorned with chromed dials and trim. It was much like the one Frank had owned in the seventies, which had fed him delights such as Led Zeppelin and Pink Floyd. But from the shadows, the label on the LP Terry was playing was just a blur.

Only a few whispered teases of sound reached Frank's ears before Terry turned the volume dial. Then he stood at the mirror with his drink in hand and the wonders of Mozart building behind him with winding woodwind arpeggios. Two heavy, sustained orchestral chords struck loudly through the glass. The space between the notes seemed to fill the void between Terry and Frank. It was the opening of Mozart's Don Giovanni opera. The piece was a favourite of Frank's.

It was meant to end this way.

All those years of lies, deaths and resentment, it was all leading up to this moment. The underdog would be the last man to stand.

A framed picture of Bradley Thomson stood on the mantelpiece. It was the focus of Terry's attention. The look in Terry's eyes evoked a peculiar disposition in Frank, who was a voyeur to his enemy's suffering.

Terry raised his glass to his dead son as he stood alone. Meanwhile, Mozart faded into the soft tones that marked the halfway point of the overture. Wind instruments replaced heavy strings, and delicate tones clung to the ceiling and the walls. Then, slowly and softly, the string section increased in depth, building with each bar. Frank was transfixed. It was a solo performance, a monologue of death taking place before his eyes. The music sang the unspoken words of Thomson's expression with eerie synchronicity. The pace of the orchestra increased with the intensity of Terry's suffering.

Frank thought of the times he too had broken and worn the very same look. Times when he was alone. Times when the smallest detail reminded him of his wife. The time soon after her funeral when he'd walked mud into the house. He'd cleaned the mess before she had a chance to find it, knowing full well that she never would. He'd wished she could find it. Frank had knelt on the floor picking up pieces of loose mud, using a damp sponge to clean the rug her mother had bought them. He'd broken then, and countless other times in countless other places. At the foot of the stairs, he'd curled into a ball and sobbed like a baby. He'd cried to the point where he found his own weapon in his own hand against his own head with no recollection of the events.

The connection Frank felt for Terry grew in bitter strength as he looked on at his enemy's mourning and felt his pain and loss. He saw himself standing before the mirror, and the feeling cast a shadow over his plan. As Frank raised the gun, eying the man he'd hated for so many years, a drop of cloudy doubt fogged his sight. To pull the trigger no longer carried the same weight.

His hands began to shake. His eyes lost focus. His desire to kill the man was countered by knowing the bullet would be easing his pain and suffering. Terry deserved to suffer. The two emotions gripped Frank's finger in an emotional tug of war. He could bear it no longer and his hands shook with the tension. Lowering his weapon and wiping the tears from his eyes, Frank stared through the glass at his final failed mission.

The gun fell from Frank's hand and clattered to the ground.

He watched Terry turn his back to the fire and face the doorway. His lips moved, silent to Frank but audible to the shadow that passed before the window. A shadow with a knife in its hand.

No fear seemed to engulf Terry as the intruder stepped closer. Instead, a look of defiance shone from his dark eyes and taut mouth, betrayed only by a single tear. Then, as if welcoming death, Terry opened his arms wide, raised his face to the heavens and closed his eyes.

Moving with the confidence of a man who lived for death, the shadow stepped into full view. He placed the tip of his blade onto Terry's heart, but paused, as if offering the man a final word.

Mozart spilled through the glass. Lips moved like a silent movie.

And steel cut flesh.

But as the first trickle of blood stained Terry Thomson's robe and the crescendo of Mozart's masterpiece faded into the songs of whimsical flutes, Terry bore down on the hands that teased him with death. Gripping them inside his own, he forced the blade through his heart. Terry took the life from his body as if it was his final wish to die by his own hand.

Eyes opened wide and gritted teeth flashed white as Terry Thomson placed one foot into the next world. Somewhere deep inside Frank's heart, a part of him died. But in his mind, a cloud of fog lifted as the body of Terry Thomson crumpled to the floor.

And Frank took one step onto the path of freedom.

CHAPTER THIRTY-SIX

A SMALL SUITCASE STOOD BY THE DOOR TO JOHN'S HOME office and the smell of coffee filled the air.

"It's done," said Harvey from the doorway.

"I can see, Harvey. It says so right here on the front bleeding page. The papers don't mess about, do they? Probably couldn't wait to tell the world that Terry Thomson, gangland crime lord, was killed," said John, as he looked away out of the window. "All these years we've been enemies, Harvey. You know, I think I'll miss him."

Harvey didn't reply. He allowed his foster father a moment of reflection.

"He burnt down my first bar, you know?"

"The one with the booth? Where you found a child? And a baby in a hamper wrapped in blankets?"

John glanced back but couldn't meet Harvey's eye.

"No." A hint of anger faded on John's face as quickly as it had appeared. "A different bar. Terry Thomson reckoned I was on his patch. I weren't. On his patch, you know?"

Harvey didn't reply.

"Funny, isn't it?" said John.

"What's *funny*?"

"Life, Harvey. *Life*."

"It depends on your sense of humour, John."

"Come to think of it, I can't remember the last time I saw you laugh, Harvey. Not properly."

"I don't remember complaining about it."

"No, of course not. You never complained about anything, really. When you were a little boy, you laughed at *everything*. Always smiling, you were."

John turned to meet Harvey's cold stare.

"Did I do okay, Son?"

"When?" asked Harvey.

"You know, as a dad. Was I a good dad?"

"Like I said, I don't remember complaining."

"You had everything you needed. Right?" asked John.

"For a while."

Sensing the reference to Hannah, John pushed the conversation on as he always did.

"I'm going to miss you, Harvey. Honestly, Son. I love Donny, of course. I love you both. But there's something about you. You've got this something inside you. A way about you that any dad would be proud of. You're a special guy, Son. Don't ever let anyone tell you otherwise."

Harvey didn't respond.

"When are you leaving?" asked John.

"Depends."

"France?"

"I've found a farmhouse."

"After all this time looking? I'd say it was meant to be. Wouldn't you?"

"If you believe in all that, maybe," said Harvey.

"What are you going to do when I give you the name?"

"Do you really want to know?"

The question hung in the air like the smell of brandy in the old house.

"No. No. It's probably best I don't know," said John, straightening his cuffs and forcing a posture of strength, despite the news he was about to deliver.

Another silence fell.

"The guns?" John asked, his eyebrow raised.

"Twelve of them. In a van in the garage. You'll need to get rid of it."

"Good. Good work. Are you sure I can't convince you to stay, Harvey?"

"No. It's time."

"Okay. Okay. So you want the name then, I imagine?" said John.

He stood and walked to his liquor cupboard. It was early, but the day was already full of loss. John poured himself a finger of brandy over three ice cubes then set it down on the desk before stepping up to Harvey.

"Give your old man a hug, Son. Before I go," said John.

His arms opened as Terry Thomson's had the night before. The smell of alcohol was strong on his breath, as was the smell of Terry Thomson's. Relenting to the whims of the man who raised him, Harvey gave John a hug, breathing in the odour of coffee and brandy one last time.

They broke off. But as he walked back to his chair, John stumbled and caught the edge of the desk before finding his seat. Then he sipped at his brandy, puckered his lips, and linked his fingers as he so often did.

Harvey didn't move a muscle.

"You know who it is already, don't you?" said John.

"I have an idea," replied Harvey. "But I want to hear the words from your mouth."

"Who do you think it is?"

"This isn't a game."

"No, Harvey. It is not a game," said John, his voice rising with emotion. "It is the wish of a father saying goodbye to his son for the very last time and clinging to every word he says so he can remember the boy's voice in his old age."

"Sergio."

It was as if saying the name out loud carved the letters in stone. A verbal epitaph.

"How come you never acted on it then?" asked John. "If you knew."

"Nobody ever confirmed it. You always protected him."

"I'm sorry, Son," said John, nodding as if arguing the fact was futile.

John sat back in his chair and sipped at his brandy. He looked at Harvey no longer through the eyes of his boss, or the man who controlled his destiny, but as a father should, with kindness in his eyes.

"Sergio has served his purpose," said John. "And I suppose, to some degree, I've served mine to him."

"Where is he now?"

"I don't know," said John. "At the office probably."

"Message him. Tell him to come here. Then leave."

"Is that what you want?" asked John.

Harvey didn't reply.

"When are you leaving, Son?"

John hit send on his phone, placed it on the desk and sat back.

"I'll be gone by the time you get back," said Harvey.

For the first time, he looked away at the sight of John's moistening eyes.

For the last time, John Cartwright stood in front of his foster son, admiring the strength in the boy he'd raised. He reached up, and with a gentle touch that had eluded Harvey all those years, John touched his cheek.

"Bye, Son."

CHAPTER THIRTY-SEVEN

A SLEEK MERCEDES ENTERED THE GROUNDS OF JOHN'S house, but Sergio didn't drive slowly, as a man who knew he travelled towards death might.

From John's chair at his desk, Harvey watched with curiosity as the lean man climbed from his car, collected his laptop bag then hurried into the building. Demonstrating haste supported the facade Sergio had developed over the years. Ever the keen, hardworking and reliable employee.

"Harvey," said Sergio in surprise, as he entered the office.

He stopped in his tracks and searched for John.

"Today's a special day, Sergio," said Harvey.

"Where's John?"

Sergio clung to the door frame, unsure if he should step inside or run back to his car.

"Out, I guess," said Harvey. "So it's just you and me."

"When will he be back? He asked me to come. I came all the way from the office."

"What's the matter? You seem a little jumpy, Sergio."

"I asked you a question, Harvey. When will John be back?"

"I don't think it matters when John will be back. Does it?" said Harvey, pushing himself from the chair.

Sergio flinched at the movement. Still standing in the doorway, he eyed the front door then returned his attention to Harvey, tracking every move with fearful eyes.

"Why don't we go for a little walk, Sergio? Just you and me."

"No. I need to stay in case John comes back."

"Sergio, you and I are going for a little walk."

"I want to leave. I will call John."

Harvey stopped Sergio as he turned to leave. "You can do this the easy way. Or you can do this the hard way."

"What do you want?" asked Sergio.

He stood in the hallway with his back to Harvey.

"You *know* what I want, Sergio."

"You want money? I can give you money. I have access to it all. Everything."

"Money doesn't really interest me, Sergio. It's you I want."

"How about this?" said Sergio, reaching into his bag. "I can give you this."

In the seconds it took Sergio to pull a handgun from his bag, turn, and aim, Harvey had snatched his own from his waist, aimed, and fired a single shot into the side of Sergio's knee. The man fell to the floor and a wild bullet flew into the flock wallpaper behind Harvey.

A scream, wild and shrill, echoed through the huge house, deepening into the growl of an animal, cornered and scared, then the muted whimper of a man who knew it was over.

"Stop. Stop. No," cried Sergio, holding his ruined leg in both hands.

The handgun lay useless on the floor beside him. Grabbing Sergio's foot, Harvey wrenched it sideways, feeling the satisfying crunch of gristle and shattered bone. An ear-splitting scream flew from Sergio's lips with droplets of spittle until the pain overwhelmed what strength remained and he slipped into unconsciousness.

It wasn't until Harvey had reached the kitchen, dragging Sergio behind him by the remains of his leg, and opened the small wooden door to the basement, that consciousness returned in its weakest form.

An eyelid fluttered.

Recognition fixed Harvey with a silent plea for mercy. Realisation woke Sergio fully.

Harvey placed the sole of his boot against Sergio's back then shoved him forward onto the cold, hard concrete steps. Harvey watched with intrigue as Sergio bounced from stair to stair, his damaged leg bending awkwardly off the walls. He landed in a crumpled heap on the floor below. Harvey followed, his steps slow. It was a time he had dreamed of for so many years. He would cherish the moment.

The basement ceiling was ten feet high with thick oak beams running the full length of the building supported by oak columns of even greater thickness. At the edge of the room, dust sheets covered decades of the Cartwright's belongings, heirlooms, toys, kitchen equipment and boxes of memories that nobody wished to remember.

Tied to one of the wooden uprights, with his ankles and wrists bound tightly, Shaun Tyson was sitting in soiled under-wear, drugged and silent, with his forehead resting against the wood.

Sergio received a similar treatment. He was stripped to his underwear and bound to the upright beam, unconscious with his head hanging back, his mouth wide open and his ruined leg at an unnatural angle with a riot of deathly colour forming across the skin.

In front of the two men and the upright beams to which they were bound, an antique copper bathtub with grotesque, gothic, clawed feet and a rolled edge took centre stage.

Beneath it, Harvey had placed a row of powerful gas burners, turned on to their maximum with bright blue flames heating the shiny, copper surface. The water inside that was filled to the brim was beginning to steam. A single light bulb shone a dome of dim, yellow light over the tub as if the main act waited in silence for the unwilling audience to arrive.

The first bubble burst on the steaming surface of the water.

A pair of eyes opened.

Harvey smiled the rare smile of a man whose dreams had come true.

CHAPTER THIRTY-EIGHT

"CARVER."

Frank held his desk phone to his ear and stared up at the image of Julios Saville. It was one of two new photos added to his pin board.

"Sir, you've been requested to join the chief in conference room two," said the secretary.

"I'll be right there. Thank you."

Frank sat back in his chair, took a deep breath, and thought about his wife whose framed photo stared lovingly at him from the desk. She would have been proud. She had always supported him even though she hadn't understood the ins and outs of his work. But she had always been there for him to vent. She had always been there to cheer him up during those tricky times when Thomson's games had him caught in a web of lies.

He pulled on his jacket, checked his shoes were clean, and made his way to the elevator. Nerves whisked his thoughts into a jumbled mix of memories and possibilities. He stared at the digital readout on the elevator, barely noticing the stares, smiles and admiration from colleagues who'd all heard the news.

In the conference room, the chief stood at the head of the room dressed in an expensive, tailored suit, white shirt and gleaming shoes. Melody Mills, Reg Tenant and Denver Cox all sat on one side of the table. Mills was sitting ramrod straight with her notepad, pen and smartphone arranged in a neat fashion. Tenant slouched in his seat, his head buried in his phone. Cox picked at the sole of his boot.

"Frank, come in," said the chief.

His boss stepped towards him and offered his hand. Frank shook it then selected a seat opposite his team.

"Thank you all for coming," began the chief. "This won't take long. I know you are all as busy as I am. I'd like to thank you all for your recent efforts. As you are all aware, we've managed to close several unsolved crimes, most of which, thanks to your diligence, were the result of finding Julios Saville. It would have been a real pleasure to bring him in with a pulse. But, beggars can't be choosers. By good police work or good fortune, you've managed to close more unsolved organised crime cases in the past day than we have in the past six months."

While the chief took a sip of water, Frank's team glanced at each other with pride.

"Next up," continued the chief, "not only did you bring in one of the most wanted men in Britain, but you also managed to find twelve missing Heckler and Koch MP5s. If I'm honest, they shouldn't have been missing at all. They were British service weapons, and all eyes were on them. So well done. Bloody good show."

Mills, Tenant and Cox smiled at the thanks from the chief. Frank stared at the wall, avoiding eye contact.

"Lastly," said the chief, "we have the case of one Mr Terry Thomson. I don't need to go into his record, but needless to say, the man was a menace and had evaded prison for far too long. I can't credit his death to you, Frank, but your actions have caused the downfall of this murderous family and consequently made our streets a safer place. Damn fine work."

"I couldn't have done it without my team," said Frank.

"There's no room here for modesty, Frank," said the chief. "You did a damn good job, all of you."

Beneath the shining appraisal, a sickening guilt began to turn inside Frank's stomach. Another lie to cover a lie. Thomson's final stab reached out from the grave and cut the pleasure Frank so deserved.

"So, here's what I'd like to do," said the chief. "I have a proposition for you."

"For me, sir?" said Frank.

"No, Frank. For all of you. You see, while the force continues to increase resources in counter-terrorism, there's been a rise in domestic organised crime."

"Gangs, sir?" asked Mills.

"That's right. While the country fights a war against terrorism, these criminals are taking liberties. It's like the eighties all over again. You remember the eighties, Frank?"

"The best days of my career, sir," said Frank with a weak smile.

"Good. Because if you play your cards right, you'll be running a domestic, covert special ops unit whose sole focus is to combat organised crime in London. How does that sound?"

"And my team?" asked Frank.

"You can have the pick of the bunch, Frank. Anyone out there, you name them, and I'll make it happen."

"Anyone?"

"Pretty much. Within reason," said the chief.

"What about resources?" asked Frank.

"You'll build a report with a budget. Be gentle, of course.

We can see about getting you more next year. Tell me what your team would look like."

"Well, I'll need someone smart," said Frank, his eyes fixed on Mills. "Someone dependable, brave, intelligent, and who can shoot the arse off a fly at a thousand yards."

"Good," said the chief. "I've got just the person in mind. Who else?"

"I'll need tech research. In fact, I'll need the finest techie the force can offer," said Frank, looking at Tenant.

"I'm sure that can be arranged," replied the chief, making a note on his pad.

"Anything else?"

"Logistics," said Frank. His eyes moved to Cox. "I'll need a world-class driver and one of the best helicopter pilots we have."

"That's a push, Frank," replied the chief. "I can get you the driver, but a pilot would be well above your budget."

"You don't understand, sir," said Frank, smiling at the three individuals who stared back at him, red-faced but beaming with pride. "I have my team right here."

CHAPTER THIRTY-NINE

SUCKING IN AIR THROUGH GRITTED TEETH, SERGIO REELED with pain and reached for his leg with his bound hands, but failed.

"Harvey," said Sergio between rasping gasps. "Harvey, untie me now. Why are you doing this?"

But his efforts at authority faded as his voice fell to a child-like sob. It reminded Harvey of a time when, as a child, he had crept into the kitchen in the early hours, drawn by the whimpering of innocence. He remembered the screams with audible clarity. He felt the bite of the cold, tiled floor on his young, bare feet. He remembered how he'd dared not move as a figure emerged from the basement, satiated, as the crying and whimpering started over with renewed vigour.

"I saw them, Sergio," said Harvey. "Your eyes."

"What? What are you talking about? Let me go, damn it."

"I saw them at her funeral. You were *shamed*, not sad. It all makes sense now."

"Whose funeral, Harvey? Just tell me what you want."

"You remember her, don't you? Hannah?"

Sergio didn't reply.

"Ah, I thought so. You remember her *well*."

"I don't know what you're talking about, Harvey. Of course I remember her. She was your sister."

"But you remember her better than most, don't you? Not *Jack* of course. He remembered her as well as you do. But he doesn't remember her anymore. He doesn't remember anything, does he? You do remember Jack, don't you, Sergio?"

"Harvey, I don't know what you want from me. But tell me. You can have it. Please, Harvey."

Sergio was fighting for breaths between sobs. His body convulsed as he cried. It was a scene Harvey had seen more than a dozen times when the guilty face justice and retribution.

"*Please*, Harvey. All these years I've taken care of you."

"All these years, Sergio, you've lied to me."

"What? Tell me what you want. You can have anything."

"There's nothing you can volunteer, Sergio. The only thing I want is your suffering."

"I *am* suffering, Harvey. Look at me. I'll never walk again."

"You'll never do many things again," snapped Harvey. Then he checked his emotions as Julios had always instructed. "You're going to die a very painful death, Sergio."

Harvey strolled to the tub and felt the water temperature with his finger. The water was warming. Not hot yet. But not cold.

In a rush of panic, Shaun came to consciousness. Finding himself restrained and semi-naked, he fought his restraints for a few brief moments but soon gave up.

"What the...Where am I? Who are *you*?" he said to Sergio. "What's going on?"

Harvey shot him a glance, and Shaun silenced as recognition set in.

"You woke in time for the show, Shaun. Do you know Sergio?" Harvey presented Sergio with an open palm.

"No, I...I don't think I do. I know *you* though. You're the man-"

"Shh, keep the noise down, Shaun. This is a civilised show. We don't want the cast spoiling it for the audience, do we?"

Shaun searched the shadows. "Where the bloody hell am I?"

"You are both about to suffer for your sins," said Harvey, using his left hand to present the bathtub to the men. "Who's first?"

As expected, neither man spoke.

"Should *I* choose?"

"Harvey, you sick son of a bitch. You can't do this. John won't allow it. Your *father* won't allow it."

"Oh, Sergio, you know me better than that, don't you? Do you honestly think I'd do anything to upset the family business?"

"See, so you can't kill me. I know too much. The business won't run without me."

"I can assure you John has everything he needs to continue without you, Sergio. In fact, I think he'll be pleased to get rid of you." Harvey paused. "So shall we get started? Seeing as neither of you wants to go first, we'll have a competition."

The two condemned men glanced at each other in confusion.

"Let's start with Shaun. I feel we ought to get to know you a little better. Confess."

"Eh?"

"Confess, Shaun. Do I need to explain the definition of the word confess?"

"No."

"What does it mean then?"

"To own up."

"Good. Now confess."

"To what?"

Harvey didn't reply. Instead, he stood, turned the chair around and straddled it, then leaned forward on the back of the chair with his chin on his arms, ready for the show.

"The more you confess," said Harvey, "the easier I will make it on you. Whoever offers the poorest confession is the loser, and losers bath first. Does that sound fair?"

Once more, the two men exchanged glances.

"Okay, I'll *tell* you," said Sergio.

"No, no, no, Sergio. You had your chance. But don't worry. That was just a warm-up round. You'll get another go soon enough," said Harvey, offering the man a wink and a glare.

"I was young," began Shaun. "I was raped."

"That's not really a confession, Shaun," said Harvey. "That's an excuse."

"I know. But that's when it all started," said Shaun. "Ever since then, I've had these urges."

"Urges?"

Harvey leaned forward with interest.

"Tell me about the first time you had one of your urges, Shaun."

CHAPTER FORTY

"Tell me what you'd need," said the chief.

Pondering the question, Frank, who had never considered such an opportunity, tried to think on his feet. But the truth was, he was overwhelmed. He was unprepared and still reeling from the glowing appraisal that, if the truth came out, would all come crashing down like a house of cards.

"We'd need an HQ, sir," said Mills, sensing Frank's struggle with words. "Somewhere to set up, keep our kit, and run the operations."

"Couldn't you do that from here?" asked the chief.

"Not covert, sir. Plus, you can't do anything here without it being all around the cafeteria by lunchtime."

"Agreed," said Frank. "It doesn't have to be huge, but close to London City Airport for domestic flights, and near to the A13 to access London and the motorway network. Oh, and close to the River Thames."

"In case you decide to ask for a boat next year?" asked the chief with a grin.

"I'll need dual, dark fibre connections to the internet and Metropolitan network, sir," said Tenant. "Plus, unhindered access to satellites and some hardware. I can get you a list. It'll be long but practical."

"Right," said the chief, making notes in his pad. "And what is it you intend on doing with all this, Tenant? Build a super-computer?"

"Yes, sir. Exactly that," replied Tenant, matter of fact.

Frank shrugged, smiled and glanced across at Denver Cox, inviting him to voice his requests.

"I'll need a workshop," said Cox. "Somewhere I can work on the motors."

"Motors?" said the chief. "Plural?"

"We don't need anything too fancy, sir," replied Cox. "A saloon, fast and sleek for undercover work, an Audi or something. Plus we'll need a new van."

"I thought your team has a van?"

"No, it's beat," said Cox, before Frank could interject. "For an operation like this, we'd need something new. Something a bit more reliable."

"Okay," said the chief, adding the request to his list. "How about you, Mills?"

"I won't need a lot, sir," she replied. "Two Diemaco assault rifles. The C8 is a good option with the underslung grenade launcher. Half a dozen Heckler and Koch MP5s. The seven-point-six-two, if possible. For handguns, we'd need a good number of Sig two-two-eights and two-two-sixes. Plus we'd need an armoury to keep them locked up, fireproof, of course. Then for surveillance, I'd need a few pairs of Steiner binoculars. None of the autofocus type. I prefer manual focus. A few NV kits would be good. A set of body armour each. Plus listening devices. Standard issue is fine."

The room was silent when she finished; it continued that way while the chief noted her requests as fast as he could write them.

"You gave that a little thought, didn't you, Mills?" he said, eventually.

"It's my dream armoury, sir. Everything a girl needs to keep the boys in their place."

The comment brought a smile to the chief's face.

He announced the meeting's closure with a snap of his notepad.

"So there we have it. But there's one last thing before I go upstairs and put my neck on the line."

"What's that, sir?" said Frank, sensing a curveball.

"You found twelve of the missing MP5s, and for that, I'm very grateful. Believe me, there's only one thing worse than wars being fought on British soil, and that's people being killed with weapons that belong to the British military. You can imagine the position it puts me in."

"We can," said Frank, speaking for the team. "I don't envy your responsibilities."

"No," said the chief. "So before I go and potentially make myself the laughing stock of the force, and before you all get your dream headquarters, you're going to go out there and do whatever it takes to bring those weapons back home."

"You want us to find the other twelve MP5s?" said Frank, more in disbelief than for clarification.

"You find me those weapons, Frank," said the chief, raising his glass of water as if it were a champagne flute, "and I'll get you all your dream jobs."

CHAPTER FORTY-ONE

"Do you feel better for that, Shaun?" asked Harvey, breaking the silence following his confession.

With his legs curled around the beam and his head resting on the smooth oak, shame fell from Shaun's face in little drops. He started to say more as if by vocalising his crimes, somehow everything would be okay.

"Now, now, Shaun," said Harvey. "It's Sergio's turn."

But Sergio just stared at Shaun, horrified at the story he'd heard.

"Come on, Sergio. You had plenty to say a while ago."

"What? What do you want to know?"

Harvey's eyes narrowed.

"What's the worst thing you ever did?"

"I never killed no-one."

Harvey stared, impassive.

"I set fire to a dog once?"

Harvey didn't reply.

"I was just a kid."

"Stop there, Sergio. Did you hear what Shaun just told us?

Did you hear the shame in his voice? The conviction in his voice?"

The silence was broken by Shaun shuffling around the beam, seeking comfort on the cold, hard floor and a better view of Sergio, whose confession was imminent.

"Jack found her," said Sergio. Then he paused.

"And I found *Jack*, didn't I?" said Harvey.

"He went first," said Sergio.

"*Sergio*, come on. Tell me a story. I want the details. How did she get down here?"

"She was getting a drink of water. It was late or early. Night time." Sergio closed his eyes, reliving the night for the thousandth time in his tortured mind. "We'd been playing cards in John's study, gambling and drinking, when we heard someone on the stairs outside. The last step always creaked."

"It still does," said Harvey.

"We heard her footsteps. They were loud in the quiet night. So Jack got up and looked around the door to make sure it wasn't John's wife."

"My foster mother?"

"Yes. Barb. She didn't approve of us gambling in the house. But Jack grew excited, waving us over from the door. We stepped out into the hallway like naughty children, giggling and whispering. She was wearing a nightshirt with little panties, and well..."

"Well? Well what?"

It was sorrow rather than shame that Harvey saw in his eyes. The shame came after the fact. It always did.

"She was a half-naked young woman, and she was...beautiful."

"She *was* beautiful, Sergio."

"Jack led us into the kitchen. We followed like sheep. I sensed something was wrong. It all felt wrong. He crept up behind her and grabbed her by the waist to surprise her. But she fought him off. Although he was only playing, she resisted. He kept going, tickling her and squeezing her."

Never before had Harvey heard the words of another man with such clarity. It was the one story he'd never wanted to hear, but it was the one story he had needed to hear since he'd been a small boy, since the night that had changed his life.

"He took it too far and felt her chest. So she slapped him. Hard. He slapped her back harder, and she fell down, hitting her head on the tiled floor. But something came over Jack. He was different, almost enchanted. He bent down beside her, running his hand along her leg and..."

"And, Sergio?" said Harvey, imagining the scene with sickened distaste, forcing himself to endure what Hannah had endured, to understand the root of the misery that killed her.

"He *touched* her," said Sergio, closing his eyes once more and reliving the nightmare.

He was in the dream, as was Harvey.

"He called us over. 'Sergio, get the door,' he whispered to me. Then he lifted her so her long hair hung from his arms, and he carried her down the steps to this place."

Sergio nodded his head to the steps.

"He laid her on the bench that was there and stripped her naked like some kind of wild animal, tearing at her nightshirt. He was overcome with awe. There was no talking to him. We tried, but he just kept touching her, feeling her smooth skin against his rough hands. He was taken by her, Harvey. He always had been."

It was Shaun's turn to stare aghast at the story. He sat with his mouth wide open, listening with horror at the events that had destroyed Harvey's family. Harvey noticed him, the expression on his face and compassion in his eyes.

"He was on top of her when she woke," continued Sergio. "She tried to fight him, of course. But he was a strong man, too strong for a girl. But still, she fought until Jack hit her and she passed out again. The next time she woke, all her courage and strength had been taken. She just lay there crying and letting him..."

"And when he finished?"

"Jack left," said Sergio, nodding once more at the steps.

"And you?"

Sergio looked up at Harvey. His mouth was turned down in an arc of disgrace and shame.

He nodded. "Yes," he whispered.

"Yes?" said Harvey, feeling the familiar touch of a talon in the pit of his stomach.

"I raped her."

A stab of the beast added finality to the words Harvey had been waiting for his whole life.

"Tell me, Sergio," said Harvey, feeling the release of adrenaline into his body and the racing pulse of his heart flash behind his eyes. "Tell me what you did."

"I hit her again. I knocked her unconscious," said Sergio. Then he paused, but he'd gone too far to stop. "I raped her. Your sister. It was me. The man you've been looking for. I'm so sorry, Harvey. I'm so sorry."

Once more, the room was filled with the whining sobs of shame, guilt, and as Harvey stood from the chair, fear.

"I think we have a *winner*," he said.

An audible sigh escaped Shaun's lips, but he watched with horrified joy as Harvey untied Sergio's bindings.

"You're letting me go?"

For a brief moment, a flash of hope showed itself across the lines on Sergio's gaunt face.

But Harvey was only just beginning. He took slow steps to

the corner of the room, savouring the waking beast's sharp claws and the tingle in his limbs. Fetching a coil of rope, he cast one end over a high horizontal beam and then tested the temperature of the bubbling water.

"I think we're ready," said Harvey, allowing a thick wave of steam to engulf his face in the dim light.

With a practised hand, Harvey tied one end of the rope to Sergio's wrists, finishing the knot with a sharp snatch. Then, like a curious child might follow a trail of sweets, Harvey traced the rope's length to the bath, and up and over the beam where he found the loose end.

He pulled once, taking the slack and snatching Sergio to one side.

"Don't do this, Harvey. I told you what you wanted to hear."

Harvey pulled again and again, feeding off Sergio's wild complaints, until Sergio's feet rose above the bath and steam engulfed him, teasing him with the flavour of heat below.

"Are you watching, Shaun?" said Harvey.

"Yes, sir," said Shaun, transfixed by the sheer terror of the scene.

"I want you to watch, Shaun. I want you to think about what he did," said Harvey, tying the rope off to the clawed foot of the bathtub. "Are you thinking, Shaun?"

"Yes, sir."

"What are you thinking?"

"About what he said he did."

"No, Harvey. Stop. Please," said Sergio.

"Tell me what he did, Shaun," said Harvey, overpowering Sergio's feeble pleas for mercy.

"He raped your sister," said Shaun, as if by uttering the words, he cast guilt upon himself.

"Do you know what she did *after*, Shaun?"

"Harvey, stop."

"No, sir."

"Harvey, *stop* this. It's stupid," Sergio begged.

"Tell Shaun what Hannah did after you raped her, Sergio."

"Harvey, come on. It's hot. This is not a game."

"Tell him, Sergio," said Harvey, his voice a whisper in the steam.

"She killed herself. Is that what you want to hear?"

"But what did she do, Sergio?"

"She cut herself. Let me go, Harvey. I'm slipping."

"She cut herself, Shaun. Sergio, tell Shaun where she cut herself."

"Ahh, Harvey. *No.* Stop. My foot, it's burning," cried Sergio, as his hands slipped further through the knot, wet with the condensed steam on his skin.

"Tell him, Sergio. You remember, don't you? Of course you do."

"*Everywhere*," Sergio shouted. "Everywhere we'd been. She cut herself to ribbons. Now let me go, Harvey. Please."

"I'll put an end to it soon, Sergio."

A jolt, as the rope eased further along Sergio's hands, stopped at his purple knuckles. But unable to raise his ruined leg, his foot submerged in the frantic water. The room filled with a fresh scream, louder than before.

"I need one more answer, Sergio. Then it's bath time."

"What? Tell me what you what to know. Just let me go."

"You said *we*."

"What?" replied Sergio. "When?"

"In the study, Sergio. It was quite clear. Jack called *us* over."

Sergio slipped lower. His entire foot stirred in the boiling water, turning an angry red, and blistering with almost immediate effect.

"It was a mistake, Harvey. I was scared. I don't know what I was-"

"If you tell me, Sergio, I'll end it now," said Harvey, his cold tone cutting through the heat of the boiling steam. "Who was the third man?"

Sergio didn't reply.

"I can end this now, Sergio. Or I can make it a whole lot worse for you," said Harvey, drawing his knife from the sheave on his belt. He ran it across Sergio's groin, which hung at head height. "Tell me who it was."

"Ah, I *can't*," sobbed Sergio.

With a flick of his wrist, Harvey turned the blade, digging the sharp point at the bulge between Sergio's legs. He jabbed up lightly but hard enough to remind Sergio of his predicament.

"Ah, *no*."

"Sergio."

"No."

"*Tell me*."

"I can't."

"Sergio."

He pushed the knife harder.

"*Donny*. It was Donny. He was the third man. He went after me. It was his first time."

The words came at Harvey like a blow to his gut. He stepped back, dizzied, dropping the knife to his side, and sucking in a lungful of hot steamy air.

"Thank you, Sergio."

Then Harvey paused to take one last look at Hannah's killer.

"Thank you."

He'd imagined the moment a thousand times.

But now his imagination was completed. The faceless man that had suffered at Harvey's hands in so many dreams was now real. He could reach out and touch him, hurt him, feed off his fear.

Instead, he swiped once with the knife. The blade slashed through the manila rope with ease. Peace fell over Harvey as Sergio, who moments before had begged for life with wretched cries, writhed and struggled in the searing, angry water, begging for death.

CHAPTER FORTY-TWO

LOUD SOBBING AND WHIMPERING LIKE THAT OF A CHILD sang out from somewhere far away as if a tortured soul was constrained to the house for eternity, existing in the old walls and shadows and feeding off the lifeless air.

To the right and left of the two huge front doors were two rooms equal in size. The first was an office with a large desk, matching bookshelves and a drinks cabinet, on top of which was a silver platter containing a crystal decanter and two upturned crystal tumblers. One held traces of amber liquid in the bottom. Lowering his face to the glass, Frank inhaled the rich scent of brandy, teasing himself. Then he stood, his eye catching a single bullet mark almost concealed within the pattern of the flock wallpaper.

Instinct popped open the strap that secured his weapon in the holster beneath his arm. But he did not remove the gun. He preferred to take in the feel of the building. Still, the cries came like the waves of an ocean, whispered and tantalising.

The adjacent room held little interest. It had a dining table, rarely used judging by the dust, and couches that might have come from the set of an eighties television show. What once might've been the scene of opulent dinner parties had faded to near ruin. A snapshot in time.

A large double staircase was the central feature of the grand hallway. It curved like two snakes ready to strike those who dared pass between.

Frank dared.

To the rear of the house, a large kitchen with terracotta tiles seemed to be the only room graced by sunlight. Large windows ran from left to right, old-fashioned pots and pans hung from oak beams, and to Frank's right was a doorway. It stood open a few inches, releasing the cries of the tortured soul. A part of the house itself.

Frank stepped inside.

Below, at the foot of a set of hard, concrete steps, a dim light shone across a floor of bare concrete and a thick, acrid smell of death and human waste tainted the air Frank breathed.

With each step, the dim light revealed more.

Two hideous cast iron feet.

The sobbing had stopped as if Frank's presence had been sensed.

A copper bathtub, an antique, its sides gleaming and its top edge finished with a marvellous roll by the skilled hand of a smith a century before.

A human arm, swollen and white with death, the skin melted and stuck to the side of the bath like candle wax.

With slow, quiet movements, Frank unholstered his weapon and stepped onto the concrete floor. Staring back at him, with eyes boiled white and skin seared, a boiled man lay partly submerged and motionless.

"He's dead."

The voice from the corner of the room startled Frank,

who raised his weapon with shaky hands, aiming at the source of the voice.

"Don't shoot. Don't shoot," said the boy, who cowered behind the single oak upright beam he hugged.

Checking the shadowed corners of the room with renewed fear, Frank returned to the boy, who watched his every move and held the wooden upright as if he would never let go.

"What's your name?" asked Frank. "What *happened* here?"

The boy didn't reply.

Only when Frank stepped closer, eyeing the boy's stained underwear, did he see the bindings on his wrists and ankles. Two eyes stared up at Frank. But they weren't the pleading eyes of a captive. Nor were they the harrowed eyes of a survivor. They were the eyes of the shamed, riddled with guilt.

A single object caught Frank's eye, out of place in the room where it seemed time stood still. On an old cabinet that had been covered with a dust sheet was an audio recorder sitting on top of a folded note.

He gave a glance back at the boy then to the bath where death stared back at him, and then to the recorder. Frank pushed the play button and the tiny tape kicked into life. The background noise was hissy and busy. There were no voices. Just the sound, Frank assumed, of boiling water.

"What's the worst thing you ever did?" said a man's voice.

Frank hit stop as footsteps behind him on the stairs grew closer. He turned, aimed, and came face to face with Mills, who lowered her weapon and sighed with relief.

"Sir?"

"Mills," replied Frank, lowering his gun. "How did you find me?"

"Tenant, sir," said Mills. "What happened here?"

"That's exactly what I'm piecing together."

"You found Shaun Tyson?" said Mills, nodding at the boy. "How does he fit into all this?"

"You know him?" asked Frank.

"Sex offender, sir. Skipped bail earlier this week."

"Call uniforms to take him away and get the boy a blanket or something," said Frank.

As Frank and Mills walked through the two huge front doors and into the grounds of the house, savouring the sweet smell of fresh air, three police cars sped through the gates, skidding to a halt in the gravel. The rhythmic thudding of an approaching helicopter killed any remaining peace as the uniforms approached the front doors. Flashing her ID, Mills pointed to the kitchen.

"Basement," she said, then returned her attention to Frank. "Well, a sex offender wasn't quite what I was wishing for, sir. But it's still a win."

"Follow me," said Frank.

With his hands in the deep pockets of his overcoat, Frank strolled away from the house and onto the wide expanse of lawn to a large single-story building with a row of three double garage doors at the front. The last one was open as if inviting them inside. Approaching with caution and with their weapons raised, the two scanned the interior. Frank walked along the front of the car collection and Mills took the rear.

"There's no-one here, sir," said Mills.

"No," replied Frank. "I didn't expect there to be. He's long gone."

"So what's the significance?"

Between an immaculate E-Type Jaguar and an old Triumph Spitfire was a white van.

"I found a note," said Frank. "In the basement."

"From him?" asked Mills.

Frank nodded.

"What did it say?" asked Mills, as a child might pester a parent.

"Two words," said Frank. "A gift."

"A gift? Is that all?"

"So Shaun Tyson was a gift?"

"No. Shaun Tyson is a lucky boy. He'll serve time, for sure. But my guess is that whoever that is in the bath was the cause of our man's issues."

Mills considered Frank's words then summarised.

"So he no longer needed Tyson? He found what he'd been looking for?"

"That's what I think," said Frank, stopping his slow pace at the rear of the van.

"So what was the gift?" asked Mills. "The dead guy?"

But Frank just shook his head.

"Are you ready for this?" he asked.

"Ready for what, sir?" she asked.

With a smile that conveyed the end of a journey and so much more to come, Frank gestured at the van.

"Open the doors."

43

CHAPTER FORTY-THREE

TALL, WILD GRASS EDGED A FINE BEACH OF GOLDEN SAND. Long, finger-like clouds stretched from the horizon across the expanse of blue sky. The rushing tide of the sea crashed forward, dispersed, then retreated back to join the ranks. At the edge of the beach near the long grass, Harvey Stone lay in the sand, feeling the warmth of the French sun on his face.

In his hands was an English newspaper. It was several days old. The headline story reported a diamond heist in the north of England that detectives were investigating. No shots had been fired. No blood had been spilt. No sign had been found that the robbery had even taken place, save for a tunnel that had been concealed by a large painting, revealed only by a few crumbs of broken concrete.

Investigators estimated that the thieves had been tunnelling for at least three weeks in advance of the diamonds' arrival in Manchester, where the gems were being held overnight. The plan had been carried out with meticulous perfection. Once more, a rare and beautiful smile crept over Harvey's face, as he lay back, thought of Stimson with the diamonds, and felt the sun wash across his eyelids.

Dreams of a small boy chasing his sister through the long, wild grasses at the edge of a beach came to him. This time, the boy caught her, and they rolled, laughing as children do.

The sunshine on Harvey's eyelids fell into shadow. The temperature dropped a degree or two and a presence woke him.

"You're in the light," said Harvey.

"I *am* the light, Mr Stone."

Had the words been uttered at any other time in his life, Harvey may have felt the threat. But he sensed a confident smile in the man's tone.

"Would you mind shining somewhere else then?"

"You're not an easy man to track down."

"I'm not exactly hiding."

"I followed you from Essex."

"I'm not exactly running either," said Harvey, countering the man's statements, waiting for the bite.

"Thanks for the gift," said the man. "But why?"

"I'm done with it all," said Harvey. "It's finished."

"Is that why you spared Tyson?"

"It was never about him. Or the others."

"So you're *finished*, are you?"

"I am."

"It's a shame. You're an interesting man, Mr Stone."

Footsteps in the soft sand preceded the return of the warm sun on Harvey's face.

In his mind's eye, Harvey pictured a man, mid-to-late fifties with grey hair and a paunch. The man had turned to face the sea. It was an invitation for Harvey to run. But concealed in the stranger's confident tone was an underlying message that he would find him wherever Harvey ran.

"How do you want to do this?" the man called, raising his voice above the crashing waves and cool breeze. Soft remnants of a Scottish accent hung at the end of his words.

Rolling onto his side, propped up by an elbow, Harvey opened his eyes and found the man, silhouetted against the sky, his long overcoat flapping in the breeze. Harvey plucked a blade of long grass from the sand and rolled it between his fingers, pondering the words.

"There's another way, you know," said the man. "It doesn't have to end the way you imagine."

"It has ended," replied Harvey, "exactly how I imagined it would."

"I need someone," continued the man.

He turned to stare down at Harvey, faceless with the sun behind him.

"Someone who isn't afraid to get his hands dirty. Somebody with a very particular skill set."

Harvey didn't reply.

End of Book 1

STONE FURY

The
Stone Cold Thriller Series
Book 2

CHAPTER ONE

In the relative quiet of a West London back street, Harvey Stone found the stage door unlocked and slipped inside. As he let the door close behind him, his eyes adjusted to the soft, flickering, fluorescent light. Years of damp had poisoned the air and a century of backstage debauchery had left a stain on the very core of the old theatre.

The slap of bare feet running on linoleum-covered concrete floor echoed through a maze of corridors, which began where he was standing. A corridor branched off to the left and there was a shorter hallway to the right. The giggling girls were loud and shrill. Doors boomed against hard walls then hushed before another door slammed soon after. In Harvey's mind, the girls were running from room to room with post-show excitement and childish amusement.

According to the research Mills had carried out, the hallway to the right offered dedicated suites and personal space for the stars of the show, while the main cast occupied shared dressing rooms and bathrooms to the left. It was the perfect layout for Harvey's plan. Finding the correct room with little effort, he slipped inside, closed the door, and got to work.

Somewhere far away, behind many thick curtains, an audience applauded the performance.

The show was over.

"Two minutes," said Mills over his earpiece, a communication device worn by the entire team.

Harvey didn't reply.

Possessions lay sprawled across a makeup bench beneath a long mirror edged with bright light bulbs. On the bench, two lines of cocaine had been prepared and a rolled-up twenty-pound note was lying ready. A packet of cigarettes, a lighter and some loose change were also sitting beside the lines.

The room was divided into two areas by a temporary screen, the type that Marilyn Monroe or Rita Hayworth might have changed behind way back when lines of coke and rolled-up banknotes were only available to wealthy and successful performers. Behind the screen was a small couch. It was cheap and stained from years of parties, makeup, alcohol, bodily fluids and general disregard. Beside it, a laptop had been left on a small coffee table.

"Found the laptop," said Harvey. But he didn't wait for a reply.

Opening the laptop, he was presented with a Windows login screen. It was a problem he had been warned he would encounter. He took a small USB transmitter from his pocket and inserted it into the side of the computer.

"It's all yours, Reg," he said.

After a few moments of silence, there was a crackle of static before Reg confirmed he had remote access.

"I see it."

A series of asterisks appeared in the blank space as Reg worked on hacking the password, leaving Harvey to prepare himself.

A large walk-in wardrobe filled the space to the right of the entrance, along with a small toilet and shower. Inside, Harvey opened a cupboard below the sink and found some cleaning utensils and a small tub of insect killer. Using a piece of tissue paper, he wiped the cocaine into a small wastepaper basket then prepared two identical lines of insect killer. The powder was off white. But his victim had been keen enough to prepare two lines in advance for after the show, so Harvey imagined he wouldn't notice the difference.

"Bingo," said Reg. "I found the files."

The laptop displayed four video icons. Harvey inserted a second USB drive.

"Ready to copy," said Harvey.

The files all began to copy to the thumb drive.

"Okay, Harvey," said Reg. "The files are copied. You can remove the thumb drive. I'm turning the webcam on so we can get a visual. The screen will go black but don't close the lid."

"Copy," said Harvey, slipping the tiny USB drive into his pocket.

A man's voice sounded through the hallway outside along with a girl's laughter, both growing louder as they approached. Harvey glanced around to make sure nothing was out-of-place then stepped into the walk-in wardrobe, clicking the light off just as the door opened and two people fell into the room, laughing and hugging.

The girl came stumbling through first. She kicked off her shoes on her way to the makeup table where she admired her appearance. Then she unfastened her costume jacket, which was brightly coloured, shiny and barely reached her hips. The jacket slid from her arms to the floor, revealing long gloves and a tight, bright red dress, from which extended a long slender leg.

Closing the door with an exaggerated flourish, the man

who followed her inside danced across the room to join her beside the table. He slid his hands along her leg then span away as only a professional dancer knows how, coming to a stop to unbutton his shirt.

"Did you see Julie in the final scene?" the girl asked him, reaching for the small clasps on the back of her dress. "Here, help me, would you?"

The target stopped unbuttoning his frilly shirt, only too happy to help the girl with her dress.

"I did. Wasn't she wonderful?" he replied. "I thought the whole audience was going to simply burst into tears, she was so very convincing."

"That's what happens when daddy sends you off for private tuition, darling," said the girl in a mock upper-class accent.

She pulled her long gloves off her long arms then raised them and let the dress fall to the floor, revealing her near-naked body, which she admired in the mirror.

"Maybe this daddy could give you a little private tuition?"

The man stood behind her and joined in the admiration. He ran his hands from her waist to her chest, cupping her breasts, then buried his face in her neck, planting tiny kisses along her skin, soft at first, then harder as he began to grind himself into her, working himself up.

"Maybe this little girl needs punishing. She didn't do *any* of her homework," said the girl, offering a naughty schoolgirl look with one finger in her mouth. "Not. One. Bit." She accentuated each word by moving her hands to her hips in time with her speech. Then she finished by sliding her panties down to her ankles, pushing herself into the man as she did.

"Oh dear, Miss Norman. You *have* been a very, *very* bad girl indeed," said the target, allowing his hands to explore her body.

Harvey stood motionless in the dark while the charade played out before him.

"Wait," she said, as the man wrestled with his costume trousers. She bent to collect the rolled-up banknote. "I've been looking forward to this."

In one single snort, she sniffed the line of poison clean off the old wooden bench then passed the rolled-up note to the man. He had stripped naked and was occupying himself while she was bent over the bench. Passing the note and dropping to her knees in a single, fluid movement, she stared up at him.

"Are you ready for the encore?" she asked.

The man watched her for a moment, his eyes darting from her mouth to the line as the performance began.

But the scene was cut short.

Coughing once then twice as the insect killer worked its way down the girl's throat, she resumed with practiced professionalism. On the third cough, however, she dry-heaved, and gagged as a trickle of blood ran from her nose.

From the wardrobe, Harvey looked on with fascination.

"What's happening in there, Harvey?" asked Mills over the comms.

Harvey didn't reply.

The girl recovered, moaning as she returned to finish what she had started. But with almost immediate effect, she coughed and gagged once more, spraying blood from her throat across the man's naked body.

"Angie? What's wrong?" the man asked in a whiny, panicked tone.

A look of horror spread across her face. Her eyes widened as she fell to the side, supporting herself with one arm and wiping away the stream of blood from her nose with the other. Then, as if acting in some gruesome death scene, a flood of blood oozed from her mouth onto her chest and she fell back onto the floor, spraying coughs of fine red mist into the air.

Wide-eyed and aghast at the scene, the target began to panic.

"Angie," he called, lifting her head from the floor. "No. *No.* Don't do this."

Angie Norman's body twitched once in spasm as the fluid that blocked her airway filled her lungs, and she drowned in her own poisoned blood.

"Oh, God. Oh, God," said the target. "Angie, no. No. Don't do this. Come on, Angie."

The realisation of the situation hit him. He dropped her head to the floor. Backing away from her naked body in a state of panic, he stepped towards where Harvey waited in the shadows. But the man stopped three feet from the edge of Harvey's blade, which was poised and ready to slice his throat.

"Oscar? Are you coming?" a female voice from the far side of the door called.

"Come on, Oscar. We're heading to the bar for the after-party," said another voice.

"I'll, erm...I'll be right there," he replied, his voice wavering. "I'll meet you at the bar."

"Well, don't be long," came the reply.

"Apparently he won't be, not according to Angie anyway," said the second girl, and their laughs faded to a distant whisper as Oscar Shaw prepared to sniff the last line to get rid of the evidence.

Harvey smiled in the darkness.

But then Oscar had a change of heart. He collected the waste bin from the floor, found a scrunched-up piece of tissue paper inside and bent down to wipe the line away.

"I wouldn't do that if I were you," said Harvey.

"Who's there?" said Oscar, spinning around in surprise.

Harvey took a single step forward into the light.

"What the hell? Who are you?" said Oscar, dropping the bin and the tissue as if denying any involvement.

"Who sets the girls up?"

"Who sets *what* girls up?" said Oscar, covering his modesty. His voice was angry but high with fear.

"I don't think you need to worry about covering yourself after what I just witnessed, Mr Shaw."

"I didn't do it. You saw? You *saw* what happened," said Oscar, backing up to the table. "She overdosed."

"You didn't do *that*. But you did *this*."

Harvey held a flash drive between his finger and thumb.

"What is it?" asked Oscar.

His eyes flicked from the laptop back to the thumb drive.

"The end of your career," replied Harvey.

"Who are you?"

"Who sets the girls up for you, Oscar?"

"I don't know what you're talking about."

"The hookers," said Harvey, still holding the thumb drive.

"How do you know they're hookers?"

"There's something special about these particular hookers though, isn't there, Mr Shaw?" said Harvey, ignoring the question.

A silence ensued as Oscar's panicked mind sought a way out.

"What are you going to do?" he asked.

"Tell me who sets them up for you," said Harvey.

"I can't," said Oscar. "I won't."

"So you have two choices," said Harvey.

"Choices?" said Oscar, his face twisted in confusion.

"One," said Harvey, stepping over the body of Angie Norman. "You don't tell me, and the police find you here with the videos."

"No," said Oscar. "You can't."

"Do you know what they'll do to you in prison, Oscar?" asked Harvey.

"Not that. I'll do anything," said Oscar, backing himself into a corner and searching for an escape, but finding none. "What's the second choice?"

"You tell me who set the girls up for you, and I kill you quickly."

"Tell me who you are," said Oscar, scrambling against the wall. "How do you know me? You don't know me. You don't know anything."

"You've got three seconds to decide, Oscar," said Harvey.

"I don't know anything. I swear."

"One," said Harvey.

"You won't get away with this. You don't know who I am."

"Two."

"Stop," said Oscar. "Just stop it. You can't."

"Three," said Harvey, and took a single step forward.

"Okay, okay," said Oscar, falling into a crouch against the wall. "I'll tell you."

Harvey didn't reply.

"My phone," said Oscar. "There's a number stored with no name."

"I'm accessing his phone now," said Reg over the comms.

"What's his name?" said Harvey.

A puddle of liquid had formed at Oscar's feet and he cowered in submission.

"I've told you all I know," he said.

His voice broke as the realisation that death was moments away hit home.

"Got it," said Reg over the comms. "Good work, Harvey. Let's leave him for the police."

"Stand up," said Harvey.

But Oscar just stared back at him, frozen with fear.

"Harvey, it's okay. We don't need him anymore," said Mills, her voice steeped in authority.

"Up," said Harvey.

"Harvey, what are you doing?" said Reg. "Leave him."

The open communication channel became frantic as both Melody and Reg explained that the operation had been a success. The job was over.

With a single flick of the tiny switch on the earpiece, Harvey silenced the chat.

Oscar Shaw rose to stand, cowering and still hiding his nakedness.

"You killed two girls," said Harvey.

"I-"

"Tell me, Oscar," said Harvey. "Do you deserve to live?"

The words seemed to break the barrier that had retained the man's tears.

"Do you?" said Harvey.

Oscar shook his head, wiping his eyes.

"Do you want to die quickly?" asked Harvey, turning his blade and sending reflected light dancing across Oscar's naked body.

A single nod and more tears.

"I can make it so fast," said Harvey, dragging the point of the blade across Oscar's groin.

"Just do it," said Oscar, breaking mid-sentence. "Just kill me."

Harvey slipped his knife into the sheave on his belt and closed the gap between them.

Oscar cowered away, his arms raised in defence expecting the blows to begin.

But taking Oscar's hand in his own, Harvey stretched each of the man's fingers out one by one until his trembling open palm faced the ceiling above, glistening with sweat.

Then, with his face inches from Oscar's, Harvey placed the rolled-up note in the man's hand and closed his fist around it.

"Sniff the line," whispered Harvey.

CHAPTER TWO

THE AUDI SPED THROUGH LONDON AS FAST AS THE SPEED limit allowed. As they crossed the River Thames over Waterloo Bridge, neither Harvey nor the driver, Denver, enjoyed the view of the Southbank, which was lit up, with its reflections spilling into the water.

Denver turned left off the bridge, followed the river downstream, and entered the Blackwall Tunnel. Ten minutes later, they pulled up outside the headquarters of an unofficial, organised crime investigation unit. It was a dark arm of SO10 housed in a brick building adjacent to the Thames Barrier. Built in the eighties and designed as a flood protection system for the Greater London area, the Thames Barrier consisted of a series of mechanical barricades that opened and closed to control the flow of water in and out of London.

The unit was led by Frank Carver, who had directed his team to success by capturing two crates of missing Heckler and Koch MP-5 sub-machine guns, taking out one of the leading organised crime families, and killing a wanted murderer who had been on the run for more than thirty years. Frank had also captured a known sex offender who had confessed to offences going back more than five years and who had taken the rap for seven victims.

The team was unofficial because the public simply couldn't know they existed, let alone know about it being a dark ops unit. Many operatives of SO10 were not even aware of the team. While the unit was in its infancy, it would remain unofficial until such a time when its success gave the chief grounds for wider exposure.

The HQ was situated in a perfect location next to the Thames for easy river access into London. The unit itself was shared with the team of engineers that managed the Thames Barrier. The building was far bigger than their needs required and had been split into two separate departments specifically to host the dark ops team. The barrier engineers were housed on one side of the building and Frank's team on the other. The two groups rarely met. The building was perfectly sized. There was a helipad on the roof. It was ten minutes away from the Blackwall Tunnel and fifteen minutes from the A406 and M11. Plus it was less than five minutes from London City Airport, where a small passenger jet had been seconded for their use.

The large warehouse doors slid open and Denver pulled the Audi inside without stopping. The doors were closed behind him by Reg, the tech guru. He'd been watching their journey on one of the twelve twenty-four-inch screens that were mounted on the wall in front of his desk in, what he liked to call, his command station. His central screen had a game session open and paused, while the surrounding screens, which all connected to various servers and computers, showed maps, audio recordings, video feeds, network health monitors, and Reg's favourite medieval TV show. All the devices that powered the screens were connected to a single KVM switch that allowed Reg to use just one keyboard and mouse to control the entire set-up. It was the set-up of his dreams, and he had finished it off with a large, comfy, leather office chair.

Denver parked the Audi between the old VW Transporter, which served as the team's mobile unit, and Harvey's BMW motorcycle in the small workshop area to the left of the large doors. The workshop comprised of three shoulder-height, snap-on tool chests, which contained every tool Denver required to maintain the vehicles, as well as an engine hoist and an overhead hoist, which was fixed to a mobile gantry and large workbench. It was the set-up of Denver's dreams.

Denver was the team's engineer and mechanic. He was also a world-class rally-cross driver and pilot. Harvey looked through these talents and saw only a solid, reliable pair of hands. Denver had been given a choice as an adolescent to either face prison for his multiple car thefts or enter into the government's rehabilitation program. He'd selected the second option and had since worked his way up through the ranks and departments.

Beside the workshop in the far left-hand corner was a caged-off area that, according to Frank's strict instructions, was to be kept locked at all times. No exceptions. The cage was twelve feet by twelve feet. Three of the four chain link walls had lockable steel armoury cabinets. The cage was Melody's domain, and she prided herself on her stock of weaponry and the cleanliness of her weapons.

Melody took credit for the operations of the team. She was a trained sniper and surveillance expert. Beside the cage was Melody's desk. It was a simple set-up with a laptop and a desktop printer. Next to her chair was a cabinet where she stored the surveillance equipment. In addition to the basic communications gear, the team used the surveillance hardware because, if used correctly, it provided eyes and ears wherever they needed. All they had to do was plant them.

A mezzanine floor ran along the right-hand wall and across the back of the unit. Upstairs was Frank's office, a meeting room, a kitchen area, and a mess.

Harvey had been allocated a space on the ground floor in the far right-hand corner, away from the large doors and beneath the mezzanine. It contained a punch-bag and a chair with a small table to one side. Harvey had few possessions.

Frank's office upstairs mirrored his previous office in London's Southbank, which he'd occupied before he'd been offered the chance to head the new team. It was a fairly large room with windows opposite the door that looked out over the Thames Barrier. His desk was central to the room. Behind it was a large pin board, the only possession he had taken from his department office when he had relocated.

On the pin board were photos of known organised crime families and groups. They were collated in various areas of the board according to the relationships amongst them. Some had a large cross drawn through them. Others were linked together with string. Six months ago, Frank had managed to put three crosses through long-standing faces on the board. It was a personal best for one bust.

The analogy Frank used to describe being a cop was that a city needs a method of disposing of garbage. If it doesn't have a method, the streets become dirty and hazardous. Society will never be garbage free because a new batch of garbage gets created even as the old one is being collected and taken out. Criminals are that garbage.

Frank heard the main entrance slide open and the heavy doors of the Audi as they slammed shut. He heard the voice of Denver calling out to Reg, in what was probably a childish insult.

Frank stepped out of his office and leaned on the handrail. He looked down at his team.

"Stone, have you got a minute?"

Frank's Scottish accent was soft and subtle. Yet it still held an underlying tone that meant anyone he beckoned didn't know whether they should prepare for a bollocking or praise. It wasn't a deliberate trick on Frank's part. It was just his voice.

Harvey looked up from the workshop floor. He had just started to fiddle with his motorbike's panniers, but he stood instead and walked towards the metal steps.

"Close the door, Stone. Take a seat."

Harvey did as instructed then stared at Frank. Harvey had a crop of dark hair, which he kept short at all times. He had an athletic build and stood at just over six foot tall. He maintained a shaved face, but other than that, he underwent no other grooming. The most striking feature of Harvey Stone was his presence. He had a way of telling you what you needed to say without moving his lips or uttering a word. It was a trait he had learned from his mentor, Julios.

Julios had taken Harvey on when he was very young. He had channelled the anger inside the boy and developed him into a killer. Harvey had been hunting the men who raped and killed his sister since he was twelve years old. The first man had been easy to find; he'd worked for Harvey's foster father. Julios had helped Harvey find him and take him out. Six months previously, Harvey had found the second man and tortured him, only to find out that Harvey's foster parents' real son, Donny, was the third man. Donny had been right under his nose all along but had fled to the Maldives following an attempt on his life.

Julios had been killed in the build-up to the event which left two people on Harvey's list: Donny Cartwright and the unknown man that killed his mentor and friend, Julios.

The first lesson Julios had taught Harvey as a boy had been a simple one that he continued to practice in every element of his life: patience, planning, and execution. It was an art. For now, Harvey could wait; he'd find his targets eventually, and his executions were typically immaculate.

"Debrief," said Frank.

"Debrief?" replied Harvey. "What do you want to know?"

"I sent you to do a job. Your debrief should be an account of the job's success level plus information on anything else that I need to know."

"Shaw is dead," replied Harvey.

"Shaw is dead? That's your debrief?"

"I killed him. Well, technically, I allowed him to kill himself. I just didn't stop him."

"And I presume you didn't stop Angela Norman from killing herself either?"

"No, I didn't. That was interesting. I wasn't expecting her to show up."

"Interesting, Stone? She was one of the country's most promising stage actresses. You let her die."

"It would have compromised the investigation if I'd stopped her."

"Listen, Stone, I know you're new to all of this, but you need to remember you represent the other side of the law now. You're no longer a criminal. We have ways of conducting ourselves, and there are also ways we shouldn't conduct ourselves. Allowing an innocent actress to die is not one of the former. Is that understood?"

Harvey didn't reply.

"This isn't a bollocking, Stone."

"I don't care if it is a bollocking."

"This isn't a bollocking. But you do need to remember that I have a file on you that would see you put away for more years than you have left in your body."

"Is that a threat?"

"No, Stone, it's not a threat. It's a demonstration of the lengths I had to go to keep you from being tossed into a six-by-four cell for the rest of your life. Have some respect. You're a talented man, Stone, but you don't intimidate me. You have an opportunity here to do a fantastic service to your country and repay some debts. Use it wisely. These opportunities are few and far between. Understood?"

"Repay some debts?"

"Yes. Repay some debts."

"You mean you have a noose around my neck and you're waiting for me to step out of line?"

"I *do* have a noose around your neck, but I'd like to *help* you take it off."

Harvey looked at his team leader. He was neither angry nor upset at Frank, who was just doing a job for the government, and Harvey was just doing a job for him. It was black and white.

"The bodies were found. The stage manager called it in around fifteen minutes ago. I don't have a full report yet. They're probably dusting for prints and running forensics. The only detail I have was that they were naked and looked like they drowned in their own blood." Frank's face turned into a look of disgust. "Why would they have drowned in their own blood?"

Harvey remained impassive. "That's what happens when you start messing around with drugs, Frank. Bad things happen."

"But why were they naked? What did you do to them?"

"They were naked of their own volition. They took drugs of their own volition. I just happened to switch their lines of coke for lines of something else. The unit is in the clear. There's no trace back to us. No cut throats, no torture, no gunshots."

"Good." Frank took a breath. "Listen, Stone, you're an asset to this unit. I want this to work, and I understand that you're not used to the formalities. But I can help you there."

Frank took a sip of water and watched Harvey's emotionless face. "In the future, do you think we can work out a way of you giving me a debrief after each case? Without me having to chase you, that is."

"Debrief?"

"Debrief."

"Reg has the number. There's your debrief."

"What number?"

"The number of the man who arranged the hookers for Shaw."

Harvey left the room, and Frank shook his head in disbelief.

Leaving the warehouse, Harvey took a walk down to the riverside, letting the cold breeze tug at his shirt and pimple his skin. He loved the river at night.

Harvey was still in a state of transition, and he was struggling. Until six months ago, he had essentially been a hitman for his foster father's web of criminal activities. Now he worked for an informal arm of the very people he'd been avoiding his entire life. What a mess.

He walked down to the river and stared at the water that flowed around the Thames Barrier leaving deadly whirlpools in its wake that would suck a man into the darkest depths. It was an endless cycle of power, always hungry, always alive, and always moving.

John Cartwright had been just as hungry, always planning a job and moving around in an endless cycle of power. He was Harvey's foster father. John and his wife, Barb, had taken on Harvey and his elder sister when they'd been left in his bar one night. Barb had wanted to foster them as they only had one son, Donny, and couldn't have more children. When Harvey had inquired years later, he learned that his real parents had killed themselves in a double suicide and left a note inside baby Harvey's hamper.

John had always been surrounded by his men, his endless cycle of power. The men saw Harvey and his sister, Hannah, grow up from babies. Julios, John's minder, had a soft spot for Harvey. He play-wrestled with him and taught him how to sneak and be quiet. Looking back, Harvey realised that the lessons in being quiet were more for Julios' sake.

Hannah was older by a few years and had been developing into a young lady, much to the admiration of John's men. Harvey woke one night and found her bed empty. He had sneaked down the long and winding staircase into the kitchen where he heard the violent whimpers and grunts of the men raping her in the basement.

Harvey had hidden in the shadows. He was just a boy. But he saw one man emerge from the basement. He remembered the man's profile in the moonlight like it had been scratched onto his eyes.

Less than a week later, Hannah had taken a kitchen knife and slaughtered herself in the night. Harvey had lost the only friend he'd ever had, and the only person he had truly loved. For her to do such a thing to herself was unthinkable. She'd been a happy girl until that night. She had shone.

Harvey had turned his grief into violence, viscously attacking bullies at school, and even hospitalising some of them. Eventually, John had to pull Harvey out of public school and invite private tutors to teach Harvey at their huge three-hundred-acre estate in Theydon Bois, Essex.

John had also asked his minder, Julios, to take Harvey under his wing and channel his aggression. Soon, Harvey was immersed in Julios' trainings. Lessons in self-defence and psychological control grew to incorporate martial arts, which Harvey absorbed. He began with defensive techniques, such as judo and aikido, then progressed to taekwondo. Harvey was amazed at how easily Julios was able to side-step a punch and use the attacker's momentum to throw them to the floor or disable them using only one hand.

Less than a year into his studies, Harvey had adapted and taken on Julios' mantra: patience, planning, and execution. He considered it in every element of his life. It was around that time that Harvey had recognised the man whose profile was etched into his mind, the man from the kitchen on the night of Hannah's rape. He'd been one of John's men. Julios had understood Harvey's needs and guided him through his initiation.

Harvey had been patient. He had planned. He executed the man with just a blade.

He'd been twelve years old.

In the years to follow, Harvey and Julios became a cohesive team, carrying out the jobs for John that nobody else could do, mostly taking out rival gang members or sending a message to people that stood in John's way. John had men to do dirty work, but often these jobs required a delicate touch, which was a little more refined than six guys kicking in some doors and opening fire.

Deep down, Harvey always had two goals on his mind: to find his sister's other rapist and to discover the truth about his parents.

He'd trained while he searched. For close to thirty years, Harvey had been isolating his own victims. He'd targeted sex offenders out on bail or released from prison. Scum. People that society wouldn't miss. He'd honed his skills in reconnaissance, surveillance, espionage and, above all, killing a man with his bare hands, as he had done many times.

A force to be reckoned with, Harvey was an incredibly gifted and ruthless killer.

Six months before the night that Harvey looked down at the water that swirled before the great Thames Barrier, Julios had been killed. It had been a botched job organised by

Sergio, John's adviser, accountant, and lawyer. In a turn of events, Harvey had learned that Sergio had been the second rapist, the man he'd been hunting for all of his adult life.

Harvey caught him and boiled him alive.

During his slow and painful death, Sergio had told Harvey of a third man in an attempt to bargain for survival. The third rapist was Donny Cartwright, Harvey's foster brother.

Sergio's death had been horrible; he'd truly suffered exactly as Harvey had intended. But Harvey was thirty-two years old, and despite a life of dishing out justice, his own problems remained unsolved.

He was still unaware of the story of his real parents. Harvey didn't know how they died or where they were buried. He didn't even know their names.

His best friend and mentor had been killed. But Harvey hadn't found the man that pulled the trigger.

Finally, his sister's death had not been fully avenged. Donny Cartwright was out there somewhere.

Harvey would find him if it was the last thing he did.

Harvey had tapped out of the criminal world. He rode his motorcycle to France to buy a small property and live out his days in the sunshine, somewhere he could focus on finishing his life's work.

That's when Frank stepped in.

Harvey's options had been slashed from endless possibilities to just two choices: prison for the brutal murder of Sergio and anything else they could find on him, or the chance to transform his skills and work for Frank.

He sighed and stared at the water. Everything had changed. Harvey turned back and looked at the bleak brick building. It was a far cry from the little farm he'd bought on the south coast of France, a twenty minutes' walk to the Med surrounded by green fields and smiling faces.

Sure, he liked the team. They were okay. Frank was alright

too, deep down. But the transition to the other side was diffi-cult. The threat of prison loomed over Harvey like a shadow on his heart. But it wasn't the tough life of a category A prison that kept Harvey awake; he could handle himself and his association with John Cartwright would place him fairly high on the inside ladder. But the knowledge that he'd never get a chance to find Donny, understand what happened to his parents, or find whoever killed Julios, that's what would taunt his sleepless nights.

CHAPTER THREE

FRANK STOOD AND WALKED TO THE LANDING OUTSIDE HIS office.

"Mess room. Now. Everyone."

Denver had just started to drain the oil from the VW Transporter. It was jacked up, and he was lying underneath removing the sump bolt. Oil had begun to flow into an empty container. "Great timing, boss," he muttered.

Reg was leaning back in his reclining office chair. He had his wireless keyboard on his lap and was typing commands into a secure shell terminal hosted on a virtual computer in a data centre in St Petersburg. He was attempting to hack into his own system. Lines of code filled two of the twelve screens. Each red line was followed by one blue line in a series of attack and defence. His automated systems were working, but not fast enough. He was attempting to pull the resources from the firewalls with continuous attacks to prevent them from operating efficiently. This particular denial of service attack would never allow a hacker inside the network; the attempts were too weak. But it would give the hacker an indication of the resources a network had so that he or she could tailor a more sophisticated approach.

"Reg, let's go," said Melody, as she walked past his desk.

Melody Mills was five foot eight with dark hair and a cute exterior. She wore cargo pants, tan boots and a tight-fitting t-shirt. She was the little sister of the group but could hold her own in a physical or verbal confrontation.

Denver walked behind her, wiping his hands on a rag. He wore overalls that were fairly clean and a baseball cap with the emblem of a little-known, British, high-performance car manufacturer that he admired.

The three of them sat in the mess room with Frank, which was around thirty feet long. One end had been arranged as a lounge with two dark, two-seater sofas and a large TV on the wall. The end near the door had a dining table that doubled as a meeting table. Two large whiteboards hung on the wall behind it. It was an efficient use of the space.

Reg sat on a sofa with his feet on the coffee table in front of the TV, which was turned off. Denver perched on the arm of a sofa while still wiping his hands with the rag. Melody stood near the coffee machine waiting for it to finish filling the pot.

After a few minutes, Harvey quietly walked into the room and sat at the table. He didn't lean backwards or forwards. He didn't make himself comfortable. He just sat upright and waited.

Then Frank walked into the room.

"Ah, we're all here. Good." Frank placed his files on the table and picked up a whiteboard marker. "We have a development in the human trafficking case."

All four of them knew of the case but didn't react. Dead hookers turned up all the time, but the team had received further intelligence. Not only were girls being brought into the country to serve as hookers, but a certain gang were bringing them in and offering wealthy men the opportunity to torture, rape, hurt and kill the women in exchange for vast sums of money. Oscar Shaw had been one of those men.

"Reg, I believe you have the number of a possible lead? I want to know who the number belongs to and the frequent numbers called and received."

"I can give you a location of the phone, plus SMS details and any email or service accounts that are associated with the number," said Reg.

"Perfect. Let's get as much as we can. Melody, please work with Reg to build up a profile. Once you have the name, I want his history and any information we can get on him, known associates, previous records, anything."

"It's probably a burner, sir," said Melody.

"*Anything* you can find. Denver, how's the fleet?" asked Frank. "We need to be in a position to move at a moment's notice."

"The fleet is good, sir. The Audi is brand new and I've just replaced the exhaust and suspension on the VW. New wheels should be arriving any day now."

"How about inside?"

"Why don't I show you? I'm rather proud of it."

"Okay. I'll take a look when I come down." Frank smiled briefly. He knew that whatever Denver had done to the van would be impeccably over and above the team's requirements.

"Mills, as soon as Reg has a fix on the location of that phone, I need a recce. I need to see numbers, who's going in, who's coming out, and who's not coming out."

"No problem, sir."

"Stone, work with Mills. You're going to need a way in. No drama. I need video feeds set up for Reg so we can take this down. We are *not* looking to take them all out. We need arrests not toe tags."

Harvey didn't respond.

"Right. Get to it," finished Frank.

Melody left the room first, she was eager to get started on the surveillance equipment.

Denver followed, keen to complete the oil change on the VW.

Reg walked directly to his desk. He used the virtual KVM switch and rotated the order of the screens. His security test was shifted to a higher screen, and an empty window was dragged into the central screen in front of him.

Harvey left the room last and walked back down the steps and past Reg.

"Got ya," Reg said to himself. Harvey stood behind him and watched him work. He saw the interface of Shaw's phone on Reg's centre screen.

"The number was in his messages. He said he didn't save it as a contact," said Harvey.

"Okay. So here are his messages. What's this one?" Reg opened a message from an unidentified number. The message read, *Thank you for last night. Let's do it again sometime*. "I'm guessing neither of the dead hookers sent him that."

"They're not dead hookers, Reg. They're the *victims* here, remember," Melody chimed in, defending camp female.

"Yep. Right. Not hookers, victims. Got ya." His eyes were blazing over the screen. He zipped in and out of messages, and opened and closed threads until he whispered, "Bingo."

Reg switched the window to his left-hand screen and opened a new one on the centre screen. He typed a command and a small program opened up with a search box in the top-right corner. Reading the number from the phone, he typed it into the search box and hit enter.

The program ran some checks and a progress bar showed up below the search. Reg sat back and breathed out sharply as if his work had been on a timer and he had just beaten the clock.

The search results began to show.

"Okay. The phone's last known location was here."

Reg pointed and copied the GPS coordinates into the satellite imagery program. Then he dragged that into the right-hand screen in the centre row. He let the image render and turned his attention back to the phone.

"And the last known callers are here," Reg continued. "Incoming up top. Outgoing down below." He dragged the tab to the screen next to the satellite imagery. "Next, we have messages." Reg hummed a few bars of some indistinguishable tune. "Okay. Let's put these here." He dragged the messages window next to the window with the callers. "Now for the fun part."

"We have wildly different definitions of fun," said Harvey.

"That's why I'm the master technologist sitting behind an array of hardware performing all manner of incredible things, and you're..."

"I'm Harvey Stone."

"That's right, Harvey. What *is* it you do for fun again?"

"That's a truth you're not ready for."

"Right." Reg sensed he had stepped too far.

"So?"

"So what?"

"So what's the fun part?" asked Harvey.

"Ah, yeah. We know where he was last, we know who he's spoken to, and we know who's been messaging him. Now to find out who *he* is."

"This is the part where he finds out it's a burner," called Melody from across the room. "He won't be able to trace the owner."

"Ah, damn it."

"It's a burner?" asked Harvey.

"Yeah. Untraceable."

"What about the numbers?"

"That's all we have to go on," said Reg. "Let's make it work."

"So you can search each number that the phone has been in contact with and come up with a list of names and locations?"

"Yeah. As long as they aren't burners too."

"Can you put a list of names together with a map of the owners' addresses or last known locations? We might be able to find a common denominator. Use that map as the central point and place the..."

"Customers?"

"*Customers* around that location. We'll build a web."

Melody had walked over to them and was looking at the collation of the data. "That's a great idea," she said.

Harvey turned but didn't reply. He acknowledged her comment with the slightest of nods and turned back to the screens.

The satellite image showing the phone's location had finished rendering. The image displayed a spot in the Essex suburbs outside East London. Reg zoomed into the location and found a small cluster of buildings off Pudding Lane near Hainault.

"Essex countryside, Reg. It's rife with crime."

"Apparently so," replied Reg.

They were referring to the bust that had landed Frank and his team with the new dark ops unit. It had happened at Harvey's foster father's converted farmhouse, which was also in the Essex countryside. Harvey had tortured and killed Sergio and left a wanted sex offender and twelve missing Heckler and Koch MP-5 sub-machine guns for the police to find.

"Okay, we have a location, Melody," said Reg.

"Send it through to me," she said, walking back to her desk.

"On its way. Now let's put some faces to some numbers."

"Last caller was one Mr Shaw, would you believe it? Next, we have a Barnaby Brayethwait. Cool name."

"Can we run a match on any common numbers between them?"

"That's happening as we speak. Right. Next we have a Mr Cartwright, Donald."

Harvey was looking at the profile of Barnaby Brayethwait on the left-hand screen when the last name registered.

"Stop."

"What's up?" asked Reg.

"That last name."

Reg read it off the screen again, "Mr Cartwright, Donald."

"Find me the location of that number."

"Well, yeah, I can do, but I'm building a database here. As soon as we've been-"

"Stop the database. Find me the location of that number."

Melody heard the tension and rose from her desk. She began to walk over. Harvey stepped across to his bike and pulled his leather jacket from the handlebars.

The satellite image began to render as Harvey walked back to Reg.

"What's happening here?" asked Melody.

"How recent is this location?" asked Harvey, pulling on his helmet and ignoring Melody.

"It's live. He's there now."

The image showed the exact same location as the burner.

"Harvey?" asked Melody.

He swung his leg over his bike, turned the key in the ignition, and nodded at Reg to open the doors. Then he turned to face Melody.

"There's something I need to do."

Harvey felt the constant vibration of his phone in his inside jacket pocket during the thirty-minute ride to the spot where the satellite image had shown Donny's location. Harvey pulled into the car park of a nearby pub called The Maypole to stop and deal with the team. He needed an update from Reg, anyway.

He called Reg's phone.

"Are you alone?" he asked as soon as Reg answered.

"The whole team is here. You're on the loudspeaker," Reg replied.

"Donald Cartwright, what's his location?"

"It's not as easy as that, Stone," said Frank. "You don't get to run free and take care of your own personal projects, especially when they compromise the entire case."

There was a long silence.

"I need to do this," said Harvey.

"You're either with us or against us, Stone. There is no half-way point."

Harvey didn't reply.

"If you come back now, we can work this case together. You might even help us arrest your brother."

"Foster brother."

"Well, like I said, if you choose to go your own way, you'll be on the ten most wanted list in under an hour. Every cop in the country will be onto you. I can't have rogue agents, Stone. I can't just watch you go after a known suspect. We need the man behind the operation, the source, and that isn't Donny."

Harvey didn't reply.

"Harvey, what do you say?" said Frank. "Come on back and let's do this together. We want you in this team."

"I can't. I need to do this."

Harvey disconnected the call and pocketed the phone. He pulled his helmet back on then turned right out of the car park. He took the turn into Pudding Lane three hundred yards later and rode slowly along the quiet, narrow road. Harvey knew the lane well and recognised the group of buildings he had seen on the satellite image. The area used to be a large farm which had been divided into smaller plots and bought out. The buildings had been converted into small business units over the years and were now independent of the farmland that surrounded them. Harvey took a slow ride and approached the long driveway.

He had no intention of entering the property but he wanted to get a lay of the land. He needed somewhere close by so he could park up and wait for Donny. The buildings were four hundred yards away. He could see a few cars parked outside. One of them, in particular, caught his attention. It looked like a black Mercedes. Donny had a black Mercedes before, back when they were brothers, back when Julios was alive.

Harvey rode on slowly and found a turn off that led nowhere. It was two hundred metres past the entrance to the old farm on the opposite side of Pudding Lane. He pulled in and turned off his engine. Then he removed his helmet and considered the move he'd just made.

He was torn. Part of him had enjoyed working with Frank and the team. It was structured and organised and played into Harvey's methodology. A large part of him had, however, longed for freedom. He'd never actually had time to enjoy the place he'd bought in France. Frank had caught up with him within a week and laid the options on the table, to work for him and put his skills to good use, or go to prison for a very long time.

Harvey had spent his entire life doing two things: working for his criminal foster father, John Cartwright, and hunting the men that had raped and killed his sister. One of those men was Donny Cartwright.

Donny was now less than a mile away. Harvey could just walk in there and wring his neck. But he knew that Reg and the team would be tracking and watching his every move. He would be taken down before he could get away. Besides, the death would be too quick. The scenario left no room for suffering, and Donny needed to suffer. Instead, it was best to just follow Donny to see where he lived and notice his habits. Harvey would take the fight away from the scene. Patience and planning.

Donny would be treated the same way as Harvey's targets, using Julios' methods. Harvey knew that they were the key to success. During the years he had been hunting for Sergio, Harvey had honed his skills on known predators. The media always announced them one way or another. Harvey had cleansed the world of thirty-three sex offenders. The number would have been thirty-four, but he'd donated the last one to the law before he made his escape to France. Frank had claimed that victory when he'd found the boiled remains of Sergio along with a recorded audio confession from both sex offenders.

The black Mercedes cruised past the turnout where Harvey was parked. Harvey pulled on his helmet, started the bike, and drove to the end of the road. A silver Nissan SUV followed directly behind Donny, which worked in Harvey's favour; Donny would have recognised the bike and the rider in his mirror.

Harvey followed the cars at a distance for fifteen minutes. When Donny turned into an underground car park of a swanky apartment block, Harvey carried on straight without stopping. The Nissan pulled into the car park behind the Mercedes. They were together. Harvey rode on.

Stopping at a petrol station, he ordered a salt beef and mustard bagel from the sandwich counter inside. It was more to pass the time than to quench any grumblings of his stomach, and Harvey didn't know when he would next eat.

Harvey gave Donny and his accomplice time to settle in whilst he developed a plan in his head. The best strategies developed in his head over time, which he was rapidly running out of.

His bike was recognisable to Donny. He needed something he could use to get closer. The team's Audi would have been ideal.

He was sat in a side street, hidden from passing cars, while he ate with his helmet off. Pulling his phone from his pocket, he ran a search for Barnaby Brayethwait. Harvey preferred to use a secure VPN when performing searches on targets. But he had no choice.

There were a surprising amount of Barnaby Brayethwaits. According to the search engine, one was a plumber in Manchester. Another was a musician. Then Harvey found the man he was looking for. Barnaby Brayethwait was a local Labour MP. He looked to be mid-fifties, slightly overweight, with a full head of thick grey hair and a false smile. He was definitely a politician.

Harvey thought about finding him. He no longer had the luxury of time, a laptop, or Reg's resources. Running a search for Brayethwait's name and address would leave a direct trail to Harvey's phone, which was linked to the unit and would compromise the team. He hated that he thought that way. Was he turning?

Instead, he searched for the Chigwell Labour office and found that the jurisdiction fell under Redbridge. The website pointed him to Epping where the office was based. He made a mental note of the address and shut down the search.

It was getting late. The office would be closed. Harvey needed to think.

He found an Airbnb nearby. It wasn't ideal, and the lady was slightly put off when she showed him the room and he closed the door on her without so much as a thank you. He showered in the en-suite and lay on the cool sheets. His SIG lay next to him on the bed. His clothes were neatly piled on a chair and his leather jacket hung on the back.

Harvey stared at the ceiling, planning.

5

CHAPTER FIVE

WHEN FRANK FINISHED THE BRIEFING, HE RETURNED TO his office to mull over the potential flaws in the plan. He often did this while the team carried out research. He prepared and created a list of potentials that would question the integrity of the plan they devised.

Frank heard the shutter doors open and Harvey's bike start so he rose and went to stand at the handrail.

Harvey was sitting on his bike. Melody stood nervously watching him. Reg reluctantly opened the doors. There was a tension in the room. Frank was about to call out when Harvey revved the engine and rode out of the unit.

Reg closed the doors behind Harvey.

"What just happened?" Frank asked.

Melody turned in surprise and looked up at him. "Harvey, sir, he just left."

"Yeah, I saw that. But why? Where's he going? What's going on?"

Reg Tenant sat back in his chair and began to pull up LUCY on the central screen. LUCY was Reg's creation. It was a combined hardware and software solution that, among other functions, monitored the satellite and GPS tags that he had planted on the team. They all knew about the chips in their vehicles and phones except for Harvey. It was a security protocol Frank had instructed Reg to carry out in case Harvey disappeared.

Reg had built and developed LUCY himself. The system was an extremely powerful software and hardware solution that officially stood for Location and Unilateral Communication Interface, or LUCI. However, Reg preferred the unofficial name of Lets Us Catch You, so she had been christened LUCY. In Reg's eyes, she had a full personality.

In terms of hardware, LUCY was a combination of four servers: one master and three slaves. Each server contained twenty-four multi-core processors plus one hundred and twenty-eight gigabytes of memory.

LUCY's interface ran on a virtual operating system. So if the system ever crashed, a new instance would fire up on a slave server to ensure continuity and zero downtime.

The database was striped across several block-level storage systems with a combined storage potential of one hundred and twenty-eight petabytes in a RAID one plus zero configuration.

LUCY was powered by one high-powered, interruptible power supply with three identical UPS in passive mode. Beyond the UPS power, a backup generator stood ready to kick in.

LUCY's capabilities included the ability for Reg to view and manage multiple pieces of software to provide a single view for satellite imagery. He could then identify the location, speed, height above sea-level, and temperature of the digital tracking chips that monitored the team and their suspects.

In addition to the tracking chips, which were just five millimetres square, LUCY had the ability to monitor mobile phones on virtually any network internationally. This allowed

Reg to not only hear the conversations but access a live view of a smart phone's interface, which provided access to messages, calendars, contacts and more.

LUCY also managed the comms system the team used on operations. Tiny earpieces were worn by the team that linked with the headquarters using various communication methods, including VHF radio. The earpieces had a tiny button for push-to-talk. Or, if the operative wanted to open the comms, they could keep the button pushed in for two seconds and the channel would remain open. Anybody else on the encrypted comms system would hear everything.

Through LUCY, Reg could group the tiny chips and assign a particular group to a particular person. Once assigned, habits were monitored, patterns were analysed, and the information was stored in a database to be called upon faster than manually identifying trends in the individual's habits. He could even set alerts that identified if a person being tracked deviated from their usual habits. He knew that Melody visited Starbucks every morning without fail. When she didn't get a coffee one morning and drove straight to HQ, Reg asked her if Starbucks had been closed. He also knew it had freaked her out, because she'd told him so.

"Tenant, show me-"

"Already on it, sir."

Reg browsed the groups in the directory tree on the left of the window and expanded the view to find Harvey. Harvey had four chips: his phone, his bike, his leather jacket and his wristwatch. The wristwatch had been the hardest to plant as Harvey only ever took it off when he trained. Even then, it was always in clear view. If Harvey had caught him, Reg imagined the consequences to be quite severe to his physical health. But he had pulled it off with the help of Frank, who had called Harvey to his office while he was beating the crap out of his punch bag.

LUCY dialled in on Harvey. All four chips were travelling at seventy miles per hour on the A406 North Circular Road. They watched as the speed reduced every now and then as Harvey slowed for the speed cameras. They watched him all the way.

The team said nothing, but the tension grew as Harvey drew closer to Pudding Lane. When he was coming through Hainault, Frank said, "Get him on the phone."

Reg used the on-screen digital phone application to dial Harvey's number. He routed the audio through the speakers and the mic that he used to communicate with the team through their earpieces.

The call rang out. A woman's voice told them that the number they had dialled had not responded.

"Again," said Frank.

Reg tried again. On the third attempt, they saw the bike slow and stop in a pub car park at the top of Pudding Lane. The call rang out again. Once more, they heard the dull tones of the automated woman.

"One more time," said Frank. "Denver, is that van ready?"

"Wait," said Melody. "He'll call us on his terms. Just wait."

Reg's audio system started to play the default ringtone through his speakers.

"You alone?" asked Harvey.

"The whole team is here. You're on the loudspeaker," Reg replied.

"Donald Cartwright, what's his location?"

Frank stepped closer to the screens. Though he couldn't see a microphone, he spoke loud and clear. "It's not as easy as that, Stone. You don't get to run free and take care of your own personal projects, especially when they compromise the entire case."

Frank turned to Melody who nodded.

"I need to do this," said Harvey.

"You're either with us or against us, Stone. There is no half-way point."

Harvey didn't reply.

Frank pushed a little harder. "If you come back now, we can work this case together. You might even help us arrest your brother."

"Foster brother."

"Well, like I said, if you choose to go your own way, you'll be on the ten most wanted list in under an hour. Every cop in the country will be onto you. I can't have rogue agents, Stone. I can't just watch you go after a known suspect. We need the man behind the operation, the source, and that isn't Donny."

Harvey didn't reply.

Frank pushed again. "Harvey, what do you say? Come on back and let's do this together. We want you in this team."

"I can't. I need to do this." He disconnected the call.

"Shall I call back?" asked Reg.

"No," said Melody. "That's enough for now."

Denver joined the rest of the team at Reg's workstation. "The van will be another hour. I'm halfway through an oil change."

"Okay. Finish it fast. The three of you are going on a recce. Mills, surveillance. Tenant, LUCY and comms. Load the van now. You're out of here as soon as Cox is finished." Frank turned to walk up the steps.

Reg had a flight case with everything he needed inside. It was ready on the floor by his desk along with a large sports bag. He continued to watch Harvey on the screen.

Harvey seemed to be parked up in a dead end turning past the entrance to the old farm. Reg hit refresh on the satellite imagery of Donald Cartwright's phone. Cartwright was still at the location. Then the icon began to move across the screen.

"Wait. Cartwright is on the move."

Frank turned and joined Reg again. They watched as Donny drove past Harvey, who began to follow him at a distance. The movement of dots on the screen looked like a cheap eighties video game.

When Donny's phone lost its signal, Harvey continued on for another mile, and then stopped at a petrol station.

"What's he doing, Tenant?" asked Frank.

"Not sure, sir. Did he see Cartwright turn or was he too far behind?"

"Harvey wouldn't be too far behind. He's a pro," said Frank.

Reg set an alert to sound when Harvey's phone was unlocked so he could monitor it. Five minutes later, LUCY announced activity. Reg hit the green *Voyeur* button he had created and the display on Harvey's phone appeared on Reg's screen. They watched Harvey search for Barnaby Brayethwait.

"Barnaby Brayethwait?" said Frank.

"Second name on the list, sir. He messaged the suspect's phone shortly after Donny. I read his name out before Cartwright's. Harvey must have remembered his name and is looking for another way in."

"Mills, get me everything you can on this Barnaby guy. What's he doing now, Tenant?"

"Well, sir, the average bloke would just search for the name and the accompanying address. But Harvey-"

"Isn't the average guy, is he?" finished Frank.

They watched Harvey search instead for the local Labour office. The address of the building in Epping came up on Harvey's phone.

"Barnaby Brayethwait. Fifty-three. Local Labour MP for Redbridge Labour. He's been voted in three years running. Divorced. Two children. One seventeen and one twenty. Both girls. The girls both live with his ex-wife in Walthamstow E17.

He lives on his own in Upminster, Essex. Drives a blue BMW M3."

"What time does he finish work?"

"No time stated. But the office closes at three p.m. Presumably, if he's been voted in three years running, he's not the type to cut out early."

"But he is apparently the type to visit an illegal brothel and murder a prostitute?"

"Just not in working hours, sir," remarked Reg, with a smile that faded as Frank's glare grew.

"Harvey's not hitting him tonight," said Melody.

Frank followed her eyes back to the screens. Harvey was searching for an Airbnb.

"Good," said Frank. "He'll hit him tomorrow morning and you three will be there to make sure nothing goes wrong."

He turned and walked up the steps to his office.

CHAPTER SIX

HARVEY LEFT THE AIRBNB IN THE EARLY MORNING. ON THE ride from Chigwell to Epping, he took a twenty-minute slow cruise through the lanes. It was a fresh morning, and the sun rose behind a blanket of clouds as he made his way through the winding roads.

The high street was growing busy with the early morning traffic. People walked to the train station with their hands stuffed deep into their pockets, their heads down, and their chins tucked into the neck of their coats or scarves.

Harvey knew the street well, so he didn't need to do a recce of the Labour office. It was one of the main roads out of town. He drove instead to the coffee shop that he and Julios had once used for one of their meets. The café was warm inside. He chose a seat by the window with his back to the wall. Old habits.

He didn't recognise the waitress. It had been six months since he was last there. While waiting for his coffee, Harvey went over the plan in his head. He would park up near the Labour office and check out Brayethwait when he arrived to work. It wasn't much of a plan, but it was early doors and ideas were brewing.

His original plan had been to wait for Brayethwait to finish work and follow him home, then Harvey would have more time to extract the information he was looking for. But time wasn't on his side. The team would be following his every move. So Harvey made the evening option plan B and moved onto the morning option, plan A, which was more brutal but would be more effective.

At seven thirty, he made his way to the offices, looking for somewhere inconspicuous to park his bike. Finding a discreet spot on the pavement, Harvey tucked his helmet into the motorbike's back box, locked it and strode off on foot towards the Labour office car park. He found a suitable place to stand and wait, mimicking a man waiting for a ride to work.

Brayethwait was the MP for the area. He would wear a suit to work and probably drive a nice car. A Mini pulled into the car park. It wasn't him; the car was too small. A man of Brayethwait's stature would drive a large four-door vehicle less than three years old. Several more cars arrived, only one of which was a possibility but was driven by an Asian man. Harvey was patient. He didn't question his plan.

The entrance to the car park was a small alleyway between the office and the next building. There were no gates that would close and lock, only a parking metre. Presumably, the workers would have some sort of method to get discounted parking. Harvey wasn't sure. He'd never had a real job. His work with Frank was his first real job, and it wasn't really a job. The unit didn't pay him directly. He didn't have a National Insurance number and hadn't been recognised by any authorities. Frank was able to move money from the unit's consumable requirements to pay Harvey, and he was lucky to get that. He could be earning five pounds a week mopping the floor in Pentonville.

Harvey stood at the front of the building on the main road. He watched the traffic drive past: buses full of school kids and minivans driven by tired mums. Men walked briskly along the pavement. Most people didn't even notice Harvey. People were often like that; they don't see what they aren't looking for. Harvey was the opposite. He saw what he wasn't looking for. So when the blue BMW pulled off the main road into the car park, not only did Harvey catch the face of Barnaby Brayethwait, but he caught the shape of the VW Transporter that pulled over two hundred yards away. He pushed off the wall and followed the BMW into the car park. Before Brayethwait had a chance to open his driver's door, Harvey casually opened the passenger's side and climbed in.

"Drive."

"What the-"

"No questions. Drive. You're in danger."

"Who are you?"

"Just drive, Mr Brayethwait. I'm an associate of Mr Cartwright."

"Donny?"

"Just drive. No time for questions now."

Brayethwait had just announced his involvement.

"This is most-"

"This is the last time I'm going to tell you. Put the car in gear and drive. Turn right out of the car park."

Brayethwait did as he was told. His hands had begun to shake, and he fumbled with the double clutch gear box.

"You're going to tell me who-"

"You're right, I am going to explain everything. For now, just drive."

Brayethwait took his phone from his pocket and began to search for a recent number. Harvey reached across and took the phone from him. He wound down the window and tossed it into a refuse truck.

"What the hell are–"

"Shut up, Mr Brayethwait." Harvey raised his voice and Brayethwait was silenced. "You do not call the shots here. You do not ask questions. If you want to live until lunchtime, I suggest you keep your mouth closed. Take the next right."

Brayethwait was taken aback but made the turn. It led to a small car park for dog walkers, bird watchers and anyone who enjoyed the nearby forest walks.

"Park over there and get out of the car."

Brayethwait did as he was told.

When the driver's door closed, Harvey got out and ordered Brayethwait to the front of the car.

"Lock it. You can't trust anyone around here."

Brayethwait locked the car with the key fob.

"Right. Now walk." Harvey motioned to a footpath that led into the forest. "Give me the keys."

"Now, come on. This–"

Harvey made eye contact with him and Brayethwait handed him the keys. Unspoken words.

They walked for fifteen minutes to a spot where the trees grew thick and the undergrowth was full. The footpath faded to nothing and merged with the forest floor. Harvey spun the man around several times. Brayethwait had to hold on to a tree when he stopped to steady himself.

"Belt."

"Belt?"

"Off."

"This is an outrage," said Brayethwait, as he slid the leather belt from the loops.

"Yeah, yeah. Socks."

"My socks?"

"Are you going to repeat everything I say, Mr Brayethwait?

Because it's going to make what's left of your life very miserable if you do."

Brayethwait slipped off his expensive shoes and pulled off his socks, offering them to Harvey.

"Throw them over there." Harvey nodded at to the ground to his left. "Okay. Now we are ready to talk. But before we start, I think it's only fair that you know a little about me," began Harvey. "Why don't you sit down?"

"I'm just fine standing."

"Sit down."

Brayethwait sat with his back against the tree. Harvey took the belt and wrapped it around both the tree and Brayethwait's neck. He made a new hole with his knife to make sure it was tight.

"That's not necessary."

"No, you're right. It's not. I am a very dangerous man, Mr Brayethwait. I have done things that would horrify you. I have done things that would give you nightmares. Do you understand? I've been doing these things since I was twelve years old and I've got a knack for getting secrets out of people."

Brayethwait's eyes were wide with fear. His hands pulled on the belt, easing the pressure on his throat, but he couldn't possibly reach the buckle on the far side of the tree. A damp patch appeared on his tan pants. Harvey looked down at it then back up at Brayethwait.

"That doesn't worry me. They all do that."

Brayethwait began to cry. Harvey let him cry. He would talk soon.

"It's gone too far. I can't stop them," sobbed Brayethwait.

Harvey didn't reply.

"It wasn't meant to be like this. They were only supposed to offer-"

"Sex, Mr Brayethwait? They were only supposed to offer sex?"

Brayethwait nodded. His eyes were shut tight. He sniffed and a run of snot fell from his face.

"Have you, Mr Brayethwait?"

He looked up at Harvey.

"Have I?"

"Yes, Mr Brayethwait. Have you?"

"No. No, I would never-"

"Is that right? So you just go to the farm and what?"

"I funded some of it. That's all."

"So you haven't even had sex with the girls? Come on," said Harvey. "A divorced man. A high-pressure job. Surely a man like you-"

"Okay. *Okay*. I had sex with one girl. But that's all."

"Tell me, Mr Brayethwait. Why did you choose *her*?"

Brayethwait looked confused.

"Surely there were many girls to choose from and you could have had any one of them. You funded it, right?"

"Part funded. There were three of us."

"Right. So why *her*?"

"I don't know. She was pretty. She was quiet with nice eyes and a nice body. Why do men choose *any* girls?"

"All different reasons, Mr Brayethwait. Trust me. It takes all sorts. Was she young?"

"Younger than me," he replied stonily.

"Younger than you? How old *are* you, Mr Brayethwait?"

"I'm fifty-three."

"So how old is younger than you? Forties? Thirties? Twenties?" Harvey paused and watched Brayethwait's face crumple. "Younger?"

Brayethwait nodded. His face was screwed up in a tight grimace.

"Eighteen?" asked Harvey.

The sobs became audible and spittle burst from Brayeth-wait's mouth. He began to pant then struggled against the restraint around his neck.

"Younger still?"

Brayethwait didn't respond. He just sobbed.

"Mr Brayethwait, was this girl younger than sixteen?"

Brayethwait was crying uncontrollably. He nodded.

"Say it. Say it loud and clear. You'll feel better. They all do. Confession is a glorious thing."

"She was..." Brayethwait paused. "Fourteen or fifteen."

"And how do you know? Was it because she was developed, Mr Brayethwait? Is that it?"

"Yes. Yes," he burst. "She was mature. She was just *young*."

"I understand, Mr Brayethwait. She was still petite and small. Did it make you feel like a big man? Is that it?"

"I didn't hurt her. I wasn't violent with her."

"Okay. So you treated her well? Did you stroke her hair? Did you caress her skin? Did you wish that she could be yours? Tell me, Brayethwait. What was her name?"

Brayethwait spoke softly as if he was remembering it all. "Her name was Anastasia. She was lovely. Perfect in every way."

"How many times, Mr Brayethwait?"

He looked up. His eyes begged for understanding and empathy. "A few."

"I have one more question for you and then all of this will be over."

Brayethwait knew what was coming and broke once more. When the words came, they hit him as hard as ever.

"Is Anastasia still alive?"

Brayethwait wrenched at the belt. "*Let me go*. Get me out of here. You can't do this."

"Tell me, Barnaby."

"No. No, she's not. I did it. I killed her. Is that what you want to hear?"

"How?"

Brayethwait settled, defeated. "Gently," he said softly.

"Gently?"

Barnaby looked up at Harvey and stared him in the eyes. "I smothered her face. I suffocated her."

"While you were raping her?"

Barnaby nodded.

"Say it, Barnaby."

Barnaby hesitated then gave a deep sigh. "I suffocated her while I was raping her."

"Thank you, Mr Brayethwait."

Barnaby kept his head down. His face was a mess of snot and tears.

"Mr Brayethwait?" said Harvey.

He looked up.

"Tell me where I can find Mr Cartwright."

"The farm," he snivelled.

"Thank you. And what is his role in all of this?"

"He brings the girls in from Eastern Europe. He has contacts. I paid for the farm, he brings the girls and-"

"And?"

"Jamie brings the clients."

"Like Oscar Shaw?"

Barnaby nodded.

"Jamie?"

"Jamie Creasey."

"Where does he find these clients?"

"She."

Harvey didn't reply.

"Jamie is a woman," said Barnaby.

CHAPTER SEVEN

MELODY WAS SAT IN THE PASSENGER SEAT OF THE VW Transporter, Denver Cox was driving, and Reg Tenant was in the back manning the surveillance equipment. He had LUCY up on one of the screens and monitored Harvey's chips.

They were parked on the side of the road and had just watched Harvey follow the BMW into the car park on foot. Reg watched as the chip on the motorcycle and the three on Harvey's person split.

"Harvey Stone down to three chips," he confirmed.

Two minutes later, the blue BMW pulled out of the car park and drove past them into the oncoming traffic.

"No point hiding. Let's go," said Melody.

Denver pulled into the traffic then turned into the entrance to the car park. He reversed back onto the road, eliciting angry blasts from the horns of commuters. Denver ignored them and joined the traffic. They could just make out the bright blue BMW in the distance.

"Be my eyes, Reg," said Denver.

"On it."

The morning traffic made for a slow chase, and by the

time they pulled into the car park in the forest, the BMW was parked up and locked. Harvey and Barnaby Brayethwait were nowhere to be seen.

"According to LUCY, they're on foot moving fast through the trees in that direction." Reg indicated west and returned his attention back to the screens.

"Okay. You two stay here. I'll go alone," said Melody. She checked the magazine in her SIG and holstered it.

"You wearing a vest?" asked Denver.

"Of course. But Harvey won't shoot me. If you see him, get me on the comms. Reg, I'm walking west. Guide me when I need it. Otherwise, let's keep radio silent. I don't want chatter while I'm listening for them."

Melody stepped out of the van and shut the door behind her, pulling her short jacket over her weapon.

"Okay. You're looking at about a mile. He's stopped moving. Keep in that general direction. I'll steer you in," said Reg over the radio.

Melody clicked twice on the earpiece and ran through the forest as fast as she could. The track veered off south-west by an old oak tree, where there stood a wooden bench seat for resting walkers. The trees were spread out at first in a mixture of beech and oak and some birch trees. But before long, the density of the trees thickened and the clumps of bushes between the trunks grew wilder and denser, which made travelling difficult.

"Eleven o'clock, Mills."

She tapped twice on the earpiece and adjusted.

"You're two hundred yards out, Mills," said Reg quietly. "Hold on. Stone is on the move. Repeat. Stone is on the move. He's heading in a south-east direction, coming underneath you back to the car park. He must have seen us. His phone chip hasn't moved. He's left his phone behind."

"Reg, Denver, are you carrying?"

"We're both carrying," said Reg.

"Good. Don't let him get away."

"You want us to *shoot* him?" asked Denver incredulously.

"Not if you can help it. But if you must."

"That's like poking a sleeping lion, Mills."

"Just don't let him leave. Okay. I have a visual on Barnaby."

Melody walked into the copse of trees and found Barnaby tied to a trunk. He'd soiled himself and looked up pleadingly at Melody.

Melody kept her weapon aimed at him.

She saw Harvey's phone on the floor and bent to pick it up. It was unlocked and had the audio recorder app open. She pressed play. Barnaby hung his head in deep shame. She zip-tied his wrists and released the belt then walked him out barefoot without saying a word.

There was some commotion on the radio.

"Come in, boys. What's happening out there?"

"Erm, we have Stone. Hurry back, Mills."

She picked up the pace and forced Barnaby Brayethwait to walk painfully across the forest floor through nettles and thorns. His comments on the discomfort were met with zero compassion.

"Okay. Update. So we *don't* have Stone. Come on, Mills. He's getting away," called Reg over the radio.

In the distance, she heard the BMW start and its engine rev loudly. Then Melody heard the whine of the car's reverse gear and the crunch of tyres skidding on loose gravel. She burst through the trees in time to see Harvey pull a J-turn around Denver, who had tried to block his escape in the van. The BMW narrowly ducked around it with just inches to spare.

Reg saw Melody approach with Brayethwait and opened

the back door. She shoved him into the van and dove inside, shouting to Denver, "Go, go, go."

Denver didn't need telling twice. He found first and slammed down the accelerator. The rear-wheel-drive van reacted instantly, and they shot forwards. He over-steered onto the main road with a long screech then straightened up and homed in on Harvey in the BMW ahead.

Melody reached up, closed the rear door, and zip-tied Brayethwait's ankles before climbing over into the front passenger seat.

CHAPTER EIGHT

HARVEY STOPPED THE RECORDING ON THE AUDIO APP. He placed the phone on the ground away from Brayethwait in a clear patch of dirt so that Melody would find it easily.

He checked Brayethwait's restraint and turned to face him.

"Six months ago, you'd be a dead man. Consider yourself very lucky."

Harvey turned and ran south then cut east back to the car park from a different direction. He burst out of the trees and used the key fob to unlock the BMW. The indicators flashed once, and he heard the door locks pop open.

Fifty yards down from the BMW was the VW Transporter. Reg had the side window open and his SIG hung out in the open air, pointed directly at Harvey.

"Don't move, Harvey. I'm really sorry. But I can't let you go."

Harvey froze and lifted his hands. He turned to face the van. He was expecting some sort of effort to stop him.

"Nice try, Reg." He lowered his hands and opened the car door.

"I mean it, Stone. Don't make me do this," Reg called from the window.

"Do it, Reg. You couldn't hit a double-decker bus from that distance."

Harvey climbed into the car and fired up the engine. He heard a gunshot and, as predicted, Reg fired high.

Selecting reverse, Harvey gunned the throttle, spinning the wheel to drive backwards out of the car park. If he drove forwards, Reg might have a better chance of getting lucky and hitting him through the windscreen. But still, the odds were slim.

He wound the engine up and reversed towards the rear of the van, just as Denver reversed to block his attempt at getting past. Harvey was expecting that too. Denver was a far better driver than Reg was a marksman. Harvey spun the wheel, braked, and slid the stick into first gear, performing a textbook J-turn and narrowly missing the rear of the van. He straightened up and kept the throttle down as he joined the road. The rear end of the car slid out nicely as the BMW's computer system controlled the power to the wheels. He shifted into second gear, third, then fourth, and settled in for the drive.

The van emerged from the car park in Harvey's rear-view mirror. He knew that Reg would have LUCY open, and they'd find him regardless of how fast he drove. So he took it easy on the winding lanes, maintaining his distance and keeping the van in view.

Harvey felt along the seams of his jacket as he drove and reached deep inside the pockets. Finally, he found a small lump in the stitching by the zip. He reached around and pulled his knife from its sheave on his belt then cut through the thick leather with the sharp blade. He tossed the small chip out the window then put his foot down.

Harvey took the turn into Pudding Lane in less than

thirty minutes and began a slow crawl to the entrance of the driveway. A game plan was formulating in his head, but there were so many variables and unknowns, it was too early to execute. He had always been able to run scenarios through his head, possible outcomes, pros and cons. It was one of Julios' influences. But sometimes, the old Harvey shone through, and he went with his gut.

He was four hundred yards from the farm entrance when a silver BMW X5 nosed out of the driveway. He flashed his lights to let the car out. A female hand waved a thanks through the passenger window, and Harvey could just make out long, curly hair through the rear window. He hung back to allow the woman to drive out of sight then pulled into the farm. Harvey drove up the bumpy track and stopped outside the old wooden barn.

The small area where drivers obviously parked outside was still devoid of cars. Brayethwait had reverse parked his car outside the Epping Labour office, so Harvey reverse parked too. People generally notice small breaks in habits. The parking area was around thirty metres by thirty metres with a faint track that led off behind the buildings.

Harvey climbed out of the car. The buildings were in an L-shape. The front one was small and derelict with two floors, and the second building was more of a barn come warehouse. It had a small door on the right and two large sliding doors to the left for farm machinery and trucks to reverse up to.

Walking to the smaller door, he studied the keys on Brayethwait's bunch and selected the correct key first time. He pushed the door open with a gentle squeak and stepped into the dim light.

He noticed the smell first of all. It was an air freshener, sandalwood. Harvey thought it odd that somebody would choose to freshen the smell of what was essentially an old barn. He quietly closed the door behind him and let his eyes adjust to the shadowed room. Throughout the old building, jagged light infiltrated the many gaps in the structure's joints. The barn's contents were clear, but the details were vague in the semi-darkness.

He stood still and listened, but heard nothing. There was a small flashlight in his jacket pocket, a two-cell torch that was small and light, and he barely even noticed it was there. Harvey turned it on.

Sitting just inside the large sliding doors was a small digger. It was a rental and had the number of the firm on the side of the boom fixed to the bucket.

Along the back wall was a series of old stables. The low stable doors had been replaced with much newer and larger ones that offered no view into the six pens. Each was locked with a padlocked hasp and staple, and a deadbolt into the floor.

A long steel beam ran through the centre of the building from end to end. It looked like it may have been used to shift hay or horse feed from one end of the room to the other using the small rope block and tackle that hung from a trolley fixed to the beam.

In the space beside the sliding doors, there was a pile of blue plastic sheets. They weren't the cheap type sold in hardware stores; they were thick and heavy. Beside them on the floor, a hose was curled up and fixed to the single tap on the wall.

To Harvey's right was a spacious area with some old couches. Somebody had made an effort with the arrangement, but the fabric had deteriorated in the old barn.

A door to the left of the couches was left open. Inside, Harvey found a kitchen. Its cleanliness in such a building was impressive. It was like somebody had recently put a lot of effort into making it presentable, perhaps somebody who was charging clients a lot of money for the services they rendered there. Harvey thought of Donny and his fine taste.

A smaller door led off the kitchen. Harvey pushed it wide open. The room was pitch dark inside. His torchlight fell onto screens that had been fixed to the wall. Each one had a glowing LED light indicating the on button. The hum of a computer showed that it was running.

He reached up and turned on the first screen. The red light turned to green, and the display lit up. It showed a dreary, monochrome image of the BMW out front. He turned on the second screen. It displayed a small room with what looked to be an iron-framed bed in the centre of the space. At the edge of the room was a bucket and a plastic container, presumably to hold water. On the opposite side, Harvey saw a bench and items hanging on the wall. The camera angle was poor so he couldn't see exactly what they were, but he guessed there would be rope, chains, various sharp implements and other sick devices.

The third screen was the same. The fourth screen was a little different. It showed the monochrome image of a similar small room with a similar bed in the centre. This room had two buckets by the wall, no bench with torture devices, and three girls sitting and lying on the bed.

One girl sat with her knees drawn up underneath her body. Another lay with her back to the camera. The third stood up and began pacing the room. Harvey turned on all the screens. Of the six stables, only two had girls inside. Stables three and four had three girls in each. Three of the stables looked as if they had been made ready for guests. The last looked the same as the ones that held the girls. But it was, for the time being, devoid of life. Harvey guessed why.

He turned the screens off and walked back to the main

barn. He touched one of the six locked doors with the flat of his palm. There was life behind the solid wooden panel. But that particular life was not Harvey's concern. Donny was Harvey's concern. Once he'd dealt with Donny, then he could help free the girls. If he tried to free them now, he risked losing Donny for good.

As he walked to the small door, Harvey heard a car arriving. Its tyres crunched on the dirt outside. The BMW X5 had just pulled into the entrance and was slowly making its way up the track. Harvey looked around the room, and then up. He ran and jumped, grabbed hold of the steel beam that ran along the ceiling, and pulled himself up. He balanced on it and walked to the end where it met the wooden truss of the roof. Making his way across the network of joists, he stopped above the kitchen in the darkness of the ceiling space.

He heard a heavy car door close outside. Then the door to the barn swung open. The person wasn't hiding their arrival. The sound of heels on the poured concrete floor stopped.

"Barney?"

There was no answer.

Harvey watched as the woman stepped slowly over to stables three and four and pulled firmly on the padlocks to make sure they were locked. She was tall for a woman and the heels made her even taller. Her thick mass of loose curly hair bounced as she walked. She wore a two-piece suit with a frilly blouse that protruded from the collar of her jacket. Her skirt was shorter than knee length, and she looked to be in good shape. Harvey judged her to be in her late thirties.

"Barney?" she called again, like she was summoning her dog.

Again, there was no answer.

She stepped into the kitchen and out of sight. Harvey tracked her footsteps through the gypsum ceiling. He imagined her walking to the control room. She wouldn't start with screen one and work across. Instead, she would start with screens four and five to check the girls were there and alone. Then she would turn on the others. But nothing. No sign of him. She wouldn't find Barnaby Brayethwait anywhere.

Harvey tracked her as she walked back out of the kitchen and stood in the centre of the open barn. She pulled her phone from her handbag and called a number. Harvey noticed that there were just three clicks: the phone app, recent calls and the number. He was too far away to see if the phone displayed a name.

"Hey. Is Barney with you?" Harvey heard the one-sided conversation. "No. His car is outside, but he's nowhere to be seen. I thought he'd be having his way with one of them, but the girls are all in three and four, and the other stables are empty." She moved to the doorway and stood looking out at Brayethwait's BMW. "No. I'm going to feed them then get back to work. What time will you be here?" There was a pause while the other person talked. "Okay, and Bruno? I'm not doing the buckets again." Another pause. "Okay. I'll lock up. Maybe he's just left his car here. I'll be back tonight around seven. Can you ask Bruno to muck the stables out and hose the girls down? I have a client coming at eight and I want them clean. When are the new girls arriving? Tomorrow? What time? Okay. I'll make their room up. I'll see you tonight."

The woman stepped into the kitchen and Harvey heard the sound of boiling water. Cupboards opened and closed, and crockery was moved about. Five minutes later, she emerged again with a tray of three bowls of what looked like porridge. She set them down outside room three, opened the door and placed the tray inside without a word. She locked the door and did the same procedure for room four before returning to the kitchen, retrieving her handbag and walking to the barn exit. Harvey heard the lock click into place and the rattle of her keys as she stepped away to her car.

Harvey walked across the wooden beams and stepped along the steel joist. He then hung down and dropped to the floor. He unlocked the door and opened it a fraction. It was all clear. So he stepped outside and locked the door behind him.

Moving quickly, he unlocked the BMW, climbed in and started the engine. Then he tore along the bumpy driveway. He turned right out of the farm entrance, in the opposite direction to where he'd seen both Donny and the woman turn. He drove directly to Epping, through the town centre and passed where he'd parked his bike earlier that day.

With no sign of the VW, he pulled the BMW into the car park of a nearby supermarket and walked casually back to his bike. He was careful to avoid direct exposure to the cameras that were sporadically fixed to street lights.

Harvey unlocked the back box, removed his helmet, and within thirty seconds was joining the light traffic on the road out of Epping. It felt good to be riding again. Harvey wasn't a fan of cars. They felt too claustrophobic.

He ran through the scenarios in his head. Ideally, he would find Donny in the farm on his own. But the mention of Bruno, who Harvey assumed was the man driving the Toyota SUV behind Donny the previous day, gave Harvey doubts. If Bruno would be mucking out the stables, then presumably he was not intellectually involved in the operation. He possibly provided some level of security. That was Donny's style. He would give the impression of wealth by having a minder to disguise his cowardliness.

In an ideal situation, Harvey would have surveillance hardware from the team. But he couldn't exactly call them up and ask to borrow some binoculars and a Diemaco sniper rifle. Hopefully, the capture of Brayethwait had stroked Frank's temper a little.

Harvey decided to overshoot the farm and spent the remaining daylight off-roading. He worked his way through the fields to reach the farm from behind. If he could find somewhere to stash his bike, he could then sit and watch the play.

He would practice patience.

Julios, his mentor, had drilled into him the importance of patience and planning. Harvey would need to know routines, schedules and habits. He would need to identify the players, work out the pecking order and find a way to isolate Donny. It would be easy to pull up alongside Donny's Mercedes at traffic lights and shoot him through the glass. But the suffering would be minimal. Harvey was not an unkind person. But, in his mind, the only way to pay penance for evil was to suffer in a similar fashion. It brought a certain balance to the world.

The house where Harvey and Donny had grown up, and where Harvey had boiled Sergio alive, wasn't far from the farm. It was perhaps fifteen minutes away. Harvey was very familiar with the area and knew a way into the farmer's fields behind the barn.

His BMW motorcycle was as capable off-road as it was on tarmac. Soon it was spitting mud from the back end as Harvey wound his way along the edges of the surrounding fields. A thick copse of trees stood behind the farm. It was perhaps five hundred yards from the buildings, which meant that Harvey would have to crawl five hundred yards.

Harvey pulled his bike into the trees and removed his helmet. His view of the barn was far from perfect. He would definitely need to get closer. The fence that ran behind the barn spread far across the fields. All along the underside, there were thick wild grasses, nettles, and occasional black-berry bushes.

Lying on his front, Harvey made his way along the fence and pulled his weight with subtle movements of his feet and forearms. Each movement gained four to six inches. It took him two hours to reach the barn. But when he did, he was confident that nobody from any direction had spotted him. He parted the grass slightly, which gave a clear view of the barn's front side from thirty metres away. Even if somebody walked up to the fence, he would remain unseen under the growth that grew beneath it.

At six, the BMW X5 turned into the farm's entrance and headed slowly up the track. Jamie climbed out. She was unlocking the single door of the barn when the Toyota SUV turned in and made its way up the drive in a far more reckless manner. It bounced in the potholes and large dust clouds formed in its wake.

Jamie didn't wait for the other car to arrive. She disap-peared inside. The Toyota skidded to a halt in the dirt in front of Harvey. The dust cloud followed it a few seconds after so Harvey closed his eyes and covered his face with his shirt.

By the time the dust had cleared, the driver was already out of the car and opening the door to the barn. Harvey caught a glimpse of the man. He was big. Very big. That didn't frighten Harvey. Not much did. It just meant that if he came to blows with the big man, Harvey's approach would need to be tailored to suit his size. Large muscular men tended to have beef protecting their organs, so a throat attack was often more suitable. This was slightly trickier as a forceful blow to the man's throat could kill him. Harvey didn't necessarily need to kill him, unless, of course, he deserved it. Time would tell. For the time being, the man was just a barrier between Harvey and Donny. It made the challenge all the more interesting.

Another thirty minutes passed before Donny's gleaming Mercedes came into view. Donny took the bumpy track, slowly manoeuvring the large saloon around potholes. He came to a stop in the spot nearest the door. The engine was cut, the door opened, and Harvey saw his foster brother for the first time in six months.

CHAPTER NINE

SIX MONTHS EARLIER, WHEN SERGIO HAD BEEN FOUND AND tortured by Harvey, he had given up Donny's name. Donny had, at the time, been in the Maldives pretending to be dead following an attempt on his life by a rival family, the Thomsons.

It had been the perfect timing for John Cartwright to stage his son's death, which effectively took the Cartwright family out of the running for the diamond heist that was being planned.

The heist attempt had not gone ahead. The Cartwrights had lost their weapons, and John had gone missing. Donny returned a month later to find his best friend, Sergio, killed, his father missing, and his father's house a crime scene. The northern job was successfully carried out by an unknown, and the family business was in ruin.

With what little capital he had left, Donny had to make a new start on his own. Without the financial backing of his father and the support of his family resources, it had been a struggle. But he'd met an old friend, Barney, who, in turn, introduced him to Jamie.

Donny still had a giant target on his back in the criminal society. So he'd hired some protection in the form of Bruno, a former bare-fist knuckle fighter in East London's underground scene.

Bruno wasn't just a bodyguard. He was Donny's conduit to the outside world. Before Donny went anywhere, Bruno would arrive up to thirty minutes beforehand to make sure the route was safe, and the location was secure. If it wasn't, Donny would not move.

Bruno stood at nearly six foot eight and out-reached most men in the ring. He weighed a formidable one hundred and forty kilos, most of which was solid bulk. His one flaw was that he was slow by boxing standards. His last few fights had been with smaller and faster opponents, and he'd taken many blows to the head. He'd still won, but his brain had taken a beating. He often landed only one or two punches, but that was all that had been needed.

His career had left him slow in the head. He had some money, enough to live on, but it wouldn't provide a lavish lifestyle by any means. Donny had seen him and stepped in, offering the huge man a way out.

Bruno's slow mental ability did not affect his instincts or his eye for danger. After nearly two decades on the underground scene in East London and South London, he'd had his fair share of vicious attacks from bottles, knives and guns. Men who had lost money in Bruno's fights often waited for him in the car park of the pub or in a dark back alley. He had a sense for danger and an immensely powerful body.

Donny was a business genius, but a shallow coward. The two were well suited.

Donny stepped into the barn. His aftershave overpowered the sandalwood air freshener that neutralised the odour of fifty years of horses and four months of Eastern European girls using buckets for toilets.

"Ah, you're here," said Jamie from the couch area of the barn. She had her laptop open and was finishing an email.

Donny ignored her.

"Bruno, where are we?" he said.

"Just finished mucking out, boss. I need to hose them down though, yeah?" Bruno said with a grin.

"That's right, Bruno. The client will be here in half an hour. Let's get them cleaned up."

Bruno smiled and unlocked stable four.

"Knock, knock, ladies. It's bath time," he said in his slow, baritone, lazy grumble.

Donny turned to Jamie. "Who's the new client?"

"Some hotshot lawyer from the city. He has a place out in Ongar. Said he heard about this place from a client of his."

"Who? Are we running checks on these people? We're not letting any old Tom, Dick and Harry in, are we?"

"We are certainly *not* letting in any old Tom, Dick or Harry. He's been vetted, Donny. He paid up front in cash. He said if it's what he expects then he'll make it regular."

Bruno walked out of the stables with three girls in tow. He held a brown leather strap that was fixed to the first girl's neck, which in turn was attached to the next girl, who was attached to the third. They could easily unfasten the collars, but they knew better than to try. They had all been stripped of their clothing and walked behind the huge man, ashamed and embarrassed, to the far wall where Bruno removed the leather strap.

Donny stood and watched as Bruno handed each of them a bar of soap. Then he uncoiled the hose from the reel on the wall and tested the pressure.

"Are we ready, ladies?" he asked.

The first girl was dark haired with dark features but pale white skin. She was physically flawless. She had no fat on her body whatsoever. Her chest was small but pert and her legs were slender. She was just sixteen years old, the youngest of the girls. She was also tough. She stared hard at Bruno as he turned the hose on her.

"Get washing. Come on. You need to wash those bits and bobs for Uncle Bruno and his massive-"

"Bruno, come on, mate. He'll be here soon. No time for fun and games. *You* can have a go later once the client has gone," said Donny.

"You can't keep letting him do that. He'll ruin them," whispered Jamie in a harsh tone.

"Oh, come on, Jamie. He doesn't get many pleasures anymore. Look at him. He leads a simple life, does our Bruno. It keeps him going. Look how happy he is."

"Hey, Bruno."

Bruno turned. "Boss?"

"How happy are you right now?"

Bruno gave a low, clumsy laugh followed by a large intake of air into his huge lungs.

"See what I mean? Leave him alone. He'd never hurt them."

"I think Barney has been visiting a little too often too. Honestly, how you expect the girls to be in any decent condition by the time you guys have all had your way, I do not know."

"Oy," said Donny, holding his hands up defensively but smiling. "*I* haven't been tainting the goods. I don't need to, thank you very much. Anyway, where is Barney? I haven't heard from him all day. It's not like him."

"I saw his car earlier, and I messaged him, but I haven't had a reply."

"Let me know if you do hear from him. I'd like to get the budget sorted out. I'm thinking we should expand the operation."

"Expand?" said Jamie. "Into *where?*"

"A new place, Jamie. I'm thinking we should keep the location moving. Always into a bigger place. See if we can get six months' rent on the next place and double the number of rooms. Then do that again after six months."

"I thought this operation was only for a year so we could all make a quick few quid. It's not exactly a career for me, Donny. I can barely sleep at night."

"Jamie, it's not my ideal career either. I can assure you. But let's face it. We can do this *and* earn well. Or we could go work in an office for peanuts."

"The money isn't *that* good, Donny. I mean, it's good, but it's not going to make us millionaires. We keep having to buy new girls."

"Bigger picture, Jamie girl. I want to bring more girls in and up the quota. Right now, we've got six rooms. Two of them are bedrooms. The others are for the clients. So we can have four clients come in at any one time. I want to put the girls out to farm first. Have them earn their cost. So clients who don't want to go for the premier package, as it were, can still get their rocks off. Once the girl has earned her cost back, she can move to the next room, ready to be offered to the premier clients. Then it's the big bucks."

"It's a *barn*, Donny. It stinks."

"I'm putting the prices up too," said Donny, ignoring her. "Premier is seventy-five thousand. The pikey package will be a grand for an hour. She'll only need to do ten pikeys. Then we can offer her to a premier client, Jamie. Come on. You don't look impressed."

"Did you hear what I said?" Jamie put her hands on her hips and furrowed her brow as she looked at him. "It's a barn. It stinks."

"Well, so what? We have to start somewhere, Jamie. Look at Bill Gates. He started in his parent's basement or something. We can turn it into some kind of Wild West theme.

That way, we wouldn't have to do a lot to it. Maybe have a bar as well? Punters would love that."

"He was making computers, Donny. You're offering prostitution services to wealthy gentlemen who get their kicks from killing the girls. The idea behind prostitution is one that has stood the test of time. Girls sell their bodies for sex, over and over. It's a reusable commodity. Your whole methodology sucks. Are you going to implement some kind of just-in-time inventory management? How do you plan on keeping a steady flow of girls coming into the country?"

"Jamie, you bring the clients and I'll bring the girls. I told you. I have a good contact and he hasn't let us down yet, has he?"

"The last batch were nearly dead when they got here. How the bloody hell is he getting them into the country?"

"Jamie, do I ask you how you get your clients?"

"Yes. As a matter of fact, you did about ten minutes ago."

"Okay. Well do I criticise your methodology?"

"What's to criticise?"

"Did you hear about Oscar Shaw?"

"Oscar Shaw?"

"The very famous stage actor who was in here about three weeks ago. You remember him?"

"Yes. Of course I remember him. He tipped very well. He had two girls, didn't he?"

"He bloody died. Police found him in his dressing room naked with some actress. They'd snorted ant killer or something. Anyway, police found a flash drive with a video of him here with the two girls."

"No way."

"Yep. It was in the papers."

"Can they trace it back to here?"

"No. Impossible. He called a burner."

"Boss, I'm done. They're all clean," called Bruno from the other side of the barn.

"Righto, Bruno," Donny replied. Then he lowered his voice again. "Just relax, Jamie. Trust me. I've been on the wrong side of the law my entire life. It's in my blood. And I'm not stopping until my bank account says I don't have to work another day in my life."

He left her with a serious stare then turned to Bruno.

"Good work, Bruno, my son," said Donny. "Good work." The six girls were lined up and connected by their necks again with the leather straps. "Right, ladies. Let's see those smiles then. Who's going to be the lucky one tonight then, eh? Which one of you beautiful girls is going to meet the man of your dreams tonight? Because you do know the rules, don't you?"

They looked at him, scared but defiant.

"Whoever gets picked, gets to go home. You get to say goodbye to your little family here. So, go on. When the client arrives, make him welcome. Won't you?"

Bruno stood behind him grinning. Donny noticed him. "Okay, girls. A new approach. Whoever doesn't get picked tonight will have to take this fella on, and I wouldn't want to be on the receiving end of that, I can tell you."

Jamie grinned at his joke from the other side of the barn and caught Donny's eye. He's a sick bastard, she thought.

The sound of tyres on the dirt outside silenced the room.

"Bruno," said Donny, with a slight movement of his head.

Bruno left the barn to stand guard at the door.

Jamie slipped out beside him.

"Ah, Mr Narakimo. How are you, sir? Did you find us okay?"

CHAPTER TEN

"STONE IS DOWN TO ONE CHIP," SAID REG FROM THE BACK of the van. "He must have tossed the one in his jacket."

"It's okay. I figure we know where he's going," said Melody.

"How about us? We can't drive around with *this* guy. Can't we drop him off at a police station or something?" Reg was forced to sit with Brayethwait lying on the floor behind him.

Melody called Frank. He picked up on the first ring.

"Carver."

"Sir, we have a one IC-1 male in custody, name of Barnaby Brayethwait. We have an audio confession pertaining to the rape and murder of a minor. It also highlights Cartwright and one other, a Jamie Creasey."

"Good work. Well done. What's the plan now?"

"Observe and report, sir."

"Excellent. Keep me informed at all times. Where's Stone?"

"We believe he is heading to the farm, sir."

"Is he going to blow this whole thing apart?"

"No, sir. I do not think he is. He had the opportunity to

finish Mr Brayethwait and chose to leave him for me to find. I think he knew that it would buy him time."

"What's the plan, Mills? Once Stone goes in, you'll need to go live."

"Sir, we need to get Brayethwait to a police station so he can be formally charged under the correct procedure. If we drive him around in the van all day, his lawyer will kick up a fuss."

"Okay. Where's the nearest station? Where are you now?"

"We're heading out of Epping. We are in pursuit of Stone. However, Tenant has him on screen so we can keep an eye on him. I suggest we take Mr Brayethwait to Chigwell, sir. We can be back on Stone's trail pretty quickly after that."

"Okay, Mills. I'll call ahead so they're expecting you. I look forward to your next report."

"Yes, sir."

"Oh, and Mills?"

"Sir?"

"Work *with* Stone. Watch him. If he let this Brayethwait guy live, maybe he'll leave us some more crumbs. Hole up and observe."

"Yes, sir."

Frank disconnected.

"To Chigwell, Denver. Let's get rid of this guy."

They took the drive out to Chigwell and found the police station quiet. A desk sergeant greeted Melody with a half-smile. The paperwork was ready for her to sign, and Barnaby Brayethwait was led off to start a new life behind bars, his head hung low in shame.

Melody climbed back into the van.

"Sit-rep, Reg?"

"Okay. So Harvey drove straight past the farm into Loughton. Then he turned around and went straight back. He is currently inside the barn."

"He's inside?"

"That's what LUCY says."

"He's crazy."

"Find us a spot we can hole up in. Somewhere close by."

"Got it. I found the perfect place. Denver, let's go," said Reg, rearranging his chair now that Brayethwait had been removed. "Mills, let's pick up some snacks or something. Last time we holed up, all we had was petrol station food."

"Shame you don't have a stove back there. You could cook for us as well," said Melody.

"You wouldn't want my cooking, Melody. But I do make a mean cheese sandwich."

"A cheese sandwich? That's literally just cheese, bread and butter."

"Yep."

"And what is it that *you* do differently to the rest of the planet that makes *your* particular cheese sandwich worthy of the *mean* award?"

"Get me to a store and I'll show you."

"Denver, you heard the man. Let's find a mini-mart or something. Then we'll hole up. Reg, how's our man doing?"

"He's still inside. I need eyes on the building though."

"It'll be too risky in the daylight. I can do a recce when the sun goes down and maybe fix a camera to watch the door."

"Ah, we'll see," said Reg. "I may be able to help there."

They drove past the entrance to the farm and Melody looked up the track as they passed.

"There's two cars there. Brayethwait's car and a BMW X5. He's not alone."

Denver took the next right. It was a small dead end that led into fields. But the foliage around the lane offered plenty of cover for the van. It was an ideal spot to stay away from prying eyes.

"What's he doing? You don't think he–"

"No. I don't think he's in there tearing the place up. I think that other BMW belongs to our friend, Jamie Creasey, and Stone is taking notes and waiting for his brother to arrive."

"Foster brother," Reg corrected.

"Okay. So maybe I can cut through this field in front when it's dark and plant a few bugs on the outside. If we can capture audio, we can build up the case from there."

"Why don't we just put a camera on the front door? Then we can see people going in and out."

"That's fine, Reg. Why don't I sneak carefully through the field and plant the audio bugs while you take a stroll up the front drive and install a camera? They might even make you a cup of tea if you ask nicely."

"Nah, I prefer to work at my desk. You know me. However, have I introduced you both to Sneaky-Peeky?"

Denver turned in his seat. "What are you talking about, Reg?"

"Sneaky-Peeky, Denver." Reg lifted up a modified, radio-controlled challenger tank with over-sized tracks and a camera in the place of the turret. "See? It peeks while it sneaks." The lifelike scale model of the tank was two feet long and weighed just fifteen kilos.

"No," said Melody. "Too risky."

"Ah, come on. You haven't even seen the best bit." Reg reached down into one of his sports bags. "I'm still working on this, but I think it'll save millions of lives."

"Millions of lives?"

"Well, yours at least, Melody. But we have to start somewhere."

Reg pulled out an elasticated olive-green scrim net that fit perfectly over the tank without getting caught on the oversized tracks. It had a hole in exactly the right place for the turret cam.

"See? We can just stuff a load of grass under this and drive slowly. Slowly is the key to stealth, remember. If we go tear-assing up the drive with this, it'll be spotted a mile off. But sneaking isn't about going fast. Sneaking is about being sneaky, isn't it?" Reg looked very proud of himself. "Hey? Come on. It's brilliant and you know it."

Reg slid open the top of the VW and let a chill into the van. He stuck a magnetic antenna on the roof and extended it as high as its telescopic sections would allow then connected the cable to a VHF port on his computer's network card. He opened the back door, pulled up some grass from behind the van and began tucking it under the netting.

"Sneaky-Peeky reporting for action, ma'am," said Reg, mimicking a soldier.

Melody smiled at Denver who was shaking his head and holding back a grin. "At ease, soldier."

The silver BMW X5 drove past the dead-end lane where they were parked, heading away from the farm.

"That was the car in the farm. I'm sure of it," said Melody.

"So Harvey is in there alone?" asked Denver. "Shall we go get him?"

"No. Frank just wants us to observe. Harvey will do one of two things. He'll be on her tail, if that is indeed Jamie Creasey, or he'll hightail it out of there and wait for Donny Cartwright. My money is on the latter."

Melody cracked the window.

"How are we going to know if we can't see the driveway?" asked Reg.

"Shh," said Denver. "That's the sound of a BMW M3."

They heard the distant engine in the quiet countryside.

"How do you know that?" asked Reg disbelievingly.

"Shh," Denver hushed again. "Unmistakable. Definitely an M3."

The engine noise faded away.

"Looks like he's gone to find Donny. Reg, how's he doing?" asked Melody.

Reg glanced up at the screen from where he stood at the rear of the van tinkering with the tank. "Yeah, he's on the move."

"Reg, how close does the tank need to be?"

"I'd say two or three hundred yards. But one hundred would be better. It has a seventy to three hundred mile lens and will capture 4K video at thirty frames per second."

"Okay. Get that tank into position. I don't know how long this window will be."

"Roger that."

CHAPTER ELEVEN

HARVEY WAS LYING STILL BEHIND THE FENCE. HE FLEXED his feet and fingers to keep the circulation going. The cold ground made his clothes damp and uncomfortable, but he'd waited for longer in far worse conditions. He'd once stood in a park near Stratford in the freezing cold snow for an entire day waiting for a known sex offender who had been released from prison. Harvey had watched him over several weeks and found no pattern at all in his timings. But the man had taken the same route whenever he walked his dog. Harvey had bit the bullet and waited from the dark morning to the dark evening before the man finally came along. Harvey had done what he needed to do and then taken the man's confused dog to a vet.

A large Bentley Continental turned its broad, elegant nose into the long driveway and drove slowly along the track. Its large wheels managed the potholes with ease, and eventually, it took a wide circle to park alongside Donny's Mercedes.

The driver got out. He was a short Japanese man whose horizontal frown matched his unsmiling mouth. He walked to the passenger door and opened it like it was second nature, offering the passenger a curt and discreet bow.

"Thank you, Hiroki-San," said the second Japanese man, as he climbed out the sleek car.

The driver then returned to the vehicle and climbed back inside.

The barn's single door opened and the large man stepped out. He was a man who looked like he was always ready for a fight. He looked questioningly at the small Japanese man who stood in front of him.

Jamie Creasey slipped out of the door and stood beside Bruno.

"Ah, Mr Narakimo. How are you, sir? Did you find us okay?"

She had the ability to please people. She was a saleswoman.

"Come in, please," she continued. "We have the girls ready for you. Have you travelled far?"

"I have a modest house in Ongar," said Narakimo. "I use it when I am in London. I do very much enjoy the English countryside." His English was very clear with no sign of his Japanese heritage.

Jamie and Narakimo stepped inside. Bruno glanced around the area, which was growing dark, and pulled the door closed behind him.

The driver remained in the car. This was an issue for Harvey. He needed to get close but couldn't arouse suspicion. Making a mental note of the number plate, he worked his way along the fence until he was out of sight of the cars. He swiftly jumped over the wooden fence, being careful not to disturb the grass that grew naturally underneath the wooden cross beams. Any flat ground would leave a sure sign that someone had been there.

Harvey stepped up to the rear of the barn. There were no

windows, no doors and no gaps in any of the wooden panels that clad the old building. There were also no visible cameras. The security had been tight on the inside and at the front, but anyone could stand at the rear.

He put his ear to the wall and listened. Nothing. Harvey stopped and thought. The Japanese man would likely want the most privacy. So stable one would probably be his room of choice. Harvey judged the distance and listened to the wall. Nothing. The thick wood absorbed any sound from inside. Harvey stepped back to look up at the roof. Perhaps there was a way in, but he couldn't recall seeing a skylight. His foot sank into soft soil, much softer than the surrounding ground.

He glanced around and noticed the patch of ground where he stood was freshly dug. The darker patch of earth was roughly eight feet by four feet and not symmetrical or neat. It was the hole of somebody who had used a small rental digger but hadn't quite mastered the skills.

At least one more body would be buried tonight, thought Harvey. Then he crept back to the fence and jumped over. He dropped to the ground and crawled slowly back to his original position. No change in the scenery.

Harvey planned.

The Japanese man would leave. Harvey imagined it would be Bruno's job to dig the hole. Donny wouldn't carry out manual labour himself. Harvey's plan all depended on who left the farm first. Jamie or Donny.

Harvey lay beneath the fence that ran behind the farm. He had a clear view of the long driveway, the side of the barn and the doors, and the fence that ran fifty metres adjacent to the track, connecting the road to where Harvey lay.

Movement caught his eye. Dusk was fading to darkness and shadows had a habit of playing tricks on the mind. He watched the area of wasteland between the track and the fence. Someone or something was moving towards the barn. But he couldn't quite place the position. Each time he looked, the area looked slightly different. Something was out of place.

He checked his surroundings. Maybe the team were closing in. That would only leave Melody. The other two clowns wouldn't stand a chance of not getting caught.

He glanced back at the waste ground. Something moved. Just fractionally. Harvey locked onto it. It was small and covered in grass, which made it hard to spot. He moved along the fence until he was in line with it then jumped over into the waste ground. He had seen the view of the cameras and was sure that camera one didn't reach any further than the cars. He crawled over to the movement and came up behind it. It was a radio-controlled tank.

Reg.

He smiled.

Harvey crawled up behind the tank. He heard the soft whir of the tiny motors that operated the turret. He pulled back and returned to his spot. Occasionally he glanced at the tank. It sat completely camouflaged in the long grass.

Less than two hours after Narakimo had entered the building, the door opened once more and he stepped out into the cold night. The lights from inside lit the surrounding ground. Narakimo wore a business suit with no tie, a knee-length Kashmir coat and a long silk scarf. Donny and Jamie stepped outside with him.

"Well, I hope the experience lived up to your expectations, Mr Narakimo."

The man paused and looked around into the darkness. "Yes, Mr Cartwright, it most certainly did. It was a..." He sought the word. "Thrilling experience."

"I am pleased. And did Anna accommodate your needs?" asked Jamie.

"What if I said no, Ms Creasey? How would you punish her?" He offered a cruel grin.

"Well, I was just seeking feedback for future experiences, Mr Narakimo," said Jamie, sheepishly defending her statement.

"I can assure you both that I am more than capable of providing adequate feedback." He smiled. "I like the set-up here. It could be more elegant, but I think the primitive decor rather matches the offering."

"Thank you, Mr Narakimo. We're actually planning on expanding. Perhaps we can offer you a return visit?"

The little Japanese man laughed. "Please, do not offer me a coupon. It's not a coffee shop."

Donny smiled warmly. "No, Mr Narakimo. But for valued clients such as yourself, we could perhaps improve the value you receive. As we get to know you more, we can tailor the experience. You may find your tastes develop each time."

"Ah, Mr Cartwright, you have a head for business. I shall return. Do you mind if I bring guests?"

"Of course not, Mr Narakimo. But please do give us advance notice. We like to ensure that each of our clients has choice and, as you can imagine, we do like to make sure that our operation remains a safe and discreet place for us all."

Narakimo nodded. "Mr Cartwright. Ms Creasey. Good night."

The Japanese man made his way to his car. His driver must have been listening as the driver's door opened the moment Narakimo said good night. The Bentley moved off and made its way back along the long, bumpy driveway. A satisfied customer sat inside.

"Bruno, let's go. We have a hole to dig," Donny called, and clapped his hands.

Harvey remembered Donny's whiny voice from his child-hood. Donny would use the same tone to call his father, John, when Harvey had done something wrong. "Dad, Harvey broke the window. Dad, Harvey won't do what I tell him to."

John hadn't risen to the whines of his spoiled son and had often turned the information on Donny himself. A life of crime had hardened John to grasses or informers, and he had tried his best to ensure that his own son didn't become one.

Donny hadn't grown up to become a grass or informer. He had learned the lessons. But he still had the traits of a man who led a very wealthy childhood and had never gone without.

Harvey had never gone without either, not in monetary terms. John had seen to that. But he had lost his sister at a young age. He now knew that was because of Donny, which made his foster brother the last man on Harvey's list. His time was growing near.

Harvey had also never fully been told about his parents. John had always said that he and his sister had been found in John's bar. Harvey had been in a hamper with a blanket. His elder sister, Hannah, sat beside him.

John's wife, Barb, had wanted to adopt them, having only one child of their own. So Harvey and Hannah's discovery had not been reported to the authorities. Instead, they had been driven back to the family house where, over time, the life of money and crime had become a way of life for Harvey. For Hannah, it had become the end. The desires of John's closest men had proven too much for the teenager.

Harvey had vowed for her vengeance and was closing in on his final target.

The sound of the mini-digger's diesel engine starting up broke Harvey's thoughts. He checked his surroundings. The tank was still sat in the long grass. Jamie had gone back inside. Her car was on the driveway. Donny was stood outside and the two large sliding doors screeched open allowing Harvey a clear view of the barn interior. The bright lights that hung in the eaves of the barn shone unnaturally onto the ground outside. Harvey checked the tank. He couldn't see it, but he knew it was there. From where Donny stood, it would just look like a clump of long grass. It was, however, moving slowly backwards. Reg had obviously thought the same thing about the lights.

Sitting in the small seat of the digger was the massive frame of Bruno. He looked ridiculous, like he was using a toy. He pushed two levers, and the tracks began to roll forwards out of the barn with a loud grumble that reverberated through the ground to where Harvey lay. Bruno steered the heavy digger out of the doors and turned right around the corner to the rear of the barn where Harvey had stood an hour before and found the soft ground.

The diesel engine revved angrily and filled the night. The two lights fixed to the top of the cab swung above Harvey as the machine passed by where he lay. The digger's engine turned off and Harvey heard Bruno starting the job with a shovel.

Donny picked up one of the plastic sheets from the floor and dragged it open. He positioned it in front of the doors in Harvey's direct sight and in front of the tank which sat patiently amongst the long grass.

Once the plastic sheet was pulled out, Donny stood in the open and breathed in the fresh air. Jamie joined him.

"It's so peaceful out here," she said, alerting him to her presence.

Donny gave a soft snort of irritation and looked back at her.

"Yes. It is. I can almost hear the sound of fifty-pound notes landing in our bank accounts."

"Do you ever think about anything else but money?"

Donny stepped forward and leaned on the fence directly

above where Harvey was lying. Harvey stayed perfectly still. He was tucked under the growth of grass and thorns.

"Yeah, I do," he said sullenly. "Often."

"What goes through that mind of yours? What eats you?"

"Ah, Jamie. We've done a good job so far of keeping our relationship purely business-like. Let's not get too familiar, eh?"

"What are you hiding, Cartwright?"

Donny took a breath and held it. "We all have our skeletons, Jamie. Where do you keep yours?"

"I'd love a skeleton or two, Donny, but that would mean letting people in. Something I was never good at."

"You don't need to let people in to have skeletons. Sometimes they arrive uninvited. Then they destroy everything you have."

"Sounds painful."

"It is." Donny sounded subdued. "My father had it all. You know that?"

"Yeah. Everyone knew John Cartwright."

"He started with one bar and built up an empire. Pretty soon any bar in East London that was worth having either belonged to, or owed money to, the Cartwrights. That's where I learned about business, from my old man. I stood to inherit all of it. I would have been set up for life, Jamie." He laughed. "What a joke, eh? Now look at me. I'm in the bloody prostitution business. My old man would do his nut if he could see me now. He hated hookers."

"What actually happened to him?"

Donny looked across at her suspiciously. The question had been quick. "No-one knows, Jamie."

"Yeah, yeah. I know that's what your lot say when someone's in hiding."

"God's truth. The Thomsons had me marked. They were-"

"The rival family, yeah. That was all public knowledge."

"Right. Well, they put a hit out on me. Nearly worked as well." Donny reached up and touched the scar tissue on one side of his face. "I survived though, and my dad saw it as a good time for me to pretend to be dead. So I was sent off for a few months. By the time I got back, it was all gone. The bars, the banks, the men, the houses. And my dad. There was nothing left."

"You haven't heard from him?"

"I doubt I ever will, to be honest. He's either dead or working on his tan. He won't be back either way."

"But you're his son. How could he just forget about you?"

"Listen, Jamie. When you're up to your eyeballs in the life we lead, the moral compass gets a bit off balance. Know what I mean?"

Jamie nodded.

"We did things that none of us were proud of. Things that we never spoke about again. We never really stopped to consider what would happen if the truth were to come out in the open. Or if the people we cared about found out those terrible things. We didn't even consider the consequences of those things ourselves, let alone how they would impact the people around us." Donny took a lungful of air and noisily blew it out through his nose. "My old man has long gone. I don't deserve anything he could offer, anyway."

"That's a shocking thing to say, Donny." Jamie almost had a caring tone to her voice.

"Don't *pity* me, Jamie. What doesn't kill us makes us stronger. I'm coming back. I'm making my own money." He turned to face her. Half his face was lit by the bright white lights from the barn. His scar was hidden in shadow. "And that is what will make my old man proud of me more than anything else in the world."

The lazy starter motor of the mini-digger broke the

night's silence. Donny and Jamie turned to see Bruno's massive bulk inside the small windowless cab. The arm of the machine dug greedily into the soil.

The two walked away and Harvey breathed out. Donny had been his foster brother for as long as he could remember. But he'd never witnessed any kind of emotion from him other than hate, spite and anger. The feelings had been mutual. Harvey was the lost kid who inadvertently stole his father's attention when they were young. If Donny had scored a goal at football practice, John would have missed it because he was tying Harvey's shoe. If there was any extra meat at dinner, Harvey would have it because, although he was younger, he was already bigger and needed more food.

When they grew older, Harvey was still treated differently. Harvey didn't cry, whine or complain to John. He dealt with his own issues while Donny wondered why nobody heard his cries. It was by Donny's own design that he was kept at arm's length.

Then the final straw had been when Donny and Sergio had raped Hannah with Jack. Hannah had brutally killed herself. John had known what happened. Not much got past the old man. But he protected both Donny and Sergio from Harvey. He needed Sergio to run the business and Donny was his own flesh and blood. But the incident had caused John's wife, Barb, to leave him. John hadn't fully trusted Donny ever since, choosing to nurture a relationship with Harvey instead. He chose someone more deserving of his trust and fatherhood.

Harvey understood now. Donny's perspective had slotted things into place. Donny would still die a slow and awful death, but he had unwittingly answered some of Harvey's questions.

He checked the tank. It was still sitting there. As far as the investigation was going, Melody and the boys would have indisputable evidence of Mr Narakimo going in and Mr Narakimo leaving, and then a hole being dug for a body. The evidence against Mr Narakimo would not be irrefutable. But Donny, Jamie and Bruno would be in a very bright spotlight. Plus there was always DNA to fall back on.

When the digger was turned off, Harvey watched Bruno stumble in the darkness then shuffle into the barn. He disappeared and re-emerged carrying the young girl's dead body. She was dark haired, very petite, and her limbs hung loosely from the man's strong arms. Bruno laid her on the plastic sheet and folded one side across the body. Then he rolled her until the lump in the sheet was unidentifiable and folded both ends of the roll inward, securing them with gaffer tape. He placed the tape back on the shelf then hoisted the long blue parcel onto his shoulder.

Harvey was sickened. He had seen death for most of his life. He'd even played the role of death and dealt it out with his own two hands. But that had been to people who had, in Harvey's mind, deserved pain and suffering. The girls that the brute was dumping in the ground deserved nothing of the sort. Harvey would seek their retribution. He would make sure the sins against them were paid in full.

Harvey heard the dull thump as the body hit the ground. Then the scraping of soil on the shovel began as Bruno began to fill the hole. He worked slowly in the dark. His only light was the two harsh lamps from on top of the cab of the digger.

Donny and Jamie had disappeared inside the barn.

When he was done, Bruno once again broke the silence of the night and drove the digger back to the barn. He switched off the engine and silence resumed.

"Boss, all done," he announced.

"Great. Let's go home, Bruno."

"But, boss..."

"Sorry, buddy. You can have some fun with them tomorrow," said Donny in a quiet voice so that Jamie wouldn't hear. Bruno's face lit up. He'd become a simpleton and Donny was manipulating him. That was Donny's style. "Lock those sliding doors up, Bruno."

"Jamie, see you tomorrow," Donny called.

She came out from the kitchen. "You're leaving?"

"Well, yeah. What else is there to do?"

"Maybe wait for me?" she said.

"Ah, Jamie, you're a big girl."

Bruno pulled the two large sliding doors closed. The space outside was plunged back into the darkness of the country-side and Harvey heard the metallic sound of locks. Then the single door opened and Donny and Bruno walked outside. They both got into their separate cars. Donny didn't wait for Bruno. He started his long and bumpy trip in his Mercedes while Bruno pulled in behind him. The Toyota SUV handled the bumps just fine although Harvey saw that the driver's side was considerably lower.

Harvey watched as Donny and Bruno drove away. He needed Donny alone, but Bruno was always there by his side.

The single door to the barn opened and Jamie stepped out. She clicked the button on her key fob. The BMW's indicators flashed once, the locks popped open, and the interior light slowly came on. She was about to lock the door when she noticed the light was still on so she stepped back inside.

Harvey vaulted the fence.

He ran quietly to the car, opened the passenger door and slipped his watch under the passenger seat. He saw the lights turn off, so he shut the door quietly and crouched down low, slowly moving back into the darkness of the waste ground. He turned and motioned to the tank, tapping his wrist with two fingers.

Jamie climbed into the car and the interior light dimmed.

She tapped out a message on her phone then dropped it into the centre console, selected drive, and accelerated away.

Harvey took a walk around the back of the barn again to see where Bruno had buried the new body. He wondered if he was making new holes or just dumping fresh bodies into the same pit. He found the fresh dirt. Bruno had dug a fresh hole next to the first one. The job wasn't neat.

Harvey thought about digging a hole for Bruno, an extra-large one. He might even make him dig his own hole. Then he'd bury the man alive while the girls watched. The thought process was all part of Harvey's planning. One thing was for sure. He would make sure the guy paid for his sins.

12

CHAPTER TWELVE

MELODY CARRIED SNEAKY-PEEKY TO THE ENTRANCE OF the driveway. She set it down in the grass to the left of the track. Reg immediately took control, and the tank began to trundle away towards the fence that ran adjacent to the driveway.

She headed back to the van unseen and walked around the rear to where Reg was sat with the large single rear door wide open. He sat on a modified office chair that had the casters removed so it wouldn't roll around on the wooden floor of the van.

In front of him were two screens and a laptop. The laptop showed the main interface of LUCY. In the centre of the screen was a satellite image of Harvey's tracking chips. It was a mess. His watch chip was in a field behind the barn. His motorcycle chip was nearly a kilometre away several fields behind his watch. His phone showed as being exactly where Melody stood, which it was, holding the audio confession of Barnaby Brayethwait. The chip from Harvey's leather jacket was on the side of a country lane in a ditch around five miles away.

The main screen showed a high-resolution live feed of Sneaky-Peeky's turret camera. It was moving extremely slowly through long grass beside the fence.

"That's a pretty clear image," said Melody.

"I modified a DSLR. Sneaky-Peeky has two built-in SD cards and a 70-300mm telescopic lens. It's capable of recording 4K resolution onto the SD cards and providing live feed at full HD, which I can record from this end. It gives us a little bit of resilience against the loss of Sneaky-Peeky itself." Reg grinned.

Melody sighed. "Okay, Reg. I know you want to tell us more. Go on."

"Thought you'd never ask." His smile was nearly as wide as his face. "Not only can it operate for close to five hours, due to the configuration of batteries, but I tore some of your surveillance hardware apart and integrated the technology with the DSLR." He continued to grin and waited for Melody to ask more.

"Well?" she said. "What does all of that mean to simple folk like Denver and I?"

"I stole your NV goggles and stuck them on the turret with the camera. It's fascinating inside those things. I'll take a closer look when I get a chance."

"You stole my night vision goggles?" asked Melody.

"Only one pair. You still have another pair," he replied, defending his actions. "Besides, now Sneaky-Peeky has night vision, and you can sit in the nice warm van." He turned to her, beaming. "Sometimes, Melody, you can almost taste my genius."

"Eyes on the road, genius," she said, nodding at the screen. "Or you'll be tasting the sweet scent of grass because it will be you that has to run down there to ask for your toy back."

"Oh, how she mocks. Denver, are you hearing this?"

"I am," said Denver, who was watching the road in front for any sign of traffic that might be slowing for the turn into the farm. "But I wish I wasn't."

"Do you both honestly think that I would send Sneaky-Peeky, my beloved creation, into the wilderness without a map?"

Melody raised her eyebrows.

"Sneaky-Peeky has a built-in GPS. I just plug in the coordinates and hit go and it'll go straight there. I can enter sets of coordinates if I want it to follow a particular route. Or, if we have the CAD file of a building, it can read the directions from LUCY."

"Can we send it to Burger King then?" said Denver.

Melody smiled at the dynamics of the two. "Where exactly *are* you sending it?"

"Right here where the two fences meet." Reg pointed at the spot on the screen. "From there we'll have an uninterrupted view of the front of the barn."

"We need eyes on the driveway. I want a heads up when cars come in or out."

"I only have one Sneaky-Peeky, Melody. But soon I shall have a fleet." He said the words with a sinister undertone and winked at her.

"Looks like I am going for a walk after all," she said, and left to prepare herself. She slid open the side door of the van and pulled her kit bag from under the passenger seat. She took an extra clip for her SIG, a small Maglite, and fitted her earpiece before pulling on a tight, black, woollen hat. She grabbed her jacket from the front seat and pulled it over her black Norwegian army sweater. Then Melody stuffed her NV goggles into a small pack.

She turned away from the van and took a few steps then tapped the earpiece button. "Comms check."

Her voice rang clear from the speaker next to Reg's laptop.

"Received. Repeat," he replied.

"Loud and clear," she said. "Okay, boys, have fun without me."

"Wait," said Reg. He found Melody's tracker chips in the directory on the left of LUCY's interface and ticked the box next to her name. All of her chips showed up on the satellite image. "Good to go. Three chips live. Phone, watch and purse," said Reg. "You're up on LUCY."

"Okay. I'll just be across the road there with eyes on the driveway. I won't get close as the tank-"

"Sneaky-Peeky," Reg corrected.

"Sneaky-Peeky has the front covered."

She slipped away and the two men watched her cross the road and duck into the thick tangle of bushes that lined the far side.

The light was fading as she made her way along the fence. She pictured the eyes on the barn. The tank was at the front looking directly at the doors. Harvey was behind the fence to the side of the doors. He would have a clear view inside if the large doors opened.

Melody tucked behind the fence, staring at the side of the barn with no windows or doors. The sky grew dark until she could no longer make out the shape of the building. She moved closer and found a spot hidden from view. She could see the driveway clearly but not the doors. Reg would need to handle that.

Three cars arrived within thirty minutes of one another. The BMW X5 arrived first with a female driver. That was Jamie Creasey. Melody reported it over the comms and Reg confirmed. Then two more cars arrived: one SUV and a large, black Mercedes saloon.

"Confirm. The second car is Donald Cartwright," said Reg.

"Who's in the first car?" Melody asked.

"Hold on. I'm just on Sneaky's night vision. I don't have a name for him, but holy crap, he's big."

"Say again."

"I said, the man is big. He just had to turn sideways to walk through the door."

For the next thirty minutes, Melody sat in the dark. It was frustrating not being able to see the doors, but she knew that nothing was happening there either. The action was on the inside.

Another car turned into the driveway.

"It's busy tonight."

"Can you see the plate?" asked Reg.

Melody read the plate number to him as the car drove past her. She heard it come to a stop and two doors opened and closed.

"The car belongs to one Narakimo. Unmarried. Owner of several Japanese export firms. He has offices in Threadneedle Street, EC2. He's of Japanese descent and has a net worth of...Wow." Reg went quiet.

"What's wrong, Reg?" asked Melody.

"I'm counting zeros."

"Okay. So he's rich?"

"That's a fair statement."

Melody heard the door bang closed.

"You think he's a client or a partner?" she asked the two men.

"Client," said Denver.

Melody was intrigued. Denver rarely voiced an opinion. He was the strong and silent type.

"What makes you say that, Cox?"

"How much is he worth?"

"Many, many zeros," replied Reg.

"Okay. So the guy's a successful businessman. Clearly, he has a head for the ins and outs of business."

"Right. Where are you going with this?" said Melody quietly into the mic.

"Do you honestly think that a guy with that many zeros after his name would start a brothel? And would he start a brothel with a known criminal?"

"You're right. He's just a sick and twisted rich man," said Reg.

"So, if he's a client who wants sex, why come to a barn in the middle of nowhere? Why not have hookers sent to his plush apartment in the Docklands?" asked Denver.

"Because what he wants to do can't really be done in his plush apartment," said Melody. "Guys, I can't sit here while a girl dies in there."

"Melody, we're observing, remember? Sit tight."

"No, Reg. How can I honestly live with myself knowing that I sat behind a barn when on the other side of this wall someone was being raped and murdered?"

"Rein it in, Mills. Come on. No emotions here. Put them away," said Denver, the voice of reason.

"Cox, someone is going to die here tonight. She might be dying now."

"If we blow this and they get away, then the girls who have already died did so for nothing. Come back to the van, Mills."

"Since when do you give the orders, Cox?"

"When you're out of control. Get back to the van and let's talk it out. If it makes sense, we'll call Frank, and he'll get us back up. But right now you need to get back to the van."

"Cox-"

"These comms are recorded, right?" asked Denver.

"Yes. Direct to file," replied Reg.

"So there's a direct order on file, Mills. We have all the

authority. It's a closed loop. If one of us loses control, the others can take action. Come on now. Come back to the van. Let's talk it out."

"But the cars-"

"I have all the information on Mr Narakimo we need, Melody. I also have a file auto-populating on Bruno Mason," said Reg. "He's the big guy. Sneaky's in place to capture video. They have to get rid of the body through one of those doors and Sneaky will record it."

"If another girl-"

"If another girl dies, Mills, we'll deal with it. Get it together," Denver cut in. "If we compromise the operation and they get away, more girls will die."

There was a silence.

"Mills, do I have to call it in?"

Melody fell back into the field and made her way along the fence to the road. She climbed through the hedgerow and walked casually across the dark, empty lane into the dead end turnout where the van was parked two hundred yards down. Reg slid the side door open as she approached.

"I'm not happy about this one bit," she said, slinging her small pack into the back of the van. She began to remove her hat and coat while Denver and Reg waited for her to calm down.

"No-one is asking you to be happy about it, Melody," said Denver. "Listen, I'm sorry I had to do that. But we're not equipped to go kicking doors in and making a bust. There's three guys in there and one woman. Any one of them could be carrying."

"Harvey's there too."

"Yeah. We know Harvey's there. But our objective is to observe. Harvey is no longer on the team."

"Yes he is. He wouldn't have left Brayethwait alive if he was off the team. You heard the confession. You know Stone."

"What makes you think Stone would back you up?" asked Denver. "He's a villain deep down. Besides, he doesn't care about the girls or Creasey. He's after Cartwright. That's where his head's at."

"He would have backed me up," replied Melody, reaching around to retie her hair back. "He's one of us now."

Denver turned away, shaking his head, then looked back at her. "You really think so?"

"Of course," she snapped. "We *have* to think that. We *have* to believe he's on our side. Or what else have we got? Nothing is what. We can't alienate him."

The two men fell silent.

Then Denver spoke. "Take the comms off."

Melody pulled her earpiece out and Reg paused the recording. He nodded at Denver.

"If you want to believe that Stone is on our side, then we need him to *know* that we're on his side. Otherwise, he'll just think we're out to bring him in and that Frank will put him away."

"How do we get a message to him? I have his phone and he doesn't have comms."

"Sneaky-Peeky to the rescue," said Reg cheerfully from the back. "Talking of Sneaky-Peeky, the camera just went dark. Small glitch. We're back up. Not sure what that was."

Melody and Denver were watching Reg work the tank's camera. He focused on the large Bentley and zoomed in on the dark windows. "There seems to be someone still inside the Bentley."

"Mr Narakimo's driver maybe?" said Denver.

"Possibly. Hold on. It's moving. Hey. *I'm* not doing that."

The camera shifted from the car to the double doors.

"What *was* that?" asked Denver.

"Stone," said Melody, with triumph in her voice. "Does that thing have a speaker we can talk to him through?"

"Erm, no. But I'll make a note. Sneaky-Peeky *Two* will have."

They waited for it to move once more or for Harvey to show himself on the camera. But enough time passed for them to realise he was gone again.

"We have action," said Denver.

They watched as Mr Narakimo stepped out of the barn followed by Jamie Creasey and Donny Cartwright. They stood and chatted for a while. The body language suggested that Mr Narakimo held the power while Creasey and Cartwright tried to please him. Reg tracked him as he walked to his car. The driver emerged and opened the passenger door before returning to the driver's side. The night vision picked up the heat from the engine, glowing brightly in contrast to the surroundings.

The Bentley pulled away and then the whole scene turned white.

"Turn the NV off," said Melody.

Reg switched off the night vision and turned the turret back to the barn. The double doors were open, spilling light out onto the forecourt. The big man, Bruno Mason, sat at the controls of a digger, filling the cage that served as a cab. Two bright lights fixed to the top of the cage came on and the digger's exhaust began to emit clouds of black diesel smoke.

The digger rolled out of the barn and turned right around the back of the building. Its two bright lights bounced through the darkness and then out of sight.

Cartwright stood by the fence at the edge of the screen and looked out into the night. He was joined by Creasey. They talked inexpressively for a while until the big man returned from the rear of the barn and entered the double doors. He dragged a blue plastic sheet to the open space at the front and then disappeared. He reappeared with the limp, dead body of a young female.

Melody gasped.

"Easy, Mills. We knew what we were getting into here. Reg, is this recording?"

Reg double checked. "Yep. We have video evidence of three suspects disposing of a dead body and one more who has just left the building, who I am sure will have left some kind of DNA on the victim's body."

The three were transfixed as the huge man causally wrapped the body in the tarp and tied it off with gaffer tape. He worked quickly and efficiently then easily hoisted the body up onto his shoulder and walked past Creasey and Cartwright back behind the barn.

Before long, the lights of the digger bounced back along the narrow walkway between the rear fence and the building. Then it turned left into the barn. The engine was killed, which kicked out a chuff of black smoke, and the lights switched off.

Five minutes later, the two men left the woman. They drove away in separate cars. Jamie Creasey prepared to leave. The headlights of the two cars flashed past the top of the turnout where the team were parked.

"Okay. I have Cartwright's phone via GPS. I can follow him home," said Reg.

"Good. Track his every move. But we also need eyes on Jamie. She's the low hanging fruit," replied Melody.

The lights of the BMW flashed on then faded as the interior brightened. Jamie fumbled with the barn door then disappeared inside once more.

"What's that?" said Reg. "See that shape?"

They saw the passenger door of the BMW open and watched Harvey's silhouette place something under the seat. He closed the door again and the shape faded away as the barn door reopened and Jamie came outside. She locked the barn then climbed into the car. There was a short pause then she pulled away. Sneaky-Peeky was left staring at the empty barn.

"Switch to night vision," said Melody.

Reg switched the night vision back on.

Harvey stepped into view and walked to the building. He glanced back at the camera then slipped around the back to where the digger had been working.

"Shall I follow him?" asked Reg.

"No. Wait a minute. What's he doing?"

Five minutes passed. Then ten. Harvey did not re-emerge.

"Okay. Bring Sneaky back, Reg," instructed Melody.

Sneaky's extract was much faster than the journey in. It was pitch dark and there was little chance of anybody returning. So Reg set the tank to return to their GPS coordinates. He watched the screen as it made its way along the country lane and turned to drive towards the van. As it drew near, he opened the rear door and stepped out.

Immediately, his arm was twisted behind his back. His body was turned and his face was pushed hard onto the wooden floor of the van. He went down with an audible grunt.

"Hands on the roof."

Melody and Denver both turned.

"Hands on the roof. I won't ask again."

"Stone, did you enjoy the show?" asked Melody.

"Hands on the roof or I break his arm."

Denver and Melody slowly raised their hands to the roof of the van. Harvey increased the pressure on Reg's arm.

"Ow. *Ow*. You're hurting me," whined Reg.

Melody and Denver pushed their palms flat against the roof.

"Okay. Do I have your attention?"

"Undivided," replied Melody.

"Good. I'll do you a deal."

"A deal, Harvey? Why don't you just come back and we finish this together? It's not too late. I can talk to Frank."

"I'll talk to Frank myself."

"Frank won't be in the mood to talk to you if you hurt one of us, Stone. Come on."

"I'll give you the girl. You give me Donny's location."

"You know where she is?"

"Roughly. You know where he is?"

"Roughly. Why should we trust you?"

"Because you're still alive," said Harvey.

"And Brayethwait?"

"A gift."

"A gift?"

"From me to you. To get some brownie points."

"We can all do well out of this if we do it right, Harvey."

"Doing well is not my objective, Melody."

"What's your objective?"

"Same as it's always been."

"Hannah?"

Harvey didn't reply.

"Reg, are you okay there?" asked Denver.

Reg's face was held against the floor. "I've been better."

"Are we recording?" asked Melody.

"No. We turned it off." Reg spat dust from the floor away from his mouth.

"Okay, Harvey. But it's bigger than this. We want you on the team. I'm talking long term. Once all this is over, we can go back to normal. You're an asset. I can help get you back in. We all can."

"I need to do this."

"I know. You've spent your life chasing this. I can't imagine how that must feel to be so close. But hang in there. Trust us."

"Trust you?"

"I know that it's hard, honestly. But we can do this and all get what we want." Melody paused. "How about you let Reg go? He's a bit fragile."

Harvey didn't reply.

"Okay. Have it your way. How about we give you Donny, but you help us take this down? Rescue the girls, nail Creasey and the Jap, and plug the hole where the girls are leaking in from?"

"I don't need you to give me Donny."

"No. But you need us to give you freedom. Frank will have you put away for this. For everything you've ever done. You know he has that power. But I know he doesn't want to. I know he wants you on the team, just like we do. Right, boys?"

The boys each grunted affirmatively.

"I'm taking Donny anyway," said Harvey. "We can talk after."

"You don't know where he is."

"He's on the screen."

"What about Creasey?"

"What about her?"

"You give us Creasey. We give you Donny. Right? It's what you said."

"You find her when the *time* is right."

The pressure on Reg's arm relaxed and he slumped to the floor rubbing his shoulder.

"What's that supposed to mean?"

Harvey didn't reply.

CHAPTER THIRTEEN

ONCE HARVEY HAD RETRIEVED HIS MOTORBIKE FROM THE copse of trees in the field, he found the road in the dark and made his way to Loughton where he'd seen Donny on the screen. Donny was inside the small apartment block that Harvey had seen him and Bruno enter the previous day. So he parked his bike in a back street, stashed his helmet in the back box and continued on foot.

It was gone midnight, midweek, so the streets were quiet. Cabs owned the roads in the early hours, carrying drunk businessmen returning from the city after a night with clients or colleagues, who would probably need to steal into their homes to avoid waking their spouses. Then tomorrow they'd do the same thing. It was an endless cycle.

Harvey liked his freedom. He preferred not to become tangled with the same woman. Too many questions. Too much emotion. Once you spent your life being trained to dispel emotions and set them aside, it's hard to call them back. He'd tried to have a girlfriend several times, but each time they got heavy, and Harvey would back off. They'd complain he was too cold and didn't show affection. He'd treat them right, more than right. He'd show them a good time, take them to nice restaurants, and enjoy walks in the wild. He even took one on a weekend break to the Lake District so they could walk in the mountains and see the beautiful lakes. But they always wanted more than what Harvey had to offer.

The apartment block was situated on a corner where a small side road ran onto the high street. It was four floors high and had a tall wall around the property. To the rear, trees poked above the brick wall. Harvey imagined there was a lawn, flowers and some kind of outdoor seating for the occupants to enjoy on rare sunny days. If the property had been in France or Spain, there'd be a pool.

The entrance to the underground car park was at the front of the building to the right of the main doors. Harvey walked past the building once and found the cameras without breaking stride. By the time he had walked two hundred yards further and turned back, he had a plan.

A building like that rarely employed a full-time security guard. The cameras probably weren't manned, but were there for the footage to be called upon should an incident occur. In Harvey's mind, that was ridiculous. He could get into the building, rob an apartment, or worse, and then leave. Sure the camera might have his face on file, but he'd be long gone.

A lesson he had learned from Julios was that acting like you were doing nothing wrong drew less attention than trying not to be seen. So he walked casually up to the top of the entrance ramp and strolled in around the barrier. There were no whistles, no alarms and no security guards calling after him. He walked to the bottom, turned into the car park and looked around for Donny's black Mercedes.

It was parked next to the silver Toyota SUV that Bruno had been driving. Donny must have had his bodyguard living there full time, which meant he was waiting for something to happen to him. Or he was just plain paranoid. Donny had never been paranoid before. He was overly confident, if anything. He had a brilliant mind for business but no backbone.

Six months previously, after Harvey had been asked to take out the son of the rival Thomson family, they had retaliated by putting a hit on Donny. John Cartwright had seen this coming and asked Harvey to shadow Donny. Harvey had managed to pull Donny out of a burning car and probably saved his life. He didn't do it for love. He didn't do it because he cared about his foster brother. He did it because that was what John had paid him to do. It wasn't until after the event that Harvey discovered Donny was one of three men that had gang-raped his sister, Hannah. If he had known Donny had been involved, Harvey would have taken pleasure in watching him burn.

The Mercedes was parked in space thirty-five. The Toyota sat in thirty-four. On the wall behind each of the vehicles was a small sign with the apartment number the parking lot belonged to. Harvey guessed this was to stop other residents using the wrong spaces. The sign behind the Mercedes and the Toyota read *Apartment 204.*

He strolled casually over to the glass door of the hallway. Two large elevators had their doors closed. The digital numbers were still. The building slept.

The door was locked and had a small electronic card reader. Flashing a security card in front of the device would release the magnetic lock. Reg would have the door open in seconds. No doubt, he'd be able to hack into the building's security system, find the network where the doors were located and release the locks. Maybe even control the lifts as well.

Harvey was not as technically gifted as Reg. Harvey had a much simpler approach to life that required minimal technology. Of the team, Harvey related to Denver more than Melody or Reg. But he was growing to like them all. They were all different. They'd led different lives. But he respected their skills.

Melody was fantastic at what she did. She had a great mind. She was tough and could shoot better than any of them.

Denver had been a villain himself until the government put him into a program to nurture his skills in an environment more conducive to doing good. His proudest moment was having two police helicopters and more than a dozen police cars chase him across the country. The chase had made the news, and he had eventually outsmarted every police driver and both the pilots. He got away.

Sadly, people with great technological minds like Reg had installed speed cameras. Denver's image had been captured in a stolen Ferrari. He was arrested for the theft of over eight million pounds worth of high-end supercars and given the ultimatum to either join the rehabilitation program or go to prison for a very long time.

For Denver, the choice had been simple. He ended up being trained by the country's top drivers and pilots and taught how to use his skills to create a legitimate career. He'd been a real success story.

Harvey stepped around the walls of the car park until he found what he was looking for. The breaker box was locked, but the lock was just a plastic key insert and a weak metal barrel. Harvey ripped it open. The catch on the inside fell to the floor by his feet. The building was designed for use by private residents, which meant that the public areas had to conform to British standards. One of the standards defining the safety and security of electricity circuits stated that each device or outlet in a public space must be labelled with the circuit number and identifier. Harvey found the circuit that matched the label on the card reader and flipped it off.

Another British standard that defined the fire evacuation protocols stated that, in the event of a power outage, all magnetic locks must release, allowing doors to open without hindrance. Presumably, this was so that people weren't trapped inside a burning building.

Harvey strolled back to the door and pushed it open.

He stepped inside and pressed the button to call the lift. He heard one of the lift's mechanisms clunk into life. The other remained dormant and in power save mode.

Harvey rode the lift to the third floor, stepped out of the elevator and found apartment 304. It was likely that 204 was directly below, with both floor plans being identical. So Harvey had a good indication of the layout of the building. The apartment was to the right of the fire escape at the end of the hall.

A quick walk down the fire escape stairwell brought Harvey to the second floor. He opened the door a fraction and saw the front door of 204 at the end of the hallway. He half expected Donny to have the big guy sitting outside like a guard dog. But the hallway was apparently empty.

He slipped out onto the soft carpet. The hallway was nicely decorated with ornate patterns in the mouldings and coving. The lights were modern and the carpet was thick and expensive. It was the type used in hotels that are designed to withstand heavy foot traffic but remain aesthetically pleasing.

Harvey walked slowly and quietly along the hallway. The apartment door was fifty feet from the fire escape. Along the way, Harvey found service doors. A cupboard with cleaning implements had been left unlocked. Another door marked *Telephony* was locked. The last door marked *Electricity* was also locked. He reached the end of the hallway and stood in front of the door marked 204.

He had several options and several plans, all of which were a risk. He ran through the scenarios in his head. Option one: set fire to the front door. The other residents might hear the alarm, leave and be safe. But Donny would burn. This was a drastic option and relinquished control to the ferocity of the fire. There were too many variables plus collateral damage. Harvey preferred his victims to die deservedly where possible.

Option two: set off the fire alarm. When Donny came running out, Harvey would slip into the apartment and wait for him to return. This option also had flaws. Nobody listened to fire alarms. They went off accidentally too often. Also, he had a greater risk of being seen by other residents.

Option three: ring the doorbell.

14

CHAPTER FOURTEEN

REG CLIMBED BACK INTO THE VAN, LEAVING THE REAR DOOR open. Melody came around and checked his arm for breaks.

"You'll be fine," she assured him.

He winced as he pulled his sleeve back down and exaggerated his pain as he lifted his arm to the bench.

"Let's have a sit-rep, Reg. Take your mind off your arm. Where are the players?"

He took the mouse and refreshed the screens.

"Okay. According to LUCY, Cartwright is two miles away in Loughton."

"That's his home, right?"

"I believe so. LUCY shows regular prolonged visits and there's no indication of him having a partner."

"Creasey?"

"We don't have her number yet."

"Stone?" she said hopefully.

"One mile away in Hainault. Travelling fast."

"That was quick. Denver, let's go."

Denver started the van. Melody picked up Sneaky-Peeky and placed it inside the vehicle. She closed the rear door, walked around and climbed back into the front passenger seat.

"Why are we tailing Harvey?" asked Denver.

"Well, we know Cartwright is at home sleeping. My guess is that Harvey won't go near him with Bruno anywhere nearby. So Stone is probably on the tail of Creasey. He said he knew her whereabouts. He'll lead us straight to her."

Denver put the van in gear and entered the chase.

They drove in silence. Denver concentrated on the road, speed cameras and efficient driving. Reg guided him with infrequent updates on Harvey's movements. Melody stared out of the window, deep in thought.

She tried to empathise with Harvey. He was throwing away his ticket to freedom. But would she do the same? How must it feel to have chased somebody your entire life and be so close to finding them? Harvey had lost his parents at an early age and had never found out the truth behind their deaths. He had witnessed the rape of his sister and waited twenty years before finally learning it was his foster brother. His foster dad had known all along, which made it worse. Just one of those things would have broken most people. But all of them together? What damage does that do to somebody?

Melody had seen the remains of Sergio, the second man of the three that had gang-raped Hannah. Harvey had boiled him in an antique copper bath. She remembered the claw feet and Sergio's clawed hands gripping the bath's rolled edge.

Harvey was a stone-cold killer. But Melody saw something else in him. She saw the good. He was turning. He had left Brayethwait for Melody to find. A crumb. If he *was* after Creasey, would he leave her for the team too? It made sense. With Creasey out of the way, only Cartwright remained, which meant a far greater chance of getting him alone. But the team needed to plug the hole. They needed the source of the girls. Stopping Cartwright would only mean that the source would probably find a new conduit. It wouldn't be a solve, and subsequently, more girls would die.

They'd been on the road for forty minutes when Melody snapped out of her thoughts. She focused on her surroundings and saw the One Canada Square tower out of the passenger window.

"We're going to the Isle of Dogs?" she asked.

"We're just following Harvey," said Denver.

"Actually, yes," said Reg. "We're going to the Docklands. He's stopped outside a club there. It's called Marco's according to LUCY. You think Creasey is in there too? It'll be a hell of a place to have a showdown."

"I don't think he'll take her out in a bar. Too many eyes. He's observing. Planning. Have you seen him work?"

"Harvey? Of course. He's a psychiatrist's dream."

"It was part of his training. He told me once when we were sparring. Patience, planning, and execution."

"You sparred with Harvey?" asked Reg incredulously.

"Yeah. A few times. He's good. He's-"

"A killer. He's a killer, Melody."

"He's a good fighter. He lets you attack him and watches your every move. It's like *he* knows what you're going to do before *you* do. It's the most frustrating thing. He knows that. He lets you get frustrated and studies your strongest side and your weakest moves. Then, out of nowhere, he pounces."

"Like a wolf," said Reg.

"Like a lion, Reg. Patience. Planning. Execution. That's what he told me. His whole life is run by the same mantra. Every time we've sparred, he has thrown just one move and taken me down. I would have thrown dozens at him, all effortlessly blocked or avoided with almost no effort."

"I hear admiration," said Denver.

"Don't you?" asked Melody. "Admire him, I mean?"

"He gives me nightmares," said Reg from the back.

"Denver?"

"I admire his control."

"There's more to him than that," said Melody. "We can turn him around. But we all have to want it."

"Like I said, he gives me the willies," said Reg.

"There's no need. Learn him. Get to know him. I bet if you knew him you'd never feel scared of anything ever again. With someone like him on your side, you wouldn't have to worry about much at all."

"If you weren't gay, Melody, I'd say you had a crush on him."

"I *can* admire somebody without needing to bring sex into the subject, Reg."

She turned to him and smiled.

"Who mentioned sex?"

"Right. We're here. The club is around the corner. What's the plan?" asked Denver.

"You two stay here. I'll go in alone."

Melody pulled the visor mirror down and began to apply lipstick. She dropped her hair from its elastic tie and let it fall into a cute, bouncy style that rested on her shoulders. She applied a little more makeup to her eyes and cheeks then turned to the two men.

"How do I look?"

"How did you do that?" asked Reg.

Reg passed Melody an earpiece from the back, which she fitted before hanging her hair over her ear.

"I'm observing only, remember. But be ready for me."

"Go get them, kiddo," said Denver.

Melody blew them both a kiss, got out of the van, and strutted away, hips swaying from side to side and hair bouncing gently with her stride.

Reg and Denver looked on in disbelief.

CHAPTER FIFTEEN

THE CLUB WAS LAID OUT WELL. IT WAS SMALL SO MELODY could view most of the seats from the upstairs area, where she feigned being stood up and leaned on the handrail alone, glancing from her watch to the doors. There was a small DJ stand on the far left of the club with a dance floor. A few girls were dancing but most people were either sitting or standing around the high tables.

A long bar ran across the back wall serviced by five staff. They were all between twenty to thirty years old and most had some kind of piercing or tattoo proudly on show.

Melody checked the dark areas in the corners of the club and saw no sign of Harvey, only men in suits with loosened ties and shirts slightly untucked, and women with large handbags. They'd all come straight from work. Drinks flowing and the chat was thick. It was a weeknight so the emphasis was more social than the weekend, which Melody assumed would be busier, more chaotic and with more people dancing.

She casually looked around for Creasey but realised that the woman would be perfectly camouflaged in a place like this with her expensive skirt suit and heels. Melody considered her own clothes and felt like she stood out like a sore thumb, being in tight black pants and a black t-shirt. She leaned on the railing and peered down onto the dance floor and seating areas.

Three men in suits stood at a high table talking to one woman in a blouse and skirt. The talk looked serious at first. Melody focused on trying to read lips and judge the tone of the conversation. The men leaned in to hear the woman talk. Then they all nodded at once in agreement with what she said.

"Haven't seen you before," a man said, leaning on the rail beside Melody.

She groaned inside.

"Haven't seen you either," Melody replied.

She was watching the woman at the table below and carrying out a process of elimination. There were two women who, in Melody's opinion, could have been Creasey. The woman directly below her with the audience of men and one that was sat by the bar alone with her back to Melody.

"So what brings you here? Do you work around here?"

"Yeah. Not far," Melody replied without looking up at the man.

"Let me guess." The man stood back and eyed her. "You work in admin for a local finance company."

"Oh wow, you guessed."

Melody hadn't even looked at the man yet. She continued to watch options one and two. Option two by the bar was busy on her phone.

"Okay. Let me go deeper. You're not HR. You don't look finance. Are you one of those cute girls that is into IT?"

"No way. How did you do that?" said Melody flatly. She had decided to keep the guy talking to her. It made her look less obvious.

"I wish our IT staff looked like you. I'd be reporting problems every day."

"Yeah. I bet you would."

"Are you one of those nerdy girls that watches shows about dragons and likes Lord of the Rings?"

"Oh, I'm a *huge* dragons fan," she replied. "Can't get enough of them."

"I bet you watch it in bed on a Saturday morning while you eat breakfast."

"You want to get a drink?" asked Melody.

The man was taken back. "Yeah. Sure. I'll get them. What do you want?"

"It's okay. I'll come with you. Let's go to the bar and chat."

They made their way down the long curved staircase and walked over to the bar. Melody led to make sure they ended up near option two. She pulled out an empty stool three down from the woman. Option two had long, brown hair, loosely curled, and matched the image she'd seen on Sneaky-Peeky. The guy sat down next to Melody.

"What can I get you to drink?" he asked.

"Just a soda water for me."

"Is that it? No wine or anything?"

"No. Not for me."

"Cheap date," he commented, then called one of the bartenders.

A girl with piercings in her nose and bottom lip came over. She had a single dreadlock in a bush of thick tangled hair and wore thick black eyeliner in an attractive way.

Melody glanced at the options again. Two women had joined option one and the whole table was laughing and joking. One man had his hand on her hip and was rubbing affectionately. They hadn't just met. They were together.

Melody ruled out option one.

Option two still sat alone. She was messaging somebody on her phone. Her eyes barely left the screen. It was only when somebody walked behind her that she pulled the screen to her chest so nobody could see what she was typing.

Melody settled on option two but still saw no sign of Harvey.

The drinks came and the man beside her lifted his beer to cheers Melody. She obliged with a chink of her water bottle.

"I hope you don't mind me saying but you seem a little distracted."

"Do I?" said Melody. She was still watching option two.

"Yeah. Shall I just go? Leave you to it?"

Melody turned and looked at him, perhaps for the first time. She couldn't remember. "No. Stay. Sorry. I thought I saw somebody I knew."

The man seemed eased and leaned his elbow on the bar. "So, now that I have your attention, can I get your name?"

"Sure. It's Kelly. And yours?"

"Miles."

"Miles? Nice to meet you."

They shook hands and, like most men do when they shake a woman's hand, he gave a limp-wristed version of his usual handshake. Melody didn't expect a bone-crunching elbow jerk. But she liked a little effort put into a greeting.

"So what is it you do, Miles?"

"Oh, I'm an underwriter for an insurance firm." He gestured his thumb over his shoulder, which Melody took to indicate he worked in one of the large towers in Canada Square.

"Sounds interesting," she lied.

"It pays the bills." He grinned.

Melody looked past Miles as a man joined option two at the bar and pulled up a stool. They shook hands formally. Melody noticed the firm but polite handshake. The man looked European. He wore a dark blue sports jacket with smart jeans and brown shoes. An inch of spotless cuff showed from the sleeve of his immaculate jacket, along with the glimmer of an expensive looking silver watch strap.

The man called the bartender over and ordered two waters. Then he cast his eyes around the club. He settled on Melody's gaze and stared. Melody returned the stare with a smile and looked back to Miles. The look fed the man's ego and he began to talk seriously with option two.

Melody continued to observe the pair while she made small talk with Miles. She noticed that during the chat, neither of them smiled. Option two did most of the talking and used her hands to express herself. The man nodded and his eyebrow raised every now and then. He asked a question and she replied. He nodded. She sipped her drink. Then the cycle would begin again: question, reply, nod, eyebrow, drink.

She was selling.

A group of four people approached the bar. Melody made a show of moving down to make room for them so they could sit together. She was one seat away from option two.

Miles continued to tell an anecdote about a recent business trip. Melody slipped the LUCY chip from her pocket and held it between her fingers. Option two's bag was open a fraction and hanging on the back of her stool, and she was distracted typing a message on her phone.

Melody pretended to be listening to Miles and waited for the punchline of his story. She laughed out loud and turned sharply to pick up her drink, purposely knocking it over. The bottle rolled towards option two and the man. Melody reached out to stop it. Option two pushed her chair back in time for the bottle to roll off the bar and hit the floor by her feet. Melody slipped the chip into the bag and picked up the bottle.

"I'm so sorry. I'm so clumsy. Did I get you wet?"

"No, it's fine," she said dismissively, then pulled her chair back to the bar.

As Creasey leaned forwards on the stool, Melody caught a glimpse of her phone's screen. The woman straightened up and hit send. Then she gave a curt glance around to see if anybody had seen the message.

Melody turned to Miles. "Okay. I guess that's my cue to leave."

"Already? Okay, well, I don't suppose-"

"Sorry, Miles. You've been fun to talk to but I have to go."

She began to walk away. He followed.

"Hey, is that it? I don't even get your number?"

"Well, how about this? If I come back to this club and you see me in here again, you buy me another drink. I promise you'll get more than just a number. You win." She gave him her best dirty look. "But if I don't come back, and you *don't* see me, I win."

"Oh yeah? Tell me more about this prize."

"Well, when you get home tonight, why don't you use your imagination?"

Melody walked off briskly. As soon as she left the club, she hit the button on her earpiece three times. "Reg, you there?"

"Yep. How did it go?"

"I slipped the chip into her bag. But there's no sign of Stone."

"He's still in the car. Hasn't moved a muscle. We did a drive-by. Her BMW is parked across the street from where you're walking right now. He must be inside."

Melody glanced around at the empty street. "I'm going to take a quick look."

"Be careful, Melody."

She strode across the street and looked in the back seat and the boot. Nobody.

"He's not in there." She carried on walking.

"Oh," said Reg.

"What's up?"

"We'll find out when the time is right. That's what Harvey said."

"His watch," said Melody.

"That's what he was doing when he opened the car door at the farm," said Reg.

"So where is he now?"

"Harvey or Cartwright?"

"My guess is that they're both back in Loughton," said Denver.

"Pick me up. Creasey has a new client. They're heading to the farm now and I think she messaged Cartwright. I want to be there before them."

"Sit tight. We're thirty seconds away," said Denver.

"Another client? It's a bit late for all that, isn't it?" said Reg. "It's one a.m."

"Yeah, well, if Harvey is on Cartwright's tail, he'll be there too."

CHAPTER SIXTEEN

HARVEY CHOSE OPTION THREE.

He walked to the side of the apartment door, put his finger over the spy hole and raised his hand to push the bell. He heard the jingle of keys behind the door and lowered his hand. Men's voices approached from the other side. He looked around and ran the few steps to the cleaning cupboard, stepped inside and pulled the door closed after him, just as the front door opened.

From inside the cupboard, he could see through the crack in the door. Donny and his goon waited for the lift to arrive. He saw Donny's scarred face. It looked worse than he thought it would and gave Donny an evil look. Once they were inside the elevator, Harvey bolted to the fire escape and ran down the stairs.

He ran from the apartment's main entrance before Donny and Bruno had started their cars. By the time they had pulled out of the car park onto the road, Harvey had turned his bike around and was ready to follow them.

He crept to the end of the road and nosed out. Once they were a safe distance in front, he pulled out behind them.

The Mercedes and Toyota turned into Pudding Lane so Harvey knew they were going to the farm. Harvey drove past the turning and diverted to the hidden spot in the fields. He bounced through the terrain with his headlight switched off, feeling the way across the rutted land cautiously. Reaching the copse, he ditched his bike and helmet then ran across the field in the pitch black. He crawled the last two hundred yards to the spot behind the fence where he'd waited before. He let his breathing settle. But this time, he had no intention of sitting and waiting for long.

Donny and Bruno's cars were already there. The single door to the barn was open, spilling light onto the small area outside. As soon as the goon was out, Harvey would step into action.

Two more cars turned into the long driveway and Harvey cursed at the lost opportunity. He recognised the BMW as Jamie Creasey but didn't recognise the car behind. It was a Range Rover and it turned to park next to Jamie. A man stepped out and shut the door.

"A barn? Is this some kind of joke?" he said, as Jamie opened her car door.

"Not just any barn, Mr Stokes. I can assure you."

"Looks like a barn to me."

Donny had heard the arrival and stepped out of the barn to welcome the visitor.

"You must be Mr Stokes. Welcome." He offered his hand. The man took it and shook it, but kept looking around.

"You're perfectly safe here, Mr Stokes. Nobody knows we're here and there isn't a neighbour for miles," said Creasey.

"Come in. Meet the girls," said Donny. "You're going to fall in love tonight, Mr Stokes."

"If I wanted to fall in love, I wouldn't be *here*, Mr Cartwright."

"Love is temporary, Mr Stokes," said Donny, smiling as he stepped into the barn.

Harvey watched as the single door was pulled closed behind them. He sat back and waited for the tank moving through the shadows, but couldn't see it anywhere. The team would surely know of the new development, and if they'd been smart and followed Creasey like he'd planned, then they might even call for back up.

Less than an hour later, the double doors slid open. A plastic sheet had been laid out on the floor inside and the digger's diesel engine fired up, coughing black smoke noisily into the air. Harvey watched, waited and planned. Execution was imminent.

Mr Stokes emerged from the single door. He abruptly shook hands with Donny and Creasey and walked to his car.

"Was it what you expected, Mr Stokes?"

"I'm not entirely sure what I expected, Mr Cartwright. But yeah. I can see your little enterprise taking off, given the right exposure to the right people." He began to walk away again. "Of course, you'll need to find somewhere else. This place just won't do."

"Are you suggesting you might know of some potential clients, Mr Stokes?"

"I'm saying you should get in touch when you're not based on a farm. Don't get me wrong, it works, but if you're going to charge seventy-five grand a pop, I imagine people will want to relax with the girls, you know, somewhere stylish with champagne and more girls serving the drinks. I love the nude thing by the way. No animosity." He opened the car door. "Anyway, thanks for the evening. Like I said, call me when you're set up properly and we'll see where we can help each other out."

He started the engine quickly and pulled away, ignoring the waves from Creasey.

The goon pulled the digger out and turned behind the building. Harvey waited for Donny and Creasey to disappear. He stepped up with one foot on the fence and was about to pull himself over when Bruno walked back around the corner into the light.

He was carrying somebody on his massive shoulder. It was Melody. She was limp and hung over his huge body like he was carrying a wet towel from the shower.

"Boss," he called, stepping into the barn. "We got ourselves a visitor." He dropped Melody onto the plastic sheet and pulled her SIG from his waistband. "She was carrying this."

Donny took the gun from him. "Take a torch. Look around."

Creasey joined him and they both stood over her.

"I know her," said Creasey. "She was stood beside me at the club."

"What club?"

"Marco's. Where I'd arranged to meet Mr Stokes."

"Did she come into contact with you?"

"No. Wait. Yes. She spilt her drink and-"

"Check your bag and pockets."

"What for?"

"For something that isn't supposed to be there."

Their voices were raised. Harvey heard everything from where he sat fifteen metres away.

"Do you think she's police?" asked Creasey.

"I think we got ourselves a new girl," said Donny, smiling. "Strip her and put her in stable number six."

The goon walked back into the barn. "No sign of anyone else anywhere, boss."

"Okay. Carry on digging the hole, Bruno. Get rid of that body."

Bruno was watching Creasey unbutton Melody's shirt.

"Bruno?" said Donny.

"Yes, boss."

Bruno walked back out into the darkness and disappeared behind the building. Harvey now knew that Donny was carrying and watched his every move.

Creasey pulled the chip from her bag. It was the size of a small SIM card.

"Bitch," she muttered.

"I'll take that," said Donny. He threw the chip on the concrete floor and grabbed a hammer from where it hung on the wall with other random tools. He destroyed the chip with three direct hits.

By the time he had vented his anger on the small device, Creasey had stripped Melody to her underwear and was uncoiling the hose from its reel on the wall. As she turned the tap, a stream of cold water spewed from its nozzle. She turned it on Melody who immediately woke and rolled over, holding her head. She covered herself as she stood but didn't say a word. Donny had her gun raised at her.

"Who are you?" he said.

Melody didn't reply.

"You will tell us," Donny said.

"Maybe she needs a little solitude? That might encourage her to talk."

"Room six is all made up for you." Donny motioned with the gun to the line of doors. "In."

Melody stood resolute. She stared at him. Harvey could see the hatred on her face from where he sat. He felt helpless. Without a weapon, he stood no chance of helping her against the three of them.

Melody moved out of sight and Harvey heard the bang of a door being slammed then the jingle of keys in a lock. Donny came back into view and stood beside Creasey in the doorway of the double doors. She turned to him.

"She's not alone. There'll be more. They're onto us," she hissed.

"Calm down. There's-"

"Calm down?" she interrupted. "Don't tell me to calm down. Who the hell *is* she? And why does she have a gun?"

"Bruno swept the place. If there were more of them we'd have found them, and no doubt they would have kicked the doors in."

"You're saying she's alone?"

"Maybe. Let me think. We can't afford to make any rash decisions. My father used to attack problems with a cool head."

"*You* can think all you like. *I'm* out of here," she said, picking up her bag from the floor. "I won't be back until all this is over."

"What?" cried Donny. "You can't leave just because of this. You're the one that brought her here. She obviously followed you."

"I didn't bring her here, Donny. I brought clients here. Two of them in one night. That's two hundred grand. We should cut our losses and get out while we can. We haven't seen Barney for days. Do you think maybe that's why? You think he's been-"

"Jamie, shut up. You're hysterical. Get a grip. No-one will do a thing while we have her. She's our guarantee." Donny smiled cruelly.

"Guarantee, Donny?" She started to raise her voice. "So you're into hostages now, are you?"

He walked over to her. They were five metres from where Harvey sat. Donny gritted his teeth while he spoke.

"If you leave now, you cowardly bitch, I'll keep every penny. There's four hundred grand in there." He gestured to the kitchen. "If Barney has been caught, he's either dead, or he's not talking. So that's two hundred grand each. You walk and I'll keep the lot. Your choice." He turned away from her.

Creasey stood staring at him. "I can't do it anymore, Donny." Her voice broke.

"I thought you had more balls than that, Jamie."

Her face was screwed up, not with hate but with fear. Harvey knew the look. He'd seen it on the faces of his targets and he'd seen it on Sergio's face before he'd boiled him alive.

"We'll move them tomorrow," he said.

"Where to?"

"I'll find somewhere. We'll torch this place."

"And the cop?"

Donny paused and looked her in the eye. "We'll get rid of her. Leave no traces."

Bruno came out from the darkness and went to the stables to get the body.

Donny looked at him and gestured with his thumb as he emerged from the stable carrying the dead girl. "It works, Jamie. You can see for yourself. You heard Stokes. There's potential here. We just need to be more careful."

"I'm *scared*, Donny."

"Of what, Jamie? What is it? Prison? There's no chance of prison. There's two outcomes here. You'll either end up dead or rich. Give me six months."

"Six months? I can't take another six months of this, Donny. I'm at breaking point."

"Alright. Six months and half of Barney's cut."

"What about Barney?"

"He's out. I just severed the tie."

"What if he grasses?"

"Chances are he's dead already. If he isn't, what's he going to say? He's not likely to just tell the police that he's involved in..." Donny chose his words carefully. "All this. Is he?"

"Six months."

"Six months or a million each. Whichever comes first."

Creasey nodded faintly in the bright light.

"Go. Get some rest. We'll take care of all this." He gestured over his shoulder.

Jamie turned and Harvey watched her leave. Bruno was wrapping the girl in thick, blue, plastic sheets. Donny stood looking out into the night as Bruno walked past him carrying the bundle.

"Good work, Bruno."

"Thanks, boss."

Donny pulled his phone from his pocket, dialled and listened.

"Michael, it's me," he began. "I know what time it is. We have a problem." He listened to the voice then began in a defensive tone. "No. It's not *like* that. No. Just a week. I need to find a new place. It's all on top here. We found some bird creeping around outside with a gun." He lowered his voice to a hiss. "What? You can't keep them *here*. We're moving the operations tomorrow. *Jesus*. Michael, have I ever let you down? I'm not letting you down now. We need to move the girls. I'll have a new address tomorrow. You can deliver them *there*. You're on your way now? *Five a.m.*? It's three a.m. now, you can't-" The man disconnected. "Ah, Christ."

Harvey overheard the one-sided conversation but could fill in the blanks. Another batch of girls was two hours away, and Melody was in serious trouble.

Harvey watched as Donny nervously began fingering the scar on his face. He was planning.

If more girls were arriving in two hours' time, the place would be full. Melody would be stuck in there. Donny would need to go and find a new place and leave the farm unprotected. That gave Harvey an opportunity to get Melody out. Then he'd wait for Donny to return. But he'd need a weapon.

17

CHAPTER SEVENTEEN

HARVEY TAPPED ON THE WINDOW OF THE VW Transporter van and saw Reg nervously jump and turn around. He fumbled for his weapon. Harvey opened the rear door and stepped into the light. The smell of fresh coffee hit Harvey.

"It's me. Put it down, Reg."

"Stone," said Reg. He lowered his gun. "Melody-"

"Yeah. I saw it. I need a weapon."

"A weapon? I'm not sure-"

"We can't give wanted criminals weapons, Harvey," said Denver from the front. He was turned in his seat and faced Harvey. Harvey saw a cool boldness in his eyes.

"You want Melody back?"

"Sure we do."

"Are you two about to go in there and save her?"

"We're not trained for that sort of thing."

"I am. So give me a weapon."

Denver stepped from the van and walked around the back to join Harvey. He held out a hand. Harvey studied him and then shook it.

"You back then?" Denver asked.

"Have you called it in yet?"

"Melody? No. Not yet."

"What's your plan?" asked Harvey.

"Whatever it was, rescuing Melody wasn't part of it. We can do this together, Stone."

"Did you hear the phone call?"

"Cartwright's?" said Reg. "Yeah. It's a burner."

"He's the source. This Michael guy. Donny was scared. There's a new batch of girls arriving at five a.m."

"That gives us a little over one hour," said Reg.

"No. Donny and his goon will need to go and look for new places. They're going to torch this place and move operations."

"Torch it?"

"Fire, Reg," said Harvey. "Lots of it."

Reg looked away.

"So, we wait for the delivery," said Denver. "Then once Cartwright leaves to find a new place, we go in and get Melody out."

"No," said Harvey. "More detail. The success is in the detail."

Denver and Reg stared at him.

"The girls will arrive in a lorry or truck of some description. The lorry will need to be tracked. Do you have any of those LUCY chips left?"

"Sure," said Reg.

"Okay. Your job is to make sure that lorry gets a chip. Once it leaves here, it'll take us right to the source. That'll please Frank."

"Got it," said Reg.

"The girls will be stripped and thrown into the stables with the others. The truck will be out of there as fast as possible. They won't hang around. Donny will leave to go see the new place, which he's probably researching right now. Reg, can you tap into the internet in there?"

"It has internet? It's like something from The Waltons."

"There's a control room and cameras in every stable. If you can get the video feed, there's your case right there. That'll also please Frank. Donny will go and find the new place. We go in and get all the girls out. I wait inside."

"What?" said Denver.

"I came for Donny. I'm taking him out. He'll come back from the trip and I'll deal with him. You guys have Jamie on screen still?"

"Yeah. Thanks for the clue," said Reg.

"Okay. You keep an eye on her, Denver. She's terrified and won't be back for a while. But if she does come along, you guys take her off the road and put the cuffs on. Frank will be happy three times in one day. Frank gets Creasey and the source, Michael. Plus, the girls live. I get Donny."

"Sounds like a plan," said Denver.

"Plus, Sneaky got the plates of Mr Narakimo. We'll find him. And who's the guy that just left?" said Reg.

"Stokes," replied Harvey. "Two killers, the salesman and the source."

Reg handed Harvey an earpiece. "Welcome back, Harvey. We missed you," said Reg with a grin.

Harvey fitted the earpiece. "Reg, are you inside that internet yet?"

"Yeah. Donny's looking at nearby commercial rental properties."

"Would the CCTV be on the same network?" asked Harvey.

"If a dumbass installed it, yeah. Why?"

"There's a bunch of screens on the wall in the control room. There're cameras in every stable."

"Okay. Well let's see." Reg went into Reg mode and began

to talk to himself as he worked. "Cameras are usually UDP based and will require a server or gateway."

"What's UDP?" asked Denver, regretting the question before he finished asking it.

"That's a good question, Denver. User Datagram Protocol is a method of transmitting data over the internet that doesn't re-send lost packets-"

"Okay. We don't really have time for this. Save the IT lesson for when we're back in HQ, eh?" said Harvey.

Denver glanced up at Harvey. "You are coming back then?"

"Let's just say my options are open right now," said Harvey.

Denver nodded at him and they banged fists.

"Okay. If you guys have stopped being so cool, let's do some pinging over ports seventy-five and eighty. Hmmm, there's the internet gateway there." He pointed to the screen. "And hello, there's the media server. So if I browse to the IP address over port eighty. Aha." He stopped muttering. "We have a log in screen. We just need the username and password for the CCTV system. Let's try admin and admin."

Reg entered the default credentials and the screen went blank. Then eight small thumbnails appeared with one larger window above showing the Mercedes and Toyota sitting at the front of the barn.

"I'm impressed, Reg. That was under a minute," said Harvey.

"If you teach me how to kill with my bare hands, I'll teach you how-"

"I'm not that impressed, Reg. What's on the cameras?"

"Camera one. Front exterior." Reg made a note on his pad.

"Camera two." He clicked the next thumbnail. "An empty room."

"That's stable one. Make a note," said Harvey.

"Presumably, this is stable two then," said Reg, making another note. "Oh dear." He looked up, horrified at the image on the screen. Three girls sat huddled on the single bed. They were naked.

"That's stable three," said Harvey. "Stable four will look the same. Melody is in six."

Reg hovered the mouse over the thumbnail for stable six and looked back at Harvey and Denver. They nodded.

Melody was in her underwear, her wrists were bound, and she was working her way around the room looking for weaknesses in the walls.

"Oh crap," said Reg.

Denver looked away.

"Does she have comms?" asked Harvey.

"Of course. But she went radio silent as soon as she was caught. We don't know if it fell out or if it was knocked out. Or if she's just plain too embarrassed to respond."

Harvey and Denver stepped away from the van. They both had a deep respect for Melody and seeing her in her underwear on a camera felt highly inappropriate. They stood in the quiet night and looked towards the direction of the farm. It was obscured by the trees that hid the van. But somewhere over there, less than a kilometre away, was their friend, and she was in a world of trouble.

Harvey pushed the button on his earpiece. "Melody, it's Harvey. Can you hear me?"

They turned to the screen and watched for her reaction. She didn't respond but stopped feeling the walls and let her head drop between her arms.

"Do you think she heard?" asked Reg.

"Melody?" said Harvey over the comms.

Melody didn't respond.

"Keep your eye on that room, Reg. Anybody goes in there

and messes with her, I want to know. We'll put plan B into action."

Harvey reached for Melody's over-sized Peli-case and pulled it across the wooden floor. He flicked the two metal catches and opened the lid. Inside was a Diemaco L119A1 along with a laser sight and three loaded magazines. All the items had the foam insert neatly and precisely cut out around them. The Diemaco was one of Melody's favourite weapons.

"And what exactly is plan B?" asked Denver.

"I kick the door in and tear the place apart." Harvey inserted a magazine and slammed it home. "That will *not* please Frank."

CHAPTER EIGHTEEN

HARVEY WAS IN POSITION BEHIND THE FENCE BY THE TIME the lorry turned into the long driveway. It bounced over the potholes, but the driver didn't slow.

It was a four-ton truck with an electric tail lift fitted to the rear and a sliding shutter that rolled up to the lorry's roof. It turned among the cars and reversed up to the double doors of the barn. Clearly, the same driver had delivered the first batch of girls. He was familiar with the system.

Harvey called the plate number over the comms and Reg ran a search for it.

Sneaky-Peeky sat in the long grass, further back than before, as daylight was brightening the gloomy sky. Sneaky gave Reg and Denver a clear view of the front of the barn. It was recording. They also had a picture of inside the barn from the CCTV cameras.

The driver stepped down from the lorry and banged on the double doors. Harvey placed him in his mid-forties. He was slightly overweight, but not too much. In his heyday, he would have been a well-built guy. He could probably still handle himself. He had on clean work boots and jeans with a checked shirt over a plain white t-shirt. His head was shaved and a large tattoo reached up from under his collar on the back of his neck in the shape of a claw of some kind.

The man's banging was answered by a tired-looking Bruno who slid the doors open. The lorry was reversed in halfway by the driver and the barn's sliding double doors were closed onto the sides of the truck. Harvey presumed this was an attempt to stop any girls from running and to prevent any prying eyes looking in.

He heard the tail lift's motor whine into action and slowly lower the large metal plate down to the floor. Harvey heard the sound of the shutters being thrown up. Then began the chorus of whimpering girls.

Another car pulled into the driveway. It was another Mercedes, similar to Donny's but silver.

"Reg, have you got eyes on the driveway?" asked Harvey.

"Not yet." Reg hit a button and turned Sneaky's turret. "Unknown. Maybe the source? It can't be another client, surely."

"Yeah. It's unlikely the main man would travel in a lorry with a load of illegals. Run the plates."

"The lorry is a rental. I could have guessed that. Registered in Norfolk."

"The Mercedes is registered to a Michael Murray, Ipswich."

"They're bringing them in on the East Coast somehow," said Denver.

"Whoopsie. I just lost the live feed," said Reg.

"They turned the cameras off?" Harvey whispered.

"I can't even hit the router. They turned everything off."

"How about the tank?"

"Sneaky's still running."

Harvey launched himself over the fence and ran to the side of the building. He took a glance around at the front of the truck that stuck out from the doors and edged closer. He slipped silently to the front of the lorry and fixed the chip's magnetic side to the inside of the wheel arch.

Inside the barn, the shutter was pulled down with a screech and the tail lift's motor began to whine back into life. Harvey ran for the fence, jumped over it and sank down just as the doors opened. He peered through the bush. The driver casually climbed in like he had just delivered a bunch of fruit and veg. He started the truck's diesel engine and pulled out of the barn. The driver took even less care as he bounced the truck across the bumpy driveway.

"Reg, you tracking that truck?" Harvey whispered.

"I am. But wait. Melody's moving too with the truck. She's bloody *inside* it."

"What?" asked Harvey. "Repeat."

"Mills is *in* the truck."

Harvey leapt over the fence once more, dropped to the ground and scrambled to the Mercedes. He checked inside to make sure it was clear. Then he popped the boot lid, climbed in and closed it on top of him.

Reg watched on Sneaky's camera. "Harvey that's not the best idea you've ever had."

"Got another one?"

"Hmmm, no."

"Reg, track that truck. She's going to need you close by in case the truck and car head to different locations."

"You could have just come back here and we could all drive together?"

"You tracking me?"

"Yeah. Your new chip is pulsing on LUCY. It's flashing red for *crazy fool*."

"Okay. Denver, I'm going to need you right behind," whispered Harvey.

Harvey heard footsteps approaching the car. He drew his

SIG and aimed above him, ready in case the boot was opened. The Diemaco lay by his side but the barrel was too long to bring up and use inside the tiny boot compartment. Plus it would probably deafen him. Harvey heard the driver's door open and felt the suspension take the weight of a man. The heavy door was closed and the engine purred into life.

Harvey held tight as the large saloon drove slowly along the driveway. He was leaving Donny behind but had little choice. Melody was in serious danger now. At the farm, they always had plan B. In the truck, the scenarios were too numerous to imagine.

Harvey made himself as comfortable as he could and judged his location by the turns of the car. They had turned right out of the driveway and had been going straight for some time. When the driver had relaxed into the journey, he turned music on. It was soft, stringed music, something John would have listened to. Harvey didn't know the names of musicians or composers. He didn't have a favourite band. He listened to music when he worked out and he either liked it or he didn't.

The music gave him a chance to contact the boys. He tapped three times on the earpiece.

"Loud and clear, Harvey." It was Denver. "We are one mile behind you, out of sight but not out of mind."

"Melody?" he whispered.

"Melody is ahead of you. Less than a mile. You're catching her."

"Location?"

"We are on the A12 eastbound heading towards Ipswich."

Harvey didn't reply.

"Harvey, key the mic three times to confirm."

Harvey tapped on the earpiece three times and settled in for a long ride.

An hour passed slowly.

He felt the car slow but not stop, like it had pulled onto a smaller, slower road.

He tapped three times again on the mic.

"You still with us, Harvey?" It was Reg.

Harvey's throat was dry and cracked. "Copy," he whispered.

"You want the good news or the bad news?"

Harvey didn't reply.

"Okay. I'll give you the bad news. We're in a place called Mistley about twenty minutes from Ipswich."

Harvey waited for the good news.

"The good news," Reg continued, "is that the sun is shining, and we're by the seaside. Perhaps we can rescue Melody and then grab an ice cream on the seafront afterwards?"

"Melody?"

"You're in the lead car. Melody is directly behind you. We're hanging back one mile."

"You have a plan, Harvey?"

"I always have a plan."

The car stopped and the driver's door opened. Harvey heard the sound of a gate being opened then felt the driver return and the car pull inside the gates. The engine was cut. Harvey closed his eyes and tried to picture the scene.

He heard the loud hiss of the truck's air-brakes beside the car then the muffled voices of the two drivers. He focused. The gates were dragged closed, steel on concrete. The sound of the driver's shoes told him it was a rough concrete floor. There was a faint echo but also a breeze that blew against the car. He pictured an open-sided warehouse with a large metal roof, perhaps with a small port-a-cabin for an office or storage. He heard water, softly, and the sound of birds, gulls. Maybe it had been designed to be a place to offload fish.

The whine of the truck's tail lift broke his concentration once more. The screech of the rear shutter bounced around the warehouse. Harvey could place the truck, the water and the men.

"Get her straight in the boat, Roger," one of the men said. He had a thick country boy accent. "We don't want anybody seeing her. Fuel up and give me a shout. I'll go get changed. We can do a spot of fishing while we're out there."

"Denver, come back," Harvey whispered.

"Copy. We're outside the gates. You're under a large roof in a compound. I can see the car through the gap in the gates. The truck is next to it, but the shutter's open and we can't see Melody."

"Does this place back onto the water?"

"Yep. I'm looking at satellite imagery," said Reg. "It has a private dock to the rear that leads out to a public beach. There is one small fishing boat docked."

"Denver, we're going to need to borrow a boat."

"Borrow?" said Reg.

"Melody is being taken out to sea. I think they'll throw her overboard."

"What are you going to do?" asked Denver.

"Adapt my plan," said Harvey. "Let me know when you are floating. Oh, and Denver?"

"Stone?"

"Best make it a fast boat, eh?"

Denver chuckled. "If I'm going to steal a boat, you can bet your ass it's going to be a fast one."

CHAPTER NINETEEN

HARVEY PULLED THE EMERGENCY RELEASE ON THE INSIDE of the Mercedes and the boot lid raised. He caught it before it had a chance to swing up, rolled out of the trunk and crouched behind the car. He reached in and grabbed the Diemaco then lowered the lid.

The surroundings weren't far from what he had imagined. He was stood in the centre of a warehouse that was open on two sides. On one end were the gates, which had been locked from the inside. The other end had a small fishing boat rocking gently on the water by the private dock. The concrete floor had channels running front to back every twenty feet, presumably for the water used to hose down the floor after it had been filled with fish.

One man emerged from the cabin in the hull of the boat. It was the lorry driver, Roger. He closed the hatch of the cabin and fiddled with something that Harvey presumed was the lock. Harvey ducked low behind the car and watched the man prepare the boat.

"How you getting on, Roger?" a voice called from the far side of the warehouse. "Ready to head off yet?"

"Aye, Mike. That we are," he replied.

Harvey watched the man named Michael walk down from a small wooden hut at the end of the warehouse. He'd changed out of his suit and into yellow waterproof fishing trousers and long rubber boots. He had on a thick woollen jumper. His clean-shaved face made him look like he was going to a costume party as a fisherman. His clothes were too clean and his face too fresh to pull off the seaman look.

Roger, however, did look like a sea-faring man. His red face and thick growth suited the overalls and beanie hat that he wore. Plus, he moved around the boat with a casual ease like he'd been around boats his entire life.

The big diesel engines fired up and idled.

Harvey took aim at the boat. It was within range. The vessel was only thirty feet long. It was white with a central helm under a solid canopy. The cockpit seated two people and the rear of the boat had a bench all the way around it. The door to the cabin in the hull was between the two cabin seats. Fishermen could also walk around on the stern of the boat where the rail opened up to a small stainless steel platform designed for fishermen to stand on when playing a large fish.

Michael untied the bowline knot that secured the craft to the dockside and lifted the fenders up out of the water. Roger expertly turned the vessel in the small space then surged forwards, maintaining the five miles per hour limit and no wake zone inside the River Stour's narrow estuary.

Harvey didn't have a clear shot. When the boat powered off, he ran to the water's edge only to see them disappear around a corner.

He glanced up and down the long concrete dock. It had been split into private docks but no other boats were tied up. Further along, in the open stretch of water that led out to the estuary, small boats rocked gently in the calm and protected water. Harvey made his way along the edge of the dock towards the beach.

He jumped down from the concrete harbour onto the stony ground. It was quiet so he waded out to the first boat he saw with the rifle hidden behind his body as best he could. The cold water bit into his skin like sharp needles. He dropped the weapon over the edge and pulled himself into the boat. He lay flat on the floor then waited a standard minute, soaked and cold.

Harvey forced himself up to his feet and sat in the captain's seat. An ignition switch much like that of a car's was to the right of the helm. No key. Harvey had never stolen a boat before but figured it couldn't be too different to stealing a car.

Harvey searched the boat and found something that would work. An old, heavy fishing gaff with a hollow pole handle similar to a scaffold tube was fixed to the top of the cabin, presumably so the fisherman could reach it from whichever side he was playing a fish.

He smashed the fibreglass panel surrounding the ignition with the heavy gaff then slotted the tube end over the ignition barrel. With a small amount of leverage, Harvey was able to snap off the ignition barrel, which left him with a square hole roughly half an inch wide. A small flathead screwdriver he found on the centre console fit the square hole easily. He turned. The engine tried to turn over but didn't fire into life.

Harvey found the primer, gave it a few pumps, and then tried the ignition once more. The heavy engine slowly stuttered and shuddered into life. Harvey had never driven a boat before so he familiarised himself with the controls.

He hit the button on his earpiece.

"Reg, Denver, copy?"

"Copy, Harvey." Denver's voice was faint and lost in the noise of a loud engine.

"You get yourself a ride?"

"Copy that, Harvey. We are ocean-bound now and out of the estuary."

Harvey looked out at the estuary but couldn't see them.

"Comms are weak, Harvey..." Static rushed across the channel and swallowed Reg's voice. "Away from the van."

Harvey guessed that the comms relied on the aerial attached to the roof of the van, which was connected to the repeater.

Harvey looked around the cab. Above the captain's seat was a small VHF radio. He switched it on. It gave several beeps then the LED screen settled on channel four. He pulled the handheld mic down from its cradle. It hung from a long curled cable like an old telephone handset.

"I'm on channel four," he said over the earpiece. "Do you copy?"

A series of broken signals came back at him loud and sharp in his ear. Then the radio burst into life.

"Broken stone, broken stone, this is Denver's dream. Come back."

"Denver's dream, this is broken stone. Are you ready to go fishing? Heads up. There may be somebody already in our spot. But I'm sure if we ask nicely they'll move along."

"Broken stone, this is Denver's' dream. We're looking forward to getting our hooks into something big today."

"Not if I hook it first, Denver's dream. Out."

Harvey liked Denver. He was switched on. On an un-encrypted radio, anybody could be listening; Denver had communicated well.

There were only three controls: two throttles and a wheel. No pedals. Harvey pushed the two throttles forward and the front of the boat raised up and began to shift forward faster than he had expected. He hung onto the wheel and retained his balance. The boat clumsily leaned over to one side when

Harvey turned the wheel too hard to the left and water sprayed out from underneath. The loose items on the boat slid across the deck.

Harvey corrected the move with a turn to the right and, after a few more bumps and splashes, straightened out. He cranked the throttles forward until the engines sounded like they would blow then dropped them down a fraction. Harvey learned to use small corrections of the wheel and soon found himself between buoys that led to the centre of the river's estuary. He sped out to sea.

The choppy open water hit the boat's hull hard. He felt the little boat slam into the water so he eased down the throttles a little and scanned the horizon for movement. There were plenty of fishing boats and they all looked like the thirty footer Melody was trapped in.

Harvey searched inside the cabin and found some old binoculars in a plastic case. He killed the engine and stood upon the prow, scanning the boats.

Men were dragging nets, pulling ropes, and casting rods, but none of them wore yellow fishing trousers. He wiped the dirty lenses on his shirt and did another scan of the boats out at sea. One small white boat was moving fast way out beyond the stationary fishing vessels. To the left of it, a fifty-foot cruiser easily cut through the rough, deep water. It was much larger than the fishing boat and held a faster speed.

Harvey was sure it was Denver at the wheel of the cruiser. They were running adjacent to the fishing boat but not directly in its wake. Harvey stepped down to the helm and slammed the throttles forward. The little engine surged back into life. He pointed the prow at the white fishing boat in the distance and held his course. The hull slammed continuously into the water and shook the entire boat each time.

Tearing between the other fishing boats, Harvey sprayed

surf high into the air above them. He ignored the calls and shouts of angry fishermen. He was locked onto a target.

He left the fishermen far behind. The land became dark as did the distant strip on the horizon that split the white sky and black ocean. Denver's dream was far out to his left. Harvey guessed it to be a kilometre away. Directly in front of Harvey was the little white fishing boat, maybe two kilometres away. It had stopped and turned side on. Harvey turned right to circle the boat then killed his engines.

The little craft rose and fell with the waves, which made using the binos difficult. Harvey found the boat and focused. Then he looked on with dread. Melody was stood on the side of the deck. Her hands were bound. She was dressed in only her underwear and looked absolutely broken. Her posture had lost its usual strong and defiant rigidness. Her shoulders hung weak and limp, framed by the frigid sky beyond. The man in yellow rubber trousers held her arm and was shouting at her.

Then he shoved her into the water.

20

CHAPTER TWENTY

HARVEY REACHED FOR THE DIEMACO AND TOOK AIM. BUT the ocean swells and the distance made it an impossible shot. He shoved the throttles forwards and aimed at the fishing boat.

He smashed the front glass with the butt of his rifle and turned his head away. Fragments of glass bounced off his skin and t-shirt. He took aim through the broken window.

One of the men turned and saw Harvey approaching. He called to his mate and the little boat immediately took off, leaving Melody in the freezing water, barely able to keep her head above the surface.

Harvey took aim, fired, missed, fired again, and missed again. There was too much movement. He closed in and killed the engines then quickly switched the rifle's selector into burst and fired off the magazine in groups of three.

The two men remained standing but black smoke began to pour from one of the engines. Harvey turned his attention to Melody. He found her. She was a small dark spot in an already dark ocean. Aiming the boat at her, he slammed the throttles into full once more. As he drew near, she sank lower out of sight. He steered the boat past where she had been moments before, slipped the rifle onto his shoulder, and hurled himself into the ocean.

He crashed into the hard water and spun beneath the surface, rolling in a world of tiny bubbles. Forcing his eyes open, he searched around him. Looking down, he saw Melody's bound hands reaching up, sinking further. Harvey turned, kicked and reached. He held his nose and equalised then kicked harder. His lungs screamed. He just needed to inhale. The urge was overwhelming. He told himself one more kick. Then another. One final kick and his fingers grazed hers in the darkness. He reached down further and gave every bit of energy his body could muster. His hands found the ties on her wrist. He pulled and straightened up.

Harvey kicked hard, breathing out the spent air. His legs were burning. His boots and the rifle were heavy and his clothes dragged in the water. But he kicked harder, faster, urgently, until he finally broke through the surface. Inhaling huge lungfuls of air, he gasped for breath, straining to stay buoyant.

Melody did not gasp for air.

She remained silent with her eyes closed and mouth open with pale white skin.

Harvey held her head above the water. Her skin was ice cold. He waved over to the incoming boat and shouted, "Hurry!"

Melody's hair clung to her face. Harvey brushed it away. He was fighting to stay afloat but managed to feel for a pulse. Nothing. He felt for her heartbeat. Nothing. He breathed into her mouth. The boat was closing in on them. Harvey couldn't perform CPR bobbing up and down in the ocean. It was as much as he could do to keep them both afloat. His breaths into her did little to help. But he wasn't a trained first aider. He was just doing what he could. He pulled her bound hands over his head and lay on his back, kicking towards the boat.

Reg and Denver approached. Reg was stood at the back of the boat on a little platform. Denver killed the engine and expertly coasted to a stop, swinging the rear of the stolen forty-eight-foot fishing boat towards Harvey.

Harvey held Melody's head above the water and swam on his back, fighting the current with one arm. He kicked with his heavy boots but the weight was taking its toll on his legs. Harvey reached for the platform and held fast to one of its handles. He let his aching legs drop into the ocean below and clung to Melody with his free arm. Reg bounded back down to the platform with a blanket he'd found and helped pull her out. Her skin was shockingly white and she was cold and weak. Her body had released its energy trying to fight the cold in the back of the lorry, and then in the boat. Then finally in the water, it had given up.

Harvey dragged himself up out of the water onto the platform, slipped the rifle from his shoulder and pulled off his wet shirt. Then he knelt beside Melody.

"Come on, Melody. Fight."

He banged on her chest, tilted her head back and pinched her nose. He gave her one full breath and saw her chest rise as the air filled her lungs. Harvey moved to her chest and placed the heels of his hands over her heart, interlocked his fingers and straightened his arms. He pumped.

"I heard it's fifteen pumps to one breath," said Reg. He began to pull the blanket over her legs.

"Come on, Melody. Help us," Harvey called. He slapped her face then returned to her mouth and gave one more deep breath.

Reg stood with his mouth open, unable to help. He was mortified. Harvey continued to pump her heart.

"Melody, we need you. You can't leave us now." Harvey

pumped. "Twelve, thirteen. Melody, hurry up. Come on. *Wake up*."

Harvey was shouting now. Melody's lips had a tinge of blue around the edges.

Harvey tilted her head back, pinched her nose, and breathed one more full breath into her. Her chest rose and sank as the air escaped, and Harvey returned to pumping her chest.

"I can do this all day if I have to, Melody. But you are not leaving us now."

A little water spurted from Melody's mouth as Harvey pumped and was immediately followed by retching and coughing. Harvey rolled her onto her side.

"Oh, thank God," said Reg, who knelt opposite Harvey and pulled the blanket over Melody.

The two men carefully sat her up then Harvey heaved her up into his arms, stood, and walked her into the cabin, keeping close to her to share his body heat. He laid her down on the long bench that ran along one side of the cabin.

"Denver, do you have a visual on them?" asked Harvey, as he approached the helm with Melody in his arms.

"They're gone. They headed back to the port."

"We need to get her to a hospital," said Reg.

"I don't need a hospital," interrupted Melody weakly. "I need some damn clothes."

She was hugging the blanket around her and breathing hot air down onto her chest. She wiped her eyes and sniffed. Harvey laid her on a bench with a blue, plastic-covered foam cushion.

"Reg, check down below. I'll see what I can find up here. Denver, get us back to shore."

Harvey ripped up the other seats and looked inside the storage compartments. He found emergency equipment, flares, first aid and a life raft that looked older than the boat.

Reg stepped up from the cabin below carrying an old sports bag. He bent down next to Melody and spoke softly.

"Hey, girl, you're in luck. I found a bag of old clothes. It's almost like one of the Kardashians left their overnight bag. Here, look at this. There's a thick woolly sweater. The itching will be a reminder of how fab you look." Melody broke into a smile and an involuntary laugh broke through her tears. "And looky here. These are simply stunning, darling. The latest line of knock-off Nike tracksuit bottoms. And last, but not least, thick, woolly socks. Boy, does this guy like his wool and look at the size of them." He held the sock up. "Melody, you could literally curl up inside that." She laughed again and he handed her the bag.

"Can you help me?"

She wrapped the blanket tight around her and lifted her arms. Reg fed the thick sweater over her head and pulled her arms through so she could pull the top down. Melody pulled the blanket away from underneath. Reg opened up the track-suit pants and helped her feed her feet into the holes. He then helped her with the socks, which were far too big and slippery on the deck. But she needed the warmth so she kept them on. She pulled the blanket back around her and dried her hair with it then pulled her knees under her chin on the bench seat and closed her eyes.

"Should she be sleeping?" asked Denver. "Isn't it dangerous or something?"

"Leave her be," said Harvey. "We need to find her a hot shower."

"And some decent clothes," Melody added from under the blanket. "I look like a Russian hobo."

The three men all smiled. Melody would be okay.

"We can't go back to the same port in a stolen boat," said Denver.

"Yeah. I made a few locals mad," said Harvey. "Probably

not a good idea. What *happened* to my boat?" He looked around the horizon. There was no sign of it.

Denver was looking out to sea. "You leave the throttles open?"

"Yeah. There wasn't time to park it." Harvey smiled.

He looked down at the ignition by the wheel, expecting to see similar destruction to what he had done to his stolen boat. But there was no damage.

"How did you do that?" Harvey asked Denver casually.

"Do what?"

"Start the engines without damaging the ignition."

"I'll teach you someday," said Denver.

He turned the wheel and gently slid the throttles forward. The boat responded and soon the rhythmic lull of the hull cutting through the ocean swells sent Melody off into a deep sleep.

Harvey stripped the Diemaco and the SIG and cleaned them as best he could with whatever rags and tools he could find. Reg was lost without his tech. But he sat by Melody and held her steady in case she was thrown from her seat on the rough seas.

When Harvey was done, he stood next to Denver who was navigating a different river estuary looking for a safe place to ditch the boat. Many of the smaller docks had security that would question why three men and a girl might arrive at a dock with no identification in an ensemble of clothes and an automatic weapon.

He found a marina that looked nearly empty of life and pulled the throttles back to neutral, letting momentum carry the boat forward. He gave a slight tickle of one engine to push the boat into the dockside. Harvey had kicked the fenders out and was ready with the rope when the boat gently nudged the concrete. Harvey tied a neat bowline and reached down to help Melody out.

The rifle was wrapped in the blanket, much to Melody's annoyance. They walked up the path towards the main road where a security guard came from out of nowhere and stood before them.

"Good morning. Can I see your paperwork please?"

"Paperwork?"

"Paperwork. Boat registration-"

He hadn't even finished his sentence when Harvey's arm came thrusting out from under the blanket, hard and fast. The man's legs turned to jelly and he crumpled to a heap on the ground.

"Let's move. Now."

The four moved fast towards the road. It was quiet so they walked away from the little port, heading north.

"How did you do that?" asked Denver.

"Do what?"

"He's unconscious. How did you do that so quick?"

"I'll teach you one day." Harvey grinned at him.

21

CHAPTER TWENTY-ONE

THE TEAM WALKED SIDE BY SIDE INTO THE SMALL TOWN OF Brightlingsea. It was the first time they'd been together and on the same team for only a few days. But it felt like weeks.

They flagged the first cab they saw and rode in silence northbound back to Mistley. It was a twenty-five-minute journey made longer by the early morning traffic and the cab driver's reluctance to use first or third gears. Denver struggled to contain his frustration at the man.

The Diemaco lay across Melody's knees wrapped in the blanket. Harvey sat in the front. They drove past the VW Transporter and asked the driver to stop five hundred yards further along the road. The gates of the warehouse looked closed and locked, but they wanted to be sure. Denver walked back on foot and drove the van to pick them up while Reg, Melody and Harvey stood off the main street.

"How does it look?" asked Harvey. "Any sign of life?"

"I heard some banging but couldn't see anything. The Mercedes was gone. I could see it through the gap in the gates earlier, but not anymore. There's just the truck."

Reg opened the rear door to climb inside. He was already firing up the computers.

"Hey, wait," began Melody. She looked at all three of the men in turn. "I just wanted to thank you all for what you did." She looked humbled but grateful. "You all saved my life back there, each of you, and I can't put in words-"

"We only did what you would have done for us, Melody," said Harvey.

"That may be so. But hey, I have to tell you how I feel. It's the way I was raised." She hugged Harvey, turned to Reg, smiled, and put her arms around him, then embraced Denver. "I'm just glad we're back as a team now. We missed you, Harvey."

Harvey looked directly at her but said nothing.

"Are we done with all the loving?" asked Denver. "We've still got two men to find."

"Donny and Bruno?" asked Harvey.

"No. We need to find Michael and his friend, Roger, first. Donny comes after," said Melody. "They can't be too far away."

"The longer we take looking for them, the further away Donny gets," said Harvey.

"But we're right here, Harvey."

"Yeah, and they're right there," said Harvey pointing back inland. "But for how long?" He stepped back from the van.

"You're *going* again?" said Melody, hurt. "We only just got you back."

Harvey didn't reply.

"You can't *keep* quitting on us." She raised her voice at him.

"I have to do this, Melody," replied Harvey flatly.

"Harvey, come on, man," pleaded Denver. "Help us take these two clowns down, and we'll *all* go and get Cartwright with you. Surely we're stronger as a unit?"

"Where are they now?"

"Who?"

"The country bumpkins."

"I don't have any information other than the chip on the lorry and that's in the compound five hundred yards away."

"You don't have their phones' GPS?"

"We don't have their full names or numbers yet," said Reg flatly. "I can get them in a few minutes from Cartwright's phone."

"I can take Donny down and be back here in a day. It'll take you that long to find your two guys."

"Yeah, with collateral damage," said Melody. "If you leave now Harvey, that's it. I don't understand why you'd throw all this away. Look at us. We're a great team."

"I'm not asking you to understand. I'm telling you. I'll be away for one day."

"What do we tell Frank? I have to check in soon," Melody lied.

"I don't care what you tell Frank."

Melody climbed into the passenger side and pulled the door closed. Reg sat down in his seat and Denver walked to the driver's door shaking his head. Harvey watched the van start and pull away from the curb. It disappeared around the corner. Harvey was left alone holding the Diemaco bundled inside the blanket with a wet shirt and boots.

He carried the bundle in the crook of his arms and walked in the opposite direction until he found a bench to sit on. He needed a plan. Sitting on a main road in a wet t-shirt with a military grade weapon wrapped in a soggy blanket wasn't a good place to start.

He needed to find a car, preferably something old but fast.

CHAPTER TWENTY-TWO

DENVER STOPPED THE VW OUTSIDE A SMALL HOUSE WITH A sign that read *Bed and Breakfast*. Melody hopped out with her pack and walked casually to the door. She was greeted by a middle-aged lady who looked her up and down with compassion.

"I'm so sorry to bother you, but my friends and I were just in our boat and I fell overboard. We have a long drive back to London and I was hoping to have a shower and change my clothes." She held the bag up and gave her best feminine smile.

"Oh, you poor thing. Come on in here." She ushered Melody into the house who looked back and winked at the two men in the van. "Are those your friends?" the lady asked.

"Yes. They didn't get wet. They're okay. I'll pay full price. I don't mind. I-"

"I wouldn't dream of it. Get yourself up to room three, first floor. There are towels on the bed." The lady had a mother's kind but instructive tone. Melody turned back to Denver and Reg and gave a thumbs up. "Do your friends want to have some coffee? It's quiet this time of the year and I have a full pot."

Melody signed the international hand sign for a drink and pointed in the house with her thumb. The van doors were open and closed before she'd turned back around. She headed up the stairs and heard Reg and Denver's voices greeting the old lady as she closed the door to room three.

The bedroom was small but cosy. It was the type of place her nan might have liked to stay on holiday. The bathroom was clearly a refurb with exposed plumbing and a small shower stall, toilet and washbasin laid out in an efficient use of space. It was everything somebody would need for a short stay on the coast.

The water was hot. It was everything Melody needed right then. Her fingers came back to life as the blood began to flow freely and her skin revelled in the steam.

She dressed in the clothes she carried in her pack. Overnighters were frequent for the team so the spare clothes stayed in the van. Reg and Denver also both had packs in the back but chose not to change.

Melody pulled on socks, cargo pants and a clean, tight t-shirt then pulled her Norwegian sweater over the top and finished with her pumps. She didn't have spare boots. But pumps were better than the hideous over-sized socks Reg had found on the boat.

By the time she walked downstairs, she felt brand new. The others all sat in the kitchen. Reg was in the middle of an anecdote about a childhood seaside visit. Melody hoped it wasn't the one where he had rigged the slot machine to empty its quarry and had been escorted back to his parents by the local police.

"You think it's time to head off?" Melody asked the two men.

"Oh, dear. That's better. Look at you now. Such a pretty girl," the old lady began. "Here. I've made you some toast."

"Oh, I-"

"Come on. I won't hear another thing said about it. Sit down. Do you drink tea or coffee? I always find tea makes me wee a lot."

Reg sat with his back to the lady and smirked.

"Coffee, please. That'll be lovely. What do we call you, ma'am?"

"Sorry, dear?"

"What do we call you? What's your name?"

"Oh, you can call me Dot. Dot Glass."

"Is there a Mr Glass?" asked Denver, being polite.

"No. He buggered off *years* ago, about the time I had the change. You know?" She looked at Melody with raised eyebrows. "Couldn't take the heat."

Reg had his lowered his head and was visibly shaking trying to control his laughter.

They eventually left the house with full stomachs and Melody was warmed through. They climbed into the van and Reg fired up LUCY.

"Right now I don't know if we're catching evil villains or if we're off to bingo," he said.

"Catching evil villains, Reg. Can you get the boatyard on satellite?" replied Melody. "Let's get back into this." She turned in her seat as Reg zoomed in on the warehouse. "Is this live?"

"No. There's around ten to twenty seconds delay depending on the location of the satellite," said Reg.

The little boat was sat at the dock once more. But there was no sign of life. Any activity would be under the huge metal canopy.

"I need to get inside," said Melody.

"Melody you've been dead *once* today already. Can't you just relax?" said Reg.

As he said it, a silver Mercedes nosed out of the side street in front of them. It pulled off and headed away out of town.

"Did you guys see that?" said Denver. He was already starting the van.

"Reg, do you have anything on that Mercedes?"

"Only that it belongs to Michael Murray. I have no phone. Nothing yet. I tried to get it earlier but couldn't get onto Cartwright's phone."

"The new Mercedes pretty much all have inbuilt GPS," said Denver. "Can't we somehow find the–"

"Serial number of the radio unit using the vehicle's plate number to find the chassis number," Reg cut in. "Then we could find the model of radio and then find the satellite identifier via the dealer's database. Yeah, we could do that. But I'll need to tap into my control centre back at HQ."

"You can do all that?" asked Melody.

"Already on it. All electronic devices with any form of network connectivity essentially use the same technology and most of them come from the same few factories in Asia. The chassis number will be linked to the other electronics in the vehicle, probably in some kind of database in the dealership. So if I can tap into that database, I'll find the chassis number and linked devices."

"You ever done that before?" asked Denver.

"No. But it's much the same as any other database. Okay. Here we go. I have the device's GPS identifier. I'm just initialising a remote session into HQ to find the right satellite. The scanner on the van doesn't have the range or the power."

Melody turned in her seat to watch him dart around the screens. "You seriously taught yourself how to do all this?"

"Well, yes and no, really," Reg said without stopping or looking up. "I taught myself how to do it all but the Ministry of Defence kept catching me. I had to find new ways to achieve the same results. So essentially, they taught me how not to do it."

He looked up at her and smiled his best childish grin.

"Right. Okay. I'm in," said Reg.

"You found the serial number already?" asked Melody, shocked at the speed at which he worked.

"Not only have I found the serial number of the stereo, Melody, my friend, but I have targeted the stereo via the inbuilt GPS and found the Bluetooth identifier that is currently connected. I searched the devices with that range of identifiers. Each manufacturer of Bluetooth devices would have a range of serials allocated to them per batch," he explained. "Then I found the phone's UID and its own GPS signal and I am now looking at..." He turned the screen to Melody. "Mr Murray's mobile telephone."

Reg sat back. He put the keyboard on the bench and smiled. The screen showed a live view of the iPhone. The other screen showed LUCY's satellite image of both the car's and the phone's GPS.

"We're joining the A12. If you have eyes in the sky, Reg, I'll hang back. Don't want to scare him off," said Denver.

"Good call," agreed Melody.

"He's picking up speed, anyway. We can't tail him without drawing attention to ourselves."

"You think he's going back to the farm?" said Reg.

"Well, he just got shot at by a nutter on a boat and his own boat is out of action. If you just delivered a lorry load of illegally imported girls to an underground prostitution ring and then got your boat shot at, what would you do?" said Melody.

"I can honestly say I've never considered it, Melody," said Reg.

"He's going to be questioning the security of his phone. So he probably won't make a call that will incriminate him," said Denver.

"Right," agreed Melody. "But he's mad as hell because-"

"The girl Cartwright asked him to dump in the ocean-" said Denver.

"Was just rescued by the men in boats that shot at him," said Reg.

"*And* put his boat out of action. Right?" finished Melody. The team all came to the same conclusion. "Murray is heading to the farm for sure. He knows we're onto them all and wants his cash so he can run."

"Sever the ties," said Reg. "Except, we've got the footage of him at the farm from Sneaky."

"We have footage of him getting out of the truck and walking into the barn. We don't have anything that will put him away," said Melody. "Prosecution wouldn't stand up."

"What do we have?" asked Denver.

"We have Cartwright, Brayethwait, Creasey and Bruno Mason. Bang to rights," said Reg from the back.

"Yeah. But Harvey isn't going to leave us much of Cartwright, if anything," said Melody.

"And he'll probably need to take Mason down too to get at Cartwright," said Denver.

"So we have Brayethwait and Creasey," said Melody.

"We also have Mr Narakimo," began Reg. "He's in the same video as the one of Bruno wrapping the dead girl in the plastic sheet. Same for Stokes."

"They'll get murder for sure. The bodies will be exhumed. Plus they'll find DNA."

"It's not enough," said Melody. "We've been gone more

than two days. I'll need to call Frank today and he'll want more than just two customers plus Brayethwait and Creasey."

"He's going to need the source. The board won't be happy otherwise."

"Exactly," said Melody. "Let's also offer him the lives of a dozen girls."

She dialled Frank's number and straightened in her seat. Her eyes were fixed on the silver Mercedes a thousand yards in front of them.

"No answer. He always picks up," she said to herself and the team. "It's eleven a.m. He'll be at HQ for sure. He's going to want a game plan. So how about this? We wait for Murray to get into the barn and incriminate himself. Taking the money should do it. Reg, can you get eyes inside the barn?"

"If they turned the internet back on, yes. But Cartwright's moving the operations. Right?"

"There's no way anyone can make a deal on a commercial unit, sign the paperwork, hire a lorry, and move the girls to a new place in..." She checked her watch. "Eight hours."

"What would you do?" asked Denver.

"Find somewhere close? Maybe he knows someone. He is from the area," said Melody. "How about you?"

"Well, personally, I'd rent a truck. Keep the girls in the back until I found somewhere more permanent," said Denver. "Park it up some place nobody goes." Denver shrugged his shoulders. "He knows someone's on to him and he's a fool if he thinks that killing you will stop whoever we are."

"Of course," said Melody. "That's why I was driven all the way out to the sticks. They knew you'd follow and he'd have time to get the lorry and move the girls. Damn." She slammed the dashboard. "Stupid. Why didn't we question *why* I was being moved?"

"We were worried about you. It wasn't until we saw you

being put on the boat that we had any idea of what they were going to do to you."

"Okay. We need a new plan," said Melody. "Even if Murray meets Cartwright at the barn, or wherever, and takes cash off him, it won't stand up. It's just cash, right? There's no context."

Just then, Denver swerved into the outside lane and the sound of a roaring engine filled the space inside the van.

"*What the-*" cried Reg, barely managing to hold on to his bench.

"It's the truck," called Denver.

He then dropped a gear and pushed ahead. The truck swerved into the back of the van and caught the bumper, which was pulled off and crumpled under the truck's wheels. Denver fought to keep straight and had to ease off the throttle to stop the tail end bouncing around. The truck slammed hard into the rear of the van. Reg flew off his chair and the back window shattered glass over him. He curled into a ball and protected his face.

Melody snatched off her seat belt, turned, and pulled her weapon.

"Stay down, Tenant," she shouted over the racket of the road, engines and screeching tyres.

Denver was swerving all over the road to try to force the truck driver to make a mistake. Melody aimed over the back of the seat and fired three rounds. The first hit the windscreen and the last two found the truck's radiator. Steam billowed out, but the driver gave one last attempt before the engine blew. He slammed the heavy truck once more into the smaller van.

They felt the van tilt onto two wheels. Denver felt the weight shift on the steering wheel and accounted for it with a sharp, jerky steer. The van came crashing back down on four wheels. Once more, Denver fought to keep control but saw traffic stopped dead ahead. He slammed on the brakes and pulled the van off the road, narrowly missing a tanker lorry stopped dead in the slow lane.

There was a huge crash of twisted metal and broken glass as the truck behind them slammed into the back of the lorry. The truck stopped dead, the driver smashed his face on the steering wheel, and the fibreglass sides of the truck's cargo space tore open with inertia, crashing down around the tanker.

Denver took the van down the steep embankment. The vehicle bounced on the rough ground and the long grass scoured the underside. The van broke through a wooden fence that lined a farmer's field and came to a stop in the dirt.

Melody was out of the van immediately. She tore up the embankment and along the shoulder past people who had climbed out of their cars to see the commotion behind.

The passenger side of the truck was embedded in the rear end of the tanker. The driver was slumped over the wheel. Melody had her SIG aimed at the man and walked cautiously around to the driver's side. Cars were stopped in the traffic beside her. They'd been lucky not to have been hit by the wrecked truck. A man in a suit was climbing out his car and froze when he saw Melody's gun. A family in a saloon behind him sat perfectly still. Just their heads and eyes followed her.

She approached the man slowly then sniffed the putrid air. She saw the steady dripping of whatever fuel was in the tanker pooling on the tarmac. The tanker's driver was stepping down rubbing his neck. Denver emerged from the embankment. Melody saw him through a small gap between the vehicles.

"Denver, clear the area. Fuel."

Denver looked at the puddle of fuel on the ground. It was trickling backwards and had formed a stream underneath the truck.

Denver heard Melody yelling at the family to get out of the car. He ran forwards, banging on car windows. "Get out of your car, sir." He had his weapon drawn and had pulled his vest over his t-shirt when he left the van. "Come on. Everyone out. Get out of your cars."

People were reluctant at first. But when the first few men and women began to emerge from their cars and huddle together on the side of the road, a few more followed like sheep.

"Not *there*. Away from the tanker. Get away from the tanker into the fields."

The crowd of people began to move quickly down the embankment and through the broken fence. A young girl was crying and stood alone next to her family's car with her thumb in her mouth.

Denver rushed to her, scooped her up and bolted down the embankment. A worried mother held her arms open to take the girl off him. The husband stood beside her holding a baby. Neither said thanks to Denver, but he knew that under pressure, most humans went into self-preservation mode before group preservation mode. The girl was mad at them for leaving her but hugged the woman who was stifling her tears.

There were close to one hundred people stood along the foot of the embankment looking up at the carnage. Denver ran up to the road and waved his hands, indicating that everyone should go back further. The crowd paid attention and slowly walked back into the field.

Melody had cleared the cars from the fast lane and edged back towards the ruined truck. The driver was groggily lifting his head. He was dazed and looked around him. He rubbed his face and winced when he found some glass lodged in his forehead.

"Get down from the truck, Roger."

"Who the hell are you?" he asked. His voice was weak and tired.

"Get down from the truck and I'll explain. But right now you're sitting on a time bomb. The tanker could go any minute."

He looked down at Melody's gun, at the tanker, and then at his position.

"My legs," he began. "They're stuck. Crushed."

"You need help?"

He was fighting the pain. Melody could see it on his face.

"So you can arrest me and jail my crippled ass?"

"Let me help you down. We can-"

"No. Shut up," he spat. "It's over."

"What are you saying, Roger?" said Melody. "Nothing is over yet."

He reached into the inside pocket of his jacket with his right hand. His left hand hung uselessly by his side. He took a cigarette and placed it between his dry and cracked lips.

"It's over for me."

He lit the cigarette. Melody began to move away from the fuel at the sight of the flame. Roger took a drag on the cigarette, inhaled deeply then slowly exhaled through his nose.

Then he looked down at Melody, blinked once, and flicked the cigarette through the open windscreen.

23

CHAPTER TWENTY-THREE

HARVEY CAME TO THE TOP OF PUDDING LANE IN A STOLEN BMW. It was an old model without an immobiliser from the days when stealing a car was easier than finding somebody's address. These days, cars were harder to steal but finding someone was simple with the internet. Finding people was one of Harvey's specialities. Stealing cars was not.

It was early afternoon when he turned into the lane, which was typically empty. He approached the driveway to the farm, dropped into second gear, turned and lifted the clutch. As he tapped the gas, the rear end slid out taking him neatly into the driveway sideways but at speed. He skidded to a halt and dipped the clutch when he saw the silver Mercedes parked at an angle beside the barn.

The BMW's exhaust grumbled as the engine idled. Harvey planned.

He slipped the gearstick into first and popped the clutch with a healthy amount of throttle. The rear wheels spun in the dirt and Harvey fought to keep the car straight as it bounced across the bumpy track.

He was halfway up the driveway when he saw the first sign

of smoke coming from the barn. Then he saw a figure dart from the barn to the Mercedes. Harvey stopped the BMW four hundred yards away from it. The two German cars sat facing each other across the desolate stony soil.

Smoke began to billow out from one side of the barn, thick and black, as the blaze took hold of the old wood.

Harvey let Murray make his move first. He was patient. He planned. When Murray put his foot down, Harvey executed.

The large Mercedes fishtailed onto the driveway spraying up dirt and stones across the front of the barn.

Harvey lifted the clutch and spun his rear wheels.

Murray steered the Mercedes onto the rough track heading directly at Harvey. The torque of Harvey's BMW and the power from the rear wheels on the loose surface sent the car crabbing along the drive, its tyres fighting for purchase. Harvey slammed the gearstick into second and floored the throttle again.

Murray held fast. The gap was closing.

Harvey hit third gear and pulled his SIG.

Murray's view ahead was obscured by dust brought up from Harvey's wheels. He could see the front of the BMW as it approached.

For a split fraction of a second, Murray saw Harvey's face. Then he saw the gun hanging from the driver's window.

Harvey fired.

Murray snatched the wheel right and the front of the car left the track. The nose of the BMW slammed into the rear quarter of the Mercedes, tearing off the bumper and shunting the rear wheel into the chassis, crippling the car.

The Mercedes spun once before the front right wheel dug into a pothole and lifted the left side of the vehicle into the air. The Mercedes slammed down on its roof and rolled twice before coming to rest in a hiss of steam and smoke in the long grass beside the perimeter fence.

The front left corner of Harvey's much older and stolen BMW tore clean off on impact with the larger, newer and better built Mercedes. The car spun immediately, slamming Harvey's head hard against the door frame. The force of the spin pulled Harvey left then right again until he slammed once more into the door.

The spin stopped when both the front and rear right-hand wheels dug into the soft earth and the car flipped over. It rolled once, twice then, after the third roll, it landed with a hard crash on its roof. The wheels turned uselessly in the air.

There was a silence in the driveway. Just smoke and steam rolled across the barren wasteland.

Harvey hung upside down and dazed in his seat belt. Blood dripped from a long wound across his forehead.

The creaking of another car door nearby brought Harvey's focus back from the spinning and rolling and crashing. He reached for his knife, which was permanently in the case fixed to his waist, and cut the fabric of the seat belt. He crashed down onto the inside of the car's roof.

Feet were approaching, upside down. They staggered through the long grass towards him.

A gunshot rang out. Then another. It was loud in the silence. More shots. Louder. Closer.

Harvey pulled his legs back and kicked out hard at the passenger window. It took two kicks to shatter the glass into tiny fragments that fell around his legs. He shuffled awkwardly towards the window until his feet found ground. More gunshots nearby. One shot hit the dashboard and ricocheted through the windscreen, shattering more glass onto him. He scrambled faster and rolled free of the car into the long grass. There was a figure on the driveway to his left two hundred yards away. The upturned BMW stood between

Harvey and Murray, who was now returning fire at the other person.

Harvey checked around. One end of the barn was fully ablaze, the furthest end. Harvey staggered towards it. The girls would perish in the smoke before the fire reached them. Sirens sounded far off in the distance. Black smoke belched across the land obscuring Harvey's view of Murray and the other figure. Harvey turned and ran as best he could towards the barn.

He broke the single door in with the heel of his foot. It swung back and crashed into the wall behind. He aimed his SIG and stepped inside. Smoke stung his eyes and tore at his throat. He lifted his shirt up to cover his face. He needed to act fast. Kicking in the door to stable six, he swept the room with his weapon. It was empty. In the main room of the barn, the far wall began to crumble as its old dry timber was eaten by hungry flames.

He kicked in the door to stable five. It was also empty. Harvey continued. Kick, sweep, check, move along. Stables three and four had a single bed in the centre of each room and a rancid bucket that had been used for a toilet. Stable two had nothing. He approached stable one knowing it would be empty. The heat from the burning wall next to stable one was excruciatingly hot. He held his arm up to protect his face and kicked down the door. Nothing.

The kitchen and control room was at the far end of the barn beside stable six. He ran to the door and slipped inside. Everything was gone, the screens, the computers. Everything had been removed.

He turned to walk out but as he spun around, a burning wooden beam that ran the length of the barn up in the eaves came crashing down and smashed into the partition wall of the kitchen, blocking his exit. He tried to pull debris from the wall out of the way to escape. But the beam had trapped the gypsum boards beneath its immense weight. Smoke began to fill the tiny space inside the ruined kitchen.

Harvey moved back and looked around him. The kitchen was against the rear of the barn where there were no windows. The exterior wall was far too thick to smash through. He coughed with the smoke but tore the cupboards from the wall and revealed the gypsum partitioning. Then Harvey began to kick his way through. He found a gap between the wooden studding that formed the frame of the partition and smashed through it urgently.

He'd managed to break through one side when more of the burning wood fell into the barn outside the kitchen. Harvey felt the heat suddenly increase. The fire was even closer now. He had only a few minutes before the ceiling gave way.

The smoke had also increased. He fell to his knees and sought the layer of cool, clean air on the cold concrete. But there was none. He rolled and sat on the dirty floor. Blood from his head wound ran into his eye. Harvey wiped it with his arm, leaving a red streak across his face.

In front of him was a hole. He'd broken through one side of the thick partition wall. He weakly raised his leg and began to kick but he hadn't the strength. The urge to roll onto his side, curl up and close his eyes was overwhelming.

More timbers crashed onto the floor outside and a huge dust cloud joined the smoke inside the small space. The ceiling began to buckle with the heat.

Harvey gritted his teeth and searched deep inside himself. One kick at a time, he brought his leg back, growled with fear, fury, and anything he could, and smashed his heel into the gypsum in front of him. Again and again. On his fifth kick, he felt the gypsum give way. Then his sixth broke through.

The heat from the smashed kitchen doorway was intense.

His eyes stung from the smoke and blood.

He'd made a hole as large as his foot. He moved his face to it and breathed. It was still smoky but felt cooler. He pulled his arm back and punched in the plaster around the hole, making it larger with each punch.

Then he plunged his head and body through the hole and dragged his legs through just as the ceiling came down inside the kitchen. He lay on the floor. But he wasn't clear of danger. Devastation was happening all around him. The smoke was growing thicker.

Harvey looked up from the floor. He was inside stable six. He'd closed the door behind him when he'd kicked it in earlier and was now trapped in a larger room with high walls and no ceiling. The exposed roof trusses above were obscured by thick black smoke and the shimmer of heat. Flames licked out at the fresh wood above him from inside the main barn.

Harvey touched the door handle tentatively. It was red hot. There was no way he was getting through the door. As he turned to find more options, the barn's burning wall fell to the ground with an almighty crash. It was followed by a searing roar of flames that licked at every empty space in the barn. Harvey heard the suck of air into the fire's lungs and the heat intensified even more.

The blood continued to run across his brow. He wiped it across his forehead. It seemed to be getting worse. He heard the crack of timber as the weight of the fallen side wall began to pull on the three remaining walls. A small crack appeared between the timbers behind him. The exterior wall was opening. If it came down in the room, it would crush Harvey and destroy the partition that separated him from the fire. His eyes were watered by smoke and blood from his head wound. He kicked at the timbers around the crack until the small break became big enough for his arm.

It felt cool outside and he lingered there. He searched

around once more and pulled a large, six by four timber through the hole from the kitchen. He smashed the end of it into the crack which widened it a little but not enough. So he jammed the timber in at an angle and heaved on it to lever the crack. It was working. But it would surely bring the wall down.

He had to carry on. The timing would need to be perfect.

Harvey readjusted the lever and pulled back on the timber. When the wall finally caved in, the rest of the roof would drop. He'd have moments to escape before being crushed and burned alive.

The crack was widening. Harvey studied it. He looked at the ceiling hanging lower as he levered its supporting wall away. The partition wall behind him was bulging with heat and browning with the fierce fire it held back.

He heaved, just once more. It was final. Harvey heard a loud splinter and fell forwards with the timber, throwing himself into the crack. It was wide enough for his torso but he couldn't pull the rest of his body through. If the wall fell now, he'd be cut in half.

Harvey forced himself back inside and tried another angle. But he was stuck. The timbers cut into his leg. Splintered shards of the one-hundred-year-old oak jabbed into his thigh. Harvey reached down to the ground outside and grabbed hold of whatever he could. Thick bunches of long grass pulled out of the ground in his hands. He found bigger bunches then pulled. The skin on his thigh split and the wooden shard connected with bone. Harvey growled and pulled, harder than before, harder than he knew he could. The shard snapped off its timber inside his leg and fell to the ground.

Harvey rolled away, sucking the cool air into his lungs as he heard the sound of twenty tons of oak crash into the fire below. There was a whoosh of energy as the fire rose higher in a display of power.

He crawled across the ground, across the soft patch of fresh earth, where who knows how many bodies had been hidden, to the fence that ran along the rear of the property. Harvey slipped between the horizontal bars to the relative safety of the field. Cool air licked his scorched skin like a puppy licking its owner.

The sound of sirens outside came loud and true over the roar of the blaze. But the thick smoke from the destroyed barn blocked any visibility.

His leg throbbed and his head pounded from the crash and the smoke.

Harvey gripped the long shard of old oak that stuck from his leg like a mummified compound fracture and felt the searing stab of nerve endings screaming through his limbs. Without releasing his hold, he growled, gritted his teeth and pulled on the shard. With each inch of wood that came out, the pain subdued, until finally, he was able to drop the huge splinter onto the ground and lay back, panting with exhaustion.

Another wipe of blood from his eye brought firefighters into his vision. Hoses and fire trucks surrounded the blaze. Blood ran from his wound in pulses with his heart. His entire right leg was soaked with sticky red blood.

Harvey gritted his teeth once more and tried to stand. Keeping his right leg straight, he managed to get himself upright and winced as he began to limp through the field. Anxious not to be seen by the firefighters, he tried to hurry. But pain and fatigue overcame the desire to remain hidden, and he strode as best he could through the dry mud.

Eventually, he fell through the trees and clung to his bike. He was able to perch on the seat and look at his leg.

His t-shirt sleeve was ripped so he pulled the tear and

wrapped the fabric loosely around his leg. Then, with his knife, he made a small cut in the inside of his jacket, which still hung on the bike's handlebars where he'd left it. He tore out some of the cotton wadding that lined the pockets and placed it between the material and his leg then tied the homemade field dressing tight.

Harvey pulled on his helmet carefully, avoiding the sliced skin across his forehead. Then he faced the challenge of getting onto the bike. His leg was too painful to swing over the back and he couldn't stand on it to lift his good leg. He settled for lying across the bike and, very ungracefully and painfully, manoeuvred into position.

The bike purred into life and he smiled faintly behind his visor. His leg had to be dragged into position onto the foot brake. Then he wormed his way out of the trees and back across the fields.

The discomfort of his leg eased with the pressure of the bandage. Applying the rear brake with his leg became easier but his head leaked blood into his eye. The helmet prevented him from wiping it away.

Before re-joining the road at a small break in the hedgerow, Harvey stopped and pulled a plastic water bottle from the bike's panniers. He removed the helmet and cleaned his face up before ripping off his other shirt sleeve and placing it over his head. The rest of the water, he poured onto his leg wound, which stung badly. But it felt better for some coolness.

Thankfully, he hadn't severed his femoral artery. It was a nasty gash that would need to be cleaned. But that could wait until after he'd finished with Donny.

CHAPTER TWENTY-FOUR

THERE WAS SILENCE. THE WORLD MOVED IN SLOW MOTION. Melody saw the cigarette being flicked from Roger's hand. It spun through the air like a firework and hit the ground at the front of the truck. The pool of fuel ran in a small but steady stream less than a foot from the burning ember.

A soft breeze, which would have been welcomed at almost any other time, gently rocked the trees on the edge of the fields, and prickled rather than stroked Melody's skin, rolled the cigarette into the fuel.

The vapour caught the fiery end of the cigarette before the Marlboro even reached the liquid. The rush of flames popped into life like a magic trick.

Roger gazed down at Melody from the cab of the truck. He smiled the smile of a man who had won.

Melody turned and ran. She jumped from the road onto the embankment and ploughed into Denver who was sending people back into the fields. They both tumbled down the unkempt grass and over rocks. They landed together with a bump in a drainage ditch at the bottom of the small hill when the flame found its way into the source of the fuel, and the tanker exploded.

A searing fireball reached out, reached up and licked everything in its reach before mushrooming into an ungodly black cloud. The noise was deafening.

Melody and Denver turned their backs. The angle of the embankment protected them but they felt the heat wash over their bodies. The flames rushed past just metres away.

Immediately the crowds began to scream and children started crying again. But the people were safely in the fields spectating. They watched as their cars and vans were engulfed in the giant fireball. The closest cars caught alight and joined in the blaze. Possessions were lost but lives had been saved.

A coolness came over Melody and Denver. When they opened their eyes and glanced around, the surrounding land had been scorched to smoky and charred tufts of grass. The pair rose and ran back into the fields to a safer distance. The blaze was strong. The surrounding cars would likely explode when the pressure built inside their fuel tanks.

Melody and Denver went towards the large crowd who stood huddled together like frightened livestock. One man began to clap his hands as Denver and Melody reached safety. He was joined by another and soon the chorus of applause increased as the whole crowd began to softly clap their hands in gratitude. There were no happy expressions. There was none of the joy that would typically accompany such a moment. It was just a sombre demonstration of appreciation.

"Is everybody okay?" Melody called to the crowd, her hands held high to get their attention. "Is anybody hurt?"

"Is anybody missing?" Denver followed.

The crowd shook their heads and held their families tight. Small groups of husbands, wives and children stood touching each other. A few men stood alone and one woman. They'd been travelling solo and now joined other people who had been travelling alone.

"Where's Reg?" asked Denver.

They both turned to face the blaze. Thick smoke poured from the vehicles and ran above the motorway. The scene looked like a locomotive had passed through it. The traffic stood motionless. There was another crowd of people stood on the motorway itself, much further along than the blast.

"You think he's there?" said Melody.

"I didn't actually see him get out the van," said Denver.

They ran to the VW that Denver had stopped just fifty yards into the field. The single window in the back had been smashed by the truck, but the van had thankfully not been hit by the fireball. They peered into the windows but Reg couldn't be seen. Melody wrenched the rear door open and Reg's limp body began to roll off the van's wooden floor. Denver caught his arms before he hit the ground and pushed him back up.

He had a serious head wound, which had leaked blood across his face and pooled on the wood. A lump had formed on his forehead the size of a child's fist. Sirens in the distance kicked Melody into action. She pulled out her phone and dialled emergency services, stepping away from the van to talk to them.

Denver pulled the first aid kit from under the driver's seat. He straightened Reg out and began to clean the wound, wiping the blood from his head and face. He used an open water bottle from the floor and his t-shirt to clean Reg's eyes before the blood dried and glued them shut.

Reg had a pulse and his airways were clear so Denver made a pillow for his head. He put it in a position where the fresh blood that leaked from the wound ran away from Reg's eyes and face. Denver began to check for breaks and foreign objects. He started with his head, worked down his shoulders, just running his hands across his skeletal frame. Most fractures would be felt through the body's thin skin membrane. Reg's ribs were intact. Denver began to ease any thoughts of serious damage. Broken ribs often tore into lungs or caused internal bleeding, which was a common cause of death. A first aider had no way of spotting early signs of internal bleeding.

Melody joined him once she had made the call. Denver was just finishing checking Reg's legs.

"No sign of broken bones or internal bleeding. Just the bump on his head," said Denver. "His spine feels okay but let's keep him straight until the medics arrive." He began to apply a field dressing from the van's first aid kit to the head wound.

Two fire trucks made their way along the hard shoulder. Seemingly without words, the firemen sprang into action. Each of the firefighters expertly performed their own part of the effort to ready the hoses, build the pressure, and keep the crowds away, who had since moved closer out of curiosity. The distant thump of a helicopter came over the empty fields. Then the bird emerged from the smoke and began to circle. The pilot brought the helicopter down into the field a few hundred feet from the van.

The helicopter was yellow with a green underside. *Essex Air Ambulance* was written in large green letters across both sides.

Denver stood with his feet together and his arms up to form the letter Y, the international sign for help.

The first medic saw him and pointed his partner in their direction. Two men in green uniforms ran the short distance carrying a stretcher between them and an emergency medical pack.

"Thank god you're here. He's been out cold for..." Melody thought about how long it had been since Denver had avoided the queue of traffic and hurled the van off-road. "Ten minutes. Maybe fifteen."

"He's hit his head and has a large bump and a gash on his forehead. I've checked for broken bones and his spine feels okay," began Denver. "He nearly fell from the van when we opened the door. So we straightened him out. That's the only time he's been moved."

"Good. Thanks. What's his name?" asked the medic. He was a middle-aged man with greying and thinning hair. But he had a kind face. He pulled on a pair of latex gloves and checked Reg's eyes and airways.

"Reg Tenant. He's twenty-seven, I think," said Melody.

"And are you his friends?" asked the man.

"Yeah. Well, we're colleagues but we're close."

"Can you tell me what happened here please?" the second medic asked, pointing back to the blaze with a jerk of his thumb. He was younger than the first guy with a full head of neat brown hair in a side parting. Melody thought he couldn't be too long out of training. But he still had a confident way about him.

"The cars in front slammed on their brakes. We had no time so I pulled off the road," said Denver.

The medic looked behind him and turned back to Denver with raised eyebrows.

"The truck behind us crashed into the tanker."

"Seems like a bad day for driving," said the younger medic. "There's another crash about a mile in front this one. Apparently someone smashed into the car in the next lane on purpose and then took off. Caused a hell of a smash."

"Did they catch him?" asked Melody.

"Not that I heard. There was a family in the car that was hit. They crashed into the central reservation and rolled. There's another chopper there now dealing with the scene."

"Any description?" asked Melody.

"We don't get descriptions like that, miss. We just pick up the pieces."

"Right. Let's get him onto the stretcher," interrupted the older medic. He'd finished his assessment. "Okay. Reg, we're going to move you now if you can hear me. Let me know if you feel anything."

Melody and Denver stood back and let the two men carefully ease Reg from the van onto the stretcher. The older man signalled to the helicopter pilot and the blades began to turn slowly.

"Can we come with him?" asked Melody.

"There's not much room," said the younger man, taking the back end of the stretcher.

"That's okay. I want to be with him."

Denver shut the rear door and pulled the keys. "I'll join you in a second."

"Need to be quick. This man needs a hospital."

"Get him loaded," said Denver. Without looking back, he ran to the nearest policeman who was a hundred yards away. He was asking a man in a suit questions. The man had obviously lost his car in the blaze and was giving his account of what had happened.

"The insurance *will* cover it, right? It's my livelihood, mate," he was saying when Denver came to a stop beside them.

"You'll need to deal with the insurance company, sir," replied the policeman.

"Sir," began Denver. "I need a word in your ear."

"I'm conducting an interview, sir. You'll need to wait. There's a lot of you to get through, I'm afraid." He turned back to the man in the suit.

Denver pulled his ID, something he didn't like to do. "Officer, I said I need a word in your ear."

"Oh, I see. I'll just be a moment, sir," he said to the man, who then gave a look of annoyance at the disruption.

"That's my van in the field. We're with SO10. Our colleague was hurt. We're escorting him to hospital. I need the van protected." Denver passed him the keys.

"I'm afraid I-"

"The van is full of highly sensitive equipment and key information in a high profile investigation. If we lose the van or the contents, the suspects go free, and it'll be you, officer, that shoulders the blame." Denver made it clear he was reading the number on the policeman's shoulder.

"I'll see what I can do."

"You'll do more than that. You'll get the van into a police compound with twenty-four-seven protection. I'll be back to get it later, officer." Denver spat the last words and the policeman understood.

Denver turned and ran to the chopper as Melody was climbing in. She looked back and held the door for him. He climbed in beside her and pulled the door closed. The medic passed him a headset. Reg was on the stretcher at their feet and the two medics were opposite monitoring his vitals. A strap ran across Reg's chest to keep his body steady.

The helicopter rose into the air. Melody looked out of the small window at the devastation below. The scene looked even worse from above. They flew over the long queue of cars following the smoke and saw the emergency services dealing with the cause of the traffic. Three cars were piled up blocking the motorway. The first vehicle was a minivan on its roof. Even from two hundred metres above, Melody could see the sparks made by the firefighters' cutting tools.

She sat back. "Which hospital are we going to?" she asked into the headset.

"Broomfield Accident and Emergency," the medic replied.

She looked down at Reg. He looked peaceful. She thought that if the positions were changed and she lay on the stretcher, Reg would probably be making jokes and annoying the medics.

Reg opened his eyes and looked up at the ceiling. His neck brace prevented him from moving his head. He tried to move his arms, but the straps held him fast. A confused look spread across his face. Then he felt a bolt of pain as his head began to pound. The medic held him still.

"Mr Tenant, you're okay. You're in an air ambulance. Your friends are here with me. They're okay. But you've had a nasty bump on your head."

Reg tried to sit up but the medic held him down.

"Reg, try not to move. Can you hear me?"

Reg mouthed something inaudible.

"Okay, Mr Tenant," the medic shouted over the noise. "I need you to move your fingers for me."

Both hands and his fingers contracted and straightened.

"And your toes, Mr Tenant."

Melody put her hands on his feet and nodded to the medic that his toes were moving.

"Okay. Do you have any pain anywhere other than your head?"

Reg tried to move his head from side to side then said, "No," softly and kept his eyes closed.

"Okay. You're going to be just fine. Just relax and try to stay awake. I'm going to keep talking. I want you to keep responding. I can't let you fall asleep."

Melody gently took hold of his hand. "Reg, it's me." She gave a little squeeze. He returned the squeeze. "That's it, Reg. Just keep squeezing, hard as you can if you like."

Reg gave a soft squeeze. He lay on his back, totally disabled. His eyes were looking down at Melody. She smiled back at him.

She held his gaze as the helicopter circled the helipad and

turned to face the wind. Then the pilot gently set the bird down. The rotors began to wind down immediately and the medics jumped into action.

The doors were flung open and the older medic jumped down. In one smooth motion, he pulled the stretcher out. The younger guy followed with the other end. The legs were kicked down and the stretcher rolled across to the open door where a team of men and women in white jackets stood to meet them.

Denver held Melody back with his arm.

"What are you doing?"

"Just wait," he said.

The pilot emerged. Denver pulled his phone out. He nodded and said thanks to the pilot as he walked by. "Just making a quick call to his wife. We'll be in in a sec."

The pilot nodded and carried on walking. Denver watched him disappear through the doors.

"Come on," he said, and ran towards the helicopter.

"What are you doing?" Melody called.

But Denver was already pulling open the pilot's door. He climbed in and waved her over through the window. She opened the passenger door at the front and looked across at him sternly.

"We are *not* stealing a helicopter," she said matter-of-factly.

"We're not stealing it. We're borrowing it. Come on." He began to flick switches and familiarise himself with the controls.

"Denver, no. This is ridiculous. We could lose our jobs."

He stopped and faced her. "If we don't, we're out of the game. Murray gets away. More girls die."

The rotors began to turn.

"Denver, no. I can't."

"Melody, Reg is in safe hands here. Get in." He took on a

serious look. "More girls will die if he gets away. He'll just find another Cartwright someplace."

Melody glanced back over her shoulder then begrudgingly climbed in. "You better know what you're doing in this thing," she said, pulling on the headset.

Denver began talking through his own headset. He read out the helicopter's identifier to control. "Control, this is Essex and Herts Air Ambulance KO-33. Come back."

A crackled voice came over their headsets.

"KO-33, this is control. Please identify yourself." The control centre knew the regular pilots and hadn't recognised Denver's voice.

"My name is Denver Cox. I am a pilot with SO10. We have just dropped our colleague here at Broomfield and I am commandeering this helicopter in pursuit of a suspect. Out."

"KO-33, you can't do that. I suggest you step away from the helicopter before-"

"Control, this KO-33. We don't have time for that. I suggest you ask your superiors to contact SO10. They'll verify my authority."

"KO-33, this is control. What's your flight plan?"

"Pudding Lane, Hainault, Essex. Out."

He switched channels back to private so he could hear Melody's shouting.

"What the hell was that?" she shouted. He'd never seen her so mad. "That's it. We won't just lose our jobs, we'll go to prison ourselves, you idiot. Why did you have to tell them who we were?"

"I couldn't lie to them, Melody."

"You couldn't bloody lie?" she shouted. A little spittle flew from her lip. "You can steal a helicopter but you can't lie?" She released her strap and reached for the handle but Denver took the weight of the chopper on the rotors. It began to move. He eased off, taking the bird higher than the surrounding buildings then checked the compass in the centre of the dials and banked.

Melody fastened her straps again. "You bastard."

Denver smiled. "Sit back. Enjoy the ride. How often do we get to do this?"

"Go to prison?"

Denver ignored her and monitored the controls. He checked the fuel, temperatures and pressure. Then sat back and looked out.

"Murray has a forty-five-minute head start on us. He'll be there by now. I'll cut across country."

"I'm not happy about this, Denver."

"Listen. If we get him, they'll thank us. If we don't and we land ourselves in deep-"

"If?" cried Melody.

"If it happens, I'll take one hundred percent of the blame. I'll tell them I forced you into the chopper."

"Damn right you will." She crossed her arms and turned away from him.

"Melody, we can do this. But I need your help. Put that to one side right now and focus." He paused then leaned over to her and held her arm. "We stand a much better chance of success if we work together. Trust me. I can fly this. We can nail him."

"How long?" she said.

"At a guess? Fifteen minutes."

"We'll probably be shot down by then anyway," she said.

CHAPTER TWENTY-FIVE

THE COLD WIND BIT INTO THE SCRAPES ON HARVEY'S HAND caused by punching through the plasterboard. His head throbbed and his leg ached. He couldn't remember the last time his body had taken so many hits.

He rode for the sake of riding and to distance himself from the crime, the blaze, and the bodies. But he had no idea where to find Donny.

A chopper hovered in the direction of the fire. It seemed to hang in the air, which was swathed in smoke.

Harvey rode away from the blaze and continued along the country lane. He'd need to go back to basics, back to before he had the team with Reg's tech, Denver's reliability and Melody's tenacity and attention to detail.

Before he knew them, he'd done all his own spadework, often just sat alone at his kitchen counter on his laptop. It was all so basic then. But he'd got the job done, whatever it happened to be. Often he had been researching known sex offenders to target so he could hone his skills. It had been therapy, piecing the puzzle together and tracking their movements until he managed to have them fall into his trap. Then, little by little, he could restore some kind of peace to the world by removing some of the poison.

Another little part of Hannah could rest.

Another family could begin the long healing process.

Harvey had never been to see a shrink or a therapist, or whatever they were called. He often wondered what they might think of him if he began to tell his story. Where would he start?

Would he start with Hannah?

Or would he start with his training with Julios? That was when the world Harvey knew had been born. The real Harvey. The little boy that was found wrapped in a hamper on a bench seat in a grimy bar in East London had died when Hannah had cut herself to ribbons. Julios had reached inside the boy's corpse and pulled out a man, kicking and screaming at first. Harvey had wanted to fight the world and all those that deserved to be punished. But Julios had tamed the beast. He'd focused Harvey's attention on a small subset of evil. Now, he was a psychiatrist's dream.

And now Harvey needed to refocus. He needed to concentrate on one tiny part of the greater evil. Donny. One man. Harvey imagined a pin pricked into his skin with relentless, unchanged pressure. He imagined his life without the sharp stab of pain. How clearly he would see the world.

If he was Donny where would he be? What would he do?

Donny would need to move quickly. He'd need to find a new place. It would be close. It had been less than a day. Nobody could find somewhere and move a bunch of girls and all that tech in less than a day. It would take a week to sign the lease. Unless he had friends. But what friends are going to lend him a commercial property for his illegal prostitution business? Besides, Donny had only one true friend, and Harvey had boiled him alive six months ago.

He pulled into a lay-by to remove his helmet and wipe his

face. Adjusting the make-shift bandage, he tidied up his leg dressing. His hand stung, but they were just scrapes. It had been a long few days and he hadn't slept.

A lorry trundled by, heavy and cumbersome in the country lane. Harvey hung the helmet on his handlebars and leaned forwards. He was able to stretch his leg now. It hurt but felt good to move it. It would be dark soon, maybe an hour, maybe less.

Harvey ran the possibilities over in his head.

Donny would need to get the girls out fast. He'd need somewhere to take them and some way of taking them there. He couldn't take them in his car or Bruno's Toyota. He'd hire a lorry. He would have to. And he could do that in less than an hour. Once he had them out, he could take as long as he needed to find somewhere.

Harvey sat forward on his bike. Where would he park a lorry full of girls? He couldn't leave them alone at night. Someone might find them. He'd have to kill them. If he set them free, they could go to the police. The description of a man in the area with a burned face and an accomplice that resembled a five-hundred-pound silverback would be easy for the police to track down.

A caravan park? A campsite?

Cogs shifted into place.

His foster father's old house. It was close by and had been derelict since Sergio's murder.

John had disappeared soon after the Sergio incident. His accounts had been closed and all communication had been through his lawyers. It was the lawyers who had closed the bars down, laid off staff, and put the house up for sale. The price had dropped after six months on the market. Nobody wanted it. The news had been national. A man had been brutally killed there and a known sex offender was found tied up in the basement. Nobody would buy the place.

Harvey fired up the bike and pulled on his helmet.

CHAPTER TWENTY-SIX

HARVEY WAS CLOSER TO LOUGHTON THAN THEYDON BOIS. So he decided to make a pass by Donny's apartment before riding on to the house. It was early evening. The streets were busy with people heading home from work and kids returning from school. He glanced up at the building and found the window of Donny's flat. The lights were off in the corner of the second floor.

Harvey parked the bike in the same spot he had before and stashed his helmet in the back box. His SIG was in his waistband. His knife was fixed to his belt.

As he turned the corner near the ramp to the car park, a couple walked out the main door. He held it open for them so the husband could get the pushchair through the entranceway.

"Thank you," the man said.

"You're welcome," Harvey replied with a friendly smile.

Then he walked into the lift lobby. He was sure Donny wouldn't be there. Donny wouldn't be back. He knew the rules. Never return to the scene. As far as Donny was concerned, he had caught Melody but still had no idea what organisation, if any, she belonged to. Brayethwait had disappeared and who knows what level of communication he'd had with Murray since Harvey had shot at his boat and Melody had been dragged from the water.

Donny would be moving. John may not have been the world's greatest father. He hadn't sat with them or helped with their homework. But he had taught them to be street savvy. As weak and spineless as Donny had been when they were younger, he had picked up on that. He had gone on to become John's operations manager across his chain of bars.

The door to the apartment stood at the end of the hall. Harvey saw that the cleaning cupboard was locked this time. He stood off to one side of the door and placed his finger over the spy hole. Then he rang the bell.

He had his knife in his right hand, ready to jab up into somebody's throat if the door opened. But it didn't.

The door was light oak. It was solid and intricately decorated with beading and an ornate design like a fleur-de-lis symbol, but with more branches of interweaving plants.

The door lock cracked with a well-placed heel of Harvey's boot. He pushed it open. No movement. Harvey closed the door behind him. He swept each room before settling in Donny's bedroom. Donny had few possessions. The apartment looked like it was rented and came furnished. None of the furniture was Donny's style. It wasn't extravagant or expensive enough.

Double glass doors off the bedroom led out onto a small balcony with a table and chairs for two people. Harvey pulled the drawers out of a cabinet. There was no point being discreet. He emptied the contents of each drawer onto the bed. He didn't know what he was looking for. A clue to John perhaps. A clue to another property. But there were no clues in the bedroom.

He moved into the lounge. It was small but contained two

large sofas and a small dining table for four. The drawers in the TV stand were empty.

It was like Donny had no previous life. He just rocked up at the place with nothing. A fresh start.

It had been a fresh start. Donny had been sent away when Thomson had put a hit on him and failed. John sent him to the Maldives. Most people would have found somewhere a little cheaper and with more people. Some places are easier to hide. Asia, for example. India or Thailand would have been better choices. But Donny didn't think that way. Sitting on an island with only a handful of other guests would have been his idea of hiding.

He must have returned from the Maldives when the calls from Sergio had stopped and his money had run out. Donny would have found John's empty house. Harvey wondered if John had contacted him. John was the one link to Harvey's real parents. He would be the next piece of Harvey's life puzzle once he'd dealt with Donny.

The kitchen was empty. Harvey took a cursory glance around the apartment as he stepped to the front door. It had been a waste of time. He had gleaned an insight into what Donny had become. A nobody. Donny wouldn't live like that by choice. It meant he hadn't the money or position to splash out on a lavish home.

A single door stood behind the front door. It was storage for a vacuum or ironing board, perhaps. Harvey swung it open. It was dark inside, but it did indeed have an ironing board, plus some boxes for electrical appliances, along with an iron, microwave, toaster and kettle.

And a small rucksack stuffed at the back.

Harvey reached for the pack and unzipped the top. Inside were old photos. They hadn't been neatly stored or placed in the bag like cherished memories. They had been slung inside in a hurry. Some of the photos were bent in half. Some were in frames. But most weren't. Harvey recognised a framed photo that stood on John's bedside. It was of six people: John, Barb, Donny, Julios, Harvey and Hannah. Hannah was in a child's swimming costume and Harvey was in shorts with wet hair. Donny was fully dressed. He never joined Harvey and Hannah even in the pool. Julios was stood off to one side. Harvey looked down at Julios' unsmiling face. His hands were folded in front of him. He was on guard. The photo was taken during the days before Harvey's training, when Julios had been John's minder.

Harvey faintly remembered the day. It was a shot of the family. To an onlooker, it gave the impression of happy memories by their pool during a summer long ago. In reality, Barb had spent the day sitting in a chair silently reading a book. John had been working in his office and Donny had been off with some friends. It was Julios who had spent the day with Harvey and Hannah entertaining them. But John and Barb had insisted on the family photo so people could see how happy they all were. Harvey looked again at Julios' unsmiling face and began to understand more.

He touched the photo. "One day my friend," he said to himself. "One day I'll find out who killed you. For sure I will."

Harvey zipped up the pack and pulled it over both shoulders. He glanced around the room then opened the front door. A large fist hit him square in the face.

The blow sent Harvey staggering back into the apartment and onto the floor. He scrambled to his feet. The doorway was filled with the giant frame of Bruno. He was silhouetted against the bright hallway lights.

Bruno came at him with hard and fast jabs. Harvey ducked and slammed a hard uppercut into the big man's ribs with no effect.

Harvey had fought men as big as Bruno before. Their organs were protected by a layer of muscle and fat which narrowed the points of vulnerability down to the face, groin and throat. Many men Harvey had fought had placed a kick between the legs, thinking it would surely take down any man. But Harvey knew otherwise. A cheap shot between the legs would leave him open, standing on one leg, fully exposed and off-balance.

Bruno swung. Harvey dodged and felt the air move across his cheek. Bruno was fast for a big man. Perhaps not as speedy as most boxers, but the guy was still fast. Bruno threw two more punches in quick succession. The first was a left jab anticipating Harvey to move into the follow-up right hook. Instead, Harvey stepped back and let both punches miss. A missed punch takes a lot of energy and sets a man off-balance. Harvey was learning how Bruno fought before he made his move. Patience, planning and execution.

Bruno rushed at him, leaving no room to dodge. But Harvey ducked beneath his sweeping arms and stood with his back to the front door. Bruno grew mad. It was exactly what Harvey had been waiting for.

Bruno threw three wild swings at Harvey who was able to dodge, duck and skip out of their way. Harvey bounced from foot to foot, ready to move in any direction at any moment. Bruno ended up by the dining table and hurled two chairs at Harvey, who was again able to avoid the attack. But Bruno came at him while he moved from the last chair. He caught Harvey in his strong hands and pinned him against the wall. His breath was foul. Harvey landed several blows into Bruno's gut. But the giant man just laughed and squeezed tighter.

Harvey tried to pull at the man's huge fingers but they were solid.

Bruno was trained and had learned the hard way how to street fight. His body was turned away to protect his groin.

Harvey felt his air supply being cut off. Bruno saw the life draining from Harvey's eyes.

Then he made his mistake.

He gloated.

Bruno put his face next to Harvey's and sneered. Then, in his deep East London accent, he grumbled, "Any message for your brother, Stone?"

In a fraction of a second, Harvey snapped his mouth open and chomped his teeth on the big man's nose. He bit down with everything he had. But Bruno didn't let go. Harvey felt his teeth sink into Bruno's skin. The irony taste of blood ran across his lips and down his face. He bit harder, growling and twisting, until finally his teeth connected. He'd bitten completely through.

Harvey snatched his head back to tear the flesh clean from Bruno's face and spat it at him. Bruno was clearly in pain, his eyes were drawn tight and his mouth closed against the blood. Yet he still somehow managed to hold Harvey against the wall. He was almost inhuman. Bruno opened his eyes and swung his arm back. A blow from him at such close range would destroy Harvey. It would be like a sledgehammer breaking open his skull.

Harvey saw the opportunity and jabbed his right hand up and out, his fingers straight and locked. They connected with Bruno's Adam's apple and he immediately released his grip. The larger man reached up to his throat, gasping for air. He fell to his knees, eyes wide. Blood poured from his ruined nose.

Harvey delivered the final blow.

CHAPTER TWENTY-SEVEN

DENVER FOLLOWED THE SMOKE.

"Well, he did say he would torch the place."

"You think the girls are out?" asked Melody. "Surely he wouldn't burn them all alive. It would link straight back to him."

"You're right. He'll take them someplace else," said Denver. "Someplace he thinks nobody will find."

Denver took the helicopter above Pudding Lane as they made their approach.

"That's Murray's car on the grass," said Melody.

"Who's that down there? That's not Harvey."

It was an impressive scene. Two cars were on their roofs. One of them was Murray's. The other was unknown. The barn was burning ferociously, pumping out thick, black smoke across the driveway. Murray was crouched behind the second car and shooting towards the end of the driveway where another man was crouched down. The man shot, ran a few steps forward, then crouched and shot again. At the end of the driveway, parked in the lane, was a dark Volvo estate.

"Is that–"

"Frank," finished Melody. "Get me down there."

Denver pushed the cyclic forwards and lowered the collective. The helicopter surged and dropped down to fifty feet where Denver levelled off.

"Denver, over there. Take me down."

Denver continued on his path straight towards Murray.

"What are you doing?" cried Melody. "Take me down."

"Hold on. I've got an idea."

Denver brought the air ambulance in to hover directly above Murray and the upturned BMW. He dropped the collective some more and the helicopter began to descend.

Two gunshots pinged off the fuselage.

"We're going to get shot in the-"

"Trust me," shouted Denver.

His face had a look of total concentration and steely determination.

Dust and smoke flew up all around them. Denver was pulling in the thick smoke through the suck of the chopper blades and sending it down onto Murray along with dust and debris.

"I can't see anything," called Melody.

"Neither can Murray," said Denver. "It'll give Frank a chance to get closer."

Denver continued the onslaught of smoke and dust and made small adjustments on the collective. Then he saw a faint Frank-shaped figure disappear under the helicopter.

Denver gently dabbed the right yaw pedal and the fuselage turned to face the driveway. Then he slowly pulled up on the collective, bringing them out of the dust and smoke.

He moved the helicopter away from the fire and began to bring the chopper down on the driveway when he saw two fire trucks pulling in. He pulled the collective and took them back up out of the firefighters' way.

The smoke and dust had cleared around the upturned car.

Frank had one knee on Murray's back and was putting cuffs on him.

"I'd say that was quite successful. Wouldn't you?" Denver said with a smile.

"Whose is the other car?" asked Melody. "There's no-one around."

"Harvey," replied Denver.

"How can you be so sure?"

"That's an eighties BMW," Denver called over the radio. "If I had to steal a fast car in a short amount of time, I'd have chosen the same."

"You think he's in the barn or the car still?"

"Neither. He's a survivor. Besides, he has another mission."

"Cartwright."

"What about Frank?" asked Denver.

"We should talk to him. He'll be happy with the arrest so now is as good a time as any."

Denver brought the helicopter down softly beside the driveway. Police had arrived and an ambulance had also turned up. The scene was a riot of swirling lights in the fading darkness. The rotors wound down and spun to a standstill.

They watched Frank hand Murray over to a uniformed officer then turn to walk towards the chopper. Melody opened her door and stepped down to the ground. It felt solid, sturdy and reassuring in comparison to the roller coaster chopper ride.

She called out to Frank as he approached, "You got the source."

"The source?"

"Yeah. That's Murray. He's the guy bringing the girls in."

"You have proof of that?"

"In a way. We were hoping for something stronger but-"

"*I've* got him for attempted murder of a police officer."

"That'll buy us time to pull the human trafficking evidence together."

Frank looked across at Denver who was still sat in the pilot's seat. "Let's discuss the elephant in the room, shall we?" He smiled. "Or should I say the helicopter in the crime scene?"

"Commandeered, sir," said Denver.

"Commandeered?"

"From Broomfield."

"How do they feel about their helicopter being commandeered?"

"I'm sure they'll feel better when they hear about it being used to capture the leader of a human trafficking ring."

"So they know who took it?" asked Frank.

"Of course, sir. Do I look like a helicopter thief?" Denver said with a smile.

"Cox, you were brought into the rehab program as a habitual car thief."

"That's just it, sir."

"What's it?"

"I'm rehabilitated. I turned my powers into good."

Frank turned away from Denver and looked at Melody. "You have an update for me, I hope?"

"It's bad, sir. Worse than we thought. Cartwright was in a gang of three running an illegal prostitution racket."

"Are there *any* legal ones?"

"They were killing them, sir. Shaw wasn't the first or the last."

"The others?"

"With Cartwright? Barnaby Brayethwait and Jamie Creasey. We have Brayethwait in custody in Redbridge."

"How long do we have him for?"

"Life, sir. We have an audio confession placing Cartwright and Creasey in the spotlight too."

"Where's Creasey?"

"We planted a chip. But without Reg, we have no way of knowing where she is."

"Where's Tenant?"

"Reg is in Broomfield, sir. Head injury."

"Head injury?" Frank was beginning to wonder what the hell had been going on.

"Yes, sir. From the crash."

"What crash?"

"Murray's man rammed us in a truck. We came off the A12 and ditched in a field."

"Where's Murray's man now?"

"Burned, sir. He's dead."

"Burned?"

"In the explosion."

"*Explosion?*"

"Petrol tanker, sir. The truck rammed right into it. We evacuated the public. No collateral."

"And Stone?"

"He left us, sir. On the coast."

"The coast?"

"We caught Murray and his man dropping off more girls. We followed them back to a town near Ipswich."

"Want some intel?" asked Frank.

"On what, sir?"

"Stone."

"You know where he is?"

"He crawled out of the BMW and ran into the barn."

Melody looked across at the blaze. The crumpled old building had been reduced to a pile of burned timbers.

"Did he come out?"

"Nobody came out." Frank sighed.

"He was one of *us*. I thought you'd be a little more upset," said Melody.

"He had one foot in," Frank defended. "He ran out on us. Stone was going to prison and he damn well knew it."

Melody was hit hard with the news. Frank carried on talking but she just heard a mumble of emotionless dribble. Around her, the firefighters were dousing the remnants of the old barn. Blue lights flashed atop police cars at the end of the driveway. Police officers had begun a sweep search of the property.

"Mills?" said Frank.

She looked up, teary eyed. "Sir."

"We just need Cartwright. You in? We can talk about Stone when we're done."

"Sir, I hope you don't mind me saying..."

"Go on."

"You're a cold bastard, sir."

She looked past him. A police officer was carrying Sneaky-Peeky towards his colleagues who were stood at the rear of a patrol car. They all looked at it with confusion.

"Denver, Sneaky-Peeky."

"What's-" began Frank.

But Melody had already begun to walk across the grass. She returned two minutes later with the radio control tank and set it down on the ground.

"One of Reg's creations, I presume?"

"Yes. We may have some footage on here that would secure Murray's conviction. We just need Cartwright. Then, as soon as Reg is up and on his feet, we can scoop up Creasey." Melody looked up at Frank. "Cartwright either locked the girls in the barn and Murray has killed them or Cartwright's taken them somewhere else. He's had about twelve hours so far to find a new place to run the operations."

"Twelve hours? That's not a lot of time. I doubt he'd even get to see a place let alone sign a lease."

"Does he have friends nearby?"

"All the Cartwright allies went with John. The scene has been quiet for months." Frank thought on it. "He'd need a truck or a van, right? To move all the girls, I mean."

"Yes, sir."

"So presumably, he'd need somewhere to park the truck overnight. It'd be too risky to park it on the side of a road somewhere."

The barn was, by then, reduced to a pile of old burned, smoking timbers.

"Let's have a quick look around," said Melody. "There's something I want to see."

She hoped there were no bodies. If there were, they'd be charred beyond recognition. They left Sneaky-Peeky sitting on the ground by the helicopter. The three of them walked towards the smoking remains of the barn.

"There were two double doors here and a single there." Melody pointed. But the doors were completely gone and fallen timbers lay in their place.

"What's that?" said Frank, looking through the smoke.

A pile of wooden timbers lay across something unmovable. Yellow paint was just visible in the grim blackness of the scene. Water from the firefighters, who were still dousing the barn, landed in a jet around the tall pile. Frank motioned for the firefighters to hold off for a second.

"That's a digger, sir," said Denver.

"A digger?" said Frank. "What did..." Then it dawned on him why they would need a digger. "Oh, God. No."

"We saw it being driven out of the barn and around to here," Melody said, as she walked behind the barn. She could still feel the heat of the burned wood. But the fire was entirely out. The stink was unbearable.

She looked around her. It was the spot where Bruno had caught her earlier. She remembered the soft earth but had only seen it in the dark before.

"Hey," she called to the firefighters. "Do you guys have spades?"

"Yeah. Sure we do," said one firefighter who stood waiting to continue dousing the fire.

"Think you can get us some?"

He called over his radio and two shovels were brought across by a man with broad shoulders and black smeared across his face.

"Thank you, sir," said Melody. She took the shovels and passed one to Denver. Then she began to dig.

"Hey, we can do that for you," said the firefighter.

"No. It's okay. In fact, I think it's best we clear this area."

"Are we okay to carry on now?"

"Yeah, sure. Thanks for your help," said Frank. He turned to Melody. "Is this going to be what I think it's going to be?"

"We didn't have eyes back here but look at the soil. It's freshly dug."

There were four freshly dug areas. They stood at the one furthest from the barn. Melody presumed it was the first.

She began to dig carefully. Denver joined in.

Within twenty minutes, they saw a hint of blue come through the dirt. The smell of decaying flesh was stronger than the stench of the burnt barn. Melody gagged.

"Okay. No more," said Frank. "We're going to need forensics on this. Get the local unit to tape the whole area off and get it guarded. I'll talk to the chief." Frank began to walk away.

Melody's phone buzzed in her pocket. She pulled it out and saw a message from an unknown number. The message read, *Gift, Aptmt 204, Loughton Heights.*

"Sir, it's Harvey," said Melody. She smiled broadly. "He's alive."

"Stone?" Frank's mind ran through various scenarios. "Follow me."

They walked away from the smoky graves towards the driveway where Frank's car was parked.

"Where is he?" Frank asked.

"I don't know where he is now. But he's left us a gift. It looks like Cartwright's apartment."

"You think it's Cartwright?"

"No, sir. That won't be a gift."

"Okay. Get this place sealed off and get a local cop to drive you down there. Denver, make the arrangements to have that chopper picked up, please, so it can actually be used to go rescue people." He climbed into his car and started the engine. "I have an idea of where Cartwright might be. I'll call you if it works out."

CHAPTER TWENTY-EIGHT

FRANK NOSED HIS VOLVO INTO THE DRIVEWAY OF JOHN Cartwright's old house in Theydon Bois. It was fifteen minutes from the farm in Pudding Lane and would be an ideal place for Donald Cartwright to keep a truckload of illegally imported prostitutes while he sought a new venue for his despicable enterprise.

The long gravel driveway remained as Frank remembered it. The grass was unkempt and covered in leaves. When Frank had last been there, the lawns had been immaculate. The little groundsman's house near the entrance, which was where Harvey had lived, had been a delightful little cottage. The gardener had maintained its appearance as it was the first structure a visitor saw when entering the gates. When Frank had last been there, a man had also been boiled to death in the basement.

Kids had since smashed the windows and spray-painted graffiti on the door during its six months of being derelict. The media had reported the property as being the scene of horrendous crimes, which made it highly undesirable for potential buyers and a magnet for kids looking for a place to hang out.

Frank saw no rented truck at the front of the house so he pulled in and drove slowly up the smooth gravel driveway. He parked by the few steps that led up to the two huge front doors.

The right-hand door had been left ajar, no doubt by the same vandal kids that had broken the windows of Harvey's little cottage. Frank un-holstered his weapon and moved slowly inside. The house was deathly quiet and eerie. The door creaked when he pushed it open. Frank stood and waited for the noise to settle. Inside the great hallway stood two staircases, one on either side of the room, each leading up to the first floor in long winding arcs. Between the staircases was the doorway to the kitchen. On either side of the hallway was a room, each a mirror image of the other in size and shape.

Frank had been in John Cartwright's office before. He had stood alone in there and smelled the history of the Cartwright family's business plans, fuelled by brandy and cigarettes.

Frank wasn't interested in those two rooms. He stepped onto the hallway's parquet flooring and walked slowly and quietly between the grand staircases into the kitchen. The door to his right was closed. It was the door to the basement.

Frank pictured the scene he had found six months previous. He had walked down the stone steps slowly with his weapon raised at it was now. The cast iron claw feet of the antique bathtub had come into view. A warm damp smell of steam had hit him halfway down the steps.

The tub had begun to show itself as Frank descended. It had several gas burners placed underneath it to boil the water, but far more than was necessary to heat a bath.

Then he'd seen the hand. His initial reaction was that

somebody was indeed taking a bath, but the hand was unnaturally red and fixed in a tight, gripping position.

Sergio's pained death had been etched onto his wrinkled face.

Frank opened the door to the basement and listened. Hushed whispers silenced in the darkness below at the sound of the door. He pulled his flashlight from his jacket but kept it turned off. His gun was in his other hand poised ready to fire. He stepped down one more step then turned to check the door was still open.

The sole of a boot caught him directly in his nose and he tumbled down the hard stairs onto the concrete floor below. His torch rolled off into the darkness and his weapon was gone. He'd dropped it on the stairs.

He lay in the darkness and heard footsteps grow closer. Slow, deliberate steps. They were the steps of a man who had all the time in the world.

The basement was pitch black. Frank silently fumbled for his weapon but all he found was the cold hard floor. He searched behind him and grabbed a naked foot, which flinched away at his touch with an audible gasp. He crawled on his hands and knees away from the foot and the whispered gasp and was met with a hard blow to his face.

He spat blood and searched frantically around for the source of the attack. But the dark was so pure, there was no variance in shades. Just blackness.

Frank reached for his phone and pulled it from his pocket. But as soon as he hit the home button and the screen lit up, it was kicked from his hand. The phone scattered across the concrete floor and fell dark. Frank was sure his fingers had broken.

"Cartwright," he growled, "you're not making this any easier on-"

Another blow to his face. He felt his jaw move sideways

and he crumpled to the floor. The metallic tastes of adrenaline and blood mixed in the back of his throat. He panted with anxiety but forced himself to stand.

A boot stood on his back and slammed him back to the floor. He spat and sucked in the dust and stale air. His lips lay on the dirty concrete.

Hands tugged at his arms. He felt the bind of zip-ties and the bite of the plastic on his skin. Although he heard them being tightened, his hands had lost sensation. He could no longer trust his senses. The darkness, the fall and the blows had disturbed his balance. His ears rang. Or was it the sound of silence? His eyes saw only the darkness.

A harsh light flickered then burst on, filling the room with clinical white light and blinding Frank. He squinted but saw nothing. Hands dragged him across the room and pulled him to his knees. Then they pulled a rough and scratchy manila rope over Frank's head. Somewhere close by, the hands pulled the rope tight. Frank was forced to his feet then up onto his toes, gasping for breath.

He tried to talk but the rope cut deeper. His jaw shot pain into the side of his face from the kick. He growled with fear and fury.

Frank's vision settled and he opened his eyes. His sight focused on the wooden beam that his rope passed over, just like Sergio's had been. It was the same beam. The tight rope prevented Frank from looking down. But he could see many other ropes along the adjacent beam. He tried to count but he couldn't. It was too many. Thin slender wrists and limp hands were bound to the ceiling joists opposite him. He was central to them. More than ten, perhaps twelve, pairs of bound hands hung in the air at the bottom of Frank's eyesight.

"You remember this place?"

"Of course I do," he rasped.

"I grew up here, you know? This house. So many memories."

Frank thought of the room. Hannah. Sergio. Shaun.

"I used to play down here if it was raining outside. Cook used to bring me my lunch and I'd play with my toys. I remember my train set. It was spread across three big long tables. Those things are a work of art, you know? The detail was incredible. I had a mountain with a tunnel, trees and grass-"

"Sounds great. What every boy dreams of, I'm sure."

"Some of us dream of bigger things than train sets," said Donny. "Some of us dream of not having to share our families with scum like my foster brother and his little slag of a sister."

"So you were lonely?"

"No. Not lonely."

"And Harvey?" asked Frank. "Wouldn't he play with you?" Frank was buying time.

"No. I wouldn't let him. He'd go off with *Hannah*. They had their *own* games. Childish games."

"You were older though, weren't you?" asked Frank. "Didn't you have friends?"

"I still am older. Wiser too, perhaps." Frank heard the grin in his voice. "I'm still Harvey's big brother."

Frank forced a laugh. "You won't get away with it, Donald. The police are on their way." The rope bit tighter into Franks' throat and the last words trailed off.

"The police aren't coming. You came alone, didn't you? You wanted the bust for yourself. Couldn't resist it, could you?" Donny raised a handgun to Frank's temple. "I'll make it quick. As you can see, I have a lot of work to do tonight."

"Is that the best you can do?" said Frank. "A bullet to the head? Your brother was far more imaginative."

Donny slammed his fist into Frank's gut. The older man sucked air in through his teeth as much as his constrained throat would allow. "You want imaginative? Why don't I show you how imaginative I can be?"

A gunshot sounded. It was loud in the closed room. A chorus of muffled screams began.

"Quiet!" shouted Donny. He aimed the weapon at another girl. They were immediately quiet. Only their heavy breathing could be heard.

"Is that imaginative enough for you?"

"I can't see what it is you've done, Donald. Why don't you tell me what you did?"

The rope went slack and Frank dropped to the floor. The noose was still tight around his neck but he gulped in air while he still could. Frank saw the line of naked girls and their hands on the beam. They had been bound by the wrists and hung from their bindings to the ceiling joist. Frank counted twelve girls. At the far side of the line, the last girl's head slumped forwards and thick gloopy blood dripped down her body to the floor beneath her.

"One down," said Donny cruelly.

"How many rounds do you have left?"

"Enough," said Donny. "Do you like what you see? Pretty, aren't they?"

The girls were all below twenty years old and trim. Two of them looked almost starved. Frank could clearly see their ribs. They had all been bound and gagged.

"You want to see some more?"

"If you stop now, I'll see to it that you're looked after."

"Looked after?" Donny screwed his face up.

"Inside. You'll go to prison for sure. I can't stop *that*. But I *can* make sure you're looked after inside. You'll be comfortable."

Donny laughed bitterly. "Is that supposed to entice me?" Donny breathed and composed himself. "You'll need to do better than that, old man." He paused. "What's your name?"

"Me?"

"Of course you. What's your name?"

"It's Frank. My name's Frank."

"Ah, you look like a Frank." Donny moved towards the girls in front of Frank then turned back to him. "This one's my favourite, Frank," he said, and ran his hand along the inside of the girl's leg.

She twitched and squirmed but couldn't move away. Tears began to roll down her face. He traced the outline of her ribs with his fingers, softly and slowly, and then her breasts, which were full and firm. He took one in his hand.

"People pay a lot of money for this, Frank. Her skin is so soft." He traced the outline of the girl's nipple. "And she smells so..." He searched for the scent with his nose. "Feminine."

"Let her be, you sick son of a bitch." Frank looked away.

"I thought you wanted me to be more imaginative, Frank. How am I doing?"

Frank turned back slowly. He knew what he would see, but his eyes confirmed. Donny gently nuzzled the barrel of his gun between the girl's legs. He smiled at Frank, whose eyes began to run. Then Donny turned the gun upwards.

"What do you say, Franky?" Donny hissed. "Creative?"

"You're sick. Take it away."

The girl's bladder released a thin stream of liquid that ran down her legs. It pooled beneath her so Donny stepped away.

"She's dirty now, but it's okay. We have a spare or two."

"Is it worth it, Donald?"

"Donny. Call me Donny. All my friends do."

"You have friends?" asked Frank.

"Some."

"I thought your brother killed your only friend?"

Donny was silent.

"Sergio," began Frank. "Yeah. He was a coward too, wasn't he? No wonder you got on so well."

Donny stepped away from the girl and yanked on Frank's rope. Frank was dragged to his feet once more. The rope bit into his throat.

"What do you know about Sergio?" asked Donny. He raised the gun to Frank's forehead.

"I was the unfortunate bastard that found him," said Frank. "Right where I'm standing."

"Found him?"

"He was taking a bath. Didn't you hear about that?"

"Sergio was dead long before I came home," said Donny.

"Oh, so you aren't aware of Harvey's last great act then?"

"His last great act?"

"He works for me now. Did you know?"

"You lie. Harvey would *never* work for the police."

"It's the truth," said Frank. "*He* came to *me*." Frank paused then spoke calmly and softly. "And do you want to hear something very special?"

"Special?" said Donny.

"Special," replied Frank. "He *knows*."

"He knows what?"

"He knows your secret."

"*What* secret?"

"The one you and Sergio were hiding all this time. All those years. All those sleepless nights wondering what he'd do if he found out."

"We didn't have any secrets. Harvey knows nothing."

"Your father told him a few home truths and, I have to say, it certainly explains all this." Frank gestured at the girls. "You're sick and perverted, Donald. You need locking up."

Donny looked interested. "What home truths?"

"Let's just say that John Cartwright let slip about Sergio raping Harvey's sister."

Donny inhaled through his nose.

"Harvey brought Sergio down here. It's almost ironic that you hung me from this beam. It's the very same one as…"

"As what?"

"The one Sergio was hung from."

"Harvey hung Sergio?"

"No. Not properly. That was just to stop the little weasel running away. Much like you've done to me."

Frank paused to time his next sentence just right.

"Harvey boiled Sergio alive."

Donny looked distraught and incredulous. "He did what?"

"Remember the old copper bathtub that was here?"

Donny did. He glanced around for it.

"The police took it away a long time ago, Donald. Evidence. See what I mean by his imagination? He's so much more *creative* in his work."

Donny was silent.

"Like I said, Donald, I had the misfortune to be the one who found him. Sergio, that is." Frank moved his neck in the tight scratchy noose. "His skin was peeling off."

"Stop it."

"His eyes had even boiled white. I'd never seen that before."

"Shut up."

"He was all puffed up like a balloon. Thought he'd pop, we did."

"Lies."

"Truth, Donald. Truth." Frank softened his voice. "I heard the recording."

"What recording?"

"The one Harvey made."

Donny looked at Frank.

"Harvey recorded it all, you see," continued Frank. "I found the dictaphone on the little table over there."

Donny turned to see the table. It was covered in dust.

"You want to know Sergio's last words?"

"No," said Donny. His mouth had an upturned grimace of pure hatred. "I want to know what yours will be." Donny raised the gun and stepped back.

"He cried, of course, like a child," Frank continued.

"He was weak," said Donny.

"Yes. He was, Donald. He wailed and sobbed. Will you cry?"

"When?"

"When Harvey comes for *you*?"

Donny didn't reply.

Frank was running out of time. "His last words, Sergio's, you want to know what he said? You want to know what Sergio told Harvey as he hung right here from bound hands with the boiling water waiting below, ready to take him, to swallow him and cleanse him of his sins?"

"No."

"You *should* know."

"Don't say it."

"He was your friend?"

"I'll kill you *right* now." Donny's hands trembled.

"It was Donny."

Donny stepped back further.

"You hear me, Donald?"

"You're filth. You lie."

"He's been hunting *you*, Donald," hissed Frank. "You're the last one on his list."

"No. I know things, things he'll want to know. He won't be able to kill me," said Donny, almost convincing himself. "He'll need me alive. I have the answers to his parents and Julios. I'm the only one left who knows about Julios' mistake. I'm the only one who knows about Adeo."

"The reason he was sent away?"

"You know about that?"

"I've been around a long time, Donald."

"It doesn't matter. The secret dies with us both."

"Oh, I don't know about that, Donald. But you know what I do know?" Frank smiled.

"What?" Donny was breathing heavily. Frank had wound him up like a clockwork toy. He'd been easy.

The lights went out.

The basement plunged into darkness once more. The girls all gave a harmony of stifled whimpers.

"*He's here,*" whispered Frank.

Donny heard the grin in Frank's voice.

CHAPTER TWENTY-NINE

DONNY PANICKED. FRANK SAW THE LOOK OF TERROR IN HIS eyes. He knew Harvey and what he was capable of.

"I know it's you, Harvey," shouted Donny up the stairs. "You come down here and I'll kill them all. Every one of them."

Frank heard Donny's frantic breathing.

"You hear me?"

Harvey didn't reply.

"Answer me, you coward."

Harvey didn't reply.

"There's no escape, Donald," said Frank softly. "Stone, it's Frank," he shouted as loudly as he could with the restricting rope around his neck. "Don't come down here. Donald is going to lay his weapon down and untie me. I'll bring him up to you and you will not harm him."

Silence.

"That's it," said Donny. He moved towards Frank and roughly pulled the noose from his neck. Frank stood and rolled his head, freeing the built-up tension.

Frank felt the gun on the back of his head.

"Move." Donny's voice had become cold but scared.

Frank stepped cautiously to the stairs in the darkness. "Harvey, I'm coming up. Don't shoot me."

He took the steps slowly. The gun never lost contact with his skull.

They reached the top of the stairs and Frank turned left into the main hallway.

"Harvey, it's us. We're coming out," shouted Frank.

"Shut up. You're a hostage," hissed Donny. "Walk faster."

Frank picked up the pace just a little and strode into the hallway. Both front doors stood wide open and leaves scattered the floor. It felt like days since Frank had walked through the entranceway.

"Stop."

Frank stopped.

"Harvey, where are you?" called Donny. "Don't cock about."

The soft, stringed introduction of an orchestral tune that Donny recognised faded gently into the room. It came from John Cartwright's old office.

Donny turned sharply at the sound as it grew in body, strength and warmth. The cellos began to add their weight to the ensemble. Frank felt them through the wooden parquet floor.

"I know it's you, Harvey. Show yourself," shouted Donny. The music grew louder.

Donny shoved Frank forwards, who turned and looked him up and down.

"Open the office door," said Donny. "Don't do anything stupid."

Frank stepped over to the door. With each slow step across the huge hallway, Frank expected the blow to his head.

It didn't come.

He reached the door, turned his back to fumble with his bound wrists and awkwardly gripped the doorknob. Frank turned it and pushed it open before stepping clear of the door. He faced Donny, who stood with his gun raised at the empty doorway. He was visibly shaking. The gun moved in his hands.

With the door open, the music rang out clearer. The intensity increased with every phrase, every bar and every beat. Violins straddled the soprano and tenor rhythm and danced delicate melodies through the ever-increasing baritone body sung by the cellos.

The crisp string tones ran from the empty room through the open door and danced their way to freedom and beyond, through the front door and up the winding stairs where great paintings had once hung majestically. Sad-looking, empty spaces now stained the yellowing walls as only memories remained of the paintings that had been sold off separately. They now hung on foreign walls in some happier place.

"Harvey!" shouted Donny. "Harvey, stop playing games."

Frank stood motionless against the wall.

A loud thud came from the kitchen. Donny jerked his head. He was twitchy. He would snap soon.

"No. No!" shouted Donny, his voice rasped with fear. He stepped back away from the kitchen and towards the front doors.

The dead girl, number twelve, lay on the cold wooden floor at the top of the steps to the basement. She'd bled dry. Frank could see the top of her head. Shards of skull stood bright against the dark red insides.

Donny stepped closer to the girl's body. His head flicked back to Frank who stood still against the wall.

"Follow me," he said. Then he called out again to Harvey. "I know you're down there, Harvey."

Donny stepped across the body and rushed to the top of the stairs, his gun aimed into the darkness below. He fired off three shots into the shadows and stood waiting and watching for Harvey's body to slump to the floor.

Harvey didn't slump to the floor. He wasn't there.

30

CHAPTER THIRTY

HARVEY WAITED IN THE SHADOWS OF THE DIMLY LIT kitchen. He sat in the same place he had once before, a long time ago.

"I know you're down there, Harvey."

Harvey heard Donny call out down the stairs. Then he heard him fire off three rounds that would hit the hard floor and ricochet off to nowhere.

Harvey stepped up silently behind the door and stood tall behind his foster brother. He reached back and drove the sharp end of his blade through Donny's knee cap. It was a move designed to immobilise the victim by destroying the cartilage and knee joint. Donny would never walk on two legs again. Donny screamed and reached down at the pain instinctively.

Harvey was ready. He grabbed Donny's gun hand, twisting the weapon and his fingers. Donny tried in vain to squeeze the trigger but couldn't move his twisted fingers. His ruined leg gave way and he fell onto the top step.

Harvey kicked out hard at the back of his foster brother's head. Donny fell forwards, cracking his face against the concrete. He bounced from wall to wall and landed with a thud as his head gave a final bounce on the last step.

Frank walked slowly towards Harvey. He turned to show his bound and empty hands then stood by Harvey's side. Frank noticed Harvey's discomfort then the dark patch of blood and gaping hole in his cargo pants.

The two exchanged a glance but said nothing of the wound.

Frank peered down into the darkness then turned back towards the front door. Sirens wailed as police cars skidded across the tired lawn and ground to a halt on the gravel driveway.

Harvey closed the basement door.

"It's over, Harvey," said Frank.

Harvey didn't reply.

"Where are *we*, Harvey?" said Frank. "Are you on your own?"

Harvey looked from the darkness into Frank's eyes.

"This needs finishing, Frank."

"And then what?"

"It's over."

"And what do I get?" asked Frank.

"You got Brayethwait?"

"Yeah."

"You got Murray?"

"I did."

"You have Creasey?"

"We can find her," said Frank. "She's chipped."

"Do you have the clients?"

"Apparently so. An unexpected bonus."

Harvey opened the basement door wide and called down, "Come on. Let's go."

A nervous head appeared at the foot of the stairs.

Harvey waved her up. "Come on. It's okay."

The first naked girl was joined by others and they walked up the stairs together, but not like the scared children they had been, timid and afraid. They walked now with purpose, as a group, and with the confidence of women.

"You're setting them free? They are illegal immigrants."

"No, they're victims of human trafficking," said Harvey. "I gifted them to you."

"Gifted?"

"Gifted, Frank. They'll identify Murray as the ringleader if you treat them right. You've got your case."

There was silence as, one by one, the girls emerged from the stairway. Harvey stepped back to allow them room. The first girl walked out, covering her nudity with bloodied hands. Harvey's eyes followed her as she stepped out into the hallway and found Melody stood at the two great front doors. Harvey jerked his head in greeting. She stepped inside and took off her coat to cover the girl.

The rest followed slowly and shyly, each of them with their bloodied arms wrapped around themselves. Melody had them wait in the hallway then took the coats of the uniformed policemen outside and gave each girl a jacket before leading them out into the dark night. Flashing blue lights lit each one rhythmically as they were led down the steps to the warm, waiting police cars.

"How do we do this, Stone?"

Harvey didn't reply.

"We had a deal. You *stop* the killing, work *with* us, not *against* us, and you *don't* go to prison. You're putting me in a very difficult position."

"Donny raped my sister."

"I know, Stone. It must be hard to know that he's lying down there and all you have to do is walk down those steps and finish the job."

Harvey didn't reply.

"Think about *this*. Whatever mode of suffering you have in mind for Donny, whatever slow and painful death you're dreaming up right now, it'll be the last one. The last person you'll ever stop. The last person you'll save." Frank stepped around the dead girl on the floor and went to walk out the room. "If you choose to do that, it's the end."

Frank turned and walked away. Harvey watched him leave. He saw the blue lights lighting his long coat and greying hair.

"Carver."

Frank stopped and turned.

"Sometimes, people are meant to suffer. Sometimes, their sins are so great that a good man can't take another step in his life without knowing that he fulfilled that obligation when he had the chance. To make the sinner suffer. To help the sinner repent. It's an obligation to society, to those that fell because of him, and to those that, in some other circumstance, would fall at some other time, a month from now, a year, however long it is. We can't let those people walk the streets as free men."

"That's right, Stone. That's our job."

"But sometimes, Frank, it's those who have been wronged *themselves*, and have suffered at the hands of that monster, been humiliated, frightened and come close to death, who get the chance at retribution. The chance to fulfil their obligation. And it's the victims that *deserve* that chance, Frank, more than anyone. They're the ones who *need* the opportunity to repay that suffering. The chance to walk free, knowing that the monster that once destroyed their lives suffered a cruel and painful death."

"What are you saying, Stone?"

"It's a balance, Frank."

Frank began to walk towards Harvey.

"Do you understand, Frank?"

"I think I'm beginning to."

Frank looked down the dark staircase.

"Sometimes, Stone, a man who has a debt to pay needs to pay that debt to the people he owes."

"And sometimes, Frank, a man's vengeance is satiated from knowing that the debt was paid by someone who deserved it more."

Frank looked back at the cars waiting outside. Pale faces stared from the windows, ghostly in the night. He turned back to Harvey.

"If we go down there, what will we find?"

"A debt repaid."

"And who repaid the debt?"

Harvey glanced back at the police cars outside. Pale, scared faces stared back at him.

"Those who were owed. Those who were obligated and had suffered the most."

CHAPTER THIRTY-ONE

FRANK STOOD IN THE OPEN-SHUTTER DOOR OF HIS UNIT'S HQ. The smell of the Thames was strong and the cold morning breeze whipped between the building and the perimeter wall.

The first vehicle was arriving. It was Melody, of course, in her little sports car. A coffee in hand, she climbed out of the car and smiled.

"Good morning, sir."

Frank returned the smile. "Good morning, Mills. One of these days, you'll bring me one of those."

"One of these days, you'll ask nicely." She stood beside him.

"You have a report for me, Mills?"

"I'll type it up first thing. It was a late night, sir."

"You have an informal report?"

"On the case? We got them, sir."

"We did. How about the team?"

"The team, sir?"

"I've been here since two a.m., Mills, and you know what I've been doing?" Frank was standing tall, his hands deep inside the pockets of his long jacket. His breath fell away in clouds.

"Writing reports, sir?"

"No. I've been gathering other people's reports, Mills."

"Sir?"

"Two stolen boats?"

"Ah."

"One stolen BMW?"

"That was Harvey, sir."

"A stolen *helicopter*?"

"Not really stolen, sir. Commandeered."

"Do you know how many cars were written off in the fireball on the A12? The fireball you lot caused."

Melody puffed her cheeks then exhaled. "A few, sir."

"Nine, Mills. Nine cars written off. More were damaged, of course. And then there's the tanker full of petrol. Not to mention the VW."

"Ah, yeah. That's going to need-"

"Throwing in the river, Mills. That's what that's going to need."

Another engine drew nearer and Harvey's bike turned the corner.

"Oh, thank God for small mercies," said Frank under his breath.

Harvey rode past them and parked his bike inside beside the tools. Frank and Melody watched him remove his helmet and hang it on the handlebars.

He strode over to join them in the doorway.

"Stone," said Frank in greeting.

"Frank."

Melody just smiled at him. Harvey raised an eyebrow at her in return.

"Sleep well, Stone?" said Frank, without turning to face him.

"I didn't sleep yet."

Melody turned to him. "It's been days, Harvey. You must be shattered."

"I'll grab some rest when this is over."

"It *is* over. We did it, Stone."

"Not the job, Frank."

"What then?"

"The bollocking, Frank."

"The bollocking?"

Harvey didn't reply.

"There won't be any bollockings today, Stone. That I can assure you."

A loud engine approached with a scraping metallic sound. The ruined VW Transporter trundled around the corner with Denver at the wheel. Its exhaust dragged along the concrete floor beneath it. Frank, Melody and Harvey stepped out of the way to let Denver past. He parked next to Harvey's bike.

"Morning, team," said Denver, as he stepped out the van carrying a coffee. "Got my own thanks, Melody."

"What? Am I supposed to supply the coffee now?" she said defensively.

Denver walked around with a skip in his step and opened the rear door. It needed a hard push to open fully as the back of the van was smashed in from the impact with the truck. The shattered glass window had been replaced with a plastic sheet.

As the door opened, a friendly face appeared inside the van.

"Reg," cried Melody. "Oh, it's so good to see you." She hugged him as he climbed from the rear of the van.

"Welcome back, Tenant," said Frank, shaking his hand.

Reg turned to Harvey and Harvey held out his hand. Reg pushed it away then grinned and went in for a hug. Harvey was shocked but laughed and slapped his back.

"So you're all better? That was quick," said Melody as they walked towards the stairs for the debrief.

"No. I discharged myself. Had to sign some papers–"

"What? Why?"

"No internet. No TV. Nothing. I woke up with a banging headache. Then I waited four hours for a nurse to bring me something to eat." He pointed to the bandage. "I have to change this every day and I'm not supposed to look at TV or screens."

"Yeah, right," said Denver.

"I'll be okay. Severe concussion, they called it." He rattled a bottle of pills as he walked up the stairs. "But as long as I take these, I'll be okay."

"So you got airlifted out for a headache?" said Melody.

"And had a nap," said Reg. "I feel quite rested, actually. So what's been going on here then?"

Melody turned to Harvey who was walking behind her.

"Oh, not much, Reg," said Melody. "Not much at all, really."

32

CHAPTER THIRTY-TWO

FRANK STOOD BY THE WHITEBOARD AT THE HEAD OF THE room. Reg and Denver were on the comfy couches. Melody sat at the small table facing Frank and Harvey stood with his arms folded leaning against the wall by the door.

"Okay," began Frank. "The players?" He pulled the lid off his pen.

"Brayethwait," called Melody. Frank wrote *Brayethwait* on the board and then asked, "Status?"

"Custody," replied Melody.

"Who caught him?"

"Harvey," said Melody.

"You put the cuffs on him," said Harvey.

"Well, *you* didn't *kill* him," replied Melody.

"I presume there's a story behind that?"

"Erm, yes, sir," said Melody. "Along with the audio confession nailing Creasey and Cartwright."

"Good. I want that in your report. Next?"

"Creasey," said Denver.

"Status?"

The team looked at each other.

"She's chipped, sir."

"Tenant, I need you to find her on LUCY and coordinate with Essex Police."

"Yes, sir. First job."

"Next?"

"Cartwright," said Denver.

The room fell silent.

"Status?"

"Deceased," said Harvey.

Frank turned to Harvey. "How? For the report, I mean."

"Repaid debt."

Frank nodded. Melody looked at the two men in wonder. She picked up on something between Frank and Harvey, something strong, a bond or understanding.

"Next?"

"Mason," replied Reg.

"Mason?" asked Frank. "Who's Mason?"

"Cartwright's minder, sir," said Melody.

"Status?"

"In custody," said Harvey.

"And a wheelchair for the rest of his life," finished Melody.

Frank raised his eyebrows and looked between Harvey and Melody. "I'd suggest we leave the details out of that if need be," said Frank.

"Next?"

"Roger," said Denver.

"Roger?"

"Murray's accomplice."

"Status?"

"Deceased, sir."

"The fireball?"

"Yes, sir."

Frank wrote *Deceased* next to Roger's name.

"Next?"

"Murray."

"Status?"

The team were silent.

"Aha, yes. That one was my bag. The big fish. My quarry." Frank looked smug. "Nice to know I can still bag 'em while my team is off stealing helicopters, boats and BMWs."

"Well done, sir," said Melody, smiling.

Frank wrote *In Custody* beside Murray's name on the board.

"How many boats, helicopters or cars did *I* steal to catch him?" he asked.

The team didn't answer.

"How many explosions did I cause to catch him?"

Silence.

"Good. That's what I like to hear." He turned and smiled to let them know he was playing. "Okay. So hostages. We haven't had a hostage case for a while."

"Eleven girls were freed, sir," said Melody. "Saved."

"Good. Reports from forensics say they found four bodies buried behind the farm. Plus one in the house. It looks like the girls will point the finger at Murray for a free lift home to wherever it was they were from."

The team were smiling. Melody looked around her. They were a bunch of misfits, but she felt at home with them.

"Good work, team," said Frank. "I might add that, if we do plan on commandeering any mode of transport in the future, we run that decision by me beforehand. It'll save a lot of explanations."

"Yes, sir. We're sorry, sir," said Melody.

"What about Stokes and Narakimo?" said Harvey.

Frank raised an eyebrow and turned to Reg.

"Reg, can you-"

"Yes, sir. Work with the local units and bring them in."

"Thanks, team. That's not a bad result. Messy. But still a good result," said Frank, drawing a circle around the list of outcomes on the board. "I want all your reports in by close of business."

Denver stood. "Sir," he began, "the VW, it's pretty much fu-"

"We need a new van, Cox, do we?" Frank cut in.

"Yes, sir."

"I might be able to help there."

All eyes fell on Harvey, who lifted his rucksack from the floor and threw it to Frank.

Frank caught it and winced at his fingers that weren't broken but were still sore. He looked at Harvey questioningly.

"Should I be concerned?"

Harvey didn't reply.

Frank unzipped the zipper and looked inside. He tipped the contents of the bag onto the large table at the head of the room. Bundles of bank notes fell out of the bag and piled high across the surface.

"How much?" asked Frank.

"Three hundred grand, give or take."

"Three hundred thousand pounds?" Frank sounded surprised.

"Give or take."

Frank paused. "Stone, can you take a walk with me?"

"Do I have a choice?"

"Stone," replied Frank, "haven't I always given you choices?"

CHAPTER THIRTY-THREE

FRANK AND HARVEY STOOD SIDE BY SIDE LEANING ON THE railing beside the river. The air was frigid and Frank's jacket flapped in the wind that ran across the choppy water.

"We had a good result," said Frank. "Much of it was down to you, I hear."

Harvey didn't reply.

"You're an asset, Stone. I want you on the team. You've come a long way. I want to take you further."

"Further?"

"Further from your past."

Harvey didn't reply.

"You had unanswered questions. Are they behind you now, Harvey?"

It was the first time Frank had called Harvey by his first name.

"We all have questions, Frank."

"But *you* needed answers. Some of us move on. Some of us get over it."

"My sister killed herself, Frank. Did you expect me to move on and get over it?"

"No. Part of me understands."

"Part of you?"

"My wife died three years ago. I still don't understand."

"I never knew."

"Nobody does," said Frank.

"What if you knew somebody out there had the answer? Would *you* look for it?"

"Maybe, Harvey. Maybe not. We had many years together, my wife and I. So many good times." Frank gazed across the water. "It took a long while for me to move on, to get over the bitterness and to enjoy life again."

"Do you enjoy life, Frank?"

"No. Not really. But I appreciate what we had. It doesn't really matter what happened now or how she died or by whose hands. Nobody can take those memories away from me. They're mine."

"We're all different."

"Yes. We are, aren't we? Especially you, Harvey. I've met some cold bastards in my time, ruthless killers."

"I probably knew them."

"You probably did. In fact, you probably killed some of them too in your past life."

"Maybe. I didn't make a list."

The truth was that Harvey didn't need a list. He remembered the faces of them all.

"You have a quality, Harvey. You're a talented man. Like I said, you're an asset. But you have this good within you. I've tried to find the word before but there isn't one. You're not a bad person. People like a man who stands up for society's weaker members."

"I'm not sure where this is going, Frank. If you want me, I'm back on the team. But you need to take the noose off."

The mention of the word noose sent vivid images of the basement into Frank's mind.

"Noose?"

"Yeah, noose. I can't have the threat of prison hanging over me. You can't expect me to jump with both feet if my head is in the noose."

Frank sighed. "You're right. But I can't take the noose off until I *know* you've left your past behind, Harvey."

Harvey didn't reply.

"You still have questions, don't you? You're still seeking answers."

"My whole life has been a lie. One big web of deceit. How would you feel?"

"I'd feel angry, I guess."

"I'm past angry, Frank."

"I understand."

"Do you? Where were you born, Frank?"

"Near Edinburgh."

"And your parents?"

"Frank and Carol Carver."

"Are they alive still?"

"No. They died a long time ago, Harvey. They led a very quiet life. My father was a farmer. He didn't earn much, just enough for them to get by."

"Old age?"

"Yes. Peacefully in their sleep. Both of them."

"Nice."

"You could call it that."

"What if somebody told you one day that all that was a lie? That everything you've ever been told about them had been a lie."

"What do you mean, Harvey?"

"There never *was* any Frank and Carol Carver near Edinburgh and they *didn't* die peacefully in their sleep."

"I see."

"Do you?"

"You want the answers?"

"I'll *find* the answers. One way or another, Frank."

"So the noose stays on, does it?"

"If the noose stays on, I keep one foot out," said Harvey.

"What if I helped you?"

"Help me? Do what exactly?"

"Find the answers, Harvey. Us. The team. We have the means. You have the motivation, as it were. I don't see why we can't do some digging. It might make it quicker."

Frank turned to him. He stood two feet away. Harvey turned to face him.

"I don't want to be the one to remove the noose," continued Frank. "But I'll help you remove the noose yourself. Like you said in the house, sometimes it's those who need to repay the debt that should be given the opportunity."

"And then the noose is gone?"

"And then the noose is gone."

"How do you plan on helping me? I've searched my entire life and I've just hit walls every step of the way."

"Well, not so long ago, I had a noose around my own neck, Harvey. A man stood before me as I stand in front of you now. He knew that death approached. He heard the footsteps in the darkness." Frank's eyes softened. "In his frantic despair, and as death loomed over him, a tall and fearless figure, he spoke of your parents, Harvey, and the answers you seek."

Harvey didn't reply.

End of Book 2

STONE FALL

The
Stone Cold Thriller Series
Book 3

1

CHAPTER ONE

TWO MEN SAT IN A BLACK CAB OUTSIDE ST LEONARD'S Primary School. The driver looked like any other black cab driver and took the same fare every day. He was dressed for comfort in trainers, a t-shirt and jogging bottoms, just like he did on most days. The other man sat in the large rear space with an open newspaper and flicked through the trashy photos of celebrities. He wore a pair of jeans and a loose jacket over an open-necked polo shirt.

All around them were mums and friends chatting while they waited to collect their children from school. The women stood in groups of two or three making idle small talk between glances at the front doors of the large brick building. They were waiting for the first opportunity to break away from the meaningless chat and get back home to their lives.

Among the mums were several men, not dads, but drivers, who stood unsmiling beside their cars. The school was private, well-regarded and extremely expensive.

The driver had parked a hundred yards back from the main gate, close enough for the little girl to see the cab, but far enough away from the eyes of prying mothers.

The main doors opened, and dozens of uniformed kids ran out towards the waiting arms of their mums. They showed pictures they had painted during class, some opened tupperware boxes to display the cakes they had baked and passed their mums their bags to carry for them. Other kids met their drivers and simply climbed into the back of the car without conversation.

"You'll never get away with this," said the driver to the man in the back. "She's just a kid."

"Relax, she is merely a pawn," said the man in the back seat. "Just like your family, Mr Bell. I have no use for them, but sometimes we need a little…" he paused, "encouragement. I have far greater ambitions, Mr Bell, than anything to do with the lives of young children. I deal in nations. So much grander, don't you think?"

"But she won't recognise you, you'll scare her," the driver replied.

"Inshallah, by the time she opens the door it will be too late."

The intuition of the man in the rear paid off. A short while later the door was opened by a little girl, and she climbed in.

"Hey, who are you?" she said.

"Oh, you must be Angel?" said the man in the back. "It's okay, I am helping Mr Bell today. Why don't you close the door, it's cold outside, yes?"

Angel turned and pulled the heavy door closed, before settling herself onto the seat.

"Do you need help with the seatbelt?"

"No, I can do it myself, I do it every day."

"Oh, well you must be a very clever girl then, Angel. Drive on."

The driver indicated, pulled away from the curb and joined the slow moving traffic.

"So," said the man in the back, "tell me about your day, Angel. Did you make a painting? Or cook a cake?"

"You don't make a painting, you paint a painting, and you don't cook a cake, you bake a cake."

The man laughed. "Such a clever girl, you know when I went to school, we didn't learn such things."

"Where did you go to school?"

"A long way from here, Angel. Somewhere very far away, but it is always in my heart, and I can find my way home with my eyes closed. Is this place in your heart, Angel?"

"My school?"

"Yes, your school, your friends and the city. Do you love them?"

"I love my friends, but not my school."

"And the city, Angel? Do you love London?"

"I don't know, I haven't been anywhere else, so I don't know what's better."

"You really are a very clever girl for somebody so young."

"How do you know how old I am?" Angel asked.

"Oh, Angel, we know all about you. And your Mum."

"Where are we going? This isn't the way."

"I must be honest with you, Angel, we are going for a little holiday. Perhaps afterwards you will know if you miss your home or not."

The man was busy pouring a liquid from a small plastic bottle onto a handkerchief.

"Where are we going? What's that you're doing?" asked Angel. "I want my mum."

"Little girl, you have asked too many questions. It's nap time."

CHAPTER TWO

Ordinary people walked past where Harvey sat, they led ordinary lives, had ordinary jobs, wore ordinary clothes and had ordinary reasons for being there.

Harvey was far from ordinary. He wore casual clothes, tan boots, black cargo pants and a plain white t-shirt underneath his leather biker's jacket, and he sat in a coffee shop amongst ordinary people on Queen Victoria Street in the city of London. But he was looking for the extraordinary.

He'd been sat for over an hour, observing.

His ear-piece was barely visible unless somebody was looking for it. It crackled into life.

"Stone, how are you doing there?" It was Melody Mills, his colleague.

He scratched his face and discreetly tapped the button twice to confirm nothing had happened yet.

"We're doing another pass along Cannon Street, keep your eyes open and shout if you see him."

He was looking for an ordinary man in an ordinary world with an extraordinary reason for being in London.

A group of four women walked past the coffee shop,

where Harvey sat by the window in the corner with his back to the wall. Protecting his back was an old habit, part of his past life, back when he'd looked over his shoulder more than he looked in front.

The women laughed and joked at something one of them was showing on her phone, and they walked on carefree.

Two men in suits passed them walking in the opposite direction. One of the men, a short, stocky man in a tight suit and long heavy jacket casually turned to admire them walking away then continued on. The man turned to keep up with his friend and bumped shoulders with another man in jeans, trainers and an oversized fleece jacket. His hair was shaved bald, and a tattoo crawled up his neck. He carried a rucksack slung over both shoulders and walked with his hands in his jacket pockets at a faster than average speed.

Harvey stood up, left the coffee shop and began to follow the bald man along Queen Victoria Street. The man crossed over Bread Street, where he passed the group of girls without looking or admiring, then crossed to the other side of Queen Victoria Street. Harvey stayed on his side of the road, but matched the man's pace, giving the impression he was heading somewhere ordinary like the hundreds of other people in view. It was London and hiding in plain sight was fairly simple if you acted ordinarily.

The man turned into Lambeth Hill, a quieter road that led down to Upper Thames Street. Harvey crossed the road after him, dodging between taxis and cars as the man disappeared from sight. He sprinted across the last few lanes of traffic and up to the corner of Lambeth Hill then resumed his brisk walk. He turned the corner but saw nothing ahead. Harvey discreetly checked around him, in doorways and alleyways, nothing. The street was empty of cars and people. Harvey began to run.

"Stone, you're on the move, we saw your tracker, you have eyes on him?" said Mills.

Harvey began to jog. "Lambeth Hill, heading down to Upper Thames Street, he's on foot moving fast, jeans and a blue fleece, shaved head and carrying a rucksack."

"Reg has you on-screen, we're on Puddle Dock coming onto Upper Thames Street now."

"Target has disappeared," said Harvey.

"You lost him?"

Harvey didn't reply.

Harvey picked up the pace of his run. He rounded a corner and caught a glimpse of the man ahead turning onto Upper Thames Street, heading toward Mills and the team. He was running.

"I've got eyes on him, he's onto me, he's running toward you on Upper Thames-"

"Okay, we have a visual."

Harvey heard the roar of the team's Audi a hundred yards away, followed by the screech of tyres on tarmac. He sprinted to the end of the road to see the man running across the four-lane street, then disappear into a cobbled road between two buildings that led to the waterside. Angry drivers honked their horns, and other cars skidded to avoid crashing into the mass of stopped traffic. Harvey leapt across a car bonnet and narrowly missed being hit by another vehicle skidding to a halt in the next lane.

Melody was a hundred yards ahead, running away from the man into an alleyway to cut him off.

Harvey reached the riverside, he looked left then right, and saw the tattooed man running across the Millennium Bridge above him. Melody was fifty yards behind him sprinting hard between groups of tourists. Harvey carried on running and made his way onto the bridge but by the time he reached it, he was well behind Melody and the man.

By the time Harvey reached the centre of the bridge, crowds of people blocked his path. He called out to them, "Move, move, move," and barged through the barrier of pedestrians. He reached the middle of a crowd where people stopped and were staring, men and women held their phones up making a video of the scene. Harvey broke through to find the man standing with a machete to Melody's throat.

"Let her go, Victor," said Harvey. "What's she done to you?"

"What's she done to me?" Victor replied. "You think I don't know you guys have been watching me?" Victor was shaking, he was at breaking point.

Harvey didn't reply.

"It ends now, right here."

"*You* don't tell *me* when it ends, Victor."

Victor looked surprised.

"You think I'm going to play into your hands?" began Harvey. "You think I'm going to tell you what you want to hear, Victor? You think this is a movie? Well it's not, you're holding a machete to my friend's throat, and you have two possible outcomes." Harvey stopped and stared at him, then spoke calmly at the man. "You drop the machete, she arrests you, you live-"

"And if I don't, you're gonna take this off me and kill me in front of all these people?"

"I haven't decided if you die yet, Victor," replied Harvey, "that's your gamble isn't it?" Harvey gave an almost imperceptible nod to Melody, who smashed her head back into Victor's nose. The man released his hold just enough for her to move away from him and twist his left arm back in one smooth action. But Victor was stronger than he looked. He pulled Melody's arm away, released her grip on him and grabbed her hair. He wrenched her head back, and with his right hand swung the machete back, ready to land the blade on her neck.

Harvey pounced forwards and tackled Victor while his arm was swung back. He pinned Victor against the railing and crunched his forehead down onto the man's nose. Victor swung again, this time at Harvey, but Harvey stepped into the swing, blocked Victor's arm and ripped the weapon from the bald man's hands. Harvey turned the blade and, with a flick of his wrist, jammed it down into Victor's arm. The sharp, heavy knife sliced through the man's wrist like it was cutting bananas from a tree. The hand fell uselessly to the floor.

Victor doubled over in agony, and Melody reached out to cuff his good hand, but he saw it coming and stood upright, sucking in air between his gritted teeth.

"Are you coming easy, Victor?" said Melody. "Don't make this any harder than it needs to be."

Harvey pulled his SIG. "On the ground, now," he shouted at Victor.

"I have to," said Victor. "They have my son," he reached for the bloodied cuff of his ruined arm.

"Don't move, Victor, put your arm down now," shouted Harvey. "Melody get those people out of here," he continued, not releasing his eyes from Victor's.

"Who has him, Victor? We can help," said Harvey.

Melody turned, and shouted to the crowds, "Move back, get out of here, come on, move back."

"They'll kill him if I don't-"

"Victor, talk to me."

The noise of the crowd control fell to a distant hum in the background of Harvey's concentration, only the dull thud of his heartbeat in his ears played in his mind. Victor stopped with the fingers of his left hand inside the right-hand cuff. Harvey glanced down and saw the small switch and two thin wires.

Tears began to roll down Victor's face. He looked up at the sky, and his fingers stumbled in the sticky mess.

Harvey fired.

Two shots in Victors' forehead. It had been a risk. Victor could have still hit the switch, but if Harvey hadn't fired, he would have definitely hit the switch.

Victor fell to his knees, his hand still on the little bundle of wires that stuck out of his cuff. Before his body had a chance to fall to the ground and possibly blow them all sky high, Harvey stepped forwards and caught him, then with a grunt, he hoisted the man over the handrail.

The dead body plummeted to the river below and landed face down. There was no explosion. There was no surge of water. There was no more Victor Hague.

CHAPTER THREE

FAISAL BIN YASSER AL SAYAN LEANED AGAINST A STOLEN black taxi in a mechanic's garage in Stratford, East London. There were three taxis in total, all parked side by side in the narrow space. The warehouse was an open space, cluttered with car parts, such as gearboxes, exhausts and engine blocks, arranged in no particular fashion. To the right-hand side of the space were four rooms built from concrete blocks with heavy wooden doors. Each room was twelve-foot square. Door number one stood ajar, door two was locked and doors three and four were also open.

Stood beside Al Sayan was Angel. She looked up at him and then around at the dirty garage.

Al Sayan took a phone from his pocket and dialled a number from memory. The ringtone was answered quickly, but no voice offered a greeting.

"I know you're there," said Al Sayan, "I can hear you breathing."

"Where is she?"

"All in good time," said Al Sayan.

"Who are you?"

"Oh, you'll know me when we meet, but until then-"

"You're messing with the wrong person."

"Is that correct?" asked Al Sayan. "I believe it is me who will call the shots, as you say. Let's keep the childish threats out of this, it is purely business, something I understand you are extremely good at."

"What do you want? Money?"

"Do not insult me, I am no petty criminal."

"Tell me what you want, it's yours, but harm her, and I'll make sure you suffer."

"How very boring," said Al Sayan. "We have a mutual friend. Or should I say, we had a mutual friend? Until this morning."

"Hague?"

"Ah, so you watch the news, it was exciting wasn't it? He was supposed to complete a task, after which I would release his child," said Al Sayan. "He failed his task, as you know."

"And his child?"

Al Sayan tutted. "Such a waste of life."

"Tell me what you want, I haven't failed yet."

"I know, Victor spoke very highly of you, I believe we shared a shipment."

"He's got a big mouth."

"He had a big mouth," corrected Al Sayan. "He also told me you are planning something. I'm not a collector, but I am very interested in ancient artefacts."

"So go to the museum."

"No, not my style. Something as valuable as the item you have your eye on could fund my little project."

"Your little project?"

"Let's just say, I'm cleaning this city, this country. It is filthy."

"So leave, go back to wherever it is you came from."

"It is not that simple I'm afraid. I just couldn't sleep at night knowing of all the sinners walking freely here." Al Sayan paused. "You could help me. We'd make a great team."

"I won't help you,"

"Then I am afraid little Angel here will die a very painful death." He looked down at the little girl who cried out. "You hear her?" said Al Sayan.

"I do, let me talk to her."

"No, you need to earn that."

"You're a sick son of a bitch."

"Wrong again, what I am is dedicated."

"So I do the job for you, and you give me my daughter back?"

"That's the gist of it, but there is one more thing," said Al Sayan. "An obstacle."

"What is it?"

"How closely did you watch the news of our mutual friend?"

"I have an eye for detail."

"So you would have seen the hero?"

"He's known to me."

"I know he is. He's your obstacle, I want him out of the picture," said Al Sayan, "and his friends, they're already too close."

"How do you expect me to do that?"

"I have already made plans for Mr Stone, he has ruined my plans once too often. He will be running now, so you should find it easy. The buddha arrives today and will be locked in the vault. The auction is in four days. In exactly two days time I will be creating quite a large diversion, somewhere close to the auction. The chaos will provide a means of escape for you and your team. Your death or capture will result in our little Angel here growing wings earlier than expected."

"Don't you-"

Al Sayan disconnected the call.

CHAPTER FOUR

FRANK CARVER STOOD OUTSIDE HIS OFFICE ON THE mezzanine floor in the team's headquarters. He looked down and watched as his team arrived. Headquarters was a brick building beside the Thames Barrier in Silvertown, East London. It stood alone in a compound surrounded by a high wall and electric gates. The team occupied half the building, the other half belonged to the team of engineers that ran the barrier on a daily basis.

Frank's team was a specialist black ops team that reported to the Home Office, via MI5. They were not the balaclava-clad assault team that would abseil down buildings and storm into hostage situations or terrorist cells. They were a very small team of highly skilled individuals. Each of them was a specialist in their own field, and collectively they worked domestic organised crime investigations, while SO10 and other units dealt with the rising terrorist threats. The thinking behind Frank's unit was that while the well known and well-funded black ops operatives stormed buildings and kicked the doors in of terrorist cells, the organised crime world was left wide open for gangs and criminals to run amok. The growth in organised crime since 9/11 and 7/7 was big enough to warrant charging a few highly skilled operatives with the task of keeping the organised crime world at bay. The team let these criminals know that they didn't have free rein. Taking down the ringleaders and, most importantly, shutting the doors of sources to prevent crimes happening again was their main objective.

Denver Cox drove the brand new VW Transporter into the HQ building. He parked between Harvey's BMW motorcycle and the team's Audi in the engineering area immediately to the left of the large sliding shutter doors. The engineering area was his own domain. He was the driver, the mechanic and the engineer, plus he was an expert pilot in both fixed-wing aircraft and helicopter.

Denver had joined at the bottom and worked his way to the top. He'd been a car thief and was just fifteen when he was arrested for the theft of a Ferrari, which led to him being found guilty of stealing several million pounds' worth of supercars. Denver's case had been kept out the public domain and was investigated by the Home Office. Eventually, after little persuasion, Denver's parents were given a choice. He could to go to prison, where he'd serve a few years at Her Majesty's pleasure, although his record would mean he stood little chance of success when he got out. Or, he could join an adolescent rehabilitation programme for promising youngsters.

Part of the rehabilitation programme had involved Denver receiving track time to further his driving skills, which then led to him pursuing his pilot's licenses. The right people in the right positions working for the government had seen his skills and saw the talent within the young rehabilitated offender. He was turned from being criminally minded into one of the good guys. But he wasn't just good, he was the best driver and pilot on the force. He'd worked with all the major crime divisions within the MET, and the Home Office had seconded him to various other government factions. He was a rags to riches success story.

Denver stepped out of the brand new van and stretched. He'd been in the seat for the entire day. The van was black with tinted windows and had been significantly fixed up by Denver. He'd dropped the diesel engine out and replaced it with a four-litre V6. He'd upgraded the suspension, put bigger wheels on and improved the brakes. From the outside, it looked like a standard VW Transporter, but with Denver at the wheel, it could keep up with most cars on the road. It was an ideal team vehicle.

Each team member had a specific skill set, and the Home Office had furnished them all with the tools required for the job. Denver had his engineering area, three large snap-on tool chests, an engine hoist, power tools and an overhead hoist capable of lifting over a tonne. The engineering section was Denver's ideal workshop.

Melody Mills was a surveillance expert and sniper, plus she was as smart as they come. She had aced every exam she had ever taken and worked her way up from entry level constabulary. After spending a few years as a detective, she was then pulled into SO10 where she met Frank. She was thirty years old and led the team's operations. Her space comprised a caged-off area, twelve feet square and full of lockable secure storage cabinets containing Diemacos, Hecklers and Koch MP5s, as well as a SIG Sauer P226 and P228s, plus enough ammunition for a team of twenty.

Melody climbed from the passenger seat and walked to her desk which stood beside the cage. Next to the desk were two more lockable storage cabinets, containing Steiner binoculars for the team, bugs, mics, cameras, transmitters and receivers. The two containers were Melody's cache of surveillance equipment. She meticulously cleaned every item on a weekly basis. The rifles, the handguns, the sights, and the magazines were all oiled. The surveillance equipment was removed from individual cases and cleaned, to ensure it was in tip-top condition. Her desk was bare save for a lamp, her laptop and a desktop printer.

Denver opened the rear door for Reg to step out. Reg Tenant was just closing down his two computers that lived permanently inside the van. He climbed out and walked over to his command centre which was immediately to the right of the sliding shutter doors. Twelve twenty-four-inch screens were mounted to the wall in three rows of four. Beside Reg's seat was a lockable server rack that housed the hardware displayed by the monitors.

Reg was the team's tech genius. He too had been taken into the adolescent rehabilitation program for promising youngsters, though his skills were very different. By the time he was twelve, Reg was hacking into major oil companies, causing enough havoc for shares to drop. The company would launch their own investigations, which again failed, due to Reg watching their every move. He then moved onto the MoD and created such a disturbance that the security training that each employee underwent was rewritten to include network security and protocols. Reg highlighted holes in the defence system time and time again, which caused the entire MoD dark fibre network to be overhauled. Several million pounds later, Reg was caught trying to access the upgraded MoD firewalls and his parents, as Denver's had been, were given two choices.

Frank led the team. He was a highly experienced investigator who had worked his way through the constabulary and several detective units, eventually leading an organised crime division of SO10 before being given the chance to run a team of specialists. He was in his fifties, and if he wasn't thinking about the case they were working on, he was thinking about his retirement.

The team performed almost the same function as his SO10 team had, but without the restrictions of a government organisation. He was answerable to the Home Office and MI5, but aside from that, nobody knew of them. The team's existence wasn't public knowledge. It couldn't be, if the public were aware of them, there would be uproar. They weren't licensed to kill, per se, but they were licensed to get the job done.

Frank was happy with his team. It was still early days, and they needed a little guidance, but they worked well together and got the job done, and that was important for both the team's success and Frank's retirement.

Six months previous, the team had taken down a human trafficking ring, in which the perpetrators had been offering Eastern European girls for sex, and allowing the clients to kill them. It was a niche market tailored to the sick and twisted but had been growing quickly. The prostitution and murders were not necessarily on the radar of the team, but the human trafficking element had placed them on the scene. The investigation had taken a few weeks, and the operation to shut them down had taken three days. The team had come together well.

Harvey Stone, the team's loose cannon, had gone AWOL as the operation had gone from investigation phase to operational. Frank was well aware that Harvey had spent many years chasing the man who had raped and killed his sister. Then, when the rapist's name had shown up in the human trafficking investigation, Harvey had gone solo.

Eventually, and only when Melody Mills had been taken hostage by the offenders, Harvey had shown his true colours, and dropped his own agenda to save his colleague. That was when Frank knew Harvey was a good fit. Passionate, tenacious, and loyal to a T.

Harvey, however, was in Frank's opinion a lost soul. His parents had both been killed when Harvey was a baby, and he still never knew their names, how they died, or why they died. He and his sister had been found and fostered by the leader of one of the largest crime families in East London, the Cartwrights.

When Hannah was raped, Harvey had sat outside and listened to the screams as a child. He'd seen one of John Cartwright's men leave the basement where it had taken place and remembered the face that had been silhouetted in the dark kitchen window. Hannah had eventually killed herself at fifteen years old, and Harvey had been taken under the wing of Julios, the family's hitman.

Harvey had been trained to kill by Julios from a young age, and as soon as he was ready, at twelve years old, he'd killed the man who he knew raped his sister. The next twenty-two years had been spent training for the day he found the other men. He had become Julios' underling. His protege. He'd become a formidable killer. It had been down to Harvey's skills as a killer, and the flow of good blood that ran through his veins, that he'd been given the choice to join the team, or go to prison.

Frank hadn't always been an honest cop. In fact, he barely remembered the days when he'd been green and keen. He'd been tangled up in the criminal world's web of deceit for far too long. Often, a favour from one criminal led to him risking his job in return, which required another favour from another criminal. The cycle had been endless. Until, twelve months previously, when he'd watched through a window in the blackest of nights, as Harvey killed the man who held Frank's balls in his hands. The man had been Terry Thomson, the renowned East End villain.

Shortly afterwards, Frank had discovered the body of a man that Harvey had boiled to death, laying in an old copper bath in the basement of Harvey's foster father's house. It had been the man Harvey had searched for more than twenty years; his sister's other rapist. Sitting beside the corpse on the cold stone floor was the missing sex offender that Harvey had left to Frank as a gift. He had been tied to a wooden beam in the cellar alongside the still-steaming, old copper bath.

On the grounds of the estate, Frank had also found a transit van full of Heckler and Koch MP5s that he'd been looking for, another gift from Harvey.

A bad man would have killed the sex offender, sold the guns on the black market and continued his life of crime. But Harvey had left all those gifts for Frank then retired to a little farm in the south of France. He'd escaped the life of crime, that was how Frank knew that Harvey wanted out. It was how he knew that the good inside him was stronger than the evil. It had been at a time when Frank was forming the team. They had the brains, sniper and surveillance. They had the driver, pilot and mechanic. They had the tech guru. But they had needed someone with the skills that can't be taught. Someone who didn't mind getting their hands dirty, for the right reasons. That someone had been Harvey.

So given the choice of prison or working for the team, Harvey had opted to work for the team. It had been a difficult transition. Harvey had spent his entire life surrounded by criminals and avoiding the law, and now he was adjusting. Harvey was guided by his moral compass, which was true and straight but lacked experience of the formalities. Frank was helping him adjust.

The mastermind behind the human trafficking case had been Harvey's foster brother, Donny Cartwright who, as it turned out, had been one of the men on Harvey's list. Donny had been the last man that had raped his sister.

Donald Cartwright had been killed during the trafficking investigation, eventually torn to pieces by the very girls he'd enslaved. But Harvey still had unanswered questions in his life. There were still men on his list, though the list had no names, just empty spaces to fill then tick off.

Frank had promised to help Harvey find out the reasons behind his best friend Julios' murder and his parent's deaths, their names and where they were buried, so that Harvey could move on with his life. Until then, Harvey was on a leash, and prison loomed over him like an angry black cloud.

Frank watched Harvey step from the van and walk casually over to his desk. He was a fearsome man, Frank thought. Harvey wasn't an oversized muscle head, he was athletic but strong. His confidence carried across the room wherever he walked, and people stopped and stared like the devil had passed them by.

Harvey didn't have large, wall-mounted monitors. He didn't have a tool chest or cabinets with automatic weapons and surveillance equipment. Harvey had a small desk holding his laptop with a desk drawer containing his nail clippers, which he used to trim his nails at any opportunity. Behind it was his punch bag, which hung from the mezzanine floor above. Harvey's needs were basic.

"Stone, Mills, my office," Frank called down to them.

CHAPTER FIVE

"DEBRIEF?" SAID FRANK, LOOKING AT HARVEY.

Harvey didn't reply.

"So we lost Victor Hague," said Frank. It wasn't a question. He had overheard the comms between the team, and then he'd seen the resulting explosion of media on the news. 'Breaking news. Unknown security organisation tackles terrorist with an explosive vest on London's Millennium Footbridge.' The video had been captured by a nearby tourist.

"He was loaded, sir," said Melody, "his backpack-"

"I can imagine what he was wearing, Mills," interrupted Frank, "but now we've lost our way in to the explosives supplier, and will need to start again."

"He would have been gone anyway, sir. He was going to blow something up, people, it's the city, sir. It would have been a disaster."

"Agreed, so what do we have to go on?"

Harvey tossed a plastic shopping bag onto Frank's desk.

"What's that, Stone?" asked Frank, keeping his tone calm, but secretly outraged by having somebody throw a bag onto his desk rather than pass it to him in a more civilised fashion.

"Hague's hand," replied Harvey.

"His what?"

"His hand."

"You cut it off?"

"It was either that, or he would have cut Melody's head off, in front of hundreds of members of the public," said Harvey.

"He put a machete to my throat, sir," said Melody, by way of confirmation.

"Yes, I saw the footage, someone recorded it and sent it to the BBC. Nice of them, eh? They didn't show the hand, oddly enough."

Harvey and Melody were silent.

"What's the plan with it?"

"With what, sir?"

"The hand, Melody, are we going to stuff it and stick it on the wall?"

"No, sir, but we thought it prudent to take it away from the general public."

"Can Reg do anything with it?"

"Just prints, sir, but we already know what Hague was involved in, I can't see it telling us anything else."

"Okay, print it, and send it off to wherever they have the rest of him. Then get everyone in the meeting room."

A short while later the team walked up the stairs to the meeting room and assumed their positions. Reg sat on one of the sofas, Denver sat on the arm of the other sofa, Melody stood near the coffee machine, and Harvey leaned on the wall by the door. Frank stood at the head of the room by the two whiteboards.

"Firstly, team, thank you all for your efforts this morning, we managed to avert a potential disaster, and there is one less bad guy on the loose. However..." Frank inhaled deeply. "There are two pieces of slightly not so good news." The team were all listening intently. "We cannot take credit for today's actions. We are, as you know, informal, we don't exist. SO10 will take the credit. Secondly, and far more importantly, we no longer have an in into Hague's world, and ladies and gentlemen, without Hague we won't know when the next shipment will be coming. But we can be quite certain that the first shipment has been distributed."

"How does that concern us?" asked Melody, "Surely that's a job for Customs and Excise."

"Typically, yes, however one of the buyers is known to us and falls under our jurisdiction," replied Frank.

The team thought on who might want explosives.

"Want a clue?" asked Frank.

The team were quiet.

"My theory is that the explosives sold to our man will be used to blow a vault door."

"Not people then?" asked Melody.

"No, Mills, not people, that would be terrorism, and as you pointed out earlier, that does not fall under our jurisdiction." Frank put the whiteboard marker down and walked to the front of the table where he sat back and leaned on the edge. "Hague had his fingers in many pies, all different flavours. Our particular pie is quite straightforward. I had Reg analyse Hague's phone records. Lots of data, most of it useless. Untraceable phones, unknown owners, short calls, coded messages. Mostly garbage." Frank cleared his throat. "However, one number that Hague had been talking to had contacted somebody we all know, who has evaded us for many years. Somebody who targets diamonds and art, and somebody who, with the right amount of plastic explosives, could get into any vault."

"Who, sir?" asked Reg. "The suspense is killing me."

"Not yet, Tenant," replied Frank. "First, I want to paint a picture." Frank hit the space bar on his laptop, which was connected by HDMI to the TV in the room. A photo of a small, green Chinese buddha appeared on the large screen.

"Can anyone tell me what this is?" asked Frank.

"A scented candle?" said Reg.

Melody smiled. "It's a buddha, sir. By the colouring, I'd say it was jade, and by the condition, I'd say it was old."

"Good," said Frank. "It is, in fact, an ancient jade buddha. How old?" He offered the question to the room.

"Five hundred years," said Denver.

"Older."

"Seven hundred and fifty," asked Reg.

"Older."

"Fifteen hundred?" asked Melody, her eyebrows raised in doubt.

Frank looked at her, then paused. "Older," he said quietly.

"Two thousand years?" asked Denver.

"Give or a take a century, experts can't date it accurately."

"This is fun," said Reg. "What's the next question?"

"Why am I showing you it?" asked Frank.

"It's a target," said Melody. "You think somebody's going to steal it?"

"Two points to Mills," replied Frank. "The two-thousand-year-old jade buddha is going up for auction later this week."

"Where?" asked Denver.

"Cornish House, out in deepest darkest Essex according to a website I found this morning."

"Essex?" said Denver, "Why there?"

"You'll see when you go. It's an old English manor house, surrounded by miles and miles of greenery with no tunnels, a large vault and no possible way of escaping. The owner is of English gentry and is a keen collector of art."

"So how do we know it's going to be stolen?" asked Reg.

"You'll see," said Frank. "How much do we think it's worth?" Frank offered the question to the room again.

"Ten million?" asked Denver.

"Twenty million," said Reg.

"You're both wrong," said Frank. "The item has never actually been bought or sold. It's been passed down through generations in a particular family of the aristocracy, and the starting bid price has not yet been disclosed."

"So how does anyone know how much money to bring to the auction?" asked Reg.

"For somebody so intelligent, you do ask some stupid questions, Tenant," said Frank. "Buyers of this type of artefact do not turn up to an auction with any money at all. In fact, the only people invited to the auction are ten of Europe's biggest collectors, all with a combined net worth greater than many small countries."

"So there's no price?" asked Melody.

"Not yet, but it's known that all of the buyers want the piece, just how far they'll go is yet to be seen."

"Crazy," said Denver.

"So that's what, where and why," said Harvey, speaking up for the first time.

Frank turned to face Harvey. "Who do you think would want this more anything in the world?"

"Only one person I know who *could* pull the job off."

"Go on," said Frank, smiling at the suspense.

"Stimson," said Harvey.

"Adam Stimson. Bonus points to Stone," said Frank, smiling. "Hague's phone records showed contact with one number that is in direct communication with Adam Stimson on a daily basis. What does that tell us?"

"Stimson's active. He's smart," said Harvey, "He won't contact anyone himself, he has men that do things like that for him."

"So if Stimson needed a little bang for his next job-"

"He'd have his closest man arrange it, he wouldn't trust anyone else," said Harvey.

"So if we add two and two?" asked Frank.

"Stimson needs explosives for a vault, and coincidently a priceless buddha is up for auction," said Melody.

"Your job is to recce the manor house. There's a restaurant attached so maybe you can go for breakfast," began Frank. "I want to know exactly how you'd get in and out. Once we have our own grounding, we should be able to put plans into action to stop Stimson. Maybe this time we'll actually catch him."

"What about the source of the explosives?" asked Denver.

"Good question, it's a great question in fact, but alas, it's not our problem."

"Customs and Excise?" asked Melody.

"Yes, we need them on our side, they're already on our case about the human trafficking ring. If we find any information on the source, we pass that on to them, I don't want internal enemies." Frank stood, put his hands in his pockets and waited for the team's attention. "Tenant, you'll be here in headquarters, I want information on Stimson's man. Stone, Mills, and Cox, you'll be visiting the manor house tomorrow morning. Like I said, I want to know exactly how *you* would do the job." He addressed the last part of the statement to Harvey.

"Lastly," said Frank as he opened the door and turned back to the room, "the auction is in four days. We have no information on when the buddha will arrive, so assume that the robbery will take place any time between now and then. Any questions?"

The room was silent.

"Good. Go get me Adam Stimson."

6

CHAPTER SIX

"OKAY, REG, ALL ON EYES ON YOU RIGHT NOW, I'M AFRAID, get us something to start on," said Melody.

There were standing at Reg's command centre.

"Righto, Melody, so let's recap, we're putting eyes and ears on Stimson's man. And I guess you all want a visual of the manor house?"

"Stimson will be in the last phases of his plan, we're well behind already," said Harvey.

"How can you be sure?" asked Melody.

"Well, Stimson is a known criminal, not just by the police, but in the world of the criminals too. He's extremely good at what he does, he's a planner. You know how I feel about planning–"

"Failure to plan is planning to fail," the team chorused.

"Exactly," said Harvey, ignoring his colleagues' efforts at making fun of him. "So you need to be aware of a few things here. Adam Stimson has never been arrested, he's never been to prison, and likely never will."

"Because he's too good?" asked Reg.

"Yeah, and he's careful, Reg," said Harvey. "He wouldn't

even buy moody fags from a bloke in a pub let alone make calls to an explosives dealer. But there's one thing that I do know for certain."

"Go on," said Melody.

"He's a glory hunter," said Harvey. "He'll want the job done so precisely that he'll be on it himself. He doesn't just send men out to do jobs for him, he's involved. It's his plan, it's his way, or not at all. He's one of the smartest strategists you'll come across and will have back up plans for his back up plans. We don't just need one way of doing the job, we need to think of every way we'd do the job, and we don't have much time. Stimson's had the luxury of time."

"What makes you so sure?" asked Reg.

"A year ago, the Cartwrights and the Thomsons were both planning to do a diamond heist, you all know the one?"

"Right, yeah. The Stimson's got away with it in the end, didn't they?"

"Yep, the diamonds are still missing. You know why the Cartwrights and the Thomsons didn't actually succeed?"

The team looked at each other.

"Didn't you kill Terry Thomson?" asked Denver.

Harvey didn't reply to the question. Instead, he continued. "Because Adam Stimson is smart. He knew that the Cartwrights and the Thomsons would go after the diamonds, so he arranged for twenty-four Heckler and Koch MP5s to be lost, and end up in Thomson's possession. The Cartwrights bought twelve of them, leaving the other twelve with Thomson. This led both of them to believe they had the hardware to do the job, but each of them was so engrossed in stopping the other from doing the job, a gang war started. Meanwhile, guess who digs a neat little hole somewhere nobody thought of digging and walks off with the diamonds?"

"Adam Stimson?"

"Not a single shot fired," said Harvey. "He's a smart man."

"So do we have Stimson's phone?" asked Melody.

"Yep, we do as it happens," said Reg. "I've been monitoring it for ages, but nothing ever happens."

"Of course nothing happens. As long as Stimson knows we're listening, that phone will be clean," said Harvey.

"It's encrypted actually, I can see and access everything, but can't hear the calls. Military grade hardware, way out of our league without significant investment."

"Did you ever meet Stimson?" asked Melody. "You know, in your-"

"In my days as a criminal, Melody?" finished Harvey. "Nobody ever met Adam Stimson, even John Cartwright never knew what he looked like. I told you, he's smart."

"But we have his phone, he can't be that smart."

"You have his phone because he lets you have his phone, that's why you won't find anything incriminating on there. Yeah, we'll get contacts, and we can isolate the links from his trusted inner circle to external contacts in the outer circle. But we'll never nail Stimson like that, and he knows we won't bother arresting his inner circle when it's him we really want."

"Smart," said Melody. "So who is his inner circle?"

"Who's the guy that made contact with Hague?" asked Harvey.

"Lucas Larson," said Reg. "Lifetime criminal. His last stretch was five years in Belmarsh for intimidating a witness and perverting the course of justice."

"Is that the only name we have to go on?" asked Harvey.

"So far," replied Reg. "I've got LUCY analysing his records to show his most frequent numbers to see what we've got. But I'm going to need some more time here to build a full picture," said Reg.

Harvey and Melody took the hint and walked away, each going to their own desks in opposite corners of the room.

Melody sat and unloaded her SIG Sauer. She placed the

unused rounds back in the little cardboard box inside her ammo cabinet, then stripped the SIG. She turned on the lamp and pulled her cleaning kit from her desk drawer. Each weapon Melody fired was meticulously cleaned before being returned to the armoury.

Harvey put his own SIG his desk, cracked his neck left then right, and stretched his arms up and around. His body felt tight after sitting in the coffee shop all morning. He turned and landed a left jab into the punch bag, followed with a right hook that sent the bag swinging up to a nearly horizontal position. It swung back towards him and Harvey stopped its return dead with an uppercut. Jumping up, he took a wide grip on the steel joist that supported the mezzanine floor above him. He did a few pull-ups without counting, then dropped to the floor.

"How's that research coming on?" asked Frank from upstairs. "Doesn't sound like much is happening."

"I think I've found something," said Reg.

Harvey looked at his watch, it had been less than two minutes. He strolled over to Reg and stood beside him, Melody and Denver came to see what he'd found.

"Most common dialled numbers from Stimson's phone are here." Reg outlined a group of numbers pasted into a text file on the far left, lower screen. There were three numbers.

"Family?" asked Melody.

"I don't suppose Adam Stimson is much of a family man myself, but, he does appear to enjoy talking to his mum. This is her number here, not a burner, it's even registered to her name." Reg highlighted the number. "He calls her at least twice a day. The evening calls seem to be the longest, morning calls are probably trivial mother and son stuff. Would you agree we can eliminate this number?"

"I'd agree with that," said Melody. "Harvey?"

"I'm not sure what's meant by trivial mother and son stuff, but I'll take your word for it," said Harvey.

Melody sensed the awkward reply. It was an area that the team usually avoided as they knew Harvey had been searching for his real parents' killer for many years.

"I call my mum at least twice a day unless we're on a job someplace," said Denver. "I can hear it in her voice that it makes her day, so I just can't bear not to anymore."

"How often do you see her?" asked Harvey.

"Three or four times a week. She does a curry for us all on the weekends and usually has a little something for me to take home if I swing by during the week."

"A curry at the weekend? Don't you have a roast dinner, Denver?" asked Reg.

"A roast? No, my mum's vegetarian, we get a killer curry, rice and homemade naan bread."

"In all this time I don't think I've ever heard you talk about your family," said Melody.

"You never asked before," said Denver.

"How about you, Reg? How often do you see your mum?" asked Melody.

"Oh, pfff, maybe once or twice."

"A week?" asked Denver.

"No, not that often."

"A month? You only see your mum once or twice a month?"

"No, a year, give or take."

"A year?" cried Melody.

"Yeah, what's wrong with that?"

"How often do you call her?"

"Once a month, maybe."

"Reg, the woman brought you into the world, take some time out and go see her."

"Most blokes are the same, except Denver," argued Reg.

"You only get one mum, Reg, look after her," said Denver.

"Maybe if she cooked for me, I'd go round more often."

"Maybe if you went round there-"

"Are we actually going to look at these names?" said Harvey.

"Sorry, Harvey, bit insensitive of us," said Denver.

"Not insensitive, but if we're going to talk about family lives and what we're doing for Christmas, I'll go home early. I've got better things to be doing than stand here listening to a load of old women talking."

"What exactly do you do at home, Harvey?" asked Reg. "I imagine you go home, sit down and stare at a blank wall, but I bet in reality you have a really crazy hobby that you keep secret, like knitting or something."

"I think about you a lot, Reg," said Harvey.

"Me? Really?"

"Yeah, with no skin on. Now show me what you found."

Both Melody and Denver smirked. Harvey was really beginning to take his place in the team. He filled a hole that needed filling but brought much more to the table than just muscle and bravado. Melody looked at him with one hand on the back of Reg's chair. She thought about how different he was than the guy Frank had described when he first put the idea of bringing an ex-hitman, who was born and bred to live on the wrong side of the law, into the team.

"So all these numbers here," said Reg, "are out. But these two here are still in the game." Reg was in his element, he loved pulling information out of nowhere and presenting his skills to the team. "This number especially gets dialled an average of fourteen times per day, that's Larson's."

"Fourteen times per day, who calls anyone fourteen times per day?" asked Denver.

"A rich man who has a number two. He's someone Stimson delegates to. A trustee," said Melody.

"Who does the other number belong to? And what else do we have on Larson?" asked Harvey.

"Well, Lucas Larson. No previous, forty-five years old, born and raised in Munich, then moved to Britain when he was eighteen," said Reg.

"So Stimson calls three people frequently, his mum, Larson, and who else?" asked Denver. "Would he even need anyone else?"

"Yes," Harvey cut in. "Stimson has Larson, who's probably highly intelligent, and capable of running the show himself, but is held to Stimson for some other reason. This other number is someone very unintelligent, but is likely pretty handy and never too far away from Stimson."

"His bodyguard?" asked Melody.

"I'd say so. If we're going to get to Stimson, we'll need to take this guy out. But if we're going to catch Stimson, we'll need to be all over Larson," said Harvey. "I'm telling you, if we get Larson, we'll stand a much better chance of getting a shot at Stimson. Where does Hague fit into this?"

"He doesn't anymore, he was just the explosives supplier," said Reg. "Larson's contact."

"Okay, but remember what Hague said? He was going to blow himself up, and he told us he *had* to do it, they had his boy," said Harvey. "Is this two different crimes or what? Who had his boy? He was carrying a bag full of explosives, are we forgetting that?"

"We're talking about going after a diamond thief who is buying illegally imported explosives to perform domestic organised crime," said Frank, who was leaning over the railing above them and listening, "which is exactly why this team exists. Nothing else concerns us."

The team looked up at Frank.

"So what do we have?" asked Frank.

"We have a location, a motive, and a link to Stimson, via Larson," said Melody.

"I also have Larson's phone monitored."

"Who's the third guy?" asked Frank. "The third number on Stimson's phone."

"An unknown. Harvey thinks it's a bodyguard."

"Makes sense," said Frank. "Now what?"

"I'd say we take a visit to the manor house tomorrow morning, go for breakfast, scope the place and work out how they're going to do the job," said Melody. "Until we get out there, this is all speculation."

"We're tracking all three phones, so we'll know if they're on the move."

"The auction is in four days," said Frank. "Harvey, if you were going to rob the place, when would you do the robbery?"

"As soon as possible."

CHAPTER SEVEN

"I NEED SOME AIR," SAID HARVEY. HE STRODE TOWARDS the single door beside Reg's command centre and stepped out into the cold November air. The wind off the river a hundred yards away bit into his skin as he walked down to the riverside to lean on the railing and watch the water.

"Penny for them?" said Melody, who came and stood beside him.

He turned to her. "We're missing something."

"It's always like this at the start of an investigation, we're still gathering intel."

"We're making up theories. We should be out there, gathering facts."

"Yeah, well, a little extra time on the intel makes gathering the facts a lot quicker. It's okay." She held a steaming cup and offered him some. "Coffee?"

"No thanks, I'm going to go for a run soon. Something's missing, I need to clear my head."

"You know," began Melody. "I never said it before, but I owe you thanks. Actually, I owe you a few thanks, you saved my life." Six months ago, Melody had been captured in the human trafficking investigation. She'd been stripped of her clothes, had her hands tied and been dumped in the freezing ocean to drown. Harvey had dove in and rescued her.

"You already thanked me for that."

"You came back to us," she said. "I never thanked you for *that*."

"You know why I'm here?"

"In the team?"

"Yeah."

"Go on."

"Frank gave me a choice, either I stay and work in the team, or I go to prison."

"For what?"

"I boiled a man alive, Melody." Harvey looked across at her, and she nodded. She'd found the body with Frank. "Plus, doubtless Frank would heap on as many unsolved crimes as he could."

"So you're not here because you *want* to be here?" Melody was taken back.

"I wasn't, not at first." Harvey smiled. "I kind of like you guys, it's a big change for me, I never had people on my side like this before. It was always dog eat dog."

Melody moved away. "No, Harvey, it's wrong. You need to be with us one hundred percent. We're a team, we're all one hundred percent invested in this, and if one of us isn't, then that person is putting the rest of our lives in danger."

"Hey, I'm here. I made the choice, didn't I?"

"It wasn't a particularly *hard* choice, was it? Let's face it."

"Yes, it was a hard choice, Melody. All my life, I've been hiding from people like us, people like Frank. How easy do you think it was to do this? But you know what, it's been a nearly year now, and we're a damn good team. I like it here."

"So could you walk away right now?" asked Melody.

Harvey didn't reply.

"Frank still has you, doesn't he?"

"He said he'd help," replied Harvey. "Frank won't take the noose off until all my questions are answered, and I can focus."

"What questions? You *found out* who raped your sister."

"My parents, I need to know who they were, why they were killed-"

"And who killed them?"

Harvey didn't reply.

"Jeez, Harvey, we all have questions, we don't all go around moping about them, you have to move on."

"When I have the answers, Frank will take the noose off."

"And *then* what?

"And then I get to choose, I guess."

"Between?"

"Freedom."

"And? Freedom and what, Harvey?"

"Boredom?"

Melody moved closer to him, "This is freedom to you?"

"I've given it a lot of thought, Melody."

"And?"

"I'm doing what I always did, what I'm good at. Only now I'm doing it for the good guys."

"Is that all?"

"No, I'm also doing it with people I like and respect."

"Like friends?"

"I guess you could call it that. I've only ever had one friend, so I'm not one hundred percent sure."

"What happened to him?"

"He was killed,"

"Tell me about him."

"What can I say? Julios was the only one that was ever there for me. He was my foster father's bodyguard, then when Hannah died, he became my mentor, he trained me."

"Trained you to be a *killer*?"

"Yeah, but not at first. I was only twelve right, it wasn't a career move. But I was angry, he channelled my anger, taught me self-defence, aikido and all that. He helped me grieve."

"He showed you how to kill though?" asked Melody. "And not get caught."

"He showed me how to do many things, Melody."

"And you know who killed him?"

"I will do. If it take me another twenty years, I won't stop, Melody. I'll find him just like I did the men who raped, Hannah."

Melody was silent for a moment. "So, if we're friends, tell me something. About *you* I mean. Something that doesn't involve killing."

"Like what?"

"Like where you live, where you go, what you do. You're a mysterious man, Harvey Stone, and we're, well we're a curious bunch. Maybe if we knew more about you, we could all be better friends?"

"This is what I do."

"And where do you go? At night I mean, where's home?"

"Not far."

"You're being coy," said Melody. "Okay, is there a potential Mrs Harvey Stone?" Melody smiled, she was enjoying watching Harvey be uncomfortable.

"Not really, women never really worked out for me, they asked too many questions they wouldn't like the answers to."

"You have your eye on anyone? I mean, come on, we all need an outlet right?"

"There's no-one, Melody."

"Okay, nice to know. Maybe I can set you up with one of my friends?"

"That won't be necessary, Melody."

"Okay, I can see this is making you uncomfortable, let's

leave it there, but I am going to learn you, Stone." She looked up at him. Harvey looked back. Then, over her shoulder, he saw a huge black plume of smoke erupting from the Isle of Dogs, which was visible just a few miles along the river. It was followed by the faint, dull thump of a distant explosion a few seconds later. The noise was deep and angry-sounding, rumbling towards them and beyond.

"What the-"

"Back inside, let's go," said Harvey.

They ran the hundred yards back to the building and walked inside. Denver was underneath the van, Reg was tapping away furiously on his computer keyboard, and Frank was nowhere to be seen.

"Reg," said Melody, "get me the satellite of the Isle of Dogs."

"Eh? What for-"

"Just get it up, there's been an explosion." She called upstairs, "Frank, you need to see this."

"See what?" he called from inside his office.

"Explosion. Isle of Dogs. It's a big one."

Frank stepped from his office and looked down. "How long?"

"One minute ago, Harvey and I saw it from the river."

"Looks like Canada Square, but the smoke's too thick to see where exactly," said Reg.

"Reg, get us a news broadcast, we may as well see what's happening."

In true Reg style, he dragged multiple news feeds across several of his screens, muted two of the channels and played the audio of one over the speakers. According to the presenter, a video had been sent in by a member the public who had captured the scene on his phone. Media teams who were also in the area were setting up. All three of the separate news broadcasts showed breaking news at the bottom of the screen, and after a few minutes, live video feeds began to show what the team saw on the satellite imagery. Thick black smoke and people running from the buildings. A reporter on the scene stood amid the chaos of crowds, ambulances, police cars and fire engines, all working hard to evacuate the public and close off the area. A few teenagers could be seen taking videos on their mobile phones behind the reporter. Another news channel repeated the video footage from moments after the blast, sent into them by another member of the public. Smoke poured from the ground floor lobby of One Canada Square, an iconic tower in London's Canary Wharf.

Ten minutes had passed, and people were still emerging from the smoke-filled building. The reporter stopped talking to allow the cameraman to film the remaining workers walk away. Most came out coughing and ran past the firefighters who stood outside ready to douse any fires that emerged. The evacuated workers held shirts and rags up to their faces. A group of women held their shoes in their hands and ran along the street barefoot, directed by the police to an assembly point away from the building. The assembly point was down some steps in a small square beside the river. One man casually strode away, his coat and bag hung over one arm, in his other other, he held a small boy's hand tightly. The man was Asian, the boy was Caucasian.

"That man there, watch that man," said Frank.

"What do you see?" asked Reg.

"The man with the boy. He's too casual, he looks out of place. He's not scared, plus look how he's clutching his bag and the boy's hand, he's heading for the kill zone."

"The what?"

"No, stop him," said Frank to the screen. "Reg get me someone on the scene. I can't be the only one seeing this."

"Who do you want? The officer in charge?"

"No, his phone will be crazy, get me the Isle of Dogs fire department, quickly, Reg."

The phone rang over the speakers and, a few seconds later, a woman answered hurriedly. Frank spoke over her introduction. "Sorry, lady, this is DI Frank Carver from SO10, I understand your units are attending the blast in Canada Square?"

"Who are you? Yes, they are–"

"Good. Get hold of your officer in charge, there's a male IC6 currently walking from the scene towards the assembly point, and he's loaded. Do it now, you can make a note of this number and call back for confirmation of my credentials, but I urge you act quickly. We can iron out your questions later."

"This is most–"

"Lady, there's a man with a bomb in his bag walking towards the assembly point. Make the call."

"Disconnect the call, Reg."

Melody, Reg and Denver all looked across to Frank who stood transfixed, staring at the screens. "Stop him, come on, someone." He spoke to the screen as the suspect, just meters away from the reporter, remained within the cameraman's frame. Another broadcast showed a group of firefighters stood beside the truck. The team watched as one of the men took a call over his radio and began to look around.

"There's our man," said Frank. "He's spotted him." The firefighter shouted a uniformed policeman over to him and began pointing towards the suspect. A group of several hundred people had congregated in the assembly point five hundred yards from the building. The policeman immediately got on his radio, and another one appeared from the steps, heading down to the assembly point. The policeman was small in the picture in the distance behind the reporter, but the team could easily see him emerge from the steps and hold his hand up to stop the suspect with the bag. He returned a call into his radio.

More people emerged from the building and ran towards the assembly point.

"No," said Frank. "Get away. For god's sake, take him down."

There seemed to be an argument between the cop and the suspect, who was indicating that he wanted to go down the steps to the assembly point. But the uniformed policeman blocked his path and was struggling to hear his commanding officer over his radio.

Then the broadcast went bright white, immediately followed by a *Signal Lost* message across the screen.

The team were silent. Reg folded his arms over his head and rested it on his desk.

"Oh my god. Did we really just see that?" said Melody, her head in her hands.

Harvey and Denver stood silent.

Frank lowered his head, removed his glasses and rubbed the bridge of his nose. "Team, take as long as you need to digest what you just saw. We reconvene in the meeting room as soon as everyone is ready." Frank turned and walked up the mezzanine stairs his office. Harvey watched him wipe his eyes as he closed the door.

The white screen was directed back to the news studio. Melody had walked backed to her desk to be alone. Reg held his face in his hands, and Denver and Harvey stood transfixed at the shocking news.

The news reporter began to talk with a broken and emotional voice. "We have just witnessed a tragedy. A cold-blooded attack on our nation's capital has just taken place. Ladies and gentlemen, a hotline is being set up for those who want to communicate with loved ones who may have been at the scene. We are still waiting for a damage report-"

"This is disgusting," said Denver. "I feel sick."

"It's cowardly," said Harvey. "I wish I could get my hands on the sick bastard."

"You and half the country, mate."

"I feel so helpless, stood here watching it on the news. We're supposed to be fighting this sort of thing."

"No mate, that's not us," said Denver. "We need to focus on what we're doing, we're not trained for this sort of thing." He paused. "How many do you think were-"

"Killed?" asked Harvey. "Who can say? We'll find out soon enough. But what does it matter? If it's one or one hundred, it's still a loss, it's still an attack."

The news reporter broke the tension between the two men. "And this just in, the BBC have just received information from known terrorist, Faisal Al Sayan, claiming responsibility for the blast. He has made no threats, no demands." The screen showed a photo of a Middle-Eastern man in a white headscarf with a hooked nose and thick beard. The reporter continued. "The Afghani man, who is at large in the UK, has claimed the blast a victory that, in his own words, will send a message to the city. He claims he will cleanse London, and make it a beautiful, sinless place once more."

8

CHAPTER EIGHT

FRANK WAITED PATIENTLY FOR THE TEAM TO ARRIVE, HE allowed them time to sit and settle, then began.

"I think it's prudent to observe a one minute silence for those who were lost in the tragedy we all just witnessed.

The room was already silent and remained so for the minute's entirety.

"What we all just saw is truly the height of what we are up against in modern day Britain. Such a cowardly attack is just one example of the war we are fighting. The people you saw congregated in the assembly area and running along the streets are those we serve, those we are sworn to protect."

The team nodded.

"However, this unit is *not trained* to fight the war on terrorism. There are others that are fighting that particular war. We fight alongside them, yes, and behind them, for sure." Frank took a deep breath and focused on each of the team individually.

"We are professionals, we *must* remain professional, and we must continue with our work as hard as it is in times like this. I *know* the urge to go and offer assistance is high, but *trust* me, *now* is the time we need to be vigilant. *Now* is the time that criminals attack, when all eyes are looking elsewhere. *Now* is the time that Al Sayan will be moving, planning, and preparing for a follow-up attack. But Al Sayan is not our concern, our target is Stimson. We *must* remain emotionally intelligent. *Do not* let the horrors that unfolded today obscure your vision. Or else we will lose this battle. Is that understood?"

The team nodded.

"I do *not* want any heroes. Is that clear?"

"Yes, sir," said Melody. Reg and Denver both grumbled a confirmation.

"Tenant?"

"Yes, sir," said Reg.

"Any questions?"

"No, sir."

"Good, well done, guys, get to it. I have every faith in you all."

9

CHAPTER NINE

THE MOOD WAS SOMBRE AS THE TEAM PREPARED.

Melody began loading the back of the van with her kit. She had Peli cases containing binoculars, a small tripod that held a sighting scope, and another for the DLSR camera, along with various lenses. Each item, including the binos, camera and scope, had the foam insert carefully cut out around it to ensure a snug fit.

Reg had given her a bag of chips, which LUCY was able to pick up and communicate with once they were activated. Melody didn't intend on getting too close to Larson, but if the opportunity arose, she would slip a chip into his pocket or his car. The chips themselves were tiny, and if placed correctly, the carrier wouldn't even know they were there.

LUCY was an extremely powerful software and hardware combination that Reg had built and developed himself. Officially, LUCY stood for Location and Unilateral Communication Interface, which produced the acronym, LUCI. But Reg had given her the unofficial name of Lets Us Catch You, so she remained LUCY.

There had been no expense spared on the design and

build of LUCY. The interface ran on a master server which was water cooled, had twenty-four multicore processors and one hundred and twenty-eight gigabytes of memory. In addition to the master server, LUCY called upon the resources of three slave units with identical specs to the master. The software ran on a virtual operating system so that if at any point the master server crashed, a slave unit would step up and take its place.

LUCY's database was striped across several block-level storage systems, giving her a combined storage potential of one hundred and twenty-eight petabytes. The entire system was powered by four high-powered, uninterruptible power supplies and a backup generator.

The immense power and speed of the software merely provided the infrastructure for LUCY's interface. Her capabilities allowed Reg to link together various other pieces of software to provide a one-stop shop for satellite imagery to identify the location, speed, height above sea-level and temperature of digital trackers that could be placed anywhere. The chips were five millimetres square, which meant that they could be put in a mobile phone, items of clothing or even, as Reg had done to Harvey six months previously, hidden inside a watch.

In addition to the tracking of chips, LUCY could monitor mobile phones on virtually any network internationally. This allowed Reg to not only hear the conversations but access a live view of a smart phone's interface, which provided access to messages, calendars, contacts and more.

LUCY's primary function had been to monitor communications on suspects and monitor operatives' whereabouts. However, due to the success of the system, Reg had been granted an additional budget to enhance the system to include the security of the building, the comms system, and the digital telephone system. Reg had taken the upgrade to the next level and was able to control headquarters within the system. He could open and close the shutter doors, change the temperature, manage the alarm system and control the lighting. These additional features didn't provide any value to the unit, but made life easier for Reg.

Each of the team had various chips on their person at all times. Reg had installed them in their phones, in case the signal was ever lost, and in their vehicles and coats. LUCY was able to detect anomalies in behaviour and provide alerts. If a carrier had a habit of driving a particular route at a particular time of day, LUCY would alert Reg if they one day took a different route. He could set various thresholds per carrier to provide alerts should an operative veer off course by a given distance.

Denver wiped his tools and put them back in the relevant drawers inside his tool chests. He'd been doing maintenance on the van which was brand new and needed little effort to upkeep, but it was what Denver did. It was Denver's responsibility to ensure that the vehicles were maintained and that routes were planned. If somebody needed a drop off or extract, he would know the potential exit routes, times, speeds, and safe places to tuck themselves away. It was a far cry from his days as a teenager when he would be chased across the country in a stolen supercar. He'd been trained by the best, and although his defensive driving and tactical driving were impeccable, he knew the safest thing to do if being chased in a town is to hole up out of sight. Being in a car and trying to get away in the age of the internet was just asking for failure. Having several locations near to an extract, where he knew he could get out of the sight of satellites and the public eye, was key to a good exit strategy. Usually, when the chaos had died down, a slow drive out a city or town was safer than driving at over one hundred miles per hour trying to outrun someone, which would be like waving a flag to whoever is doing the chasing.

"Okay, guys, here's your location, I'm sending it across to your phones now. You're looking for a place called Wethersfield, about fifteen minutes from Braintree in Essex. I've got Larson, Stimson and our mystery man on screen, and I'll update you first thing if the location changes," said Reg.

"Thanks," said Melody. "You going to miss us, Reg?"

"While you guys are out on a joy ride, I'll be busting through World War Two on my new game."

"Is that right, Tenant?" said Frank from above him on the mezzanine.

Reg looked startled at Frank's voice above him. "Well, it's not precise, sir, but I'll be thinking about it."

"Mills, Stone, stay in touch with Tenant."

"Will do, sir," said Melody. "We set?" she said to Denver.

"We are, I'll drop you home then pick you up in the morning. Harvey, you want a ride home or you taking your bike? Looks like the weather's going to get awful nasty out there."

"I'll take my bike and meet you in Wethersfield, we might need two vehicles."

"Suit yourself, say six am?"

"I'll be there."

"Let's do it," said Denver, and he started up the van. He listened to the van's engine purr for a few seconds then climbed into the driver's seat. "Reg?"

Reg looked across the floor of the headquarters with his eyebrows raised.

"Door?" said Denver.

"I'm a doorman is what I am," said Reg, hitting a button on his keyboard. "An over-qualified doorman," he called to Melody as her downcast face passed by, and Denver put his foot down. Harvey followed the van out on his bike and Reg hit the door button again, causing the sliding metal shutters to close.

The three news channels still showed the devastation of the bomb scene at Canary Wharf, but the sound was down. Reg switched them off.

"You don't want to know what's going on, Tenant?" said Frank from above.

Reg stayed looking at LUCY's interface on the screen in front of him. "It's not that I'm not interested, sir. It's just that we have a job to do, and as much as it pains me, going after Al Sayan is not part of that job. I'm not a violent man, sir, as you know, but I bet there isn't one Brit that wouldn't like to get his hands on that guy right now. I dread to think what would happen if Harvey got hold of him."

"Thankfully, Harvey won't have a chance."

"How did you know, sir?"

"Know what, Tenant?"

"About that man in the suit?"

Frank thought back to the horrific scene that had played out. "Do you know what a kill zone is?"

"I've heard it being talked about, but-"

"What happens when a bomb goes off, or a shooting takes place?"

"How do you mean?"

"Well, what would *you* do if you were in that situation?"

"I'd run I guess, I hope anyway."

"Exactly, and where would you run?"

"Away from the bomb or the shooter."

"Right. So a nasty, despicable, tactic that terrorists use is to create a second bomb in an area they know that people will congregate. For example, the emergency evacuation assembly point for Canada Square was that little flat area by the water, where the cameras were pointing. So once the first bomb had gone off on the ground floor, the bombers knew that the evacuation procedures would lead the workers all to that point. Simple. Send the second bomb to that point. There's a few hundred people, maybe more all huddled together."

"That's sick, sir."

"It's modern warfare I'm afraid."

"But how did you know it was him?"

"When all this is over, I'll play the recording back, you'll see for yourself. He had telltale signs."

"You've seen that kind of thing before?"

Frank hesitated. "Many times. Over and over, Tenant. Each time I watched the people all run to what they thought was safety."

"Sir?" said Reg. Frank was staring.

"Sorry." Frank roused himself. "God forbid you're ever in a situation like that, Tenant."

10

CHAPTER TEN

DENVER DROPPED MELODY HOME AND TOOK THE SHORT ride to his own home. He kept the music off, absorbed by his own thoughts of the images he'd seen that day. It wasn't the first terrorist attack he'd witnessed. He'd seen the reports of the 9/11 attacks in New York, and the subsequent 7/7 attacks in London. He even vaguely remembered the IRA attacks in London when he was younger, but that was the first time he'd actually seen the bomb go off. It was horrific. Lives had instantly been lost just as they had in other attacks, but witnessing the blast somehow made it more real. Maybe because technology was more efficient, it allowed the media to broadcast faster. Whatever it was, Denver had been hit hard. His eyes moistened as he drove. Sorrow, hate and all kinds of emotion consumed his mind.

It was late in the day when Denver arrived in Barking, Essex. He had a little two-bed house in front of a park. The ride to work was under thirty minutes, and the location was far enough out of town for him to feel away from it all. That day he felt closer than ever, but that was the job. He loved the team. He and Reg worked well together, and

Melody was hardworking, which pushed Denver to perform. Harvey had been difficult to get used to, but during the human trafficking case, when Melody had been kidnapped, Harvey and Denver had a few moments that brought them closer. Harvey was a good guy. He'd done some terrible things that Denver could never empathise with or even forgive, but it wasn't his place to judge. From what he'd seen so far, Harvey had a stronger moral compass than any of the team.

Denver stopped at the church at the top of the road. There was no service on, but Denver liked to sit in the quiet. He'd been misguided as a youngster and considered himself fortunate to have been set on a new path, a good path, with a career that allowed him to do good things. He was certain that if the opportunity hadn't arisen to join the force, he would be in prison by now. Reg had said once that maybe that's why Denver liked Harvey so much because they both had a background of crime. But Denver had argued that while he had graduated from stealing old Ford Capris and Escorts to high-end Ferraris and McLarens, Harvey had been immersed in a criminal world as a child and had killed his first man at twelve years old. It was a different league. There was no crossover.

A few people sat alone in the church pews. Candles lined the altar rails and cast weak shadows on the cold stone walls, lost in the gloom that hung above the wooden beams high above. Denver walked slowly and quietly to the front pew where he sat and bowed his head. He wasn't devoutly religious, but his mother was, and an element of her religious spirit carried with him. It guided his morals, as a blind man might use a cane. When a blind man's cane hit something solid, the blind man would stop and feel around for the right way to go. When Denver found something that itched his sense of right and wrong, he'd stop and ask himself what his mother might do. It was his way of asking himself what god might do, but without directly being reliant on religion.

Aside from the morality guidance, Denver enjoyed the peace and harmony of the old church, which often sought following the horrors of his job. They were expected to be hardened to horrific scenes and evil people, and were asked to perform actions that crossed so many lines of morality. The church allowed Denver to reposition his actions; it cleansed him.

Denver lit a candle for those who had fallen earlier that day. He thought of their families and their suffering, although they would never know that, out there, a man unknown to them was grieving and sharing their pain. Denver left the church and drove the short distance home. After parking the van in his driveway, instead of going inside, he walked the one hundred yards to his local grocery store. The store was cheaper than supermarkets and more convenient for Denver's erratic routine. A small price to pay for the quality of life he led.

"Mr Denver, sir, how are you?" said Ali, the grocer.

"Mustn't grumble, Ali," said Denver. "How's the kids?"

"Oh, they're fine, they're upstairs playing on their video game. It's quieter down here I think. All those car races, explosions and guns, I sometimes wonder how they sleep."

Denver thought on that; it sounded like a typical day at work. "New generation Ali. Gone are the days of conkers and hopscotch." Denver was filling his basket with a small loaf of bread, avocados, bananas and spinach. He picked up a few tins of soup and some tea and walked to the counter. Ali emptied the basket and placed the items in a plastic bag.

"All in one bag, Ali, no need to separate them."

"Same every time, Mr Denver."

"Save the planet, Ali." Denver smiled.

"It all helps. Is this on your account?"

"I'll settle at the end of the month?"

"That's fine, Mr Denver, your credit's good. Enjoy your evening."

"You too, Ali. Thanks." Denver walked out the store and heard the little bell above the door. He took a slow walk back to his house, locked the front door behind him and placed his bag in the kitchen. It was an old house built just after the Second World War, when babies were booming and industry had started to pick up again. The Ford factory less than two miles away had provided jobs for many of the local men. But in recent years, the British automobile industry had steadily declined, and the houses now provided homes for a vast variety of people and cultures.

Denver poured a tin of mushroom soup into a pan and set it to boil. While it cooked, he halved an avocado and scooped out the delicious fruit with a small spoon onto a plate.

His living room was small with a TV in one corner, a selection of DVDs on a shelf, and a large couch with a coffee table in front. There wasn't much room for any more furniture and Denver didn't need anything else. He rarely had visitors, unless he brought his mum home for Christmas, but typically he'd go to hers. Her house was more of a home than his own. He turned the TV on with the remote and found a nature documentary straight away. He didn't flick through the channels as he knew that many of them would be showing the day's horrors. Denver had quietened his mind, he didn't need reminding.

He sat on his couch and ate the soup, followed by the avocado, then set about washing his plates and the pan in the small kitchen sink. He placed the items on the drying rack where they lived. He rarely used anything else in the kitchen, and it was pointless putting them away each night.

He showered and dressed in tracksuit bottoms and an oversized t-shirt, then took the loaf of bread into the garden to scatter crumbs for the birds. His garden was small but stylish. There were no overhanging trees so there were no piles of leaves, just well-trimmed bushes and hardy plants. A small lawn area stood in the middle, and a little table with one chair sat by the back door. In the summer months, he'd drink his morning tea in the garden and watch the birds. The high walls around his property gave him all the seclusion he needed. It wasn't a perfect home, but it was his home, and it was as nice as he could get until retirement.

Denver dreamed of St Lucia, where his family home stood near long, perfect beaches that lined the turquoise ocean, heated by the incessant, golden sun. He'd travelled there before with his mum, when her own mum had died. He'd lain beneath palm trees on his grandfather's hammock with a book and enjoyed the tropical breeze. That's how he'd spend his final days. It was all he needed to drag him through the horrors of the modern world.

The nature show was still on when Denver sat back on the couch and heaved his legs up. He settled down with the remote on his chest and his phone by his side, then pulled a thick blanket over himself. He fell asleep to the soothing voice of David Attenborough and woke to the harsh shrill of his phone's ringtone.

"Harvey? What's up? It's late."

"I have a problem."

CHAPTER ELEVEN

Harvey pulled into the driveway of his house in Buckhurst Hill. It was a rental. He only owned one property, and that was in the South of France. He'd owned it for a year and had only spent a few nights there when Frank had caught up with him and put the noose around his neck.

The little house in Buckhurst Hill was enough for Harvey. Frank had the rent covered, but Harvey had to pay the bills. It was a good deal, all things considered.

He clicked the button on the electric garage door that he'd had fitted himself and watched it open. He never left his bike outside the house for a number of reasons. Firstly, he'd grown up in Theydon Bois not far from Buckhurst Hill, and knew that the affluent London suburbs were a target for small criminals from less affluent areas. Harvey had been on the wrong side of the law his entire life and had seen the people that openly spoke about heading out to Buckhurst Hill, Ongar, or Theydon Bois for a quick buck. They'd spend a few days sitting and watching then, when they knew the owner's habits, they'd empty the house. Not violent criminals, but heartless bastards who destroyed memories. Secondly, Harvey had owned his bike for nearly ten years. He'd done enough jobs with it for anybody who was anybody in the organised crime world to know that the silver BMW belonged to the infamous Harvey Stone. Harvey didn't want those types of people knowing where he lived.

He rolled the bike in and clicked the garage door closed, then put his helmet in its protective bag and hung it from a hook. The garage was bare except for the bike and a rack of three hooks fixed to the wall beside the door into the house.

The house itself was built in the 1930s. It was solid brick with a bay window to one side of the front door, which a person could sit on and watch the world go by. A large chimney breast and fireplace was the feature of the lounge. The house had originally been one much larger house, but an opportunistic landlord had split it into two properties some years back.

Harvey had chosen the house because he was familiar with the area, and it was only twenty-five minutes to head-quarters on his bike. Frank had suggested an apartment closer to headquarters, but Harvey preferred to live in a building with a ground floor. He could defend himself more easily in a house than in an apartment with only one exit.

The house was old and cold, but Harvey seldom used the heating system. He kept his jacket on and sat at the island counter in the kitchen on a bar stool. His MacBook was the only sign of modern technology in the house. The lounge had no TV, just a single armchair and a sofa he'd bought more to fill the empty space than to sit on. He slept in the armchair frequently.

Harvey had many nights where his mind would go over and over the facts surrounding his parents. He'd sit in the armchair in the darkness, his mind a whirl of possibilities. One day, he knew that one of those possibilities would be plausible, and he'd be able to delve deeper. But for now, his only knowledge of his parents was the cock and bull story his foster father had told him, verbatim, for close to thirty years.

Harvey pictured John telling him the story with a tumbler of brandy in his hand. Three ice cubes chinked to the side of the glass as John recalled his fable to repeat it once more.

"We only had one bar back then, we did things ourselves, your mum and me. We served drinks ourselves if the barmaids were off, we put orders into the brewery, and we even cleaned the bar at close up. That was when we found you both. You in a little picnic hamper wrapped in blankets with a note. Hannah sat beside you, wide-eyed and scared."

The note had said that Harvey's parents had killed themselves; life had got too much for them. John and Barb had fostered Hannah and her baby brother, Harvey.

Harvey had been researching his birth parents, based on John's story, for as long as could remember. There were no records of anybody named Stone in Plaistow, where the alleged bar had been, not that matched the ages that Harvey's parents would have been, anyway. There was no record of a single suicide in the area at the time, let alone a double suicide. There were no marriage records, no mortgages, not anything that pointed to something of any use. The only consistent thing Harvey had discovered was the story that John had told him time and time again.

Harvey opened his laptop and stared at the little box the search engine. It was as empty as the results it would produce. He closed the lid without typing anything and rested his head in his hands.

His mind wandered to the blast they'd seen earlier that day. It had been shocking, disturbing even. Harvey was a ruthless killer. He'd done things to people that would make most people vomit with disgust. But even he was hit hard by the images they'd seen that day. It was so much worse because they'd seen the killer walking nonchalantly towards the huddle of innocent people.

Perhaps that was it, perhaps that was why Harvey was disgusted. He'd always stood up for the weak and innocent. He'd always preyed on cowardly bullies that ruined peoples lives. During the time that he worked for his foster father, he and Julios had been hitmen. They'd done things that required a certain skill set and a very specific mindset. Things that John's other men could have done, but they would have been messy, and brought retaliation to the family's operations.

It was during Harvey's time as a hitman that he'd taken on training, in preparation for the day when he met his sister's rapist. He would scour the news for early releases or arrests of sex offenders, rapists or molesters, and target them. He honed his skills on the bullies. He would track them, watch them and learn them, then plan their suffering and execute his plan with brutal force. He'd seen many a man suffer, and watched them as they fell from the lofty heights of self-assurance to weak, soiled and pitiful victims. They all cried, all thirty-three of them. They all pissed themselves in fear. They all died a prolonged and agonising death.

Harvey couldn't shake the image of Al Sayan from his mind. Crimes such as robbing a priceless buddha were not harmful to anybody. In another life, Harvey would let Stimson do what he wanted, it was no skin off his nose, nobody was hurt. But when victims' lives are ruined, and pain and suffering are brought upon the weak and helpless, Harvey couldn't help but feel the anger inside him grow. Yet the politics surrounding the good side of the law placed Al Sayan in the jurisdiction of some other team.

Harvey moved from his kitchen to his lounge and fell into the soft armchair. He put his feet up on a footstool and linked his fingers on his stomach. He sat for a while and tried to steer his thoughts towards his parents. What might they look like? How old would they be? What did his father do for work? But each time, his mind took a U-turn and brought him back to the photo news broadcasts had shown; the bearded, unsmiling face of Al Sayan.

Peace wasn't ready for Harvey that evening. His mind raced with the blast, the beard, the crooked nose, and, of course, his parents. He decided instead to go for a run to try and clear his mind of everything. He changed into shorts and a hooded sweater and started with a slow jog from his door. Harvey ran every morning except when he was on an all-nighter with work. He never ran the same route, a lesson he'd learned from Julios.

Epping Forest was once a vast area that covered much of the county, but was now reduced to a few miles of woodland. In Buckhurst Hill, it was still a great place to run. Harvey followed no trails, he just ran where his feet took him. He hurdled fallen trees and streams and sprinted up hills. By the time he was finished, he'd run six miles, and warmed down by walking the last two hundred yards from the end of his street to his house. It was a quiet night.

He closed the front door behind him and slid the bolt across, an old habit, then kicked off his running shoes and walked up the stairs. He reached behind the shower curtain and turned the shower on; it usually took a few minutes to get hot. Then he stepped into his bedroom, which was the smaller of the two rooms at the back of the house. He preferred it; the view of the forest was calming and familiar, and there was less chance of people looking in.

He stripped off his sweaty clothes and strode naked to the bathroom. Steam clouded from inside the shower, and the mirror was already beginning to fog. He slid the shower curtain back, looked down and stopped at what he saw.

Harvey turned the shower off, quietly stepped back to his bedroom and retrieved his SIG. He swept the house, checked the spare room then ventured downstairs. There was no sign or trace of anybody. The front and back doors were locked with no signs of forced entry, as were the windows.

Harvey crept back up the stairs and dressed in clean cargo pants and a plain white t-shirt. He picked up his phone and dialled Denver's number from memory.

"Harvey?" said Denver. "What's up? It's late."

"I have a problem."

12

CHAPTER TWELVE

At four am, Denver and Melody stood in Harvey's bathroom looking down at the dead body that lay in the bathtub.

The man had been in his fifties by the look of his grey hair and the paunch that protruded from his midriff. He wore a pair of cheap running shoes, blue jeans and a dark grey cardigan over a checked shirt.

Two small dents in the bridge of his nose suggested he'd worn glasses, which may have been lost during his attack. A laminated identity card hung around his neck stating that Arthur Bell worked for Hackney Carriages as a black taxi driver. The card gave Arthur's driver number and showed a photo of the man much like a passport photo.

Harvey stood in his kitchen and watched Melody and Denver walk down the stairs to join him. Melody picked up the coffee she'd walked in with and leaned against the kitchen counter holding the cardboard cup in both hands.

"I'm guessing you don't know him?" she asked.

Harvey didn't reply.

"It's a bit random isn't it?" said Denver. "I mean, what the hell?"

"Well, it's not the first time you found a dead body in the bath," Melody said to Harvey. She was referring to the Sergio incident when Harvey had boiled his sister's rapist alive. "Sorry, that was uncalled for."

Harvey didn't reply. He had learned from his training with Julios a method of communicating without words. A look, a gesture, or sometimes no response at all could express his thoughts.

"Shall we tell Frank?" asked Melody, moving the conversation along. "We need to get the body out of here."

"I don't see what Frank would do," said Denver, "except call the police, and have it dealt with the same as any other murder. Then Harvey will be arrested and out of action until he clears his name."

Harvey looked up at Denver.

"Let's get Reg on it," said Melody. "He can do some research on Arthur Bell for us. Find out who he is, his history, and probably even the last fare he had."

Just then, there was a hard knock on the door, three taps. Denver and Melody looked at Harvey, who put his finger to his lips and crept toward the door. He looked through the spy hole and edged back to the kitchen.

"Police. I'm being set up. Back door, quick." Harvey picked up the rucksack he'd packed the previous night and quietly opened the back door. They stepped out into the dark morning. The sun was still way below the horizon and the trees from the forest cast a gloom over the long, narrow garden. There was no side entrance to the house so any police looking to cover the rear would have to walk to the end of the street and find their way along the fence in the forest.

Harvey peered over the fence into the trees. He saw no movement, so quietly opened the back gate and let Melody and Denver out. As he closed it, he heard the sounds of the front door being forced in. Lights came on in the house.

Harvey led his two colleagues into the forest and took a wide circle back to the high street, five hundred yards from the entrance to his road. Once clear of the house, the three walked like they were walking off a Sunday roast. Melody cradled her coffee, Denver strolled with his hands in his pockets, and Harvey walked calmly and quietly. They reached the tree line where the forest met the main road.

"Denver, tell me you didn't park the van directly outside my house?"

"Give me some credit, Harvey. It's parked on the main road. We walked the five hundred yards down to yours."

"Okay, Melody and I will wait here in the tree line. You want to grab the van and get us? If I'm being framed for murder, then my face will be on the minds of every cop around here."

"Sure, I'll take a look down your road and see what's happening too."

"I can tell you what's happening, Denver. Uniformed police have found Arthur Bell, have called in the brain squad to deal with the body, and also put a call out to all units to be on the lookout for an IC1 male that fits my description."

"At least it solves your problem," said Melody.

Harvey looked across at her.

"You don't need to worry about getting rid of the body anymore." She smiled apologetically.

"Is the house clean?" asked Denver.

"Yeah, of course," said Harvey. "Everything I own is here apart from my bike." He gestured with his thumb to the backpack. "I can't go back there. I'll need to find somewhere else, at least until we find out who did this."

"Right, sit tight, guys, I'll be a few minutes," said Denver and strode out of the forest. He looked both ways then walked towards the van.

"To work out who did it, we need to understand why they did it," said Melody. "Any old enemies?"

"How many fingers you got?"

"Okay, are there any old enemies that you have seen or been in contact with recently?"

"None, I cut free of all that. The only thing I've done recently that links me to anything is what I've done for Frank and you guys. And we-"

"Yeah, we locked everyone up who you didn't kill," said Melody straight-faced.

"I don't think it's that," said Harvey. "Someone's getting me out of the picture."

"And framing you in another?"

Harvey didn't reply.

"But what's framing you for a murder going to achieve?"

"Is Reg online?"

"Bit early for him, he'll be there in about half an hour. Why?"

"We need his research skills."

Denver pulled over to the side of the road beside the trees. He checked in front and behind then gave them the all clear. Melody and Harvey walked out of the trees. Melody climbed into the passenger seat, and Harvey laid down in the back of the van out of sight.

"Cheers, Denver, let's go, mate. Let's get out of here before they shut the place down."

Denver indicated and pulled off into the empty road. The houses opposite Harvey's road behind them flashed blue every second. Harvey imagined the road chock-a-block with police cars. The neighbours would be at their windows. Discretion was not on the MET's priority list when it came to murder.

"Good morning sunshines." Reg's voice came across the radio. "How are we on this splendid day at such a fine hour?"

Melody picked up the handset and looked back at Harvey who shook his head.

"Is Frank there yet?" asked Harvey.

"And good morning to you, Reggie, you're bright and breezy this morning," said Melody over the handset.

"Well it's nearly five am, and I'm sitting at my desk alone in the dark. If I don't keep myself happy, I'll gladly fall back to sleep."

"No Frank yet?" she asked.

"No, he said he'd be in later, said he'd give us time to get some results."

"That's kind of him. Listen, Reg." Melody turned back to Harvey, who nodded and held up his thumb and first finger, indicating that she tell Reg only what he needed to know. "We need you to look something up for us, but hey it's only a stab in the dark, so keep this one on the down low."

"Wow, early morning mysteries, what you got?"

"If I gave you the registration number of a black cab driver, could you do some digging? We're still about an hour from the manor house."

"Yeah, I'll see what I can find. Is that it? It's a bit vague."

"Right now that's all we have, Reg."

"Okay, you going to let me in on how you came about the number or why you want me to do this?"

"Yes, we will do Reg, of course, but right now I need you see what you can get with an open mind. When you get back to us, we'll fill you in."

"I see, out of sight out of mind," said Reg, slightly deflated.

"Reggie, come on, I just want that brilliant mind of yours to not be obscured by details. I want to see what you can find. What do you say? Thirty minutes?"

"You know how to get me going, Melody. Righto, thirty minutes it is."

"Thanks, Reg, we love you," said Melody and put the handset down.

Once they were out of Buckhurst Hill, Harvey sat up and leaned against the side of the van on the wooden panelling behind Melody. The side behind Denver was home to Reg's workbench. Two computers were fixed down beneath it and two large screens sat atop the surface with a single keyboard and mouse.

A single cable ran up to the van's ceiling and out through a grommet that Denver had drilled into place. A motorised aerial increased the effectiveness of the van's radio comms with headquarters. A small, hidden transponder and receiver spoke to the satellites, allowing Reg access to the internet from virtually anywhere. But without Reg in the van, the whole workbench and associated electronics were useless.

Harvey felt the van's speed increase and knew that Denver had just pulled onto the A12, a busy four-lane motorway that ran from East London to the East Coast. Braintree was about thirty to forty minutes up the A12, so Harvey settled in and closed his eyes. He didn't know when the next sleep was coming.

CHAPTER THIRTEEN

"D<small>ID YOU SEE OUR LITTLE MARTYR</small>?" <small>ASKED</small> A<small>L</small> S<small>AYAN INTO</small> the phone.

"You sick bastard-"

"Now, now. You are forgetting yourself," replied Al Sayan. "How are your plans coming on?"

"You'll get what you want, just don't touch my-"

"Your little Angel?" asked Al Sayan. "Now that you have seen how serious I am, I hope you will apply the same level of professionalism to the job as you would any other job. The stakes are high."

"And Stone? You said he was running. What from?"

"I imagine right about now he's being locked in a cell where he belongs," said Al Sayan. "But he is a troublesome fellow, so I urge you to take precaution. You have less than two days. What are you doing now?"

"I'll run my own job. I don't need your help, it's better that way."

"Good, I'd hate to see Stone come between you and your daughter, so do tell me if you need assistance. I have men who would gladly give their lives to take the nuisance down and allow me to carry out my own plans."

"I told you I don't need your help."

"Good, so you don't need to tell you that all of your phones are being monitored by Stone's team. They are watching your every move. I'll leave you to deal with that shall I?"

Silence.

"I shall contact you again before the deadline is up."

"Wait."

There was a pause.

"I'm here," said Al Sayan.

"Let me talk to her."

"I told you before that you do not call the shots. I can assure you she is safe with me. The next time you talk to her will be in one of two potential circumstances. One, you have achieved your goal and delivered to me what I have requested."

"You'll get it."

"Two, little Angel will be trundling out of here with a little surprise in her cute little pink backpack."

"I need proof of life."

Al Sayan was silent for a moment. "Send your man to me, Mr Larson. Send him to my garage in Stratford. He will be followed, no doubt. He will see how well I am caring for Angel, and I will make sure the pests are eliminated."

CHAPTER FOURTEEN

"WE'RE COMING INTO WETHERSFIELD NOW," HARVEY heard Denver say. He opened his eyes and rubbed his face.

"Do we have water?" Harvey asked.

A bottle of water appeared over Melody's shoulder which he took, drank and returned.

"So what your game plan?"

"Reg, you there?" Melody called over the radio.

"Of course I am."

"Okay, give us some news, buddy."

"Arthur Bell. Fifty-two years old, married with two grown children. Lives in Slough, west of London. No previous record, same for his wife and kids."

The team were silent for a moment.

"So he's basically lived an average life?" asked Melody.

"Yeah, sounds about right."

"So why would somebody kill him?" asked Denver.

"For his taxi," said Harvey. "Whoever did it needs his taxi for something."

"Reg did you-"

"Check his taxi? Yeah of course. It was re-registered and

tested two months ago at Hackney Carriages, hasn't picked up any speeding tickets and has the GPS switched off."

"Reg?" said Denver.

"Go ahead, Denver."

"We're coming into Wethersfield now, can you give us a sitrep on Larson?"

"He and the mystery man are at the Manor House Hotel already, looks like they stayed in the hotel as they haven't moved since nine pm last night."

"Thanks, Reg," said Melody. "How would you guys like to get some breakfast in the manor house?"

"Oh breakfast, come to me, baby," said Denver.

Harvey was on one knee between Melody and Denver's seats as they turned into the manor house's long driveway. Frank had been right, the surrounding landscape was only fields. The sun was rising somewhere behind a wall of grey but shone enough light for Harvey to see that escaping from the place would be difficult, especially if helicopters were in the air. There were no other buildings nearby, and no other streets for miles around.

Harvey leaned forward and picked up the handset. "Reg, Harvey."

"Go ahead, Harvey."

"Send us through any details of Larson's car, and Stimson's if you have it."

"Will do, it's coming at you now."

Harvey's phone beeped an incoming message. "Larson drives a black BMW seven series." He read the plate number out.

"Hey, Reg," said Melody, "we're going into the hotel side of the house for breakfast, see what we can see, keep your eyes on Larson and tell us if they move. We're hoping to catch them at breakfast and slip them a chip."

"Will do, you want to do a comms check?"

"Will the ear-pieces work this far out of London?" asked Melody.

"Should do, I beefed up the transmitter in the van. As long as you stay in range of it, the comms should be okay."

"What's the range?" asked Melody.

"Don't go more than five hundred yards away, the closer the better obviously."

"Gotcha, thanks, Reg," said Melody. She pushed the button on her ear-piece. "Reg, come back."

"Loud and clear," said Reg.

Melody looked at Denver and Harvey, they all nodded, confirming that they'd heard him. "Yeah, copy that, we're parking now."

"Just a heads up," said Reg, "I can see Larson and Stimson's minder in the hotel."

"Thanks, Reg."

"Black BMW seven series, first row of cars, near the door," said Denver.

"Melody, you have some of them chips on you?" asked Harvey.

"Yeah, Reg gave me a bag."

"Good, first chance we get we'll chip the BMW."

The team were greeted at the door of the manor house by a well-mannered man in a very stylish three piece suit.

"Good morning, welcome to Cornish House. Are you here for breakfast?" he said.

"We are," said Melody.

"If you'd care to follow me, then," he said and headed towards a set of large double doors, which he opened ceremoniously, and stood to one side. Melody followed close behind him, and Harvey and Denver tried their best not to look out of place.

As soon as the doors opened, Harvey scanned the room for Larson. He spotted him at a table with a lady and a large man at the back of the massive room, away from the windows.

"Are there others joining your party, ma'am?" the man asked Melody.

"No, just us thanks," she replied.

"I'll hand you to our concierge, and I hope you have a pleasant breakfast." He gave a small, discreet bow, turned and left through the double doors. Another man in an identical suit as the first man's greeted them. "Good morning. Do you have a reservation?" he asked.

"No, we don't know-"

"That's perfectly fine, I have a table for you over by the window just there, if you'd allow me to show you?"

"Can I ask where the washroom is?" asked Harvey.

"The washroom, sir?" the man said. "Yes, not at all, through the double doors at the back of the room. You'll also find shower facilities and our spa."

"That's great, do you think we could sit closer to the doors?" Said Harvey.

"He's not feeling well," Said Melody, "Are you dear?" Melody rubbed Harvey's back.

"No, I'm not feeling great." Harvey agreed.

"Perhaps then I might suggest another table. Please do follow me." The man turned and walked away, and the team followed. They reached a table for four, twenty yards from Larson and his company. The man offered Harvey a seat, but Harvey chose his own, one with an optimum view of Larson. Melody sat beside him, and Denver sat opposite with his back to the targets.

"I shall ask a waiter to join you shortly, please do have a nice breakfast, and I do hope you feel better, sir."

"Thank you, that's very kind," said Melody.

"That's Larson and Stimson's minder," said Harvey under his breath.

"Who's the woman?" asked Melody.

"Not sure," said Harvey. "We need ears over there."

The woman sat at the end of the table. Larson was to her right facing the team, and the minder sat opposite him. His broad shoulders covered most of Harvey's view, but Larson was easily recognisable from the photo Reg had provided.

"Okay first things first, let's get the car chipped. Then we'll work on getting a bug closer to Larson's table," said Melody.

"You have audio bugs?" asked Denver.

"Of course, we have these new ones that Reg gave me. Apparently, he can pick up the audio through LUCY, as long as they are in range of the van," said Melody.

"Can I take one?"

Melody passed him one.

"And a chip?"

She passed him a chip. "What are you doing?"

"Taking care of the car." Denver pushed his chair back. "Order me the full English, will you?" He left the room.

Harvey and Melody sat looking at the menu until a waitress approached them.

"Good morning, how are you both today?" she said.

"We're very well, thank you."

"Are you ready to order or would you care for more time?"

"We'll take three coffees, a full English for our friend, and I'll take the healthy omelette. What would you like, dear?" Melody said with a smile.

"Just coffee is good for me, thanks," said Harvey and handed the waitress the menu.

The waitress collected the other two menus. "I'll be back with the coffees shortly." She smiled and left.

Harvey casually glanced around the room as anybody might in a nice restaurant. He looked behind him, noted the paintings on the wall, and made a show of pointing to one and talking to Melody about it. Long emerald green curtains were tied back with braided gold rope onto elegant hooks and fixed into the walls. As Harvey's eyes made their way back to face forward, they fell on Larson, who stared unabashedly at him. He gave a half smile, blinked and turned his attention back to the woman.

Harvey did the same, turning back to Melody. He put his arm on the back of her chair, as a husband might do, and pulled his right leg up onto his left knee. He feigned talking to her about what they might do that day. Reaching across her, he pulled a tourist leaflet from a little stand at the end of the table. As he leaned over, he uttered under his breath, "I think it's a trap."

Melody said nothing but leaned into him to look at the leaflet, which described a tour of the manor house revealing its history and impressive art collection. The pamphlet was tri-folded, and the inside page was dedicated to the house's fantastic collection of artwork.

Harvey made a point of skipping past the pictures of the art and glanced at the rear page of the pamphlet before discarding it on the table as if he wasn't interested.

"What have you two lovebirds been talking about then?"

Harvey realised his arm was still on the back of Melody's chair. "Just playing the game, Denver," Harvey said quietly. "You all done?"

"Yeah, the chip's in the boot and the bugs are in the front under the dash," muttered Denver. He glanced around him. "Did you order yet?"

"Yeah, it's on its way," said Melody, just as the waitress reappeared with three coffees and a small silver bowl of sugar. The three cups of coffee each had a little shortbread biscuit on the saucer beside the cup, which sat on a white frilly dolly.

"Your order will be five minutes," said the waitress. "Can I offer you some toast and jam, perhaps?"

"No, thank you," said Melody. "That'll be fine."

The waitress left.

A few minutes passed, then the waitress reappeared with another waiter pushing a small stainless steel cart. There were two large silver covers over the plates of food. They served the plates smoothly on the table in front of Melody and Denver.

"Can I get you anything else?" she asked.

"No, this is perfect, thank you very much," said Melody.

"You're welcome, please do enjoy your breakfast." The waitress and the waiter left, and Denver began to cover his breakfast in salt and ketchup. Harvey drank his black coffee and kept an eye of Larson with infrequent flicks of his eye.

Denver was halfway through his breakfast when Larson, the woman and the big guy stood. They thanked the waitress and left the table, walking behind Harvey and the team towards the exit.

"Okay, Reg are you hearing me?" said Melody.

"Loud and clear, Melody."

"Larson is on the move, he's with a woman and the minder. Are you able to identify the woman somehow?"

"I can't see any activity unless I know the number or the person's name."

"Where's Stimson, Reg?"

"Hold on, I'm just checking. He's way out, in Shepton Mallet," said Reg.

"Shepton Mallet? What's there?" asked Melody.

"A prison outside of Bristol," said Harvey. "But Stimson's a West Country guy right?"

"Yeah originally, he moves about a bit."

"Okay maybe he has a house there. Let's see if we can get a lead on the woman, Denver's chipped and bugged the BMW. We're heading out now, we'll hang behind, and you can be our eyes, Reg."

"Copy that," said Reg.

Melody paid the bill as Denver and Harvey left and stood by the front doors. They saw the big guy climb into the black BMW. The woman opened the passenger door of a little Porsche, and Larson climbed into an Audi. The Porsche pulled off and drove slowly up the long driveway. The Audi followed, and the BMW pulled out behind the other two, obscuring the plates of the cars in front.

"That didn't work out, did it?" said Denver. "Reg, they've taken three cars."

"Okay, I can see Larson on the move, the minder guy is also moving," said Reg.

"Yeah, they all climbed into different cars. We're going to need to rely on Larson's phone to follow him. Keep on him Reg, we'll be on the road in one minute," said Harvey. Denver ran across to the van and started it up. By the time Melody came out the restaurant, Denver was at the bottom of the twelve grand steps that led from the main doors to the gravel driveway. She climbed in, and Denver put his foot down.

"So we're following Larson only. The other two are of no interest to us at this point, Reg."

"Copy, I've got Larson's phone up on LUCY. He's moved ahead of the other guy, looks like he's heading into London. The other guy is following him, but much slower."

"I knew it," said Harvey. "They spotted us in the restaurant. if we try to follow Larson, the big fella will step in."

"They spotted us?" asked Denver.

"Yeah, they recognised me somehow," said Harvey. "Hang behind the BMW, let's see where this goes."

"I don't see how they would recognise us," said Melody. "Surely-"

"He recognised *me*. Larson locked eyes with me, and it was more than a casual glance. He *knows* something."

"You think Arthur Bell?"

"That's exactly what I'm thinking."

Just then, the familiar sound of a police car's siren came in two short bursts from behind the van. Harvey looked out the back window and saw the roof of the police Volvo behind them.

"Ah, you must be kidding," said Denver.

"I'm guessing this isn't a tug for a driving offence, Denver," said Harvey. "Melody, if they take me away, get Frank on the case, but carry on after Larson."

"You sure?"

"Positive," Harvey replied. "You guys don't need to be wrapped up in this."

Denver came to a stop on the shoulder of the busy A-road and stepped out the vehicle. Harvey had his hand on the handle of the sliding door but held it closed. He waited to hear the police officer speak, but Denver spoke first.

"Morning, officer, how can I help?" said Denver politely.

"Place your hands on the vehicle please, sir."

"Excuse me?"

"Place your hands on the vehicle."

Denver leaned up against the van, and the police officer performed a search of his body. Denver didn't carry his issued weapon, but it was tucked under the seat in a fixed holster, ready to pull at a moments notice. A quick search of the van would raise some difficult questions.

"You might want to check my ID, officer, it's around my neck."

"All in good time, sir," the officer replied. He took his time searching Denver, feeling behind his belt, in his pockets, in the seams of his jacket, his shoes and socks.

"Aren't you supposed to tell me what it is I've done?" said Denver.

"Can you place your hands behind your back please, sir?"

"What? What for?" said Denver, he was getting annoyed.

"Just place your hands behind your back, so I can perform a search of the passengers," said the officer. His tone was flat and calm. He pulled the cuffs tight on Denver's wrists.

Melody stepped out the van. "Excuse me, sir, I think you're making a mistake." She held up her ID and stepped towards the officer who twisted her arm back and slammed up her up against the van.

"What the hell are you doing?" cried Denver. "She's a cop for god's sake."

Harvey slid the door open and stepped out. "Stop, it's me you want." Harvey put his hands up. "Let her go, officer."

The police officer stepped back but held onto Melody's wrists. He slid the cuffs on and let her go. "Stand there," he told her and pointed to a spot beside Denver.

"Harvey Stone?"

"That's me."

"Hands on the vehicle." The officer gestured with his head to the van.

Harvey turned to the van and placed his hands high on the roof. The officer stepped behind Harvey, pulling another set of cuffs from his waist belt.

"Put your left hand only behind your back. That's your left hand only. Now."

Harvey brought his left hand down and allowed the police officer to fix one side of the cuffs to it. Harvey watched him in the reflection of the van's side window. The officer looked up to his right hand.

"Okay, now your–"

Harvey drove his right elbow back into the man's face, smashing the officer's nose. Before the man had a chance to react, Harvey grabbed onto the officer's neck and slammed his face into the van three times. Then he let the unconscious man fall to the ground.

"What the hell are you doing?" cried Denver.

"Harvey, you can't-"

"He's either bent or a fake, my money's on him being fake," said Harvey.

"What makes you say that? You just beat up a police officer for god's sake, I'm not sure even Frank can help you there," said Melody.

Harvey bent down and emptied the policeman's pockets. He pulled the keys from the imposter's belt and uncuffed his colleagues.

"Denver, check the boot of that car will you?"

Denver walked to the police Volvo and opened the boot.

"You're not going to believe this," said Denver.

Melody walked over to join him.

"Is he alive?" asked Harvey, already knowing what they'd found.

"Yeah, he has a pulse," said Melody.

"Injured?"

"No. Drugged or knocked out by the look of it, but there's no blood or sign of injury, anyway."

"Well, get him out of the car, people might notice a black guy and a girl standing here with a cop in the boot of his own police car."

Denver pulled the unconscious policeman up and lowered him to the floor, sitting him up against the side of the Volvo.

Harvey put the cuffs on the fake cop, opened the passenger door and ripped out the camera. He then found the hard drive storage unit it was connected to and ripped that out too.

He lifted the radio handset from the dash. "Officer down, officer down, three miles out of Braintree on the A131, assistance needed." He replaced the handset. "Let's go," he said to the others. Harvey climbed into the van and sat back down, putting the dash cam and hard drive on the floor beside him. "Now, people, let's move."

Melody and Denver walked back to the van, and within five minutes they were clear of the scene and on a back road heading towards the A12 into London.

"What the hell just happened there?" asked Denver.

"Fake cop, two objectives," said Harvey, "delay us, and take me out of the game."

"Reg, you there?" said Melody.

"I'm here, I heard it all. Everybody okay?" replied Reg.

"We're all good," said Harvey. "I'm going to call your number from the fake cop's phone, tell me what you know about it." Harvey dialled Reg's number.

Reg's phone lit up. "Okay, I have it, give me a sec."

"You still haven't told us how you knew he was a fake," said Melody.

"He didn't give a reason for tugging us, he was too rough with Denver and then you, then when he knew my name and didn't call for assistance, I knew it had to be fake. I'm wanted for Arthur Bell's murder right now. What policeman is going to try to arrest me and two other suspects on his own? Besides that, what policeman carries three sets of handcuffs unless they know they are going to be cuffing three people?"

"Okay I have it," said Reg over the comms. "It's a burner, but the call history has is interesting."

"One of Stimson's?" asked Harvey.

"Without a doubt," confirmed Reg.

"Thanks, Reg. What's the update on Larson?"

"He's on the A12 heading into London, he's five miles out."

"Is Frank in yet?" asked Harvey.

"Not yet,"

"Good, how do I turn all this stuff on?"

"What stuff?" asked Reg.

"The computers in the back of the van. There're two computers, and I have a hard drive I want you to access."

"Power up the one on the left and plug the drive into the USB port on the front."

Harvey leaned across and did as instructed. "Done."

"Okay, sit tight, I'll need a few minutes to access the computer over the satellite link," said Reg.

"Okay, we need a sitrep," said Melody. "Frank sent us out to confirm Larson's location and do a recce on the manor house, and so far Harvey's wanted for a murder he didn't do, Larson has met with an unknown woman plus Stimson's bodyguard, and now the woman has disappeared and Larson and the goon are heading into London. Not a great report, even by our standards."

"Someone wants me out of the game," said Harvey. "They tried to frame me for murder, then tried to kill me."

"Kill you?" said Melody.

Harvey leaned over into the passenger seat. "He was carrying this." He handed her a Glock handgun.

"He's not linked to the forces then," said Melody. "They wouldn't use this plastic crap,"

"Reg, it's Harvey."

"Go ahead."

"How many chips are on me right now?" Reg was known for planting hidden chips on the team so that Frank could see where they were at all times. Frank had asked Reg to plant as many as possible on Harvey, who had a habit of finding them and throwing them onto buses or into the handbags of passing women. There was nothing malicious meant by it, it was just Harvey's way of rejecting the noose around his neck.

"Five, Harvey," said Reg, like he was admitting he had a drinking problem.

"Five?" said Harvey, incredulous.

"Five. Your phone, your jacket, your shoe, your gun and there's one inside your ID."

Harvey didn't reply.

"There's also two on your bike, but I can see that's still at your home."

"What's your plan, Harvey?"

"The plan is coming," he replied. "For now, just keep following Larson."

"Ah, I can see the hard drive," said Reg, "it's video footage."

"How long is it?" asked Harvey.

"Looks to be about an hour's worth of two-minute clips. I think they roll the footage around, so it overwrites the earlier data with new data."

"Okay, can you watch the last thirty minutes? Let me know what's on there."

"I'm watching it now," said Reg. "It's like watching a really boring episode of that TV show about police chases."

15

CHAPTER FIFTEEN

HARVEY SAT IN THE BACK OF THE VAN WITH HIS BACK against Melody's seat. He held his phone to his ear. "Frank?"

"Stone, talk to me, I'm hearing strange things from above, being asked questions I don't know the answers-"

"Get me on the comms, Frank, my phone is compromised."

Harvey disconnected the call and turned the phone off. Melody turned in her seat.

"Compromised?" she asked.

"How else would they know where I am and where I live?"

"So we should assume all our phones are compromised?" asked Melody.

"Turn them on when you really need to, otherwise we use the comms."

"Reg, are the comms encrypted?"

"Yes, they are. The phones are not though, it's a public network, so I don't control them. The boss is here, sit tight."

"Stone, I need an update. It's not looking good from my end," said Frank.

"I believe Stimson or Larson has managed to get my identity," said Harvey. "I found a body in my house last night, then the police came knocking, serious crime squad, and about thirty minutes ago, one of Stimson's guys tried to kill me. He took out a traffic cop, dumped him in the back of his patrol car and pulled us over just as we were tailing Larson."

"Do we have proof of that?"

"Of the body? Not yet."

"Of the kidnapping and the alleged assault of the police officer?"

"We have enough to keep the guy in custody. We cuffed him and left him on the side of the road, then called it in. I imagine he's getting a hiding in the back of a meat wagon as we speak."

"Where are you all now?"

"On the A12, sir," said Denver. "We're thirty minutes out from the city, maybe less."

"How would they of got to you?" asked Frank.

"It's not impossible that they have their own Reg," said Harvey.

"Whoa there," said Reg, "There's only one-"

"What about Mills and Cox?"

"Larson saw us together in the manor house, sir," said Melody. "We have to assume we're known to them as well."

"Where's Larson now?" asked Frank.

"He's off the A12, heading into Stratford. He's being followed by Stimson's tough guy."

"His minder?" asked Frank.

"Yeah, we caught them having a breakfast meeting in the manor house, Larson, the goon and some woman."

"A woman?" asked Frank.

"Yes, sir, an unknown," said Melody.

"This is getting complex," said Frank. "Come back to base, we'll discuss."

"Negative, Frank, we're on the heels of Larson, and he's

heading somewhere he doesn't want us to know about. We need to see what he's up to, and who he's with."

"Stone, you're aware that every policeman in East London is looking for you right now?"

"The story of my life, Frank."

"Harvey, tell me straight," began Frank. "Anything you want to tell us?"

"As it happens, Frank, yeah there is."

"Go on, I'm listening."

"I'd like to tell you I'm getting bored of having you poke your finger at me every time someone gets killed. We're on this guy, and for the first time, he doesn't know it. If I'm right and he's been watching our every move, then this is the first time he won't know we're coming."

There was a silence while Frank thought.

"Okay, go," said Frank. "I'll be watching you all, and remember, we don't want any action, we're just observing."

"How come every time the boss tells Harvey and Melody to just observe, all hell breaks loose?" said Reg.

"Not this time, Tenant," said Frank. "I'm holding you accountable. If you see or hear anything that deviates from my orders, I want to know, and you'll be just as guilty as they are."

"Ah guys, look what you did," said Reg. Melody and Denver smiled at his remark.

"Sir?" said Melody.

"Go ahead."

"The manor house."

"What about it?" asked Frank.

Melody nodded for Harvey to explain.

"It's the perfect place to hold an auction of a priceless artefact. It's surrounded by miles of green, has no underground tunnels, and if they have airborne security, the chances of an airborne getaway are even slimmer," said Harvey.

"What are you saying?" asked Frank.

"I'm saying that the place is impossible to rob."

"Good, we might actually catch them then. If Larson is heading into town, he might be meeting the crew. It sounds like the breakfast was a recce, and he's pulling the team together now."

"Agreed, sir," said Melody.

"Okay, stay on them, report back and don't deviate."

"Copy that, sir," said Melody.

"Okay, Larson and the goon have both stopped at a warehouse in Stratford," said Reg. "There's nothing more conspicuous than a gloomy East London warehouse, right?"

"Send us the location, Reg," said Denver.

"You're looking at Tutbury Lane, it's off-"

"I know it, I know the warehouses too," said Denver. "You got a unit number?"

"Not yet, I'm zooming in, looks like it's the end unit of the first row, facing the main road."

"Any cars outside?" said Harvey.

"There's a few, looks like it's a busy place maybe a mechanic's garage. You can park on the road outside and see in through the fence. Don't drive in, it's a dead end, and probably full of yardies."

"Copy that, Reg," said Denver. "Thanks for the heads up."

"So what do you reckon about you having a bit of competition, Reg?"

"What do I reckon about what?"

"Competition, Reg. You know, whoever it is Larson has tracking our phones. Sounds like you might have some competition."

"Oh, come on, any fool can track a phone," said Reg. "I mean if they were that good, *I'd* know about them."

"You sure about that?" asked Harvey. Harvey rarely got involved in the banter with Reg, but it was fun, and the team needed a lift in morale. "I mean, they must be pretty good to, first of all, find out where I lived, hack my phone, and get my name."

"Child's play, Harvey, child's play."

"That gives me an idea," said Melody. "If we turned Harvey's phone on, could you see if it was being tracked and from *where* it was being tracked?"

"You're talking to the master, Melody."

"Okay, when this is done, and we're out of Stratford, you can have a go. We might find out where they're working from."

"Good call, nerd warfare," said Denver. "In the meantime, we're nearly there. Get yourselves set up. There's a shop over the road from the warehouses, we can park outside it and watch the play."

Denver reversed up onto the pavement and killed the engine. They had a perfect view across the road at the front of the warehouse. Melody set up her DLSR and zoom lens. Harvey used the scope. They both watched, but nothing happened.

"I don't see the BMW anywhere," said Melody.

"Inside maybe?" said Denver, who was keeping watch for passers-by, to make sure nobody looked in and saw the big camera and sighting scope. In East London, if someone saw a van parked up with surveillance taking place, the word would get around like wildfire that the police were closing in on something. A block of flats stood a few hundred yards away and would have been home to countless drug dealers, stolen goods, and probably hookers. It wasn't the nicest part of Stratford, and in those parts, people were street savvy.

"I'm going to take a closer look," said Harvey. He pulled his jacket on and slid the door open.

"Harvey, no. You heard Frank," said Melody.

"Harvey, don't do it," said Reg over the comms. "I'd have to get Frank, and he won't be happy."

"Give me five minutes," said Harvey. "If I'm not back, call it in, tell him I've been a bad boy."

"Oh Jesus, why is it every time we try and do something, we have to step off the line?" said Melody.

"Because staying on the line is not going to get us anywhere is it, Melody?" said Harvey. "Look across the road, the doors are shut. They're hardly likely to leave them open and let us watch them planning a robbery are they?"

"Even so, Harvey, we need more intel, and how we get intel is by being patient and planning. That's your mantra, right?"

"Yeah, that's right, Melody, it's what I live my life by."

"So why do you go off it all the time?"

"Because sitting here isn't going to give us a plan. Me going over there and taking a look will give us the intel we need to create a plan."

"Guys, guys, stop," said Denver. The shutter doors of the warehouse slid back a few meters, and the goon stepped out. Melody grabbed her camera and started to snap away. Harvey climbed back into the van and slid the door shut. The goon walked along the small lane outside the row of warehouses and checked the cars, then walked back to the shutter door and slid it open.

"He's checking the road's clear," said Melody. "Somebody's coming out."

The shutter door slid open further, and there in front of the team was the rear end of a ten-year-old black taxi.

CHAPTER SIXTEEN

SITTING BESIDE THE TAXI WAS THE BLACK BMW. THE BMW's reverse lights came on as soon as the shutter doors were fully open and the big saloon reversed out onto the concrete. The goon pulled the doors closed again. The screech of metal on metal carried across the road to the van.

"Did you see that?" asked Melody.

"Yeah, that's not good," said Denver.

"When that BMW pulls off, I'm going in," said Harvey.

"Harvey, what is it you expect to see in there?" said Melody.

"Answers." Harvey checked his SIG and slid it into his cargo pants. "I'll just have a look around, give us a head start."

"Remember, Harvey, you know I'll have to call this in don't you?" said Reg over the comms. "The big guy'll fry me if you go in."

"Are you a grass now, Reg?"

"Oh, please don't make me be the bad guy," whined Reg.

"The BMW is on the move," said Denver. He started the van and reversed it up behind the wall so it was completely out of sight.

"That's Larson. The goon is leaving too," said Reg. "How big is he? Is he as big as the last guy?"

"Bigger, I'd say, reminds me of Julios."

"And Julios was your teacher from killing school, right?" said Reg.

"Julios was my best friend, he taught me a lot of things."

"Yeah but he also taught you how to kill, didn't he?" said Reg. "My teachers just taught us maths and the gross domestic produce of some place I'll never go to."

"Reg, I get the impression you're lonely in there on your own," said Melody, breaking up the dead-end conversation.

"I'm not on my own, Melody, I've got Chief Inspector fun buckets sitting upstairs waiting for me to call him as soon as Harvey does something wrong."

"So you are a grass then?" said Harvey. "You know what they do to grasses in prison, Reg?"

"I'm guessing they don't get extra food?"

"You're right, but they do get a nice little cuddle in the evening," said Denver.

"That sounds nice," said Reg.

"You should try it," said Harvey. "I can even arrange it for you if you keep on going the way you are."

"Changing the subject, the BMW and the goon have left. They both turned left out of the warehouse compound. Are we going after them, or are we getting into trouble?" said Reg.

Harvey had slid the door open and had one foot out on the concrete.

"Harvey, get back in the van, we can come back," said Melody. "That's an order, let's go back to HQ, regroup and reassess. If you really want to get back here, we'll do it at night, on my terms, and I'll even come with you, but we need to brief Frank."

Harvey paused and looked across at the garage. "I'll hold you to that, Melody Mills," said Harvey, sliding the side door of the van closed. "If Larson wants me out of the picture so much, he won't stop now. He couldn't get me arrested, and he couldn't kill me the first time, but who's to say he won't try again?"

CHAPTER SEVENTEEN

REG HIT THE BUTTON SHORTCUT ON HIS KEYBOARD TO OPEN the shutters for the van to pull in. He closed it again and stood to pop the rear door open for Harvey.

"Hey, team. I missed you guys."

Harvey climbed out, stretched his arms upward, then folded to touch his toes. He clung to his feet for a few seconds, then slowly eased himself up, releasing a long breath. Reg looked on aghast.

"If I tried that, I'd get stuck and end up staring at my crotch for the rest of my life."

Harvey didn't reply.

Frank called down from the mezzanine, "Debrief, let's go."

The team didn't reply. Instead, they walked up to the meeting room and took up their usual positions. Reg sat on the couch, Denver sat on the arm of another couch, Melody stood by the coffee machine, waiting for it to finish filling the pot, and Harvey leaned on the wall by the door.

Frank stood by the whiteboard at the head of the room.

"Welcome back, team. Things are moving. What did we learn? The manor house?"

"Perfect for auctioning a priceless artefact," said Melody. "With the right security, there's little chance of it being robbed by a small team. The place is full of expensive art, Caravaggio, ancient pottery. You could use the frames of some of the painting's *alone* as a house deposit. Do we know how the buddha is being transported?"

"Not yet, there's no talk of it at all, it might already be in the country. Did you see the vault?"

"No, sir. We were preoccupied with Larson and his crew," said Melody.

"Okay, Larson. Tell me what you know."

"The photo's accurate, he hasn't changed his appearance. The phone we are tracking is correct, plus we bugged and chipped his car."

Frank turned to Reg. "Tenant, anything on the bug?"

"Not a bean, I pulled a WAV file from it and literally all we have is road noise. He hasn't uttered a word."

"Okay, who was he with?"

"Big guy, still an unknown, Stimson's minder."

"Another big man? Is he going to be a problem?" asked Frank to Harvey.

The team looked across to Harvey who rolled his eyes. "No, probably not."

Melody grinned.

"Are we tracking the big guy?" asked Frank.

"We have his phone," said Reg.

"Yeah, when they left the manor house they split into three cars," began Melody. "Larson took an Audi, the goon took the BMW, and the woman was picked up in a little red Porsche. The only one who isn't on LUCY is the woman."

"We tailed Larson, but the goon was hanging back so we

couldn't get close. That was when we got pulled over, sir," said Denver.

"Okay, so stop there, before we go any further." Frank began to write on the board. "Manor house is perfect for an auction but almost impossible to rob. In my mind that makes it an ideal target for Stimson, he'll be all over that. You agree with that, Stone?"

Harvey didn't reply.

"Good. Larson isn't running the show, he's a puppet, a powerful puppet. Would you agree with *that* Stone?"

Harvey didn't reply.

"What if Larson *is* running the show?" said Melody. "How can we be sure that-"

"If Larson was there with Stimson's minder, I would imagine the minder is Stimson's eyes and ears. There's no way he's going to go to the manor house he's about to rob to have breakfast with the team he's getting to rob it." Frank paused. "Would you agree with that at least, Stone?"

"I agree with what you're saying, Frank, you don't need to ask. Trust me, when I don't agree you'll know about it."

"No ambiguity there then. Stone, if you were robbing a priceless buddha from the manor house, how would you go about it?"

"I thought about that. The vault is probably underground, there'll be a heavy security detail, but the buddha isn't there yet-"

"How you can so sure?"

"We could have walked out with any one of those paintings or pots with a toy knife. There was a poncy butler on the door, and no cameras. If I was Stimson, I'd take it in transit. Failing that, I'd wait until the place was empty of the public, which I'm sure it will be on auction day, and full of men that are collectively worth more than a small country. Men who have everything to lose and cash to pay for their lives."

"Hostages?"

"Yeah, hostages. I'd go in armed, hard and fast with enough men to cover the auction room while two or three more blow the vault. I'd stash the buddha inside the house, somewhere open to the public. If anyone gets caught, I'd make it look like the boys were stealing money from the rich buyers. The buddha would be hidden and not found on any person, and it can be picked up during a nice little breakfast with some friends a few weeks later when the whole thing has calmed down. If I was Stimson, I'd have found a few places behind wooden panelling or somewhere to stash the buddha."

"You thought hard about that?"

"Yeah, there's no possible way you'd get away with the buddha once the alarm has been raised, and there's no way the crew would get away either. They'd get a few years for armed robbery and would need paying off, but there's a load of guys out there that would risk that for their families, and Stimson isn't shy when it comes to spending money on something he wants. The crew will be lifers, men Stimson can trust, who know they will be looked after inside, and have their families looked after on the outside.

"No, he's not afraid to splash the cash." Frank gave Harvey's plan some thought. "What about Stimson? Surely he wouldn't be prepared to go away?"

"No he wouldn't, not with dedicated men like that, he'd have an exit, he may even go in as a buyer. A bystander as it were."

"Good analysis," said Frank. "Tenant, see what you can find on the security for the manor house, any locals firms, mobs or whatever."

Frank put Reg's name beside the manor house on the whiteboard.

"Moving on, so you were pulled over by traffic police? I want the full story. Mills, go."

"We were out of Braintree, heading for the A12, when the Volvo came from behind us. He gave two short blasts on the sirens and indicated for us to pull over-"

"First sign," said Harvey.

"Denver got out of the van, and the policeman told him to put his hands on the vehicle, without explanation, then he cuffed and searched Denver."

"Second sign," said Harvey.

"I got out and showed him my ID, and he shoved me up against the van and cuffed me."

"Third sign."

"That's when Harvey stepped out and gave himself up. He already knew Harvey's name and had him up against the van with the cuffs in his hand. That was when-"

"That was when I was sure he was fake," said Harvey.

"Why?"

"Two short blasts on the sirens on a quiet A-road? Not a traffic cop's style, they keep them off unless the roads are busy or it's high speed. The way he handled Denver, too rough, plus he gave no reason for the tug. He was rude and rough with Melody and cuffed her despite her ID and for no reason, then he knew my name."

"You're sure he knew your name?"

"Yeah, positive. Why would a white hat in the sticks know my name?"

"Because of the dead man in your bathtub?" asked Reg.

"No, we're talking deepest darkest sticks, not much chance of it being at the top of a traffic cop's priority list out there," said Harvey. "Lastly, the cop had three sets of cuffs on him. Pretty unlikely he carries *them* every day, right?"

"Right. So what did you do?" asked Frank.

"I told him what I thought."

"You told him what you thought?

"I put the guy down and cuffed him. Then unlocked these guys' handcuffs."

"That's when we found the real cop unconscious in the boot of the car, sir," said Melody.

"And what did you do with him?"

"Sat him on the ground leaning on the car," said Harvey. "I gave a call over his radio, took the dash cam and hard drive, and we got out of there."

"So nobody saw you?"

"Whoever drove past might have seen us, but no police saw us."

"What's with the questions, sir?" asked Melody.

"Well, Mills, every time you lot go out, I have to pull answers out of my backside for the mess you make."

"This wasn't us being cavalier, sir," said Melody.

"No, you're right. So I hear now your phones are compromised?"

"Only Harvey's for sure, but ours are off to be safe. We're relying on the comms until Reg can confirm the phones are safe to use."

"What's the plan to check that?"

"I'll go out, away from here. I'll turn my phone on, and Reg will be able to see if it's being tracked, and where the tracker is," said Harvey.

"Tenant, you can do that?" asked Frank.

"In my sleep, sir."

"So why isn't a basic security protocol like that in operation all the time? Is it something we can do constantly?"

"Okay, I'll get it set up," said Reg, slightly perplexed at his oversight.

"Has my phone been compromised?" asked Frank.

"I'll check," said Reg. "In the meantime, it's best to turn it off."

"Good. This is the type of thing we need to get better at, people. Now, talk to me about the warehouse."

"Stratford, sir. Old warehouse, rough part of town," said Denver.

"We followed Larson and the goon there," said Melody, "They weren't there long and then they left again."

"But?" said Frank. "I can sense a but coming."

"We got a glimpse inside, sir."

"Tell me what you saw."

"A black taxi, sir. Reg has checked the plates, it was Arthur Bell's taxi."

"What else did you see?"

"Nothing, sir, the door was only open for a moment while Larson pulled his car out."

"He either picked something up or dropped something off, Frank," said Harvey. "I'm going back tonight."

"Are you? I thought it was me that gave the orders, Stone."

"Not when it comes to people trying to kill me, Frank. With all due respect." Harvey spoke the last words slowly and clearly.

Frank stared at Harvey for a second. "Okay, let's make it worthwhile. Mills, you're going in with him. Cox, Tenant, you'll both be outside. What's security like?"

"There's a guy on the gate, easily avoided, he's more likely there to stop pikeys getting in," said Harvey. "There's a single door on the warehouse with a pull-down shutter over it and a large sliding door."

"Plan?"

"I'll get into the single door. The large door screeches and will wake up most of London."

"Alarm?"

"Doubt it, Frank. There's a stolen taxi inside that

belonged to the dead guy the police found in my house. If I had that taxi, I wouldn't be setting an alarm."

"Anyone inside? Security detail?"

"Only one way to find out."

"Okay get in, have a look around, bug it and get out." Frank turned to address the whole room. "Anything else I need to know?"

"Actually, sir, yes," began Reg. "The dash cam Harvey ripped out of the police car had some pretty quite surprising footage on it."

18

CHAPTER EIGHTEEN

IT WAS FOUR AM WHEN HARVEY SHEARED THE LOCKS ON the shutter door. Harvey quietly put the car jack he'd used to one side, and pulled the shutter up, revealing a single door with a glazed upper panel. The wood was soft, cheap and old, and gave easily when Harvey slipped his jimmy bar in and leaned a little weight on it. The lock remained in position, but the entire door was forced away from the frame and opened easily.

Harvey stood in the doorway listening.

"What are you waiting for?" Melody whispered.

Harvey tapped his watch and held up one index finger. Melody noted his frown and look of concentration. She stepped back and checked behind her; the compound of warehouses and garages was clear of people. The security hut a hundred yards away was lit softly from inside, allowing the guard to read his book.

Melody checked across the street and saw the van parked outside the shop. She couldn't see any movement or lights from inside, the tinted windows hid Denver and Reg well. Even Reg's screens didn't light the interior of the van.

She sensed movement in the corner of her eye, Harvey was moving in. She stepped slowly behind him, watching for an attack to come from the shadows. The warehouse smelled like a mechanic's garage; the air was thick with the smell of motor oil and dust.

Melody had her SIG drawn and held it in two hands aiming beyond Harvey into the darkness. Harvey stepped out the little hallway into the large warehouse space and disappeared into the gloom. Melody stood in the doorway listening for his footsteps but heard nothing. She lowered her night vision goggles and saw Harvey standing to her left beside the taxi. Harvey didn't wear NV. He allowed his senses to adjust to the darkness. When he was happy that they were alone, he motioned to Melody to turn the lights on. She found the switches on the wall beside her. Even in the green NV she could see the grime on the switch.

She closed her eyes before flicking the switch and lifted the goggles before opening them again. The warehouse looked like a far different place than it had with the goggles on.

"Stay near the door, in case security see the light."

Melody stayed put, but planted three audio bugs in various places nearby while she waited; one on top of a large space heater, one below a workbench beneath the light switch, and one on a rack of metal shelving behind her. She leaned against a wooden crate and watched Harvey move around the taxi. The space around the parked car was empty, save for a few hessian sacks that were sat on the dirty floor. An old tool chest stood open, and an array of tools had been thrown inside it. It was a far cry from Denver's set up and his meticulously clean working environment. A stack of wheels stood in the corner beside the shutter door and a large hydraulic car jack sat beside them. In front of the taxi was a pile of car seats, semi-covered in thick blue plastic sheets, and behind that was an old, battered forklift truck.

Harvey placed a bug inside the black cab. "Rear seats have gone," he said, just loudly enough for her to hear.

"They're there in front." She nodded with her head when he looked at her. "They're stripping it down to hide the murder?"

Harvey glanced at the pile of seats and stared back at the taxi. He stepped over closer but didn't move anything. Harvey glanced back at Melody.

Melody looked at the crate she leaned on. It was a heavy wooden box fixed to a wooden pallet. She stood away from it to read the sides, but the language was foreign. Whatever it said, it was written in German.

"Harvey?"

Harvey saw Melody looking at the box and joined her.

"German," she said.

"Car parts?" said Harvey.

"You know what's made in Germany?"

Harvey stepped back to the tool chest and found a large flathead screwdriver. He rejoined Melody, who was taking photos of the writing.

She hit the button on her ear-piece that opened comms, "Reg."

"Go ahead," came Reg's reply.

"Sending you a photo, need it translated quick smart."

She hit send on her phone, then turned it off quickly. She watched as Harvey worked his way carefully around the top of the box, easing the lid up without leaving marks in the soft wood. He prised one end up enough to slip his fingers underneath, and yanked the lid upwards, then carefully lowered it to the floor.

"Direct translation is a bit confusing, Melody, but it basically says, *Highly Volatile*."

Harvey was carefully lifting a plastic sheet that covered the contents of the box. Melody held out her hand to stop him.

"Did you hear Reg?" she asked.

Harvey didn't reply. The frown deepened on his face. He lifted the plastic fully and stared down at the mass of plastic explosives. He raised his eyes to Melody.

"That's a lot of explosives," said Melody.

Harvey pulled the lid back on and hammered it closed with his fist.

"Let's go," he said. "Denver, extract." They stepped outside and heard the warble of the van's exhaust from across the street.

"Go, I'll catch you up," said Harvey, as he turned to pull the shutter door down.

Melody turned and ran to the wall she and Harvey had climbed over. She checked behind her to make sure the coast was clear, then pulled herself up and waited for Harvey to join her.

Harvey sprinted from the shadows and leapt up. He caught hold of the top of the wall and was down the other side in matter seconds. Melody took a final glance back towards the warehouse, but as she did, headlights appeared at the entrance to the compound. She laid low on the top of the wall. More headlights appeared after the first, another car. Melody lowered herself down and stood beside Harvey as Denver pulled the van up on the street.

The sliding door slid open, and they climbed in. "Go, go, go." Denver pulled away as the door pulled shut, and the team sat in silence for a while until they were clear of the area.

Melody was the first to speak.

"We're too late," she said. "The explosives are already here, and it looked like two cars just arrived as we left."

"How much?" asked Denver.

"PX5? Enough to blow a hole in London big enough to fit another city in. About a hundred kilos."

Denver's eyes widened. "A hundred kilos of plastic explosives?"

"Sitting on a pallet in a warehouse in the arse-end of London," said Melody.

"Not for long," said Harvey. "That's what the cabs are for."

"What?" said Melody.

"It's obvious. They didn't strip the cab down to hide the murder, they stripped it down to fit the explosives inside." Harvey took a breath. "That cab's going to be driven through London and detonated somewhere busy."

"Stimson?"

"Sadly, yes."

"Why would Stimson do that? He's a diamond thief, not a terrorist," said Melody.

"I know, it doesn't make sense."

"Reg, can you get us a list of all known auction houses in the city of London? Not West London, in the city," said Harvey.

"Easy," replied Reg.

"Then tell me which ones have a day scheduled as closed in the next few days, should be on their website."

"What are you saying, Harvey?" said Melody.

"I'm saying the auction isn't happening in Wethersfield, that's a decoy. Stimson planted that intel to lead us away from the real auction."

"Frank got us that information," said Melody.

"Where from? His phone?" said Harvey. "We've already seen my phone is compromised." Harvey let that information settle in, then said, "The robbery will take place at the same time as that taxi drives into London and detonates. They'll be so much chaos that getting away with a tiny little statue will be easy."

"There are a number of auction houses in the City of London itself, but notably, there's one on Queen Victoria Street, which happens to be directly behind St Paul's Cathedral. It's closed in three days time for a private event, according to the website's calendar."

"Queen Victoria Street? That's where we found Hague, he was on foot heading towards St Paul's," said Harvey.

"You think the buddha has been there all along?" said Melody.

"It makes sense," said Harvey. "Imagine it, they tried to do the heist with Hague as the decoy, but we nailed him, foiled their plan, so they aborted the heist. They found out who we were from the bloody videos people took on the bridge and set up a decoy auction out in the sticks. Meanwhile, their tech guy hacked my identity, they planted a body to get me arrested, then tried to take me out in Essex." He paused. "And now this. They know we're getting closer."

The team sat silently and thought on Harvey's synopsis.

"Denver," said Harvey, "let's go see this auction house."

"Copy that," replied Denver.

"Even Stimson wouldn't stoop so low, would he?"

"That depends doesn't it," said Harvey.

"On?"

"His Motive."

"His motive?"

"Yeah, what's driving him to pull such a crazy stunt."

"The priceless buddha?"

"The Stimsons are responsible for the biggest heists in recent history. They've been doing this for as long as I can remember," said Harvey. "And you know what?"

"What?"

"They've never killed a single person in any of their heists."

"Not a single one?"

"Nothing more than the butt of a rifle in a security guard's face. So why would they change that habit now and potentially kill hundreds of people?"

"His motivation's changed," said Melody.

"It looks like it, but there's more."

"More?"

"Think about what you just saw, Melody."

She turned to face him in her seat, "The taxi?"

"And?"

"The wheels?"

Harvey didn't reply.

"The seats?"

Harvey raised his eyebrow.

"There was a pile of seats," she said, then her eyes widened. "Too many for one taxi." Cogs fell into place. She gasped. "There's more than one taxi."

19

CHAPTER NINETEEN

"How far, Denver?" asked Melody.

"We're coming up to Liverpool Street, less than three minutes away," Denver replied.

"What's the plan?" asked Melody.

"I just want to take a look, see the auction house, see what Stimson is likely to do," said Harvey.

"Looking at the satellite imagery," said Reg, "from the auction house, they'd have a clear run down to the river, if they had-"

"A boat waiting," finished Melody. "They'd be away in no time at all, they could have a car waiting at literally any point along the river."

"I was going to say that, you always steal my thunder, Melody," said Reg. "I'll call Frank, and tell him what we're doing, he should be in HQ by now."

Reg dialled Frank's number and waited for him to answer.

"Wait," said Harvey. "Your phone is on?"

"Well yeah, it works better when its-"

"Turn it off!" shouted Melody.

"Tenant?" Frank answered the call. "What's the update?"

Just then a car slammed into the side of the van, forcing it into oncoming traffic. Denver's head crashed into the door and shattered the glass. Reg was thrown back off his seat and onto Harvey who was sat on the floor behind Melody.

Denver pulled the van back to the correct side of the road, but the car held its nose into the side of the van. The two vehicles were locked, neither one dropping their throttles. Smoke rose from the screeching tyres and the smell of burning rubber filled the air.

"It's a taxi," called Denver.

Harvey jumped up and slid the side door of the van open, but it was jammed by the damage and the front wing of the taxi. He pulled his SIG and fired two rounds through the small gap into the taxi's wheel. The taxi slowed a little, allowing Harvey to shove the door open, but the door's rails were smashed, and it fell off onto the road. The taxi bounced over it, accelerated again and slammed once more into the side of the van, nudging it further and further sideways.

Harvey put his SIG into his waistband and leapt from the van onto the taxi's bonnet. He grabbed hold of the windscreen wipers. They twisted and bent under his weight, but he held on, his legs swinging across the front of the car's rounded bonnet.

The sound of the two battling engines was all Harvey could hear, and the road was filled with smoke. People ran from the sliding wreckage. The van drove on with the taxi wedged into its side, both engines fighting for control.

Harvey let go with one hand and pulled his SIG once more, but the driver yanked the steering wheel just as he aimed, and Harvey's legs swung across to the passenger side. His feet scraped the road just inches from the tyre. Denver saw Harvey's struggle and turned hard into the front of the taxi, pushing it off the road to stop Harvey from being crushed. The driver held the wheel firm. As the taxi careered into the roadside barrier, Harvey was dragged off the car.

The team watched in horror as Harvey's body disappeared from view and the taxi bounced; its rear wheels drove effortlessly across Harvey's leg. Melody turned sharply in her seat to see Harvey roll into the middle of the road. The taxi came to a stop. Denver was out the van like a shot. He forced his driver's door open as Melody opened hers. She ran back to Harvey, frantically trying to raise Frank on the comms, while Denver yanked the taxi's driver door open.

The Middle-Eastern driver had smashed his face on the steering wheel when Denver had forced him off the road. He raised his bloodied face and looked ahead of him, confused. He turned and looked up at Denver as Denver's fist connected with his jaw. Denver stood upright, held onto the open door with one hand and the roof of the taxi with the other, then brought his foot down hard on the man's face again and again.

Sirens sounded in the distance, and the taxi driver roused himself at the sound. He raised his arm to stop Denver's attack and looked behind him. Then he smiled cruelly at Denver. Denver saw the man's left hand reaching across to the passenger floor. A tangled mass of wires was connected to a home-made switch. He glanced into the back of the taxi and saw that there were no seats.

Denver threw himself into the driver's seat on top of the man and wrestled his arm from the wires, but the man was strong and held on. His fingers were slowly working towards the switch while Denver tried to pull him away.

With no other choice, Denver stamped on the gas pedal. His right leg dragged along the ground as he steered the taxi away from the van and the team. The Middle-Eastern man struggled harder, but Denver pulled his foot in and pushed back on the driver, pinning him to the seat. He held the driver's wrist and tried to pry the wires from his bony hand but the man held fast. With his right hand, Denver steered the accelerating taxi away from other traffic. The wing mirror smashed off as he passed too close to another car and the driver got out and began to shout.

Denver rounded a long, sweeping bend and came to a straight. He held the steering wheel with his leg and began punching the driver's head furiously. The man was shouting in a foreign language, repeating the same sentence over and over.

Grabbing the wheel once more, Denver slid the taxi around a corner too fast. It bounced off the curb, but maintained its speed. He rounded the long chicane of Queen Victoria Street where the road merged with the embankment, and, seeing no other choice, aimed the speeding taxi towards the river.

The high curb tore the front wheel off the chassis and the car's rear end bounced hard, launching into the air. Denver braced for the impact. The crazed driver seized the opportunity he'd been waiting for and lunged for the switch as the car crashed into the water.

The river muffled the explosion, but the blast rocked Blackfriar's Bridge, shook the surrounding trees and smashed the glass of cars passing by. A rush of water surged high into the air.

Within moments, the river had returned to its steady flow of brown water. The only sign of the taxi was the thousands of bubbles that surfaced then dissipated, disappearing as quickly as the taxi had been destroyed.

CHAPTER TWENTY

HARVEY LAUNCHED HIMSELF FROM THE SIDE DOOR ONTO the front of the taxi that was wedged into the side of the van. Both vehicles were powering through the crash, each driver battling to bring the other to a stop. Harvey clung to the wiper with one hand and with the other reached behind him and pulled his weapon from his waist. He brought it up to fire, but the driver pulled hard on the steering wheel, sending Harvey to the far side of the car's bonnet. His leg fell off the smooth surface, and his foot dragged perilously close the wheels scraping the floor. His felt the burn of the rubber through his thick boots.

The taxi ploughed on with one blown tyre. The driver straightened up, and Harvey clung on for his life, desperately trying to keep his foot and leg from going under the wheel.

Denver saw his chance and steered the van into the taxi's path, trying to stop the cab from crushing Harvey into the railings, but it was too late. Harvey was dragged from the car, and his hand ripped off the sharp metal wiper arm. The rear wheels bounced across his thigh, and Harvey rolled to a stop face down on the tarmac.

His leg pounded and his hands were wet with warm sticky blood. All he could do was close his eyes and rest his head on the hard road.

It felt like an eternity, sleep washed over him, deep and welcoming. He was no longer laying on the road but was warm in fresh, clean sheets. All around him were featureless white walls and air so clean he could taste the sea. He imagined a long, empty beach with the sea far off to his right. Long wild grass grew in clumps to his left, beyond was a blur of pastel yellow and green. He ran on the sand. He ran so fast he thought he would trip and stumble, but she held out her hand. It was Hannah, enticing him to catch her, faster, faster, her long legs bounded easily over the sand. Her bare feet barely left a mark.

He was closer now; the sun was stronger; the light was brighter. He squinted but ran harder. Tears streamed from his eyes. He reached out, step after step, bound after bound in the soft sand, then, at last, he felt her hand slip through his fingers. Harder, faster, he pushed, his breathing in time with his effort, blinded by the bright light he ran on and on. He could hear her laughing. "Run, Harvey, you can catch me."

He growled loudly and pushed harder than ever. His little arms pumped wildly and his legs were numb, but all the power in his child's body surged through them. Reaching out once more, he felt her fingers, long and slender. He held his hand there, groping in his blindness as he pumped his other arm and legs. He growled again, long and hard and pushed with everything he had.

His hand found hers, and gripped it tight, like a man's grip. She laughed in the light then stumbled and they fell together and rolled. He came to a stop on his back, and she laid across him, panting. "You did it, Harvey, you caught me." He was no longer a boy, he was a man. But his sister retained her youth, her perfect skin and welcoming smile. Kindness shone from her eyes and the wind ruffled her long, blonde hair.

"You did it, Harvey." She smiled up at him.

CHAPTER TWENTY-ONE

A COLD WIND RUSHED OVER HARVEY. HIS BODY SHOOK AND his muscles convulsed. He tried to curl up but his leg wouldn't move, and a dull ache set into his back. Something wailed in the distance. The sound grew closer. The bright, white walls and the clean air turned to grey. He licked his parched lips and tasted grit and blood.

He opened his eyes.

"Harvey?" A silhouette kneeled over him. "Harvey, talk to me." He closed his eyes again.

Harvey clenched his fist and felt the stab of pain across his palm, but clenched tighter and harder, squeezing the blood from his grip.

"Don't move, Harvey, stay there, it's okay, there's help coming."

The realisation that he was lying on a road struck him, and he rolled painfully onto his back.

"Don't move, Harvey. Can you talk? Can you hear me?"

He opened his eyes once more and saw nothing but the dome of St Paul's Cathedral, black against the grey sky.

"Here, take some water." The woman held a bottle to his

mouth and poured him a sip. He wanted more and reached for it, but she held him down. "Stay there, Harvey." He swallowed and felt the water release the tension in his throat.

"The taxi?"

"It's gone," said the woman. "You nearly killed yourself."

Recognition came to him, and he stared at her. Her long hair rested on his neck as she leaned over him. "I know that smell."

"Harvey, you've had a serious accident, stay down, just relax."

"I know you," he rasped.

"Of course you do." She put her hand on his face and wiped moisture from his eye with her thumb. "It's me, Melody."

"Melody," he said. The wailing grew louder. More people stood around him. Melody spoke loudly to them. "Move away, give him space." Harvey saw them holding their phones. A man in a bright yellow jacket helped her move people away, and the ambulance parked alongside him. Two men in bright green knelt by his side.

"Mr Stone, can you hear me?" said the first man.

Harvey didn't reply.

The man stared into Harvey's eyes. "Can you hear me? Can you tell me where it hurts?" The man was feeling along Harvey's legs for broken bones.

"Come closer," said Harvey.

The man leaned into him so Harvey could talk into his ear.

"Get me up."

"Oh no, you're going on a stretcher my friend, you won't-"

"Get me up, now," said Harvey. He turned his head to find Melody, his eyes wild. "Get me up, Melody."

"Harvey, no. Let them do their jobs."

"What's your name?" said Harvey to the second EMT, the

older of the men who was filling out a report on a tablet. He looked down at Harvey.

"My name's Jim, Mr Stone."

"Jim, tell your friend to stop checking for broken bones and help me up."

"You're clearly a brave man, Mr Stone, but as my colleague-"

"I'll do you both a deal." The two men listened. "If you help me up and I begin to fall, you can stop me falling and put me the ambulance. But if I don't fall, and can stand, I walk away with my friend here."

"Sir, unfortunately-"

"Am I a grown man?"

"Yes, Mr Stone."

"So let me make a grown man's decision. If you don't help me up, I'll damn well get up myself, and that'll be the end of it."

"Harvey, you can't-"

"I can do what I like, Melody," he said calmly but sharply. "Are you going to help me up?"

The older of the two nodded at the first one, and they knelt either side of Harvey. Harvey bent his good leg and felt them pull his shoulders up. He pushed against them and felt the blood rush to his head, dizzying him.

"Easy now, come on, sit in the ambulance." The two men each held an arm.

"Okay," said Harvey. "Let me go."

Melody stood in front of him shaking her head. Harvey put the weight on his bad leg and breathed out, letting the pain in, controlling it, dominating it, as it scoured his leg for new places to hurt. He put more weight on and the pain increased. Still he stood, defiant.

"Thank you, both," said Harvey.

Melody stepped across the road and stood beside Harvey

as the two EMTs moved away. She put her arm around him, and he rested his arm on her shoulders. He limped across to the van where Reg stood.

The look on Reg's face was sour. Tears rolled freely from his eyes.

"Reg, where's Denver?" asked Melody.

Reg didn't reply. He just stood and stared, shaking his head. He stood paralysed, looking dumbfounded between Harvey and Melody. They stepped in closer. Harvey put his other arm up to Reg's shoulder, and Melody did the same. The three of them stood like that for several minutes, holding each other. The emotion ran through the group. At first, Harvey felt he was holding his two colleagues in a time of tragedy, then he felt the anger and loss wash over him, and felt as if it was them that held and comforted him.

Policemen broke up the huddle and took them to one side of the street. Melody discreetly showed him her badge and asked him to wait for Frank Carver to arrive. She and Reg slumped to the ground, but Harvey stood leaning against the wall. He put more weight on his bad leg for longer periods each time. Melody rested her head against his good leg and closed her eyes.

Harvey knew the power of adrenalin, he knew it would render the team powerless once its magical effects wore off. He kept himself charged and ran through the events in his head. Everything had changed. It was all different now. He looked up at St Paul's Cathedral across the street and wondered what might have been.

The team's sleek Audi drew up beside them. The driver side door opened and Frank stepped out the car. He pulled his long jacket around him and tied the belt, then folded his collar up against the wind. It was only then that Harvey realised the wind was strong and cold. His leather jacket had saved his skin and bore the brunt of the fierce British winter breeze.

Frank stood before them.

Melody looked up at him, but didn't stand. "I'm sorry, sir."

"You've nothing to be sorry for," said Frank with strength in his voice. It was just the four of them on the pavement opposite the cathedral. Frank waited for a full minute before speaking.

CHAPTER TWENTY-TWO

"WE JUST LOST A GOOD MAN, THE WORLD JUST LOST A GOOD man, and Denver's family just lost everything," said Frank. "We need to act now, grieve later. I know it's hard, and if you want out. Now's the time to leave."

They were all silent.

"Let's recap what we've got," said Frank.

"We believe that the auction isn't going to take place in the manor house, that was a diversion from Stimson," said Harvey.

"Okay," said Frank. He was engaged and listening.

"We believe the auction will take place at an auction house on Queen Victoria Street, that's a hundred yards from where we're standing."

Harvey saw the cogs turning in Frank's head.

"We also believe that the buddha is already there in the vault."

"So the explosion was meant to be a distraction for the robbery?" Asked Frank.

"Yeah, we found Arthur Bell's taxi inside the warehouse, the seats had been stripped out ready for the explosives."

"And?"

"Plus the seats of of at least two more taxis."

"And?"

"About a hundred kilos of plastic explosives."

"There's two more taxis rigged to blow?" asked Frank.

"We believe so, sir."

"This is Stimson we're talking about, loud explosions are not his style."

"Harvey thinks his motivation has changed," said Melody.

Frank nodded. "I'd agree with that, the entire strategy has changed, but he's been through a lot of trouble to get us out of the way. The manor, the cop. Are the phones still compromised?"

"We believe so, sir. They knew exactly where we were," said Reg.

"And probably where we are now," said Harvey.

"Exactly," said Frank. "So we need to move fast before they strike again. The taxis were stolen, they're hard to spot, easier to transport explosives. No-one would look twice at a taxi driving through here."

"But *we* needed to be diverted," said Melody.

"Yes, but not killed. Stimson isn't a killer remember," said Frank.

"So why were we attacked and nearly blown up?" asked Reg.

"The motivation got stronger," said Harvey. He pushed himself from the wall and winced as he limped to stand closer to the others. Melody put her hand on his arm, but he nodded to reassure her that he was okay standing on his own. "Whatever pressure is on Stimson to get that buddha, it recently got a lot stronger. Whatever is driving him to do the heist has recently become more pressing." Harvey thought on his own words. "Time is running out."

"Time is running out?" asked Melody.

"Reg can you tell us if the auction house is closed now?" asked Harvey.

"Sure, I'll fire up the computers and see if I can-"

"Or you could walk around the corner and see if there's anything outside, like a timetable. Public auctions often have a notice behind glass like a courtroom," said Harvey.

"Oh, okay, that's easier," said Reg.

"Keep your comms open," said Frank as Reg walked away and disappeared around the corner.

"So, I'm guessing you'll be starting at the top, and finding out why Stimson's motivation has stepped up?" asked Frank.

"Seems like a good place to start," said Harvey.

"And how exactly do you plan on doing that? Time *is* running out, after all."

"There's three players here, not including Stimson, because he never leaves the house it seems."

"Right."

"Larson, clever bastard, one step ahead the entire time."

"Agreed."

"The goon, who doesn't really pose much of a threat until we come to take Stimson out, which isn't the top priority here is it. Our priority is stopping the bombs going off so the auction can run, and the buddha can be removed from the vault safely and taken away someplace else."

"I'd agree with that loosely. Who's the third player?"

"Al Sayan."

"I told you not to go there, Stone."

"You want me to finish this, you need to trust me. Al Sayan is the key. Do you honestly believe that Stimson is responsible for what just happened to Denver?"

Frank looked at Harvey, sighed, then nodded slowly. "That changes everything," he said.

"While we waste time chasing Stimson and Larson, Al Sayan is picking us off, making it easier for them," said

Harvey. "We need to turn our attention here to the one who's calling shots."

The team were silent.

"First job," said Harvey. "We need to lure them out. Go somewhere easy to find, somewhere we can't run away. Once we see who comes after us, we'll see who's calling the shots here."

"That's a terrible plan, it doesn't make sense," said Melody.

Harvey smiled. "Did you see the taxi driver?"

"Yeah."

"British?"

"Middle Eastern at a guess."

"Right," said Harvey. "We'll get out of here, go somewhere with an open space and fewer people, somewhere a bomb could go off and not hurt anyone but us."

"You've lost the plot."

"They're tracking us, we're being hunted. Don't you see it?" said Harvey. "Let's not take the mountain to Mohammed, let him come to us."

"You have a plan I presume?" said Frank.

"I take the phones, stand in the middle of a field or a car park or something. Then two things will happen."

Melody was intrigued, but concerned.

"Reg will see the phone's interception."

"And?"

"Someone will turn up, possibly in the second black cab."

"And what good will that do?"

"Two things, if the driver is British, which I doubt he is, Stimson's running the show, and we prod the driver for information. My speciality."

"And if he's-"

"If he's Middle Eastern, he won't talk, but he won't need to."

"Why not?"

"Because if he's one of Al Sayan's men, it means that it is Al Sayan increasing the pressure on Stimson. We have a direction."

"You're putting yourself in the line of fire, Stone."

"Denver just drove a taxi rigged with explosives into the Thames so we could live. Let's make it count. You have a Diemaco in the van?" Harvey asked Melody.

"Sure," said Melody.

"You can take him out."

There was a long pause. Melody and Frank both knew the plan would give them direction. It was a loose plan, but it was all they had.

"What happens if the phones aren't intercepted?" asked Melody.

"Plan B."

"What's plan B?"

"Make a new plan," said Harvey. The comment wasn't meant to be funny, it was a statement that perfectly summed up their predicament. They had only one option.

"How are you feeling, Stone? Are you sure you're up to this?" asked Frank.

Harvey stared at him.

"Well, just let me know if you need anything, you look like crap, are you guys-"

"We'll be fine, sir," said Melody. "Are you going to see-"

"Denver's family? Yes."

"Please pass on the condolences of the team, sir. We all loved him. I can't believe he's gone," said Melody.

"I'm supposed to go down to the river now. There're more questions to be answered I'm sure," said Frank.

"What's to say?" said Harvey. "Denver's a hero. If it wasn't for him that four-hundred-year-old cathedral standing there would be levelled, and none of us would be stood here talking."

"He's a hero alright, but that doesn't make the news any easier to break to his family."

"He was close to his mum," said Melody. "Would you like me to go? You know, it's sometimes better coming from a woman."

"That's kind of you, Mills. But there are some things that need to come from me. You three have enough on your plate."

Reg returned from around the corner and walked towards the rest of the team. Frank turned to him and watched the small-framed man scurry along in the cold.

"There'll be a service?" asked Melody.

"Of that I'm sure," replied Frank glancing back. Then he turned to face St Paul's Cathedral. "We'll all be there."

Reg returned to the group. "Closed, no sign of anything, security in reception."

"Good, we still have time," said Harvey. "Let's do this."

"Did I ever tell you all about my wife?" asked Frank as the team made ready to go.

"No, sir," said Melody.

"She was a lovely woman really, caring and the rest. Did the things for me most men wouldn't do for themselves. Looked after me. We had a good many years together too. We travelled, we ate well, saw things some people only ever seen in photos. Jan was a good woman, the best. Salt of the earth. You know what I'm saying?"

The team nodded slowly.

"I lost her, three years ago. Some bastard felt that the time was right to destroy the lives of those around him." Frank stared at them with watery eyes. "You remember the Bow Street bomb?"

Melody's eyes widened. "She was on that?"

"Same carriage. She didn't stand a chance."

"That was Al Sayan too. What exactly are you saying, sir?" asked Melody.

"What am I saying? I don't know, really." He huffed. "Loss? Hate?" He sighed. "Someone I respect a great deal once told me something that I'll never forget." Frank looked up at the sky and searched for the words. "Sometimes a man does something so bad, so evil, that society has an obligation to seek revenge, to right the wrong. And sometimes, those who have been so badly wronged are owed so much that they earn the opportunity to enact that revenge. For it's those that suffer the most who most deserve the closure that retribution brings." Frank turned to Harvey. A tear ran freely from Frank's eye.

Harvey gave an indiscernible nod.

"What am I saying?" said Frank, turning to Melody and Reg. "Go get them. For Denver."

CHAPTER TWENTY-THREE

THEY STRIPPED THE VAN OF EVERYTHING THEY NEEDED AND loaded it all into the Audi Frank had left for them. Reg removed his laptop, a mobile antenna and the mobile comms receiver.

Harvey helped Melody remove her Peli cases, surveillance equipment, two Heckler and Koch MP5s and her favourite, the Diemaco. It was a 7.62mm calibre assault rifle with a telescopic scope. The rails on the underside could hold either a red-dot laser or a grenade launcher. It was an awesome-looking weapon and Melody's choice of weaponry for long range. The rifle also had a selector that changed the action from single shot to three-round bursts or full auto. Melody preferred the accuracy of single shot, but would quickly shift to three-round bursts if her position was compromised.

Frank spoke to the officer in charge at the scene and arranged for the van to be taken to headquarters. He then tossed Harvey the keys to the Audi. "I'd wish you luck, but..." He paused, unable to find the words. He knew he was sending his remaining team off into the unknown, short-handed and emotionally scarred, but there was little he could do in such a short amount of time.

"For Denver, sir," said Melody.

"For Denver," replied Frank. He turned and took the longest walk of his life down to the river where divers and investigators tried to piece the puzzle together, and scared onlookers filmed the scenes on their mobile phones.

Harvey tossed the keys to Melody.

"Why am I driving?" she asked.

"It's got four wheels," replied Harvey.

Reg had begun to set himself up in the back. He placed the small antenna on the roof and ran the cable down beside the rubber door trim. His laptop sat on the seat beside him and he placed the comms unit on the parcel shelf with the headphones plugged in and hanging on the headrest.

Melody's equipment was loaded into the boot and several pairs of binoculars and her scope were unboxed and kept loose beside Reg.

"Okay, before we move, let's do a comms check," said Reg.

"Stone," said Harvey pushing the button on his ear-piece once.

"Copy."

"Mills," said Melody.

"Loud and clear," confirmed Reg. "Comms are good. My connection to the satellite will be slow without the powered v-Sat unit the van had, but I'll see what I can do with the modems I have, and create an SSL VPN back to headquarters. This laptop won't run LUCY so well, so I'll be using the power of the command centre and just viewing the visual over the link to keep the bandwidth down, it should mask our IP as well."

"Sounds technical, Reg," said Harvey. He slid the action back on his SIG and chambered a round, flicked the safety on, and put the weapon back in his waist. "Yep, that works."

Melody climbed into the driver seat and pulled the door closed. She started the engine and pulled her seat belt across her chest. "Where are we going to do this?" she asked.

"Somewhere with little to no people, but close enough that we can get back here, quickly," said Harvey. "Reg, tell me what you see on satellite."

"How big does the space need to be?"

"Big enough for a car to explode with no collateral damage."

"Okay, the nearest large empty space I can see is Wanstead Flats. There'll be a dog walkers, maybe even some dogging action, but we can probably park out of the way."

"Which way?" asked Melody.

"A13, A406," said Harvey. "We'll be against the traffic this time of day."

Harvey slid his belt across when Melody put her foot down. The Audi's powerful engine kicked in, and before he knew it, they were leaving the city.

"Where are your phones?" asked Harvey.

Melody pulled her phone from her pocket, and Reg passed his forward over Harvey's shoulder.

"Here goes, Reg are you ready?"

"I'm activating the scanner now, it'll effectively use LUCY's tracking mechanism, and provide a bandwidth monitor. If somebody else starts tracking the same phone, my tracking bandwidth will be affected, then I can start identifying the source."

"In English, Reg?"

"It's like water running through a pipe. If you turn one tap on, you'll get full flow, but if a second tap is turned on, the flow of the first tap will decrease."

"Okay, sounds easy enough," said Harvey, glancing across to Melody with his eyebrows raised. "Turning on the first phone now."

Harvey turned Reg's on first, then five minutes later turned Melody's on, and then another five minutes later, he turned his own on.

"Last phones on, Reg. You got them on screen?"

"Yep, all clear," replied Reg. "I have three flashing operatives and three bandwidth monitors running. I've set audio alerts up to sound when the bandwidth drops below a certain threshold."

"Right, next can you look for missing persons?"

"Missing persons?" asked Melody.

"Missing persons," confirmed Harvey. "We've still got two taxi drivers missing. It'll be useful to see if we can get the number plates, so we don't stumble upon some poor old cabbie eating his sandwiches."

"You think they'd keep the plates on? I would have thought they'd swap them out," said Reg.

"Might do, might not. No harm in knowing, is there?" replied Harvey.

They pulled into a parking area in the wide, open space of Wanstead Flats within less than thirty minutes. The car park sat on the edge of a large triangle of grass, which was bordered on all three sides by roads. There was a lake near one corner and a few clumps of various trees spread sporadically across the expanse of grass.

"No taxis in sight," said Reg.

Then the laptop omitted a soft beep.

"Bingo," said Reg. "It's Harvey's phone."

Beep.

"There's yours, Melody, bandwidth just plummeted on the tracker."

Beep.

"Three for three," said Reg. "He's locked on."

"Okay, we don't have long," said Harvey. "I'm not sure what we're up against here. I'm expecting the second taxi with another lunatic behind the wheel, but we should be ready for the cavalry. These aren't skilled killers, but they are ruthless and will do anything for their cause. They won't even need to get close to me with a car bomb."

"This is insane," said Melody. "You have no idea what they're capable of."

"No, you're right," said Harvey, "I don't. But neither do you and this way we'll find out sooner rather than later." Harvey finished stuffing all the phones into various pockets of his cargo pants. "Melody, can you set yourself up discreetly in those trees there?" Harvey pointed to a copse of trees surrounded by long wild grass.

Melody climbed out the car, retrieved her Diemaco from the boot, tapped on the car window as a gesture of good luck to Reg and Harvey, and walked away carrying the Peli case. She needed to get into position, put the rifle together and calm her breathing down.

"Reg, keep your head down, stay out of sight and shout when you see something. You get the plate numbers?"

"Yeah, I'm working on it now."

"Good you'll need them more than us, let's hope we can do this and get to them before they end up like poor old Arthur." Harvey opened his door and stepped out. "Keep the comms open," he said, then closed the door, glanced around him, turned, and walked calmly across the expanse of grass. His limp was clearly visible but much better than it had been an hour before.

Harvey walked slowly to the centre of the open land. He saw Melody drop into the long grass five or six hundred yards to his right, and carried on walking for a minute to give Melody a chance to put the rifle together. Then he gave her another minute to calm her breathing. Emotions were high, her adrenaline would only need a little hint of action, and her heart would start pumping fast.

He glanced across at her and saw no movement. So he stopped, folded his arms, planted his feet shoulder width apart, and stood ready for whatever was about to happen.

He could have been wrong, his theory could have been way off. The whole strategy was based on assumptions which themselves were based on guesses. But what else did they have? If they waited for facts to arrive, they'd get nowhere.

Harvey stood for twenty minutes, turning every now and then to change his viewpoint. A few men walked past more than a hundred meters away. Some walked dogs, another just walked with his hands in his pockets, cutting across the grass to get somewhere. A group of teenagers sat on a bench a few hundred meters away, two on the seat, three on the back, They passed a joint between them and kept their hoods up to stay out the wind that blew unobstructed over the patch of wild.

The wind was gusting. When it dropped, the world seemed silent, but when the gusts came, the cold wind was loud in Harvey's left ear. His right ear was protected by the ear-piece, which was silent. Even Reg wasn't making any jokes. Tensions were high in the team.

Two hours had passed when a man walked to Harvey's right alongside the lake. A casual glance told Harvey the man had a beard, was below six feet and wasn't in a hurry. He was foreign, judging by the skin tone. Harvey looked passed him but kept his eyes focused.

A taxi drove into the car park and pulled up beside the team's Audi.

"Guys," said Reg.

"Reg, did you get the plates of that taxi?" said Melody.

"I'm running them now. They belong to a blue Ford, they're stolen plates.

"Ah, christ," said Melody.

The man with the beard was a hundred yards away from

Harvey. He adjusted direction slightly and began to take a route that would lead him close to Harvey and on towards the taxi.

"You guys seeing this?" said Harvey.

"Harvey, can you take a step to your right?" said Melody. "You're blocking my view."

Harvey causally kicked the grass around him and moved three paces to his right.

The man adjusted his course, he was typing something on his phone as he walked.

"And again, Harvey, he's changed his course again."

"He knows you're there," said Harvey. "He's using me to block your shot."

The bearded man suddenly stopped and looked up from his phone. His eyes were wild, pumped full of adrenaline, fear, hate, and whatever else. Harvey could see the man's chest moving with his heavy breathing. He was thirty meters away. If he was wearing a vest, Harvey would be obliterated at that range.

"Oh, Jesus," said Reg. "I have him in the binos, he's fumbling for something in his sleeve."

"A vest?" said Melody

The taxi revved its engine. Reg kept low but adjusted his position. The taxi driver's face was obscured by a long white headscarf.

"You guys," said Reg. "This taxi's getting ready to play."

"Mr Harvey?" the man called. He brought his hands together and pulled his cuffs down over his hands.

"Reg," said Harvey. "Does beardy have anything in his hand?"

"Left looks clear, although his right hand is clenched."

"Melody, you ready for this?" asked Harvey.

"Copy. Drop on my count when the wind drops. Reg, get ready to run like hell."

"What do you want?" called Harvey to the bearded man. "Hold fire, Melody," he said under his breath.

"You've been busy," he replied,

"Not as busy as you."

"Did you honestly think that luring me out here would put you in a strong position?"

"I've seen your face now, that's the only position I need," replied Harvey.

"How is your friend?"

"My friend?" Harvey replied. "I don't have friends. You need to check your intel."

"Oh, Mr Harvey. You surely remember Arthur?"

"Name doesn't ring a bell," said Harvey. He glanced across at the taxi four hundred yards to his left. He could hear the diesel engine being revved. "Is that your mate? Sounds like he's having trouble."

"He's just fine, Mr Harvey."

"I bet he didn't do the knowledge either did he?" Harvey was referring to the extremely stringent test of London that all black cab drivers had to get through, in order to earn their right to drive a black taxi.

"That is a blessed man," said the bearded seriously. "Do not mock him."

"Guys, I'm in a spot of trouble here," said Reg over the ear-piece.

"Okay, Reggie, don't panic, I'm watching him," said Melody.

"So is he," said Reg. "He's looking right at me."

"Reg, stay focused. Have you got tabs on that tracker yet?" said Harvey quietly.

"It's coming."

"Don't play games, Mr Harvey," said beard. "We do not need to hurt your friends, but we will if we have to. I'm sure you have seen what we are capable of."

"Capable isn't the word I'd have used."

"You're going to walk towards my friend, Mr Harvey. Then you are going to sit inside the taxi."

"And where is it exactly I'm going?"

"Your destination depends on how nicely you decide to play, Mr Stone."

"If I play nicely?"

"You will see."

"If I don't play nicely?"

"Somewhere special."

"Will you be coming with me?"

"I'm ready to go to either destination, Mr Harvey. I've been ready for a very long time."

"And if I don't?"

"Your friend, Reg, isn't it? He will most certainly die."

"He's not my friend," said Harvey.

"He's not your friend?"

"That's right, he's not my friend."

"He looked like a friend this morning when you all learned about poor old Mr Denver. I watched you all, it was very touching."

"You should have joined us, we could have touched you."

"Enough of the small talk, Mr Harvey. Walk."

Harvey turned away from the man and muttered to Melody, "Melody call the distance, let me know if he closes in."

"This is crazy, Harvey, we should just take them both out."

"Too risky, Reg you have me on screen?"

"Three times."

Harvey stopped in front of the taxi and stared through the windscreen at the driver. The driver stared back grinning. His front tooth was missing. Harvey continued to stare.

"Closing in, ten metres," said Melody.

Harvey spat on the windscreen.

"Five."

The man stared back and lifted his hand. Two wires hung from his fist, and he dropped down to the floor on the passenger side. He continued to grin.

"Two metres."

"Hands on the bonnet, Mr Harvey."

"He's stopped, two paces behind you."

Harvey saw beard in the windscreens reflection.

"Listen carefully to me, Mr Harvey, you will do exactly what I say."

"Will I?" Harvey continued to stare at the driver.

"Yes, Mr Harvey, you will. Do you know what is special about this taxi?"

"It's not a blue Ford?"

"Very good, Mr Harvey, what else?"

"I'm guessing it stinks by the looks of the driver."

"The taxi is rigged with explosives, Mr Harvey, but you already knew that didn't you?"

"I had an idea."

"You're a smart man, Mr Harvey, I won't insult you with games."

"Too kind."

"Can you tell me what will happen if you do not get into the taxi?"

Harvey stared at the driver.

"What do I win if I'm right?"

"You don't win anything, I'm afraid, Mr Harvey," beard chuckled. "It's just a game."

"You said you wouldn't insult me with games."

"There is one more taxi waiting for its next fare, its final fare."

"Let me guess, it's also loaded with explosives and is parked somewhere close to a bunch of people."

"Very good, Mr Harvey, it is loaded with explosives, but it

is not parked near lots of people. I would hope you think a little more of me than that. I am somewhat resourceful and, I like to think, creative too."

"I don't think anything of you. You'll just be another dead man when all this is over, and I'll be thinking about more important things. Like getting a coffee, or washing your blood off my fingers."

"Would you like me to tell you?"

"Go for it."

"You'll never guess."

Harvey didn't reply.

"Ask me for help, Mr Harvey."

Harvey didn't reply.

"Would you like to, how do you say, phone a friend?"

"I already told you I don't have friends."

"Do you think Frank will know where it is parked, the other taxi?"

Harvey didn't reply.

"You seem to have gone quiet, Mr Harvey, I was enjoying our little chat."

Harvey stared at the driver. He heard Melody over the comms talking to Reg.

"Reg, do you copy this?" she said.

"Yes, Melody, I'm piecing it together."

"Can you get onto the CCTV in HQ?"

"I'm opening the webcam of the command centre."

"Tell me what you see," said Melody. "Harvey, I have this man, clean shot, no problem."

Harvey didn't reply.

"With your left hand, Mr Harvey, using only your finger and your thumb, I want you to slowly remove your weapon and throw it on the floor."

Harvey did as instructed. He threw the SIG down on the ground, out of reach of both him and the beard.

"Good. You may now step into the vehicle."

"Can I ride up front?"

The beard chuckled again then stopped abruptly. "No, you ride in the back."

"Doesn't look very comfy, you removed all the seats."

"I'm sure you'll find a way, but please be careful, plastic explosive is quite volatile."

Harvey stepped towards the door, he caught sight of Reg who sat wide eyed in the rear of the Audi.

"Harvey, say the word and he's gone," said Melody.

"You're not going to like this," said Reg.

"Go ahead, Reg," said Melody.

"Well, there's a black taxi parked in Denver's workshop."

"As I thought," said Melody quietly.

"Some hairy guy is in my seat," said Reg.

"He's what? The tech guy?" asked Melody.

"Yeah, he's using the power of my command centre, no wonder he's one step ahead of us."

"Can you see what he's doing?"

"Not yet, I'm working on it," said Reg.

Harvey turned to the bearded man. "Before I get in, my friend drives away."

"I thought you said you didn't have any friends, Mr Harvey."

Harvey didn't reply.

"Go ahead, he's of no use to us."

"Reg," called Harvey over the taxi. Harvey saw Reg lift his head from his laptop at the mention of his name. "Go, leave. Now."

Reg slowly opened the rear door. He took a tentative step toward the driver's door.

Harvey nodded at him. "It's fine, Reg. Go."

Reg looked across at Al Sayan, who turned to face him.

"Before you leave, Mr Reg,"

Reg had one leg in the car. He didn't reply.

"I see you met my friend," said beard. "Handsome isn't he?"

Harvey looked on proudly as Reg stared the man down and stood resolutely.

"He tells me you have quite an impressive setup. LUCY isn't it? How cute. I hope the old man is comfortable."

"What's he talking about, Reg?" said Melody over the comms.

Reg didn't reply.

"Okay, if you won't tell Mr Harvey, I will tell him."

"They have Frank," said Reg.

CHAPTER TWENTY-FOUR

HARVEY SAT ON THE FOLD-DOWN SEAT OF THE TAXI. HE had his back to the driver. Al Sayan sat down beside him in the adjacent fold down seat, and pulled the door closed. The taxi began to reverse, and Harvey heard the automatic locks click into place.

"You know the danger you are in, Mr Harvey?"

Harvey didn't reply.

"You are sat in a confined space with twenty-five kilos of plastic explosives, plus some other things we found."

"Other things?"

"Yes, you know, nails, screws, ball bearings. Small things. Much pain, Mr Harvey, for the man who gets too close."

"What about the innocents?"

"Innocents? Mr Harvey, I have been in this country a long, long time now and I am afraid I rarely see innocence. Ignorance, yes, I see this. But innocence? No."

"What would happen if I attacked you now?"

"If you attacked me, Mr Harvey, why would you do this? I have been polite have I not?"

"You know me?"

"I know a great deal of things, Mr Harvey. You are a very interesting man."

Harvey glanced out the window and saw they were heading back into London. He needed to buy time, he needed answers.

"Am I? You must live a very boring life if you find me interesting Mr Sayan."

"Ah, you have worked it out. My name."

"I had an idea it was you. Then I smelled you, and knew it had to be."

"You insult me, Mr Harvey? That's not playing nicely," said Al Sayan. "I have followed you with interest. I believe we have a mutual friend."

"Stimson?"

"You are highly regarded, and your history is a tragedy." Al Sayan looked pathetically at Harvey. "Your poor sister, what an awful ordeal for such a young girl to go through. Tell me, was it two men or three men, Mr Harvey, that so callously raped her?"

Harvey tensed, but Al Sayan saw the trigger and raised his hand with two wires trailing from his fist. "Ah ah ah, Mr Harvey, I must warn you." He smiled and bared his dirty brown teeth. "I must confess I am wearing a little jacket I made myself. Extra security. I'm sure you understand. If I release my grip, the vest will be detonated, the explosion will be significant on its own. But inside here? It will also detonate our little passengers." Al Sayan gestured at the long strips of PX5 that sat between the seat frames.

"It was three, wasn't it? I remember now, you always thought it was two, but then you learned of your brother's, if you do not mind me saying, unforgivable involvement in the ordeal." Al Sayan paused and studied Harvey. "How did it feel? To catch him? I heard that Donald Cartwright's body was quite literally torn apart. His throat was ripped open, his eyes ripped out and his genitals stuffed in his mouth. That's impressive, Mr Harvey.

Harvey didn't reply.

"And then there was Julios, what a man. I saw a photo of him once, and I thought to myself, wow. This man was a strong and capable man, Mr Harvey." Al Sayan leaned back onto the door behind him. "Am I right? Was he as strong and capable as he looked?"

Harvey didn't reply.

"You're not much fun, Mr Harvey. Why you don't talk?"

Harvey didn't reply.

"I heard that Julios was the man who trained you, and that you were so very close. Am I right, Mr Harvey? Were you so very close?"

Harvey didn't reply.

"Ah, I am right. I can see it in your face. There is much pain in your eyes. You really are a sensitive man, Mr Harvey, surprisingly sensitive."

Harvey didn't reply.

"So if you don't want to talk about your poor sister, or your good dead friend, Julios, perhaps you'd like to talk about your parents?"

Harvey stared at Al Sayan.

"Yes, now we strike nerves, Mr Harvey. Look at the anger in you, so wild." Al Sayan leaned forward. "I cannot imagine the anger I would feel if I knew that my life had been full of so many secrets and lies, Mr Harvey. I understand your rage, truly. To have the one man you trusted and respected keep secrets from you, when you so clearly and plainly were looking under every stone you found, it must be a very difficult thing to deal with."

"I didn't trust or respect him, we had an arrangement. So think what you like. Are we nearly there? I'm getting tired of this."

"Ah, Mr Harvey, I do seem to have touched on something sensitive. You cannot avoid talking about it. In fact, talking is sometimes the best way to overcome your anger. Humour me, Mr Harvey."

Harvey didn't reply.

"So you didn't respect him or trust him, yet he was your best friend? I find that hard to believe, Mr Harvey."

"John wasn't my best friend," said Harvey. "He was my foster father and my boss. That's as far as the relationship went."

"Oh, Mr Harvey. I am not talking of John Cartwright. Oh, no. I am talking of Mr Julios, of course. He was your mentor, am I right? He trained you?"

"Yeah, he taught me a few things."

Al Sayan laughed. "A few things? You are a master, Mr Harvey, a dangerous man. You were carved by Julios like a sculptor carves a stone statue. He chips away at the stone, one tiny piece at a time." Al Sayan flicked Harvey's shoulder lightly. "Then he will stand back and admire his work, he will check the balance of his creation, and maybe chip a tiny piece off from this side." Al Sayan touched Harvey's cheek.

"You getting dangerously close," said Harvey.

"I am merely describing how Julios, your mentor, your best friend, your sculptor carved you, shaped you, created you. Stone from Stone, Mr Harvey."

Harvey didn't reply. He took a deep breath through his nose.

"That's right, Mr Harvey, control your breathing. Let the anger flow through you, not out of you. Just as Julois taught you."

Harvey didn't reply, he stared at the plastic explosives in a row.

"So it must have destroyed you when you learned of your sculptor's treachery?"

The squeal of brakes as the taxi slowed for traffic lights was loud in the back. Harvey rocked in his seat.

"Do you think he would have done it if he knew?" said Al Sayan. "Do you think that if he had known what a great and dangerous stone statue he would create, he would still have killed them, Mr Harvey?"

Harvey didn't reply.

"Do you think he savoured the moment? When he stood over your mother and father? Do you think he regretted it afterwards?" Al Sayan laughed out loud.

Harvey pushed up with his legs and held Al Sayan against the glass with his forearm. Harvey brought his head back and smashed his forehead into the man's face. The driver broke, and Harvey lost his balance, he stumbled and fell against the glass partition. Al Sayan shoved him back to his seat and held his face with one hand. Blood ran from his nose through his fingers. Al Sayan nodded to the driver, and the taxi drove on.

Harvey was limp in his seat. His mind swam, confused, dizzied with memories of Julios standing over his faceless parents. The kind and nurturing smile on Julois' face as Harvey swam in the pool, and Julios lifting him out as a young boy. The moments they had shared after a sparring session, when they had both laid on their backs on the rubber mats in John's gym, panting and sweating. The times Harvey had discussed his efforts at finding his parents' killer. Each time, his mind came back to Julios' huge frame standing over his dead parents.

"How does it feel, Mr Harvey?"

Silence.

"Perhaps you need some time to consider what you just learned."

Harvey sat with his arms resting on his knees. He stared at the grooves in the wooden floor of the taxi. His heart was racing, he needed air.

"We are here," said Al Sayan.

Harvey felt the taxi slow and turn sharply to the left. He looked up out the window and saw the Stratford warehouse on his right. The driver got out, and a few minutes later the sliding shutter door screeched open. Then the taxi pulled inside, and the shutter door slammed shut. The locks on the doors popped open when the driver hit the switch in the cab, and Al Sayan stepped out but kept his eye on Harvey. Harvey was limp and despondent.

"Out you come, Mr Harvey, we have a tight schedule."

Harvey didn't reply. He didn't move.

The driver opened the door on Harvey's side and pulled two plastic zip ties on Harvey's wrists, binding them together. Harvey stepped out and took in his surroundings. The warehouse looked gloomy even in the daytime. The weak strip lights that hung from thin chains left the sides and corners of the space in shadow. The pile of seats still sat under the tarp, and the wheels were still stacked in the corner with the car jack. The large wooden box had been removed. A plastic tarp was pulled out flat behind the old forklift. It was three metres square, and on it stood a tripod and a video camera.

"You've been here before, Mr Harvey, we found your little listening devices." He tutted. "Such devious behaviour. Did you honestly think that I am a caveman? I think you will find that we are far more sophisticated than you give us credit for, Mr Harvey." Al Sayan walked away towards the back of the warehouse. "Follow me, Mr Harvey, I'm sure I don't need to prompt you anymore."

Al Sayan stopped at the far end of the warehouse and opened the door to a small dark room. "I hope you will find it comfortable in here. I'm afraid the building just isn't as equipped as I would like it to be, but it is only temporary."

Harvey felt the gun in his back. The driver stood behind him. Harvey smelled his warm, stale breath. He stepped forward. Rooms ran the length of the right-hand side of the warehouse. The walls of each room were built from thick concrete blocks, and the doors were of thick wood with metal plates fixed front and back as reinforcement. There were four identical rooms in total. The first was open. Harvey glanced inside as he walked past, roughly eight foot by eight foot with no window. He presumed the other rooms would all be the same.

The next room along was closed, as was the third. Al Sayan held the door to room four open for Harvey.

"Goodbye, for now, Mr Harvey. Perhaps one day we will meet again."

"Leaving so soon?" replied Harvey.

"I'm afraid I'm a workaholic. My friend here has a pressing engagement to keep. He is about to change the face of London." Al Sayan smiled cruelly. "You're witnessing history, Mr Harvey."

Harvey didn't reply. Instead, he took a deep breath through his nose and stepped into the cell.

"I would urge you to leave any thoughts of escape to one side. You're a smart man, Mr Harvey, I'm sure you have worked out that our little garage here has been suitably prepared. It will be several days before they find any of your remains."

The door slammed shut, and a series of locks and bolts clicked and slotted into place.

A silence fell in the dark room. Harvey could barely make out the door. He stood for a moment, then began to plan.

He heard the shutter doors open at the far end of the warehouse. The taxi's diesel engine started and the shutters closed again.

Harvey mulled over what Al Sayan had said. Over and over, Al Sayan's words repeated in his mind. How true was it? How had he known about Hannah? He'd saved the final blow until they'd arrived at the warehouse. Al Sayan had known the news of Julios would knock Harvey for six, but he still couldn't believe it, didn't believe him. Yet he knew deep down that it was true.

It made sense. Harvey's attempts at understanding had been blocked time after time, downplayed almost. Even Julios had known something, and steered any conversation of his parents, away to something else. Harvey thought back to the last conversation he'd had with Julios. They'd been buying a van load of automatic rifles from the Thomsons and had been waiting at the spot. Julios had made a mistake, he let slip that he'd known something, then brushed it off.

Harvey sank to the cold stone floor. He leaned against the wall and brought his knees up to his chest. He pulled his bound wrists over his knees and buried his face in his legs.

Being alone was something that Harvey was used to. Even if he had chosen a career in an office, doing some mundane, ordinary job, he'd still be the same. His very nature made Harvey a solitary person. But he'd always had one friend. For most of his childhood that friend had been Hannah. Julios had been in the background and was friendly, but his one true friend had always been Hannah. She'd never let him down. Then, when she'd died, Julois stepped in.

Was it because Julios felt guilty? Was that it? Was that why Julios had suddenly became so involved in Harvey's life? Did he pity Harvey? He didn't need pitying, he was Harvey Stone. He was strong and resilient. He pulled a boot lace from his tan boots. Then, in the darkness, he tied a large loop in both ends of the long cord.

He didn't need friends. He was Harvey Stone.

He pulled the lace through the two zip-ties on his wrists.

So what if Julios had lied? His whole life had been a charade anyway. People had watched him try to understand

and fail for as long as he could remember. What was the point in trying to understand now?

He pulled a loop over each boot.

So what if I'm alone. Don't they know who I am?

He leaned back and lifted his legs, working his feet back and forth, the lace heating and wearing through the plastic zip-ties.

Al Sayan can't stop me with words. I'm Harvey Stone.

The lace cut through the first zip-tie.

I'm Harvey Stone.

Snap.

The second zip tie fell to the floor. Harvey replaced his bootlace, rubbed his wrists and stood up.

"Come on then, Harvey Stone. Since when did a closed door stop you?"

He stood and stretched. He closed his eyes to the darkness and breathed calm, deep breaths. He filled his lungs with the stale air and pictured the room before Al Sayan had closed and locked the door.

Breeze block walls, hard and thick. Solid wooden door with steel reinforcement in the form of a plate on each side of the door. The wooden frame. Harvey imagined the frame being screwed into the concrete blocks; strong but not impossible to shear off.

He walked towards the wall with the door and felt along until he found the wooden frame. His hands felt the wood in the darkness. He touched the door handle, cool in the cold warehouse.

Then he felt the hinges on the weakest side. He had heard the many bolts being slid into place into recesses drilled into the concrete blocks. The hinges, however, would just be drilled into the door frame.

He stepped back with his left leg. It still throbbed, and Harvey knew without looking that it would be badly bruised.

He'd been lucky, the taxi had been empty, and had bounced over his leg. The tissue would be damaged, the muscles sore, but the bone was intact. It just needed time to heal.

Harvey slowly raised his right foot to the hinged side of the door and judged a solid kick with the heel of his boot.

He lowered his foot, stepped back and kicked.

Thud.

It was solid.

Thud. Thud.

He thought of the taxi making its way into the city.

Thud.

He heard a small shower of dust fall from the concrete blocks surrounding the door frame.

Thud. Thud.

The taxi driver's dirty, toothless grin.

Thud.

The wires that ran from the plastic explosives in the rear.

Thud.

People crossing the street, stepping back to take photos of St Paul's to show their families when they got home.

Thud.

Ordinary people wearing ordinary clothes going to ordinary jobs.

Thud. Thud.

More dust.

Al Sayan.

Thud.

His cruel smile.

Thud.

Julios.

Thud, thud, thud.

Standing over his dead parents.

Crack.

The lies.

Crack.

The explosion.

The door frame split at the top and light spilt into the small room.

Thud.

More light.

Thud.

I don't need anybody.

Crack.

Julios.

Crack.

Al Sayan.

Crunch. The door fell away. Its lower hinge held true but twisted under the weight of the wood and steel plate.

Harvey stood, closed his eyes, took a deep breath and stepped out into the warehouse.

Dust had filled the air from the crashing and banging and it hung in swirling beams of light from the extractor fan that span slowly in the centre of the warehouse's rear wall.

Everything else remained as it had. Harvey strode towards the two exit doors. The shutter had been pulled down over the single door. A small repair job had been done, and Harvey saw the new wood where he had broken the door with Melody.

The large sliding shutter doors were locked, but Harvey had a plan.

He passed the other rooms and noted the locks. He stepped back to room three and put his ear to the door.

He knocked.

Nothing.

He knocked again, slightly harder.

Then faintly, he heard a voice. "Hello?"

CHAPTER TWENTY-FIVE

MELODY WATCHED THE TAXI LEAVE THE CAR PARK, THEN popped up to her feet, grabbed the rifle and the Peli case, and ran to the Audi. Reg moved out the driver's seat and climbed back into the rear. Melody snatched open the boot, dumped the Peli case inside and carried the rifle to the passenger seat. She made the rifle safe, then set it down and wedged it between the seat and the door so it wouldn't move.

"How's HQ looking?" she asked, "How many do we have there?"

She slammed the car into reverse and accelerated through the empty car park.

"Melody?" said Reg, looking out the rear window with concern on his face.

"Talk to me, Reg. What's HQ looking like?"

She slammed on the brakes and spun the wheel, dipped the clutch, and found first gear. As she slammed the accelerator down once again, the car spun and its momentum from the spin and power from first gear sent the rear wheels sliding out across the gravel. Small stones pounded the bodywork and the underside of the car.

"Reg, come on." She accelerated away from the car park and settled in for the ride, pulling her belt on and checking her mirrors.

"The taxi went the other way, Melody," said Reg.

"Harvey will have to look after himself. Headquarters?"

"I'm looking at my webcam, there's only one man there as far as I can see.

Melody took a final glance in her rearview mirror and saw the taxi disappear from sight. "Good luck, Harvey."

Reg heard her, and glance behind him. "You think he'll be okay?"

Melody sighed. "I don't know, Reg. We need to get Frank."

"I'm looking at Frank now. He's tougher than he looks."

"He's been through enough."

"I honestly have no idea how I'd react if that were me." Reg stared at the image. Frank was sat behind the man at Reg's computers. He was gagged and tied to a chair. It was the chair from Harvey's desk. His legs were bound, and his wrists were tied behind him.

"I saw you back there, Reg," said Melody. "You held your own."

"The driver though," said Reg. "What the hell goes through these people's minds? He looked crazy. *Surely* they feel *some* kind of remorse? He was pure evil."

"It's exactly as Frank said, Reg."

"What?"

"It's what we're up against. There's no respect for life."

"This is too big for us, Melody, we need to call it in."

"Call it in? What do you think will happen, Reg? I'll tell you, the taxi won't be stopped and the driver won't be arrested, he'll detonate the car. And Frank? They'll detonate that taxi too. We can do this, Reg. What would Harvey do?"

"Normally? Torture them or something."

"No, he wouldn't, you talk about him like he's a monster, Reg. He'd wait, then he'd make a plan, and then he'd execute."

"We don't have time to wait. Do you have a plan, Melody?"

"Are you controlling LUCY?"

"Not controlling, observing. If I make a move, he'll know I'm there and kick me out."

"That's good, stay out of sight, but watch him."

"What are you going to do? We can't go kicking the doors down and storming in."

"We have to believe that Harvey will be okay, and if Harvey's okay, that means he'll take care of the taxi. Our focus is Frank, HQ and the other taxi. Pull up the satellite of HQ and find me a roof."

"A roof?"

"Somewhere I can get a shot in."

"Okay, there are flats in the next road, but-"

"Can we get on top?"

"I guess so, but-"

"That's all we need. If Harvey takes his taxi out, they'll need the one in HQ to do the job. We can take them out from the roof. It's a gamble, but if I can make the shot-"

"Oh no," said Reg.

"Tell me, Reg."

"I'm watching him. He's smart. He's taken control of the CCTV in the city."

"How's he done that?" asked Melody.

"He's into the Bishopsgate control centre. That's where the police monitor the city cameras from."

"What's he looking at?"

"Looks like Queen Victoria Street. Have a guess where?"

"The auction house?"

"White van parked outside. Crew of workman beside it."

"The buddha."

"To be honest, they can take the buddha, I don't care anymore."

"Reg, come on, we need to focus on the taxis."

"There's only two of us, Melody. Denver's gone, Harvey's been captured, and Frank is tied up next to a ticking time bomb."

"Reg, stop it," said Melody harshly. "You're the best god damn tech guy I know. Think clearly, what can we do? I'll tell you what we can do, one thing at a time. That's what we can do. That's all we *can* do."

"One thing at a time."

"One thing at a time, Reg," replied Melody,

"Right, time to get LUCY back," said Reg.

"What are you going to do?"

"I'm going to show this bastard exactly how powerful LUCY is."

Reg began to type frantically on the laptop.

"First of all, I need to get him off of her."

"What are you doing, Reg?"

"I'm logging on to LUCY's admin console and disabling his phone to start with. He won't know until he tries to use it."

Melody looked in the rearview mirror and saw Reg with the tip of his tongue between his lips, concentrating.

"Right, now let's freak him out a little,"

"What you got in mind?"

"Just ringing a few phones around the building. The digital phone system has a test feature that can ring all the phones at once. I'm even setting the ringtone to Rule Britannia, boom, there, now he's wondering what's going on."

"Don't piss him off, Reg, we don't want him to detonate."

"I'm just toying with him. If he's any kind of specialist, he'll try to resist me before it comes to that."

"Okay, if you're sure."

"I'm sure, Melody. There we go, his account is disabled, and his screen is locked. From LUCY's admin console I can capture his keystrokes."

"What will that do?"

"That'll enable me to get his password, so I can undo whatever damage he's done once we're done with him. He'll likely be trying to access the system, so LUCY will capture everything he does. I can also pull a report on everywhere he's been in the system with that user account."

Reg hummed to himself, a sign he was pleased with his efforts.

"Right, next, remove the trackers from our phones, they're all in Harvey's pockets right now, but he may have given another system access."

"We're nearly there, Reg."

"I'm nearly done, I'm just going to shut the screens down, and then..." Reg hit the keyboard with finality. "Turn the lights off."

"Nice touch, have you ever seen how dark it is in there with the lights off?"

"Yeah it's creepy,"

"Is that the road there?" Melody pointed to a side road close to the HQ turning.

"That's the one, the flats are at the end on the left."

Melody stopped the car outside the flats on double yellow lines.

She grabbed the rifle and the magazine from the passenger side, climbed out and slammed the door shut.

Reg opened his door.

"Stay there Reg. I need eyes."

Reg pointed to his ear-piece and cupped his hand around his ear. "If you use the comms this close, he'll hear, use code."

Melody was aware that she was standing in the middle of a road with an automatic rifle. It was a dead-end side street that led down to the river, so it was quiet, but people still had windows.

"Before you do anything, Melody," began Reg, "I'm taking my LUCY back."

"I'll give two clicks on the ear-piece, Reg. On the first one, I want you to sound the alarms in the building."

"Copy." Reg was listening intently and realised the plan as Melody explained her requests.

"Second time, I want you to open the shutter doors. I'll take care of the rest."

She turned and saw a teenager run from the flats and disappear around the back of the building. Clean white trainers, tracksuit bottoms and a thick hooded sweater; it was probably a paranoid drug dealer that happened to see Melody out his window. Melody caught the door as it slowly swung shut and took the stairs. The flats were low rise, five stories. She ran all the way up and kicked through the door at the top. Pigeons scurried away in a chaotic bid for escape. The roof was covered in gravel, bird droppings and aerials. She sank to the floor and crawled across the stones and crap to the low wall that faced HQ.

She chanced a glance over the wall. To HQ, it was a six hundred yard shot, not easy with the wind off the river below. She was protected by the walls so couldn't feel the wind, but the trees and clothes that hung from washing lines further along the road told her it was gusting still, and quite strong. Five or six knots. She'd need to time her shot right.

She brought the rifle up and sat the fold-down bi-pod on the wall, then pulled the rifle butt into her shoulder and stood until the green metal shutter doors of HQ came into view through the scope.

She was relying on human instinct. She was relying on gut feeling. She was relying on hope.

Melody clicked once on her ear-piece.

A piercing alarm sounded from the building. The flashing light above the doors began to spin and cast an orange glow even in the daylight. The alarm sound would be deafening inside. Melody remembered that when it was installed, they all had to leave the building; the noise was intolerable.

She clicked a second time.

The shutter doors cracked open then, as the motor took up the slack in the concertina doors, they slowly dragged open. Melody imagined the man inside holding his ears, then trying to find the door override, a large red button on one side of the shutters. The door was open more than a metre now.

Melody calmed her breathing. Her focus through the scope was in the centre of the gap in the shutter door. The noise of the alarm was loud, even from six-hundred yards away. Nothing.

"Come on, you bastard. Show yourself."

Then a foot appeared in the scope's magnified view.

It shuffled sideways. Black business shoes and black suit trousers. Frank. Behind him was Al Sayan's tech guy.

Melody lowered the butt of the rifle a fraction and saw Frank, gagged and blindfolded, his hands behind his back. The man was standing behind him with his arm around Franks' neck, pushing him towards the shutter door.

The Arab stood directly behind Frank. There was no clear shot for Melody.

Melody kept Frank's head in view, knowing that the terrorist's face was just behind. She just needed Frank to move, but the other man was cautious or afraid. Determined.

The door stopped moving when the Arab hit the big red button. One more push began its closing action. Melody's heart raced as the door slowly crept into view from the right-hand side of her scope.

Frank, whose ankles had been untied to walk him to the

door, suddenly bent forward and slammed his head back into the man's face, then bent double all the way down. The terrorist was caught off guard and brought this hands up to his bloodied nose.

Time stood still.

Melody opened her free eye and saw the trees still. The bright white shirt that hung out to dry hung freely and motionless. Melody squeezed the trigger, and before the man's hands reached his ruined nose, the back of his head exploded in a shower of bone, blood and brains.

Frank fell to the floor and was still, blinded by the rags the man had tied around his head.

"Kill the noise, Reg," said Melody. "Target is down."

The alarms fell silent.

"Open the doors."

The shutter doors began their slow opening action. The electronic motors pulled on long chains, winding them onto the chain spools. The light filled the floor of headquarters. Melody could see Denver's workshop area. The taxi, the blood. The pristine tool chests and workbench, the dead man on the floor.

"That was for you, Denver buddy."

26

CHAPTER TWENTY-SIX

HARVEY FOUND A LONG CROWBAR, AND AFTER A FEW minutes had successfully ripped the door off room three. He stepped to one side and let the door fall to the floor, then stepped into the empty doorway.

The room was the same as the one he'd been locked in. No furniture or shelving around the edges, no windows and a dirty, dusty concrete floor. The only difference was the chair that stood in the centre of the room. Sat on the chair was a small girl. Her long, blonde hair hung across her eyes. She'd been unable to move the chair because her hands were tied, as were her ankles. She wasn't gagged or blindfolded, but there was no reason to in the small dark room.

Harvey saw the dirty face that stared up at her, scared and trembling. She had cried so much that her eyes were puffed. Dried tear marks ran down her face and cut through the grime like water on the walls of a limestone cave. Two eyes shone from swollen eyelids, big and blue.

No words were needed.

Harvey stepped closer with his hands held up in a gesture of peace. He bent down to untie her, but she fought and struggled. Harvey didn't bother to try and calm her, he would untie her and then she would calm down. She struggled the whole time, and when he had finished, she sat still.

"My name's Harvey," he said. "I'm going to get you back to your mum. Would you like that?"

The girl nodded.

"Okay, let's get out of here. I don't like it here at all, do you?"

The girl looked up at him with her big eyes and shook her head.

"What's your name?"

The girl didn't reply.

"That's okay, you don't have to tell me, but let's go somewhere safe."

He held out his hand, which she took before slipping off the old wooden chair to the floor.

They walked to the large shutter door that the taxi had used.

"I need to find a way to open the door. Will you help me and stay there, while I have a look around?"

The girl nodded and hugged her arms around herself.

"Good girl, I'll just be here, I won't leave you." Harvey stepped across to the big pile of junk by the seats that had been ripped out the taxi.

He stepped back and bumped into the girl.

"Hey, I thought I asked you to stay by the door?"

The girl didn't reply.

"That's okay, we can look together." He took her hand. "We're looking for something long and strong." Then he saw it, an old scaffold tube leaned up against the wall. Harvey bent down, picked the girl up and sat her on his hip. He stepped over the junk, car parts, gearboxes and heavy tools, grabbed the scaffold tube with one hand and walked back to the shutter doors. He set the girl down a few meters from the door. "This is going to be a bit noisy so put your fingers in your ears like this." He motioned putting fingers in his ears and squinted his eyes shut.

The scaffold tube was two feet long. He turned to face the doors and pulled the tube back behind him. Then, before he swung, he gave her a quick look. "Are you ready?"

She nodded.

Harvey launched into an attack on the bottom part of the door and wedged the tube between the main unit and the smaller leaf section. Once he had the end of the tube through, he used his weight to lever the door open at the bottom. The mounts broke one by one, and the bottom corner began to open outwards. Once it was open enough, he turned to the girl.

"Are you ready to get out?" He held his hand out to her.

She nodded.

"You're a brave girl," he said. "That's it, just climb through there." He lowered himself down and looked up at her. She looked down at him. "You be sure to tell me if anybody comes, okay?"

She nodded.

Harvey picked up an old screwdriver from the floor, laid down and pushed his arms through the hole. His head followed, and he wriggled until his hips caught the side of the doors. He had to pull and squeeze himself through, and the metal scraped the skin on his hips. Eventually he broke through, pulled his legs out, and rolled to stand beside her.

"See, easy," he said with a smile.

She looked up at him and lifted her arms to be carried.

"Let's go see about finding your mum eh?" he said. "Are you going to tell me your name?"

The girl rubbed her eyes then held on to his t-shirt. "Angel," she said in a soft, girly voice.

"Angel?"

She nodded.

"That's a pretty name for a pretty girl."

She buried her face into his shoulder.

"Okay, let's go. We need to find a car though, Angel," said Harvey. "Which one do you like?" Harvey pointed to the two oldest cars he could see. "Do you like the blue one or the black one?"

Angel pointed at the blue one, it was an old Ford with rusted bodywork and missing number plates. The bonnet was a lighter shade of blue than the rest of the bodywork, as if it had been replaced at some point.

The car was parked beside a van with flat tyres and was hidden from passers-by. Harvey pulled the scaffold tube through the bent shutter door and walked to the old Ford. He set the girl down and tried the door handle. It was locked. Harvey worked his fingers into the top of the driver's window and forced the glass down as much as he could. Older cars without electric windows worked on a mechanism. The winder mechanism wound a belt that raised or lowered the frame that the glass sat on. Harvey knew that the belts on old cars had slack in them from years of use, especially the driver's door. The window had dropped an inch, it wasn't enough to even get the girls arm inside.

He looked around and found a wooden wedge behind the wheel of the van. He used the scaffold tube to force the wedge out from beneath the tyre and prised the top of the driver's door open enough to slot the scaffold tube inside. Any further and he risked breaking the glass. He asked Angel to help him. She put her arm in and pulled the lock up.

"Good girl, that's a great job," he told her. She looked proud that she'd helped.

Again, Harvey tried the door, and it opened.

Next, he smashed the plastic cover beneath the steering wheel and tore it off, exposing the ignition barrel. He snapped off the barrel using the scaffold tube, leaving him with a square hole. Harvey put the flathead screwdriver from the garage into the hole and turned until the ignition lights came on, but the engine didn't turn over.

He dropped the handbrake and lowered the window. The car had a clear run of twenty meters in front of it. Harvey rocked the car back and forth. It didn't feel like it had sat there for long, the starter motor had probably died and was sat outside to be repaired. Harvey glanced at the black Vauxhall and thought it probably worked fine, was unlocked with the keys in it, but Angel had chosen the blue car.

He climbed out the car and held the door frame. Grunting, he gave the car a push to start it in motion then ran harder and faster. He worked up a quick run of short steps, jumped into the driver's seat mid-run, selected first gear and bump started the little Ford.

He didn't brake in time and crashed the front of the car into the large bins outside the warehouse. He dipped the clutch, gave it some more gas then reversed up alongside Angel.

Harvey leaned across and opened the door for her. "How did you like that then, Angel?"

She laughed. "You crashed."

"Yeah yeah, you need to get in the back and put your belt on, okay?"

She climbed in and crawled between the front seats to sit on the back.

"You set?" He turned, she nodded. Her head barely reached the top of the glass, she would probably need a child seat, but that was the least of his worries. "Okay, let's go find your mum, then shall we?"

He pulled off and turned out of the compound. He worked the old car up to fourth gear quickly and relaxed into the drive. The little motor felt ancient compared to the team's Audi, but needs must. He considered dropping Angel at a police station, but the possible consequences were entirely unknown. He couldn't risk the delay. She'd have to go with him to London. With any luck, Melody would be there and would know what to do.

The A12 led Harvey from Stratford into the city and the steering wheel wobbled all the way. Harvey felt like the wheels would fall off at any moment. He checked in the back infrequently and Angel seemed content looking out the window at the sky and buildings that went passed.

"So, what did you say your mummy's name was?"

Angel didn't reply.

"Do you know where you live?"

She shook her head.

"That's okay, we can find a policeman who can help us. Would you like that?"

Angel nodded her head and looked back out the window.

Harvey considered his predicament. He was in a stolen car with someone's kid. His team had fallen apart, one was dead, another kidnapped and the two functional members could be just about anywhere.

He needed to find the taxi, he needed to stop the bomb, and he needed to get the kid to her parents, plus prevent the buddha being stolen, but that was way down his list.

He found his way onto the highway into London. It was a slower route that bypassed the iron circle protecting the City of London, which was manned by police twenty-four seven.

He passed the Tower of London and found Upper Thames Street. From there, he turned into the side street where Hague had run. Harvey ditched the car and took Angel in his arms.

"Okay, Angel we're going to run now."

Harvey ran to the pedestrian crossing and hit the button to cross. Normally, he would have just run across the road between cars, but he was very conscious of carrying some-body else's kidnapped kid. He crossed the road and ran up a side street in the direction of St Paul's. Then it dawned on him that he was running toward a potential bomb carrying a young girl. The odds were stacked heavily against him.

There was a sandwich shop on the side of the road. He considered taking her inside and asking the owner to take care of her, but this was London. It wasn't an option; the police would arrive in seconds. He'd taken responsibility for her and would have to deal with it.

"Okay, Angel, we're going to see some people, and I need you to stay with me okay?"

Harvey made a plan. If a cop came along, he would just say he found Angel walking the streets and hand her over. He didn't want her to be hurt, but a lot more people might die if he didn't stop the taxi.

He stood on the corner of Queen Victoria Street and Peter's Hill then turned to look about him. The auction house was around the corner, he couldn't walk any further without passing it and potentially being recognised. And he definitely couldn't do that with Angel.

He scanned the cars that drove past for the taxi. He was concentrating so hard on trying to see it that when the Volvo stopped beside him, he barely recognised Reg and Frank.

"Stone, what the-"

"Long story, Frank." Harvey bent down and looked through to Reg at the wheel. "Where's Melody?"

"Getting set up on the roof behind you. She watched you walk up from Upper Thames Street and got us on the comms."

Harvey opened the rear door and put Angel inside.

"Angel, these two men will take care of you. They're policemen, so you'll be safe, okay?"

"No, they don't look like policemen."

"Do you trust me?" he asked.

The girl hesitated then nodded.

"Okay, good girl. I need you to be grown up now, be strong for me. The man with the grey hair here is called Frank, he's a very important policeman. You can ask him all sorts of questions."

"I don't want you to go," cried Angel.

"I'm sorry I have to, but I'll be back." He closed the rear door and turned back to Frank and Reg. "You got an ear-piece for me?"

"You're in luck, Harvey," said Reg, and he handed over the little ear-piece. Harvey placed it inside his ear. He hadn't liked them at first, but over the past year he'd been working with the team, he'd gotten used to wearing them.

"You might need this as well, Stone." Frank handed him his SIG. Harvey discreetly checked the chamber and the magazine.

"What's the deal here?" said Harvey. "Last I heard you weren't doing so well."

"Headquarters is secured, the taxi has been disarmed, and Reg has LUCY under control again."

"So there's one taxi left?" asked Harvey.

"We believe so," replied Frank. "You've been busy." Frank gestured at the girl in the back of the Volvo.

"So have you, looks like a hell of a tea party."

"You should see the mess we made. Do we know the mother?"

"Not sure about the mother, but something tells me she's linked to all this. Reg are you tracking the taxi?" asked Harvey.

"Yeah, it stopped for a while at a mosque in Bow. They've been on the move for twenty minutes, currently working their way through the city, ETA six minutes."

"Direction?"

"Westbound. Melody is watching Cannon Street with her Diemaco."

Harvey stuck the weapon in his waist band under his t-shirt. "And the heist? Stimson?"

"Larson and a team of men are around the corner waiting for the explosion. If we hit them now, Al Sayan might be watching. LUCY ran some calculations. If the blast of twenty-five kilos of PX5 goes off right outside the cathedral, the surrounding buildings and the cathedral itself will be destroyed, but the auction house will be fairly well protected. It might lose a few windows, but Stimson will have a getaway on the chaos."

"And the priceless buddha?"

"Not if we're quick," said Frank. "I want you in position ready to take them down as soon as Melody takes the taxi out."

"Welcome back, Harvey," said Melody over the comms.

"I hear you need a hand?" replied Harvey

"I can handle it, but if you want to come and have some fun, you're welcome."

"Shout when you take the shot. If you miss, I guess we'll all know about it."

"If I miss and it detonates, I'll be toast."

There was a silence as the team all thought about Denver.

"Yeah, well," said Harvey. "That's not going to happen."

"One minute," announced Reg.

"Get her out of here," said Harvey to Reg, then ran off, ready to slip around the corner.

"I have the driver in my sight," said Melody coolly. Harvey pictured her with one eye closed and her finger resting on the trigger. She'd be beginning to work the trigger into the crook of her index finger.

"Hold on, there's two of them," said Melody. "They've stopped, and the passenger has got out. He's walking towards the auction house on your side of the street, hundred yards."

"Al Sayan," said Harvey. "He's a decoy, where's he gone?"

"I can't see him, he's between the buildings."

Harvey ran to Cannon Street. St Paul's loomed above him. He turned right and scanned the pathways for Al Sayan. The taxi stood at the end of the road, parked as if it was waiting for a fare.

"I have the driver in my sight. Am I taking him down or what?" said Melody.

Harvey didn't reply.

"Harvey, talk to me," said Melody, keeping her voice calm and her breathing relaxed.

Just then, Harvey heard screaming coming from his left. He looked across the road at St Paul's and saw smoke pouring through the open door of a pub on Cheapside, the road that ran behind the cathedral.

People ran from coffee shops to get clear of any blast that would follow the smoke. A car swerved to the other side of the road when the driver saw people running and slammed into a young couple who were running away. Crowds came running down towards Harvey. They ran in the road, on the pavement and across the grass, anyway they could to get away from the scene.

"Kill zone, Melody. Same as Canary Wharf."

"Where's Al Sayan?" asked Melody.

"He's disappeared," replied Harvey,

"Okay, Harvey, taxi is moving."

Harvey watched as the taxi pulled slowly out from the lay-by and drove directly towards him.

"Take him down, Melody." Harvey ran towards the taxi. If Melody only wounded the driver, he could still hit the switch. Harvey pulled his SIG as he ran. The driver saw Harvey and accelerated. "Anytime, Melody."

"I don't have a shot," Melody replied.

Harvey stopped on the road with one hundred yards to go and aimed his SIG with two hands. He calmed his breathing and fired. The windscreen shattered, but the taxi carried on accelerating.

Fifty yards.

Harvey began to see the driver's face.

He fired his weapon again, and Harvey saw the man lurch into the back of the seat. The taxi rolled to a stop twenty meters from Harvey. If it detonated, he would be torn to pieces along with the dozens of people that were still running from the smoking pub across the street.

Harvey stepped forward slowly. With each step, Harvey kept his gun on the man. More people ran from the smoke, saw Harvey standing with a gun and stopped. A group was forming. Harvey glanced across at them. "Move, go, run." He couldn't form a sentence.

He turned back to the driver just as his head began to move, then his face caved in. Harvey heard the report of Melody's rifle, and again. The man's chest opened up from the 7.62 calibre Diemaco almost instantly.

Harvey stepped to the side of the car and wrenched the door open. The man had his hand on the switch, but would never be able to push the button or anything else again. Harvey carefully pulled the switch from his hand and laid it on the seat. Then he dragged the ruined body from the taxi. He stepped away backwards as he saw policemen running toward him. Sirens grew louder from all directions.

"Target is down," said Harvey. "We've lost Al Sayan."

CHAPTER TWENTY-EIGHT

"THE AUCTION HOUSE," SAID MELODY.

Harvey turned and ran along the narrow lane between the buildings opposite the cathedral. The auction house was a single five-story brick building that was surrounded on all four sides by smaller lanes. It had an industrial look and was rounded by offices buildings, coffee shops and small restaurants. It had two basement levels, a little loading bay and a modest reception. Harvey stood in front of the reception. He doubted Stimson and his men would use the main entrance, they would be behind the building.

Harvey checked the doors anyway, they were locked. He walked around the side of the auction house, turned the corner and saw the front end of the white van sticking out. He put his weapon away and pulled his t-shirt over it, then pulled out one of the phones and pretended to be typing a message while he walked.

He turned the corner by the van, expecting to be confronted by Stimson's men, but it was empty. The van was locked. A small set of steps led down to a service entrance of the building. The door was ajar.

Harvey put the phone away. If he walked in, there would be no pretending.

"Harvey, where are you? I'm at ground level," said Melody over the comms.

"Service entrance, back side."

He stepped slowly down the steps and opened the door fully. He saw that the biometric security panel had been shorted and the double doors had been forced in.

A small corridor, ten meters long, was in front of him. It led to a T junction. He walked to the end and drew his weapon again, looking both ways. To the right, a set of concrete stairs led down, and a small ancient elevator with black wrought-iron gates sat beside it. To the left was a series of room entrances and one large set of doors. Harvey guessed the double doors led to the rear of the auction house back stage, and the other doors were perhaps storage rooms or offices.

Harvey turned right and stood at the top of the stairs. He peered down. He could see two floors below between the iron bannister. The lowest floor was lit dimly by a yellowish glow. Harvey began the walk down the steps, slowly and quietly, as Julios had taught him all those years ago. He kept to the shadows where possible. The first floor was clear. But as he stepped onto the stairs that led to basement two, he heard the faint muffled sound of men's voices.

He checked back up the stairs, he was still alone.

He stepped to the concrete floor of basement two and into the yellow light. Another biometric panel had its wires pulled from the bottom of the unit on the wall. The lights on the security panel were off.

The lights that lit the dark corridor were a string of bulbs fixed to the ceiling beside the wall. They cast two or three shadows of Harvey as he made his way along. The walls were tiled like an old underground station. The white tiles took a yellowish glow from the dim lights above, and every sound he made was echoed in the still space.

There was only one set of doors at the end of the corridor. They were large windowless double doors, with yet another biometric panel and three heavy duty locks at the top, middle and bottom. The doors opened outwards judging by the closers, so Harvey stepped to one side and listened. He waited a full minute, another of Julios' lessons.

The voices he'd heard were clearer now, but still hushed and urgent.

"Stimson just messaged me, go, go, go."

"Okay, I'm going as quick as I can."

"We should have been in and out by now, what's taking so long?"

"You can't rush this, Lucas. If this doesn't go right, it'll be all bang and no buddha, know what I mean?"

"If you don't get it right, all bang and no buddha will be written on your headstone, pal."

"One minute, why don't you clear the room, give me some space," the second man said.

"What happened to the explosion outside we were waiting for?"

"I don't know, do I?" said Larson. "But Stimson said go, so just bloody go."

"Move out the way, I can't see anything in here."

Harvey removed his belt and quietly fastened it around the two door handles so it couldn't be opened from the inside.

"I'm not leaving you alone, Johnson, you don't exactly have a great track record do you?"

"You hired me to do a job, Lucas."

"So shut up and do it."

"How good are you at running?"

"Why?"

"Because in twenty seconds this vault door's coming off, and I have no idea how big the bang will be."

"I thought you'd done it before?" Larson's voice was anxious.

"I have, well, I've seen it done, but we didn't use as much as this."

"What?"

"Ten seconds, run."

Harvey heard banging on the doors. "It's locked. Let us out. Help!"

Harvey took a slow walk back to the staircase, casually checked up the stairs and walked up to the dark first floor. He ignored the screaming and banging and waited for the blast with his ears and eyes covered.

The explosion was deafening inside the tiled space. It came with a wave of power that seemed to rock the building. A cloud of dust found its way up the stairs, and Harvey saw the yellow lights had been blown out. It was pitch dark. The noise had been deafening, a jumble of audible carnage. Harvey pulled his shirt up to his mouth and walked back down the steps.

The air was black, dust and grit stuck to his watering eyes, and the smell of concrete and lime was heavy in the air.

He stepped off the stairs, and his foot found a large piece of broken concrete in the darkness. Harvey pulled a phone out his pocket to give him some idea of where he was treading. He cursed himself; he normally carried a Maglite in his pocket, a small two-cell torch that had been more than useful on several occasions. But it had been lost, maybe in the taxi crash, he didn't know.

Slowly working his way along the short corridor, he stepped over the broken double doors and around the concrete blocks that had formed the wall. He drew closer to the vault. The huge, thick steel door had been ripped from the vault by the hinges, but the lock still clung to its counterpart, so the door itself leaned up against the entrance.

Harvey saw a leg on the floor beside the vault. He knew the room must be covered in body parts, but there was no need to look. He'd seen dismembered bodies before and it wasn't pretty. He shone the phone into the vault.

The space was ten feet by eight feet inside, Harvey guessed. On one side were shelves, which were only hanging by the fixings on the far end. The ends of the shelves closest to the door now sat on the floor among scattered paperwork. On the left-hand side was a rack that held paintings. A felt base formed the plinth for the large frames. Dividers kept the paintings from touching and held them upright. There were only four paintings, each one was covered in a shiny purple cloth. Harvey had expected to see more of a haul, but he guessed the reality was that vaults in auction houses didn't store valuables for long, the idea was to move them on.

There was a small wooden box on the floor below the broken shelves, partly hidden by the fallen shelves. It was ten inches square and beautifully finished. A layer of dust had already begun to settle on its surface.

Harvey bent, picked the box up and felt the weight. He guessed at three or four kilos, not heavy, but solid. He opened the two small brass catches on the front and lifted the lid. The box was lined with a soft cushioning and a small square of fine green silk lay over the centre.

Harvey lifted the corner of the material and exposed the perfectly smooth, ancient, green-stone artefact underneath. The two-century-old, little, fat buddha laid cross-legged in the box and stared up at Harvey. It was only six inches tall and perhaps four inches across the belly.

Harvey looked around the vault, then made his exit. Outside would be crawling with police by now. He stopped at the bottom of the stairs and considered his options. He was wanted for murder, a car with his prints on had been suspiciously abandoned outside, and now he was walking into the street where the police would be looking for him, with an ancient priceless buddha.

He took one step onto the stairs.

"It's a dilemma isn't it, Mr Stone?" said a woman's voice. It was the voice of a confident woman who was used to having her own way.

"Not really."

"You can't walk out of here with that," she said.

Harvey searched the darkness above him for the source of the voice.

"Why don't you let me take it off you?" she said. "You might get away, you might not. I just hope the police don't shoot you on sight before they know you're one of them."

Harvey didn't reply. Patience.

"You should respect your betters, Harvey, I thought John would have taught you that."

"He taught me you need to earn respect."

"And haven't I earned it?"

"I don't know. Why don't you tell me?"

"Ah come on, Harvey, we both know where the brains lie."

The woman stepped into the light from the ground floor above and looked down at Harvey. It was the woman from the manor house.

"Bring me the buddha, Harvey. This'll be over soon, and you can go back to playing cops and robbers."

"I think we're playing a pretty good game of it right now."

"I'm not your average robber, Harvey."

"I'm not your average cop."

"You're not the average anything, are you?"

Harvey didn't reply. Her voice was mature yet had a youthful element of fun. She was well spoken, like she was used to being around wealthy individuals, but hadn't been born into wealth.

"I've always wanted to chat with you. I always thought it would be nice to sit and talk one day, Harvey, you know? Really talk."

"I'm not really the talkative type."

"And that's what makes you intriguing. A man like you could do well with a girl like me."

"I've managed pretty well without you so far."

"Join me, Harvey. Don't you miss it? The chase? This thrill of the hunt?"

"I never stopped hunting."

"But you feed someone else now."

"I feed myself."

"But where's the next meal coming from?"

Harvey didn't reply. The woman stepped down onto the first step.

"There you are," she said, "in all your glory. I've watched you for years, you know? Admired you."

"I would have remembered you."

"Oh, you remember me, Harvey. I'm the one that was always one step ahead of you."

"Nobody springs to mind."

"I have friends too, friends that may be of interest to you."

Harvey didn't reply.

"Come closer."

Harvey walked slowly up the stairs to the first floor then stood still.

"That's it. Such a powerful man. Tell me how it felt."

"How what felt?"

"Oh, so many things, Harvey, where to start? Tell me about our mutual friend, Thomson."

"Terry Thomson?"

"Yes, Terence, not his spoiled little whining son. Terry was a king, how did it feel to destroy him?"

Harvey didn't reply.

"Did you feel his power?"

"Not really."

"No? That surprises me, Harvey. Did he fight?"

"No, he opened his arms to it."

"He didn't cry or beg?"

"One of the few that didn't."

"I hear respect."

"No, you don't. He was in the way. He needed stopping."

"I'm glad you did, stop him, that is. He was messing up my plans, he was always interfering."

She knew him. Harvey's memory for faces was good, but he couldn't place her past the manor house.

"And Sergio? That was messy, Harvey, even by your standards."

Harvey didn't reply.

"Are you at peace now, Harvey? I hear Mr Sayan filled in a few blanks for you. Was it the answers you've been searching for, Harvey?"

Harvey didn't reply.

"You must be disappointed in your friend. Do you feel betrayed?"

"I don't feel anything-"

"He taught you well then, Julios I mean."

Harvey didn't reply, but he could hear his own breathing loud against the solid tiled walls.

"Tell me how you feel now, Harvey. How do you remember Julios? As the man that carved you from an angry, broken little boy to the masterpiece you are now? Or do you remember him as the traitor that lied to you your entire life?"

Harvey didn't reply, he wouldn't be pulled down, not now.

"Was anything ever true? I can't imagine how you must feel. So much doubt."

"It won't work, Stimson."

"Ah, clever boy. You've put two and two together."

"That's why nobody ever found you, isn't it, all these years. They searched for a man, a man that never existed."

"Clever boy, I'm surprised nobody else ever figured it out, to be honest. It's not like I ever burst into an armoured van and stole cash or a bank."

"Diamonds," said Harvey. "Always diamonds and jewels."

"And anything that glitters. So pretty." She said the last words with a girly tone.

"And you never killed anyone, impressive."

"No need for that, Harvey, not if you do the job right."

"I thought this place was a little low on security."

"They're all locked away in a storeroom, alive for now, someone will find them when we're gone. No harm done."

"So why the bombs?"

The woman's face sank and her smiled dropped to an emotionless blank expression.

"Not my doing, Harvey, you know me, I'd never–"

"No, you wouldn't. It's okay, you don't have to convince me."

Stimson didn't reply.

"It's your daughter, isn't it?"

Stimson's head jerked up to Harvey.

"The buddha was never for you, it was for Al Sayan, to get your daughter back."

"It was the only way he could get it," she snapped.

"And if somebody wants something priceless, there's only one person to call, right?"

"I refused at first."

"But he took Angel, didn't he? And he took Hague's kid, a bloke like that would never convert, am I right?"

"Help me, Harvey."

"That's strong, all things considered."

"He has more, explosives, I mean."

"The warehouse is empty."

"Don't be a fool, Harvey, you saw the box."

"The box?"

"The wooden crate. You don't need to read German to know what it said, do you?"

Harvey didn't reply.

"How many plastic explosives do you think he had in each of those taxis?"

"He told me there was twenty-five kilos in the one I was in."

"And how much did the box say?"

"A hundred."

"Plus, of course, he has a small army of devout men, all just *dying* to help."

"Not funny."

"I'm sorry, poor Denver. That was unnecessary."

"Tell me what the plan was."

"The exchange?"

Harvey didn't reply.

"We meet, I give him the buddha, I get Angel back."

"She's a sweet girl."

"You saw her?"

"We shared the same accommodation."

"The warehouse?"

"She's safe."

"Safe? None of us are safe if Al Sayan *does* get the buddha."

"So let's get him first."

"I want to see Angel."

"Take me to Al Sayan."

"Angel first."

"Then what?" asked Harvey.

"You give me the buddha, and I take it to Al Sayan."

"In return for what? He doesn't have Angel anymore."

"He doesn't want Angel, he wants the buddha." She sighed loud in the stairwell. "He says it'll fund his campaign to cleanse Britain."

"What's to stop me walking out of here and handing you over?"

"You won't get Al Sayan, and he'll bomb the crap out of whatever he needs to get what he wants. Could you live with that? Knowing you had the chance to save lives?"

"You want to see Angel?"

"Or you don't get Al Sayan."

"She's close."

"So show me, I need to see her." It wasn't the demand of a scheming criminal mastermind on the brink of walking off with a priceless antique, it was the plea of a broken-hearted mother who'd had her daughter kidnapped by terrorists.

The door behind Stimson opened, and light flooded the dim corridor where she stood.

"Mummy?"

"Angel?"

"Don't move, Stimson." Melody walked through the door carrying the girl. The girl reached her hand out towards her mother. Stimson took a step towards her, but Melody moved back to the doorway. "I told you not to move."

"Mummy."

"It's okay, darling, Mummy's here. Are you okay? Are you hurt?"

The girl shook her head.

"Are you hurt? Has anybody hurt you?"

The girl shook her head,

"You've seen her, now take us to Al Sayan," said Harvey.

"Honey, mummy has to go somewhere, but this lady will look after you, just for a little while longer."

Harvey took a step up the stairs towards Stimson as her back was turned to Melody and the child. He felt the nuzzle of a gun in his back and closed his eyes.

"She'll be safe with me," said Melody. "Harvey let's go."

"I seem to have met your friend, Stimson."

"Ah yes, my private security." She looked over his shoulder at the man standing behind Harvey.

"You going to call him off?"

"I need *some* security, Harvey, I'm sure you can empathise."

"Tell him to drop the gun."

"No idle threats, Harvey."

"I don't make threats."

"He's good you know, one of the best bodyguards a girl can have."

"I'm sure he is. Call him off. We have Angel."

"Security is his blood, you know?"

"Great, call him off."

"I think you two will get along."

"Not with a gun in my back we won't."

"True. Adeo."

Harvey felt the dull point of the gun being removed from his back.

"Adeo?" asked Harvey.

"That's right, Harvey, Adeo."

"I told you it's in his blood, he comes from a long line of highly dangerous men."

Adeo gave a deep and short laugh behind him. It had the depth of a man with a broad chest, a large neck and wide shoulders. It was a laugh much like Julois'. In fact, it was nearly exactly the same.

"You can catch up later, I'm sure you have a lot to talk about," said Stimson. "Let's go."

Melody disappeared from sight back outside. "All clear," she said over the comms.

Harvey walked up the stairs. Once again, his mind rallied through his memories of Julios, who'd told Harvey his brother was dead. This time, Harvey channelled his anger. He let it flow through him, feed his tired muscles, and feed his hunger for Al Sayan.

He stepped outside into the bright daylight, still carrying the box.

The Volvo was parked outside behind the van Larson had used. The van's hazard lights still blinked. Reg sat in the driver's seat with Frank beside him. Melody had climbed in the back and was pulling the seat belt across Angel.

Harvey walked up the few steps to the pavement and stood beside the car. He turned and watched Adeo come up the steps, his huge legs hauling his massive weight. Harvey studied his face; he was, without question, related to Julios. It was like an old memory, like thinking of a face you used to know, but you can't quite place the features correctly.

Adeo had Julios' nose, his family nose, and his jawline was wide and strong like his brother's had been. But Adeo's brow was deeper, which gave him a dumb look. He was also bigger than Julois had been. Harvey remembered Julios telling him that he was the eldest of the two, and had cared for his younger sibling, as Hannah had cared for Harvey.

"Fond memories, Harvey?" said Stimson.

"Ancient history."

"Talking of ancient history." She gestured to the box.

"What's the plan?"

"I call him, he tells us where to meet."

"Then what?" asked Harvey.

"You give me the buddha, I go meet him."

"And?"

"He shows himself, you take him out, Mills here gives me my daughter back."

"Somebody needs to go to prison here," said Frank. He'd climbed out of the car and stood leaning on the Audi's roof. "You know the score, Stimson."

"I don't see why it needs to get nasty, Franky."

Frank stared at her shaking his head.

"What?" said Stimson. "Surprised you've been outwitted by a woman all these years?"

Harvey stared at her too. She was worthy of a stare. She obviously looked after herself. Harvey judged her as early thirties, his age, but knew better. She'd been on the scene since he was young, he'd heard the stories.

Beneath her long fur coat, she wore a tight red dress and matching heels. She was strikingly beautiful with a figure that most men would fall for.

"It's rude to stare, Harvey. Didn't Julios teach you that?" said Stimson, turning to Harvey.

Adeo grinned.

"Your time's up, Stimson. When this is over, you'll be taking a holiday," said Frank.

"That's right, I need a break, some time with my daughter, perhaps."

"Her Majesty's pleasure, Stimson."

"Oh, Franky."

"Work with us, and I'll see all things are considered."

"All things are considered? What things, Frank?"

"The robbery for a start?"

"Wasn't me."

"Larson?"

"Larson who?"

"Lucas Larson, your number one."

"I don't know what you're talking about. I've never seen or spoken to anyone named Larson, have I, Adeo?"

The big man shook his head and jutted his lower lip out in denial.

"You have nothing on me, Carver."

"People have died, you callous bitch."

"I don't think there's much need for that kind of language in front of my daughter if you wouldn't mind."

"You can't get away with this," said Frank.

"I take you to Al Sayan, you let me go."

"You take us to Al Sayan, you get your daughter back, that was the deal."

A mobile phone began to ring. The noise came from Stimson's clutch.

"Mind if I get this? It's kind of life and death."

She pulled the sleek looking smartphone from her bag, tapped the screen with a perfectly manicured nail and held the phone to her ear. Harvey saw the glistening earring beside the phone and the sparkling ring on her finger. He followed the contours of her body and saw the bright watch on her slender arm beneath the fur sleeve.

She pulled the phone from her ear, disconnected the call and put it back in her bag. She snapped the clutch shut with finality.

"Tower Bridge, one hour."

CHAPTER TWENTY-NINE

Melody, Frank and Reg travelled in the Volvo, while Harvey and Stimson rode in the little Porsche. The buddha rode in the Porsche's small rear seat, and Adeo followed in the van.

"He wants me alone," said Stimson.

"I'm sure he's not the only man out there that wants you alone, Stimson."

"I'm sure." She smiled, pleased at his recognition of her looks.

"I'm sure there are a few men out there ready to choke the life out of you," said Harvey. He didn't face her, he carried on looking out the window. He felt her smile fade.

"Any police on the scene and he hits the bang button," she said.

"Any idea where he's planted it?"

"He didn't say."

"Taxis?"

"He didn't say."

"So it could be nothing? He might not have anything."

"Bit of risk though, Harvey, isn't it?"

"Frank's got the river police standing by, and there'll be armed police all over."

"What Al Sayan doesn't know shouldn't hurt him," said Stimson.

"Oh, it'll hurt alright, but it won't be the police that hurts him."

Stimson looked across at Harvey. "You're not going to hand him over are you?"

"He's got a debt to pay," said Harvey.

There was a silence.

"And me?" said Stimson.

"What about you?"

"Haven't I a debt to pay?"

"Not really. It's a transaction. You give me Al Sayan, and you get your daughter back. As you said, Frank probably doesn't have anything on you, anyway."

"So he'll stand by his word, will he?"

"Most honest man I know."

"That doesn't say much, you grew up with villains."

"Pot, kettle," said Harvey.

"Pot, kettle," agreed Stimson.

"Ever wished you did something else?" asked Harvey.

"Like ordinary people?" replied Stimson. "No, I wasn't made for that life." Stimson checked her rearview mirror.

"She's still there," said Harvey. "You can trust Melody."

"She's cute."

Harvey didn't reply. Melody overtook them on Upper Thames Street and sped off to get in position.

"Some might say," replied Harvey.

"Have I come between y-"

"You've come between nothing, Stimson," snapped Harvey. "What you have stepped into though is a team of very angry people who just lost their friend because of you. And I'll be honest, I don't know how long I can keep this friendly charade up for. It's your fault we're in this, and I'm doing my very best not to lean across this car and rip your throat out."

"I had to."

"Had to what?"

"Bring you into it," replied Stimson. "You would have got wind of it anyway, you were *supposed* to fall for the decoy."

"The manor house?"

"Yes, you should have been concentrating all your efforts into understanding how on earth anyone could carry out a heist in such a place."

"That's ridiculous, I took one look and knew it was impossible."

"Ah, but impossible is my speciality, right?"

"You go for the hard to get, I'll give you that."

"Is that what you are, Harvey? Hard to get?"

Harvey didn't reply.

"If you'd have just stayed out in Essex, you'd have been fine," said Stimson.

"You dumped a body in my house."

"Al Sayan did. Killing's not my style remember?"

"Right."

"What about the fake cop?"

"Ah, that was me."

"Not very well planned, I saw through it. Plus we got you on the dash cam."

"It was last minute, you shouldn't have followed us."

"In fact, I've seen through all your plans and schemes."

"It's not been my finest hour, Harvey, I'll admit that, but the stakes were high."

"Angel."

Stimson nodded.

"You need to disappear after this."

"I know, I've made the arrangements."

"Where?"

Stimson raised her eyebrows.

"Worth a try," said Harvey.

"Join me?"

It was Harvey's turn to give Stimson a look.

"Worth a try. I bet a man like you could take care of a girl like me. There must be a lot of women out there that sat and stared at you wondering what you'd be like. Wondered how it would feel to have a beast on top of them, what it would be like dancing with the devil. A moment of taboo ecstasy, perhaps?" She paused. "How about it?"

"I'm not for hire."

"I wouldn't be paying, not cash anyway."

Harvey heard a click on his ear-piece. "Mills in place."

"ETA one minute," replied Harvey.

"Is that her?" Stimson asked. "She's a lucky girl."

"I'm not her type."

"But she's yours?"

"Talk me through the plan."

"I'll stop the car here." She pulled over in St Katherine's Way, which was on the north side of Tower Bridge and on the opposite side of the road to the Tower of London. "I'll climb up those steps, walk to the middle of the bridge and give Al Sayan the buddha."

"Then?"

"Then I come back, and your sweetheart gives me my daughter back."

"And Al Sayan?"

"Not my problem."

"Al Sayan is in position," said Melody. "I have him in my sight."

Harvey looked away from Stimson. "Sit tight Melody. He's placed something somewhere."

"Say again?"

"There's one more package. His fall-back plan."

"But there were only three taxis?"

"I'm thinking the meeting on the bridge isn't just a convenient location."

"Say hello from me, won't you?" said Stimson.

"Save the girly chat for when you see her and tell her yourself," said Harvey, getting out of the car. "Grab the buddha and let's go."

"You're going *with* me?"

"You don't think I'm going to stand and watch you walk away with that thing do you?" Harvey strode towards the stairs up to the bridge. Stimson locked the car and chased after him.

"He'll blow it up, all the people."

"*Harvey, are you sure about this?*" said Melody over the comms.

"What people?" Harvey turned and squared up to her. "So far it's all been about you, hasn't it? And if it hasn't been about you, it's been about your daughter or you not going to prison, or you trying to break me down. You just lost Lucas Larson, a taxi driver lost his life, and god knows about the other two and what about all those people in Canary Wharf? And what about-"

"Denver?" said Stimson. "Is that it? You finally lost someone too, so now you're mad. Well, good. That's what we need, that's what this *city* needs right now is for Harvey Stone to get mad and stop Al Sayan."

"So tell me where his next target is, tell me where I need to be."

"You need to be up there with me, you need to chuck the lunatic off the bridge."

"Is that what you want or is that what he wants?" said Harvey. Stimson closed her mouth. "That's it, isn't it? He wants me, and you're going to let him take me."

Stimson didn't reply.

"And with me out of the way, you can go back to being the spoiled little bitch who gets all the diamonds."

"I don't want all the diamonds." Stimson pulled a ring off her finger and threw it at Harvey. "I just want my daughter." She stood in front of Harvey looking helpless, dejected and broken.

"Let's go."

Stimson didn't move, she just stood there in the road.

"Don't give me that, pick up your ring up and get up those stairs. If you were upset, you'd have been upset before I told you she was safe."

Harvey climbed to the top of the stairs, stood on the bridge and looked along it. The shape and length of the bridge meant he couldn't see to the middle from where he stood. But he could see where Melody said she'd be, on the top section intended for maintenance. If Melody said Al Sayan was there already, then he was there.

He began to walk. Stimson had slipped off her heels and ran to catch Harvey up.

"Give me the buddha."

"No, I need to-"

"Give me the buddha, Stimson." He held out his hand.

"Wow, I like it when you're angry." She passed him the buddha. She had removed it from the box and its covering. Harvey felt it. It felt like any old ornament you might find in any old house. It was just sickly green.

"I'm not angry," said Harvey.

"What are you then? Moody, quiet, sultry?"

"I'm focused. I'm taking this bastard down, and you're a distraction. Or is that your game too? Distract me so he can kill me?"

Stimson didn't reply.

"You're smart, I know you're smart. You don't have to

prove it, I'm smart too." He gestured with the buddha. "Walk in front and walk fast."

Harvey saw Al Sayan from a hundred yards away and checked his comms were open. The Arab was unmistakable in Harvey's mind now. As Harvey walked forwards, he saw a large bag by Al Sayan's feet. Harvey hid nothing, not even with the rage that was boiling inside of him, feeding him.

"Mr Harvey, thank you for joining us."

"Let's make this short, shall we?" said Harvey.

"That's fine by me, I see you've brought me a gift, how kind."

"Stimson is blocking my view," said Melody.

"Don't get too close to him, Stimson," said Harvey.

"I'm not wearing my vest," said Al Sayan. He looked down to the bag by his feet.

"Where's the explosives?"

Stimson moved back away from him and stood beside Harvey.

"If I tell you that, I lose my upper hand." Al Sayan smiled. "Can't we just carry out the transaction without the need for all the games and power play?"

Harvey didn't reply.

"I didn't think so." Al Sayan continued. "I know you took the brat, the offspring of this tart. So I took my own precautions. If you give me the buddha, and I walk away, who's to say your other little slut friend won't shoot me in the back?"

Harvey didn't reply.

"That's what I thought, Mr Harvey," said Al Sayan. "That's why you're going wear this vest until I'm safely out of the way. I'll call Stimson's phone when you can take it off, and we can all go on with our lives."

"As long as you're here in this country, you won't be safe."

"I'll take my chances, Mr Harvey," said Al Sayan. "Put the

vest on." He slid the bag across to Harvey with his foot. "You win some, you lose some, Mr Harvey. Isn't that what you say?"

"And what is it you say?"

"I don't, I just win. Put it on."

Harvey picked up the bag off the floor carefully and unzipped it.

"It's quite safe to handle."

Harvey saw the police boat in the water below him. It had stopped other smaller vessels from passing under the bridge, Frank had obviously made some calls. The police boat was small, and an officer stood on the rear deck waving his hands to the other larger boats, which were mostly tourist vessels. Groups of people stood on the decks and happily snapped away at the attraction, oblivious to the danger as Harvey donned the vest.

"Zip it up. It's quite snug," said Al Sayan. "It's my own work."

Harvey didn't reply. He slid the zipper up to his chest. Stimson looked on at him wide-eyed.

"What the hell are you doing, Harvey?" said Melody over the comms.

Harvey stared at Stimson. "This is what you wanted, wasn't it?"

"No, it's not."

"Stimson leaves now," said Harvey.

"I don't think so," replied Al Sayan.

"Where's the detonator?"

"Hidden. Inside the vest. But it's okay, it's fully automatic. All I have to do is call the phone that's connected, and-"

"And?"

"It'll all be over," said Al Sayan.

"I'll find you."

"Maybe, maybe not," replied Al Sayan. "Now pass me my prize."

Harvey stopped. He controlled his breathing but could feel his heart racing.

He held his hand out in front of him. The jade buddha stared back at him.

"Put it on the floor, Mr Harvey. I don't trust you."

Harvey swung his hand out to his left and held the buddha over the water.

"Ball's in your court, Al Sayan," said Harvey. "Tell your man to back down."

"Harvey no, stop," cried Melody over the comms. Harvey heard the tone of her voice, she was ready to break.

"Is this what you call a stalemate?" asked Al Sayan.

"No, it's what I call you telling your man to back down."

Al Sayan held his phone up. "If I dial this number, we all die."

"That solves the problem then, doesn't it?"

"Harvey, no," Stimson pleaded. "Just give him the buddha."

"You should listen to her, she's wise."

"She's smart, not wise. If she was wise, we wouldn't be standing here."

"If you drop the buddha, more people die," said Al Sayan coldly.

"If I drop the buddha, you die."

"And then the people die."

"I guess you could call them martyrs then, because if you die too, how many more lives will be saved?"

"I'm tired of these games, Mr Harvey." Al Sayan's voice grew harsher. "Put the buddha on the floor, or the people die."

Harvey didn't reply.

"Please, Harvey, don't do this," said Melody.

"Why do you want this so badly? You don't look like a collector."

"What does a collector look like? Or another way of looking at it, Mr Harvey, could be, what is it that I am collecting?"

"You're not collecting anything, you're just brainwashed."

"Easy now, no need for insults."

"I don't get it, you people, you're all mouth when it comes to the spineless act of blowing up innocent people, but a little banter, and you get all upset."

"Mr Harvey, that will not do–"

"Don't tell me what I can and can't say. Listen to yourself. You're weak, hiding behind a bag of explosives because you don't have the intelligence to fight a war like the rest of civilisation."

"Don't have the intelligence?" shouted Al Sayan. "Who do you think orchestrated this little saga? It wasn't me that robbed the auction house, was it? No, Mr Harvey, it was you that walked out with the buddha. And who was it that dragged this whore out of her cave? How long had you been looking for her? Years, Mr Harvey, years. And you have the gall to mock my intelligence. Put the vest on, stop this nonsense."

"You put the phone down, I'll put the buddha down, and we'll fight like men. How does that sound?"

"Have you any idea what that is worth?"

"Nothing to me."

"What you have in your hands, Mr Harvey, will fuel my plans to cleanse this wretched country for as long as it takes. The war on the west will never stop until all the infidels are wiped off the face of the planet. And only those who believe in the one true god, and worship him as the prophet Mohammed said we should, are free to walk the streets. Without fear, without pain, without suffering. With food in their bellies and roofs over their heads and a future. Mr Harvey, don't you see? To change the west and to spread the will of the one true god will take more than a few small explosions. This is only the awakening, my friend. This is the birth of Islam and the downfall of Christianity, a religion that has mocked the rest of the world for far too long. When the people of London are untied with Allah, the rest of the country shall fall. And when England falls, the rest of the western world will tumble down around it."

"You make me sick."

"You will be one of the first, Mr Harvey, to fall in the name of Islam, but nobody will remember your name. Nobody will sing for the fallen hero. But they will remember me. They will remember my face as I stand upon the ashes of Christianity and build mosques so that the beloved can pray. It will be me that is remembered five hundred years from now, Mr Harvey."

"And this little statue will do all that, will it?"

"No, Mr Harvey, but that little statue, as you call it, will fund my campaign to free the west. When London falls, I will have all the riches I need." Al Sayan stopped and eyed Harvey. "How easy it would be to purchase a few passenger jets. How easy it would be to bring the once great empire of Britain to its knees. That, Mr Harvey, in your hand, is the key to the future of England."

"You won't make it off this bridge."

"Try me," said Al Sayan. He lifted his phone. "I'm growing tired of this, I'm afraid I really just make a call."

"I don't care what you do," said Harvey. "Blow me up, blow the bridge up, but there's no way I'm handing this over to you until you tell your man to stand down."

"You don't follow the rules, do you?"

Harvey didn't reply.

"Okay, okay. I will tell my man to stand down," said Al Sayan. "But you pass the buddha to Stimson first. She can act as escrow."

Harvey slowly brought the buddha back. He stared hard at Stimson, gauging her allegiance.

"Do it, Mr Harvey."

Harvey handed Stimson the jade buddha.

"Call him off. Now."

"Easily done," said Al Sayan. He turned away and looked down to the group of boats. Tourists huddled on the decks staring up at the scene that played out in front of them. Al Sayan nodded and the driver of one boat put the engines in reverse and began to move away from the pack, away from the kill zone.

"Oh my god, it's one of the boats. I have him. I have the driver in my sights," said Melody. "What do you want to do?"

Harvey watched Al Sayan's man from the bridge. The hate was brimming inside him. Over a hundred people were stood on the boats below, they'd all be torn to shreds and drowned.

"Now," said Harvey.

The shot fired before he'd finished saying the one-syllable word. The small glass window of the boat's cabin smashed and the rest of the glass was spattered with the driver's blood. He slumped to the floor and out of sight. Women screamed far below, and the police boat jumped into action. Its bow raised up as soon as the driver slammed the throttles forward.

"You just lost your bargaining power," said Harvey and stepped forward toward Al Sayan. He reached out and grabbed his neck with one hand and smashed the heel of his hand into the man's face.

"Go, go, go," Melody called over the comms, and the sound of sirens filled the air.

Harvey dragged Al Sayan to his feet. Blood ran down the Arab's face and clumped in his long, straggly beard. He smiled up at Harvey and hit the green *Call* button on the cheap Nokia.

29

CHAPTER THIRTY

MELODY SPRINTED UP THE STAIRS OF THE BRIDGE. THE space was empty; tourists had been told to leave when Frank had called it into his superiors, and the message had filtered down to the bridge's tourist operators.

Melody reached the top of the north tower. The glass floor gave her a great view down between the bridge's structures but didn't afford her the shot she needed. She pulled the Diemaco's strap over her head and climbed off the viewing platform onto the old stone walls at the top of the tower. Melody worked her way around until she had a clear view of Al Sayan, stood alone in the centre of the bridge.

"Mills in position," she said over the comms. She didn't need any reply. The plan didn't stretch any further than Melody going up and taking Al Sayan out. Then Harvey told her about the fall back bomb. That changed the outcome. She could take Al Sayan out anytime, but innocent people would die.

Patience. She thought of Harvey's mantra. Patience, planning and execution. She could be as patient as she liked, but the planning was out the window. There were too many variables. She made herself comfortable. The rifle's bipod stood on the parapet like an archer of days gone by. She held Al Sayan in her sight.

Boats passed under the bridge, tourists off to see the Tower of London's famous Traitors' Gate, where doomed convicts would be taken in from the river, unlikely to ever see the sky again. The Tower of London's history is full of stories of death and suffering, Medieval London, rats and executioners. Whatever happened in the next hour would determine if that storybook had another tale of death added to its collection.

She noted the flags on the Tower's tall flagpoles. The wind was a constant south-easterly, five to six knots. Melody adjusted the scope accordingly, moving only four clicks to account for the difference in height between Al Sayan and the flags.

She heard Harvey had switched the comms to open and Melody had heard their conversation. The conversation between him and Stimson had been personal. They were like old friends that had never met. Stimson was cunning, but her allegiance was clear. She would be loyal to no-one but herself.

Harvey was going onto the bridge with Stimson. That changed things. He was putting lives at risk.

"Harvey are you sure about this?"

He gave no reply to Melody, but she heard the argument between him and Stimson, and could do nothing about it from where she was sat.

Melody watched the two of them walk across the bridge towards Al Sayan. She watched how Harvey controlled her, and how Stimson let him. Stimson had made several comments about Harvey and Melody, including enough questions that Melody had asked herself. What would Harvey be like? But the answers were always the same. He would be selfish, cold and mean. She'd grown to love the man, he was lovable, but in the same way she loved Reg, and had loved Denver. They'd shared close calls and boring nights of surveillance in the back of the van, but that was it. It was platonic. She loved Harvey enough to be worried about him. So when she saw him put the explosive vest on, her heart began to race. Al Sayan moved up and down in her sight. She fought to control her breathing but struggled; Harvey was killing himself.

"What the hell are you doing, Harvey?"

He held the buddha over the water.

Al Sayan remained composed. He had nothing to lose. What can you take from a man who is ready to die for his cause? The ultimate sacrifice.

"Harvey, no, stop," she cried.

But Harvey didn't reply. He continued to hold his hand out over the water.

Melody tried to regain her own composure. Al Sayan still stood in her sight, but tears clouded Melody's vision. She wiped them away, but her sight was still blurred. She felt the tears run down her own cheeks.

"Please, Harvey, don't do this."

Harvey passed the buddha to Stimson. Melody wiped her eyes and refocused. She found Al Sayan. He turned away and gave a signal to somebody below. Melody tracked along and the driver who had begun to reverse a boat full of tourists.

"I have the driver in my sights. What do you want to do?"

"Now," said Harvey. His voice was calm, clear and crisp over the ear-piece. And Melody squeezed the trigger the final eighth of an inch.

She immediately brought the rifle back to Al Sayan and saw Harvey reach for him. Harvey delivered a blow and dragged the man to his feet, but then there was a pause. Silence. It was like time stood still for a second, maybe two.

Then Harvey wrenched the man close to him and launched them both over the wall, down and out of sight.

"No," Melody screamed. She dropped the rifle and ran to the far side of the parapet but could see nothing. Tourists searched in the water, and police ordered the boat drivers to disperse with frantic waving of their arms. The Thames is tidal, and the river was flowing out to sea, but its strong currents beneath the surface were violent and unpredictable. More police boats standing by joined in the search and the comms was a riot of noise as Frank and Reg began to call to each other.

A few seconds passed, then a muffled explosion shook the water beneath the bridge. A circle of power ran out from the quietened blast in a violent shock wave. It then dispersed, and the river resumed its flow.

Melody sank to the floor and dropped her head. This time she let the tears flow and released her grip on the bursts of emotion that came from inside her in uncontrollable sobs. She did love him, she had loved him. She wanted to tell him. She wanted to go back to when they had stood on the riverside outside headquarters. Turn back even further to when he had pulled her from the sea and saved her life. She wanted to see him smile, make him smile and smile with him.

She climbed down unsteadily from the top of the tower onto the viewing platform and fell the last few feet to the floor. Her vision was foggy and her head was dizzy. Pulling herself up, she leaned on the wall for stability. Slowly, she made her way to the stairs and walked down.

Reg was stood in the ancient doorway, silhouetted by the bright light outside. She knew it was Reg by his shape, his posture. He held his arms out, and she fell into him. Reg held her tight, and her tears returned. Her body convulsed as the sobs came.

"Let it out, it's okay, let it out." Reg stroked her hair.

"It's over, Reg," she said into his shoulder. "We can't go on, not now."

Melody pulled the ear-piece form her ear and threw it on the floor. She stepped away from Reg and stamped on the device, crushing it beneath her foot.

"Take a breath, Melody," said Reg in a surprisingly soft tone.

"I'm sorry," said Melody, wiping her eyes and trying hard to focus. "Where's Stimson?"

"Disappeared," he said. "She was there when..." Reg paused. "When he went over, and then she'd gone. The big guy was sitting with the girl the whole time, but by the time we realised Stimson had gone, we saw that he'd gone too, and the girl. We were distracted."

"So we lost?" asked Melody. Her mouth hung open in exhausted exasperation.

"He didn't die in vain, Melody. He took down Al Sayan."

"But we lost Stimson and the buddha," said Melody. "And we lost Harvey."

"There's nothing I can say to bring him back, Melody. But what would Harvey do now?"

"He'd kick ass," said Melody between sobs.

"So let's go kick ass."

"How? What with?" said Melody. She broke away from Reg. "We don't have anything, no suspects, no tech, no nothing." She sounded dejected and looked defeated.

"Don't do this, Melody," replied Reg. "Don't let Harvey's death be the end of you. Don't let it be for nothing."

Melody didn't reply.

"Let's go," he said, "for Harvey."

"And Denver," said Melody.

"For both of them," said Reg.

CHAPTER THIRTY-ONE

MELODY AND REG WALKED TO THE WAITING AUDI. "MIND if I drive, sir?" She opened the boot and placed the Diemaco carefully inside.

Frank got out the car and walked to the passenger side. Reg climbed into the back seat and pulled his belt on.

"You ready, Reg?" she asked, then gunned the accelerator without waiting for his response.

"Can you get access to LUCY, Reg?"

"Of course I can," replied Reg. "Easy girl," he added as the large saloon car slid into the outside lane.

"No time for easy, Reg. If they reach a plane, that's it, game over," replied Melody. The Audi's engine roared out of a bend in the road using both lanes. Melody felt the car control the slide and shift the power to the inside wheels.

"Okay, I'm inside his profile. I just need to connect to LUCY, and I can pull up the big guy's phone signal, assuming he hasn't lobbed it somewhere."

"Forget the phone, Reg," said Melody, easing the car toward Rotherhithe Tunnel. "Find my jacket."

"Your what?"

"I dropped the tracker from my jacket in Angel's pocket."

"You're a smart girl, Melody," said Frank. "I'll give you that."

"Okay, they're currently on the A12 heading out of town."

Melody swerved around a slow driver in the fast lane of the tunnel approach road, then dropped down a gear. "Hold on."

The noise of the car's high-performance engine inside the tunnel was loud enough to alert the drivers in front that a car was coming up fast. Reg looked on in horror as cars strived to reach the inside lane before the Audi reached them. Frank held onto the door handle, but remained silent. Twice Melody had to maneuverer the Audi between a lorry and stubborn driver who refused to move. Reg held his hands up to his face, unable to look at the catastrophe he was sure was about to happen.

When they finally emerged from the tunnel, Melody once again dropped down into third gear and launched though the traffic that fought for the exit lane. The Audi roared past the other cars in a blur. The A12 stretched out in front of them. Miles and miles of multi-lane fast roads led from the city all the way to Ipswich on the East Coast.

"Okay, Reg, find me all the airfields on our path."

"All the airfields?" Reg replied. "That's going to be quite a few."

"Start with the closest one."

"There's a small airfield near Upminster in Essex, not busy and unlicensed. Another in Noak Hill, again not busy, quite small and unlicensed. The main licensed airfield heading east would be Stapleford Abbots."

"Stapleford Abbots?" said Melody. "Why do I know that name?"

"It's about three miles from Theydon Bois," said Frank. "That'll be where she's heading."

"Theydon Bois?" asked Melody.

"John Cartwright's house," replied Frank. "It's where Stone grew up, where Stimson would end all this."

"What makes you think that?"

"You heard them talking, Stimson's playing games with him, she wants him. Wanted him," Frank corrected himself. "She would have had no idea that Harvey wouldn't survive. Imagine it. Harvey learns that Julios wasn't the man he always thought he was. He's devastated, lost faith in everything. Taking him back there invokes memories for him. She offers him work, freedom, answers. You don't think she told him all that crap about his life because she felt like having a chat with another old villain do you?" Frank sighed. "No, she was enticing him. She was telling him how much she knows, about him, about his past, about his life. She was going to try and take him from us. If there's a plane waiting for her, it's there in Stapleford."

"You need a route, Melody?"

"I could drive there with my eyes closed after what happened there." Melody wiped her eyes at the mention of Harvey and concentrated on the road, though her head was bursting.

"Where exactly can she fly to from Stapleford?" asked Reg. "Runway looks pretty short from the satellite."

"It's mainly small aircrafts, Cessnas and the such, but even they can make it to France easily without refuelling. From France, she could go anywhere," said Frank.

"What happens if she gets away with the buddha?" asked Melody. "What's the consequence here?"

Frank saw that Melody was stringing out the conversation, avoiding long silences where her mind could wander off to Harvey.

"Failed case? Strike one."

"Even-"

"Even if we have taken Al Sayan down? Yes."

"Where does that leave us?"

"Well we won't be shut down, the case will stay open, but too many fails and the unit will break up. The unit's not official yet anyway, so all they'll do is place you two somewhere else, and I'll take early retirement."

"Was it true what you said about your wife being killed by Al Sayan, sir?" asked Melody.

"I wouldn't lie about something like that, Mills."

"Could have been motivational."

"No, it was true," said Frank. He gave a large exhale. "She was one of the unlucky ones."

"Sorry, sir," said Melody quietly.

"What are you sorry for, Mills?"

"For pushing," she replied. "For your loss."

"It's the world where we live in, isn't it?" said Frank. "It's a cruel, cruel world. We spend most of our days saving up to retire, then when we're finally ready, things have changed so much we don't want to anymore. Not here anyway. There's no freedom and too many memories."

"And if you could change it?" asked Melody.

"I'd take freedom over comfort. Security over choice. And friends over memories, Mills."

Melody heard the words and let them roll around her mind. She looked across at him, and he gave her a smile that said *I know how you're feeling*.

"Okay, I have Melody's jacket turning off the M11 motorway heading toward Stapleford," said Reg from the back.

"We're ten minutes behind them," said Melody. "It's going to take some doing to catch them up once they're on the back roads."

"Open her up, Mills," said Frank.

"Go big or go home, sir?" said Reg.

"Something like that, Tenant."

The team made the turning off the M11 in six minutes. "Stimson is five minutes out from the airfield, we are eleven if we maintain speed," confirmed Reg.

Melody slid the Audi skilfully off the exit ramp and wound the engine back up as fast as the A-road would allow. The smaller roads in the village of Abridge meant the team had to slow for a brief time. But, as soon as they had passed through it, Melody slammed the car into third gear and wound the engine back up.

"Stimson is in the airfield. We can only assume the plane is ready for takeoff, and that she'll park nearby," said Reg.

"How fond of this car are you, sir?" asked Melody.

"Why?" asked Frank.

"They're on the runway, and we're not. I'm just-"

"Airfield entrance is coming in five hundred metres," said Reg.

"Do what you need to do Mills," said Frank.

"Copy that, sir," replied Melody. She touched on the brakes, eased into third and let the gearbox slow them down a fraction. Then, dropping into second, she spun the wheel and popped the clutch as the car started to turn out of the bend. The rear end slid nicely out. The front smashed the gates open and tore one of the wing mirrors from its hinges. Melody straightened the car up and found third.

"Reg, be my eyes, there's a hundred planes here," said Melody calmly.

"One o'clock, eight hundred yards," replied Reg without hesitation.

"That's the runway," said Frank.

"I have a visual," said Melody. "They're taxing for takeoff. Reg, pull the back seat down and grab the Diemaco from the boot. Sir, care for a drive?" Melody didn't wait for an answer.

She hit the cruise control button on the steering wheel and pushed her seat all the way back.

"Mills," said Frank "What are-"

"Left foot first, sir."

Frank moved his left leg over to the driver's side. "For god's sake-"

"You got the wheel?"

"I have it, I don't know what-"

"Okay, all yours sir," said Melody. She hit the button on the rear door and lowered the window. Frank climbed fully into the driver's seat and pulled it forwards. The car veered slightly as he took control, but he brought it back on course.

"Get me alongside them, sir. I'll take the tyres out," shouted Melody over the rushing wind from the open window.

"Let's try this my way first, Mills." Frank gave a dab of brakes to turn off the cruise control, then dropped the car into second and spun onto the runway. The little Cessna was three hundred yards ahead.

"They're leaving," shouted Reg. The little plane sat at the end of the runway and worked up its engine.

"Two hundred yards," called Reg.

The pilot released the brakes, and the Cessna began to accelerate along the tarmac.

"One hundred yards."

"Sir," said Melody, "what's the plan here? I can take the tyres out before they get airborne."

They drew level with the plane and Frank guided the car under its wing and sounded the horn. The pilot refused to heed Frank's call.

Melody ditched the rifle onto Reg, reached out the window to hold the roof bars and pulled herself up to sit on the door.

"Closer," she shouted. Frank eased the Audi in closer until

Melody could reach the wing support, made up of two circular bars connecting the underside to the fuselage. Melody gripped onto the bars and stood on the car door. Her arms were wrapped around the wing support. She pushed off with her feet and swung her legs up over the bars just as the wings began to get lift. The wind against Melody's body froze her hands and threatened to rip her off the wing, but she locked her legs in place and tightened the grip of her left arm. Reaching behind her, she pulled her SIG from her waistband, levelling it at the pilot and gesturing for him to take them back down.

The pilot turned away and spoke to Stimson. Melody saw her gesture for him to continue.

Melody fired two rounds into the fuselage near the back of the plane. The pilot began waving one arm at Stimson, who was leaning forward, telling him to continue.

Stimson stared in disbelief out of the window. Then she turned to the pilot and started shouting. He argued back. Melody could make out the conversation but heard nothing. It was clear he was simply stating that there was a woman on the wing with a gun.

The plane banked sharply, and Melody had to hold on with both arms, but the gun stopped her from gripping the tube. The pilot pulled back on the yoke. Melody was hit by extreme G-force. She fought to hang on, her legs were holding tight, but her gun arm was slipping. Her hands were frozen, and the blast from the propeller deafened her.

Then the pilot eased the plane forward. Melody wasn't ready for the change. She slid around the wing support, reached to grab the other support, and saw her SIG fall to the ground below.

The pilot saw the gun fall and eased the plane back into a steady flight. The little Cessna began to climb.

With the plane stable, Melody was able to adjust her position and began to kick the window of the plane. She tried hard to smash the perspex so she could get inside. She had no doubt that once inside, she could take control.

But before she could settle in for another kick, the door was heaved open. Stimson stood in the doorway, her long coat flapping around and whipping against her body. She looked angry but determined. Holding on with one hand, Stimson reached out to Melody. For a brief moment, Melody thought she was going help her in and was grateful. Then Stimson's hand turned from an open palm to a fierce, well-manicured claw that stabbed into Melody's hands.

Stimson dug in deep and broke skin. Melody gave a yell and gripped with her legs. Her left hand fell from the support, and with each attempt to reach for the tube, the wind and Stimson blocked her. She was forcing Melody off. Her right hand was slipping, she couldn't hold much longer. The wing support was too fat for her hands to grip properly. One of Stimson's feet came at Melody's legs, long heels dug into her shin, but she gripped tighter and her strong thigh muscles held the supports. Then Stimson made a mistake. She lunged at Melody's flapping hair, grabbed it and pulled Melody's head towards her.

Melody let go with both hands. Arching up with her burning core muscles, she took hold of Stimson's jacket and heaved backwards. She felt the jerk as Stimson's grip was pulled from the passenger handle inside the cockpit and felt the stroke of soft fur slip past her face. Then she hung upside down by her legs and watched as Stimson plummeted to the earth below. Her arms and legs flailed as she grew smaller then hit the ground in a cloud of dust.

CHAPTER THIRTY-TWO

FRANK AND REG MET THE PLANE WHEN IT HAD FINISHED taxiing. They stood beside the Audi side by side as equals and welcomed their remaining team member back to the ground with open jaws and arms.

Melody stepped away from the wing quite dishevelled, but not shaken. She reached back into the aircraft and held out her hand. Angel jumped down. She'd been crying but was quiet. She wore the same pink pyjama bottoms with a red coat and carried the same little pink backpack.

"That was insane, Melody," said Reg.

"That was above the call of duty, Mills," said Frank.

Melody breathed out long and slow, bent and picked up the little girl.

"The buddha?" asked Frank.

"Adeo," said Melody.

"The Porsche has gone," said Reg, looking at the line of cars outside the quiet airfield offices. "It was there when we came in, I'm sure of it."

Melody let her head fall back and closed her eyes.

"It wasn't for nothing. You did a brave thing, Melody," said Frank.

"It feels like it was for nothing, sir," she replied. She moved closer to Frank. "This little girl's mother just died." There was compassion in Melody's eyes.

Frank moved in closer to Melody. "This little girl's mother just caused the death of two of our team and countless others," he said, then pulled back and looked directly into her eyes. "You're a hero, and I'm damn proud to have you on my team, Mills."

"So would Harvey be," said Reg. "I don't think even he could have pulled that stunt."

"Thanks, boys," she whispered.

Angel clutched onto Melody's leg and buried her face in her cargo pants. Melody looked back at Frank, who raised his eyebrows, but didn't make any attempt to pull the girl way. Melody smiled then gave a little laugh which made Reg and Frank smile.

"I'm sorry to ask," said the pilot. "I was hired for the day, will I be needed?"

Frank's smile grew into a full laugh, hearty, from his chest. The pilot looked shocked at the reaction after what had just happened.

"Go, while you can," said Frank. "If we need you we can pull your name from the office, right?"

"Yeah, they know me, I fly here every week," said the pilot. "The name's Lord, Jason Lord."

CHAPTER THIRTY-THREE

THE FALL TO THE WATER WAS JUST EIGHT METRES, BUT IT felt like Harvey had landed on concrete. He released the zip on the explosive vest as soon as he hit the water, before he'd stopped spinning in the water's turbulence, before he'd thought about breathing and before he'd looked for Al Sayan.

Any second now.

He pulled the vest off and pushed it below him. He didn't stop to watch the current take it away. He just swam for his life.

He had to get away from it.

The explosion rocked his very core down to his internal organs. His bones felt as if they would snap. The sound of the river went quiet, and the searing pain through his head cast a black shadow over everything.

The fast flowing current rushed him away, washing him free of the place and the memories.

Harvey Stone surfaced two hundred metres down the river. The cold wind that rushed across the water woke him from death with a start, and he coughed up brown water. He felt as if his body was broken. He was unable to move his limbs and just lay on the surface taking in air.

Several minutes later, he'd travelled a mile down the river and began to shiver. Shock and the cold set in, which caused a severe reaction within his body. He shook. Not just his fingers or his hands, but his entire arms violently and uncontrollably fought to keep the circulation going. His lower lip trembled, and his lungs stung with each cold breath.

Was this the end? Had it happened already? The world glided past silently. Had it been that simple? After everything he'd done, it was over in seconds. Harvey knew he was alive. He also knew that all he had to do was close his eyes and all the pain, all the memories and all the lies would go away.

Nobody would remember him five years from now. He played a part in the game and his time was up. Could be up.

Do I have a choice?

Can I fight this?

Surely not, I can close my eyes and drift away.

I'm drifting already, it's easy. I don't have to try.

But what if there's more?

Harvey tried to stretch his arms out wide, but his joints ached and told him so by sending electric pulses along his nervous system.

My body is broken. How can I try?

He filled his lungs with air to keep him afloat.

My insides are damaged, I can't go on.

I can go on.

I don't want to go on.

You haven't tried.

But I have suffered.

You need to try. Take a step.

He began to flex his fingers.

You'll need more than fingers. One more step.

But I can close my eyes.

You're strong.

Not right now.

You've always been strong.

Let me sleep.

You can bend your arms.

Harvey slowly bent one arm beneath the water, then the other.

It's not over.

Have I made my choice?

I can do it.

There's no going back.

I've made my choice.

You're Harvey Stone.

I'm Harvey Stone.

Harvey found the movement in his limbs painful as thoughts of giving up washed over him and were taken out to sea. Though painful, his legs moved freely. He began to bend his arms back and forth. He moved his toes inside his wet boots and lay on his back to stretch his muscles. But he still shook. The water was viscously cold.

He'd come close to death, and he knew it. Harvey felt that when death held him in his hand, he was warmed. He couldn't remember the shivers, the biting cold or stinging skin. He had let death pass through him then banished him and now suffered the penance.

Harvey watched the sky pass by above him, unsure if the sky was moving or if he was moving. Perhaps both. He wondered how far he'd travelled, but didn't recognise anything when he turned his head to see. There were no tall buildings, just factories and warehouses.

How far did I float?

That was when his head hit a rock.

The dull thump sent white light across his eyes, and he scrambled in the water. Blood trickled across his wet face, mingling with the water. He felt stones beneath him. He *heard footsteps on the stones.*

Harvey span and his vision caught a second after, then a wave of blood ran through his bruised mind. Harvey focused on the stones beneath his hands. He brought a leg up and dug it into the gravel. He slowly raised his head.

Nobody was coming.

But a man was walking away.

Al Sayan.

He had survived.

Harvey pushed his body upright, bringing his head slowly up. His legs were trembling and his fingers shook. He squeezed his hands tight then flexed his fingers.

He took a step.

He's getting away.

Another step.

Come on, Harvey Stone.

Harvey's wet boots sank into the gravelly beach. His bruised thigh pumped dull aches through his leg and his muscle tensed with every step. He pushed hard. He wasn't looking at Al Sayan who was moving fast now, away from him. Harvey focused on the next step, then the next. He built a rhythm. Slowly, each step came with a short, sharp exhale of used air, spent. He sucked in more, took another step, let the pain run through him. Then more until the pain was pleasant. He welcomed the dull ache. He welcomed his body's rejection of movement. He forced his legs to move and his arms to pump, then he reached the grass. Soft, muddy grass.

Al Sayan was a distant shape two or three hundred metres away. Harvey didn't care, couldn't care. He had to keep moving away from the beach. Harvey could take long steps. They got faster. He looked ahead. Another man with Al Sayan. A small white van beside them both.

Heat.

The man went down. Harvey saw Al Sayan raise a rock high above his head. Harvey ran. The feeling was alien at first. A slow jog, but faster than the slow stumble.

Al Sayan brought the rock down on the man.

Harvey stepped faster. His legs trembled like he'd ran a marathon but his arms pumped.

Al Sayan opened the van door.

A dog barked and ran from nowhere, passing Harvey.

Harvey ran on. The dog leapt at Al Sayan and caught his leg as he was climbing into the driver's seat. Harvey heard a yelp, then the dog launched again.

Not far.

The dog snapped at Al Sayan and pinned him to the seat. Small, sharp bites on his legs and fingers. Harvey began to hear the frantic screams of Al Sayan from inside the car. His legs lashed out at the dog who relaunched his attack.

Harvey stepped up to the fight and surprised the little dog. It took one look at Harvey and moved to sit beside his owner's body.

Al Sayan tried to straighten himself up and pull his legs into the van, but Harvey stood on his foot, took hold of the door and swung it hard against his leg, again and again. The Arab bent double and reached for his leg. He didn't cry out. In Harvey's experience, men who know that death is coming rarely do. As Al Sayan reached forwards, Harvey grabbed hold of him and wrenched him from the vehicle onto the mud. The man tried to crawl away but found himself being dragged backwards.

Harvey hoisted him up into the van and slammed the doors.

The dog looked at Harvey with flattened ears, his head cocked to one side. His owner was dead. There was nothing Harvey could do. The dog was a collie. A white stripe ran the length of its nose between his eyes and ears and finished on top of his head. The rest of his face was a mix of black and brown.

"What do you say there, boy?" said Harvey lazily. "You staying or coming?" The dog looked at his owner. The back of the man's head had been caved in. "You getting in?"

"Good boy," said Harvey and opened the passenger door for the dog who jumped in and sat down. The keys were in the ignition, and the engine was still warm. Within one minute, Harvey had warmth on his feet and legs and some semblance of human feeling returned to him.

Harvey found first gear and took the little diesel van along the bumpy track that led away from the river towards the road. Road signs told Harvey where he was and he made his way through the town of Rainham, then Hornchurch, then Romford. The sights became more familiar, the trees seemed greener, and the fields of Essex soon replaced the dirty buildings of London.

CHAPTER THIRTY-FOUR

It was a typically overcast day at the East London cemetery. Melody and Reg stood either side of Frank, and together they stood among the friends and family of Denver Cox. His mother sat at the front dressed in a smart black dress, a black hat and veil, and black gloves.

There was no coffin, no dug earth. There was just a headstone to remind the world of Denver's existence, and give his mother and his family a place to go and visit him, to talk to him, to remember him and grieve.

Melody would need no headstone to remember Denver. He had been a solid man, true and reliable. She stood and listened to the vicar reading from the Bible and remembered how Denver had talked her down from bursting into the barn when Donny Cartwright had been running a human trafficking ring. Denver had always been quiet until push came to the shove, and then he always stepped up.

Denver's family took turns to talk of him, and Melody delighted in hearing about her friend, things he'd done as a child, antics, his passion for speed and adrenaline. Even at a young age Denver went go-cart racing and displayed an almost fearless trust in his own capabilities. His mother explained how she had watched him take corners at high speeds and had to look away.

Nobody spoke of Denver's love for supercars, and how that passion had come very close to putting him behind bars. There was no need to mention it. He hadn't gone to prison and had formed a career from doing the things he loved the most.

The vicar asked the assembly if anybody else would like to say a few words.

Frank stepped forward.

He addressed the gathering of friends and family but spoke directly to Denver's mother.

"I've met many men in my time in this world in many countries, cities, and towns. Some come and go, while others stay a while. Denver was an honest man, true to his word and one of the most reliable," said Frank. Denver's mother nodded. "I firmly believe that the people we meet, new faces that enter our lives and share our time, fall into three categories. Some we meet for a reason; some twist of fate guides the purpose of the meeting for the benefit of them or me, and then they move on, or I move on. Fate is fulfilled. Denver does not fall into this category." Frank took a breath and paused to let the words sink into the engaged crowd.

"Others, we meet for a season; a brief period of time, summer, winter or a year or two, where two people become friends, enemies, colleagues, and then fate again sends one or both of us along a different path. Denver does not belong in this category." Frank cleared his throat and stood strong, though Melody could see that he was holding his emotions together.

"There's some people we meet that do not cross our paths for a reason or a season, they join us for a lifetime. These people are few and far between." Frank took his eyes away from Mrs Cox and looked at Melody and Reg. "But these people are exceptional, and some subconscious inside us, in our very cores, knows that we will love these people forever, and no matter what happens, we will be by their sides when times are good, and we will offer our shoulders when times are difficult. Regardless of the circumstance, and regardless of the outcomes, we will be together, and that person will be a part of our lives forever. Denver Cox is one of those people. I'm proud to say he will always be a part of my life, for as long I still breathe."

Mrs Cox wiped tears away as Frank stepped down from the small astroturf podium to rejoin Melody and Reg. He put his arm around Melody's shoulder. Melody wiped her eyes with a small handkerchief.

The congregation were invited to join Denver's family at their home for his wake. As soon as the people began to move, Denver's father stood and approached the team. He stopped directly in front of them all and shook their hands one by one, looking each of them in the eye.

"Denver died doing what he loved the most," said Mr Cox.

"He's a hero, sir," said Reg. "I'll never forget what he did."

"You were there?"

"I was, sir."

Mr Cox nodded and put his hand on Reg's shoulder. He turned to Frank.

"Thank you for the kind words, Mr Carver."

"It was nothing that isn't true, Mr Cox."

"So you're the team he spoke about then, are you?" said Mr Cox, in an attempt to cheer the conversation. "I thought there were more of you?"

"We were five," began Frank. "But we lost-"

"We lost the best driver and pilot I ever met," said a voice from behind them. "He was a hell of a man."

Melody spun around at the sound of the voice.

"I'm sorry, who are you?" said Mr Cox.

"Stone, sir. Harvey Stone." Harvey held out his hand for Mr Cox. "I'm very sorry your loss. Denver was one of my closest friends."

CHAPTER THIRTY-FIVE

THE TEAM SAT IN THE MEETING ROOM OF HEADQUARTERS. Reg sat on one of the two couches, Melody stood by the coffee machine, and Harvey leaned against the door. There was a hole in the room where Denver used to sit on the arm of the other couch.

The dog had visited the team individually and received pats on the head. He'd got a lot of cuddles and attention from Melody, then went to sit at Harvey's feet.

Angel sat beside Melody on a little chair. She was colouring in a pad with an array of pens and pencils, oblivious to the people around her. Melody had bought the young girl a new dress and had cleaned her from her ordeal as a prisoner.

Frank addressed the team.

"Today's debrief will be slightly different, aside from the addition of our two guests," said Frank. He shifted his feet, looked up and stared at the team, one by one.

"I'm taking Angel to the child services today, sir," said Melody. "They've found a home for her."

"Good, she'll need a lot of care after what she's been through."

"She's a strong kid, sir."

Frank turned to Harvey.

Harvey didn't reply.

"And have you found the mutt a home, Stone?"

"Yeah, as it happens, I have."

"Good, I'm glad," said Frank, then turned back to the room. "Today's discussion will not involve us mourning Denver, though we all do mourn him inside. The day will not even involve us celebrating his glorious death, though we are all grateful for his heroic actions." Reg leaned forward in the seat, and Melody stared at Frank, hanging on his words.

"We will, of course, assess our successes, our failures and compile our reports. It's part of the job, but I'd also like to hear from you all. I'd like to know where your hearts are, and where we stand as a team." The last sentence was spoken softly.

There was silence.

"Let's start with a recap of suspects." Frank picked up a whiteboard marker and turned to the board.

"Stimson," he whispered to avoid letting Angel hear her mother's name.

"Nailed," said Reg. "Courtesy of Melody Mills." Harvey looked across at her and nodded his approval. Frank wrote beside Stimson's name *Deceased*.

"Larson, status?"

"Nailed," said Reg. "Courtesy of our very own, back from the dead, Harvey Stone." Reg hammered out a drumbeat on his knees.

"Hague?" asked Frank, ignoring Reg's enthusiasm.

"Deceased, sir," said Melody.

"Not doing too well so far, are we?"

"Adeo, Stimson's minder," called Frank. "Did we find him?"

Melody and Reg were silent.

Frank turned back to face the room. "And I assume we believe the priceless jade buddha is with him?"

"That's correct, sir."

"So the case remains open." Frank stared at Melody. "Until further notice." He turned to Harvey. "I want the man found."

"Yes, sir," said Melody.

"You should know," began Frank again, "that your actions, though unrecognised with respect to Al Sayan, have not gone unnoticed where it counts."

"Sir?" asked Reg.

"We found the missing two taxi drivers in a locked room inside the Stratford warehouse. They were alive, and we've been credited with their release. My superiors sent an email thanking us for our efforts throughout the entire operation and also sent condolences for the loss of Denver."

"Sounds cold, sir," said Melody. "Would have been nice to hear it from the horse's mouth."

Frank didn't reply to Melody. Instead, he carried on with his talk.

"Okay, like I said, we're going to discuss how we're feeling, where are we as a team. It's been a long few days and we've all been through more than our fair share of trauma."

Angel began to tug on Melody's sleeve.

"Not now, sweetheart," said Melody.

"Sir," began Reg, "what about Al Sayan? And the taxi driver, and the tech guy?"

"That's not our case, Tenant," replied Frank. "We can't take credit for a case that doesn't fall under our jurisdiction. He was collateral." Frank held his gaze until Reg turned away.

"But, sir-"

"No buts, I'm afraid. SO10 and SO19 took the credit for the takedown of all three terrorist suspects. Please omit them from your reports. You will, however, be asked to provide a statement surrounding Denver's actions at a later date."

The team fell quiet.

"So, how are we feeling?" asked Frank.

Nobody replied.

"Melody, you usually have something to say, where's your heart at?"

Melody didn't reply.

"Team, I'm not asking you open up here, I'm looking to gauge the motivation. And right now, quite understandably, it's on the floor." He paused. "Am I right?"

"It's pretty hard to think about the future, sir," said Reg.

Frank pointed at him. "Good, keep it coming."

Melody looked confused. "You seriously want to hear how mad we are that we lost a friend and failed to solve the case?"

"Yes, tell me." Frank was loud, excited and enthusiastic at hearing their dejected tones.

"Okay, well, we're upset we lost Denver," said Melody.

"Understandable," said Frank. "So am I. Next."

"We're mad that we didn't recover the buddha," said Reg.

"Good, *why* are you mad?"

Reg looked at Melody for support.

"It's the first case we lost, sir."

"*Yes,*" cried Frank. "Yes it was. So what are you going to *do* about it?"

The team were stunned by Frank's outburst, it had been a sombre few days.

"You're going to go find it, right?"

Melody caught on to Franks encouragement. "Yes, sir," she shouted.

"*Good,*" said Frank. "And what happens when we can't find it?" Franks voice rose in volume.

"We look harder, sir."

"Excellent, Tenant. Are we going to fail?"

"No, sir," both Melody and Reg called out.

"Fantastic. Denver doesn't want you sitting in here moping. Get out there and make it happen." Frank pointed to the door.

Angel began to pull on Melody's sleeve again.

"Angel, let me talk please."

"But look," said Angel.

Melody glanced down at the girl who had pulled some colouring pencils from her little pink backpack. "Not now, darling,"

"This isn't mine," said Angel, and shrugged. "Where did it come from?" Angel said the words slowly, as young girls do.

Frank had turned away and was summarising the status of the deceased suspects on the whiteboard. Reg was fiddling with an iPad, but Harvey was looking directly at Angel.

He smiled when he caught a glimpse of green.

Melody caught his smile and followed his gaze.

Angel stood by her side with a two-thousand-year-old jade buddha in her hands.

35

CHAPTER THIRTY-SIX

FRANK DROVE, AND HARVEY SAT IN THE PASSENGER SEAT. Harvey was dressed in clean cargo pants, new boots and a clean white t-shirt beneath his old leather jacket. They drove out of town and headed into the green suburbs of Essex. The dog was in the back seat.

"Are we heading anywhere in particular, Stone?"

"I thought we might take a stroll, Frank."

"Could have done that by the river, couldn't we?"

"I want to show you something," said Harvey.

"Sounds nice. Are you going to tell me what happened?"

"What happened?"

"We thought you were dead, Stone. We saw the explosion. Nobody could have survived that."

"It was close, maybe the closest I've ever been."

"It's almost a miracle, Stone, not just close."

"Depends on your point of view," replied Harvey. "I haven't given it much thought since. How are you feeling?"

"Feeling?"

"You asked the team how we're feeling, nobody asked

you," replied Harvey. "How are you feeling? Are you motivated?"

"Motivated enough to fight another day. Are you offering encouragement?"

"In a way," said Harvey. "Turn here."

Frank steered the car toward Theydon Bois.

"Do you have closure, Frank?"

"Closure?"

"Yes, closure. Do you feel like Jan can rest in peace? Do you feel like you avenged her death?"

"In a way, it hasn't sunk in yet. What with–"

"Denver, right," finished Harvey. "Do you feel like the noose has lifted, or relaxed a little?"

"My noose?"

"Yes, Frank, your noose. We both wore them. Yours woke you up at night, didn't it? It dragged you to work every day, and it reminded you daily that someone out there somewhere was responsible for your wife's death. It reminded you that you lived and breathed another day on the planet in the same country, city even, and that you shared the same air as him." Harvey paused. "The noose was tight, wasn't it?"

"It was, Stone, yes."

"Forget the formalities, Frank, I'm Harvey. I think we know each other well enough now," said Harvey. "Tell me how you feel, how tight the noose is. Maybe I can help." Harvey looked across at the older man. "I'm an expert at dealing with nooses, Frank. Remember?"

"You want the truth?" Frank asked.

"Of course."

"I can't remember when I last slept a solid night."

"Thought so."

"You can tell?"

"I told you, I'm an expert."

"I don't think I'll *ever* get closure. I don't think I'll ever understand how one human being can be responsible for the deaths of so many others."

"It's a cruel world, Frank."

"Yes, yes it is, Harvey," replied Frank. "How about you? You were typically quiet in the meeting."

"Planning," said Harvey.

"Planning?" asked Frank.

"And patience. The two go hand in hand in my experience. Turn right here."

Frank indicated and turned.

"You going to tell me what it was you were planning?" asked Frank.

"My future."

"Your future?"

Harvey didn't reply.

"Your future is with the unit, Harvey. We need you now more than ever."

"Perhaps," said Harvey. "Perhaps not. Whatever I decide, it needs to be my decision."

"Your decision? It's always-"

"I need you take my noose off me, Frank."

"Okay."

"You want commitment? Release me, give me a choice. You want to see what I'm capable of, set me free. Some birds are just not meant to be caged, Frank."

"I take it you got the answers you were looking for?"

"I got answers, not necessarily the ones I wanted to hear, but I can put the rest together myself."

"Did you ever suspect Julios?"

"Never, he was my one ally."

"I'm sorry."

"Don't be," Said Harvey. "He's dead, they're dead. I'm alive, you're alive."

"So how does your future look?"

"Fresh start, deeper sleep," said Harvey.

"Deeper sleep?"

"Peace, Frank." Harvey paused. "I'm not sure I ever knew what it was."

"So if it was Julios after all this time, who killed Julios? Are you any closer to finding that out?" Frank glanced across at Harvey's face, but it was typically impassive.

"I'll find him. He's on my list. But I'll take my time."

"I'm pleased for you, Harvey," began Frank, before pushing the conversation forward, "I'm pleased you finally found the answers, even if the truth wasn't ideal."

"Ideal, Frank?"

"You know what I mean," said Frank, "you got your closure. You worked hard at it, and there's plenty of people who never thought you would."

"I have you to thank, Frank," said Harvey.

"I didn't solve anything."

"You held the noose tight, that's what I'm saying. I don't need the noose anymore. It's detrimental to my future now."

"It's detrimental?" asked Frank. "But if I set you free, if I tear up the arrest warrant, would that be detrimental to the team?"

"You want the truth from me?"

"Of course."

"I feel part of something, Frank. When Denver died, I feel like we all lost something. I've seen men lost to crime. They've bled out or had their heads blown off, but I never felt loss. Not like–"

"Like Denver?"

"Yeah, not like Denver."

"Turn here, Frank."

"But this is–"

"John Cartwright's house, yes."

"What are we doing here?"

"Taking a walk, showing you something." Harvey sighed. "Letting you in, I guess."

"Letting me in?"

"You wanted to see where my noose was tied."

"I thought I held the rope?" asked Frank.

"You tightened the knot. The rope has always been tied to this place."

Frank stopped the car beside the little groundsman's house. It was where Harvey had lived when he worked for his foster father, John Cartwright.

"Needs some care and attention, doesn't it?" said Frank, looking at the broken windows, overgrown ivy and graffiti on the front door.

"Don't we all." Harvey climbed out the car, let the dog out, and started walking along the little stream that ran through the grounds of the three-hundred-acre property. Frank followed and caught up with the younger man. The dog ran ahead, drank from the dream and bounded in the long wild grass.

"Are you keeping him?" asked Frank, referring to the dog.

"Was thinking about it, or maybe gift him to Melody. They both need some love and attention."

"What you going to call him?"

"Boon."

"Boon?" asked Frank. "Why Boon?"

"It's a name, and I found him the boonies, in the middle of nowhere." Harvey paused. "This is where Hannah and I played as children," he said without looking at the older man.

"Lucky kids," said Frank.

"We made the best of a bad situation. Our parents were murdered, remember?"

Frank didn't reply.

"We used to climb that willow there and pretend to be pirates. Our names are carved in the bark somewhere."

"Fond memories?"

"The only memories I've got, Frank," said Harvey. "At least, the only ones I wish to remember."

"You're different now. You've changed, Harvey."

"Things happen, people adapt."

"No, not adapting. You really have found peace, haven't you?"

"I think so, Frank. That's why I need the noose removed."

"Okay. That's easy, Harvey."

"It's gone?"

"It's gone."

"No more threat of prison?"

"I'll tear the warrant up as soon as we're back."

Harvey didn't reply.

"Feel good?"

Harvey nodded. "Want me to remove yours?"

"My what?"

"Your noose."

"Mine's tight."

"That's what I thought, *I* can ease the knot, *you* can take it off yourself."

"How are you going to do that?"

"You remember the basement here?"

"How can I forget? Its history is full of–"

"Closure, Frank," said Harvey. "Its history is steeped in closure."

Frank didn't reply.

"Why don't you go take a look down there?" asked Harvey. "I'll wait here."

"And what will I find?"

"You remember once, we discussed the obligations of society, and how sometimes a man's crime is so severe that society is obligated to punish him?"

"I remember," said Frank. His heart began to beat harder as the tone of Harvey's voice fell into a cruel, cold tone.

"And do you remember how we discussed that, sometimes, it is those that have suffered the most who are obliged to enact that punishment?"

Frank was quiet, his breath held. "Al Sayan?" he whispered.

Harvey didn't reply.

The End.

Click here for Stone Rage, the 4th book in the Stone Cold Thriller series.

STONE BREED - FREE NOVELLA

The
Stone Cold Novella Series.
Book 1

1

KERFUFFLE

"THEY'RE A BIT BLEEDING UGLY, DOUGY, AREN'T THEY?" said Handsome. "Are you sure they're the right ones?"

Handsome's cockney whisper carried along the long, oak-lined corridor and came back at them in the quiet night.

"Shhh," said Douglas, "they can hear you a mile away. But yeah, you're right, they're not pretty, but they sure are worth a few quid."

"Says here they're fifteenth century," said Handsome. "Must have been bleak back then if this is what they called art. Reminds me of this bird I was seeing once, about a year ago. She had crap like this all over her house, she did, was like a bleeding museum, it was."

"She didn't live *here*, did she?" laughed Douglas.

Handsome whispered a laugh. "I hope not, mate. Her old man weren't too pleased to see me when he came home and found me wearing his slippers and drinking his brandy."

They both began to chuckle quietly until they heard the echoes of their laughs in the darkness. They stopped suddenly, then realised they'd only heard their own echoes and began laughing again.

"And the funniest thing was," said Handsome, grinning in the darkness, "I'd nicked a motor to go see her. Bloody great house, it was, out in the sticks. I'd lifted some car keys from some bloke's pocket in the boozer, some old banger, and parked it on her drive beside her Jag. But when her old man came home and found us both at it on the chaise lounge, I had to do a runner and left the keys upstairs on his bedside table." Handsome was laughing hard, and trying to keep quiet. "The old bill found me half way up the road, running in just a pair of paisley slippers and a tartan deerstalker, with me bleeding wedding tackle swinging about like a pair of church bells."

Douglas laughed, louder than he'd meant to, which started Handsome off again too. They'd both bent over double, laughing at the image and held their fingers up to their mouths, shushing each other.

Handsome recovered after a few moments and wiped the tears of laughter from his eyes.

"Come on, Dougy, let's get these ugly bloody things and get out of here. This bleeding place gives me the creeps."

"You're not scared, Handsome, surely?" said Douglas. "It's just a big, old, spooky house in the big, old, spooky country."

"It's just all this old crap, statues and stuff, Dougy, it makes me feel like I'm being watched."

Handsome reached up and opened the oak and glass cabinet. Its door creaked lightly.

"Shhh," whispered Douglas.

Handsome let out a loud laugh, and immediately tried to restrain it, but he couldn't.

"I don't think we should of had those beers, Dougy," said Handsome, as he reached into the cabinet. "I feel half-cut."

"You'll feel more than half-cut if you don't put your hands where I can see them," said a voice in the darkness behind Douglas.

They both whipped around to see who it was, but the dark wooden cladding and the pitch black night outside had formed deep shadows inside the old house.

"Who the bloody hell is that?" said Douglas in a hushed but angry tone.

"Never you mind, Dougy, but I think you'll find those two little beauties are coming with us. So get your mucky little paws off them and step away before I blow a hole big enough to park my car in your backside."

"You what?" said Handsome. "You're not-"

"Robbing the place, Handsome?" said another voice. "Well, we was trying to, but it looks like you two clowns beat us to it."

"Well, bugger off then. We were here first," said Douglas.

"Oh no, son. We're not going anywhere without them statuettes."

"Here, how do you know our names then?" said Handsome.

"We heard you from the bloody driveway, you pair of plums. Now move out the way, or you'll get what's coming to you."

The man's voice came at them in a loud, harsh whisper with a thick Yorkshire accent.

"Oh no, my old son," said Handsome. "We aren't giving in that easily."

One of the men stepped up to Handsome and stared out of the darkness.

"I've got a gun, and you haven't. Now get out of the bleeding way."

"Hold up, hold up, hold up," said Douglas. "I've got an idea." He held his arms out to calm everyone down.

"Why don't we just take one each?" he said. "Simples."

"Oh behave, Dougy," said Handsome.

"No way. It's both of them or nothing, son," said the northerner.

"Dougy," said Handsome, "you heard what the boss said; on their own, they're not worth bugger all, but together, they represent a small fortune."

"Okay, okay, okay," said Douglas, defeated. "I've got another idea."

"He's full of ideas your mate, isn't he?" said the northerner.

"Bleeding mastermind, mate," said Handsome.

"Shhh," hushed Douglas. "So how about we fight it out? No guns, or we'll wake the old bastard up."

"Sod off, mate," said one of the men. "I can barely see you in the dark."

"No, hold on, hold on," said Handsome. "He's onto something here. But I happen to be taking a bird out tomorrow night and could do with having all my teeth in place if you know what I mean. So how about we have a one on one here in the hallway. Dougy against one of you two."

"What d'ya reckon, Goldi?" said one of the strangers.

"Ah, for God's sake, Dopey," sighed Goldi. "Alright, you go, I'll keep watch. Make sure old Handsome over there don't run off with the prize."

"*Me?*" said Dopey. "*You're* the bloody tough nut."

"Just get on with it," said Goldi. "This is bloody stupid. We should be halfway to London by now."

"Well if you pair of plums hadn't of turned up," said Handsome, "we bleeding would have been too."

"What? In that old rust bucket you've got parked down the road?" said Goldi. "You'd be down there with the bonnet up waiting for the A-bloody-A."

"Alright, alright," said Douglas. "Are we going to do this, or what?"

"I'm game if you are," said Dopey.

The atmosphere suddenly tensed.

"Right, no weapons," said Douglas. "A fair fight. Winner takes all, yeah?"

Dopey was rolling his sleeves up and had begun to crouch and sidestep around the room, circling Douglas.

"I won't need any weapons," he said. "Goldi, get ready to go, this'll be over in-"

"Hold on," said Handsome, forgetting about the fact that they were trying to be quiet. "*They've bleeding gone.*"

Dopey and Douglas stood upright from their crouches.

"What do you mean they've bleeding gone?" said Goldi, stepping over to Handsome at the cabinet.

"The statuettes, mate," said Handsome. "They were here, and now they're not, which in my book, makes them gone."

"You took them," said Dopey. "Goldi, check him."

"I never took nothing, mate," said Handsome. "I been stood here all along, haven't I?"

"Well who bloody hell took them then?" said Douglas. "Was it you two? While we were fighting?"

"Fighting?" said Dopey. "We never threw a punch."

"You know what I mean," said Douglas. "While you were doing your little battle dance."

"*Battle dance?*" said Dopey. "That weren't no battle dance."

"Well, what was it then?" asked Handsome. "Some kind of mating signal?"

"*Bloody cheek*," said Dopey.

"You *did* look like a bit of a tit, Dopey," said Goldi.

"That was what you call owning the ring, boys," said Dopey.

"Is that right?" said Handsome. "You looked like you needed the loo, mate,"

Goldi laughed.

"Oy," said Dopey, "you're not supposed to join in."

"Who the bloody hell's down there," said a loud voice from the end of the corridor, which was followed the familiar sound of a shotgun being racked.

2

LABOUR

NEWHAM HOSPITAL ON A FRIDAY NIGHT WAS A BUSY PLACE. Drunken teenagers with drunken injuries, broken bones from drunken fights, and an odd homeless man looking to stay warm for a few hours until the security guards crazed him out the door. At the far end of the hospital, away from the accident and emergency ward, was where the miracles happened. On the first floor beside a small, peaceful waiting room, where anxious men frequently checked their watches and didn't read the magazines that they flicked through mindlessly, was the maternity ward where, over several decades, thousands of women had brought thousands of babies into the world.

At about the same time that Goldi and Dopey were plucking up the courage to tell their boss they'd lost the statuettes the previous night, one man sat alone in the waiting room of the Newham Hospital maternity ward. He didn't flick through the pages of one of the car magazines or travel brochures. And he didn't frequently check his watch. He sat with his back to the wall facing the entrance, as calm as calm can be, with his hands resting on his lap, and his eyes on the door.

Nurses came and went. They shuffled through the reception with urgency, and the receptionist spoke loudly on the telephone. All the while, the lone man sat and waited patiently for his wife to perform the magic that only women can.

"Mr Stone?" said the receptionist.

He looked up and raised an eyebrow.

"It's the telephone for you, sir," she said. "Are you expecting a call?"

Leo Stone didn't reply.

Instead, he stood, took the five paces to the reception and took the handset that the receptionist offered him.

He put the handset to his ear. A full three seconds passed before he handed it back to the receptionist.

"Is everything okay, sir?" she asked, surprised at the lack of dialogue.

"Please tell my wife," he spoke quietly, and the receptionist leaned forward to hear, "tell her, I'm sorry." Leo then turned and made toward the door. He caught the door to his wife's room opening a fraction, and saw his mother-in-law peer through the gap, a look of disappointment carved into her weathered face.

Leo stopped and stared back at her. His ability to communicate his thoughts without words was second to none. It was a vital skill that he and his partner used. Each knew from a single gesture or expression what the other was thinking, or what they were going to do.

He took the two small flights of stairs to the ground floor, stepped out of the main entrance, took three steps to his motorcycle, and swung his leg over, pulling his helmet on as he did.

Another two minutes later and Leo Stone was on the road heading towards Theydon Bois in Essex.

3

WRATH

"Nicked them?" shouted Terry Thomson. "You were supposed to bloody nick them."

"We know, Terry," said Dopey. "They *were* there, but then they weren't."

"They were there, but then they weren't?" said Terry, as if trying to comprehend the statement. "They just upped and buggered off on their own, did they?"

"We reckoned it was the other blokes, Tel," said Goldi. "They were there before us."

"What other blokes? What was it, a *party*? Did you break out the fizz? Did you have a little dance?" shouted Terry.

"Well, as it happens, Dopey had a bit of a-"

"*What other blokes?*" screamed Terry.

"We don't know who they were, Terry," said Goldi. "They were already there when we got there. We reckon they must have heard about the statuettes too, and we reckon they must have had the same idea we had."

"May I remind you, Goldi," said Terry, calmly, quietly and with over-pronounced diction, a sign that the crime boss was very likely about to blow his lid, "that first off, it was my bloody idea. It was me that found out about them. It was me that planned it, and it was you pair of doughnuts that cocked it up." He stared at the two men who turned their heads to the floor. "And secondly, you had bloody shooters. Why didn't you just take them off them? Whoever they were."

"We didn't want to wake the old man up, Terry," said Dopey.

"Wake the bloody old man up?" said Terry, incredulous. "You were robbing the stupid old bastard. Did you go and tuck him into bed? Did you sing him a bleeding song?"

"Well, no Tel," said Dopey. "But he could have called the police."

"You two amaze me, you really do," said Terry, turning away. He paced the floor of his car body shop, where he ran his operations. "I give you one simple job. It wasn't like I asked you to rob the crown jewels, was it? Eh? No. It wasn't as if I asked you kidnap somebody who might have tried to run away. Eh? No, it bleeding wasn't. I asked you go to the dirty great big house, break in, and rob the statuettes. Did they run away, Goldi?"

"No, Tel."

"Dopey? Did you happen to see them trundling off on their lonesome?"

"No, Terry, I didn't."

"Right, so who nicked them then?"

"We don't know, Terry," said Goldi.

"And who were the blokes that were there supposedly robbing the place before you pair of idiots turned up?"

"We don't know, Terry," said Dopey.

"So what are you going to do about it?" asked Terry.

"Find out who robbed them?" asked Dopey.

"And how are you going to do that?" asked Terry.

Dopey and Goldi turned to each other, then back at Terry.

"We don't know," they both said together.

"I'll tell you what," said Terry. "I'll go wake up the big guns, shall I? Maybe I need someone a little more competent on the case, and you two can go back to simpler tasks until you learn how to be a bit more self-sufficient." He turned to Goldi. "What's your boy's name again, Goldi?"

"Lenny, Terry. Little Lenny, we call him," said Goldi.

"Well, Goldi, how proud of his daddy is Little Lenny going to be when he finds out what his new job is?"

Goldi stared at the floor.

"What is it you want us to do, Terry?" said Dopey.

"What is it I want you to do?" repeated Terry. "It's a complex task, Dopey, but one that befits the severe lack of intelligence, foresight and common sense that you two plums seem to display." Terry stepped away, his hands sunk into the pockets of his Kashmir overcoat, and his eyes magnified by the thick lenses in his horn-rimmed eye-glasses. "The job I have in mind for you pair of morons will provide you with the opportunity to redeem yourselves, to show me how much you truly want to succeed, and how dedicated you are to me and our little enterprise, Dopey."

Dopey and Goldi's eyes followed Terry around the room as he paced between his cars, flicking minuscule bits of dust from the immaculate bodywork of his Mercedes.

"Are you ready to prove yourselves, boys?"

Goldi and Dopey looked at each other, then at Terry, and both chorused, "Yes, Terry."

"Good," Terry replied. "Now wash my bleeding cars while I go wake up the Bulldog."

4

GREED

THE GROUNDS OF JOHN CARTWRIGHT'S ESTATE RAN AS FAR as the eye could see. To the left of the long gravel driveway was a brook that flowed behind the great Edwardian house, and an orchard, over which the tiny village of Theydon Bois could be seen, surrounded by Epping Forest. On the right-hand side, as Leo powered through the two large wrought iron gates, was the old groundsmen's house, and beyond that were well-manicured lawns, flower beds, and John's garages, where he stored his collection of classic cars.

Leo was greeted by the housekeeper, and shown into the huge reception hall. Two grand staircases swept up to the first floor with eloquent curves like a pair of hooded cobras, ready to strike.

The housekeeper tapped gently on the solid wooden door to the right of the hallway, and she gestured for Leo to go inside, closing the door behind him as he passed through.

"Leo," said John, sitting up from the paperwork on his large teak desk, "come in. Sit down."

John stood, and began to pour two tumblers of brandy.

Leo sat in the guest chair and listened as six cubes of ice chinked home in the crystal glass tumblers.

"I hear that congratulations are in order, Leo," said John. The statement was more to break the ice than an attempt to bring Leo into a conversation. John knew that Leo wasn't much of a conversationalist. He set the tumblers on mats on the desk, and then returned to his chair behind his desk.

"She's there now," said Leo. "He hasn't made an appearance yet."

"Oh," said John. "So it's a boy, is it?"

"You called," said Leo, moving the subject on. "You have a job for me?"

John gave thought to Leo avoiding the subject of his newborn baby. "Yes," he said. "Yes, I do have a job for you. I've got my eye on a couple of little ornaments, statuettes to be precise, Leo."

"Statuettes?" said Leo.

"Statuettes, Leo," said John. "Like miniature statues, about nine-inches high, ugly as sin but worth a small fortune."

"If it's a robbery, John, you called the wrong guy."

"It's not a robbery, Leo. They've already been robbed."

"So what's the problem?" asked Leo.

"It weren't us that nicked them, was it?" said John. "If it was us, we wouldn't be sitting here having this chat."

Leo didn't reply.

"Do you know Honest Harry?"

"Yeah, he runs the betting shop off Green Street," said Leo.

"Right. If there's anything that's out there to be known, it'll be him who knows it," said John. "If there's something worth nicking, he'll know where it came from, how much it's worth, and who plans on nicking it. Start with him, Leo, shake him up."

"And when I find the culprit?" said Leo, flatly.

John paused, took a sip of his brandy, and placed it back down on the desk, adjusting the mat to be perfectly symmetrical with the corner of the desk.

"Do what you need to do, Leo."

5

BULLDOG

"It's been a while, Bulldog," said Terry Thomson. "How've you been?" His voice came through the pay phone crackly, distorted, but unmistakably Terry Thomson.

"Is this a social call, Terry?" said Bulldog.

"No, Bulldog, I only wish it was."

"Right, well time is money, Terry, and right now you're on the clock."

"I'm missing a couple of things, Bulldog," said Terry. "A couple of very expensive things."

"And what might these very expensive things be?"

"Ornaments, Bulldog."

"Ornaments?"

"Yeah, ornaments. They're things that most people like to have in their homes to make the place look nice. But I don't suppose you have those in your caravan, do you, Bulldog?"

"No use for such things," said Bulldog. "What's so special about these ornaments?"

"Oh, Bulldog, they are as old as old can be, and together, my old mate, they are worth an absolute bleeding mint."

"That's what I thought, Terry. So where do I find them?" Bulldog's Birmingham accent came through thick and heavy. He was a true Midlands man, raised by hard-working parents in hard times on rough streets, and he didn't let people forget it.

"If I knew where to find them, I wouldn't have woken you up, would I?" said Terry. "They were nicked, sunshine, from a big house in the even bigger countryside, and they could be bleeding anywhere by now."

"Two ornaments, you say?" said Bulldog.

"That's right, Bulldog," said Terry. "You want me to come and draw you a picture?"

"No picture, Terry, but what are they worth?"

"What are they worth?" asked Terry. "What do you think I am, Bulldog, an antique dealer? Did you see me on last week's bleeding Antiques Roadshow? No, Bulldog, you did not."

"So far, Terry, all you've told me is that someone stole two decorations."

"*Ornaments,* Bulldog," corrected Terry. "They're ornaments."

"Someone stole two *ornaments,*" said Bulldog, "and it wasn't you. And you don't know where they are, or who has them, and now you're telling me that you don't even know how much they're worth."

"That's why I have people like you, Bulldog," said Terry. "This is one of your skills. You're able to coerce information out of people, and then you're able to extract *other* things out of *other* people, *like bleeding ornaments*. It's not rocket science, is it?" said Terry.

"Well actually, I disagree, Terry."

"You northerners are all the same, aren't you?" said Terry. "Did you actually go to school in a coal mine or was that just a rumour?"

"I *disagree*, Terry," continued Bulldog, ignoring the insult, "because it's clearly a lot more complex than you think."

"What could be simpler, Bulldog? Find the bloody statuettes, take them off whatever muppet has them, and bring them to me," said Terry.

"So they're statuettes now, are they?" said Bulldog. "You need to paint a better picture, Terry. It's all about the details."

"Paint a picture, Bulldog?" shouted Terry. "I'll paint you a bleeding picture, shall I? You go find the statuettes, ornaments, whatever you want to call them, and bring them to me."

"So what's stopping me from finding the statuettes, taking them off whoever nicked them, and then selling them myself?" said Bulldog. "I don't see how me bringing them to you is worthwhile to me, Terry."

Terry sighed loudly. "Bulldog, you don't even know what an ornament is, how the bloody hell are you going to sell them?"

"Sixty percent," said Bulldog.

"Sixty percent?" screamed Terry. "Sixty bleeding percent? Bulldog, do you even know what sixty percent is?"

"It's like half, but a bit more, Terry," said Bulldog. "That little bit more is my cost."

"Your cost, Bulldog? What is your cost exactly? Do you have any overheads? No, Bulldog, you live in a poxy caravan. You're not even a proper pikey."

"Sixty percent," said Bulldog, "or I'll go find them and sell them to someone else. You must have some kind of idea of what they're worth or you wouldn't have called me. Don't take me for stupid, Mr Thomson. I might live in a caravan, but I've done you more favours than you've done me."

"For God's sake, Bulldog," said Terry. "Okay, they reckon about a hundred grand for the pair. But only about twenty for one. So that means I want them both."

"Hundred grand?" said Bulldog, surprised.

"Yes, Bulldog, one hundred bags of sand, which makes fifty percent. *Fifty* bags of lovely sand in your grubby skyrocket, my old son. That's my last offer."

"I said sixty, Terry."

"And *I* said fifty. Take it or leave it, Bulldog."

There was a silence as each of the men held onto their offers.

"Fifty grand and I drink in your bar for free," countered Bulldog.

"Drink in my bar?" said Terry. "You? I tell you what, fifty-five grand and you stay the bloody hell away from my bar."

"Fifty-five grand?" said Bulldog. "Done."

"Done," said Terry.

Bulldog replaced the handset on the pay phone.

"You have been," he said to himself.

HONESTY

"Bleeding hell, what do you want?" said Honest Harry from behind the counter of his betting shop off Green Street. "Look, you've nearly emptied the place."

Frank Carver turned around and smiled as most of the shop's customers recognised the undercover policeman and promptly left with their betting slips.

"The company you keep, Mr Barlow, is not the most pleasant," said Frank in his watered-down Scottish accent. He turned back to Harry, who had discreetly closed the safe door under the counter while Frank had his back turned. "If I were you, I'd be thanking me for getting rid of them. You wouldn't want to be associated with criminals, would you now, Harry?"

"Innocent until-"

"-proven guilty, yeah yeah," said Frank. "The problem with that, Harry, is that I can make anyone guilty. All I have to do is to apply a little pressure in the right spot. Know what I mean, Harry? Find a weakness and open it up."

Harry was silent, which was often the best approach when dealing with bent coppers like Frank Carver.

"That's one of the big problems with the human race,

Harry. Cracks. We all have them. Some of them are harder to find than others, but they're there. And I have a knack for sniffing them out."

"Great," said Harry. "Thanks for the introduction. Now do you mind telling what it is you want so I can get back to earning money and feeding my family?"

Frank looked past Harry, through the door into the back room, and saw Mrs Barlow and her daughter sitting at a table. He gestured to them with a discreet nod of his head.

"They're okay," said Harry. "They're family, and we don't keep secrets. Secrets become lies, Frank, and lies cause trouble."

"Who do we know, Harry, that has an eye for expensive things?"

"Do you mind being a little more specific, Frank? What are we talking about here? Jewellery? Cars?"

"Art, Harry."

"Art? You mean like a painting or something?"

"More like ornamental art, Harry."

Harry sucked air between his teeth.

"I'd love to help, Frank, you know I would, but I haven't heard a dicky about no art. But it was nice to see you. Let me know when you plan on coming back, eh? Give me time to shut the shop."

"I wonder where *your* cracks are, Harry," said Frank.

"Oh, I wouldn't worry about *my* cracks, Frank. I'm as smooth as a baby's bum."

"I wonder," said Frank. "A little pressure in the right places. I just need a big enough lever."

Harry stared at the policeman and caught Frank staring through the door behind him to where his wife and daughter sat at the table. Harry kicked the door closed with a sweep of his foot.

"No cracks there, Frank. Let's keep it clean, eh?"

Frank smiled at the smaller man.

"I'll tell you what I'll do, Harry," said Frank, "I'll give you two days to do some homework."

Frank turned and made towards the door.

"Oh leave off, Frank. I told you, I don't know anything about no ornaments," Harry called after him.

Frank opened the door a fraction, glanced outside, then turned back to Harry.

"Remember, Harry," he said, "cracks and levers."

7

PITY

LEO PARKED HIS BIKE BETWEEN AN OLD FORD CORTINA AND a Vauxhall Viva. A middle-aged man opened the door to the shop, loitered for a few seconds, then left and climbed into an old Volvo.

Leo kept his helmet on with the visor down. He waited for the Volvo to drive off, then took a few steps along the footpath and kicked open the door with the heel of his heavy boot.

He stepped into the shop and glared at the two remaining customers. They read his unspoken message, collected their belongings and left. Leo locked the door behind them.

"Wait," said Harry, fear suddenly alive in his voice. "What are you...? Who are you?"

Leo didn't reply.

He picked up a stool that was to his left and began to systematically smash the glass in all five fruit machines with well-placed swings. Then he discarded the stool and made his way to the counter.

"I'll call the police," shouted Harry. "Get out. Leave us alone."

Leo reached over the counter, grabbed Harry, who was cowering near the door to the back room, and wrenched him across the wooden surface onto the floor.

Harry curled up in a foetus position, so Leo picked up his leg, and dragged him behind the counter. A well-placed kick destroyed the lock on the door. Leo was met with Harry's scared wife and daughter who sat huddled together looking at the door, each of them deciding if they should chance making a run for it. Before they could make up their minds, Leo had made it for them. He dragged Harry into the room and dumped him at their feet.

Harry sat up, half protecting his daughter, half trying to escape the reach of Leo.

"Just tell us what you want," he said, his voice nearly breaking with fright.

Leo took a look around the room. It was much as he'd imagined the back room of a betting shop to be, shelves, crappy wallpaper, paperwork, and filth.

A few long, silent seconds had passed when Harry spoke again.

"Well?" he said. "Are you going to tell us what you want or are you just going to stand there? I suppose you'll want a bleeding tea as well?"

Leo looked down at Harry on the floor, whose bravado shrank back and hid behind his fear.

Leo reached behind and pulled a handgun from his belt. He aimed at Harry's knees. Then slowly, inch by inch, he raised the gun until it pointed at Harry's groin. Harry turned away, leaning on his wife who sat holding their daughter.

Leo raised the weapon some more. He skipped over Harry's face and settled on the wife for a few seconds. Terror struck her and her daughter, and they cowered to the floor with Harry until Leo moved the weapon off the frightened woman, and let it fall upon the daughter.

He stopped.

"What?" screamed Harry. "Just bleeding talk to me. Tell me what you want."

Leo pulled the cocking lever back with his thumb.

"No," said the woman, defending her daughter. "No, just leave. Can't you see we've done nothing wrong?"

Leo didn't reply.

"It's those bleeding statues, ain't it?" said Harry. "Is that what you're after?"

Leo lowered the gun and stared at Harry.

"Well I ain't bleeding got them, so get out of here."

The daughter was crying audibly. The mother tried her best to move in front of her from where they were pinned.

Leo raised the gun once more.

"Whoa, whoa," said Harry. "Okay, okay."

Leo returned his stare to Harry.

"I heard about a job, and that maybe someone wants shot of them. I said I might be able to help them out. But I don't know who he is."

Leo didn't reply. He held the gun straight and true at the daughter's forehead.

"But I know where you can find them, maybe."

Leo thought for a few seconds, then lowered the weapon.

"Okay," said Harry, "I'll tell you. Just leave them alone, please. Please."

TAILING THE BEAST

PARKED A FEW HUNDRED FEET FROM THE RUN-DOWN LITTLE betting shop off Green Street, Bulldog sat in his black VW camper van. His process was the same each time he did a job. It didn't matter if the job was a robbery, or taking someone out, a few minutes of peace and quiet in his car to gather his thoughts seemed to calm him.

Terry Thomson was offering a lot of money, so Bulldog needed info. He knew that if anyone had details about the stolen ornaments, then Honest Harry would. If he didn't talk, then Bulldog had some tricks up his sleeve that might coerce Harry into offering a few snippets of information.

Something was up though. Something just wasn't quite right. The shop looked shut, and by mid-morning, Harry's little betting shop was typically full of down and out losers handing out their dole money for a chance at the big one.

But the shop looked empty. Bulldog sat a while longer, watching through the window until the door opened, and a man in bike leathers and a full face helmet stepped onto the street.

Bulldog saw Harry through the window, who ran to shut

the door, reached down to push the bottom lock, and then up to close the top lock.

Harry wouldn't shut up shop this early, thought Bulldog.

A tall, lean man strode around the corner with his hands in his pockets, a folded newspaper under his arm, and a hand-rolled cigarette hanging from his lip. He tried the door and expected it to open, but it wouldn't. Stepping back onto the pavement, he looked left and right, then peered through the glass. He must have seen Harry, as even Bulldog could see him clearly, gesturing wildly at someone out of view, maybe in the back room. But the man's attempts at knocking were ignored.

The man in leathers had started his bike and pulled out onto the street.

Bulldog started his van.

The bike turned left onto Green Street, so Bulldog followed. His patience had been rewarded. The man was clearly up to no good, and a betting man would have money on the fact that this biker knew about the ornaments.

Bulldog could save shaking up Harry for another day.

It wasn't hard for Bulldog to follow the biker. The road was fairly quiet, and he fell in with the traffic about eight cars behind. If the biker took the A13, the dual carriageway into London, then Bulldog might lose him, his old van wouldn't keep up. But on the back streets, he'd be fine.

The journey was short. The biker was clearly a local boy; he knew the swerves and the shortcuts that cut out the set of lights by the High Street. It wasn't long before Bulldog found himself entering the grounds of the hospital.

He turned into the car park and let the bike go on ahead. Bulldog watched him to see where he was parking. The bike rode past the accident and emergency unit and stopped near the wards.

He was visiting someone.

Bulldog parked and watched as the man in leathers entered the doors marked gynaecology and maternity wards.

Bulldog followed on foot.

9

A BEAST IS BORN

OLIVIA WAS SLEEPING WHEN LEO STEPPED INTO THE SMALL room. His mother-in-law had left. She'd taken Hannah, their two-year-old daughter off somewhere to give Olivia a chance to rest.

Leo closed the door softly and went to her side. He pulled the hair from her face. She was flushed, exhausted, but she stirred.

"You missed it," she said softly, her words mumbled from fatigue.

Leo didn't reply.

She didn't look at him, she kept her eye's closed, but a small tear leaked out, and ran down her face.

"He's healthy," she said, "in case you're wondering. He's sleeping."

"We've got a son," said Leo, "and you're okay. It's enough for me."

The words from Leo were enough to open Olivia's eyes. She rolled onto her back, and Leo smoothed her hair.

"I can't believe you weren't here."

Leo didn't reply.

"He didn't even cry," said Olivia. "He's just like his dad."

"Can I see him?"

"Through the glass," said Olivia. "But let him sleep. We'll both be awake later. Why don't you come back, eh?"

Olivia rolled back onto her side.

Leo bent and kissed the side of her head, but Olivia didn't react. She fell silently back to sleep.

Leo stepped out of the room quietly, and closed the door labelled 'Stone'. He moved along to the large window that allowed parents to view the row of cots and found the one also marked 'Stone'.

They hadn't decided on a name yet. But right then, names were not important. What was important was that Leo had a son, a healthy boy.

Leo stood in wonder at the small boy that lay, wrapped in a blanket, fast asleep, with an expressionless face. Leo saw that other babies were frowning, or looking around at their new worlds, but Leo's boy had his eyes shut, in complete peace, almost unafraid of what was to come.

"Hello, boy," said Leo softly. "I'm your dad."

Leo suddenly felt a pang of self-consciousness at his words and checked left and right to make sure nobody had heard.

"I'll come see you later, yeah?" He touched the glass lightly and left.

The reception desk was unmanned; the nurse was probably off on an errand. Just one man sat in the waiting room, flicking through a magazine. He looked up at Leo's arrival.

Their eyes met, and the man nodded a greeting.

Leo didn't reply. He opened the door, took the two flights of stairs down the ground floor, and stepped onto his motorbike.

10

EYES

FRANK CARVER WAS DESTINED FOR GREAT THINGS WITHIN the British Police Force. The London crime scene offered men like him boundless opportunities to make a name for themselves, compared to the small village in Scotland where he'd grown up.

He had a nose for trouble, for liars and for thieves, partly due to his own shady background. It had been mere good fortune that had saved Frank. If he'd been caught doing the things he'd done as a youngster, the momentum of the criminal life would have carried him far away. But as luck would have it, he wasn't caught and watching his friends go to prison enabled him to re-evaluate his life.

It had been his father that had spoken of the force. Initially, Frank had disregarded the idea. Any association with the law would be met by his friends with horror. They would turn on him, and he'd be an outcast.

His father had pleaded with him in the end, and when Frank had seen the steady income that was available to entry-level beat cops, the career had become a possibility, especially considering that Frank had almost no qualifications to his name. Twenty-five years later, Frank had worked his way up, been transferred, chased promotions, and had finally hung his uniform up to go plain clothes.

It wasn't that his brain was particularly sharper than his colleagues', or that the senior officers generally loved him. His success was more to do with the fact that he was able to think like the criminals. He'd always ask himself what he would have done. His gut and instinct steered him well.

It had been his gut and instinct to leave Honest Harry's, drive around the block, and park a few hundred feet away, hidden amongst the parked cars that lined the side street. From there, he'd sat and watched as the man on the motor-bike entered and exited the shop not long after Frank himself had left. Frank had also seen the black VW camper that had pulled out behind the motorbike.

So Frank had followed discreetly.

He parked in the hospital car park, far enough away from the camper to watch the man get out and follow the biker into the building.

Frank waited for a while. He knew that both men would exit the building the way they had entered, so he sat and watched.

The biker had re-appeared less than ten minutes later. He pulled on his helmet, straddled his motorcycle, then rode away.

The second man did not re-appear.

Frank made the decision to go in.

The single elevator doors were open, so Frank stepped in and hit the button for the first floor. Ten seconds later, he found himself in the reception of the Newham Hospital maternity ward, feeling very aware that he was neither a female, a pregnant female, or the husband of a wife who was pregnant. He had absolutely zero excuse for being there.

The waiting room was empty, so he made his way towards the stairs to make his escape.

He was halfway down the first flight of stairs when he saw the man from the camper van rushing towards the car park carrying something.

Frank tried to recall if the man had been carrying anything on his way in, but the sudden and shrill, blood-curdling scream of a broken-hearted mother suggested otherwise.

11

TEAMWORK

FRANK RETURNED TO HIS CAR. HE WAS SHOCKED AND dazed. He'd missed the van leaving, and didn't know which way it had gone. He pulled the door closed, he put the keys in the ignition, then sat back and let his head fall onto the headrest.

That was when he felt the muzzle of a handgun in the back of his neck.

Frank froze.

"You followed me," said the man in the rear seat of his Volvo. "Why?"

"You looked like a man who could help me."

"And why would I do that?"

"You looked like a man who knows a thing or two about art," said Frank. "Specifically, two recently missing pieces of art."

Frank knew that if the man deciphered his vague description, he'd likely be guilty.

"Do I look like a thief?" asked the man.

"I do enjoy the smell of leathers," said Frank.

"How about the smell of cordite?"

"Sometimes,' said Frank. "Depends on the day."

"Is today one of those days?" asked the man.

"You know, I don't think it is."

The man didn't reply.

"So, what now?" asked Frank. "Are you going to shoot me here?"

"That depends. Who are you working for?"

Frank gave a hearty laugh. "The tax-payer, son."

"You're a copper?"

"Somewhere between you and the police, my friend, is a special placed in hell reserved for people like me."

"And what do you want with the statuettes?"

"Ah, so you do know about them?"

"I don't have time for games, copper."

"Let's just say a friend of a friend wants them and is willing to pay handsomely."

"What if I don't have them?" said the man.

"Then I guess it was a dead end," said Frank. "Maybe we go our separate ways."

"Give me one good reason why I shouldn't off you right here."

"I'm observant, son," said Frank.

The man didn't reply.

"I see things that many don't."

"Is that right?" said the man. "Tell me what you saw then."

"Did you see a black VW camper parked up there on the left?" asked Frank.

"I saw it about fifteen minutes ago. It was gone by the time I came back."

"I saw it first," said Frank.

"So what? Do you want a prize or something?"

"No. Well, unless you call two lovely little fifteenth century statuettes a prize, then yeah. I'd be happy to take them if you even manage to find them."

"I don't know what you're talking about, copper," said the man. "You need to start making sense."

"Well, remember the old VW camper up there?"

"The one that left?"

"The very same," said Frank. "Being the observant individual I am, I noticed something very unique about it."

"This better be good."

"Do you want to know what's unique about it?"

"If I have to, but your time is running out."

"The man who drove that camper van followed you from your little visit to Honest Harry's."

"You know Harry?" asked the man.

"I know Harry, you know Harry, that woman over there with the two kids probably knows Harry. Everyone knows Honest Harry, and Honest Harry knows everyone."

"So what?"

"So, considering the hunt for these two statuettes, and given that our friend in the camper van followed you, I'd say he's under the impression that you have them stashed away somewhere."

"So why doesn't he ask me? I'd set him straight."

"Well, the chances are that if you spoke to him, and given the fact that you have a gun to my head, one of you, if not both of you, would wind up floating in the canal," said Frank. "Do you agree, son? You are both, if you don't mind me saying, unsavoury, to say the least."

"What makes him so unsavoury? He's just a pikey in a camper van, right?"

"Not just any old pikey, son," said Frank. "If he is who I think he is, that is."

"What makes him such a special pikey then?" asked the man in the back seat.

"Before I continue, son," began Frank, turning to face the

man behind him, "would I be correct in offering you congratulations?"

The man didn't reply.

"Your wife gave birth to a little boy earlier, did she not?"

"Who the bloody hell *are* you?" said the man, his aggression rising. "Not that it's any of your business, but yeah, today's a special day."

"Right. So if you want to see that little baby again, sunshine, you'll do well to put that gun down, and pay close attention to what I'm about to suggest."

12

BURN

THE SMELL OF PETROL WOKE BULLDOG FROM A RESTLESS night. He sat up in his camper. The baby was asleep and quiet, finally, but he was soaked. Oily liquid ran down his face and into his mouth. He spat it out, rolled off the tiny bunk, and wrenched the side door open. He fell to the floor in just his boxer shorts, and began to frantically wipe the petrol from his body.

He was parked in one of his usual spots beside the canal in Hackney. So he ran over and began to wash his body with the freezing water. He lowered his head into the canal when a large boot from behind kicked him into the water.

Bulldog sucked in the cold air and frantically tried to pull himself out of the freezing water. But the large boot then stood on his hand.

His eyes stung from the petrol, and the shadow that loomed over him in the darkness stared down at him. He began to shiver. His feet fought for purchase against the muddy bank but slipped. Bulldog hung from the bank, the boot on his wrist holding him above the surface.

"Help. Get me out of here," he called up blindly. "I can't swim."

"You want the statuettes?" said the man above.

"No, bloody keep them. Get me out of here." His lip started to shake as the freezing water began to take hold of him.

"No," said the man. "You wanted them bad enough you'd take my baby, am I right?"

"I didn't hurt him. He's there, in the van," said Bulldog.

"So what exactly was you going to do with him?" asked the man. "Blackmail me?"

Bulldog's head sank below the water, and he came up coughing. "I'm sorry," he sobbed. "Just let me out, you can keep them."

The man dropped a heavy hessian sack to the ground. It landed with a thud.

"What's that?" said Bulldog, fear now gripping his trembling voice.

"It's what you wanted."

"No, I don't want it," said Bulldog. "I just want to get out."

"So who did want it?"

Bulldog was silent.

The man reached down and in one swift motion fixed a pair of police handcuffs to Bulldog's wrist.

"What are you doing?" said Bulldog, who used his free arm to pull at the steel, but to no avail. "What's this?" Bulldog found the other cuff was fixed to rope.

He pulled on the rope, and the hessian sack moved towards him. He could feel the weight inside.

"No," said Bulldog. "No, you can't."

"I think you'll find I can do what I like."

"Stop," cried Bulldog. "Look, your baby's in the van. There's no harm done."

The man lifted the heavy sack.

"What's in there anyway?" asked Bulldog, buying time. "Rocks?"

"No, mate," said the man. "There happen to be two very expensive, and very heavy, fifteenth-century statuettes that by all accounts, a lot of people are looking for."

"Stop," said another voice from the shadows under the trees. "You can't do that, sunshine." The second man was Scottish and had an air of authority in his voice. He walked over to where Bulldog was partially drowning and freezing to death.

"Give me one good reason why not," said the first man.

"Well," said the Scot, "in that sack is a hundred thousand good reasons, and I'll give you ten thousand of them not to throw it in."

Bulldog looked up pleadingly at the man in black who stood, swinging the sack gently back and forth.

"I think they've caused enough agro, don't you?" he said and winked.

Then, to Bulldog's dismay, the man launched the sack high in the air above the water and stepped off Bulldog's wrist.

13

SHOCK

"I BELIEVE THIS LITTLE FELLA BELONGS TO YOU?" SAID Frank, as he handed the child wrapped in blankets to the man in biker leathers.

Leo didn't reply. He took the bundle in his arms and held his child for the first time.

"You're aware that a murder needs a killer, and the killer usually goes to prison?"

"Only if the victim is missed and reported as missing," said Leo despondently. "And something tells me you're not going to report it."

"What makes you so sure of that?" said Frank.

"You're in this deeper than me," said Leo, looking up from his baby. "Me? I can just ride away into the sunset, and you'll never see me again. But you? Sounds like you're *obligated* to find those statuettes."

"I think obligated is perhaps the wrong word."

"It's in your interest, not mine," said Leo.

"You could also say that it's in my interest to bring in a killer. I did, after all, just witness you murder the pikey."

"I'm not sure that's a good idea," said Leo.

"Oh?" said Frank. "And why's that then? I hope you don't think you're above the law?"

"No, mate. I'm somewhere in between," said Leo. "There's a special place reserved in hell for people like me."

Leo turned and began to walk towards the camper.

Frank remained by the canal. He smiled in the darkness at the comment, and then watched as the dark mass of black that was the man in leathers was suddenly lit up by a naked flame, a cigarette lighter.

The flame was tossed into the rear of the van, and within a few seconds, the interior was ablaze. The man in leathers stood there watching with the baby boy in his arms.

"Wait," called Frank, and he strolled toward the man, who was tucking the baby inside his leather jacket and straddling his motorbike. "So you win?" said Frank. "Is that it? You get your boy back, and I get nothing to show for it?"

"I told you that you had more to lose than me."

Frank sighed. "You just tossed a fortune into the canal, son. I can have you stopped at the top of the street if I need to."

"What do you want from me? Money?"

The blazing camper suddenly ignited, and a rush of hot air sucked the flames high into the air, causing Frank to recoil away from the sudden heat. The man in leathers remained impassive.

"You'll pay one way or another," said Frank.

"Sometimes the police need to take a backseat and let society take care of itself," said the man in leathers. "You win some, you lose some, right?"

He turned the key in the bike's ignition, kicked it into gear, and rode away slowly and confidently.

Ever cautious, Frank checked around the little grassland area to make sure the blazing camper hadn't caught anybody's attention. It was surrounded and overshadowed by warehouses on one side and a tall wall on the other side, which held the main road into London at bay. More importantly, it kept away prying eyes. Frank disappeared into the trees and took the short walk back to his car.

He thought for few seconds about the man who had been pulled to the bottom of the canal, and the statuettes that had so ironically weighed him down. He considered the horror of drowning in the freezing, pitch-black water, being disoriented, holding on until the body screamed for oxygen and the lungs felt like they burst from that first deathly inhale of water. Frank wondered how long it took for the man to drown. He wondered if he'd be missed by anybody and if the statuettes would ever be found. He considered their value if they were to be found in fifty years time, dredged up by some development firm and tossed into a waste skip with cars, shopping trolleys and bikes.

Frank strolled with his hands in his pockets, the blaze fading behind him and the sound of the fire brigade's sirens disturbing the peaceful early hours.

The peace was a good time for Frank to consider what had happened. Who was the guy in the leathers? Where had he come from? The man had such confidence. He'd killed the pikey as if it was normal, maybe it was. But who did he work for? And why had the pikey been following him?

A career in the force had earned Frank a keen sense of judgment. It was that judgment that spoke to him and told him that the man in leather would be back. It definitely was not the last Frank would see of him.

MOTHER

THE SMELL OF DISINFECTANT WAS STRONG, AND FOR A maternity ward, the corridors were silent. A nurse sat at reception and beamed when Leo emerged from the stairwell with his baby boy in his arms. He put a finger to his mouth to stop her from crying out, and she sat back down, grinning from ear to ear.

Leo quietly turned the door handle and peeped into the small room. Olivia was laying with her back to the door, but she wasn't sleeping.

"Babes?" said Leo, quietly. "There's someone who wants to see you."

"I don't want to see anyone," she replied. "I don't even want to see you."

Leo stood smiling and closed the door.

"I said, go away, Leo," said Olivia. "I'm not sure I can face it." Her voice was slurred, thickened by tears, and drained of energy.

"Are you sure, babes?" said Leo. "I don't think he'll be too much bother."

Olivia rolled onto her back and opened her mouth to snap

at her husband when her eyes fell on the little bundle of blankets in his arms. Her look of exhausted fury was replaced with shock and surprise. Then a smile crept onto her lips, and her tears of sadness were replaced with tears of joy.

She held out her arms, and Leo carefully handed their newborn baby to his wife.

"Where?" she asked, without looking up.

"Does it matter?" said Leo.

"No," said Olivia. "No, it doesn't." She reached out and took his hand, but once again, kept her eyes on the little boy in the blankets.

"Thank you, Leo," she said quietly. "Thank you for getting our boy back."

15

THREAT

JOHN AND BARB CARTWRIGHT KNOCKED LIGHTLY ON THE door of Olivia's room in the maternity ward of Newham Hospital. Leo opened the door and glanced back at his wife, who nodded for them to come in.

Barb was beaming. She rushed passed Leo, her fur coat brushing past him and leaving her thick scent of perfume on his skin. She hugged Olivia and stood admiring the little boy.

John offered his hand to Leo, and they shook, then stepped outside and sat in the waiting room.

John picked up a magazine and flicked through the pages mindlessly before he spoke.

"You found what you was looking for?" said John.

"No, I found what belonged to me," replied Leo.

"She must be over the moon, eh?"

Leo didn't reply.

"Are you coming back to work, Leo?" asked John. "You know, I'm still trying to find a couple of things myself, and could do with your help."

Leo was silent for a moment and then stood to look out of the window.

"I thought he'd gone, John," said Leo. "I honestly thought that the games we play had gone too far, and my boy was gone."

"What would you have done, Leo?"

Leo didn't reply. But John knew that the man in leather who stood so calmly at the window would have torn down every door in East London to get his boy back. The man was dangerous; he was a stone-cold killer.

"So, now you found what you were looking for, are you going to help me find what I'm looking for, Leo?"

Leo turned to face John who sat with his arms resting on his knees and his fingers interlocked.

"I wouldn't worry too much about them, John," said Leo.

John took a sharp intake of air, then breathed out slowly.

"That's funny, Leo, because you know if they were lost, say thrown into a canal or something, there would be serious repercussions." John stood to meet Leo eye to eye. "Do you know what I mean, Leo?"

"Serious repercussions?" asked Leo.

"Serious repercussions."

Leo began to pace the small waiting room. He turned and paced back to the window.

"Let's say, for example, John, that someone did, in fact, throw them into a canal in order to save something far more precious. Just, for example, you know?"

John nodded.

"And, for example," continued Leo, "let's say that the two very expensive statuettes were irrecoverable. What, in your *experienced opinion*, would be a suitable way forward from that scenario? Hypothetically, of course."

"Hypothetically?" asked John. "Well, if the two very old and very expensive statuettes were indeed lost and irrecoverable, then I would imagine that there might be two possible outcomes to that scenario, Leo."

"And they are?" asked Leo, with one eyebrow raised.

"Firstly," said John, who had stood and begun to pace the small room, looked up at the ceiling imagining the outcome, "the individual who lost the statuettes, or indeed threw them into the canal, must have had a reason."

"Like I said, John, let's imagine that reason was to save something far more precious," said Leo.

"Yeah, far more precious," said John. "Then whatever it was that was valued at such a high amount, and held with more regard than the statuettes themselves, would be fair payment for the loss of the very old and very expensive statuettes."

Leo nodded and absorbed the statement.

"Interesting," said Leo. "And what is it that you might do with something so valuable? I mean, do you value them as equal?"

John moved across the room and stood face to face with Leo. Their eyes locked in two stone-cold stares.

"Not equal, Leo, no," replied John. "But close enough."

They both stood their ground, and the empty room was thick with the electricity of testosterone. The confrontation was broken by Barb, who walked around the corner, sensed the atmosphere, and stopped dead.

"I'll meet you downstairs," said John, without looking at her.

They heard her heels fade in the stairwell.

"Why is it you want them so badly?" asked Leo in a hushed tone.

"They're precious to me, Leo," whispered John.

"They're precious to a lot of people it seems," said Leo. "In particular, to one very bent and dishonest detective."

It was John's turn to remain silent.

"Hypothetically speaking," began Leo, "if someone were to

try to take what I deem as valuable, the repercussions would be unthinkable. I'm not entirely sure of the punishment, John, but you can be sure that body parts would be removed, and the pain would be unbearable. I'd see to that. So let's have no more talk about taking what's mine and get down to it. You promised that very bent copper a lot of money for the statuettes, and if those statuettes were to have been discarded, or irrecoverable, as you put it, you would still owe him the money. Am I right?"

"Hypothetically, yes," said John.

"So here's what's going to happen, John," said Leo. "You leave this hospital, and let me be with my family. Nobody touches them." Leo held a single index finger up as a warning. He pointed it at John. "I'm not talking hypothetically now, John. I'll kill anyone who tries anything, and you know what I'm capable of."

Leo began to walk away towards the room where his family were resting.

"So that's it, is it?' said John. "I'm supposed to just take that and walk away with nothing?"

Leo stopped.

He turned to face John.

"How long have I worked for you, John?"

"Long enough to know what I'm capable of, Leo," replied John.

Leo nodded.

"Have I ever let you down, John?"

John shook head. "Not until now, Leo."

Leo nodded again, then began to move away. He stopped before he disappeared around the corner and turned back to John who was staring out the window.

"Oh, by the way, John," said Leo. "Two things."

John glanced across the room at Leo.

Leo smiled.

"You might want to go and see Honest Harry. He's not as loyal as you might think."

The comment caught John's attention.

"And the second thing?" he asked.

"Get that bent copper of yours," said Leo, "to check the back seat of his car." He winked and disappeared from view.

HARVEY STONE

"It was nice of John and Barb to pop by," said Olivia. "She was really taken with him, didn't want to put him down, she didn't."

Leo was sat on the edge of the bed holding the baby boy.

"What did he want anyway?" asked Olivia. "Surely he didn't come here to talk about work, Leo?"

"No, babes," replied Leo. "We just..." He searched for the words to use that wouldn't trouble his wife. "Came to an understanding is all."

"There's not going to be trouble, is there?" asked Olivia. "I can sense it when something's happening, you know?"

Leo looked at her, reached across and squeezed her hand. "No trouble, babes."

He stood with the baby boy wrapped in blankets and went to stand beside the window.

Leo was still for a while, as the boy began to open his eyes.

"I think he's a Harvey. What do you think of that for a name?"

"Harvey's a nice name, Leo," she replied from the other side of the room. "Harvey and Hannah, I like it."

"Well, Harvey," said Leo quietly to his son, "say hi to the world." Leo turned the boy so he could see out of the large window. "You can be whatever you want to be, son," he whispered. "It's *your* world, Harvey Stone."

The little boy stared back at his father, not with inquisitiveness, and not with hunger, but just an emotionless stare.

"He's going to be strong this one, babes," said Leo. "Are you going to be a strong boy, Harvey?"

The baby boy stared back as if in confirmation.

"Are you going to take care of your sister?" Leo smiled as the boy's eyes began to search the room. They stopped and fell back onto his father's.

"Harvey Stone," whispered Leo.

Harvey didn't reply.

End of Novella 1.
Download the next Stone Cold Box Set Here...

FREE EBOOKS FOR YOU...

As a gesture of thanks for buying Stone Cold, I'd like to invite you to the J.D. Weston Reader Group. Members of my reader group get the following:

- Three free eBooks.
- Early bird discounts on ALL my new releases.
- Freebies as and when I run them.
- News of discounts from my author friends. (there's usually one or two of them running a promo at any given time).

One thing is for sure, as a member of my reader group you will have plenty of opportunity to save some cash and get your hands on free and discounted eBooks.

All you have to do is visit www.jdweston.com and follow a few easy prompts. I hope to see you in the group.

J.D. Weston

ALSO BY J.D. WESTON.

The Frankie Black Files

Torn in Two

Her Only Hope

Run Girl Run.

The Stone Cold Thriller Series.

Book 1 - Stone Cold

Book 2 - Stone Fury

Book 3 - Stone Fall

Book 4 - Stone Rage

Book 5 - Stone Free

Book 6 - Stone Rush

Book 7 - Stone Game

Book 8 - Stone Raid

Book 9 - Stone Deep

Book 10 - Stone Fist

Book 11 - Stone Army

Book 12 - Stone Face

The Stone Cold Boxset Series

Stone Cold Boxset 1-3

Stone Cold Boxset 4-6

Stone Cold Boxset 7-9

Stone Cold Boxset 10-12

.

Printed in Great Britain
by Amazon